AF674512

The Girmitiya Saga

The Girmitiya Saga

Giriraj Kishore

Translated from the Hindi original
by

Prajapati Sah

Recipient of the *Vyas Samman,* 2000

NIYOGI
BOOKS

Published by

NIYOGI BOOKS

D-78, Okhla Industrial Area, Phase-I
New Delhi-110 020, INDIA

Tel: 91-11-26816301, 26813350, 51, 52
Fax: 91-11-26810483, 26813830

email: niyogibooks@gmail.com
website: www.niyogibooks.com

Cover Design: Navidita Thapa & Premanka Goswami / Niyogi Books

ISBN: 978-81-89738-45-7

Publication: 2010

Printed at: Niyogi Offset Pvt. Ltd., New Delhi, India

Dedicated to the memory of Late K.R. Narayanan, Ex-President of India, whose eagerness to read PEHLA GIRMITIYA could not be fulfilled for lack of an English translation …

Before the novel …

The life of Mahatma Gandhi can be divided unto three phases: the 'Mohaniya phase,' the 'Mohandas phase' and the 'Mahatma Gandhi phase'. The Mohandas phase, about which I have chosen to write, from the time he became a barrister to the time of his return from South Africa. The childhood and the adolescent phase, or the Mohaniya phase, also reappears during the Mohandas phase through Sheikh Mehtab, Kastur, *Ba* and *Bapu*, Uka and many others but the main preoccupation of the Mohandas phase is the problems of *girmitiya*s or Indian indentured labours, in South Africa.

One may well ask why I chose to write only on the Mohandas phase. In April 1995, when I travelled to South Africa and Mauritius with a view to writing a novel on Mahatma Gandhi, I had already written two hundred pages on his Mohaniya phase. My intention was to write a novel on the complete Gandhi. Had I done so, it would have been like crossing all the seas of the world. Even in writing only on the Mohandas phase, I felt I was daring to cross the Indian Ocean and I was sure to drown midway. However, after travelling to South Africa, I decided that it would be best to confine myself only to the Mohandas phase, and even within that phase only to the South African Gandhi. South Africa was for me redolent with memories of Gandhi.

It is true that Gandhi is the hero of our struggle for freedom, but it is Mohandas who is more closely attached to common man's sensibility and his experiences. The upcoming generation needs Mohandas more so that it can know how he became the Mahatma. In addition to being a moral person, Gandhi is also a social person who does not try to conceal his weaknesses. Doors to greatness open only when you are able see your weaknesses. For me, going to South Africa, seeing those places, streets, cities and contexts with my own eyes and relating to them personally was like re-living Mohandas within me. I felt for the first time that I was stepping out of myself, that there was a big, big world outside the sphere of my experience in which I was also present through the mediacy of hundreds of thousands of immigrant Indians and through Mohandas.

The struggle of Mohandas was the struggle of a stranger and of an average person in a foreign country. Whether in his own or in a foreign land, a displaced person always has to struggle, though from the points of view of time and space there may be a difference in the quality and quantity of his struggle. It is everyone's effort in his life to progress towards a predetermined, undetermined or underdetermined goal. In the pursuit of that goal, he makes sacrifices, puts up with adversity and nurses aspirations. He does whatever is possible, necessary or unnecessary. Mohandas' goal was not a well-defined struggle. It was, in my view, a case of the goal making itself clear as the caravan progressed. His path to the Mahatma-hood lay through these narrow lanes of uncertainties, sacrifices, renunciations, sufferings and humiliations.

The main character of this novel is as ordinary a man as it is possible for one to be. He was neither born with a silver spoon in his mouth nor a golden crown on his head. He sold his wife's jewellery to study law in London. When he returned as a barrister, he faced unemployment and had to depend on his elder brother. Then his moral values found themselves up against the rampant immorality of the law courts. His poor speaking skills led to his losing case after case. Whatever little he was able to earn was by writing drafts for the clients of his elder brother's lawyer friend, who also claimed a share of the earnings. Mohandas was very upset by this mode of exploitation. As a result, this barrister too had to leave for South Africa with thousands of poverty stricken, illiterate and unemployed labourers to earn a living on a one-year *girmit* (agreement), with the only difference being that, being a barrister, he would earn ten times the *girmitiya*'s wages. He landed in South Africa, a complete Indian within but a total Englishman without, carrying his mother's devotion to truth and tolerance and his father's well-meaning nature and his self-respect. On the very first day, when he entered the Durban courtroom with his mentor, Dada Abdullah, wearing a Gujarati *pheta* (i.e. a turban) in order to maintain his Gujarati identity, he preferred to leave the courtroom rather than to yield to the court's order to remove his turban. Travelling to Pretoria, he was thrown out of the first class compartment like a bundle at the Maritzburg station, was thrashed by the coachman of the stagecoach—all this became part of his unfolding destiny. There was no accounting of the times he was beaten up and bundled out. But every time it happened, his forgiveness increased, his tolerance and his well-meaning quality became stronger, and he approached the truth a step closer. His sensitivity sharpened. His insight into human nature deepened. His encounters with truth and his experiments with it multiplied. The struggle of the ordinary to become great and the struggle of the great to become ordinary intensified.

The great South African student of Gandhi's literature and life, Mr. Hasim Sedat, once told me: 'Kishorebhai, I am proud of the fact that the world's biggest diamond was found in our mines, but what we returned to you as Gandhi was an incomparably more precious and polished diamond.'

A common belief about Gandhi has been that he was a friend and sympathizer of the traders; actually he was basically a *girmitiya.* His heart cried out for them. It was they who were most affected by the three-pound tax by the Supreme Court judge Justice Searle's verdict on the illegality of Indian marriages, because they formed the majority of the Indian community and were in no position to migrate to another place. Both these factors were relatively easier to manage for the traders. In the final stage of the struggle, these were only the two items remaining on the agenda. The *girmitiya*s were with them all the way in the struggle against them. The traders were working behind the stage. In the eyes of the local whites, though, every one of them was a coolie. He was one of them—Gandhi the coolie barrister.

Mr. Hasim Sedat, whom I mentioned above, is a senior attorney in Durban. He was the first African-Indian office holder of the local Law Society. He is an acknowledged authority on Gandhian history. His personal library on Gandhi is bigger than anyone's in India. You can find here all the journals and books on Gandhi published anywhere in the world and all the old newspaper files. It was through him and through his library that I was introduced so intimately to Mohandas. I was introduced to Mr. Hasim Sedat by another attorney, Mr. Anand Jairaj. Mr. Sedat also presented me two books: a photocopy of Millie Polak's life of Gandhi and Marin Waughan's research work published in South Africa, *Gandhi: The South African Experience.* A book edited by Fatima Meer, entitled *The South African Gandhi*, was published in 1995 jointly by Nadib Publishers and Gandhi Memorial, Durban. He brought this book with him when he came to India in 1996 on my invitation. Anyone working on Gandhi is received with open arms at his place. His wife, Farida Behn, drove me wherever I wanted to go and even got vegetarian food prepared for me. Few persons I have met have her nature. She can make everyone feel so dear to her.

My experience is that South Africa has more serious students of Gandhi (than India), for example, Mrs. Fatima Meer, Archbishop Dennis Hurley, Nikki Padayachi, Sita Dhupalia, Mrs. G. Burnig (She published a selection of letters between Kallenbach and Gandhi a few years ago from Durban City Museum) and Nelson Mandela himself. They have all contributed to Hasim Sedat's book *The South African Gandhi.*

My contact with Anand Jairaj was established through Mr. Vishvanath Shrikhande, musician and former Secretary, U.P. Sangeet Natak Akademi. Like her husband, Mrs. Shirley Jairaj too has a special regard for Indians. Jairaj arranged my stay in the Asoka Hotel which is owned by a gentleman of Indian origin, one Mr. Harry. Jairaj also received me at the Durban airport. He also introduced me to Mr. Ramgobin Mewa, President of the Phoenix Settlement Trust and former husband of Ila Gandhi, grand-daughter of Mahatma Gandhi. It was Mr. Mewa who took me to Phoenix. Like Ila Gandhi, Mr. Mewa is also a member of the parliament.

Mrs. Ila Gandhi is a decent and cultured person, mostly resident in Cape Town. She happened to be in town during those days. She took me around Durban the whole day. She also arranged my stay in Johannesburg.

The visit to Phoenix with Mr. Mewa was a sad experience. Nothing is left of the Phoenix settlement. On the way, he told me many things about Phoenix, which I witnessed with my own eyes on arriving there. Everything is in ruins. Only the bare walls of the press that published *Indian Opinion* are now left standing. Only a platform of Gandhi's home remains; the rest was all broken down. The government is a silent spectator. The place is a den of underworld activities. Phoenix is in the hands of natives. Only the school building is standing. On the day we arrived there, the School Trust was holding a meeting in the school. Ila Gandhi was also present. Many natives are members of the Trust.

When the nomenclature of the school was to be decided, Gandhi had said: 'Let's call it Phoenix. A phoenix never dies. It rises again and again from its ashes.' Today Phoenix is only ashes. Let's hope Gandhi's word comes true and this phoenix rises again some day.'

In Durban, Pietermaritzburg and Johannesburg, I got to see many places which filled my heart with sadness. In Durban, Hasimbhai took me walking to Beachgrove Street. The Dada Abdullah residence used to be close by: new buildings occupy the place now. Entering the street, you come across a car parking. Showing it to me, Hasimbhai said: 'Kishorebhai, where you see the car parking, there used to be the Beach Grove Villa. There was a balcony on the beach side where Gandhi sat for a while after he returned from the court. Being a Porbundar man, he loved sea breeze.'

That house now didn't have a single brick left.

A little distance from the place was Grey Street where Congress had its hall. It now housed a shopping complex. The hall had been parcelled out into shops. There was no trace of Congress. On Fiels Street, where Rustomji Parsi had his home, there now stood a glittering multistoreyed building. That was where Gandhi, having disembarked from the quarantined ship *Courland*, quarantined because of a suspected plague attack, had arrived. The place where he was attacked by the whites was a little distance away from the Old Customs House, on West Street. That was where he had been cornered. The place which housed Police Captain Alexander's office, or the 'Burrow Police Station,' where Gandhi had been taken from Rustomji's home, is now occupied by Maidwood Garden. I also saw the courtroom where Mohandas had appeared with a turban on his head and where the Magistrate had ordered him to take it off. The place is now occupied by the local History Museum. Durban jail, which had housed Mohandas and Kasturba, has been taken down. Foundations of a new building were being excavated at the site. A photograph showed it to be a well-secured jail.

From Durban, Jairaj, Hasimbhai and I went to Pietermaritzburg. This was the place where, having been thrown out of a train, the fire had set off within Mohandas which eventually led him to become the Mahatma. Pietermaritzburg station is a good specimen of Gothic architecture. There is a clock tower atop the building. As you enter the building, you find yourself in a hall, which is all woodwork. Small candelabras hang from the ceiling. A wooden staircase leads to the top floor, which probably houses offices. A part of it had probably been burnt in a fire. The place where Mohandas fell has not yet been correctly determined. Beyond the hall is the platform. Almost directly in front lay a bench belonging to the same period. The first class compartment stopped right in front of the bench. Mohandas had fallen somewhere close to it. Pietermaritzburg was the capital city of Natal. The Supreme Court, where, despite the opposition of the Law Society, the Chief Justice had nominated Mohandas as an attorney, was located here. That building now houses a museum. Across the road is the City Hall, which is counted among the most beautiful buildings of Natal.

In Johannesburg, I stayed at Chhibbubhai's home, Lenetia, courtesy Ilaji. Chhibbubhai is a Gujarati and from a very cultured family. He introduced me to Mr. N.G. Patel. He is a leading attorney and also the Chairman of the Centenary Celebration Committee of Tolstoy Trust. Chhibbubhai took me first to Lawley station, from which it is about a mile to Tolstoy Farm. The entire land of Tolstoy Farm is now with a Dutch firm, which manufactures bricks. After the firm had bought the land and had had it surveyed, it discovered that it had once been Tolstoy Farm. The head of the firm then called some leading Indians and handed over to them the house and part of the land so that they could keep alive the memories of the Farm. The house is in a much worse condition today than it was when it was handed over to the Indians. There was a library, which is now in total ruins. The house has been ransacked and even the stone and the woodwork have been stolen. Important leaders from India often visit the place, pay their tributes, make tall promises and make their way back to India never to look back again. If the Indian government thinks it has nothing to do with places associated with Gandhi, why should one expect the South African government to have anything to do with Tolstoy Farm? South African Indians are a prosperous community and if they wished they could themselves do a lot for the Farm, but as is common with Indians everywhere, they are a divided lot. Mr. H.K. Bhasin was Director (Culture) there. He very much wanted Indians to work jointly on this project. I went to see him along with Mr. Patel and Chhibbubhai and Mr. Bhasin talked to them about it. It seemed to me that, like the Indian Gandhi, the African Gandhi too is turning into a political issue. Hasimbhai told me that later the Indian High Commissioner, Gopal Gandhi, had initiated some action in this regard.

Pretoria has the Kruger palace. More of a large house than a palace actually. Outside the house sit two very peaceable lions, as peaceable as Kruger was aggressive. It was outside this palace that the guards had beaten up Gandhi for walking on the footpath. On inquiry, I found out that no one knows about the incident any more. The first house that Mohandas was to occupy in Johannesburg was 14, Albmerry Street. It was a street wholly occupied by whites. I went to see it with Chhibbubhai. When I was there in 1995, I came across an issue of the South African magazine *House and Leisures* (October 1994) which contained many photographs of the 14, Albmerry Street house. The house is now with Michael Hearse, an architect. He wants to turn it into a tourist attraction. The site of Empire Theatre is now occupied by an opulent building. I also saw the place where Mir Alam had attacked Mohandas. The mosque where the *satyagrahi*s had their meetings is also extant. After his meeting as a prisoner, that was where Mohandas had called a meeting.

Let me also mention the limitations of this novel. In the absence of adequate information, I have had to take recourse to a writer's imaginative license at several places. If there are readers who have the desired information, they will surely find my license excessive. I must specifically quote two or three instances. First, there is the incident at Tolstoy Farm when Gandhi got the locks of two young girls cut off. I could not lay my hands on the names of the girls nor could I get the name of the boy who was responsible for it, though I remember to have read the names of the girls in a Gujarati novel. Millie, in her biography of Gandhi, has used the initials of the girls' names, which I did not consider adequate. Second, Mr. Baker had arranged for Mohandas to stay in the home of a lady baker as a paying guest. I could neither discover the name of the lady baker nor any details about her family. I have called the lady Matilda and woven a touching story about the family. There must be a couple of other such episodes too. Some ships carrying *girmitiya*s had broken up: I have included them in the novel. The names *Sudderingham* and *Fusilier* are to be found in the literature as also the incidents relating to them described here, though I have added on some elements. I had a feeling I was present there myself.

Marcel Ledue was a French businessman. He wrote a derogatory account of Gandhi's life in French, which has been translated into English by Rumi Minty and edited by the U.S. based A.D. Lazarus, grandson of D. Lazarus of Newcastle, who was a companion of Gandhi. Ledue called himself a contemporary of Gandhi. I have used him as a character in the novel. I think his character helps in highlighting the character of Gandhi. I saw the English translation in manuscript with Prof S.S. Singh in Durban. I do not know if it has been published since. It contains many references which are not only hard to believe but also an insult to Gandhi.

It would not be appropriate on my part to say anything about the quality of the novel. I am however, conscious that many questions will be raised—questions of authenticity, questions of historicity, questions about the identity of the characters, questions about places, streets, etc. Knowledgeable people will also make comments about the pronunciation and spellings of names of places, streets, people, etc. Some people may even go to the extent of saying that it is not a novel at all. They may ask: Why did the author stop short with Mohandas? Was he afraid of moving on to the Mahatma? They may also say, as is often said in the context of historical novels, that if the work is sixty per cent history, what does the writer achieve by adding forty per cent of his own? This novel, though, is more life than history. These questions will be raised because this novel happens to be about Gandhi. Being Gandhi has its problems as well as privileges. The more you try to know about him, the more you find has escaped your knowledge. However, it is not for the author to answer these questions; critics may, though critics also try to save themselves the trouble.

I can only say that I have made every effort to keep the use of the writer's license within the bounds of authenticity. It is however possible that where I had to base myself on official documents, or cite legal ordinances, the text has no longer remained as interesting as generally expected in a work of fiction. There are occasions when the evolution of Gandhi's thoughts had to be included; those portions may have become somewhat abstruse and it is possible that some readers may find them a little dense. From the writer's point of view however it was not possible to deny their essential role in the narrative.

I have also mentioned Mauritius. In 1901, *Naushera* made a halt in Mauritius for a few days with Mohandas and his family aboard. I have included that episode in the novel. But, despite the stupendous efforts of Bhai Abhimanyu Anant and the poet Pujanand Nemaha, not much material regarding Gandhi's stay there could be uncovered. But, in a sense, Mauritius has been the Mecca of *girmitiya* labourers. The South African ordinance on indentured labour was modelled on Mauritian law. It was not possible to leave that out. Some material was provided to me by Mr. Prahlad Ramsaran. There is, however, some internal disagreement among the local scholars regarding Gandhi's stay in Mauritius. I did not have to concern myself with that controversy. There is no one now living in Mauritius belonging to Gandhi's times. Durban had the eighty year old daughter of Gandhi's associate, Lawrence, but she could not speak. As a child, she used to go to walks with Gandhi, holding his finger. Rustomji Parsi's relatives are also living. The Mahatma Gandhi Institute did a lot to minimize my difficulties by offering me hospitality. I am grateful to them. I doubt if any Indian writer has tried to associate himself with Mauritius in this context. It may be Mauritius or any other country, wherever there is a bit of *girmitiya* India, Gandhi, and South Africa are as relevant to it as they were to the coolie community in South Africa. Their past too is quite alike.

Giriraj Kishore

Kanpur, April, 1999

Th

me on

of India

at great

it I had

English

Fr

Prajapat

a conscie

receive

admirer

Gandhi

seeker

many bo

years be

It

of this

determi

attention

wish to

a friend

I w

the publ

In

to Presi

to his la

Preface to the English Translation

The idea of bringing out an English version of *Pehla Girmitiya* occurred to me on June 3, 1999, when I presented the book to Sri K.R. Narayanan, President of India, at the Rashtrapati Bhavan, New Delhi. President Narayanan talked to me at great length about the novel and was very disappointed that he could not read it. I had then promised him that I would personally present him the novel when an English translation was published.

Finally, the English translation of the work is ready, thanks to my friend, Prajapati Sah, who also translated my earlier novel, *Dhaii Ghar,* and has also found a conscientious publisher in Niyogi Books, but Sri Narayanan is no longer there to receive it. While that loss cannot be made up, I am sure there are many others, both admirers and critics of Gandhi, who will want to read about the crucial phase in Gandhi's life which turned him from an English trained lawyer into uncompromising seeker of truth and non-violence, and a leader of the masses. The publication of many books on Gandhi and the release of a number of films on his life in recent years bear witness that interest in Gandhi has by no means diminished.

It was with understandable trepidation that Prajapati undertook the translation of this work, but once he had undertaken it he pushed on with it with great determination and finished it almost at breakneck speed but without sacrificing the attention to detail that is the hallmark of his work. It was a tremendous job and I wish to thank him wholeheartedly even at the risk of incurring his displeasure as a friend.

I would also like to record my thanks to Niyogi Books and its staff for making the publication of the work possible in such a short time.

In the end, I wish to make up, at least in part, for my failure to keep my promise to President K.R. Narayanan by dedicating this English translation of *Pehla Girmitiya* to his lasting memory.

Giriraj Kishore

Kanpur, October, 2009

To those Indians and their descendants
who migrated to other countries
as girmitiyas *and travellers*
forming bridges of prosperity;
and never returned.

To those Indians
whom the sea swallowed up
and to their children for whom
they continued to live
even in the waves of the sea.

To the upcoming generation of
my grandson Tanmay
and granddaughter Vanya,
for whom knowing Mohandas
will be probably of greater significance.
As Mohandas, he exerted himself
in a foreign land for the freedom
of his fellow countrymen and,
as Mahatma Gandhi,
fell to bullets in his own land
and died, with the name of Ram
on his lips.

I

The whites had their dreams.

When they seized other countries, the whites took their dreams with them.The first task they set themselves was to weed out, one by one, the dreams of the natives and implant their own dreams in their place. The land belonged to the natives, the dreams to the whites. The natives, they believed, weren't exactly born on the land either. They arrived in Natal in the middle of the seventeenth century and became natives.We arrived a little later, and stayed non-natives. Born of slaves! Actually, reduced to misery by the tyranny of the whites, these so-called natives had arrived here in the middle of the seventeenth century from the newly born country of America. America hadn't yet quite become America. The natives of the land were still being uprooted. The trees of their dreams were still being cut down by the whites. Along with the trees, those who had planted them were also being displaced. They were falling from the skies to land on trees all over the place. South Africa was one of the trees where they had landed and they were now busy making their homes there. They formed the majority of the natives. They had their own languages: Zulu, Swazi, Bush and so on. Languages formed tribes. Then came the whites. In the nineteenth century, there were about a hundred thousand whites and about five hundred thousand natives. The natives became slaves and the whites became the masters. On this land, which stretched up to the horizon, the masters were in a hurry to plant their own dreams. The slaves were dubbed *kaffirs*. The whites were of course whites. And they were the masters too.

The natives knew little about themselves, about the power they could wield or about the fertility of their lands. For them, the colour white was a flag the very sight of which made them think of themselves as powerless and of the other as all-powerful. They felt all their power being drained into the whites. They were reduced to mere 'folk'. In some sense, though, the power of their tribal chiefs was greater than that of the whites. If there was anyone after God to whom everyone in the tribe paid complete obeisance, it was the chief. His was the bread they ate, the work they did, and the glory. Before him, even the whites paled into insignificance.

Every *kaffir* had more than one wife. Mother of his kids. The more kids a wife had, the more fortunate she was reckoned. And one got an additional hand with no wages to pay. The more wives one had, the wealthier he was. The wives put in the labour, the men enjoyed the fruits. They smoked tobacco and refreshed the chief's pipe. The problem before the whites was to find someone to work in their fields. They themselves were sahibs; to work in the fields you needed labourers. The workers were to be found in the tribes. The chief could let them have the labourers, or not. It was his sweet will. He could give you a few or many. He could call them back halfway. He could ask for any sum and you would have to pay.

In their temperate clime, the whites wanted to grow crops of temperate regions. The natives only knew how to grow corn. In some places they could also grow wheat. The whites' dream of striking it rich on agriculture was falling to pieces. How far could they go on corn alone? The land was so fertile that a good crop would spout gold! How to harvest this gold? The whites could neither understand their language nor make themselves understood.They thought of Mauritius: any white who had landed there weighed himself in gold.

~

October 15, 1851, Friday, a room in Durban Government School:

One pompous white followed another! Each in his own coach. Some were drawn by two, some by four horses. The coachmen as well as the masters were white. The coach would pull up in front of the room; the white master would get off and would walk into the room.

The coach would turn around and would join the other coaches in the parking place.

The coachmen were all in a fluster; their masters were going to import coloured labour from across the seas. The natives themselves were proving to be a handful; how did they think they were going to handle the coloureds?

'Those people know magic. They'll use magic to become our masters while our masters will turn into their slaves.'

'What are you saying? Have whites ever been slaves?'

'It's all a matter of magic.'

'Magic works only with those who are afraid of it.'

'That depends on the magician.'

'Our masters too are learning magic. Black magic.'

John Miller was a big farmer. He was the last one to arrive. His coach had four horses. Everyone stood up when he entered the room. There were twenty to twenty-five whites in the room. He walked straight on to the stage and sat down on the chairman's seat. There was applause. John Miller was a man of few words. It was believed about him that when it came to farming, his was the last word. He knew and understood each and every secret of farming.

John Miller pointed towards another farmer, Evans. Evans started by badmouthing the natives. 'They are shirkers, illiterates and understand nothing about farming. The kind of farming they have been doing generation after generation is of no use to us whatsoever. They can neither fill their stomachs nor earn any money by that sort of farming. Eventually, they will just go and drown themselves in the Indian Ocean.' When he read out his proposal, everyone was stunned. It was an abusive proposal. The least harmless of his proposals was this: 'It is sheer stupidity to trust the *kaffirs* of this colony to maintain a regular supply of labour to us according to our needs. To grow temperate crops, it is essential that we import coloured labour.'

Evans' words reflected not only anger but also fear. One could see clearly how scared the whites were of the natives. The great pomp and show they put up made you feel as if they were the bravest of the brave that they could pick up the Table Mountain by their little finger and dash it to the ground like a glass vessel. Table Mountain was close to Cape Town and was known as the Friendly Mountain. Evans was of the view that forcing the natives to work for them was not free from risk. Every white citizen, no matter what his trade, needed to be provided with a gun.

Someone butted in: 'Why not import white labour?'

Evans dropped his own line and started on the mover of the proposal. He was now spewing venom on him, 'What will white workers do? What do they know about temperate crops? Are we growing apples or berries here? Do you know how much a white labourer costs? In Australia a white worker gets twenty pounds as annual wages plus two meals a day. His food bill for the year is another twenty pounds. Are you willing to pay that much?' He continued after a pause: 'A coloured labourer in Mauritius costs practically nothing. Half the wages and a lot more labour. If we hand them guns and teach them how to fire them, they will take care of these *kaffir* natives. We won't have to do anything. To tell you the truth, the coolies are the true antidote to the natives.'

Morewood had been listening silently. He could not hold himself any longer. He stood up to speak, 'Dead wrong! That we've been listening quietly does not mean you can go on saying whatever comes to your mind. I have been in this line of work for the past thirteen years. I never had to face shortage of *kaffir* labour. You deal with them kindly and they will never give you a reason for complaint.'

That day, Campbell had come to the meeting with the avowed intention that he'd keep his mouth shut. Every time he opened his mouth, he was misunderstood. But now he got so annoyed that he could not keep quiet, 'We already have so much labour available. You bring in more labour—white or coloured—and the wages will go down further. Even survival will become difficult for them. Who will be responsible?'

Dr. Johnson stood up with a serious mien and spoke very slowly, 'I agree that *kaffir*s aren't treated properly. If they can manage white labour in Europe, why can't we? I'm sure we can keep them under control the way the captain of a ship keeps his crew.'

Byron did not understand anything. He suddenly started speaking in a loud voice, 'Everyone knows a *kaffir* is a *kaffir*. He cannot be trusted. Absolutely not. Here we have the most beautiful land, ideal for temperate crops. And what are we doing? Busy sweet-talking the tribal heads! No attention to land or produce, which is what we most need to do! We need a regular supply of labour. Any bottleneck there, and we will find ourselves sitting twiddling our thumbs. It is absolutely essential that we import coloured labour.'

The concluding motion was to be proposed by Dixon, but he'd forgotten and was dozing. The Chairman had to prod him, 'Are you sleeping, Mr. Dixon?'

Dixon jumped. More than startled, he was embarrassed. He immediately started rattling off the resolution, without any comma or full stop,'Let's establish a company for the import of coloured labour. No temperate crops like cotton, sugarcane, etc., can be grown till we initiate some action in this direction. It is also essential to present a petition to the Governor seeking land and financial support.

Although the decision to import non-native, non-white labour was taken after much heat and dust had been raised, it lay in cold storage for four years. The petition was finally made ready in 1855 and was presented to the Governor by a group led by John Miller.

Among other things, the petition included a very amusing detail: 'There are thirty thousand native workers. Ten thousand of them work as servants to the whites as personal attendants, garden hands, watchmen and so on. Absenteeism is the worst trait of the natives. They work six months in a year, and rest the remaining six. For full six months, the relaxing ten thousand lie in their corrals smoking tobacco and enjoying the services of their women folk. At any given time, only ten thousand natives are at work. Tribal chiefs, leaders and old folk have to be discounted anyway: they are good for nothing. Therefore, if the whites want to have a future and grow crops, they must be given permission to import non-native workers. They must be given land and financial support. Otherwise, the white community will shrivel up like a creeper drying up on a tree.'

'Can't we train the natives?' The Governor asked.

'Even if we could, would ten thousand natives be able to meet the farm requirements of a hundred thousand whites?'

Another member added: 'If India can supply labour to Mauritius, why can't it supply us?'

'We're ready to offer better terms.'

The Governor laughed, 'We can't force them. It all depends on the sweet will of the Indian government.'

'India is a British colony. So is Natal. The whites are in power there, and so are they here. That's such a big country that it's hard to feed everyone. What possible objection can the Indian government have?'

'Only the Indian government can answer that question.' The Governor looked annoyed. The members could read the signs on his face. As the Governor stood up, so did they. Miller had been quiet. Now he spoke for the first time, 'It was not our intention to comment on your observation, Your Excellency. We are only concerned about the development of this colony and our own problems.'

The tension on the Governor's face eased a little. 'The matter can be discussed with the Indian government,' he said as he walked away.

The white farmers lingered on for a while after he was gone. Then they shrugged and withdrew, wondering when the discussions would be held and when, if at all, the workers would arrive.

'Meanwhile, we just hang around here, far from home and hearth, doing nothing.'

~

November 17, 1860. The immense water mass of the Indian Ocean rising and falling. At Eddington Port, people were straining their eyes, shading them with their hands, to figure out something towards the north.

Something, which looked like a bird, could be seen floating. People were taken by surprise. No one had ever seen a bird like this, nor had there ever been any traffic from this direction. The people clustered together and seemed to join their eyes together in a kind of communal sighting effort, in a way that suggested that if all their eyes came together they would see farther and much more clearly.

'What could it be?'

'Anything but a bird. You surely couldn't see a bird from this distance.'

'Then maybe it's a ship.'

'A ship from this direction? It's said they used to come once, but have never been seen more recently.'

'Well, it's not impossible.'

'If it's a ship, then whose ship is it? And why is it coming here?'

Everyone held his peace. No one could understand whose ship it might be. The nearer it came, the wider became its occupation of the water-space, as happens with domination, or with a squirt of colour. The shrill wail of its siren sounded as if it was challenging the sea shore. A variety of sounds began to be heard: the mass of water striking the ship, the ship, in turn, slicing the water as it surged forward. A shiver ran through the people collected there. Of course, ships did come, from the neighbouring colonies, from London, but a ship from the north was coming after a long, long time, like a stranger who had lost its way.

The ship dropped anchor a little distance from Eddington Harbour. People waited, holding their breath. More people had collected from the neighbouring places. The shore was a little distance from where the ship had dropped anchor. Little boats were dispatched from the shore to fetch the passengers ashore.

Since few ships arrived at this site, the number of boats available was also small.

Those who were standing on the shore became more and more curious.The language the passengers spoke was, of course, strange; their faces and their dress too looked quite outlandish. Their speech sounded like gibberish. Large eyes, colourful dresses. Men had their heads wrapped in cloth. Women covered their heads with the same length of cloth which was also wrapped around the rest of their body and their legs. People were wondering how they could possibly have managed this feat.

Some officials were also present. One of them declared: 'This ship is called *Touro.*'

'It's written up there on the ship. It's coming from Madras.'

'From Madras?'

'Yes, the recruiting agent had sent word that coolies were being sent on the *Touro.*'

There were two or three whites among them. One of them observed:

'Something is better than nothing. At least they won't behave like the natives.'

'It's a new place for them. They must be feeling scared.'

'Should be thrown into the sea, if they don't.'

'They can then swim back home, or make it straight to heaven.'

They roared with laughter.

~

By sheer coincidence, *Touro* had arrived on a Friday. Nine years ago when the white farmers had met in a classroom at the Durban Government School, it had been a Friday too. The sun had gone down. Shadows of trees enveloped the earth. It showed how enormously shadows grow before they die. Birds swarmed the sky as if they had just been released from their cages, had rediscovered their open sky and now flew fearlessly. They were now slowly descending and beginning to circle round their trees and the nests built in them, as if performing a ritual circumambulation before landing and seeking the tree god's permission to land. Cattle were returning from the day's grazing. There was dust all round. The passengers on the ship were reminded of their village: the cattle home after grazing, the villagers feeding the cattle, the milking to follow. They forgot they were on a ship. A few of them found their fingers moving by themselves. The swish-swish of the milking motion began to echo in their ears.

When the *Touro* announced its arrival by sounding its hooter, the birds were the ones to be disconcerted most. They took off on a steep flight as if the ship was here only to catch them and as if it was a big bird-catcher. Suddenly the sky had become a safer place for them than those trees where they spent twelve hours out of the twenty-four. After a short while, the birds had landed again, still a little frightened. Everything was now back to normal. A question however had lingered like a desire in the minds of the people on the ship: 'Will it ever be their fate to return to their country or will they return to dust on this land?'

When the ship reached the harbour, the Natal coolie agent, Edmund, was absent. The government officials present were at a loss to understand what to do next. The necessary documents were with Edmund. Those who watched the scene from the shore always felt that those who came riding the waves brought all kinds of calamities with them: death, diseases, infections, adultery! They might blow them all into their faces like chilli powder the moment they got off the ship. New people, new diseases!

Only Philip Allen was present there. Though a white, he had been posted there by the government. In the absence of Edmund, he did one good thing: he got the men he had brought with him to start constructing temporary barracks close to the harbour. He also dispatched a man to fetch Edmund. Edmund lived in Pietermaritzburg, which was the capital of Natal. Durban and Pietermaritzburg must at least be about seventy to eighty miles apart. He was under the impression that *Touro* would still take a long time to arrive. When he heard that it had already arrived, he was speechless. Edmund ordered his horse to be harnessed and took off. He rode the whole day without stopping. He did stop at night to take rest for a few hours. He refreshed the horse and resumed his journey again at the crack of dawn. Edmund reached Eddington a little after noon. Had he followed the main road, it would have taken him longer. As he occasionally chose crosscuts, he reached relatively quickly.

Two things kept bothering Edmund along the way. A horde of non-native coolies must have descended from that ship; what sort of habits would they have? How would we remember their names? What would their food habits be like? How would we understand their talk? God alone knew what language they spoke. How would he manage them single-handed? He had no staff, no office, and no furniture. Even recording their identification features would be a problem. Without such a record, even identification would be a problem. They were carrying nothing except their *girmit.* Even the *girmit*s had only their thumb-impressions. A few of them did have signatures, but the writing was strange indeed.

When Edmund arrived, Allen was already there. 'Hello, Edmund,' he said, the moment he sighted Edmund: 'So late! They are stuck on board. They keep breaking into noisy protests from time to time. As far as I am concerned, I know nothing about them.'

'I don't know much more either, Allen! I have nothing except their *girmit*s.'

'The ship has to go into quarantine first. Only then will they be able to disembark.'

'Aren't the Health Department people here yet?'

'They've been here since yesterday. They aren't letting a single person get off.'

'The Health Department certification is of course obligatory before they can get off.'

'But they have to be unloaded first. How else can they be examined otherwise? Who knows how many of them are there? In what condition? In my opinion, they must first land on the terra firma.'

'The numbers I have are based on the *girmit*s. There are three hundred and forty-two *girmit*s. I have no knowledge how many have died during the journey. I've heard when they start dying, they die like rats.'

It was only after a lot of entreaty on the part of Edmund that the Health Department allowed the passengers of *Touro* to disembark. It was, however, made clear that no passenger would leave the spot. They would be handed over to Edmund only after a thorough examination. Edmund agreed to each of their conditions. Only after an agrrement with the Health Department could Edmund start sending his boats to fetch the coolies. The boats positioned themselves beside the ship. Ropes were dangled from the ship. They would descend directly into the boats with the help of the ropes. There were children, women, and of course men. When they were told that they had to use the ropes to descend, they started to cry and wail as if they were being led to their execution or to be drowned into the sea. Their wailing drowned all other sounds. It was not possible to make them see reason.

Women tied the smaller kids to their waists and took to the ropes. The bigger kids were with the men. Every moment they felt the rope would slip from their hands and they would crash into the sea. Strange sounds emanated from them even as they slid down the ropes. Tears overflowed. Sometimes it appeared there were more tears than sea water around the place. People standing on the shore were watching this 'spectacle on the high seas' as if a play was being rehearsed. Even after the passengers had landed safely their sobs were unabated, especially those of women and children. Even as they cried themselves, they also tried to console the others.

A strange scene presented itself when the boats beached. Whites and natives had collected on the beach in good numbers. They were watching the boats keenly as if the gates of a zoo were about to open and disgorge varieties of animals. The people who actually emerged however were neither animals nor people of their kind. A mixture of surprise and disappointment washed over their faces. They found the newcomers quite ridiculous, resembling neither the whites nor the natives, now laughing and now crying. Their kids had protruding stomachs and sunken eyes. Some of the women were like that too. When they laughed, their teeth covered their faces from ear to ear. When they cried, they sniffed and snorted a lot. Their language was impenetrable. Only God could understand the sounds they produced and the meanings they tried to convey. They spoke so fast that it reminded you of an expert tailor's scissors snipping its way through cloth. Safe landing on the shores had of course produced a sense of relief on their faces, but traces of apprehension were still intact. You never knew what to expect next. The best thing of course was that they were impervious to what others were feeling and thinking about them; otherwise things would have been much worse for them. The way they flopped around, it suggested they were wearing outsize shoes.

A few of them wore Arab-style turbans on their heads. Their cheekbones were very prominent and shone from afar. Some of them had their hair tucked in. They walked stuck close to each other as if to separate would mean to lose your way. They wore colourful clothes, especially the women. The women's eyes were large, a little downcast and beautiful. One could read anxiety and uncertainty all over their faces. 'This is no place for us to be,' they seemed to be thinking. The kids, delicate, curious, handsome, like wilted flowers, held in spindly arms, gawked, as if they wanted to find out all that there was to know just by looking. They played with their mothers' long and thick hair, like tangled bushes. They seemed to belong to a different species altogether. The natives and the whites had got to know each other at least a little: each other's habits, lifestyles, joys, and sorrows; but what about these people?

Alone and far from home.

~

The second ship, *Belvedere*, reached Durban a few days after *Touro*. It came from Calcutta.There were three hundred and ten coolies on *Belvedere.* It was smaller than *Touro*. The passengers had been packed in it like sardines. There was restricted supply of drinking water aboard the ship. One or two sips were all that a coolie was allowed to slake his thirst. A small cabin had been converted into a hospital. A curtained area was the toilet where they answered the calls of nature. Bath was a rare event, and this bothered the coolies the most. They could skip a meal, but craved for a wash. They could have shower only when the ship cast anchor and the shore was close by.

At times passengers would cry out even in sleep. Even if one passenger screamed, everyone ran scared. Scare was so widespread that they seemed to be looking for excuses to get scared. One night, a doctor dragged a woman to his cabin. She screamed and people got up. But when they saw the doctor, they held back.

'She has a fit,' said the doctor.

Her husband too was begging the doctor to let her go but the doctor was unmoved. Others were too frightened to speak. They'd been told that if a ship's official was displeased, he could get you thrown over board. Better save one's own life, they thought. Right at the start, the ship's staff filled fear in people's hearts by telling them all kinds of stories. 'So and so was pushed overboard; even his body was not recovered.' Such stories left the passengers petrified. They couldn't figure out what to do: stay aboard or jump overboard.

Another problem was sickness. Every second day, someone got measles, or diarrhoea, or malarial fever. Everyone had to go to the doctor. The doctor gave you a mixture with more water than medicine in it. If you displeased him, you never knew what he might hand you, maybe medicine, maybe something else. Several times, patients had died after taking the medicine. One learnt later that the doctor had been displeased. As a result, the patient had found relief not in medicine but in the sea.

The woman whom the doctor had dragged into his cabin had screamed for a while, then had become still. No one could figure out where her voice had gone.

The ship's captain wrote in his report: 'In such a long voyage, with so many people on board, men and women constantly interacting, such incidents are not unnatural and only to be expected. It's not moral turpitude.' The Captain also said that every care was taken to lodge the women passengers in the rear part of the ship. If there was a single woman, she was lodged with married couples. Similar care was also exercised with single men. A guard is on watch throughout the night. Any single man or woman up to any mischief is never allowed to go scot-free.

The report however made no mention of the woman.

The doctor however went about with his usual airs, bullying the patients. 'Don't take me to be a run-of-the-mill doctor,' he would say. That incident had scarred the relationships so badly that no one could bring himself to speak out. People felt the whole ecology of the place had been wounded with suppressed screams of victims mixed up in it.

~

The first passenger to get off *Touro* was as dark as the natives. A dirty white wrap covered the lower half of his body. His head too was wrapped in a white cloth, like a turban. One could see his pate clearly through the cloth. At first, no one could get his name. Later, it emerged that his companions called him Devaram. A few Christian clergy appeared on the scene soon. They had found out from Edmund who the Christians were in the lot. As chance would have it, the very first passenger was a Christian and a Catholic too. The clergy beat their path to him and sprinkled holy water on him and his family. His wife and kids, following the Indian practice, prostrated themselves before the priests.

Devaram's wife was called Nagiyam. The recorded age was eighteen, but she looked weak and much older. The husband's age was recorded as thirty. The son, Kube, was four and the daughter, Elizabeth, year-and-a-half. She had just about learnt how to stand on her feet.

The next family to disembark looked as if it was walking straight out of the pages of the Old Testament. It was Abraham and his family. Abraham's registered age was thirty-six but he looked fifty. He sported shepherd-style beard and mustache. His wife, Sarah, aged thirty. Three sons, Isaac, Yakub, and Orlando, were ten, eight, and five respectively. Daughter Rachel was a little older than Devaram's daughter, Elizabeth. In the documents, her name had been entered as 'Regal'. Rachel had of course no inkling of it; in fact even her parents and brothers didn't know anything about it. If they did, perhaps 'Regal' would have become 'Rachel'. The way it happened, she stayed 'Rachel' in life and 'Regal' in the records.

Medical examination over, the two families were sent to the barracks which Allen had got ready. White farmers, big and small, arrived with their retinue to pick up coolies of their choice in the same style as people go to animal fairs to buy elephants, horses, camels or cattle. Some coolies were lucky; they were picked up in the very first round. The first coolie to find a master was Sheikh Ibrahim. His serial number in the roster was forty-nine. When his master left with him in tow, people of the barracks watched him as if God's messengers were carrying him to paradise on a plane. Sheikh himself was behaving as if a caparisoned thoroughbred was being escorted by a musical band, a thoroughbred fully conscious of his pedigree and of the honour bestowed on him. In any case, he was the healthiest of all the coolies. It was the railway company that had picked him up. Among the buyers of the Indian coolies most belonged to the Natal Railway, sugarcane farmers and hotel owners. Similarly, the first person to get a job in the second lot, which arrived on the *Belvedere,* was Muder Seeba. He was a *Thakur* from Aaraa, though his name sounded Christian. Three hundred coolies who came before him had been left cooling their heels when he was selected.

When they bought the coolies, the masters tested the goods to their satisfaction. The coolie was made to trot like a horse and run with a load on his back, and even had his mouth checked for the number of teeth. They squeezed his muscles and struck at his legs to test endurance. The moment a coolie was selected, silence descended on the place. Like a slowly dying wick, the flicker in the eyes of the people was smothered by smoke. Their knees buckled. There was no will to rise again or to lift the others. They cursed the day they had allowed themselves to be talked into leaving their own country by the agents. Every face they had left behind now called out to them as it swayed on the flowers growing on the plants around them: 'Come back! Come back!' But how could they go back? There was the big ocean to reckon with. Could they take on so much water, so much that if it so decided it could drown the whole earth? Would it spare them? They couldn't cry, nor could they laugh. They stopped looking at themselves and gazed at those whose eyes, across seven seas, were looking for them.

The Devaram and Abraham families had to bide their time in those barracks for three months, waiting for a master. It was perhaps easier to sell foul and rotten stuff than a fully functional man, with two hands, two feet and two eyes. They felt so crushed by this thought they could be the red ants that the jungle tribes crush to make chutney for themselves. Though the responsibility for feeding them till they were taken away by a master rested with the agent, they were lucky to get even one meal a day. Often they went hungry both the times. The adults managed one way or another but the kids cried themselves sick. If sometimes fortune smiled on them, church fathers delivered food for their kids. People of other religions then watched them eat even as their wet tongues slithered over their lips. Especially, Malabar Muslims and the Hindu coolies had no well-wishers around. In addition, they had to put up with humiliation all the time. They didn't know whether to cry or to laugh.

When however they saw any customer approaching, even their hungry stomachs began to sing in anticipation. A gleam appeared in their eyes, even if a blank and black screen of despair hung behind them. In their hearts, the same old script started to unfold: 'Curse the fellow who cast us in this far-off land thousands of miles from home.' But then how could you blame him? You were the one to be caught in the web of greed and temptation. Well, maybe you often went hungry, but you were at home. Here, you were not only hungry but also dying to hear a couple of warm words of your own people.

When the customers came, the coolies made an attempt to assume a posture that would display the biceps of their spindly arms, their muscles and sinews to the best advantage. If someone had some oil or cream, he applied it to his body, not to look dry and desiccated. But though a hungry stomach may still be able to sing, it does not quite make your biceps and sinews taut. When the masters asked a question in their language, they neither understood what was said nor could they provide an answer. If the sirdar happened to be around, some sort of wobbly bridge of communication between the masters and the coolies was set up, otherwise they just picked up the coolie they liked and left. The person who put his thumb impression on the *girmit* turned from a human being into a *girmitiya. Girmitiya* meant work and slavery—a lot of work, slavery and limited rations.

During all this time, Devaram was lost in thought. If his people and the folks of his religion had not cast him out, why would he come this far? After he married Nagiyam, he felt abandoned. He was looking for work all the time. If he found any, they would eat; if not, they would go to bed hungry.

~

The agents were always on the lookout: anyone sick? Starving? Famine some place? Anyone buried in debt? Wherever they located someone, they promptly showed up. In their bags they carried colourful dreams like balloons. They worked on the psychology of the people and layer after layer, they broke down their resistance, handing them a balloon at each step. They loaned them money for food. They gave them old, used clothes. On their very first visit, they served them the dream of a paradise that existed across the seven seas. To Devaram, they unfolded this dream in slow stages: 'There is a country called Natal. It lies across the seven seas. Whites and blacks all live together there. There is so much wealth, so much gold! No one is poor. No one goes to bed hungry!'

Devaram spent his whole day dreaming of the place and thinking about it. Slowly, his mind was made up, his intention ripening like a mango left in straw. When the agent saw that the iron was hot, he struck: 'I can't bear to see the plight of your children any more. Please go. I'll get the company to pay for your ticket and the expenses.' To him, the agent looked like a messenger from God, like someone leading the way in total darkness holding a lighted candle aloft. He looked around him. He felt that if he did not find a way out of it, the fire blazing so fiercely all around him would burn everything to cinders. What would be his options then? This was the time when he could still pull himself and his family out of this fire of hunger and hatred.

One morning, he made it to the agent's house quite early. There were quite a few other people present there. The agent took him aside and said: 'These people are all like you, deep in trouble. How many people can I help? The company I work for is annoyed that I pick up so many people. "This is a company, not a charity," they tell me. "We are not in the business of providing shelter to everyone." But I can't bear to see your misery. It just so happens that I like you. Tell me now what you've decided.'

'I'll go. My wife and children too.'

'Let me make one thing quite clear. If you're single, it's easy to get a job. But getting jobs for the whole family isn't that simple.'

'It's okay, sir. Even if I alone get a job, everyone can be fed. Here we've to go hungry for days.' He almost choked.

'Okay, okay. Don't lose heart. You can all go.'

Devaram was happy. Finally, he was going to the world he had dreamed of. In that world, no one went to bed hungry. There were gold mines. Blacks and whites lived together.

Abraham too had been sweet-talked by the agent into joining the exodus. Like any needy and poor person, he too was in search of a world where no one went to bed hungry and where no one was discriminated against. These agents carried with them a sketch of just such a world and they spread it in front of anyone who seemed to them to be in misery and a victim of injustice, be he a Devaram, an Ibrahim or an Abraham. There was something in that sketch which attracted them in their helpless state like a magnet attracted iron. And they let themselves be pulled without offering any resistance.

~

When the first two batches of coolies arrived on the *Touro* and the *Belvedere*, they had before them a strange and unfamiliar sea coast. The agent who had tempted them with the dream of a golden future was nowhere around; the people were so different, even the soil had a different colour. Like Noah's Ark, the waves of the sea had cast them ashore on a strange continent. Noah at least had his animals, his fellow citizens, and birds, but they were totally alone. They knew the nature of sea-waves: all their life they had seen the waves of their native sea. Those waves had been their friends. As they reached here, those waves had become quite unfamiliar and hostile. You never knew where they would cast you ashore and return laughing to the sea.

One day, a white farmer showed up accompanied by the agent's man. The man first offered him Devaram. Although short, Devaram had a strong physique. The white farmer was Mr. Crompton. The agent's man was trying to sell Devaram as if he was an animal. 'Look, what strong legs! He can walk miles with a ton of stuff. Thick neck, broad shoulders, and chest like that of a wrestler. And so intelligent!' Nagiyam wasn't a bad piece either, whether in her looks or in her body structure.

Mr. Crompton signalled to Devaram to run. Devaram kept running till Crompton asked him to come back. He was out of breath and drenched in sweat. His legs however remained steady.

Mr.Crompton asked about the kids: 'How much do they weigh?'

'Never weighed them.'

Crompton picked up each child like a pup to find out if they were light or heavy, or if they would start bawling.

'What's the diet per person?'

'The question of diet would arise only if there were food available.' Nagiyam couldn't help muttering this time.

The agent's man interpreted it to the white master. He laughed and said, 'They have good weight, the kids. The diet must be good too.'

'No, sir, the weight of poor kids is in their bones. That's what helps them survive.'

'They need rice for their meals. How much rice would five persons need for one meal?'

Devaram said in a whimpering tone, 'Elizabeth is still on mother's milk. How much rice would such a small baby eat anyway?'

'Yes, she's a baby today, but in a year's time she'll eat as much as you do.' Crompton laughed.

It was their lucky day. Bargaining started. After very hard bargaining, it was settled that they would be given half rice and half corn. Crompton would pay forty-four pounds and eight shillings for the whole family annually, although the rate was seven pounds for an adult and three pounds ten shillings for a child. Devaram did not want to let go of the chance, so they promptly agreed to go with him. They were often served boiled corn for meals at the camp too and they had to eat it without a grudge. Beggars could not after all be choosers. In the beginning, the kids made faces but a couple of days without food and they learnt fast that in the matter of food, taste came last. What came first was whether you got a full stomach or not, whether the hunger was satiated or not. If the answer to both the questions was 'yes' the food was tasty on all counts: on count of taste as well as on count of quality.

~

The two families—Devaram and Abraham—wanted to stay together. If they could get the same master, it would become a lot easier to share their joys and sorrows. If one of them got hurt, the other could apply the salve; if one of them lost heart, the other could say a few words of courage. But one doesn't get what one wants, even death, the worst thing one could ask for. He gives it to you only when He wants it. So there was another white who came and collected Abraham's family for thirty-one pounds and six shillings. Some whites found it more economical to hire whole families. That way you could get more work for less money. This white had offered a price of ten pounds, five shillings, and eight pence each for Abraham and Isaac, the eldest son. In the eyes of Indian law, Isaac was ten years old and counted as an adult.

The younger sons, Yakub and Orlando, went for six pounds each. Sarah and Rachel would only get their meals. Sarah was very lean and thin. Their master was called Captain Bishop. The Captain had managed a better bargain than Crompton. Actually the Captain was considered an expert in the matter of coolie trading. Other farmers used to engage his services on such occasions and paid his expenses. The expenses on the Captain were minimal while the savings ran into several pounds.

After spending three months together, the two families separated. They felt as if they were once again leaving their country behind. The two families were like a country now. Both were Malabaris. When they had met at the Eddington Port, the port itself had turned into Malabar for them: same language, same religion, and same identity. Only the land was foreign, but they tended to forget about it. But when they separated, everything once again turned strange to them, except the memories.

The place they were housed in was a cubbyhole in a long barrack covered with a straw roof. All coolies lived here. It was known as Coolie Lines. The whites and other biggies lived in Civil Lines. One advantage of living in Coolie Lines was that you could escape the supervision of the masters for short stretches. You could then devote some time to your household chores. If there was some space in front of the barrack, they planted some vegetables or rice, sometimes even sugarcane.

Devaram's home was no different from that of the others. There was no outlet for the smoke. There was a drain running out in one corner where they had their bath and which they also used as a urinal at night. A stink pervaded the whole house at all times. At first, even children felt nauseated. With time, they got used to it. Behind every cubbyhole there was a pit. All the water from the drain collected in the pit. Mosquitoes buzzed their way in through the drain. At times, if someone in the family happened to be sick, he was allowed to use the corner as a toilet too. Of course, things had gone so far now that they didn't feel at home unless the stink and the mosquitoes were in place.

Crompton had a very large sugarcane farm. Large farms had sugar mills attached to them. Language presented a permanent problem for the coolies, whether talking among themselves or with the masters. The Indian coolies themselves spoke different languages. Devaram's was the only Malabari family. They had picked up a few Hindustani words. The masters of course spoke English. They were not concerned whether the coolies understood their language or not: if they didn't, they'd be the ones to suffer. The masters got mad at the coolies. Sirdar was the only go-between who understood both parties and interpreted one to the other. He issued commands on behalf of the master, kept the coolies on a tight leash, foul-mouthed them, and even handed out punishment.

Devaram and his family worked twelve hours a day in the fields. First they prepared the land. The soil was dug up. This was Devaram's job. There were others too. Then drains were laid out and manure was spread out evenly. Women workers cut eighteen-inch lengths of sugarcane. When cutting sugarcane, one had to be careful that the eye of the cane was not damaged. If the eye was lost, the fertility of the sugarcane was lost, that is, the cane was lost. The sugarcane lengths were then spread out on the ground at equal distances. The eye was to face upwards, as that's where the plant budded. Then the weeds were removed, using a trowel. Nagiyam was very skilled at this job. The children too had picked up all the jobs. Elizabeth was still too young. She either just played around the place or slept on a hammock rigged up by tying a piece of cloth between two tree trunks.

Many times when Devaram returned from work tired, he said to Nagiyam, 'If I ever come across that agent I will ask him: "You'd promised to send me to a country where no one went to bed hungry; so how come you sent me to a country where I have neither food nor any identity? All that I have is humiliation and constant worry."'

Nagiyam had just one comment for every moment of sorrow: 'It's all Mother Mary's will.' She would start speaking like Hindus: 'This land was calling us, so how could we have stayed back? If we are fated to live here, we have to do what people here do.'

The children often remembered Abraham Uncle and his family. They would ask: 'Will we ever see Abraham Uncle, Isaac, Yakub,

Orlando and Auntie again?' When they received no answer, they were disappointed.

'Mom, how sweet they were—Isaac, Yakub, Auntie, weren't they?'

Nagiyam just gave a nod. She was reminded of her country and her people. Then she thought: 'Poor kids. How'd they know how much one has to leave behind in life, never to find it again? If He wants us to meet them again, He'll arrange it,' she would mutter, as if consoling herself.

Nagiyam had never liked working with mud and clay. At times when work on the farm was slack, she was assigned to serve at Crompton's house or to work at the sugar mill, digging up earth, mixing it with water, and kneading it, making bricks, drying them, and then baking them. When construction work was on, she had to prepare the cement mix. The master could not bear to see the workers sitting idle. Moreover there was no proper communication between the masters and the slaves. Anyone who understood the masters' language was the boss. The sirdars functioned as the eyes and ears of the master. The whole colony functioned like this. Everything was done in the name of the government in London. The sirdars of London were running the show.

~

Karanpillay was also a coolie. He worked on another farm a little distance from Crompton's farm. He fell sick. The rules said the master of the farm must maintain a sick-room, but everywhere the sick-room turned into a store-room. The white masters were of the view that the coolies did not need a sick-room since they were a sturdy lot. Many farms simply did not have a sick-room at all or any arrangement for a doctor. The sirdars themselves handed out pills on behalf of the master. The coolies too had come to believe that sick-room meant 'death-room'. The master's men themselves arranged this belief to be entrenched in the minds of the coolies so that they on their own became dead set against the sick-room. The masters anyway took any pleas of illness as excuses for shirking work. The *girmit*, they argued, was for work, not for illness. The five-year *girmit* had no provision for rest. The masters had to extract as much work as possible. At the end of five years, the workers could live or die as they chose. But the five years belonged to us! Life or death could claim the rest!

Karanpillay was getting worse by the day. He could barely walk. Two steps and he would begin to heave like the bellows. He became restless. The legs were getting swollen. On that particular day, he was worse than usual. He set out to work but staggered and fell. When he did not report to work, the sirdar arrived fuming: 'Where's Pillay?'

Karanpillay lay on the ground. He tried to speak but could not. Sirdar ordered his men: 'Pick him up and take him along. The scoundrels want a free ride! Malingerers!'

Karanpillay and his family pleaded with the sirdar, went down on their knees before him but he didn't budge an inch. They heaved Karan onto a stretcher and took him. At the site, he was still unable to get up. A report was filed against him accusing him of shirking work and violating the conditions of the *girmit.* He was prosecuted. The white lawyer could make out only part of what he said. White lawyers did not pay much attention to what the coolies said since they didn't have enough money to pay their fees. Their cases often went by default and they were handed punishment *ex parte.* That's what happened with Karan too. He was sentenced to fourteen days' hard labour.

In the jail, Karanpillay pleaded with every warder. He was sick, he couldn't move, his whole body was inflated. But the jailer shut him up with: 'The scoundrels are getting fat on free food, and they tell me it is swelling.'

Karan tried to explain, 'Give me some light work, something I can do sitting.'

'This is a jail, not you father's home,' he was told.

Karan was eventually given whatever work had been planned for him or whatever was covered by 'hard labour'. He just couldn't do it. The warders got tougher with him and one day Pillay collapsed. The warder was a native. The natives only repeated what the whites said. He came and kicked Pillay a couple of times. Karanpillay fell into a trough of water. 'Drink and be fresh!' The warder laughed and moved away.

Karanpillay lay in the trough for some time. When he was finally taken out, his pulse had slowed down considerably. In a little while, he lost control of his limbs. Actually, Karan too had come on the *Touro* with Devaram, but he beat Devaram to a job, although he was No. 99 on the list. Though often sick, Karan was always happy. Very sincere in his work, he had the knack of keeping his supervisors in good humour too.

Devaram was informed that Karanpillay had died in jail; that he had lain in water and no one had bothered to take him out. He had died in water. For several days, Devaram went around saying, 'What happened to Pillay can happen to anyone of us.' No one got it that Karan was a heart patient. How could anyone? He was a poor man after all.

Nagiyam had only one point to make: 'There aren't too many ways for a poor man to die. Why mourn? We all are destined to die the same way. Don't lose heart.'

But for many, many days Karanpillay kept rearing his head in the mind of everyone in that house. For Devaram especially, he had become a synonym for every coolie.

~

II

The Indian coolies had become commodities for sale and purchase much before *Touro* and *Belvedere* landed in South Africa. They were already being exported to places as far as North America.

Those were the days of voyages. The sea was the only route one could take to other countries. People died, ships sank, but the few who survived made it to their destination. The ship *Sudderingham,* laden with coolies, was on its way to Mauritius. The ocean on one side of Mauritius was so calm that it was like a mother stroking her baby to sleep; on the other side, it was so rowdy that it appeared as if millions of rocks had sprouted in the bed of the ocean, all bent upon shattering the ocean's pride and the ocean was hitting back at them with all its might.

That day the sea was in a nasty mood. The waves roared and roared. As the ship, with a load of coolies on board, nudged its way in, they were in a fury: 'Look at its impudence,' they seemed to be saying. 'It dares to intrude on our solitude!' And they let loose their full force on the ship. This was almost the beginning of the seventeenth century. The ship found itself surrounded by a storm as if it was not an ocean but a siege laid by an enemy from which it was unable to find the way out. A hole appeared in the ship. Water rushed in as if from a spring. The water level kept rising. At first, the sailors tried to pitch the water out, but when they realized that the water was unstoppable, the captain as well as others took to the boats and scurried like rats leaving the ship.

The Chief Officer told the Captain: 'This is your ship. If you leave it, it'll be orphaned with no one to look after it.'

The Captain begged for mercy: 'Please let me go. I have small kids.'

'And who will be responsible for all these lives?' Before the Chief Officer could complete his sentence, the Captain was in the boat and the boat was on its way to the shore. The Chief Officer looked at the sky and then at the coolies, who had staked their lives trying to save the ship. The women and the kids were in a bad shape. He muttered softly: 'It is Thy will, Lord. How can I leave them to die?' And he plunged into the effort.

Suddenly, there was a noise in the ship. A part of the ship had broken off. Nineteen men were swept away in the strong current. About a hundred persons survived. They floated away in different directions on planks which had broken off from the ship. Sometimes they disappeared behind the waves and then came in sight again.The Chief Officer still stood on the sinking ship, performing the duties of his Captain. Whenever a part of the ship and the people sitting on it swam into view, he waved at them. Goodbye! In his hands he had a musical instrument, which he used to play at odd times of day and night. Now as the ship was going down, he played the instrument, his eyes closed.

The other ship, *Fusilier*, was sailing to Africa with its merchandise of coolies. It was sailing and the sea was letting it sail. All of a sudden its cold waves turned into countless flaming tongues of fire. It started dancing, bouncing the *Fusilier* here and there as children bounce balls. The Captain and the seamen had no clue as to what the sea was suddenly up to. The shore was drifting away. The waves seemed to have made up their mind that, no matter what, this insolent object must never be allowed to make it to the shore. The ship cried out, in its countless voices, to be forgiven only this once: 'O God of the waves, please pardon my error!' But no one was listening. The sea was ready to hit the sky. It had gone completely mad. Suddenly, *Fusilier* broke into two. Like pomegranate seeds, seamen and coolies were flung all over the surface of the sea. A good proportion of the coolies had been wiped out by an epidemic during the journey. Those who had succumbed had been buried at sea. The survivors had thought that they might be able to find their destination.

This incident had taken place a little distance from Durban, in the Bay of Retal.

That night, the Bay had been very agitated. A little way up from the Bay, there was a big farm owned by a Dutchman. He had got a number of barracks made for his coolies on the farm itself. The farm being at a higher level, the waters of the Bay did not reach it and the people there were safe. Even so, even a little disturbance in the Bay set the poor coolies on edge. That night too, the strong winds in the Bay had kept them awake throughout. You didn't know when the barrack roofs might be blown away in the wind, leaving you standing under the open sky. One of the coolies peeped out of the window to get a measure of the sea and the wind and saw lights scattered over the surface of the sea. He thought they were spirits and was scared stiff. He called out to his fellow men: 'Look, what are those lights in the sea?'

Normally, the fellow men would not have responded to his call, but when they heard what he had to say they quickly gathered around him. Fire, water and wind had them badly rattled. Water and wind particularly had been behaving as if there was going to be no tomorrow. In a short while, they could also hear people screaming. These were perhaps screams of people in their last fight to save their lives. Their screams spoke of a fear of death and a strong craving for life. It was hard to say which element was stronger. The voices also sounded familiar.

One of the coolies spoke out: 'These are no evil spirits; they are people like you and me who are in deep trouble.'

'Maybe, like us, they are also being transported here as coolies?'

Everyone was in a fix. No one knew what to do, how to save the people. The storm and the waves were so strong that merely to think was to be surrounded by a quicksand, a bog which, with the slightest opening of its mouth, swallowed a person whole. The voices were slowly dying down. The lights too had been going, going, and finally gone.

'Where are they all gone? What happened to the voices?'

They didn't have any answers to these questions. The coolies had a sirdar. An Indian and the master's spoilt favourite. He had picked up their language. He was now as stone-hearted as any flunkey who happens to be the master's favourite. Nevertheless, he called three or four coolies who were known to be fast walkers and commanded them: 'Go at once to the master's villa. Inform him that a ship loaded with coolies has sunk offshore.'

The rain and the wind were so fierce that one's body shook and shivered like a leaf. Any conversation was out of the question. A command and its compliance are two different things. The former has language, the latter has none. It is simply compliance. The coolies left. If they took two steps forward, they were pushed back two steps. So they tried to take three steps forward, so that they had the satisfaction of having taken at least one step towards the villa. As protection against rain, they carried a leafy umbrella, which the wind almost succeeded in blowing away. But they kept walking. In their ears, there still echoed the screams and the dying voices that floated with the lights they had seen on the surface of the sea. Before them was the wind, beneath their feet the water-ravaged, faded earth. From time to time they fell, and then steadied themselves; at times they stopped, then started walking again, sometimes they chattered and wheezed.

By the time they arrived at the master's villa, it was almost midnight. Cold and fatigued, they could barely stand. It was fortunate that they were now under a shade in the rear of the villa. Here the wind and water did not torment them as much as they had done all along the way. They were quite safe. But sometimes being moved to safety from the absence of safety itself becomes a cause for misery. They were now shivering very badly. But duty stood before them like a fierce animal: you either did your duty or you died for it.

The question was how to wake up the master. How could a mere coolie dare to disturb the master in his sleep? You could afford to displease God once, but displease a white master you couldn't. There was only one saving grace: the sirdar's message. They had been here before with the sirdar's messages, but never so late at night.

One of them, in a voice so low that even a sleeping wall would not be disturbed by it, said, 'The master is very kind. Maybe when he hears of the death of so many people he will not be annoyed and will forgive us.'

'Yes, and if we go back without delivering sirdar's message, we'll annoy the sirdar. Annoying the slave is always more dangerous than annoying the king.'

'When the master gets to know later that we went away without delivering the message, he'll have us cut to pieces and served to his dogs. The sirdar will have to wait his turn.'

One of them was a Tamil speaker. He had been keeping quiet. Although each one of the four spoke a different language, the thousands of miles that separated them from their homeland and the realization that they were all slaves had so united their hearts that language was no longer a problem. Although they did not understand each other, yet they understood each other quite well.

There was no let up in the rain yet. Even as they stood under the shade of the villa, scenes of misery, their own, and their people's, swam before their eyes. God knows how many of them had survived, and in what condition, if at all. They were all impatient to get back as soon as their work was done.

A few masters had bells installed in their villas for the coolies. The bells were supposed to be proof of their kindness and love of fair play. They showed that they were always ready to listen to the coolies. The coolies stood there watching the bell for a long time. There were flares burning all around them. Their shivering bodies were now getting a little warm.

The Tamil speaker spoke for the first time, 'Let me pull the bell string. I am single. There's little chance that I'll ever be able to return home across the seas again. There's no one waiting for me here either.' The way he said it, with his expression and his gestures, all the three of them could understand perfectly what he meant. His eyes were moist. A few of the flares that were not shielded against the wind had gone out and were smoking. The smoke got into the eyes.

He stepped forward and tugged at the rope a couple of times. His face shone with a sense of achievement. He was happy. The others were stricken dumb with fright.

Nothing stirred for a little while. The master must be sound asleep, they thought. Suddenly, the door opened and they shrank back as if a lion was to appear before them.

'Who is it?' asked the master in his language.

The seniormost *girmitiya* among them could understand a good deal of their language. He stood with his head bowed down in salute and said:

'It's us, master.'

'What happened?'

In broken language, the man conveyed the matter: 'A ship seems to have sunk near the Bay of Retal. There were people screaming. From their screams it appeared the ship was ferrying coolies. The sirdar has sent us to inform you.'

'Any survivors?'

'It happened some distance offshore. We couldn't tell because of the rain and the storm. We could only hear screams. They were crying out for help.'

The master's Dutch wife now made her entry. She was shaking with anger. If she had a cane in her hand, she'd have skinned them. She shouted in rage, 'Shoot the bastards dead. Black dogs! How dare they disturb us in our sleep in the middle of the night?'

The master signalled her to be quiet: 'Please let us talk. A ship ferrying coolies has sunk off the farm in the Bay of Retal.'

'Let the rats perish.'

'They are human beings too. We can use them, if a few of them survive. We'll get a good price for them.' He paused before going on: 'You don't know. An Indian coolie is like a machine. Put him to work anywhere and he'll not budge till he's done.'

'Don't tell me you're planning to rush to save the rats at this time of the night. Those foul creatures! You must be mad!'

'You want to sleep, go ahead. I'm sorry that your sleep was disturbed. Please let me do my work. Whichever way I look at it, I see a good opportunity here.'

She stamped back to her room, gathering her gown behind her. The master turned to his dressing room to get ready.

The fury of the storm was now beginning to ebb.

The four coolies stood outside in the same state, waiting for their orders. No instructions had been issued to them yet. Should they wait or leave? In a short while, the master's horse carriage suddenly pulled up before them. The carriage had eight horses in harness. Two horsemen preceded the carriage, two followed it. The coachman was a white, and to them he too looked like a sahib. They bowed to him in salute. The coachman was fully draped in a mackintosh. The horses too wore capes. The coolies were barely covered. The coach was enclosed on all sides.

The master took his seat in the coach and the coach started. The coolies ran behind the coach. The coach jolted and bounced because of the rain and the mud. The birds nesting in the trees fluttered up and screeched repeatedly at the sounds of the coach and the horses. The horsemen who led the coach each carried a flare in his hand that it was a struggle to keep burning. If one of the flares went out, the horseman lit it with the help of the other one. The two horsemen were having a hard time keeping the flares alight, but they still managed to do it. On either side of the carriage, there was a lantern which contained a lighted candle. The two lanterns burned in tandem along side the carriage as if they were security guards. The rear horsemen were having a better time than the front ones. The coolies of course had the worst of it. They not only had to keep running but had also to fight the enemy weather. The rain sometimes lashed hard, sometimes slowed down a bit. There was a slack in the wind, but a gale-begotten wind still had some pace. Mud, of course, reigned everywhere. Actually, if rain contributes to anything it is mud or weeds. Emaciated, with half-fed stomachs and an enemy of a weather, the coolies ran behind the master's carriage. With so much breath that the chest could hardly hold it. The only difference was that running gave them the energy to fight the cold. If they stopped occasionally, the cold seized them. They had often to run like this behind the white master's coach. Whenever the coachmen lashed out with the whip, their bodies shrank as if it was they that had received the whiplash.

The master had shut himself up in the coach and lay fast asleep.

The sky was getting light blue when the coach rolled into the farm. The rain had stopped. The clouds were holding their position at the front and could start trouble any time. The agitation of the Bay had subsided somewhat. Wherever the waves had touched, they had left their mark. The marks that water and time make, it is said, are hard to erase.

The barracks in the Coolie Lines had taken the full brunt of the storm. They lay in ruins. The children and the adults all lay under the trees. No one was able to tell, and no one could understand, how they might have spent the night. They had had the experience and they were now being tossed about in the sour and sweet waves of that experience. A few young men had found shelter on top of mounds; others in caves and thick groves.

The master got down and looked around, sizing up the situation. The sirdar was following him. The master muttered, 'It was a fierce storm.'

The coolies had not yet arrived. The sirdar pointed towards the site: 'A ship sank there.'

The master focused his eyes at the spot: 'It does look like something has sunk there. Looks like the top of a sail.'

The amount of mud made the spot inaccessible, especially for the master.

'How many boats are around?'

Without waiting for the sirdar's reply, the master continued: 'Put them all to water. The coolies must be saved.'

'It's been hours. I wonder if anyone is alive now.'

The master said nothing, but he was firm.

The boats were launched. It was not as if the waves were lifeless now. They tried to stop the boats with all their might. They bounced them like balls in the hands of naughty kids, from wave to wave. Sometimes waves loomed up like walls and hid the boats. Then it looked as if a falcon had grabbed a bird in flight. The Dutch master was watching the boats intently as if the line of his sight was tied to them.

By now the four coolies had also staggered in. In their thoroughly mud-splattered state it was hard to recognize them.

The master asked, 'When did the ship sink?'

'The sun had gone down. Kitchen fires had been lighted. So strong were the wind and the rain that the kitchen fire kept going out. The kids were crying out for sleep. That was when the screams of the drowning people rose like a blazing fire.' The senior coolie had spoken in his broken Dutch. The sirdar refurbished and refined the language as much he could for the benefit of the master.

The master turned to the sirdar: 'Tell them all to leave. They are producing strange sounds.' Perhaps he never had occasion before to observe people shivering with cold, that's why the chattering of their teeth appeared strange to him.

As the master looked away, he again addressed the coolies: 'Go and ask the boatmen also to put their boats to water. They'll be paid per head for every person pulled out of water. More if pulled out alive.'

Many of them put their boats to water.

The Dutch master was right. The masts could still be seen protruding out of water. The boats looked for those drowned around them. A few bodies were stuck in the ship. Had they arrived a little later, the bodies would also have sunk to the bottom with the ship. Whatever bodies they could recover, they brought to the shore on their boats. If they didn't have nets, even these bodies would have remained unrecovered. They were all coolies. When they saw the bodies, the coolies present were reminded of their own voyage. They couldn't help feeling that they too could well have met the same fate. It was the grace of God that they had landed ashore. Not that the sea would have been any worse than this life. They were all very keen to see the faces of the dead bodies: who could tell if there might be someone among them from their own village headed here in search of a living, like themselves.

Among the dead bodies, several belonged to budding youth with fresh downy growth. Like Sindbad, they had set out on the voyage as a challenge. Now they lay on the ground, so still and innocent-looking, as if they never had anyone in the world who they could call their own, or who could call them their own. No one even knew where they had come from or where they were going. If there was anyone at all who could laugh with them or cry for them, it was the coolies. Deep inside them, the coolies felt that they were their own kith and kin, and therefore they must now do whatever had to be done. The search for a living had brought them this far! There isn't a place man leaves unexplored in his search to escape hunger and find food. He neither escapes hunger nor finds food. Death finds him instead. They all have faces but no names. It might have been different if someone knew who their parents were, what place or village they came from, but now it was as if they had fallen from the skies and into the sea. There were as many opinions as there were heads.

One of the boatmen found a leather bag floating on the waves. He handed it over to his Dutch master. It contained a few papers. Looking through them, he found that it was the Captain's coffer. Possibly, it contained the passengers' names, but who was going to read it? The Captain had gone down with the ship.

~

The morning had reached its highest point. The darkness of the night had been rinsed off completely. Whites from the neighbouring farms had also appeared on the scene. They had slept through the night of storm and the cries of drowning people undisturbed. They were laughing at their Dutch colleague; 'You lost your sleep, and so much money—all for these people?'

'They must mean a lot to you?'

'Suppose there is a fire in the forest tomorrow and the mushrooms catch fire, will you try to save them or will you burn yourself with them?'

The Dutchman said, 'The ship could have sunk anywhere, I wouldn't have bothered. But it came and sank in the Bay of Retal. That is a bad omen.'

The hearts of coolies standing around, especially of those who were familiar with the incident, were heavy with anguish. They had always said that those who perish this way never cease to exist for their near and dear ones living in the far-away country, who spend all their life waiting for that one day when, having made a lot of money, they would return. Kids grow up into old men and die, and even in their death-bed nurse the hope of their return. This strange illusion holds back the voyager from the far-away land from death, and keeps him alive—always.

The air was getting thicker with the stench. Dead bodies lay piled up one on top of another. No one had seen so many corpses together at one place. A few were stiff, a few swollen, while some had their faces flattened. Bodies had turned into rocks. There were a couple of kids too whose bodies had bloated. Women who never let their *pallu* slip were now indifferent to all the body parts. Some had their limbs chewed off by water animals. One corpse had an eye missing. In its place was a hole filled with mud and filth. The other eye was swollen so big that it looked like small, featureless face in itself. Another body had its nose and part of its lips chewed off. One woman had her breasts bitten off in places. All this had happened in a very short time.

The Dutchman, with a piece of cloth covering his nose, walked around examining the corpses, while the rest stood around with folded hands. When he had made his rounds, he told them, 'Go and get the horse carts from the farm. Load these bodies and take them to the farm.'

They were puzzled. What was master going to do with the corpses? Grudgingly, they dragged the corpses. Among them there were Muslims as well Hindus. The scuff marks the dragging left on the ground were scraping the coolies' hearts. The Dutch master kept a close watch at the proceedings.

A little later, he dispatched a few of them with spades and pickaxes to dig holes and trenches: 'Respect for the dead is a part of our religion. Burying them respectfully is better than letting them be eaten up by birds and beasts.' The Hindu coolies wanted the Hindus to be cremated but no one dared to make the suggestion to the master. Inability to make the suggestion was causing them a strange anxiety: they felt helpless and distressed. They were doing what they were told. Sometimes they felt as if they were themselves the corpses and they were dragging themselves too. At times a face seemed to them to resemble that of a relative or a friend.

A cheroot stuck in his mouth, the master supervised the disposal of the corpses. So thick was the moustache on his lips that it was hard to say whether he was laughing or sobbing. There were no *shloka*s being recited, no *fatiha* being read and no padre around. Having buried the corpses, the coolies laid down their pickaxes and stood around quietly for sometime.

Even the pickaxes had fallen silent.

When the master approached his wife, she snapped, 'Keep your distance! You smell of those coolies. I shall not allow this smell into the villa.'

'But I didn't even touch them!'

'They smell worse than dead rats.'

'But how hard they work! Living, they help grow crops, now they'll help them multiply even when dead!'

~

III

Mohandas too had his dreams. These were the dreams that had taken him to London to study law. But when he arrived in Natal, his dreams already lay in ruins. However, he had not accepted defeat. Like pieces of cream in an ill-washed pan, bits and pieces of his dreams still stuck to him. He did not wish to scrape them off. He would gather together the remains of his shattered dreams, plant them again and gather a new crop. He had done something similar with the remnants of his dreams. He was twenty-four then.

When he disembarked at Eddington port, he knew nothing at all. He didn't know where he was supposed to go, what sort of country it was or what sort of life it was going to be for him. However, unsure though he was, he was not lacking in determination. Decked up in a felt hat, frock coat, trousers, necktie and a pair of shiny shoes, his clothes made him look like a white every inch. In fact, anyone seeing him could be forgiven at least once for thinking: here comes another white man. Of course, his colour and his manner of speech did not quite confirm his status as a white man. The people who had come to receive him included a white, a Parsi and a Muslim. This also confirmed that he wasn't a white.

When he came out, it was these three he saw first, especially Dada Abdullah. He was wearing the dress of a Gujarati Muslim, a black and white beard, and a same style turban. The Parsi wore a long coat and a traditional Parsi round cap. The white of course was a white. Dada Abdullah had also guessed that he was looking at the barrister his brother had sent.

Mohandas made the first move: 'Dada Abdullah?'

'Gandhibhai!'

The first person to whom Dada Abdullah introduced him was the Parsi gentleman: 'Parsi Rustomji is a leading businessman, and a prominent member of the Indian community locally.' Then he turned to the white gentleman, who was looking at Mohandas quizzically in the true manner of a white gentleman: 'This is Mr. Marcel Ledue, a French businessman.'

Mohandas shook hands with him. Under the breath, Dada Abdullah whispered, 'What am I going to do with this white elephant?'

Mohandas looked at him.

Parsi Rustomji said: 'You are a Gujarati, aren't you?'

Mohandas took the hint. Without letting him finish the sentence, he replied, 'Yes, but this is my usual attire.'

'You are sharp …,' Parsi Rustomji laughed.

'Not quite!' He replied, looking at Dada Abdullah.

Ledue laughed a funny laugh. Mohandas observed him very carefully.

~

Abdullah Karim Jhaveri looked after the affairs of Dada Abdullah Co. in Porbandar. He was a partner in the company and also a relative, in fact, Dada Abdullah's brother. And, of course, he was a Muslim. It was he who had written to Mohandas's brother, Lakshmidas, to send his brother to Natal.

Lakshmidas took Mohandas to Jhaveri. Jhaveribhai was a talkative person. As he ushered them in very respectfully, he addressed himself to Mohandas: 'Look here, young man, you are very dear to me. I am very friendly with a number of English people in Natal. If you go and meet them and mix with them, you'll gain influence with them. If you have influence with the English, there is nothing that you can't accomplish.'.

Mohandas heard him out quietly. He wanted to say that he was going there to do a job and not to make friends with the whites. But since both of them were his seniors, he didn't open his mouth.

Jhaveribhai continued in the same vein: 'You can be of use to us; after all, you are like a member of the family. You can take care of the official communication, which is all in English. You'll be our guest there. You won't have to spend a penny. Everything is on us.'

Mohandas shoved aside all this talk like so much moss on the surface of water and went directly to the point: 'For how long, and how much?'

'For as long as you wish, and as much as you wish,' was Jhaveri's initial offer.

'I'd appreciate it if you could tell me yourself.'

So he had to tell it: 'Salary one hundred and five pounds per year. First class travel. We of course have our own ships.'

Mohandas spoke very softly, 'Please give me some time to think it over.'

Lakshmidas tried to break in: 'What is there to think about? Take it.'

Jhaveribhai, with his eyes fixed at Mohandas' face, said, 'Let him think it over, Lakshmibhai. A job that's well-thought out is a job that lasts.'

At Rajkot, in a way, Mohandas was at home, though he was born at Porbandar. Ever since his father, Kaba Gandhi, had migrated to Rajkot as the Diwan of the state, he had been living here. He had seen Kaba Gandhi's times, and now he was seeing the modern times. Practising at Rajkot, Mohandas was particularly troubled by one thing. A tax, *vighoti,* was levied on farmers. The rights of the ruler had also been curtailed. Mohandas was handling these two cases. The clients who had secured Mohandas' services were impressed by the fact that he was a barrister who had passed out from London and whose father, uncle, grandfather had all been prime ministers of the state. Being from a family of prime ministers, he was sure to be heard when he presented their cases before the administrator. The officer before whom the cases were to be argued, although an Indian, was deeply dyed in English colours. It was he who had appointed the administrator to hear the cases.

Mohandas had worked hard on the cases. He was confident that the judgment would favour his clients. However, the verdict was exactly opposite. The farmers received no relief at all, though they were the ones most in need of relief. The farmers had not expected that Mohandas' arguments would be brushed aside so completely, even though he had made relief for the farmers his sole aim.

Mohandas observed that, although an Indian, the administrator beat the English hollow in rudeness. He delivered his judgment without even listening to Mohandas' arguments. The ruler's privileges had certainly been enhanced but the farmers were going to derive little benefit from that.

A cat, they say, growls harder at another cat. The Indian officer had done the most damage to the rights of other Indians. Mohandas felt defeated. It hurts a soldier most when he loses without a fight.

~

Mohandas brought the matter up with Kastur, his wife. He showed her Jhaveri's letter and told her the details. Then he asked for her opinion.

'The children will miss you. You have hardly spent any time with them all these years.'

'And you ...?'

Kastur just smiled.

'But, listen, Kastur, what should I stay here for? I know I have shortcomings. The way the officers here shift their eyes to see me, it seems to me it'll make no difference to them whether I stay here or not. How hard I had worked in the farmers' case! Yet, what was the result? How can I stay here after that? If I cannot help win even a just case, what use is it for me stay in Rajkot?'

'I don't think you should go at this point.'

'But how long can I be a burden on my brother? After all, it's just a matter of one year. It'll pass just like that.'

'You're happy to do a clerk's job there?'

'I don't have even that here ... I have decided I'll go. Please stand by me. You and *Ba* had both supported me when I went to London. *Ba* is no more. Only you and my brother.'

Kastur's eyes were wet. Mohandas continued:

'I understand, but I can't stay here in the circumstances. My brother also seems to think I should go.'

The tears in Kastur's eyes lingered. She nodded.

The next day, Mohandas told Jhaveribhai he was ready to go. Mohandas knew that he wouldn't be practising law. His job would only be to explain the case to the white lawyers and to help in the preparation of the documents. But he was also motivated by the desire to see a new country, and to get to know and understand the people there. He also realized that talking about vegetation could not be a substitute for vegetation; to find vegetation you had to get into a garden or a forest. The world was a big place. What did Rajkot now have to offer him? Mother was dead. There was the wife, the kids, his elder brother and his family. The elder brother of course needed him, but he also needed him to earn money. The money that he had spent on him had not been recouped yet.

Mohandas was confident that the ticket and the ship would be waiting for him at Bombay and that he would not have to go through all that he had to go through when he had travelled to London. The memories of his London travel still made his hair stand on end. When he had arrived in Bombay on his way to London, the sea was ruffled. Then he discovered that throughout June and July, the sea remained unpredictable. Only when it returned to normal in November would he get to leave. His brother had already returned to Rajkot: after all, how long could he have waited? He had also been cast out by his kith and kin. They could not forgive him the sin of travelling across the seas. Even today, Mohandas could not recall the six months of hell he had gone through in Bombay then without a shiver running through his body. If it hadn't been for the Patwari family, he'd never have made it to London.

When the misbehaving sea got his London trip postponed, Mohandas had handed over the money he had raised for the journey by selling Kastur's jewellery to his sister, Raliyat and her husband, for safe-keeping. In the month of August, when he came to know that a Junagarh lawyer, who was going to England at the invitation of the London Bar, was ready to offer him a berth in his cabin, he went to his sister and his brother-in-law and asked for his money. The brother-in-law replied, 'Look, our kin have forbidden your travel. I do not wish to incur their wrath. I'll not pay you for committing an irreligious act.'

To Mohandas it was as if someone had dropped the mirror of hope that he had brought from home with him, and it had shattered. It was impossible to gather the pieces together again. It was in smithereens. If he tried to gather the pieces, the attempt would leave him bloodied all over. If he didn't, it would be all darkness for him.

Mohandas looked at his sister. She got up and walked into the house.

~

When Mohandas reached the harbour, a military band was playing full blast. An army contingent stood in salute. Spectators had gathered and watched from a distance. They didn't have the guts to step any closer. He joked to himself: 'In your honour, Mohandas!'

He stood with the spectators for sometime. A carriage drawn by white horses appeared after a while. Some of the spectators promptly hid themselves in sheer fear. A white man got down from the coach. He wore a prince's coat. Its collar had a band of silver embroidery. A similar band adorned his trousers. A sword dangled from the waist. The handle and the scabbard were both golden. He had his hand on the handle. The sword kept step with the man.

Accepting the salute, the man climbed up to the ship. A gathering of people was waiting to receive him there.

The bandsmen, with their instruments hanging like faces of disheartened people, were marching off. The crowd had dispersed. Mohandas went up to the ship and addressed a man who looked like a sailor: 'I want to meet the Captain.'

'The Captain is busy. What can I do for you?' That a white man should talk to him in this way both impressed and astonished Mohandas.

'I am M.K. Gandhi, barrister. Dada Abdullah & Co. has invited me on a one-year contract agreement. I met the agent. He says there's no room in the first class. "You can travel as a deck passenger if you like," he says. I am after all a barrister and am going to work for the company which owns this ship ...'

The man thought for a while and then said, 'I am the Chief Officer. There's indeed no room in the first class. The Governor of Mozambique is travelling on this ship with his retinue.'

'Can you help me in some other way?'

The man looked him over from top to toe and then said, 'There's a spare berth in my cabin, not intended for passengers. Since you're travelling on Dada Abdullah & Co.'s business, I can let you have that berth.'

Mohandas was amazed. What sort of Englishman was this—offering space in his own cabin to a coloured man? Something of the same expression broke out on his face that appears in the eyes of a wounded man when his wounds are attended to by a stranger. Mohandas stayed in the Chief Officer's cabin. The Captain was his friend. Whenever the Mozambique Governor came out of his cabin, there was a festive air all round. Everyone was on his feet. The Captain put everything aside to dance attendance on the Governor.

The Captain was fond of chess. He had buttonholed Mohandas on the very first day: 'You know how to play chess?'

'No.'

'That's a surprise. A barrister should be an expert chess player.'

'Maybe that explains why I'm a failure ...' Then he continued: 'Perhaps it's a game for more than ordinarily great persons.'

The Captain had laughed it off: 'And how do you rate yourself?'

It was Mohandas' turn to laugh.

'I'll teach you how to play,' said the Captain.

'Very well, I'll try to learn it like a devoted pupil. I'm an extraordinarily patient man. Be it life or be it chess, one needs a lot of patience. You are a sailor and sailors often have to conduct a dialogue with the waves. Waves are unpredictable: here one moment, gone the next; angry one moment, placid the next.'

'Absolutely correct ...' There was admiration in the Captain's eyes.

~

Lamu was the first stop. The ship stopped here for three or four hours. Either the Captain or the Chief Officer had to stay aboard the ship. At Lamu, the Captain needed to go ashore. He was anyway called the 'Master' of the ship. Most of the passengers got off the ship to take care of their little needs. Those who carried their tiffin of gram or *sattu* with them had it right on the shore, and then started a song and music session, which attracted a crowd. Everyone had been told that the ship would stay for four hours and that everyone must be back in three or three-and-a-half hours.

Mohandas had a letter to write to his elder brother. He asked his way to the post office, where he was surprised to see a number of Indians working. He had a feeling as if he was at home and knew everyone quite well. They made all writing materials available to him. When they got to know that Mohandas was on his way to Natal, they went and called two or three Africans. This was Mohandas' first face to face meeting with any African.

After the conversation got going, Mohandas asked them, 'How is life there for outsiders?'

'It's awful.Your people are even worse off,' someone said.

Mohandas said nothing but it was a jolt for him. How could a black say a thing like this? It raised a number of questions in his mind. Had he made a wrong decision? Will he have to regret it?

He plodded his way back to the ship.

~

An immense ocean on one side, an equally large and uneven expanse of indecision on the other: the set of twin conditions had produced a rich situation for a dialogue with self. As he walked back, he kept talking to himself. 'Right or wrong, having travelled this far in his journey, can anyone give up and go back? *Ba* used to say that if an ape senses danger after having made his leap, he reverses direction in mid-flight. God has not granted this skill to man. After setting out on his journey, fear of danger cannot make him turn back like an ape. No matter how aimless your journey, it does have some purpose or the other.'

The shore was right before him. During this short time, the sea had undergone a change. The waves were beginning to heave more than normal. The boat which had been sent to fetch Mohandas to the ship was a small one and had too many people on it. The waves kept pushing it back. The ship was still at some distance. The sailors were busy rowing. Mohandas was beginning to lose nerve: the time was short; what would he do if the ship set sail without him? Perhaps the others had the same fears. Their faces had lost colour. Outside, the waves were going crazy; inside, their heartbeats. The Captain stood on the deck holding a telescope to his eyes. He saw Mohandas waving a handkerchief. He was holding the bar of the boat with one hand, and waving the handkerchief with the other.

The ship's siren was keeping up its wail. Mohandas saw the Captain turning back and giving a signal. The siren stopped for a while.

A boat raced towards Mohandas' boat. It carried two or three sailors. One of them caught hold of his hand, and in a single action, pulled him over onto his boat. So steady was his hand that Mohandas didn't feel the jerk at all. In the other case, he could have fallen into the waves, which would have made a meal of him. Now the boat rushed towards the ship. The other people on the boat shrieked in unison: 'We're also coming. Take us with you too.' But a mountain of a wave rose just then soared between the two boats. The cries of those people pursued Mohandas for a long distance. He didn't even have the opportunity to refuse to leave without them, to stay behind and drift on the waves with them. He could neither turn back to look behind him nor could he see anything before him. He was wonderstruck how the sailor was managing to row the boat so calmly in such a stormy sea.

When the boat was next to the ship, ropes were dangled from her—swing-shaped ropes. The Chief Officer and his colleagues were shouting instructions about the use of the ropes, though the sailors also knew how to use them. It was the sailors who helped Mohandas climb on to the swing-shaped rope. The rope dug into Mohandas' hands and thighs. On other ropes, sailors sat as if they were swings. Mohandas was being continuously bombarded with instructions not to look down. When he did once, the feeling he had was that the waves were climbing on top of each other to get to him and pull him down. But while he still watched, they fell back and scattered. It was the first time he had seen this miracle of nature.

When finally Mohandas was aboard, he was thoroughly soaked, and shivered with cold. The thought of the boat crossed his mind, but it was impossible to locate it in that vast expanse of water. He cast a glance. The sea had grown smaller and the weakening waves were sinking like dying flames.

The Captain smiled at him: 'So, you see …?'

Mohandas heard him, but a reply was ruled out in his shivering condition. The image of that small boat tossing about in the playful waters of the sea kept returning to him. The next day, he did bring it up to the Captain: 'It wasn't right. God knows what happened to those poor people.'

'M.K., you still haven't forgotten about that? If a journey is held up, the destination shifts that much farther. The rules of a journey are different from the rules of a stopover. The successful completion of a journey is the responsibility of the Captain and it's not possible to fulfil that responsibility while trying to suit everybody's convenience.' Mohandas was staring at the Captain's face, which was wreathed in a smile even as he spoke those words.

The stopover at Zanzirabad was seven days—the longest anywhere. This time it was the Chief Officer's turn to leave the ship, but it was the Captain who did. He also took Mohandas with him. An Englishman was also with them, a personal friend of the Captain.

The Captain was so happy that he kept repeating the same thing: 'Land, finally! After so many days! I'm going to enjoy this land for full seven days. That's what makes land different from water. Water constrains, land liberates.'

Every now and then, he also kept teasing Mohandas: 'The two of us are going to educate M.K.' Mohandas kept quiet. Perhaps he should not have joined them. The Englishman also let off a barb or two at Mohandas periodically: 'You're going to be baptized today. And don't you make any excuses!'

~

The Captain's boat was rowed fast by a bunch of sailors. Mohandas watched the small waves forming and un-forming in the sea. Every now and then they started racing so fast it looked they were going to attack an enemy. But when they returned, they looked tired and becalmed, while their campaign was taken over by other little waves.

The moment they made the shore the Englishman broke off and soon got talking to a stranger. The Captain's eyes were shining. The Englishman, who seemed quite excited, beckoned to him. Now the Captain and the Englishman were trying to catch up with the stranger, who walked very fast. Mohandas was straggling, although he was walking normally. A short distance later, they entered a black colony. A peculiar meaty smell pervaded the air. Mohandas was finding it difficult to breathe. Taking a couple of deep breaths, he kept walking. He wasn't able to figure out where these two were headed. He did not find it interesting enough to rush forward and ask. His only interest at the moment was to imbibe as much as he could the incomparable natural beauty of Zanzirabad Island. The roads they had taken to reach there was very broad and full of greenery.

The man took them to a small room and asked them to wait. The ceiling was quite low and the Englishman could not stand erect. Mohandas was the shortest of them and could have stretched his arms and legs, had he so wanted. Suddenly, something flashed in Mohandas' mind: he was reminded of the Vegetarians' Conference he had been to in Portsmouth in England. Portsmouth was a settlement of seamen. Entertaining men was the trade women of many families in this settlement engaged in. Was it the same story here? The sort of conversation the Captain and his English companion carried on had created a suspicion in Mohandas' mind.

The delegates to the Portsmouth conference had been assigned to different families. The family which hosted them was considered to be a cultured one. Dinner over, they all sat down to a game of bridge. As the game progressed, the scene changed. His friend and the hostess gradually slid so close to each other that only their clothes separated them. His friend had included Mohandas in the game. One of the lady's hands held the friend's hand; now with the other one, she held Mohandas'. So warm, so fleshy was her hand that Mohandas felt something stirring within him, as in a simmering pan. He found his entire consciousness crushed under her magnetic charm.

But it was the same friend's voice that suddenly jolted him awake: 'What! Mohandas? A dark horse!' He felt it was not the friend but someone within him who had uttered those words.

An ebony-black girl, with a glint in her eyes, entered the room—full of youth and glowing flesh. She was smiling, displaying her pearly teeth. Her head was wreathed in innumerable slender plaits, her body only partially clad. Despite the deep black, her body exuded amazing physical charm.

The Captain whispered to Mohandas: 'Experience it once and you'll never fancy another woman ever again.'

A fear suddenly gripped Mohandas. He heard a voice telling him: 'Get up! What are you doing sitting here? This is not for you.' It was the same voice he had heard in Portsmouth. The other two left with the woman for another room. He sprang from his seat and ran out. Only the stars shone in the sky. The breeze from the sea tickled the trees which swished as they swayed from side to side. A long walk brought him to the road. A number of small inns and hotels stood along the road. He took shelter in one of the inns, from where he saw the whole of Zanzirabad. He had never seen such rich vegetation before. In the six or seven days he was there, he struck up such deep friendship with the trees, the pastures, the sea and the green that he could now rely on them fully. He was sure they won't let him down; they won't subject his conscience to the strain of a test.

~

Mozambique is the first port for Natal. The Governor was to disembark here. Having seen the pomp and show that attended him in India, what awaited him at the place where he was the Governor was a difficult exercise even for the imagination. All the passengers of the ship had gathered on the deck. The Representative of the Crown, the Master of a Colony was getting off the ship! Bands playing music, contingents of the army, horses and carriages, officers of the state, and noblemen in full regalia! The Captain and the other officers of the ship were also present for the farewell. The Governor shook hands with the Captain in farewell after he got off the ship. Then he plunged into the stormy sea of reception.

Mohandas observed that, even long after the Governor had left; the coolies who had come under the *girmit* could not gather enough courage to use the steps the Governor had used.

They were scared stiff. Even after the Captain gave them a scolding, they walked down the steps very gingerly, careful not to put their step where the Governor might have put his. The Governor they called the *Laat Sahib*. Who could fathom the height of a *Laat (Laat* in Hindi also means a minaret or a tower)?

At Eddington too, the ship dropped anchor offshore. The Captain had made the announcement on board in advance.

First class passengers were the first to leave the ship. They had to use the rope swings to land directly onto the boats. It was a singular and frightening experience for them. The others descended after them.

One question that kept cropping up in Mohandas' mind was where would he go after he landed? He didn't know if there would be anyone ashore to receive him. The coolies were even more nervous. One of them had a pocket-sized copy of *Ramcharitmanas* in his hands. He kept touching his forehead with it time and again. Mohandas looked at the man very closely and asked him, 'Where have you come from?'

But the man had only one answer to all questions: '*Tehi vidhi rahiye Ram, jehi vidhi raakhe Ram*.' (A [mis]quote from *Ramcharitmanas*. Literally: Be content to stay the way God chooses to keep you.) He suffixed 'Ram' to everything he said.

The horrifying strangeness of the new country had come crashing down on him and you could read it in his face. Mohandas was at least assured that even if no one showed up to receive him, he could trace Dada Abdullah as he had his address, and he could read and write. But what about these people?

They were like a drop released in the air: would it fall in the snake's mouth or would it be lost in the waves of the sea? This question made him feel very uncomfortable. The face of the man with the pocket-sized Ramayana haunted him for several days.

~

Several boats floated on the surface of the sea. As they approached the shore, a stunned silence began to descend within Mohandas, causing him to freeze like ice inside. In this very silence he could sometimes also hear Kastur, and the children whispering. These whisperings pushed him deeper into a feeling of alienation. So long as there was water around, there was a sense of journey. The water mass of the Indian Ocean connected him to the other end where he had begun his journey. *Ba*, like a time gone by; Kastur and the kids, like dreams; his elder brother, like a pillar of support; friends like Sheikh Mehtab—all of them floated to the surface like mirrors, then broke up and floated away.

Thinking of Sheikh Mehtab always left Mohandas disturbed. Nobody at home liked him, but he did. *Ba* forbade him to play with Uka, though he still did. When he returned after the play, *Ba* used to pour a bucket of water on him. But she never said anything about Sheikh Mehtab. Kastur, on the other hand, never missed an opportunity of running Sheikh Mehtab down. Mohandas had always had the feeling that his friendship was having a positive effect on Mehtab, though the opposite was really happening. Mohandas felt that his world was falling apart, that he was being stripped naked. Still, Sheikh Mehtab was his companion in joy and in sorrow. How could he forsake Mehtab just because Kastur wanted it? Why did she want it?

He had travelled a long way back, thousands of miles away! Right where he had started.

~

Dada Abdullah had arrived in Durban twenty years ago, without a penny in his pocket. Before he came to Natal, he had spent a few years in Mauritius.

By that time Mauritius had passed into the hands of the British from the French. No sooner had he landed in Durban than success, like a trained pigeon, alighted on his shoulder. He used to say, 'God smiles on those who make their own destiny.'

Abdullah & Co. was considered to be the oldest and the biggest Indian company in Natal. Financially, Dada Abdullah was the richest among Indian businessmen. He wasn't quite literate, but knew so many languages that it left the people goggle-eyed. If you have language in your throat, you can have the listener for your meal. French, English, Arabic, Persian and Hindustani—he could speak them all, but he wrote only Arabic. Dada Abdullah had stuffed himself full with modesty; with modesty came simplicity. He had learnt that, although wealthy, he still stood on the lowest rung of the local society. The whites had pushed the Indians all the way back. The only way one could survive this backwardness was through modesty and simplicity.

Dada Abdullah was a seasoned sailor. His journeys to France and England had been as a sailor. He used to say: 'I belong to the race whose ancestors had once shaken up the entire Christendom. Our flag flew as far as Spain.'

When, after the day's work, Dada Abdullah relaxed in his drawing room, a hookah was placed a little distance from him. The glittering tube of the hookah, sheathed in precious, chintzy cloth, snaked away from him. The nozzle of the tube was studded with diamonds. When he took the nozzle to his mouth, the sparkle of the diamonds flashed past the faces of the people sitting around him. Normally a man of few words, Dada Abdullah was particularly articulate at that hour, rummaging through his experiences, his views, and his past.

Marcel Ledue was a newcomer to Durban. He had opened his office in the area where the offices of Indian traders were concentrated. His father had a business in France. It was his father who had sent him to Durban. Durban in those days was a paradise for traders. Marcel thought that he could do well in business if he worked with Indian businessmen, since the other whites looked down on him. He calculated that if he could develop good relations with them, they would feel honoured and also help him do well. Dada Abdullah was a big name among Indian businessmen, so he latched on to him and started visiting him frequently.

The hookah was fresh. Marcel sat before him. Dada Abdullah took a puff and blew out the smoke. A fragrance, with a whiff of tobacco, wafted through the air. The perfumed tobacco was imported from India for Dada Abdullah. Marcel was listening to him patiently: 'My young friend! No feudal lord, however big, can have an idea of the way I spent my childhood at Nagpur. Nagpur summers are terribly hot. We used to live in cellars, with a swimming pool on top. There were thick, double walls. It was as if we were living in the hills. The taste of fresh pomegranate! Pomegranate sherbet—what a drink! And pomegranate wine—it is matchless! The favourite drink of great warriors and poets! The pomegranate blossom is a symbol of love.'

From Marcel's expression it appeared that these things were quite new to him, which greatly encouraged Dada Abdullah. Another puff at the hookah and he started again with renewed energy. Every time it was a new topic. He was very fond of the Arabic poet, Hafeez. Hafeez happened to be a great lover of flowers.

For Dada Abdullah, Babur was the greatest warrior the world had ever seen, a warrior who had crushed Rana Sanga of India with the help of only seven hundred soldiers. Talking of Babur's bravery and his poetry, Dada Abdullah went into ecstasies. Then he suddenly veered round from Babur to Sirajuddaula. The Black Hole of Calcutta was compulsory viewing for every British officer. In that small cell, Sirajuddaula had imprisoned one hundred and forty-six white soldiers, who had been asphyxiated to death. Expanding on these themes, Dada Abdullah seemed to change his own role; now and again he would be Babur, at times Sirajuddaula and sometimes Hafeez!

To Marcel these discourses sounded very exotic but he listened with complete attention.

Dada Abdullah's talk had now moved on to his travels to France and London. He was now saying, 'Mr. Marcel, during my travels to France and London, I realized that the image of Jesus varies against the background of these countries in the same way as does that of Islam among educated Muslims and Blacks. Among all religions, Islam is the one that cares most for the poor and is the most practical. It is the religion of those people who live by the sweat of their brow.'

Marcel was startled to hear this. A couple of questions arose in his mind. But he kept shaking his head. Only on one specific point he made his support explicit: 'Yes, every country has its own image of Jesus.'

That evening too Dada Abdullah was in a conversation with Marcel. Marcel had a business problem to discuss with him. Just then Mohandas entered the room.

'*Salaam-aalekum*.'

Dada Abdullah did not notice, so Mohandas kept standing. Marcel gave him an odd look and smiled. The smile revealed a shiny set of teeth but little else. Maybe a slight dip in the lips. To all appearances, he looked quite unaltered. He had noticed that Dada Abdullah was looking elsewhere.

Dada Abdullah was telling Marcel, 'You know why I wear a green turban? The green turban is a badge of that honour which reading the *namaaz* at Qaba during my pilgrimage to Mecca conferred on me. That's why I'm called a *haaji*. The turban is the proof that I'm a *haaji*.'

When Dada Abdullah noticed Mohandas, he acknowledged him by a little signal of his hand waving him to a seat. Mohandas repeated, '*Salaam-aalekum*'.

This time Dada Abdullah acknowledged the greeting: '*Aalekum-assalaam*,' and continued, 'You have met this gentleman. He's curious to know more and more about us. I hope you're doing well.'

Mohandas addressed himself to Marcel: 'What a beautiful city is Paris, perhaps the most beautiful in the world.' He spoke in English.

Marcel inquired in French: 'You've lived in Paris?'

Mohandas replied in English, 'Travelled to France on a short visit. There was an exhibition there in 1890. Messrs Cook had made all the arrangements. I was studying in London for Bar-at-Law then and couldn't get the time to learn French. I can follow it a little, though.'

Dada Abdullah put in a sentence edgeways: 'London is a beautiful city too.'

'Yes, but it's a different life altogether. The customs, the ways of living—all very different. But what a life! People are so liberated, so friendly. Here ...,' he stopped himself midway.

Dada Abdullah nodded. The arrival of Mohandas had made Marcel a little uncomfortable. He got up and without a glance at Mohandas begged leave of Dada Abdullah: 'Let's drop the matter here. I must be on my way. Please talk to Mr. Gandhi; I can come again some other time.'

Dada Abdullah nodded again and he left.

Mohandas offered his apologies: 'Dada Abdullah, I'm sorry. Maybe I dropped in at the wrong time and interrupted something.'

Dada Abdullah laughed: 'Nothing of the sort.'

Mohandas remembered what Dada Abdullah had said: 'What am I going to do with this white elephant?'

Mohandas had let it pass then. But the look Marcel had given him had let that sentence of Dada Abdullah rise to the surface afresh on Marcel's face. Troubled, he was on the point of asking what he had meant by that sentence, when he stopped himself. Placed as he was, so far from home, he could have done nothing whatever the reply. And it was not as if he didn't know what the idiom meant.

It was Dada Abdullah himself who broached the subject: 'I'm not quite sure what work you can possibly do here.'

'That's for you to tell me. Jhaveribhai must have written to you.'

'I can't think of any work which I can entrust to a highly educated person like you.'

That stopped Mohandas in his tracks. In that case, why had Abdullah Sheth come to receive him with two of his men?

Both kept quiet for a while. Then Dada Abdullah spoke: 'Gandhibhai, you live like top-class whites. Must take a lot of money.'

Mohandas thought it best to hold his peace. He just gave a smile. He was unable to figure out what Dada Abdullah was driving at.

After a short pause, Abdullah Sheth himself resumed: 'We have a lawsuit in progress in Transvaal. You know Transvaal? It's a colony like Natal. Our lawyer in that case is Mr. Baker, considered one of the top lawyers of Transvaal. Jhaveribhai has possibly sent you for that case. But so long as Mr. Baker is there ...'

Mohandas responded to the whole thing with just one sentence: 'Yes, Jhaveribhai had told me about that case. Perhaps I'm supposed to prepare the brief.'

Dada Abdullah looked at him with a bit of surprise: 'But you are so new. I'm not familiar with you or your abilities. The case is in Pretoria and I can't be present there all the time. When the other party finds out that you are alone, it can try to pressurize you.'

'You are right. You cannot, and should not, take on trust the abilities and reliability of a person you don't know.'

Perhaps Dada Abdullah was not ready for this answer. He was nonplussed. Perhaps it was for Mohandas to speak again.

'If you have also to think of the skills of presenting and arguing the case, then of course it's a different matter altogether. You already have people to do it. If they go wrong, you can punish them. But you might hesitate a little to give the same treatment to a Bar-at-Law.'

Mohandas was suddenly reminded of the white elephant idiom. He said: 'If you have no work for me, keeping me at a hundred and five pounds per year will certainly be keeping a white elephant.'

Abdullah looked at him and laughed. 'Nothing of the sort. You go and rest for now. After the hardship of such a long journey, one does require a day or two to recover. In fact, I stay in bed for several days in such a situation.'

Mohandas said his greeting and left for his room.

Mohandas was staying in the room next to Dada Abdullah's. It was clean, comfortable, and well-appointed. The first question that sprang to his mind on entering the room was: Had *Ba* and *Bapu* been alive, would they have accepted Dada Abdullah's hospitality? Perhaps not. Would it be because he was a Muslim, or because he ate meat? I have seen many Hindus in London eating meat. He himself had partaken of it in his apprenticeship with Sheikh Mehtab. How can religion be a reason for restrictions on food? Isn't it a way of finding God? Dada Abdullah too was worried on this account. That morning, he had asked him in the coach, 'Do you have any problem staying with me?'

For a moment, Mohandas had found himself in a fix. Who is he accountable to here? No friends, no relatives. Such questions arise only when you have choices before you: either this or that. But here he had only Dada Abdullah and his job. So he had laughed, and said simply: 'You mean more to me here than my own people. So what problem can there be?'

Dada Abdullah had been pleased with the answer.

~

Mohandas was fast asleep. After he returned from Dada Abdullah's room, he lay down to sleep and slept so long that he missed his dinner.At night, he woke up to the sound of footsteps outside. Still groggy, he couldn't figure out anything. He thought he was in the Chief Officer's cabin, and the Chief Officer was walking in and out. The Chief Officer often came in late at night and quite often had to get up from sleep to attend to emergency duties. But now Mohandas wondered why the ship was not moving. There was no movement of the ship, nor any rise-fall of the waves. Still wrestling with these questions, he suddenly remembered that he was actually in Durban, in the guest-house of Dada Abdullah & Co.

He got up and looked out of the window. It was dark and he could see nothing. He called out: 'Who's there?'

There was silence for a second, then a voice: 'It's me. Dada Abdullah.'

Mohandas came out: 'You? At this hour?'

'I woke up suddenly and realized it was a new place for you. You might have had difficulty sleeping. When I return from my voyages, my home feels like a ship.' He laughed.

'It was the same with me. I was seeing sea on dry land. I felt I was sleeping in the Chief Officer's cabin and not in Dada Abdullah's guest house. The Chief Officer had let me have a berth in his cabin only after I'd told him your name and my business.'

'People unfamiliar with the sea think of it as an enemy.

'For us the sea is a dear one. We were born on its shores, grew up there and quarrelled with it too.'

Dada Abdullah said, 'There's still time before it is morning. Please go back to sleep. I'm sorry that out of my ignorance I woke you up. Actually, I can't sleep very much. When I'm awake, I start pacing.'

Both of them went back to their rooms.

~

Mohandas couldn't go back to sleep for quite some time. When he had embarked on his journey from India, he had left everything behind. But, astonishingly, that everything was already present here—home, wife, kids and the whole of Rajkot. There was a question which had now attached itself to them all—had he been right to leave them to come here? This question had assumed increased importance in the context of Dada Abdullah's behaviour this morning, despite the fact that Dada Abdullah had been personally present to receive him at the Eddington docks. He had absolutely no doubt that Dada Abdullah was a good man. But what he had said that morning had raised a cloud of smoke around him. Then, again, what did he come looking for at that late hour to his room? Just to see if he was asleep? And that too in the dark? There was only a dim lamp burning outside, with maybe just enough light to see one's way. Was Dada Abdullah looking for a way to be rid of him? Every little incident was assuming the form of a question in his mind.

Mohandas didn't know when he drifted off to sleep. In the morning, everything looked fresh. What he had left behind still occasionally raised its head. Mohandas was trying to get rid of it. However recent the memories, they are stubborn enough to defy all your efforts to get rid of them. They just dig themselves in. Coming out of the room, Mohandas loved the touch of the sea breeze on his body. She was an old friend, absolutely no different from what she had been there. As pleasing and as dear. Caressing, tickling.

Next to the building of Dada Abdullah & Co. on the West Street, there was an even bigger one—a villa. It turned out that the villa belonged to the owner of the Green Harvey Ekka Co. The two buildings were so big that they could be seen from afar. Coconut trees grew as far as one could see. Their leaves fluttered like the wings of some large bird. Trams had not yet started plying. Quiet reigned all round. Occasionally, a man or two passed by, which made you feel the pulse of the street was still running. Mohandas saw two street vendors and was filled with wonder. For a moment he felt he was back in India. They were carrying shoulder-carriers.

~

When Dada Abdullah came out after the *namaaz*, he saw Mohandas standing on the verandah and approached him. Mohandas' eyes were following the street-vendor, though he was already a good distance away. Dada Abdullah laughed and said: 'Wherever an Indian goes, he creates his own India. That's what the whites complain about us, although I take it as a compliment.These peddlers are people whose period of bondage or *girmit*, is over. In lieu of their return fare, they have been given some land where they grow vegetables or keep cattle, and peddle their produce. Those who have neither *girmit* nor farming are keeping up the struggle of their lives working as labourers. But the whites don't like the freedom they enjoy, so they have found another way of skinning the cat: no vending without a licence. This is called government: squeezing the weak.'

Mohandas felt dizzy. He had always thought of the English as a noble race. He had always believed that in the British rule the tiger and the lamb supped together. That was what he had been told in the childhood. They were all subjects of the Queen, so how could there be any discrimination? But he said nothing. He didn't know how Dada Abdullah might take it.

The vendor with the shoulder-carrier had covered a great distance and was now merely a moving speck. Dada Abdullah said: 'If you're not too fatigued, I could show you the courtroom of Durban. You are a barrister. The court is your Mecca and Medina. You may have to appear there some day. The customs and practices in the two colonies are not quite the same.'

'Isn't there an Indian lawyer here?'

'An Indian lawyer?' Dada Abdullah roared with laughter. 'Come down to earth, Gandhibhai,' he said. 'In the first place, there isn't an Indian here fit to be a lawyer. Even if there was, the whites would not let him survive. Even if he survived, no complainant would go anywhere near him. An Indian can only be a complainant. More than fifty per cent of the practice the white barristers and lawyers enjoy here is due to our people. Whoever is harassed approaches the court, and it is always the weak who are harassed. Sometimes a man of power may also find himself trapped, but he always finds a way out.'

Mohandas looked at Dada Abdullah. His face wore a strangely troubled look.

Dada Abdullah said, 'Gandhibhai, for us a court is an illusion like the illusion of water at a distance in a desert. Everyone thinks it is water, but there is really no water anywhere.'

Then he continued: 'Do get ready. I'll get ready too.'

Mohandas was still thinking of what Abdullah Sheth had said. So many distinguished Indian traders and not a single Indian lawyer! And then, he didn't quite realize when a thought stole into his mind: who knows he may earn the honour of being the first Indian barrister! He couldn't help smiling. For the present at least, he was Dada Abdullah's white elephant and for him to think of being a barrister was nothing short of sheer foolishness.

~

Mohandas was putting on the bow. Before him was the mirror. He felt he was wearing on his head the same wig that he had worn when he had received the law degree in London. He shook the idea off with a shake of the head, picked up his hat, and was going to put it on when the idea struck him: it was his first appearance in the Durban court, should he be wearing a hat? Shouldn't he have something about him which would show that he was an Indian? He put the hat aside and put on a *pheta*, a Gujarati turban. It might look a bit odd with the western dress. He looked in the mirror, but he didn't feel like taking it off. After all, Dada Abdullah also wore one. When he came out, he was in a *pheta* with the western dress.

Dada Abdullah stood there, all ready to go. He saw and smiled, but said nothing.

As they came out, an attendant opened the window-like door of the horse-carriage. The coachman was already sitting on the coachbox, all set to go. The courtroom was very close by, on Aliwal Street, barely a furlong from their place. On the way, Dada Abdullah pointed out the City Hall.

Mohandas was impressed to see the splendour of the building. From West Street, they reached the courtroom via Mercury Street. Mohandas was curious to see the courtroom. He had seen the courtrooms of London, and also Bombay. He was now going to see the courtroom of Durban.

They both got down together, one from the right side, the other from the left. Dada Abdullah got down from the right side. The door on his side was opened by the coachman. As they walked, people cast curious looks at Mohandas. Some had sarcastic smiles on their faces. All around, you only saw whites wearing wigs and gowns. But it wasn't exactly a crowd. Even Rajkot had more people. The thought occurred to him once again, though he didn't know why, that if he ever started his law practice here he would have to compete with the white lawyer. There was actually no reason for him to think so. In the same context, he also thought of the regard the white people had for justice and fair play. In fact, this was becoming a refrain of his thinking. Black or white, how could one make the winning one lose and the losing one win? Then the answer came from within him: by denying a hearing, as had happened in the farmers' case in Rajkot.

The courtroom was on Aliwal Street. The court Dada Abdullah took him to was neat and clean, and was furnished in a simple European style.

'Our courtrooms are so different,' he thought for a moment. He had seen similar courtrooms in London. Dada Abdullah knew almost everyone. The whites responded to his 'Good Morning' with a pleasant smile. To see the whites' attitude to Dada Abdullah, Mohandas felt that the white lawyers and officers did not necessarily look down upon Indians. There were some who actually stopped and shook hands with Abdullah Sheth, though their gaze was regularly fixed on Mohandas' turban.

When Dada Abdullah stopped, he introduced Mohandas, 'Mr. M.K. Gandhi, barrister from England. My countryman. Joined my firm today.' They also met a couple of Indian traders, who were Gujarati. They talked to Mohandas in Gujarati. They made very eager inquiries about those people back home, whom they still remembered, even if Mohandas did not know them.

There was a case in progress. Both the lawyers were arguing forcefully. The magistrate listened very attentively. There were chairs in the courtroom for other lawyers. The only other people were complainants and defendants. The lawyer of Dada Abdullah & Co. was also there with his assistants, waiting for his turn. Dada Abdullah wished him good morning and introduced him to Mohandas. As he shook hands with Gandhi, his gaze too was fixed at Gandhi's turban. Occasionally, he also stole a glance at the magistrate.

The magistrate too had cast a few glances at Mohandas' turban. It looked like he wanted to say something. Dada Abdullah's gaze was fixed at the magistrate. Mohandas however was quite unaware of all this. Dada Abdullah pointed out a vacant chair to Mohandas to take. The magistrate now focused his full gaze on Mohandas. He signalled with his hand to the arguing lawyer to stop.

The magistrate said, 'Gentleman, this is a courtroom. Take off your turban before you enter.'

Mohandas' face turned red with rage. He got up from his seat and said, 'My Lord, this is a *pheta*, a symbol of our honour. I cannot take it off ...' and he walked out of the courtroom. The magistrate shrugged his shoulders as if to say: 'What a strange man!' Abdullah Sheth also followed Mohandas out. Both of them walked to their coach and left. There was silence for some time. When the coach reached Mercury Lane, Dada Abdullah said, 'Most of the offices here belong to lawyers. You can cut through the grounds before us to get from West Street to Gray Street.'

Mercury Lane looked very much like a part of London. The surroundings were very similar. The houses too looked almost the same—with tiled roofs. Seeing Mercury Lane, he felt refreshed.

Mohandas had not responded to Dada Abdullah's remark. Abdullah spoke again: 'Gandhibhai, it was good you didn't take off your turban.'

'But you too were wearing a turban?'

'I forgot to tell you. Only Arabs are allowed to wear turbans in the courtroom.' Dada Abdullah was looking away, while Mohandas' eyes were fixed on his face.

'Arabs?'

'Muslims are called Arabs here.'

'Indian Muslims too?'

'Yes.'

'You don't object?'

'Maybe because Islam comes from Arabia.'

'But you come from India. Clothes may belong to any fashion, but the point is who is the person wearing them?' Mohandas stopped midway.

Mohandas had kept pacing his room till quite late at night. You eat something that doesn't agree with you and you have to put in a lot of effort trying to digest it. In relation to what had transpired during the day, Mohandas was more or less in a similar situation. The Indian Muslim feels flattered at being called an Arab the way a fair-skinned Indian might feel flattered at being called an Englishman, and think of himself as being different from other Indians. Dada Abdullah had in fact said in passing that Parsis were able to escape with their caps by passing themselves off as Persian. But what should the rest of them do? There were of course some Indians who were Christians when they had arrived here, but many converted to Christianity after their arrival for the sake of a job. For them, the turban was not important. The stomach came before the turban. Mohandas felt strangely disturbed. A question kept bothering him: 'These people left so much behind them when they came here, why did they bring their differences with them?' Mohandas wondered: 'On an Arab's head, a turban is a mark of his identity; the same turban on another man's head turns into a cause for contempt of court? Had Indians not been divided among themselves, perhaps this wouldn't have happened.'

There was one thing about Dada Abdullah that Mohandas was quite unable to understand: When he had put on the turban, Dada Abdullah had seen him and had even smiled. He could have told Mohandas that wearing a turban to the court could annoy the judge. In that case, he might have put on a hat, or might have done without a head wear. In any case, all the unpleasantness could have been avoided.

Along with all this, Mohandas was thinking of his father too, though the courtroom incident had nothing to do with him. *Bapu,* Mohandas' father was a short man. Well, not exactly short, but he couldn't be called a tall man. His turban raised his height. He respected his turban more than he respected himself. When he returned home, the first thing he did was to take off his turban. He always put it on a high place where at least the kids would not be able to reach it. If there was anyone who was allowed to touch it, it was *Ba.* And she too cared for it as if it was a member of the family.

~

Memories spread like wild fire: the briefest touch is enough.

Mohandas and the middle brother, Karsandas, were getting married. *Bapu* was the Diwan of Rajkot. The marriages were being held at Porbandar, where they had their ancestral home. There were three days to go and *Bapu* had not been granted leave. *Ba* had left with the kids for Porbandar a month before. She had to look after all the arrangements, both at home and outside.

With only three days remaining for the marriages, the *Thakur* of Rajkot told *Bapu*: 'So your children are getting married! Had you decided to hold the weddings here, we too could have joined. But I know that you must go to Porbandar.'

'I'm sorry, but it makes little difference now. It takes at least five days to get there, which means I can't be present at the wedding ceremonies. Post marriage, I might just as well meet the couples here ...'

The *Thakur* laughed and said, 'Don't I know that the time is too short? But I have made all necessary arrangements so that you can be there on time. Please take my chariot. The bullocks really fly! Once they take off, they won't stop till you are home.'

The royal chariot of the *Thakur* was at the door for *Bapu*. *Bapu* was feeling very pleased that the *Thakur* had made his chariot available to him. Truly, when the bullocks raced they snorted as if they were spewing fire. They did take him there in three days, but taking him there on time was about all they did. *Bapu* was happy that he would be there for the ceremonies. The bullocks and the bullock-driver were fully aware of their responsibilities, but, you know that saying:

Look at the irony of fate
At what point did the rope snap?
(When the ledge of the roof
Was barely a hand or two away)

There was a mishap. The chariot bounced, *Bapu* was flung off, the chariot and the bullocks overturned. The driver was badly injured. *Bapu* had taken several somersaults; his face resembled a broken triangle. Knees and elbows were bruised. He had landed on his head. Had he not been wearing the turban, anything could have happened.

When *Bapu* had gathered his wits about him, the first thing he did was to check the whereabouts of the bullock-driver. The bullocks too had received injuries. The driver had had a hard time trying to disentangle the bullocks from the cart. Patting them on the back, he tried to console them as if telling them to take it easy. The bullocks were harnessed again and they resumed their journey to their destination. Despite the injuries, the bullocks hadn't slowed down particularly.

When they reached Porbandar, darkness had already descended. Everyone was waiting for them eagerly, but when they saw *Bapu*'s condition their spirits fell. It was as if someone had poured water on a heated furnace.

The first thing that *Bapu* had then done was to hand his turban to *Ba*: 'Put it away with care. It saved my life today.' He then lay down and did not get up for hours except to say one thing: 'Do look after the bullocks and the driver.'

The next day, he was present on every occasion at which the marriages demanded his presence, decked out in a refurbished and upright turban.

~

If it is night and you can't sleep, your mind turns loose. Memories never sleep; they are awake even when they are asleep. Whenever this happened to him, Mohandas thought first of *Ba*. Her persona overwhelmed the total darkness. No matter how intense the dark, light can always show up the way. Next came Kastur, her large eyes always on the lookout. Whichever way he looked, he saw those two unmoving eyes; alongside would be the two kids, their innocent, little eyes asking him: '*Bapu*, where are you? When will you come home?' Then his two brothers—Karsan and the elder brother, Lakshmidas. Karsan had settled down at Porbandar. Lakshmidas was with him. Like a coachman pulling back on the reins of his galloping horses, Mohandas too tried to pull back on himself.

Ba, of course, was no more. When he had left home, Kastur's eyes had held the same question—'How many days did you spend with me?' Those eyes would then turn into a delicately innocent face, only to turn suddenly into a face full of fury.

When Mohandas had started from home, Kastur stood behind the door. She hadn't spoken a word till the very end. Must have been thinking: 'You are leaving home every other day, why should I spoil my mood?' How much meaning lies hidden in unspoken words! Her silence was like the still waters of a lake. Images of trees, birds, and vegetation, our own images, form and un-form in still water. A slight motion, and where's everyone?

Won't even let you take a peep at your face. Like squabbling kids wiping out one another's creations on sand, it wipes out every face. Every face is defaced.

Abdullah Sheth's welcome to him was a reality. Mohandas felt that from a man he had turned into an elephant and was roaming around trumpeting. The magistrate's orders were echoing in his ears like the drum-beats of a crowd leading an animal to sacrifice. Suddenly, he spoke out loud: 'I'll not take off my turban. This is not defiance; this is my tradition and the tradition of my ancestors. This is my armour.'

Mohandas startled himself with his own voice.

'Dada Abdullah is not out for a stroll today. Must be sleeping the sleep of a carefree man. The books have been balanced. A businessman, after all.' He couldn't help smiling to himself.

Mohandas went and sat at his desk. He turned up the lamp and started drafting a letter to the newspapers. When he was practising as a barrister at Rajkot, writing drafts was his main business. That was what earned him his livelihood. After all, if you can't speak for yourself, who'll speak for you? He wrote:

> *Sir,*
>
> *I am an Indian. I have a barrister's degree from London. I arrived in Durban a couple of days ago, on May 24, 1893, on a year's contract with Dada Abdullah & Co. On May 25, Dada Abdullah took me to the courtroom. I belong to Gujarat. I was wearing a Gujarati* pheta *on my head. When we visit a place deserving of our respect, it is not our custom to take off the* pheta. *The* pheta *is a turban. It symbolizes respect for the nation as well as self-respect. Taking off a turban insults both. But the moment I entered the court, the honourable magistrate ordered me to take off my* pheta, *although the proprietor of my company and a prominent businessman of Natal, Dada Abdullah, was also wearing a turban. Dada Abdullah is an Indian but is known as an Arab here. If an Arab wears a turban, it is taken as his mark of identity; if I wear it, it is contempt of court. Why this discrimination? It was not possible for me to respect*

the orders of the magistrate. To do so would have been to show disrespect to myself, my country, and the tradition of my country. So I walked out of the court.

In India, whether it is a pheta *or a turban, it is held in the same regard by everyone. A Hindu or a Muslim or a Parsi—everyone is an Indian first. This discrimination will only help to divide Indians. Through the esteemed columns of your paper, I wish to register a protest against this discrimination, and the humiliation caused to me by the magistrate.*

Yours etc.

M.K.Gandhi

Mohandas read and re-read the draft, made necessary corrections, and then went to bed at peace with himself. The only thing that he cared for was that this should be taken as a matter of national honour and not as misbehaviour on his part. The thought however also occurred to him, as he lay in bed, that even if it was taken as misbehaviour how did it matter to him? After all, he was going to be here only for a year.

This was the first pebble cast in the pond.

~

Mohandas got up late. The first thing he did was to make a fair copy of the letter he had written at night.

Dada Abdullah was up too. Seeing him at his desk, he peeped into the room and said, 'Looks like you have been up till late at night.'

'Yes. The courtroom incident wouldn't let me sleep. I've written a letter to the newspapers. I want to register my protest. Which are the main newspapers?'

'Would you like to read it out to me?'

'Sure.'

After listening to what he had written, Dada Abdullah kept quiet for a while, then said, 'That means the first thing you want to do as soon as you land here is to annoy people, that too the white people.'

'I know, but this will also spread awareness. I hope you have no objections, because if you do, I'll ...'

Dada Abdullah hesitated a little and then said, 'What objections can I possibly have?'

'That's all that matters to me.'

Mohandas dressed quickly, got a few copies of the letter ready and set out in search of newspaper offices. Dada Abdullah offered: 'Take the coach; you won't have to walk. Or let us send it through somebody.'

Mohandas laughed: 'Unless one walks and establishes a bond between one's steps and the city, one does not make friends with the city. You go away as you come. I walked miles in London.'

Dada Abdullah gave a brief smile and shrugged his shoulders, like the magistrate. Mohandas couldn't figure out the shrug.

~

Mohandas must have covered almost the whole of Durban in his mission to deliver the letter to the newspapers. Broad roads, tall trees, vast and green parks, trams, horse carriages, and so on. The part of the city where the whites lived looked like Fort William of Mumbai. The similarity between different British colonies had struck him for the first time. The thing that he found unusual about Durban was the way it was divided up. In one direction, the hovels of the natives stretched endlessly, so densely packed that a peep from outside would reveal nothing of the insides. On the slopes outside the city was the settlement of the coolies. Like honeybees, they lived in hives. These were people who had been released from the *girmit*. In their huts, he saw India, where the majority lived in huts anyway. There were Indian traders too in Durban. They lived and carried on their businesses in small cubicles. The white government was unhappy with the way they lived. It thought they were unworthy of a civilized society and its residential colonies. They were all people on the go, that is passengers who were here on their own expense to do business, but had settled down here. It made Mohandas restless to hear this kind of talk. What could he do? A feeling of helplessness overcame him.

~

When he returned in the evening, Mohandas was quite tired, but he was happy that he had not been subjected to any disrespectful treatment during his entire sojourn in the city. Some whites did pass comments on his dress ('Look, the coolie is trying to be our equal, forgetting that a coolie remains a coolie!') but he refused to be provoked. This sort of thing, after all, happened, why, it still happens, quite regularly in India. If someone belonging to a lower caste puts on clean clothes, the so-called upper class people start bad-mouthing him. So, what right does he have to take umbrage at the comments?

~

'Gandhibhai, your letter!' Dada Abdullah had the day's newspaper in his hands. Just by looking at it, he was able to guess that it must be Gandhibhai's letter.

Mohandas took the newspaper from him. He was a little surprised to see the title, but then laughed.

'Why? What happened?'

'Interesting title: "Unwelcome Visitor!" Am I the only one? All those people whom they got over here after much wheedling and cajoling of the Indian government, have they all become unwelcome visitors after my arrival?' Mohandas paused and then continued: 'Looks like the title has been chosen after consulting the magistrate. Weren't these whites unwelcome visitors to the natives?'

Dada Abdullah tried to pacify Mohandas: 'A ruler is a ruler. No tags like welcome or unwelcome with him. It is his power that makes him welcome.'

Mohandas looked at Abdullah Sheth and said in a serious tone: 'I don't think so.'

In a deft move, Dada Abdullah changed the topic. 'I don't know how people will react to this letter,' he said. 'I only hope you don't have to regret writing this letter. We are traders. We know only the politics of prices and quotations. We've got used to all sorts of treatment. Educated and learned people use their brains too much. For them respect and dignity mean a lot. From that point of view, it might still prove to be a good idea to publish this letter.'

'Where is the question of respect and dignity yet? First, a road has to be laid to reach that goal. Continued tolerance of injustice is not the way to build that road.'

Dada Abdullah looked at him and said smiling: 'I see. So this is not just a protest against the courtroom incident. It is more!'

Mohandas said nothing.

~

At night, Mohandas suddenly found himself awake. He felt as if someone was calling him. Could be Abdullah Sheth. He came out of the room and looked around. It was absolutely quiet. A very thin and weak shaft of light escaping through a crack in Dada Abdullah's door was stuck fast to the verandah. It was two in the morning. He had perhaps gone to sleep with the lights on, since there was no question of his being awake at this late hour. He returned to his room. Turning up the light of the paraffin lamp, he picked up the newspaper by his bedside and read his letter two or three times. Two or three sentences from the original had been deleted. He was happy that his very first letter had been published by the leading local newspaper. Though he had been shocked to see the title at first, he now realized that by giving it that title the editor had stoked the curiosity of the reader. After all, a newspaper carries so many letters to the editor, you look at some, ignore others. Actually, the title really applies not only to him but to every immigrant Indian from an indentured labourer to a traveller.

Mohandas read the letter once again and smiled. To him, the letter seemed to have expanded and was covering the entire page. The faint light of the lamp seemed to have filled the whole room like a festive shadow. He himself was covering a whole wall. For Dada Abdullah too, he was not very different from what the newspaper said. Had that not been the case, he would certainly have told him how annoying the *pheta* or the turban of a Hindu could be to a magistrate. So many travellers, traders, and *girmitiya*s are sloshing around in the mud-pond of humiliation, but they are still surviving. When someone decides to venture this far, the option of escape from circumstances is no longer open to him. Questions of honour and dishonour get dissolved into the larger question of survival. At Porbandar, when people set out on pilgrimages or on the Haj, they were given ceremonial farewells with music and all. If they came back, it was well and good; if not, it was goodbye for ever. This was pilgrimage for your bread. You lived or you died—all for bread.

The thought crossed his mind that he should write to Lakshmidas telling him all about the incident, but Mohandas was uncertain what his reaction would be. Lakshmidas might actually turn on him and start asking him questions like: 'What do you think you are there for? To work with Dada Abdullah & Co. or to teach law to the British.'

A shiver ran through him as he remembered the incident. Humiliation has been a bosom friend of his. A fearsome figure took shape before his eyes. It was the figure of a white friend. Perhaps it would be wrong to call him a friend. He was an officer. The way portraits and statues often give the impression of following you with their looks, officers too sometimes give the impression that their favour is focused on you. When he was studying in London, Olivant was in London on holiday. He occupied some high position in India. He had become quite friendly with Mohandas. The two went out together and spent hours talking to each other. They talked about India; discussed things good and bad, the bad always coming from Olivant. In those days, Mohandas had only one dream—to be another Sir Pherozeshah Mehta. After coming back from London, he had practised law for six months at Mumbai. He went to the High Court every day, sometimes on foot, sometimes, when he had the fare, by tram. He came back every evening empty-handed. Later, on the insistence of his brother, he left Mumbai for Rajkot to practise draftsmanship.

~

When Rana Bhav Singh became the ruler, Lakshmibhai was his adviser and secretary. Rana had stripped the royal treasury of its gems and diamonds even before he acceded to the throne. This was conveyed to the agent in a devious way: that this had been done on the advice of the secretary and adviser. The agent could do little to the Rana, but he let the secretary have it.

Olivant was the agent.

Ever since Mohandas had returned, Lakshmidas had been going after him everyday: 'Olivant is your friend. Go and meet him. I am your elder brother. I have done for you whatever I could. Today, when my head is on the block, you are enjoying the spectacle! It's your friend who is wielding the chopper.'

Mohandas tried to explain it to him: 'Dear brother, Kathiawad and London are worlds apart. From being in London on vacation to being in a position of power in India can transform a man completely. Here he is the representative of the Crown and we are his subjects. There cannot be any comparison.'

Lakshmidas was not prepared to listen. Mohandas had to go. Olivant did show the courtesy of calling him in as soon as he was announced. He was studying a file. Mohandas kept standing.

When he lifted his head, Mohandas again wished him good morning and said, 'Perhaps you didn't recognize me: I'm M.K. Gandhi.'

'I remember you quite well.' Mohandas was pleased to hear this. He became a little more hopeful too. Olivant kept turning the papers, without paying any attention to him. It became clear to Mohandas, in fact, had been clear to him all along, that Olivant was not the ordinary individual who was home on vacation and who had roamed the streets with him. Now he was the political agent. People like Mohandas competed for his attention in hundreds. He had to continue standing: 'Sir, my elder brother, Mr. L.K. Gandhi, was secretary and adviser to Rana Bhav Singh ...'

Before he could complete, Olivant looked up at him sharply. He cut himself short. The lines on Olivant's forehead became denser and denser. He said, 'I hope, Mr. Gandhi, you are not here to encash our personal relationship.' Then, with his eyes boring into Mohandas' face, he continued: 'Your brother is a cheat. He conned the Rana into stripping the treasury of its diamonds and gems. I don't wish to hear another word about him. You may go.'

'I didn't come here to take any advantage of you. Please hear me out.'

Olivant rang the bell. Stretching a full arm towards the door, he indicated to the peon to turn him out. The peon gave him a slight push, which sent Mohandas staggering. He noticed in the eyes of the Indian peon the enthusiasm and the joy of carrying out the orders of his white master.

Outside, Mohandas scribbled a note:

Mr Olivant,

You have insulted me by getting your peon to push me out. You must apologise or I'll be forced to take legal action.

M.K. Gandhi

Olivant returned the same slip with his note on the back:

I had no alternative. You were losing your manners. You are free to do as you please.

The memory of that incident made Mohandas restless, he started pacing the room. He felt he had been standing before Olivant continuously since then, and he was getting him thrown out. The place of Olivant had now been taken by the magistrate. Now it was Olivant back again...to be replaced by the magistrate again ...the places were changing so fast.

Mohandas thought of Sheikh Mehtab. He hadn't written to him since he came to Durban, although he had promised to him that he would. What he couldn't reveal to anyone else he could disclose to Sheikh Mehtab. Mohandas missed his presence now. He could of course also speak of such things to Kastur, but Kastur had no interest in such matters. As a result, he ended up with a monologue.

He wrote to Sheikh Mehtab:

Dear Mehtabbhai,

This is my third day in Durban. I had sent a telegram to my brother telling him of my safe arrival; he must have told you about it. Yesterday, the proprietor of our company, Abdullah Sheth, took me to show the Durban court. I wore my pheta, though I was also wearing jacket and trousers. I thought the pheta on the head would be a mark of my Indianness. Don't the English do so much to honour their traditions and their culture? But the whole thing recoiled on me. The magistrate got annoyed and ordered me to take off the pheta *although the proprietor of the company was also wearing a pheta. He too is a Gujarati.*

I preferred to leave the court. I couldn't bring myself to take off the turban. My company proprietor later informed me that Muslims were allowed to wear turbans because they were known as Arabs. He could have told me this beforehand, but something must have kept him from telling me.. Could be that he doesn't like my coming here. What I quite fail to understand is why Indian Muslims, passing themselves off as Arabs, can wear turbans but not Hindus. I wrote letters to local newspapers protesting against this. I'm waiting to see what the local whites think about the issue. My company boss was not exactly enthusiastic about my writing the letter, but didn't oppose it either. Maybe he wanted to keep all his options open.

I'm also enclosing a letter for Kastur. Pass it on to her or read it out to her.

Yours,

Mohandas

~

The next day, some papers carried reactions to his letter. Mohandas had been waiting eagerly for them. Some reactions were in his favour, but most were against him. What right does a coolie, even if he is a barrister; have to defy the orders of a white presiding officer? He should have taken off his turban at once and apologized. Such people must not be allowed to remain in this colony. If timely action is not taken, the coolies will start thinking of themselves as the equals of whites. They should be whipped. One letter said: 'At least one person has stood up and raised his voice in defence of his identity. The coolies can establish their identity only by emulating this man; otherwise their status will be one day worse than that of the natives, while the excesses of the whites will keep multiplying day by day.'

Mohandas read those reactions many times. There was a kind of joyful feeling on his face. Surely, people will now begin to recognize him.

When he came out that day, he had a feeling that some people on the street were looking at him. He heard one of them telling his friends: 'This was the coolie who defied the magistrate in the courtroom.'

'Oh, so this is the coolie barrister whose letter the paper carried!'

'Hit him!'

A couple of stones also landed near him. Mohandas had a feeling that perhaps this was a good beginning for him.

~

A few days had passed since Mohandas had arrived in Durban. The spell of the stir caused by the letter in the newspaper was now dying down. A feeling of emptiness was beginning to cause him anxiety at times. Time seemed to have pulled to a stop. Nothing was forthcoming from Abdullah Sheth. What was he supposed to do? Why had he come here? How would he pass a whole year in this way? Questions like these had begun to hover around him.

Dada Abdullah sometimes talked religion. At such times, Mohandas was reminded of *Bapu*. During his last days, when he was confined to bed, people of different religions came to discuss religious matters with him: Jains, Hindus, Muslims, and Parsis. He listened to their discussions very attentively. Mohandas was young then and could think of little beyond his duties towards his father. But he still found himself interested in what Dada Abdullah had to say. Dada Abdullah could recite whole verses from the Quran Sharif. Being a Muslim was a matter of pride for him.

One day Mohandas asked him: 'I've noticed that you never get angry. Is this an occupational trait or have you learnt to control your mind?'

In reply, Dada Abdullah related to him an episode from the life of Prophet Mohammed. He passed through a narrow lane everyday. At exactly the time Mohammed passed through the lane, a woman used to throw out garbage into the lane from the roof of her house. It always fell on Hazrat Mohammed, but he kept to his path without a word and without even looking up. Once, there was no garbage for several days. Mohammed wondered why. What could possibly be the reason? He knocked on the door of the house. A very weak voice floated out from the house: 'Come on inside. The door is open.'

Inside the house, he saw a woman lying in a bed, groaning. There was no one to attend on her. So Hazrat took charge of the woman. He came everyday, tended to her needs, helped her sit up or lie down, and served her food and drink. He continued to do this till she had fully recovered.

When she was completely cured, she felt very ashamed. Mohammed told her: 'There is no need. You were doing your duties, I did mine. Each of us was only doing what he/she had to.'

Dada Abdullah summed up the story: 'If your duty is clear to you, it leaves no room for anger, does it?'

When Dada Abdullah talked in this vein, a strange kind of glow lit up his face. Often Mohandas wanted to ask a question but he stopped him with a raised hand. 'If you keep on asking why this and why that, you'll neither get a reply nor will you be able to fathom the depth of the matter.'

Mohandas pondered deeply over these remarks of Dada Abdullah.

~

One day, over breakfast, Mohandas asked Dada Abdullah: 'Why are the Indians here such a servile lot? Why don't they assert their rights?'

Dada Abdullah laughed: 'Did they ever do that in India?' He continued: 'We were born in India, we live here, and the conditions of our living are decided in London. You accept that the British government is fair and just, we too accept it, then what's the catch? It's not safe to pursue your inquiry beyond this point.' At this point, he fell silent. As the flow of his words came to an end, so did the glow on his face, the glow generated by the churning of his conscience.

Such talk left Mohandas very uncomfortable. Although simple and straightforward, the things Dada Abdullah said made him uneasy.

At times Mohandas would get agitated: 'I'm talking of a nation. When a nation awakes, morning cannot be far behind. People can be of both types; they can be weak or they can be courageous. Here, we have a whole nation of Indians, a nation of abused and frightened people.'

'You are right. We've all come here to earn our livelihood, *girmitiya*s and traders alike. That's the sole purpose of our lives. You will see that most of the *girmitiya*s have their families in India, but they themselves are here. They earn here, and support their families there. If things run smoothly here, things are pleasent there too.'

At such moments, the whole of India would unroll itself as a map before Mohandas. He just couldn't decide where to put his finger.

Mohandas had brought some books with him. They were still packed with the rest of his things. Suddenly he thought of the books. He unpacked the things and took the books out: there were the Gita, the Ramayana, devotional songs of Narsi Bhagat, altogether eight or ten books. There was a selection of Tolstoy's essays presented to him by a vegetarian Englishman in London. It was after a long time that he opened the Gita: the page on which it opened carried the following *shloka*: 'Among trees, I'm the peepul; among cows, I'm Kapila; among gods, I'm Indra, among castes, I'm *brahman*.' Why *brahman*? He thought of his childhood friend, Uka. Why not Uka? Uka suddenly stood before him exactly as he had looked in childhood. *Ba* always forbade him to play with him: 'Uka is a good boy. I have nothing against him. But I'm afraid of going against my religion. It's a sin to touch an untouchable. Sin leads you to hell.' Had the Gita instead said 'Among castes, I'm *shudra*,' it would not have been against the religion to play with Uka. Still, Mohandas played with Uka. *Ba* would pour a bucket of water on Mohandas. He would play with him again, and again *Ba* would give him a bath. He had separated the two things in his mind: playing with Uka and *Ba*'s giving him a bath. He also asked himself: Where does the Gita say that it's a sin to play with Uka? They may be *brahman*s, but why should that stop him from playing with Uka?

It appeared to Mohandas that they were all Ukas in South Africa: Dada Abdullah, he himself ..., everyone who had come from India. The whites were the only *brahman*s. He became agitated: How did India travel all the way here?

There was a knock on the door. Abdullah Sheth had sent for him. He got up to get ready. Whenever he went out, he dressed fully. Although not English, he looked a complete Englishman in his attire. In England, a white professor used to say: 'A proper dress makes an incomplete man complete. Without it, a man looks ugly. Your dress should be appropriate to the occasion and the occupation.' Mohandas followed his advice to the letter. The professor's words had made a deep impression on him.

But the courtroom incident had thrown up many questions. When he put on his dress, the questions, like the dress itself, kept tightening their hold on him. And there was no way he could take them off.

When Mohandas arrived, Dada Abdullah was issuing instructions to his assistants: 'Gandhibhai has to leave for Pretoria. Get a first class ticket for him.'

The assistant's voice was very low: 'First class is only for the whites.'

'Do you think I'll send a barrister in the van with the natives?' The assistant shrugged his shoulders and left. He was the third person to shrug his shoulders ever since Mohandas had arrived.

Dada Abdullah said: 'Good news! There's a letter from Mr. Baker. He is dealing with our case in Pretoria.' He handed the letter to Mohandas.

Mr. Baker wrote: 'Please send some trusted person or come yourself to help prepare the case.' Mohandas couldn't help laughing.

Dada Abdullah asked: 'Why do you laugh? You are the one going to Pretoria.'

'Lawyers' letters are perhaps equally brief in every country,' he said. 'But I know nothing about the case.'

'You'll learn it in a jiffy. There're the files and there's myself and you know the law. It's the case Jhaveribhai had mentioned to you.'

'Still it'll take some time to understand the case.'

'Take your time. I've sent for tickets for the next week.'

'Right now, I don't even know what my role is going to be in the case.'

'Study the file. I believe when you've studied it, you'll be able to decide on your role yourself.' Dada Abdullah handed over the file to Mohandas and said, 'Many of the papers in the file are in Gujarati. You may have to translate them into English. Neither Mr. Baker nor the court will understand Gujarati. I know that it is not a duty of a barrister to translate, but we can perhaps impose on you as you are almost a member of my family.'

~

When, after escaping from the Captain's clutches in Zanzirabad, he was living in an inn, Mohandas had struck up acquaintance with a Gujarati. Mohandas asked him if he could see the local court.

'Sure, it is not a restricted area. Anyone can walk in. Come, let's go.'

A Parsi lawyer was arguing a businessman's case. The merchant was a Gujarati. The lawyer was trying to explain to the court how Gujaratis kept their accounts. The magistrate was totally unconvinced by the lawyer's arguments. He had endless number of questions about the way Gujaratis kept their accounts. Whenever the lawyer thought he was ready to conclude his argument, the magistrate would fire a question at him which obliged the lawyer to retrace his argument from the very beginning. Actually, the magistrate was smarter in matters of book-keeping. But the lawyer was not prepared to give up either.

Bored by the argument, Mohandas walked out of the court. Accounts had always bored him. Studying the case file of Dada Abdullah, the face of that Parsi lawyer, who was arguing with all his might to win the case for his client, kept flashing before his eyes. For every step that he moved forward, the magistrate's questions pulled him one step back. One question kept raising its head in Mohandas' mind: 'I'm a barrister, so why did I walk out of the court?' He was very annoyed with himself. Had he shown some sense then, it would have helped him today.

Should he tell Dada Abdullah frankly that he knows nothing about book-keeping?

But how can he do it? He has come all this way just for this job. How irresponsible it would be of him to say such a thing! It would also be letting down Jhaveribhai.

He kept pacing up and down for a long time. Telling the truth, he felt, can never be wrong. But wouldn't giving up without trying be unfair to himself and to the times?

In the end, he decided that he would neither refuse Dada Abdullah nor tell Mr. Baker in Pretoria that this kind of work was beyond him.

Mohandas spent the whole night poring over the file. He made detailed notes. When he prepared a draft in Rajkot, he had to test every word on the touchstone of law. If necessary, he talked to the client and checked with his friends.

The first thing next morning, he went to the cashier. He was a loquacious person. Long-winded talk was a habit with him. Even before Mohandas could say anything to him, he started on his explanations: 'I have to look after everything in this firm: keeping accounts, maintaining books and records, receiving and making payments. I have built up this firm with my blood and sweat. The master knows this.'

Mohandas had to agree with him: 'No doubt, this firm would have sunk without a trace without you.' The cashier looked carefully at Mohandas: Is he making fun of me? But Mohandas was serious. He said, 'I have to ask you a few questions about this file. My questions have nothing to do with your book-keeping; they have everything to do with my ignorance.'

The word P-note occurred frequently in the file. Every time he came across this word, Mohandas got stuck. He had in fact been to a bookshop and got himself a textbook of economics before talking to the cashier. But P-note remained a mystery. He had also hunted for it in the dictionary.

The cashier was in full flow. Mohandas was meanwhile wrestling with himself: asking the cashier would mean inviting ridicule. He will go around telling everyone that the big shot barrister Gandhi doesn't even know what a P-note is. But is it a crime not to know something? He mustered all his courage and asked him: 'What's a P-note?'

The cashier's face lit up with a sense of all-knowing pride. He smiled and said, 'Gandhibhai, there are many words that you know only too well but whose usage is unfamiliar to you. That's what puts you in a fix. Many things that books cannot tell you, experience can. Take P-note. This is a word we use every day. P-note is promissory note. It is used ...'

'I got it,' Mohandas cut in.

Mohandas was laughing at himself: 'Such a simple thing and I didn't get it.'

The final round of consultations was to be held with Dada Abdullah himself. There were a number of things in the file which only Dada Abdullah could have clarified. Mohandas left the cashier to go to Dada Abdullah. He had realized that he could approach anyone for words and their meanings, but the essence of the file was known only to Abdullah Sheth. Mohandas told him, 'Abdullah Sheth, I have never dealt with cases related to book-keeping. For me this whole file is like a maze. The first problem is how to get in, and if I do get in somehow, the second problem is how to get out. Only you have the key to this maze.'

Abdullah Sheth laughed: 'Gandhibhai, I'm an illiterate person, who has picked up a few words of English in the company of people like you. Mr. Baker used to say, "Application of common sense is law." For people like me, law is something like swimming across an ocean. Book-keeping too looks like common sense to me. You have income, write it down; you have outgo, set it down. Whatever payments you make, put them on record; whatever you receive, note them down too. Whatever the losses, put them down. In other words, all give and take, buy and sell, profit and loss—if it's all recorded on paper, the structure will stand. The same applies in the present case. The goods we delivered to Tyebji, the payments that Tyebji made—everything is recorded. Whatever we are yet to receive from Tyebji too is in the books in full detail. But the other party doesn't agree. If they have any records of their own, they too can put them forward. That's the case we have presented before the court through our lawyer. All that now remains to be done is to interpret the law in such a way that the court accepts what is right as right. If what is right comes out as wrong, then, in our own eyes, we are all liars: I am a liar, you are a liar, and the law too is a liar.'

Turning the papers, Mohandas asked: 'What's your claim?'

'Tyeb Sheth is a big trader. He is also a relative. Some goods were sent to his company. Only part payment was made, and was made late. The part that remained unpaid went on collecting interest, and interest on interest. I know that not everyone has the capacity to repay forty thousand pounds. There are of course people who can. Those who can't look for escape routes. We have in our possession P-notes written by Tyeb Sheth in good times and bad times. They are substantial documents. He wants to strike at truth with falsehood. That, in short, is what the whole tussle is about.'

Mohandas saw transparency and honesty in what Dada Abdullah said. Dada Abdullah had at his fingertips the dates of the dispatch of goods, the payments made, and the P-notes issued. He rattled them off as if a math teacher was explaining problems of the principal, the interest, the gross amount, etc. to students.

Mohandas now felt assured that his work was half-done. Actually, when Dada Abdullah was explaining, he had been examining the papers one by one.

Mohandas' remarks now carried a tone of responsibility. He announced: 'Abdullah Sheth, I'm ready.'

Dada Abdullah scrutinized Mohandas' face carefully. For the first time, he got an impression of firmness from his face. He asked, 'Where are you going to stay there?'

That question surprised Mohandas. What could he possibly say? Surely, Dada Abdullah had something in mind. He rejoined with another question: 'Where do you want me to stay?'

Dada Abdullah squirmed a little, but recovered quickly and continued: 'Let me write to Mr. Baker. He will make the necessary arrangements for your stay. I hope you don't mind. I'll also give you a note for the Memon traders of my community, though I don't wish you to stay with them. Tyebji has a lot of influence with local traders. If anyone of them is able to lay hands on our papers, it'll be a disaster. We'll have to guard against such elements.'

Mohandas was somewhat surprised at what Dada Abdullah said. He thought for a moment and then said, 'This is not my country, nor do I know anyone here. But I have no problem staying with anyone, anywhere. Of course, in the first place, I'll stay wherever Mr. Baker puts me up. If he has any problem making the arrangements, I'll make my own arrangements.'

'But ...'

'I wish to request you with a full sense of responsibility that you may place your fullest trust on me. Not a single paper, not a single fact, will leak through me, even if I stay with a trader of your community. I have absolutely no intention of establishing any links with Tyebji. But, surely, it does no harm to be introduced to him, or to mix with him, in a general way?'

Abdullah Sheth was listening to him, quite unbelieving. Mohandas had not yet finished. He continued: 'Tyebji is a relative of yours. We should keep all the doors open. If there is a mutual understanding, the relationship too can be saved. Your money too will not be in danger. But this can happen only if both of you want it.'

Abdullah Sheth held his peace for a while and then said, 'An agreement is a good thing. It saves unnecessary division and destruction.'

'I have just suggested a possibility. It is not necessary that it'll come about.'

'We know each other inside out. Tyeb is not the kind of person to give up easily. You want to extract oil from a seed, you have to apply pressure.

A slight mistake and we'll find ourselves back where we'd started. Please be careful in whatever you do. I can afford to wait.'

'All I wanted to know was how much trust you are ready to place on me, and how much leeway you'll allow me. If I meet Tyebji, this is what I'll try to explain to him: the power of truth is supreme. The path may be bumpy but if you make it to the destination, there's little chance that you'll be dislodged again.'

Abdullah left the place without a word.

That night, Mohandas wrote his diary:

> *It has been a week since I arrived in Durban, but it feels as if I have been here for ages. I am so far from home that, despite its being so recalcitrant, my mind has finally reconciled itself to the place. You accept your circumstances and there are no more choices to worry about. At home, I have my elder brother and his family.* Ba *is no more. A link snapped when she died. Kastur and the two kids, so it seems to me at times, are pulling me hard and keeping up the pressure. I was never able to spend time with the younger kid. I have been on the run all the time, as if someone has tied wheels to my feet and given me a push. Once, when I wrote drafts for a living, someone had commented sarcastically:* padhe farsi beche tel *(Study Persian, sell oil = Where was the need to study Persian, if selling oil was all that you had to do?). Selling oil is all that I have been doing and all that I have to do here too. But why listen to what people say? Didn't they say all kinds of things about me and Sheikh Mehtab? So much so, they didn't even spare Kastur. Mustn't Kastur be feeling bad too, especially now when I am not there? Now that Ba is gone, it's only Kastur and the kids who are my ties to the family. But even when I'm with her, Kastur seems so indifferent. Is it only my feeling or is she really stone-hearted? Sheikh Mehtab often told me: ' Bhabhi really doesn't care for you.' Is it possible that I've also started thinking alike under his influence? Sheikh Mehtab is another weakness that I have. These are like two circles: sometimes they seem to circle separately, sometimes they start intersecting.*

Mohandas felt very tired. He put the pen aside, though there was much more he wanted to write. A thought suddenly sprang to his mind: diaries are perhaps always written at night. Like wives, they too need solitude. His lips spread in a line of smile and he went to sleep with the smile sill in place.

~

The train tickets had arrived. A telegram had been dispatched to Mr. Baker. 'M.K. Gandhi, Bar-at-Law, is arriving at Pretoria to argue the case. Please arrange for his stay. Thanks.'

Dada Abdullah had also sent a letter, which he had got someone else to write for him. Mohandas hadn't got to see it. He had also given Mohandas a few letters for his friends; also a few pounds for his expenses. Durban station was on Pine Street, which was not very far from West Street.

When Mohandas had first detrained at Durban station, he had been surprised to see the system at the station. There were separate exits for whites and blacks. The passage for the whites was clean and very imposing. The number of people using that path was also very small. The blacks on the other hand came in hordes; as a result, there was a lot of jostling and a lot of filth. The discrimination left Mohandas speechless.

The train for Pretoria left at around seven in the evening. Mohandas was ready by six. He was slightly nervous. He had made his preparations very carefully, paying special thought to the things he might need. You never knew what you might need and when. Having got ready, he came out on the balcony, pacing up and down. In a way, he was trying to put things in order within him. He still had to get his tickets from Abdullah Sheth. At about a quarter past six, he came down. He saw Dada Abdullah's horse-carriage pulled up in front. He was surprised. Dada Abdullah's carriage at this hour? Maybe, he has somewhere to go. The thought also occurred to him that maybe it was for him, but he couldn't help laughing at the idea. The Viceroy, aren't you? Company servant on a year's agreement—that's what you are! Don't even dream of a carriage; sometimes the dream itself hobbles you. The dreams will never get you anywhere.

Dada Abdullah came out and handing the tickets to him, said, 'Here's your ticket.' Then, laughingly, he said, 'Whenever we Indians set out on a journey, we prepare ourselves mentally that maybe we won't come back whole,' and looked at Mohandas' face. Though he was laughing, his face was colourless. Dada Abdullah found the laughter hollow and careworn. He quickly said: 'I didn't say that to alarm you. They all come back. So will you. Come, let me take you to the station.'

'I'll manage. Let me take someone with me to help me with the luggage. The station isn't all that far.'

'What is the carriage for? I'm not going to take you or your luggage on my back. You are going on company work. I'm not so ungrateful as not even to see you off at the station.'

'I didn't mean that.'

'Fine, so let's go.'

The luggage had been brought down. It was placed on the carriage. Dada Abdullah first got Mohandas to sit in the carriage and then got in himself. It was getting cold. Winter days were short anyway. Darkness was descending on the streets. The cold in the months of May and June was no less than the cold in December and January in India. Mohandas liked it.

On the way, Dada Abdullah asked: 'You have woollens, don't you?'

'Yes, I had some made in London. I'm still using them.'

'How did you know that it was cold here at this time of the year? It must be scorching hot in India.'

'Since I was coming for a whole year, it had to be cold at one time or the other. Good that I can use my woollens early. A lawyer's brain, anyway, is used to making all the necessary investigations before starting on any work.'

Dada Abdullah laughed.

There were lamp posts on both sides of the road. The dim light shed by the lanterns in them spread on the road like a lighted shadow. The lamp post seemed to move with you with its light for a little distance, and then sprang back to its original position as the boundary of the next lamp post started. A thin corridor of darkness separated the two lamp posts.

Abdullah Sheth said: 'Mr. Gandhi, get yourself bedding on the train. It'll cost you five shillings. You can go sleeping on the upper berth.'

'It's not necessary.'

'For one thing, you'll be comfortable against the cold; for another, you will escape the comments and questioning the lower berth may invite. You never know how the white passengers may start behaving.' As he spoke the last sentence, there was a catch in his throat, which he coughed clear.

'Five shillings is not a small amount. In times of need, even a single shilling is priceless.'

Dada Abdullah assumed a serious mien: 'It's up to you. What I mean is that you should not compromise with your comfort for the sake of money. It's our duty to see to it that all your needs are met.'

The first-class compartment was empty. Dada Abdullah's expression showed that the sight of the empty compartment had relieved him of the worry which had been weighing him down. Laughing, he said: 'You are lucky. You have the whole compartment to yourself. You'll have a comfortable, hassle-free journey.'

Mohandas did not react. He just said: 'Let's see,' and started arranging his luggage neatly.

When the train had left, Dada Abdullah said *khuda hafij*. Mohandas just repeated the greeting. Coming back to his seat, he looked around the compartment sizing it up and then settled down to his reading. Dada Abdullah had presented him a copy of the Quran.

Mohandas was feeling pleased with himself. For the first time he was travelling to another city, Pretoria, on a definite mission. So far, he had been wandering aimlessly. If he is successful in reviving the relationship between the two close relatives, it'll be a bigger achievement than even winning the case. Surely, there is a divine plan behind all this! Why should he otherwise be running from India to Natal and from Natal to Transvaal? Why should the three disparate people from three disparate corners, Dada Abdullah, Tyeb Sheth and Mohandas

Karamchand Gandhi be thrown together? South Africa did not seem as bad to him now as it had seemed at first, especially when he saw Dada Abdullah's attitude on the day when, talking to Marcel, he hadn't even offered him a seat. Marcel too had been looking at him as if he was a piece of property shared by those two. The turban episode too was still sticking to his mind like a brittle scab over a fresh wound. Dada Abdullah's not giving him the true picture also hung like a question mark before him.

He read the translation of a verse from the Quran: 'Forgiveness is God's unique gift to man.' He lingered over the verse for a few minutes. Every religion actually says this. When *Bapu* had forgiven him the sin of stealing gold from Karsan's bracelet and selling it, tears were streaming down his face as if he was washing his sin with them. His letter seeking forgiveness, in which he had confessed his crime, lay in *Bapu*'s lap and was soaked with his tears.

When Mohandas' father, Kaba Gandhi, relinquished his prime ministership of Porbandar, he had got his brother, Tulsidas, appointed in his place. Kaba Gandhi still commanded a lot of respect; in fact, not only Kaba Gandhi but his father, Mohandas' grandfather, Ota Gandhi, too. It is perhaps a man's daring and courage that is remembered more than the man himself. He had faced the guns of Porbandar's queen, whose wrath he had incurred by insisting on the innocence of an innocent man. The queen, Rupali *Ba*, had vowed to put him and his family to death. In the ensuing exchange of fire, his bodyguard, Makarani, had fought single-handed till he was killed. Burying Makarani, Ota Gandhi had flown overnight to Kutiyana, which lay in the territory of the Nawab of Junagarh.

When, after a tiring three-day journey on camel back, Mohandas reached Porbandar and asked his uncle to recommend him to Mr. Lely, the agent in Porbander, his uncle's retort was that he would not partake of a sin by recommending anyone for crossing the seven seas. When Mohandas went to see him, Mr. Lely was absent. He waited. When Mr. Lely arrived, he stepped forward and greeted him. All previous night Mohandas had spent memorizing and rehearsing a few sentences of English for the occasion. Now he delivered as many of them as he could recall, carefully and in the manner of a dialogue. Lely stood on the stairs half turned away from him. He listened to Mohandas as one listens to a beggar. He asked: 'Have you completed your graduation?'

'Not yet.'

'London is not Porbandar or Rajkot. First graduate and then ask for help. The state does not have money to waste.'

Mohandas smiled to himself. Thank God, Lely did not have him thrown out of his house. Lely clattered up the stairs, leaving Mohandas gaping after him. The first experience of humiliation is the most painful. Since then, he had had many of them.

He dozed off. It was the same house again with Hari and Mani, *Ba*, Kastur and Sheikh Mehtab. He was quite happy.

~

The train was losing speed. Mohandas woke up. He realized that he was not at home, but travelling on a train. The past too is like imagination. The train pulled to a stop. He could see Pietermaritzburg written in front of him. The station was bathed in a dim light. The temperature seemed to have dipped quite low. Simply putting your head out of the window made you shiver. There was very little activity at the station. The number of passengers was smaller than the number of staff. A few coolies stood waiting for passengers, some of them Indian. Right in front of his compartment there stood an empty bench shrivelling in cold. Behind it stood the station building. Mohandas smiled as the thought occurred to him that probably in every country the first class compartment always pulled up in front of the main gate of the building. Nowhere except in very small village stations in India did you witness such sparseness of population. And Pietermaritzburg was the capital of Natal! He looked at the watch. It was nine.

He muttered to himself: 'When it's so cold, it's cosier to sit huddled with yourself.'

The door opened and a blast of cold wind swept through the compartment. It was an attendant. He asked Mohandas: 'Need bedding?'

'No, thanks.'

The attendant got off. Another blast of wind. Mohandas thought he would probably have to travel alone in the compartment. Never mind. He spread out his legs on the berth, relaxed his body and closed his eyes.

A white man was now entering the compartment. Good, thought Mohandas, better two than one. Some whites are good company, although most of them are snobbish and prefer to keep to themselves. They considered it beneath their dignity to talk to others.

Standing in the centre, the white surveyed the compartment as if he was standing in the middle of a deserted island. Such a large compartment and empty! Suddenly his eyes fell on Mohandas. His expression changed at once, as if someone was going to attack him. He swung around and jumped out of the compartment. His sudden exit struck as peculiar to Mohandas. A little tension disturbed his carefree ease; his legs shrank and his eyebrows stiffened. However, he told himself: 'Why are you worried? Maybe he left because he remembered something he had to do.' Actually, somewhere at the back of his mind were stuck the assistant's words: 'First class is for the whites.' He had a first class ticket. The whole compartment was anyway empty. Had there been a problem, they wouldn't have let him enter the compartment at Durban itself. He felt a little better and closed his eyes or maybe he closed his eyes to feel better. However perhaps it would have been wiser to have the bedding. He had been feeling cold too, but it had become warmer now. Good that he didn't get the bedding. It would have been a waste of five shillings.

The white man was back with two white railway staff. The man and one of the staff stood at the door while the third man came and stood near Mohandas. Eyeing him angrily, he said: 'Who allowed you into this compartment? Pick up your luggage and go to the van. That's where the coolies travel.'

'But I'm a barrister.'

'Whatever you may be, you are a coolie first. How did you dare enter a first class compartment?'

Mohandas' face was blazing, but he was also trying not to get agitated inwardly. However, disappointment was writ large on his face.

'You are not allowed to travel in this compartment, do you understand?'

'I will definitely travel in this compartment.' His voice was certainly firm but his legs were shaking.

'Vacate this compartment within five minutes, or I'll have you thrown out.'

Mohandas closed his eyes for a moment. He heard someone telling him: 'No. You will not leave this compartment.'

Mohandas spoke without the slightest hesitation: 'Yes, you can have me thrown out, but you cannot ask me to leave. I consider my right to be a truth. My ticket gives me that right.'

His other white companion, who was guarding the door, stretched his neck out and shouted: 'Police! Police!' His voice was shaking in anger. None of them had thought that a member of the coolie class could talk back to them in this fashion. He would call out to the police once and then turn around to look at Mohandas as if he was a dangerous animal advancing towards him.

The first white man was tearing into Mohandas in his own style: 'I know people like you inside out. You filthy, contemptible people want to be our equals! Rotten worms, that's what you are! You should thank the goodness of our heart that we allow you to stay on here.'

'Also the fact that you need us ...,' Mohandas said very gently.

'You damned ...,' the man rushed at him as if to flatten him on the spot, but stopped after a couple of steps.

His friend had now got a policeman with him. The white passenger was looking at Mohandas cautiously as if he was going to jump out of the window and escape, but didn't speak a word.

The other man told the policeman: 'Throw this coolie out with his luggage.'

Mohandas had planted his feet firmly on the floor. The policeman was a strong fellow. He grabbed Mohandas by the shoulders and dragged him to the door. The English passenger was smiling at Mohandas' discomfiture.

Mohandas kept up his protest to the policeman: 'You cannot treat a civilized and educated person like this.'

The policeman was either deaf or such a blind follower of the master's word that his own concerns were dead. At the door, Mohandas tried to hold on to a bar, but someone pushed him so hard from the back that he fell on to the platform. He fell on his right side. Fortunately, he was able to grab hold of the bench or he would have been badly bloodied. His knees and elbows had been scraped. As he fell, his luggage too followed him in the same fashion. He got up with the support of the bench and looked at the train. The whistle had gone and the train was creeping forward, leaving puffs of smoke. The white passenger was still at the door looking at him, a triumphant smile on his face. When the entire compartment had passed him, he realized that all its window glasses had got blind.

Seeing a man being thrown out of a compartment, a few coolies rushed to the spot. Mohandas had settled himself on the bench by this time. One of the coolies said, 'This is some coolie-sahib.'

'Looks like he got into the first class.'

'What else did he expect? Comparing himself with a white sahib, wasn't he?' The other coolies too had arrived by now, some of them natives. They sniggered. One of them wisecracked: 'Wearing stripes doesn't make you a tiger.'

In the half-light nothing was visible clearly. Mohandas had no external injuries; it was the internal damage that had left the deepest wound and hurt the most. A couple of coolies came close to him and examined his face.

A couple of railway officials also made it to the scene. One of them said: 'Although a coolie, he got into the first class.' The other one issued an order: 'Deposit his luggage in the station master's office. He can collect it in the morning.'

'Look at the daring! Thinking of himself as an equal of the whites! Will never dare to enter the first class ever again.'

Two of the coolies picked up the luggage and followed them. Both of them were absolutely quiet and kept looking back at Mohandas sitting in a corner of the bench. The others too sauntered off. The cold was getting worse.

The train had left, leaving behind its smell. Utter silence had laid siege of the platform. Mohandas put his hand on the arm of the bench to lift himself up. It was freezing. His bruises were still fresh. He postponed getting up and pressed both his hands between his knees. He felt a little warm. Wounds hurt more when it was cold. He looked around. There was no one in sight. Only in the booking office a dim light was burning.

'Perhaps Pietermaritzburg is at a higher altitude than Durban,' Mohandas told himself, shivering a little.

Someone seated himself on the ground behind the bench. Mohandas paid no attention till he heard someone whispering: 'It's cold here. Let's go and sit in the waiting room.' His voice sounded cautious. Mohandas was not familiar with his language or pronunciation, but he felt as if someone had placed a warm hand on his shoulder. He got up and took slow steps towards the waiting room. He was having difficulty walking. The waiting room was the hall next to the entrance gate. The walls were all covered with woodwork as a result of which the room was not so cold. A wooden staircase led up to the clock tower directly above the hall. All night, he heard it ring out the hours. They had helped him spend the night. Even at that time the thought had occurred to him that wherever they went Englishmen were sure to set up clock towers. Maybe, this was the reason.

When Mohandas walked to the waiting room, he had thought that maybe it would provide him relief from the biting cold, but the cold continued to bite as before. The only difference was the wind. There was no wind inside; the cold had lost its breath. Mohandas wanted his overcoat very badly, but it had been deposited with his luggage at the station master's. Couldn't he get his overcoat now? He got up, but then the thought occurred to him: suppose someone misbehaves again? The station master's office was upstairs. He would probably come rolling downstairs. He sat down again, pressing both his hands under his armpits and raising his heels. His feet felt wet inside the shoes.

Suddenly, he heard the sound of shoes walking in his direction. The whole platform resounded with the sound of the shoes like a pair of drums. Actually, it had taken the platform only a short time to turn into a tautly drawn sheet of utter silence. Mohandas sat all huddled up. He gradually unwound himself: legs first, hands next, neck last. The shoulders were still stiff. A few passengers walked in. Their faces were mere shadows for one another. A small candelabrum hung from the ceiling, its light so faded that one could barely sense the walls and maybe persons. Faces are far too finely featured. The man who walked in was covered from top to toe. Looking at him, Mohandas was again reminded of his overcoat. Lucky chap, to have his clothes with him.

It was the passenger who broke the ice: 'Where are you going? There's no train due till the morning.' The way he said it, Mohandas could make out it was a white man.

Mohandas kept quiet. If he said anything, it might offend him, and like an eagle, he may rush at him and start clawing him. He had been hurt enough already.

He spoke again: 'It' so cold. I hope you have enough clothes.'

Mohandas felt he should respond, but he was afraid that his teeth might start clattering. That would be worse than making a response.

The newcomer took out a cigarette and lit it. Mohandas cringed. He might see his face in the light of the cigarette and then he would have to leave the waiting room too. Mohandas turned his face towards the wall.

The man mumbled: 'You are surely going to die of cold.'

He wanted to say: 'None of your business.' But he clenched his teeth.

It was a great relief when the man left. Now he wanted to spread his limbs. But he couldn't.. It made only a slight difference: he breathed more easily. In the presence of the man, he was feeling choked.

'What should be my next step? Should I go back?' thought Mohandas, 'But how can I? I am here on a year's agreement. My self-respect and the honour of my country are closely linked to the question of staying on or going back. But how can I save my self-respect in the present conditions?'

Mohandas got up with a jerk and started pacing the room. He realized there could be heat within you too. That heat was now making him pace the room. Thin shafts of light were streaming in and were stuck randomly on the walls like discoloured stickers. When he walked through them, the stickers jumped off the walls and stuck to his face, his clothes or his body. As he walked past, the first ones again slipped off to their original place while new ones took their place. He of course knew that darkness had a flat surface, but the passing lights made it uneven. Shadows did the same with light.

He muttered to himself: 'Is it possible that the only purpose these questions have is to strengthen the fears within me? Don't I have it in me to fight these fears? Cowardice begins to show on your face like water spilled on an earthen pitcher. It then leaves no part of your body unsoaked—not your heart, not your mind, not your blood, nor any other part. To go back will mean handing yourself over to that cowardice, to sink yourself in it. There is no bigger humiliation than cowardice. There was no personal enmity behind that insult on the train, no self-interest, only a psychological hatred, which was ubiquitous. We are all part of it. To pierce a hole in this thick cloud, you must stay with it. Don't run. You run and this hatred will chase you with renewed vigour. You stay with it, and you can run your fingers through the holes of its weak spots and tear its fabric to pieces.'

His eyes began to grow heavy. He sat himself down. The cold rose like a current within him and ran a shiver through his body. His eyes opened, and fell shut again. He huddled a little more. He wanted to but he couldn't spread his limbs.

When a train passed the station early in the morning, it woke him up. It was perhaps the first train. All night, the railway tracks were just cold steel. Then he realized suddenly that his body was warm. Had the weather changed overnight? He found that his body was covered in an old blanket.

He was surprised. How had this come about? There was no one around. He came out on the platform. Two men were sleeping on a bench under a single blanket. He remembered that it was the same bench which had saved him from serious injury last night. He thought of *Ba*. Had it been *Ba* in place of the bench, she would also have saved him as the bench had done. But how could he compare *Ba* with a bench? A bench is an inanimate object; *Ba*, on the other hand, was full of feeling and love. Maybe the bench had assumed the role of *Ba* just at that moment. Slowly, the scenes of the previous night began to re-enact themselves in Mohandas' consciousness: the white man with a smile on his face, his luggage strewn all over the platform, the train steaming out of the platform. The experience of humiliation bores into your consciousness like a slowly turning drill, although at the moment of experience it hits you like a sledge-hammer. He felt he was walking a tight rope. He tried to balance himself. The train had left, but somewhere on the tracks its departure lingered. They were shining. He came near the bench, holding the blanket in his hands. He knew that it was not his blanket, nor did he have any right to the warmth it had given him. He wanted to get rid of it as quickly as possible.

It would be still some time before he could get his luggage from the station master's office. It was a quarter past six on the clock. He stood watching the two men sleeping on the bench for some time and then returned to the waiting room. In India too people spent nights like this: hitting the bed wherever fancy took them. These people at least had a blanket with them. He went to the bathroom and washed his face. The water was freezing cold. He didn't have anything to wipe his face, so he used his handkerchief. The handkerchief got completely soaked. The clothes he wore were all crumpled, all full of wrinkles and folds. He was impatient to have his luggage back so he could change his clothes. The face was still moist and cold. Having nothing to do, he was finding it difficult to kill time. He started pacing again. He looked up at the ceiling. Several candelabra were hanging there, but only one, slightly bigger than the others, was lighted at night. Maybe that was why the dark was so cold. The morning was no longer young. He heard footsteps behind him and wheeled around. You never knew what shape the aftermath of last night's events might take. Two coolies appeared. Perhaps they were the ones sleeping on the bench.

'There was a blanket here ...,' one of them said.

'So it was yours? You suffered in the cold and gave me the blanket?'

'We had two of them. We thought here was someone from our land and maybe he knows no one here. The station master had left for home and there was nowhere to stow the luggage. So we put it in the booking office and went to sleep right here. If you lose your luggage in a foreign land, there's no one to help you out. When we came back to tell you, you were lying here all huddled up. So we put one blanket on top of you and used the other one for ourselves. We were anyway better off, being two.'

'Do you sleep at the station everyday? You don't go home?'

'We do, but we thought it wouldn't be right to leave you alone here—an educated man, harassed by the whites, with no luggage. So we thought we'd just sleep here. Makes no difference even if you go sleepless for a night.'

Mohandas thought of *Bapu*. It often happened that, while sleeping, his covers would fall off. When *Bapu* woke up, he would put them back again. They say a woman has a soft corner even for a stranger. Maybe, every man too has a woman inside him. He looked at those two walking out with the blankets over their arms. No words came out of his mouth, though there was much that he wanted to say.

Before they left, they had got Mohandas his luggage. Mohandas had decided to stay on and fight rather than make good his escape. As the day progressed, his determination too became stronger.

~

When Dada Abdullah received Mohandas' telegram, Marcel was sitting with him. When Dada Abdullah opened the telegram, his mind was full of apprehension.

Marcel's eyes were focused on his face. He asked the question that is conventionally asked on such occasions: 'Is everything fine?'

'Yes ...' He read out the telegram: 'Despite first class ticket white fellow passenger throws me and my luggage out of train at Pietermaritzburg station. Humiliated. Journey postponed. Protest telegram sent to General Manager. Please contact.' Below, it said: M.K.Gandhi.

Marcel laughed out loud: 'A good lesson. You put him in the first class; this was the only cure. The fellow was talking that day of Paris as if he had seen every street and every square. And the fellow doesn't know a word of French.'

'I don't get it,' said Dada Abdullah.

'One doesn't become a barrister just by putting on a frock coat, talking fancy and passing exams. One also needs brains.'

Dada Abdullah held up a finger to silence him and said, 'Never mind all that, Mr. Ledue. At that moment, Mr. Gandhi was going to Pretoria in the capacity of a representative of my company. Possibly, you are right that I should not have done so.'

'Oh, no, this was a godsend opportunity. You should be happy that you didn't have to tell him yourself and a way unfolded itself. He'll make good his escape. If he doesn't, you can be sure you'll never find a more shameless guy anywhere.'

'All that will follow later. Right now, we need to work to meet the demands of the moment.'

Dada Abdullah upped and left to get ready. Marcel continued to wait for sometime and then got up and left without telling anyone anything. When Abdullah Sheth returned, he was already gone. Abdullah Sheth found it peculiar that Marcel had left so unceremoniously.

The general manager's office was on the first floor of the Durban station building. It took Abdullah Sheth fifteen minutes to reach there on foot. He got himself announced and was called in at once. Mohandas' telegram and Marcel's visiting card lay in front of him.

'Good afternoon, sir.'

'Well, what can I do for you, Mr. Abdullah?' said the general manager, returning his greeting.

'Sir, Mr. M.K. Gandhi was travelling to Pretoria on my firm's business. He arrived from India barely ten days ago. I have received this telegram from him. He was thrown out of a running train. He had a perfectly valid first class ticket.'

'I know ...,' said the general manager, glancing at the telegram. 'I have also received a telegram from Mr. Gandhi. I have sent for a report.'

'Throwing out an honourable gentleman, a barrister from London, with his luggage, out of a compartment—is it justified?'

'You knew that only Europeans travel first class; why didn't you stop him?' The general manager's face was a little stern. Abdullah Sheth didn't like it. He said, with due modesty: 'He had in his possession a valid first class ticket. The Railways had sold him the ticket.'

The general manager relented a little. 'You are right, but you don't walk into a home just because the front door was left open inadvertently.'

'But, sir, a train is not a private home. It's a passenger facility that any fare-paying citizen can avail of. If someone has a ticket, which he has bought himself, then he earns the right to use that facility in a legitimate way. Mr. Gandhi is a barrister with a degree from London. This sort of thing perhaps doesn't happen there.'

The general manager's voice was stern again: 'But it does happen here. It was your responsibility to inform him of this.'

Dada Abdullah had spoken more than he would normally have dared to. After this last sentence of the general manager, he lost heart. The general manager was looking at him with a sense of triumph. Dada Abdullah mustered courage once again and said, 'I thought Mr. Gandhi has an English degree, dresses in the English way, is a barrister, maybe you'll view him differently from the ordinary Indians. I couldn't think of sending such a person in the van compartment.'

'This might have been your problem, but it wasn't the Railway's.'

It was for the first time that Dada Abdullah found himself fuming at a white officer's remarks. He got up with a start. The general manager asked him to be seated: 'You are one of our big clients. I have sent a message to the Pietermaritzburg station master that Mr. Gandhi should be sent, with due care and comfort, on the same ticket, to his destination. But this certainly doesn't mean that this is a right that belongs to Mr. Gandhi.'

Like mercury in a thermometer, Sheth Abdullah's temperature came down halfway in a single jerk. He bowed a little and with a 'Thank you, sir,' he came out.

Dada Abdullah had seen Marcel's card on the general manager's table. His irritation at the whites had grown.

Sheth Abdullah was home but he still didn't feel at ease. He sent telegrams to a number of his business friends. The message was the same in all of them: 'Mr. M.K. Gandhi, company barrister, thrown out of train at Pietermaritzburg station. Please extend all possible help. Dada Abdullah.'

As afternoon progressed, several businessmen gathered at the station. Most of them were Muslims, a few with beards. They wore a round cap or a turban. Mr. Abu Bakr was the first one to arrive. He had brought along some food and drink with him. He introduced himself: 'I am Abu Bakr. I run a small business in Pietermaritzburg. Dada Abdullah is a friend. The moment I got his telegram, I left at once, wondering whether you had anything to eat at all. I am indeed very sorry for the ill treatment meted out to you by the whites. We are frequent victims of such treatment. But how irresponsible of me to start by talking of myself! Please have something to eat first.'

'No, thanks. When this incident occurred, there were two coolies, fellow countrymen, at the station. They helped me a lot. They took my luggage the whites had thrown out in their custody and safekeeping. They covered me with their blanket in the severe cold of the night. If they hadn't, all you might have found here would have been my stiff body.' Mohandas laughed.

'It's the grace of God. He always sends his messengers in some form or the other to help people in distress.'

'They got me some tea and biscuits. I was also carrying some foodstuff.'

'That's not a meal enough, Mr. Gandhi. There's nothing here that you can't eat. I know what Gujarati Hindus eat. But if you have any qualms ...'

'What are you saying? What qualms? But ...'

'In that case, no ifs and no buts. Start eating. You know I'm your senior in age.'

Abu Bakr had brought along a servant with him, who was a Hindu. He laid out the food. Holding him by the hand, Mohandas also got Abu Bakr to join him. Although Mohandas ate very little, while eating he couldn't help being reminded of the days when, in Sheikh Mehtab's company, he had turned a non-vegetarian and always had a full stomach. When he returned home at night and *Ba* asked him to dinner, he always had an excuse ready: 'I'm not hungry.' Sometimes he had to eat, despite a full stomach. It wasn't easy to refuse *Ba* everyday. After eating meat, at least for sometime, he felt he had grown stronger. Sheikh Mehtab's observation that eating meat was making him fitter to fight the English seemed to him to be turning out right. However, internally, lying to *Ba* was making him quite as weak. Finally, he had to tell Mehtab that he couldn't continue to lie to *Ba*. Whether or not he could fight the English, meat eating had to stop!

'A penny for your thoughts,' Abu Bakr said.

'The affection with which you brought me food reminded me of a friend and of my mother ...'

Abu Bakr said softly: 'Yes, Mr. Gandhi, it happens, it surely happens. When we left our country to come here, except at work, we were always thinking of home, of our country, of our people, of their love—of nothing except these. But gradually time rose like a wall between us and hid everything from us ...'

Several other businessmen had also arrived at the station. Everyone was trying to give courage to Mohandas in his own way. Listening to them, Mohandas had to make an extra effort to keep his own courage intact.

One of them said, 'Why do we work so hard? For whom? For this country. We together have made Natal what it is today.'

Another one said, 'If we hadn't arrived, these whites would've fled from this place. The natives had already given them the thumbs down.'

The third one said, 'First and second class are not for us; they are for whites only. Even their dogs travel with them. Which one of us hadn't had the experience of being thrown out of a running train, of being kicked, and beaten? Okay, so we were illiterate and put up with the treatment! But you are a graduate from the holiest of their holy, London, a barrister, and they still treat you the same?'

'Wait a bit longer. You have seen nothing yet. Now you are a marked man!'

A funny feeling of irritation was growing within Mohandas, but he stayed quiet. All that he allowed himself to say was: 'Sometimes, humiliation and neglect can turn into strength. Please don't worry yourself.'

One of them blurted out: 'It'd be best for you to go back. They'll not tolerate educated people like you.'

'Tolerance breeds tolerance. I must go to Pretoria. Run from your responsibility once, and you'll be running away all your life.'

Mohandas had nipped the issue in the bud.

They all stayed on till the train came and left. Many of them narrated their tales of woe at the hands of the whites. 'We have suffered so much; for you, it's just the beginning.' In a way, this is what they were trying to tell him: 'Our line of woes is much longer than yours; in fact, yours is as yet only a point.' Mohandas could understand what they were trying to tell him. Deep inside him, a chain of questions was taking shape: 'Why did they allow themselves to suffer? Okay, maybe they had to suffer; there was nothing they could do to avoid it, they could have protested. Why didn't they? After all, we too are subjects of the same queen as they are. Why so much discrimination then? Even London does not have so much discrimination as the colonies.' Then, there rose in his mind an unacknowledged answer as a question: 'England is their country. Colonies are just colonies.'

Abu Bakr had been listening quietly. He was the seniormost among all of them and also the wealthiest. He intervened, speaking very softly:

'It's getting colder. Let's go home, instead of making conjectures. Only time will decide what's true and what's false.' At this sign from him, everyone made a move.

Outside the station, the land sloped away for quite some distance. Standing here, you could see right up to the point where the rows of shops came to an end. People walking down the slope looked like kids sliding down. A few of them carried canes. These made a lot more noise than the cane of God. God's cane hits you when you are least expecting it. These canes instead issued warnings. As it was already dark, a cane helped more than a light. Abu Bakr's house was the closest after the slope, so he was the first one to say *khuda hafiz*. The rest of them continued under the protection of God and kept dropping out one by one as their homes approached.

~

Mohandas hadn't been keeping the diary for quite a few days. The habit of keeping a diary he had picked up during his London sojourn. In the beginning, he wrote it in English in order to shed his inhibitions regarding the use of English, to cultivate the practice of writing in English, and incidentally to chronicle the experiences of his London stay so that, when he came back to India, he would be able to tell *Ba* each and everything truthfully. It was his dream to dedicate to *Ba* whatever knowledge he acquired along with the three vows he had taken. But when he returned, *Ba* was already gone. His dream was shattered so completely that he was never able to resurrect those dreams again, much as he wanted to.

Lying prone on his berth, Mohandas tried to write in the moving train. He wanted to give words to his humiliation so that it would remain a living presence for him. He wrote:

> *Rajkot has been with me everywhere, first because of* Ba, *now because of Kastur and the kids. Kastur can't stand Sheikh Mehtab. He is not a bad man at heart. I have to use him to send letters to Kastur. I can't send them through my*

elder brother, can I? Kastur has a feeling that I care more for Sheikh Mehtab than for her. My brother takes good care of Kastur and the kids, but she has a point when she asks if father's brother can take the place of father? The question also makes an oblique reference to husband and husband's brother. She never keeps things to herself, and never misses an opportunity to do some plain speaking if she can.

The train was now shakier and bouncier than before. It was difficult enough to write then; now it had become impossible. He couldn't form the word-shapes; instead he got crooked lines. Sleep too was beginning to weigh heavy on him. He had spent the whole of last night and the whole day today sitting. The tyranny of the cold last night had been worse than the tyranny of the whites, the only difference being that the eyes of cold did not bear the same hatred for him that the eyes of the whites did. Hate can often inflict a deeper wound on you than a knife or a dagger. This was not his own sentence: it was his friend, Uka, who sometimes said it.

The train reached Charlestown quite early in the morning. He had spent the night in peace and comfort. The fatigue which had seeped into each and every pore of his body had almost vanished and left behind only a faint remembrance of how tired he had been the previous day. He wished to forget the humiliation of the day before like a bad dream, but its memory sat heavy like a big mountain on his little finger, a big mountain which it was impossible to move even an inch.

There were still no trains between Charlestown and Johannesburg, and he had to travel by a stagecoach—a carriage drawn by six or eight horses. You got the stagecoach ticket along with the train ticket. A stagecoach ran every hour or every half-hour throughout the day. Each coach took several passengers. Mohandas' journey had been disturbed at Pietermaritzburg, so he was now carrying the stagecoach ticket for the previous day. The coach travel and the day-old ticket were causing him worry, though the ticket did not carry any expiry date.

Mohandas took the ticket to the stagecoach agent: 'Here's my ticket. I have to go to Johannesburg.'

The white agent examined Mohandas from top to toe and then scrutinized the ticket. Throwing it back to him, he said: 'This ticket expired yesterday.'

'But it doesn't carry any date.'

'Makes no difference. I know when it was sold and who brought it to me and when.'

'That's not a valid argument.'

'What I have said is final and valid.'

'But you must convince me. I have a valid ticket and Dada Abdullah must have informed you telegraphically about the postponement of my journey.'

At the mention of Dada Abdullah, the man perked up a little. People from that company were regular travellers. Every employee of the coach company knew of Dada Abdullah. The white man spoke to the fellow white sitting next to him: 'These coolies are real pests.'

'I'm not a coolie. I'm a barrister,' rejoined Mohandas at once.

'Whatever you may be, by race you are a coolie.'

'Colour is not race.'

The two whites looked Mohandas over again. This time the agent and his friend also noticed his European dress. The agent perhaps also realized for the first time that Mohandas was speaking better and more fluent English than him.

'All right,' said the agent: 'you are Dada Abdullah's man, but you'll have to sit where you're asked to. Most passengers on this coach are European.'

'That's fine. I must go today.'

As Mohandas was coming out, he heard the agent telling his companion: 'Don't let this coolie sit inside the coach. A bundle of diseases, that's what they are! What's more, they smell so awful. And act so stubborn as if they own the coach!'

The companion was actually the coach leader, the main coachman.

Outside, the coach stood ready to leave. There was space enough inside the coach. The luggage had been stowed in the rear. Mohandas wanted to sit inside the coach but the leader intervened: 'You'll sit outside in my seat on the coachbox. I'll take this seat. I told you, didn't I, that there are Europeans travelling on this coach?'

Mohandas had no desire to be thrown out of the coach again as had happened the day before. Although his ticket was for a seat in the coach and not for a place on the coachbox, the agent's words were still fresh in his ears. He had told Mohandas that he would have to sit wherever he was asked to. So he decided not to force the issue. His arrival in Pretoria had already been delayed and he did not want further delay. Mohandas tried to climb onto the coachbox by putting his feet on the footboard the way he had seen the coachman do, but while the coachman did it with practised ease, Mohandas found it difficult. So he had to put his feet on the tie-bar of the coach. He was nervous that putting his feet on the tie-bar may upset the horses. Three persons could sit on the coachbox—the leader and two of his assistants. As the journey was a long one, they took turns driving the coach. Mohandas sat in the right corner. The wind was quite strong, so he had turned up his overcoat collars. As the carriage moved, he felt lacerated by the insult, but, citing his duty and responsibility, he tried to paper over the pain. He could still feel the cold shiver of the night before. The only difference was that he had an overcoat now, and the journey was punctuated by intervals of sunshine which kept him warm. But as the bells around the feet of the horses tinkled, he felt molten lead pouring down his ears.

There was one thing that was making Mohandas happy. Inviting him, there lay all around him nature, unattached and unaffected. He felt that he was in constant conversation with her. The resounding hooves of the horses were agitating the vast expanse of forest around him. When the wind passed through the tall trees, parting the leaves to make way for itself, a smile seemed to light up the trees, but only to be gathered up quickly. It was as if the trees asked the wind not to disturb their hard-earned solitude. At some places, the forest had climbed up, tree by tree, like a bunch of naughty children, to reach a hilltop where the trees congregated, thick like a festival crowd. From the top, they leaned forward, laughed and asked others who they were. The wind whispered in the ears asking the others not to be afraid and assuring them that people who lived on top had this habit of prying and probing, and that they didn't need to worry, as they could depend on her. They were not bad at heart, only a slave of their habit.

During such breaks, when Mohandas became one with nature, he felt that whatever was past was no more; only what was present was the actual and real. It was what was truly yours. When travelling to London, in the high seas, that was how he had viewed the ocean. He had felt so close to it, as if it was talking to him. The twinkling stars of the sky at night had appeared to him like shimmering creatures swimming in the sea, as if the sea, like an elderly person, was teaching them how to swim, without letting them go.

Mohandas smiled. The games that nature plays!

'Hey, you!' Mohandas heard someone calling him.

It was three in the morning. The coach was standing at Pardekoph. The white leader had got out of the coach and was calling him out as if Mohandas was one of his assistants or perhaps a farm hand who looked after his horse.

Mohandas was groggy. He had been dozing off now and then, so was holding on to the bar of the coachbox. He kept sitting and asked: 'What's the matter?'

The man beckoned to him with a crooked finger to get down, but he kept sitting. The leader said: 'Didn't you get it? I want to have a smoke.'

'So what am I supposed to do?'

The man collected a piece of dirty-looking sacking from the coachman, spread it on the footboard and said: 'Come and sit here, Sami. I'll take that seat.'

Most south Indian names had 'Swamy' attached to them; hence, in addition to the coolies, all the Indians also came to be called 'Samis'. They didn't know the meaning of the word 'Swamy' or 'Sami'; if they did, they probably wouldn't use it. Anyway, Mohandas broke into a sweat, though it was a winter morning. The sacking smelled like horse shit. When a horse, which was pulling a cart or something, shat, that was how it smelt. Mohandas had a feeling that if the smell lasted a bit longer, he too would start whinnying like a horse. Fighting hard to keep his cool, he said:

'Mr. Leader, instead of giving me my seat inside the coach, you made me sit here on the coachbox. I swallowed that insult, though I had a valid ticket. Now that you feel like having a smoke, you throw me out like a dirty piece of cloth and want me to sit near your feet?'

'What's your problem with it? You'll sit wherever you're asked to. You are a coolie. The agent had told you everything in advance.'

'I'm not ready to sit at your feet. If you want to sit here, I'm ready to go inside, where your seat is now vacant.'

Even before Mohandas had finished his sentence, the leader fell on him. He straightaway landed two blows on his ears. Mohandas was completely at a loss to understand what was happening to him. Startled and injured, his brain had stopped functioning. He could have never imagined that God would forsake him so completely. A few people standing around the place were enjoying the spectacle of a coolie sahib being thrashed by a white man.. He tried to pull Mohandas down, but Mohandas was holding on to the brass bar which served as the coachbox railing. He was holding on with both his fists to the bar so fast that the bar could break but his hold would not. He felt darkness descending before his eyes and thought that maybe his end was approaching. One by one, the faces of *Bu*, Kastur, and the kids began to revolve before his eyes. The man was now showering the choicest abuses on him as he continued hitting him. Mohandas kept absolutely quiet but remained fixed to the bar. Go on, hit as much as you can. So what if I can't fight you, I can take all your excesses in utter silence. This too is a fight. It is a fight for one's rights by responding to excesses by tolerating them. At that moment, Mohandas realized that his capacity to tolerate had turned into his strength.

Seeing an innocent man being beaten up had slowly begun to touch the hearts of the people sitting in the coach. A few necks were now stretched out of the coach.

'Let him go. Why are you hitting the poor man? What has he done? If you want to sit on the coachbox, send him inside the coach.'

'Never,' said the leader.

Though the leader said this, the intervention of the white passengers sitting inside the coach had really unsettled him. He stopped hitting Mohandas at once, though even as he stopped beating he let him have a few more of his choicest epithets. His eyes were of course blazing with anger at Mohandas, but now he was no less furious at the people who had interfered with his benevolent task of coolie-bashing. He signalled to the farm hand sitting on the other side of the coachman, who occasionally helped with the driving, to sit on the footboard. The assistant obliged quietly. He got the coachman also to move, and then sprawled himself all over the coachbox as if it was a throne.

Mohandas' clothes were thoroughly crumpled and stained. He also had some scratches. His feet were still trembling. The whites inside the coach addressed him: 'You can come and sit here.'

Mohandas sat with them. When the coach started, the leader kept leaning over to glance at him and telling him in gestures: 'Just you wait till we get to Standerton. I'll see you then.'

Mohandas pressed his lips together tightly, shutting them like the doors of a house in times of danger. He did not want to utter a single word. His face still looked as dark as it did when the white man was beating him.

He kept repeating to himself a single question: 'Didn't the whites sitting inside the coach undergo a change of heart towards him because he let himself be thrashed by the white man without putting up any resistance?'

He didn't have a direct answer to this question yet.

Sitting inside the coach, Mohandas jostled with the idea of the danger that awaited him.

In fact, the danger was two steps ahead of him.

When the coach reached Standerton, it was evening. The shadows of the trees had lengthened and then faded. People had turned back towards their homes or were doing so now. Mohandas was the first to get out of the coach. He was quite alert. He looked around and saw quite a few Indians. From their clothes, they all looked like traders. The people who had come to see him at Pietermaritzburg had also been wearing almost the same style of clothes.

Seeing Mohandas alighting from the coach, a few of those people approached him:

'Are you Mr. M.K. Gandhi?'

'Yes,' he said, looking towards them with some degree of surprise.

'We are here to receive you.'

'You have come to receive me, but I don't know you, nor do you perhaps know me personally.'

'It was only today that we received Abdullah Sheth's telegram. He described your personal features and that's what helped us recognize you. You have anyway been the only Indian to arrive in the last two coaches.'

As he talked to them, Mohandas' eyes were constantly fixed at the leader, who was also keeping an eye on him from where he was standing near the coach. Perhaps he was waiting for the people around Mohandas to move away before resuming action. Mohandas couldn't help being impressed by the efficiency of the arrangements that Dada Abdullah had made. Had he not sent telegrams to these gentlemen, he would have found himself completely alone at this moment.

Mohandas walked in step with them. They had appropriated his luggage. Each item of the luggage had inscribed on it M.K. GANDHI, BAR-AT-LAW, LONDON.

On the way, he asked them, 'Where are we going?'

'To Sheth Isa Haji Sumar's shop. He is waiting for you impatiently.'

He kept quiet. He knew nothing of this Isa Haji Sheth. He also didn't think it proper to ask. Who might this Sheth Isa Haji Sumar be?

One of them volunteered: 'Our Sheth is a very close friend of Abdullah Sheth. Whenever Dada Abdullah visits here he is a guest of our Sheth.'

Without giving a thought to how Isa Sheth might react if he described the experience of his humiliation to him, Mohandas gave him all the details. When he was describing his experience, the Sheth's employees too gathered around, their hearts filling up with sorrow as they listened to what had befallen Mohandas. Everyone fell silent for a while.

Mohandas said, 'I want to write to the coach company about this incident.'

Sheth Isa said: 'This is a daily occurrence here. Your writing to the company will produce no effect whatsoever.'

'Effect or no effect, we must learn to oppose acts of highhandedness of this kind. If we don't do it, they will keep multiplying and then we'll have no other option but to go on tolerating them till they cross the limits of tolerance and destroy us completely.'

Mohandas wrote out a detailed account and sent it to the agent. He also mentioned that when he continues his journey the next day, he should be given a seat inside the coach.

The agent wrote back: 'The coach from Standerton is bigger. Tomorrow it will also not be carrying the leader against whom you have complained. You will be given a seat inside the coach with other passengers.'

Isa Sheth was deeply affected by this episode. He couldn't have imagined that white officers would care so much for the letter of a coloured person. He said very quietly: 'Maybe they are so oppressive because we put up with so much.'

Mohandas had said nothing then, but he had liked Isa Sheth's reaction.

~

IV

Standerton was a town on the way to Johannesburg. After spending the night there, Mohandas started for Johannesburg the next day. This part of the journey was as eventless as the journey till Standerton had been eventful. Johannesburg was the biggest city in Transvaal. After getting off at Johannesburg, Mohandas stood wondering for a little while where to head next. He had hoped that someone would be there to receive him from Mr. Baker. Dada Abdullah's telegrams had so far produced results at all places. When no one turned up, Mohandas' mind started working differently. What status could an Indian have in the eyes of an Englishman, he thought, especially if he happened to be a lawyer's assistant?

Mohandas had a list of hotels and their addresses. He had no other option but to choose one. He called a taxi. The taxi driver was a native.

'Grand National Hotel,' he instructed the taxi driver.

The driver looked at Mohandas pointedly, and smiled a little. Mohandas missed the smile. Throughout the drive, the driver kept humming something in his native language.

At the hotel, Mohandas directly approached the manager. When he was close enough, the manager addressed him coldly: 'What can I do for you?'

That took Mohandas aback for a moment: what did a manager do for a guest?

The manager was a white and wore a black bow tie on a black suit. He first smiled and then offered with extra politeness: 'Please do excuse me. The hotel is full. Most of our customers are regulars.'

The baggage of a white customer was being hauled in. Mohandas looked at the manager, who just smiled. Mohandas didn't quite understand, but thought maybe the gentleman had booked the room in advance.

As he stepped out of the hotel, the taxi driver gave him an all-knowing look, and asked, 'No room?'

He just shook his head. The taxi driver's lips spread in an extra large smile as he asked, 'Now what?'

Abdullah Sheth had given him the address of Mohammad Qasim Kamaruddin Co. To Mohandas, in his situation, that looked to be the only straw he could clutch at. He asked the taxi driver to drive him there. The Kamaruddin firm was only a short distance from the hotel. Mohandas was of course worried that he may not find Sheth Kamaruddin or Sheth may not be very welcoming. He didn't know what he would do in the circumstances. But when he landed there, he found the present owner of the firm, Abdul Ghani, waiting for him.

Stepping forward, he inquired: 'You are Mr. Gandhi, barrister to Dada Abdullah Co.?'

'Yes, but how did you know?'

'Thanks to Abdullahbhai. He makes wise men out of ignoramuses like us.'

'That means his telegraphic circular has found you too! Had I known, I'd have headed here directly.'

'So you have been visiting places, have you? Our coach had gone to fetch you, but it looks like it missed you.'

'My fault too, for which I had to pay. I have been to the Grand National. They had no vacancy.'

'So that's where you have been. Whoever told you you could get a room there?'

'Why?'

'A few more days here, and you won't have to ask.' He continued: 'This country is not for educated people like you. Only people like us, for whom respect and dignity have lost all meaning, can stay here. We die every moment. That is the only reality of our lives.'

Abdul Ghani turned out to be a real windbag. At every mention of Indians, he came out with a story or two about their condition. He rounded it off with: 'Mr. Gandhi, it's writ large on our faces , like an ad on a hoarding: "Come, insult us."No matter who you are—a famous, learned man, a rich businessman, a Muslim priest or a Hindu pundit, and now a barrister too, if you are an Indian, there is always a rich spread of insults in front of you. Transvaal is worse than Natal in this regard. Here we never get to see a first or second class ticket.'

'The fear of insult has got you so scared that that you put up with it without protest. More than the insult, it is the fear which scares you.'

'We did make a representation, but our own people turned indifferent. Okay, they argued, so we are allowed to travel first or second. What difference would it make? The whites are going to treat us the same anyway.'

Mohandas was seething. Abdul Ghani was getting emotional. To Mohandas these people looked like the wolf who had made the error of jumping into a pond of indigo blue and the blue had entered every pore of his body. He now flaunted the blue as his mark of identity.

Mohandas asked Abdual Ghani, 'Can you get me the Railway Rulebook?'

'I have it. I'd sent for it at the time we made the representation.'

Mohandas glanced through the rules. Abdul Ghani laughed and said, 'Read the rules or do whatever else you like with them, but to go to Pretoria you have to be in the third class.'

Mohandas too laughed. He said, 'You just watch. I'll either go first or if I can't, I'll take a coach. It's only thirty-three miles to Pretoria.'

'Waste of money and time.'

'It's a matter of honour, mine and my country's.'

'I beg your pardon. We are all coolies here, come here to earn a living. A coolie is not concerned with dignity or disrespect.'

'I don't think so. Will you do something for me? Please send a letter to the station master, with your signature. I'll make the draft.'

Mohandas got the draft ready. It said:

Dear Sir,

Mr. M.K.Gandhi is a barrister who has passed out from London. He is on his way from India to Pretoria in connection with a court case. Mr. Gandhi has always been travelling first class. It is important for him to be in Pretoria tomorrow. Time is short, so please do not bother to reply to this letter. Mr. Gandhi will personally collect the reply from you. I hope you will help him to get a first class ticket. Thank you.

Faithfully yours,

Abdul Ghani

After getting the letter dispatched, Mohandas said, 'You must be wondering about my reasons for sending a letter. The letter will give him a chance to think about the matter. There was a risk in asking for a written reply: if he declined, it would be difficult to get him to change his reply. When I appear before him in my full attire, he'll think twice even if he is inclined to say 'No.'

Abdul Ghani laughed: 'There's some truth in what you say. Maybe it'll have some effect.'

At the exact hour, Mohandas landed in front of the station master, fitted out flawlessly in his frock-coat, necktie, and the rest.

'Good morning,' he said.

The station master looked up at him. Mohandas took out a sovereign and placed it in front of the station master.

'A first class ticket for Pretoria, please.'

'So that letter was for you?'

'Yes. I am M.K.Gandhi. I'll be obliged if you'll kindly issue me a first class ticket.'

'I'm ready to let you have a ticket, but I have a condition,' said the station master.

'Sure.'

'If, on the way, the guard removes you from the first class to the van, you'll not drag me into the affair. You'll not sue the company for making you travel in the van after issuing you a first class ticket. You are a decent person. I wish you a safe journey.'

He not only gave Mohandas a first class ticket, he also got up from his seat and shook hands with him.

Standing close by, Abdul Ghani heard everything, his face unable to contain the joy. He was amazed: was this happening in Transvaal? He told Mohandas: 'I pray to God for your safe arrival in Pretoria. I only fear that the guard may not let you travel in peace, and even if he does, the white fellow passengers may get under your skin. Do forgive me; it's not my purpose to scare you. *Khuda hafiz*.'

'Don't worry at all. Nothing scares me after Pietermaritzburg.'

The train steamed in. Mohandas got into the first class compartment without the slightest hesitation. Abdul Ghani's face reflected both joy and anxiety. When he said '*khuda hafiz*', Mohandas could feel Ghani was praying for him. He recalled that at Durban too the train had left without a hitch, but by the time they had arrived at Pietermaritzburg, things had completely changed. As the next station neared, his legs began to tense; the calves became stiff; and his grip on the arms of the chair became tighter. The train stopped at Germiston. Mohandas edged up on his seat, as if expecting something to happen. A white man, who looked like the guard, was moving up, checking tickets. The closer he got to him, the higher went Mohandas' level of anxiety. At one point, he had the suspicion that this was one of those two persons who had joined the white passenger at Pietermaritzburg to throw him out of the train. This man however had a longer neck and longer legs too. Suddenly, he sighted Mohandas. Skipping two or three seats in between, he surfaced in front of Mohandas: 'You …?'

'How come, you are here?'

Without a word, Mohandas extended the ticket towards him.

'Over there. This place is not for you.'

Mohandas kept sitting, so he raised his voice: 'I say leave this place and go to your compartment. Should I write it on paper and stick it on your forehead?'

A white man was sitting at the other end of the berth. He got up and came close. He said: 'Why are you pestering this gentleman? When the fellow passengers have no objection, what's your problem?'

At first, the guard was taken aback. Then he moved away, muttering: 'It's no skin off my back. You want to travel with a coolie, you're welcome to it. I have done my duty. If this is the way things are to go, one day the coolies will travel first and we'll be in the van.'

The guard was still muttering when he got off at the other end.

Mohandas stood up to thank the white passenger. 'You have saved me a lot of humiliation. I was thrown out of the compartment at Pietermaritzburg. I have never been able to forget that insult.'

'I understand. Take it easy and go to sleep now.'

'I am M.K.Gandhi. Bar-at-Law, London.'

'Me, Martin.'

As the train caught speed, Mohandas' legs spread out and his grip on the arms of the chair relaxed. He suddenly felt very tired.

It was eight in the evening when the train arrived at Pretoria. The station was like the station at Pietermaritzburg: small and with very few travellers. The architecture was of course different. He got down and waited on the platform. At all the previous stations, he had been met by Dada Abdullah's messengers. He naturally thought there would be one at this station too. If none else, at least Mr. Baker's man should be here. Dada Abdullah's arrangements had never failed so far. Mr. Baker had been sent a telegram in his own presence.

One after another, the passengers all left. The platform was now deserted. He paced up and down for a while, hoping someone might turn up. As time passed, his anxiety grew. If no one turned up, where would he go? He had addresses of a few Indian businessmen with him, but, in a way, he had committed himself against staying with any of them.

Nearly an hour passed. There was no sign of anyone. The very idea of spending the night at the station gave him the shivers. The night he had spent at the Pietermaritzburg station had not been just one night: it had grown to occupy days, months, and years. Had those two coolies not covered him with blankets, there was no question of his ever making it to Pretoria. The cold had seeped into his bones like rainwater into the bricks of a wall. What a stylish send-off the manager at the Grand National had given him last night! It was indeed nice of him that he didn't get Mohandas kicked out.

In the end, he just picked up his luggage. The ticket collector was counting his tickets. He too was a white. When he had finished, Mohandas handed his ticket to him and said, 'I am a barrister. This is my first visit here. I need some help from you.'

Though he was talking to the ticket collector, mentally Mohandas was also preparing himself for any eventuality. Nothing of the sort however happened; instead the man asked him with unexpected modesty: 'Sure. Tell me what I can do for you.'

'I've come here from India in connection with a lawsuit. I was expecting my hosts to be here to receive me. I don't know what might have happened; maybe they didn't receive the message. The problem is where to spend the night. There is no one I know here.'

It's Sunday today. Everything is closed. Maybe that was why your host wasn't able to send anyone to receive you. People here don't spend weekends at home: they always go out trekking or something.'

A black American stood by the ticket collector. He now faced Mohandas: 'Looks like you are a complete stranger here, with no friends at all. I know a hotel here. The proprietor is an American. He's not narrow-minded like the local whites. The hotel is small, but good enough to spend a night. Come with me. I'm sure he'll have a place for you. After all, it is the question of just a single night.'

Mohandas looked at the black closely. He wanted to make sure that the man was a dependable one, not some conman. Strange place, unknown people! The ticket collector had left. Maybe he thought it best to leave the two coloureds together.

Mohandas decided quickly. 'Thanks a lot,' he said. 'Come let's go. I'm ready.'

The hotel was called Johnston Family Hotel. The owner was also called Johnston. He knew the black. 'Hello, Elic,' he said as he set eyes on him.

Elic had told him his name at the station, but so lost had Mohandas been in his own worries that he hadn't heard it. Elic took Johnston aside and told him something. Then, joining Mohandas, introduced him to Johnston: 'This is barrister Gandhi. He is an Indian, but a stranger here. He is here for the night but has nowhere to go. Please put him up. You know what this city is like.'

'I have one condition. You must have your meals in the room. They'll be sent up there.'

Mohandas accepted the condition: 'I have no problem. Being a vegetarian, I won't be availing the services of your kitchen too much anyway.'

'I want to assure you, Mr. Gandhi,' said Johnston: 'that I make no distinction between black and white. But all my customers happen to be white. If I serve you meals in the dining room, they may object. I may lose all my customers. My business will be ruined.'

'Please don't worry at all. You have already done more than enough by letting me stay in your hotel. In the few days I have been here, I have got some idea of the things here. I assure you that you'll face no trouble on my account. I'll find myself a place somewhere else the first thing tomorrow.'

Johnston's face glowed innocence as he gave him a smile.

It was a fair-sized and reasonably clean room. The window opened on the road, where the traffic was not particularly heavy. During winter, people tend to rush home rather than loiter on the roads, unless of course one happens to be a bohemian. Looking carefully, he could see a line of trees stretching to a great distance. Whether or not he was able to see them clearly, they certainly must be watching him as a stranger. He sat at the table, waiting for his food to arrive. Hunger, like a sharp knife, sliced through him.

Mohandas peeped out. The waiter was nowhere to be seen. He had already informed Johnston about his food. Maybe, it is not yet ready, he thought. Maybe, it is being arranged or the waiter is busy. Just then, there was a knock at the door. He opened it quickly. It was Johnston where it should have been the waiter.

'No, not you! Who wanted you here at this time?' Mohandas said to himself.

Johnston was very polite: 'I'm really very sorry,' he said and stopped. 'Maybe,' thought Mohandas: 'food could not be arranged or maybe the white guests had declared war on him. "Either him or us," they might have said. Easier to apologize and send you packing than to deal with such large-scale desertion by your guests.'

Johnston took the matter forward: 'I had told you I'd have your meals sent to your room, but later I felt ashamed. So I told my guests that I have an Indian barrister in the hotel who I have asked to have his meals in his room on account of them. They at once said they didn't mind and that you could have your meals in the dining hall. So please come and have your dinner with the others. You can also stay in the hotel as long as you like. I'm in fact glad that because of you I was able to find out what my guests feel about racial discrimination.'

Johnston looked very happy. 'Come, let's move. Your dinner has been served,' he said. 'Sometimes you have to do things which you don't want to do. After all, I must run the hotel. Please don't take it otherwise.'

Mohandas made to say something, but Johnston cut him off. 'Not a word more,' he said: 'I know I have hurt you.'

When he reached the hall, the diners all smiled their welcome. For a moment, happiness in him replaced hunger. It all looked like a miracle to him. It was like an island where people didn't know hate and were happy to see one another.

Back in his room, Mohandas was lost in thought for a long time. How had all this come about? Who had created such goodwill for a coloured man in the hearts of the whites: was it he himself, his own tolerance or a miraculous transformation in the mindset of the whites? Had Jesus filled their hearts with his own love for the non-whites? Had he lit in their hearts a desire to become better human beings by offering respect to others? He did not have any quick answers to these questions. He was so tired that his eyes refused to stay open. Time and again, his neck fell sideways, but, so deeply was he submerged in the pleasurable sensation of the unexpected regard shown to him that he wouldn't brook the idea of going to bed. Receiving regard and giving it to others make a man happy. The regard he had seen in the eyes of these whites was an antidote to the fire of hatred he had witnessed in the eyes of the whites who had him thrown out of the train at Pietermaritzburg.

~

When Mohandas woke up in the morning, the experience of last evening was still fresh in his mind. He got ready quickly and set out on his search for Mr. Baker. He had got some idea about the address from Johnston. He found the address: A.W. Baker, Attorney, was written right outside. He stood there a while. Though Mr. Abdullah had nothing but praise for Mr. Baker, Mohandas had his fears. It was hard to predict when someone might turn nasty. Mr. Baker might have been friendly with Abdullah Sheth, but it was not necessary that he would be nice to Sheth's lawyer too. Right there, Mohandas decided that he would not leave without meeting Mr. Baker even if he misbehaved on racial grounds. He put his hat on the hat stand, looked at himself in the mirror and groomed his hair. He knew that white officers had such stands placed in the verandahs precisely for such a purpose: so that when the visitor appeared before them he looked presentable. Mr. Lely too had such a stand in his house. But at that time he had been quite ignorant about their purpose.

Mr. Baker had sighted him standing near the stand. He was sitting in the room, working. He came out quickly and made a quick appraisal of Mohandas, giving him the once-over. Then he gave a smile. Mohandas wondered what it was about him that had raised a smile from a stranger. He tried to tell him about himself, but Mr. Baker forestalled him:

'Mr. M.K. Gandhi. Dada Abdullah & Co., Durban. Right?'

Mohandas was speechless, but he grasped the situation quickly.

'Mr. Baker ...?' he asked.

'Yes. That's me.'

Mr. Baker shed all formality pretty quickly.

'How was your trip, Mr. Gandhi?' He asked and continued: 'I'm sorry I couldn't send anyone to receive you. It was Sunday yesterday, and Sunday here means full stop.'

'I found a black American at the station. He arranged for my stay at the Johnston hotel. It would have been difficult for me to spend the night if he hadn't. The manager of the Grand National Hotel had sent me on my way, claiming no vacancy. I had seen a white man walk in with his luggage just then.'

'It really grieves me that colour prejudice has entered the bloodstream of people here.' He paused a little before continuing: 'Do forgive me, Gandhi, I've still not been able to arrange accommodation for you. What can I do—such are the conditions here. I know someone—a baker's wife. She is rather poor and may have you as a paying guest. It'll be a help to her. Would you consider it?'

'I have lived as a paying guest in London. Does she have a young daughter?'

Baker guffawed. 'I see,' he intoned.

Mohandas joined him in the laughter, but said: 'It makes me a little nervous …, you see.'

'Let's go and see this thing through first,' said Mr. Baker.

Both of them stepped out on the street.

The baker's wife lived close by, so Mr. Baker thought it best to walk the distance. On the way he told Mohandas: 'I know that you are a qualified barrister. I'm a little bothered that we don't have the kind of work that would suit you.'

'I know.'

'But your presence will make my work a lot easier. I should have little difficulty now in understanding what my client says and conveying it to the court. If I said Johannesburg, he took it to be Durban, though proper nouns are really not so hard to understand.' He laughed. Mohandas thought his laughter was so childlike. This was the second time he had come across such spontaneous expression of friendliness ever since he had arrived in South Africa. Last night was the first time, this the second. Mohandas had always considered laughter to be closely linked to a man's feelings. Laughter had no meaning unless it came from the heart.

Suddenly Mr. Baker asked: 'What are you?'

'An Indian,' Mohandas was quick as a shot.

'I have absolutely no doubt you are an Indian. I was actually asking about your religion. You have so many religions in your country. So have we.'

Mohandas was quite at ease with himself when he said: 'I follow Hinduism. The majority in my country follow Hinduism.'

'I know.'

'Have you read about our religion, I mean, Christianity? It's a very liberal and progressive religion. It enables a human being to live like a human being.'

'That is not a problem in my religion either. In fact, we also think of animals in the same way. But …,' Mohandas left the sentence unfinished.

Mr. Baker was silent for a minute, and then said: 'I'll give you some books to read.'

'I'll be happy to read them, though when I was living in London I had the opportunity to read a lot about Christianity.'

'That only confirms what I thought.'

'What?'

'That you are a very tolerant person. You showed a lot of forbearance and generosity of spirit in dealing with the difficulties that you had to face during this journey. The second telegram of Dada Abdullah hinted at it. That was impossible without knowledge of Christianity.'

The smile on Mohandas' face spread almost from ear to ear.

'Isn't it?' asked Mr. Baker.

Mohandas said nothing. They were at the baker's place. 'We'll talk about it later. This is the lady's house,' said Mr. Baker, pointing to the house. 'Looks like she's at home. She is a good woman. Her husband is of course a drunkard, but you'll have nothing to do with him. She has her limitations, being a woman. I hope you understand.'

Mr. Baker knocked on the door. A woman with a glint in her eyes opened the door. The sinewy calves peeping from under her skirt were evidence of hard physical labour.

'Good morning.' They greeted each other. Mr. Baker said: 'Mr. Gandhi is my guest. He is an Indian. He'll be staying in Pretoria for a few days and work with me.'

After the introduction, Mohandas wished the lady 'Good morning'. She fixed him with a steady, penetrating look, which made Mohandas feel very uncomfortable. Mr. Baker addressed himself to the lady: 'Come, let me have a word with you.'

His hand on her shoulder, Mr. Baker took her aside. Mohandas felt awkward standing in the house of a stranger. Why was he after all standing here? He could feel the passers-by eyeing him and wondering why this coolie stood there, although he found it hard to swallow the word coolie applied to himself. Suppose the lady refuses to have him as a paying guest! What then?

The lady was saying something. He tried to catch the words. She was saying: 'I never had anything to do with Indians. They call them coolies. I'm a little scared. You never know what kind of a man he may turn out to be.' Mohandas had heard the word 'coolie' applied to him before, but hearing the lady use the word filled him with rage.

Mr. Baker said laughing: 'Does this man look like Satan to you? Indians are not ruthless like Arabs. As for the rent, you'll get it from me.'

There was silence for a while. Mohandas' pulse quickened. The accumulated tension of standing there like a prowler, the uncertainty regarding a place to stay and the madness of colour discrimination were telling on him. He could have stayed on at Johnston's hotel, but for how long?

Mr. Baker came out laughing. 'You are a lucky man, Mr. Gandhi. You'll have to pay forty-five shillings a week. I'll let Dada Abdullah know. You can stop worrying now. Matilda is a great hostess.'

'I'm grateful to you both. For a total stranger like me …'

Mr. Baker said: 'Help whoever you can, that is the message of Jesus. We're all on this earth only to carry out his work.'

~

All the way back, Mr. Baker kept telling him about himself: 'I have built a church with my own money. You could call me the priest of the church; I also give the sermons and conduct the service. I do not believe in colour discrimination at all. We are all sons of the same God. I am the director of the South Africa General Mission. I practise law for a living, but for my peace I work in the Mission.'

Mohandas was listening to him very attentively. At the same time, the wheels in his mind spun continuously: 'Was it Christianity that made Mr. Baker think like this or was it a personal quality? Those people who had pushed him out of the train, the leader of the horse coach—they were Christians too.' He had been on the point of mentioning this but had not, choosing instead a smile and silence.

Mr. Baker wasn't letting up: 'Some of us, I and a few of my friends, gather every afternoon at one o'clock for prayers. A prayer, you know, has the power to take away all your ill will and to charge you with fresh energy for the future.'

We do all kinds of things, Mohandas thought, except pray.

After a pause, Mr. Baker asked: 'You understand prayer, don't you?'

Mohandas replied: 'Certainly, it forms the basis of all religions.'

'So, join us for the prayers at one o'clock everyday. It is the easiest of the routes to Jesus. Once you are with him, there is nothing but bliss.' From Mr. Baker's expression one could make out that he was soaking in the bliss.

'Sure,' said Mohandas.

~

Back in the hotel, Mohandas told Johnston, 'Your putting me up for the night proved lucky for me: I now have a place to stay.'

Johnston said with a start: 'You are not leaving, are you?'

'Yes. And, after all, you too have to run your business.'

'Your stay for the first time lifted the invisible wall of colour discrimination that was there in my hotel. For the first time, the white guests had agreed of their own accord to dine with an Indian guest in the dining room. And now you are leaving!'

'Mr. Johnston, I'm myself quite thrilled with this incident. Ever since I entered South Africa, I have been a regular victim of colour discrimination. I wonder if this can happen to me, what must be the fate of others! How large must be the burden of their humiliation! Last night's experience has actually helped in restoring my faith. These were all decent people, so they accepted your suggestion; but this is a hotel; there are new guests everyday. Who can tell whether they'll accept what you tell them? If it were a matter of a few days, I'd still have agreed to stay on. I think it'll be best if both of us froze this moment of happiness and never allowed any untoward event to cloud its memory.'

When Mohandas came out with his luggage, Johnston accompanied him to the exit. His eyes were moist. He held Mohandas' hands for a while and then walked back without a word.

On the way, Mohandas asked himself: 'What made Johnston so emotional? Was it a coloured man or was it the colour discrimination that he had exposed?'

~

Matilda had been waiting for him. It was already evening. Mohandas had seen the room with Mr. Baker and had also made advance payment for a week. Why had he then not turned up? True, the room was rather small; the furnishings were also probably not up to scratch for him; rather short on conveniences too; but the room was airy.

The moment Mohandas appeared before her, she blurted out: 'O Jesus! Thank God, you are here. I was worried. If you were to be delayed, you'd have problems. One is not allowed on the roads after 9 pm.' She of course safely omitted to say who was not allowed: everyone or persons of a specific group.

He thanked Matilda for her concern and said: 'I know. Mr. Baker had told me.'

'You must be tired. Mr. Baker had told me you are a Hindu and a vegetarian. I have vegetarian food ready for you. If you like, you can have soup.'

Mohandas hadn't eaten the whole day. He always had a feeling that every woman has a mysterious bonding with hunger. Anyone, in any form, that comes near her has his hunger attended to first.

For dinner, he had bread, butter, cheese, boiled vegetables, beetroot, a little honey, and a cup of milk.

Dinner made him feel good. His eyes closed, he thought back on the events. Thank God, he had at last arrived at the destination. But he felt as if he had arrived piecemeal, a piece at a time. The way the white leader of the coach had started on him and had persevered in his beating, South Africa could well have been his last place of rest, had the gentleman only continued with the same speed. It is of course true that the people who had saved him had also been white. Matilda too was white. And Baker too. He had of course Jesus in his heart. Why would he otherwise come all the way to help a non-white? When the leader of the coach was thrashing him, the cross on his heart was swinging wildly. Mohandas wanted to stop him to tell him that the cross might suffer injury. But never had he been given a chance. He had continued to receive the blows, he had continued to recover from them, and he had continued to see the cross being injured.

~

Tired, Mohandas fell into sleep while still in his chair. Suddenly, he woke up with a start and looked around: *Ba*,...where did *Ba* disappear? She had been asking him: 'Why are you wandering from your path?' He was bemused. Had *Ba* been around, she would surely have waited to hear his answer: 'Your Mohania was born to wander. It's not only his body, his soul is also wandering. It's his quest, nothing for you to worry about. He'll continue to wander till he finds himself. The path your Mohania has chosen is a very lonely one, a long one, and cuts through the paths of all others.'

It had been a long day for Mohandas. The sleep that he had dispelled was beginning to claim him again. He lay down. Sleep had washed and wiped his face making him look so innocent that sleep could have been *Ba* herself.

~

Mohandas was busy working when he suddenly remembered: Mr. Baker could be waiting for him. It was ten minutes to one. He rushed. The prayer room was next to Mr. Baker's chamber. Pictures of Jesus and Mary adorned the wall in front. Devotees gathered in front of them to pray. When he arrived, he found everyone waiting. Mr. Baker had already told everyone about him and had even assured them that he was certain to come. Mohandas had started to take off his shoes when Mr. Baker said, 'That is not necessary. You can keep your shoes on.'

Mohandas remembered he was not in a temple. A church does not require you to take off your shoes. As a child, he used to accompany *Ba* to temples. He always found himself standing outside, though this incurred *Ba*'s displeasure. He hated taking off his shoes. The temples were not really clean places. He liked to be in a church. They were clean and quiet places. He walked in in his shoes.

Mr. Baker introduced Mohandas to everyone. There were two middle-aged women, Miss Harris and Miss Gabb; the rest were all men. Mr. Coates looked the busiest of all. Prayer, rising like sleep, filled their eyes. He closed his eyes for a moment and wondered if he would be able to feel the prayer within him in the way they did.

They were all genuflecting now, and looked towards Mohandas. He imitated them. This was his first experience of a prayer. A prayer may be collective, but the thoughts and feelings of everyone were his own; everyone was alone. He didn't know what the others were praying for, but he could think of only one thing: Dear God, my country and countrymen are in a pitiable state. We do not ask you for anything else: give us only the right to live and earn our living with dignity.

When Mohandas opened his eyes, he was confused. What was this? *Ba* stood in place of Mary, and he was in her arms. A shiver ran through his body. A strange thing to happen! It had never happened before. Everyone's eyes were closed. Miss Harris and Miss Gabb had teardrops trembling on their eyelids. With folded hands, they were all asking God for something, even if it was peace and happiness for themselves or forgiveness for their sins. What however startled him was to hear Mr. Baker speak: 'Son of God! Lead our new brother here on the right path. Give him peace as you give peace to your own flock. Protect him the way you have protected us. Show him the true way for he has wandered from the path.'

That last sentence of the prayer was what had startled him most. This was exactly what had entered his mind last night and what he had scribbled in his diary. The same sentence was being spoken here in prayer to Jesus!

Everyone exclaimed 'Amen!' and sat there a little while longer with folded hands.

Prayer over, Miss Harris and Miss Gabb walked over to Mohandas. They greeted him and welcomed him to the prayer group. Miss Harris spoke: 'Mr. Gandhi, you are a person with a pure heart. Only pure-hearted persons seek shelter with Jesus. Mr. Baker told us that you were a Hindu. We have heard Hindus are very old-fashioned and hidebound.'

'Aren't we all?' said Mohandas.

The ladies laughed. Miss Gabb said: 'The two of us stay together. You have a standing invitation to visit us. Please have your tea with us every Sunday at four.'

Seeing signs of hesitation on Mohandas' face, Miss Harris said: 'Please do not hesitate at all. You'll be quite safe with us.'

Everyone laughed.

Mohandas recorded his thoughts and actions of the day in his diary. Any spiritual ideas that occurred to him were taken down in full. He noted the ladies' invitation to him in his diary. The question that bothered him was why they had invited him. He had no answer to the question yet.

Mr. Coates was the leading member of the prayer group. He was the first to arrive on Sundays. He made all the necessary arrangements. He narrated the week's experiences to those who arrived early at the meetings: the books he had read; the impact they had had on him. If some other member of the group happened to have read the same book, a discussion would follow. The two ladies too chipped in with their experiences. Their narrations were pleasant and sweet. They also included those topics of religious significance which had been discussed at their tea-meetings. Such topics were welcomed enthusiastically by the group.

~

Matilda knew the prayer group quite well. Whenever anyone of the group came to see Mohandas, she offered him tea, sometimes accompanied by eatables. This was on her, and she made this clear. Mr. Coates was a frequent visitor, so he had more opportunities to enjoy Matilda's tea. When she clarified that the tea was on her, Mohandas laughed and said: 'Matilda, actually, everything is on you, isn't it?'

'Oh, no,' she said: 'I charge money for everything else.'

'Money may get you things, but it doesn't get you friendship.'

She would laugh and would leave the scene smiling. Mohandas loved to see her leave with the smile on her face, her eyes shining with sincerity.

Coates was a man with an open mind and a pure heart. He was very fond of reading books. Any book that he read he also offered to Mohandas to read. After Mohandas had read it, he would discuss it with him. Most of the time, he just listened to Coates, with an occasional comment here and there. Even while discussing, he continued to do his work. Sometimes, he would be sealing an envelope or pinning together sheets of paper or folding his clothes. When someone objected to this habit of his, his rejoinder was: 'Activity helps you digest the discussion, which otherwise can cause indigestion. Discussions without an accompanying activity often degenerate into a waste of time.'

At times, Mohandas tried telling Coates about his own religion: 'Look, for us a sin is a sin. Once committed, it's forever recorded in your account. How can you erase something that has been entered in your account?'

Coates was a transparent person. He would never agree with this point. He would say: 'Jesus is the son of God. God has given him, and him alone, the power to take all our sins on himself and grant mercy to all of us. By confessing our sins, we expiate them. Jesus grants us forgiveness.'

'Can't we do this amongst ourselves? Can't we forgive the sinners?'

'God has conferred this power only on Jesus.'

'Mr. Coates, I can accept the confessional technique as mental therapy. I can also accept that, by confessing, man surrenders all his sorrow and pain, all his sins and good deeds, to God. I also have no problem in accepting that Jesus was a great soul, and he made enormous sacrifices for the good of mankind. As a teacher, he was extraordinary and out of this world. But it is difficult for me to see Jesus the way you see him.'

Coates listened to Mohandas attentively. Sometimes one could read signs of exasperation on his face. At times, he even protested: 'Mr. Gandhi, man is helpless. God has sent His son on this earth with the specific mission to deliver mankind. The grace of God is granted only to those who have complete trust in Him.'

'I have a different opinion. In my view, the strength of Jesus lay in his sacrifice and in his devotion to truth, love, non-violence and his power to forgive. It does not sound logical to me that you are delivered from your sins only if you convert to Christianity. I agree with the Sermon on the Mount when it asks us not to fight evil with evil, and to turn the other cheek; to love your enemy and to pray even for those who bring you nothing but sorrow and misery.' Then, he laughed and said, 'Didn't you all pray for me on that first day?'

Coates wanted to say something, but Mohandas cut him off with 'The enemy too is the son of the same God who is your father.'

'What do you mean?'

Mohandas laughed. 'I wrestled a good deal with questions like these when I was in London. The idea that Christians are somehow holier than people of other religions is hard for me to accept. People of other religions too have made sacrifices; they too have been ready to give up everything to preserve truth and purity. It is not as if other religions are quite lacking in what your religion has.'

That came as a severe blow to Coates. His face blazed. He reflected for a moment but could not think of a rejoinder. Then his eyes fell on Mohandas' neck. Mohandas was wearing a necklace of Tulsi beads presented to him by *Ba.* Usually, it was hidden under his clothes, but that day it was showing. Coates asked, 'What's that round your neck?'

'We have a holy plant we call Tulsi. This is a necklace made out of beads of its wood. It's called *kanthee.* Mostly it's the Vaishnavites who wear it.'

'Does it endow any physical benefit?' Coates smiled sarcastically.

'Does a necktie endow any physical benefit on the wearer? But still a necktie is now part of the European dress. Similarly, we also adopted the necklace and now it's an inseparable part of Vaishnava dress. Personally, I don't see any benefit in wearing it.'

'If you don't mind, let me break it,' said Coates and extended his hand to grab it, but Mohandas stopped him.

'No, you'll do nothing of the sort. It's a sacred gift from my mother.'

'It means you are superstitious.'

'It's true that I don't know the religious significance of this necklace. I also accept that not wearing it is unlikely to harm me in any way. But I see no reason why I should break it and throw it away, especially since my mother put it round my neck with her love and blessings. Like all things, it will also wear away one day; that will be the last day of my *kanthee.*'

Coates smiled: 'I see that there is no salvation for you till you surrender to Jesus.'

Mohandas too smiled and muttered: 'And what about the cross?'

Coates either didn't hear it or chose to keep quiet.

~

V

For sometime now, Kastur had grown quieter. She had always been the quiet type, but this South African adventure had turned her really numb. There were a couple of things which especially weighed on her. She had heard so much about England that she had got used to the country. It sounded to her to be a familiar place, like a country or a city in your own neighbourhood. South Africa, on the other hand, had been an unknown quantity. She had never known or heard about it, though there were a good number of Gujaratis there. She first heard about the place when Mohandas went there. She in fact could never recall the name Natal, and always referred to it as Africa. She heard stories about Africa that completely horrified her. The place was inhabited by Negroes, who were cannibals and ate up human beings. The flies of South Africa could suck all your blood if you let them sit on your body. Had she heard these stories beforehand, she would have put her foot down and never allowed Mohandas to go. Thoughts such as these kept her in a permanent state of fear and apprehension.

What hurt her most was his sending her letters through Sheikh Mehtab. Her husband may consider him a friend, but Mehtab meant nothing to her. So long as she was living, her mother-in-law either lapsed into silence at the mention of Sheikh Mehtab's name or simply exited the scene. She was a woman of few words, but when reference to Sheikh Mehtab became unavoidable, she did open up. She would start on stories from Mohania's childhood. As a child, Mohandas was easily scared. He had never encountered a thief or a ghost, though snakes did surface during the rains. He was scared of all the three. Ramabai was the household maid. Mohandas was very close to her. If it was late evening and he had to come upstairs, Mohania would stand at the foot of the stairs and call out to Ramabai: 'Ramabai, come and take me upstairs. I am standing here.' He would continue calling out to her till she came down. Once Ramabai got so annoyed she called out to him: 'If, instead of calling out Ramabai, Ramabai, you'd call out Ram, Ram; recitation of God's name would earn you divine favour.' Mohandas was upstairs in a few seconds reciting 'Ram, Ram.'

After his marriage, Mohandas always slept with the lights on. In the beginning, Kastur was puzzled but she soon got to know the reason. She was a braver soul. She feared neither ghosts nor snakes.

None of this talk however consoled Kastur. She would manage to reintroduce Sheikh Mehtab into the conversation somehow or the other. *Ba* would say that Mehtab was a braggart. He boasted about how he could crush a snake with bare hands. As for a ghost, he could banish him by flinging a verse from the Quran and a few drops of water at him. A thief he could handle personally. Mohania takes his word to be God's own truth.

Whenever Sheikh Mehtab delivered Mohandas' letter to her, she spent a lot of time turning it over in her hands. Then she recalled how much effort Mohandas had made to teach her to read. She simply had not bothered. Deep in her was entrenched the idea that reading and writing were a male business. A woman was supposed to look after the house. She did not need to be literate to perform that duty.

Often he would wake her up from sleep and force her to study. But while still teaching, the teacher would turn into a lover. Kastur couldn't help smiling. Her face flushed. But why blame him? Didn't she enjoy it too? Now he has been away for years and years, except for a few days after he returned from England. They only had Hari then. People do so much for their kids, but talk of him! Sometimes he would be in England, at times in Rajkot or in Bombay, and now in South Africa, where everything is so black.

~

Then she suddenly thought of that night. What a dark night it was! It was a late moon. Sickness had made *Bapu* very weak. It was Mohandas who looked after him or it was *Ba.* After he was back from school, Mohandas was constantly by his bedside, changing his dressing, giving him medicines, pressing his feet or attending to his toilet needs. That day the Diwan of Porbandar, *Bapu*'s brother, her uncle-in-law, Tulsidasji, was visiting. When *Bapu* relinquished the prime ministership of Porbandar, he had got his brother the job. It was ten at night. Mohandas was pressing *Bapu*'s feet. Diwan uncle came and told Mohandas: 'Mohania, you can go now. Your wife must be waiting. I'll be with *Bapu.*' Normally, he would not leave *Bapu*'s side, so maybe he had something on his mind that day. So off he went and straight into Kastur's arms. *Bapu* too did not ask for him. Any other day, the moment he felt a changeover in the hands pressing his feet, he would immediately inquire: 'Where's Mohania?'

They were completely lost in each other, when someone rattled the bolt on the door. They felt as if all the bolts on all the doors of the house had started rattling at the same time. They felt as if they had been wrenched out of their dream.

'What's that noise?'

Mohandas jumped out of the bed, got into his clothes, and tried to recover his breath. Then he asked: 'Who is it?'

'Open the door.' There was a horror in those words. He never heard a voice so terrified in his life again.

An old faithful servant of the family was at the door. It took Mohandas only a few moments to grasp the situation. With trembling hands, he opened the door. The first sentence that came out of his mouth was: 'How's *Bapu*?'

The servant looked at him wide-eyed and just shook his head. It was all over.

Kastur had never imagined that Mohandas would be so devastated with pain and remorse. For a moment he had been left standing there like a child whose guardian had lost him in a fair. She too was wrecked by his sorrow. She had stepped on a quicksand and could not help being engulfed by it. Mohandas rushed as he was, all dishevelled. His eyes didn't see anymore: the pupils had dissolved. Kastur too walked as fast as she could in her condition. To her it appeared that Mohandas' tongue had stiffened like dried wood.

As Kastur arrived on the scene, *Ba* told her: 'It's not right for you to be here in your condition. Please go. You will stress your stomach if you sit here.'

Ba looked quite composed even at that moment, though her face looked like a glass dish which had cracked into a thousand pieces but was still holding together. Even after all that had happened, she hadn't shattered. Mohandas was looking at *Bapu*'s body as if he himself had murdered him. He had let him die for an act so degraded that it now loomed large before him like a monster of a sin. Uncle stood unmoving on the other side. What a moment it was, he wondered, when he chose to sit by his side to press his feet. His brother, who had been like a father to him, had died even as he watched helplessly. He stood there feeling guilty. Watching Diwan Tulsidas's face, one could understand how helpless, how utterly abject the feeling of guilt can render one. Lakshmidas stood in silence. Karsan had still not been able to grasp the situation and was busy trying to pull himself together.

Mohandas shared his pain and remorse with Sheikh Mehtab: 'The sin I committed took away my father's life. Here I was indulging in carnal pleasure while *Bapu* lay there dying. His soul must have seen all. The soul permeates the whole universe like ether the moment it leaves the body, doesn't it? Oh, my God.'

Hard to say if his thoughts got through to Sheikh Mehtab or not, but he did try to console him: 'You might well have lost self-control, but *Bhabhi* should have known better.'

Kastur stood behind the door, listening. When Mohandas walked in, his head was completely shaven. In the light, the shaven pate was shining like an upturned bowl made of reflecting metal.

Kastur said: 'Even at a time like this, this friend of yours can only think of putting the blame on your wife. I certainly don't appreciate his trying to poison your mind against me in this way. And how many of your friends are going to hear this story from you? Maybe you have no shame to bother about, but what about your wife?'

'I know you don't like him. He might or might not have said anything against you but you are always ready to assume that he has.'

'*Bapu* is dead and he wants to hold me responsible for it.'

Mohandas kept quiet.

~

Kastur's first child was stillborn.

For several days, Kastur seemed to have withdrawn into a shell. It had been only a few days since the patriarch of the family had departed. The new guest to arrive did not quite arrive. *Ba* only said: '*Baba* must have detained him thinking it would be good company,' and had burst out crying. In a space of few months, Mohandas had to escort two bodies to the cremation ground. One body had arrived without life in it; the other one had been left behind by life.

Mohandas had only one refrain: 'We are paying for our sin …'

Kastur would say: 'Why do you blame your wife?'

But he would continue nevertheless: 'Had I been with father, he would not have died; nor would the child have been born dead.'

When Kastur could not bear it anymore, she said: 'What would you have done? Stopped death in its tracks? It is one thing to feel grief, another to feel guilty. It's not sin, it's time …'

Though Kastur said all this, she couldn't forget how Mohandas would set his ear against her stomach to listen to the child's heartbeats. She felt embarrassed and would push him off. Mohandas would say: 'The fellow already talks such a lot; what would he be like once he is out?'

Sometime Kastur used to experience a lot of activity going on inside her. She would report it to *Ba*, who just laughed and said: 'The child is turning on its side. How would the mother know the child is playing if he doesn't? When I was carrying Mohania, he wasn't the rowdy type at all. In fact, sometimes I worried why he was so quiet. I had a very different type of pregnancy in his case. If I told his father, he would only say: "He is sure to be a very promising child," and his face lighted up.'

Next he would say: 'You just wait and watch, Lakshmi's mother, this child is never going to stop, never. He will be on the move, always.'

'That's hardly a blessing.'

'For him, it will be a blessing.'

Ba was the silent type, but when someone mentioned Mohania, she could hardly stop talking. She told her that she had never talked so much in the presence of *Bapu* than when she was carrying Mohania; he seemed to have opened up the floodgates of her courage. 'Isn't his father on the move always?' she said: 'So how can I expect him not to be?'

Kastur felt she was reliving all this inside her. From *Ba*, she would suddenly find herself moving on to Mehtab; she didn't know why. Was he her obsession, her phobia?

Sometimes Kastur went day-dreaming and was greatly tickled by the thought that one day Hari would grow up into a young man, would learn to read and write, and would write to his *Bapu* and tell him that now that he knew reading and writing, *Bapu* could send his letters to *Ba* through him. He would read them out to his *Ba*. But *Ba* didn't like the idea. She would then take Hari in her lap and tell him: 'You must grow up fast and become a learned man like your father. When you return after your studies, I will be alive and waiting for you. I'll then be known as the wife of a learned man and mother of a learned son. I will be carrying the learning of two people!'

She would then laugh out loud at her silly thoughts and would turn sad.

Sheikh Mehtab was regaling Hari with the story of the Natal train incident that had happened with Mohandas as if Mohandas was the hero of a folktale: how the whites threw him out of the train, how he spent the whole night shivering at the Maritzburg railway station, and how two coolies had covered him with their own blanket.

Hari asked: 'How did you know all this, uncle?'

'I received a letter from him.'

Though speaking to Hari, he actually intended it to be heard by her and chuckled at the thought. Kastur was ready to cry her heart out: How hard must it have been on him in a strange country! Kastur called Hari inside. In a raised voice, Sheikh said: 'How will Mohanbhai's son ever learn how courageous his father is, if we don't tell him about his father?'

Kastur let it pass.

He continued: 'A messenger's duty is to see that the message reaches its destination. He should therefore have free access to all places. When my friend writes to me, I have to make sure that the message reaches my sister-in-law and my nephew. Moreover, when I see Hari, I see Mohanbhai in him.'

Sheikh Mehtab visited them only when Lakshmibhai was not at home, though Lakshmibhai had on several occasions hinted to Mehtab that he should call only when he is at home: 'It would be nice to have you here when I'm at home. We can then exchange gossip and have a great time.'

But what Lakshmibhai said and what Sheikh Mehtab did continued to be two separate things. He came, he laid siege of the kids and he started shooting his mouth.

Sometimes Sheikh Mehtab would carry on with Hari in the same vein: 'Do you know how much your father loved Mehtab uncle?'

He didn't. How would such a small kid know how love is measured?

So he told him: 'Your father had to go to Porbandar to seek the help and blessings of his uncle for going to London. His uncle was the Prime Minister of Porbandar. *Ba* wanted your father to seek his permission before going to London. The journey from Rajkot to Porbandar had to be performed on camelback. When a camel moves, the water in your tummy goes gurgle-gurgle.'

The idea of 'water in your tummy going gurgle-gurgle' sent Hari into a peal of laughter.

Such talk made Kastur see red. When Mehtab was talking, her ears were glued to him.

Hari of course would be listening spellbound, as if it was a story-telling session. Sheikh Mehtab continued: 'The day before Mohandas had to leave for London, we had a big fight. For poor Mohandas, it was double misery: the misery of having picked up a fight with his friend, and the misery of leaving his friend behind.' He said the last bit in a raised voice and then continued: 'He was very unhappy. At night, when he was returning with a few friends from a session of devotional songs, he didn't notice a coach heading in his direction and, so perplexed he was, he collided with the coach. Actually, he didn't like the idea of parting from his friend one bit. And he fell down.'

'Was he hurt much?'

'Yes. He lost consciousness for a few minutes. He had a poor physique; and he was also very timid.'

Suddenly, Hari asked: 'Did he lose consciousness when he fell from the train?'

Kastur called out: 'Come inside, Hari! You are always talking nonsense.'

Hari left, but the question kept bothering him: 'Had *Bapu* lost consciouness when he fell from the train?'

Hari asked Kastur. Kastur did not know what answer to give. She had no clue. Mohandas hadn't mentioned it in his letter to his brother. And she was furious about it.

She was on the verge of tears, but recovered and told him: 'Your uncle is only telling what he might have heard.'

'Uncle is not a liar. He says a Muslim never speaks a lie.'

'Okay. You do as you please.'

'I'll go to my *Bapu*. I'll hit anyone who bothers him.'

She started crying, but held back her tears and tried to laugh: 'Your *Bapu* doesn't believe in fighting, except with me. If you hit anyone, he'll be angry with you.'

~

Mohandas was pleased with Matilda's hospitality. His day was spent working with Mr. Baker, but Sundays were free. When he was free and Matilda wasn't busy, she would knock on his door and inquire: 'May I come in?'

If Mohandas was busy, he would say: 'Could we meet a little later?'

'Sure,' she would say and leave. However, this was a rare happening. Normally, he welcomed her enthusiastically.

Matilda loved to talk. For her, Mohandas was a bit of a curiosity and she was always trying to find out more about him.

'Mr. Gandhi, you don't drink, and you don't eat meat. How do you survive?'

'I don't know how I survive,' he would laugh. 'All I know is that I eat the food you cook.'

This pleased her no end and she would give a broad smile. Taking the opportunity, Mohandas would launch into his talk: 'It's up to us whether we want to turn our stomachs into a graveyard of animals or a garden. Of course you can neither see the graveyard nor the garden. It's all a matter of feeling. One gives you the feeling of freshness, the other perhaps makes you feel all bloodied. Don't you think so?'

'I have heard you can't survive in London without liquor.'

'I too had heard the same. When I was on my way to London, I had a white gentleman as a fellow passenger on the ship. He told me: "So far we have been passing through warm climes, but when we reach the Bay of Biscay it'll be so cold, so cold that you'll freeze. I'd then like to see how you survive without meat and liquor."'

She was looking at him with great curiosity. 'What happened then?' she asked.

'Well, there was little I could say. I just thanked him for his valuable advice and told him that I'd given word to my mother that I'd stay off meat and liquor. Bay of Biscay came and went but made no difference to me: I stayed off meat and liquor.'

'What about female companionship?'

'I like white women. They are not shy and all bundled up like Indian women. But beyond the point of friendship, I'm again tied to my word. In any case, when even meat and liquor make me shiver in my boots, won't the touch of a live woman reduce me to a blabbering idiot?' Matilda burst out laughing.

Mohandas joined her in laughter.

The Portsmouth scene flashed before his eyes. The pretty hostess and his own deceiving self, the warning from his friend and saviour, the saviour who then sank himself. Scared of his own self, he had started running and had kept running. He felt that the dark of the night was closing in on him in the shape of that woman. She had spoken to him but her words had been lost in the tug of war between the fear within him and the force of her attraction. For a moment, he became apprehensive that the Portsmouth scene might be about to come alive before him once again.

'Why have you turned so serious, Mr. Gandhi?' asked Matilda

'I was thinking that nothing in this world is a unit, solitary and by itself; other digits, tens and tens of tens, go on attaching themselves to it one after another, and can go on till infinity,' said Mohandas: 'contexts after contexts go on revealing themselves, causing one to wonder wherefrom such mushrooming of contexts could possibly occur. Like mushrooms in the damp, ideas keep growing in the mind, and man finds himself getting crushed like a helpless rabbit in the ever-tightening embrace of the multiplying contexts.'

'How educated was your mother?'

'Educated or not, the very fact of having a mother makes you a child. You must of course know it first-hand.'

'What I meant was if your mother was aware of the possible consequences such promises could have?'

'This issue has no connection whatsoever with being educated or not. What is it about her children that a mother does not know or understand? Anyway, the Bay of Biscay had come and gone. The passengers were all shivering with cold and plying themselves with meat and liquor, which they thought were their saviours. My saviour was the word I had given to my mother. The white fellow passenger was wondering why I wasn't dead still.' Mohandas laughed.

'Didn't you tell him?'

'After the Bay of Biscay had passed I told him I had a feeling I'd gained some weight. He was amazed. I asked him to write me a certificate to the effect that despite the cold of Bay of Biscay I was still surviving without meat or liquor. I carried that certificate with me for a long time but tore it up later. If one didn't trust my word, why would one trust the certificate?'

'But I trust your word,' she said and continued,'my husband loves to drink and I like meat. I am a bit worried now that our kids are growing up. They may also turn into fish swimming in liquor like their father. Our food and drink is controlled by our income: if we drink more, we must eat less. I don't know what to do.'

Mohandas was keeping quiet.

'Can you suggest something?' Matilda asked him.

'I can only pray. But you can stop him if you so choose.'

'How?'

'You give up what you love most: eating meat. It's possible your husband may give up drinking in exchange.'

'I don't think it very likely.'

'The fruits of sacrifice grow really fast, madam.'

~

Not a day passed without Mr. Baker and Mohandas meeting. He also met Coates and the other friends at the prayer. It was very rare for Mohandas to miss the prayer. Although everyone met him with great ardour, Mohandas realized that the initial enthusiasm was now missing. Nevertheless, some still survived.

Mr. Baker's enthusiasm had not diminished at all. His enthusiasm rivalled that of sportsmen. He had presented a pocket Bible to Mohandas which he had inscribed: 'To Mr. M.K. Gandhi—Baker.' Mr. Baker never tired of speaking: he was a lawyer, and a proselytizer to boot. Speaking was the first requirement of both. Everyone, black or white, believer or non-believer, could enter his church. It was not a Hindu temple which could be desecrated by the presence of anyone: from the same or from another religion. Nor was it a first class compartment of a railway train where only whites could travel.

It hurt Mohandas to think of the railway compartment. A searing pain ran through his body every time he thought of the humiliation he had suffered. A permanent fire seemed to smolder inside him sending out fine particles of burning ash through the holes of his skin. He often felt himself riding a train with several fellow passengers like himself. A few whites enter the compartment and push them out at every station. They climb back again, and again they are pushed out. They have all been maimed: someone has a broken hand, someone a leg, somebody is bleeding from the head. There are small kids, who perhaps do not yet understand humiliation, but are crying out of injury. By the time they grow up, the seed of humiliation will have transformed into a poisonous tree, whose fruit it will be their inevitable fate to taste.

A thought kept crossing Mohandas' mind again and again: How long will they go on like this? How long will they go on drinking hemlock from this cup of humiliation? Is there a way out? In a world where everyone is equipped with enough weaponry to crush the life out of other people, who are taken to be no more than insects, how long can a lone individual keep up his solitary fight? How long can he fight against weaponry?

The last question troubled him the most. Will all these people who are riding thc train be able to get off the train? This question often made him jump out of his sleep. The people sitting on the train and those standing outside caused a sharp divide in his sleep as if a stream of water had been sliced through the middle into an upper stream and a lower stream with the upper stream riding hard and choking the lower stream.

Like a leaping flame, the coach leader's whip flashed before his eyes. That whip was his strength. 'We fear him because there is a bloodthirsty beast inside him inciting him to kill. If we can separate the man from the beast, the weapon will become harmless. Our fear will evaporate. To be free from fear is to be free within.'

Sometimes all these ideas would appear to him to be airy nonsense; at other times he would feel that there was emerging beneath his feet the solid ground of reality.

~

Among the Sheths in South Africa, there were only two who mattered: Abdullah Sheth in Durban and Tyeb Sheth in Pretoria. Mohandas was in a peculiar fix: on the one hand, there was Dada Abdullah's warning not to mix with the traders of Pretoria, on the other was Tyeb Sheth, the doyen of Indian traders in Pretoria. If Mohandas were to stay in Pretoria, he would have to meet Tyeb Sheth. There was no way to resolve this dilemma.

After he had been thrown out of the railway compartment, Mohandas had spent a lot of time on the platform like a wounded bird thrashing about his wingless body. There must be other people like him who had had the misfortune of being thrown out of other places and who had then been unable to make it to their homes on their own feet. It is quite possible that these Sheths haven't had the occasion to experience this humiliation with the same intensity as he had had, the reason why they could afford the luxury of a private brawl. Unless he first got to understand both of them and made them understand the issue, it would be inadequate to expect that they would understand that closing the distance between their two hearts would amount to striking out a new path for the whole community. The obstacles in his path were the prohibitions issued by Dada Abdullah, the professional attitude of Mr. Baker and Mohandas' unfamiliarity with Tyeb Sheth. What could he do? Should he also just beat his path to the courts and back with the files under his arms, like other lawyers? If something went wrong with the case, as the weakest link, he would neither be forgiven by Dada Abdullah nor would he be able to forgive himself. Who was right and who was wrong were matters that could be discussed later. What was going to be his role in all this? He would close his eyes and let his thoughts drift along. Ever so slowly, his own face would start emerging before his eyes and he would be able to hear his own voice: it is the worst kind of slavery to allow yourself to be guided by the delusions of others. You know what slavery means? It means the death of your conscience. Mohandas would then feel life returning to his body. Someone was calling out to him: 'Go on try it out! Break down this wall of hatred that divides people!'

Mohandas got up and started walking. He kept moving as if he was on someone's wings, as if there were wheels beneath his feet. When he stopped, he found himself at Tyeb Sheth's doorstep. Tyeb Sheth had an impressive personality: a light beard, Turkish fez and in contrast to Dada Abdullah, English clothes. Under the fez, a bald head. Large bluish eyes.

'*Aadaab arz*,' said Mohandas, raising his hand and bowing slightly in the Muslim style.

'*Aadaab*,' Tyeb Sheth's eyes reflected part curiosity and part familiarity. Familiarity because he looked Indian; curiosity because the face was unknown. Who could he be? Where could he be from? A suited and booted, dyed-in-English colours Indian at his doorstep? The question however stayed in his eyes only. With some people, the face is so eloquent that words are unnecessary.

'I am from Porbandar. My father, Karamchand Gandhi was Diwan of the state of Rajkot. My name is Mohandas Gandhi. I am a barrister.'

The Sheth looked delighted: 'I say, you are one of us, aren't you?'

'That's so kind of you.'

'What can I do for you?'

'I am concerned about the Indians of Transvaal. I don't know the natives at all. Moreover, I am not aware of their language, their requirements or their ways of living. I know that I cannot have any communication with them. Hence I want to meet the Indians and talk to them. I know this would not be possible without your help.'

'Why would you want to do that?'

'I have been hurt so much while travelling to this place that I am wondering how much more wounded must the Indians be who live here. I want to compare notes with them about our sufferings.'

Mohandas then told him all that had happened to him. As he spoke, Tyeb Sheth listened to him quietly. The expression on his face changed with every episode: a transparent layer of tension, pity, anger, desperation and pain emerged on his face by turns.

'Tyeb Sheth, I wake up in the middle of the night. I have visions of all the Indians being herded into a field, being tethered to stakes like animals and being struck with whips. They are like dogs that can neither cry nor bark. I have visions of us and our kids being thrown out of trains like live and kicking bundles while the trains rush to their destinations. All the Indians who came here, either as travellers or as bonded labourers, or *girmitiya*s, are struggling to find only one thing: money. They think money is what will provide the salve for their wounds; they think money tops happiness, peace and respect. Why do they only respect money? Can money alone give them their identity?'

'We are here to earn a living, not to fight a war,' said Tyeb Sheth in a decisive tone.

'There is no question of fighting or surviving. We are all going down, but we can't feel it. It's fully possible that we may sink without a trace tomorrow. Or maybe survive only in the form of monkeys and dogs. The monkey turned into man; we are turning from man to monkey, aren't we? Money comes much later.'

Tyeb Sheth sat there listening to Mohandas without speaking a word. A transparent screen of silence seemed to have fallen across the doorstep of his consciousness in which he was seeing distorted images of himself. After a while, Tyeb Sheth spoke as if he was speaking with his neck protruding out of a hole: 'Mr. Gandhi, we have never thought along those lines nor do we think now.'

'Nor will you ever think in the future either, will you?'

Tyeb Sheth kept quiet. Mohandas was still at it: 'I can appreciate it about the *girmitiya*s that bread and butter is their first priority. Starvation has deprived them of the power of thinking. Why would they otherwise leave their homes to come to this hell? They had boundless love for their country and their people, but for a foreign government that love held no meaning. Your priorities are of course different those are not determined by bread alone. I hope you will forgive me for saying all this.'

'No, actually, it's not like that. I acknowledge that we must take that point of view too. We might have arrived here as travellers, but we remain basically illiterate. And there's no question but that we came here for business.' He laughed and continued: 'I am reminded of a joke. There was this man who piled up soil on his head and sowed rice on it. He would rush wherever it rained. Naturally, he harvested an excellent crop. That's what a businessman does. Wherever he finds the going good, he lands there leaving home and hearth behind. Do forgive me; I failed to ask where you were staying and if you were comfortable.'

'Never mind. Mr. Baker has arranged for me to stay in the house of a woman baker.'

The name of Mr. Baker was enough to make Tyeb Sheth sit up. Trying not to show his consternation, he said, 'I know Mr. Baker. He is a God-fearing man. He happens to be the lawyer of my opposing party in a court case.'

Without the slightest trace of hesitation, Mohandas looked directly at Tyeb Sheth and said, 'I am here in connection with the same case. I have been sent here by the other party's partner, Mr. Jhaveri, from Rajkot.'

Tyeb Sheth's eyes narrowed.

Mohandas continued: 'For me, these are two unrelated issues: the court case and the issue of Indians living here. If we can learn to settle our disputes through mutual discussions, all our problems can be solved. If we can't, this ship of ours, all decked up and ready to sail, will break up and go down like the *Fusilier*. I have only heard and read about the ship, but I carry a horrifying image of it in my mind. I don't know if you have been to the site. Three hundred and two coolies died in that mishap. When I went there, it seemed to me that the swollen carcasses of all the three hundred and two coolies were still floating on the water; that their skin, like disintegrated pieces of soaked bread, was strewn all over the area. Tyeb Sheth, we might be landlubbers, but when it's our turn to drown, even land begins to behave like the sea.'

Tyeb Sheth said, 'I am somewhat convinced by whatever you have said. I'll talk to my friends and call a meeting.'

~

The news of the meeting being called by Tyeb Sheth reached the ears of Mr. Baker. He asked Mohandas, 'Mr. Gandhi, I hear that on your prompting a meeting of Pretoria Indians is being called by Tyeb Sheth. Are you sure that it will not invite a negative reaction from Dada Abdullah?'

'This meeting has nothing to do with the Dada Abdullah case. Had Dada Abdullah been here, I'd also have invited him to the meeting. This meeting is being called to discuss the future of the Indians living in Pretoria.'

'What do you mean?' Mr. Baker stopped whatever he was doing and looked at him.

'You mean their identity ...?'

'You got it right,' Mohandas cut him short.

'The people here may not like it.'

'Do you think these people like what happens to them? You know very well that everyone has the God-given right to decide how he wants to live. It is we men who put ourselves above Him and try to interfere with what He has ordained, taking recourse sometimes to law, and sometimes to tyranny.'

'You are right. The Bible says: this world is the Kingdom of God. Know thyself in His grace. If you want to participate in the meeting, do so by all means. Have no worries on my account.'

Mr. Baker patted him on the back and shook hands with him warmly. Whenever Mr. Baker liked something, he looked at the picture of Christ on the wall and crossed himself. This was his prayer and his thanksgiving to God.

~

Most of the people present at the meeting were Muslims, more specifically, Memons. The presence of Hindus was negligible. Not only in Pretoria but in the whole of Transvaal, the number of Hindus was very small. Most of them belonged to the lower classes, working in mines, hotels and farms. A few of them had turned up from neighboring places because of the Hindu name, Gandhi. 'A barrister called Gandhi has come from India,' they had been told.

The meeting had been arranged at the house of Haji Muhammad Joosab. Haji Joosab was a friend of Dada Abdullah too. He had actually given a letter to Mohandas for Haji Joosab. He was of course a regular visitor to Tyeb Sheth's house. Although the meeting had been called by him, Tyeb Sheth had chosen to sit in a corner. As a participant walked in, he would first go to Tyeb Sheth and bow to him before taking his seat. The meeting was to be conducted by Haji Joosab. He was also the one to introduce Mohandas:

> *Brothers, Tyeb Sheth has given you the trouble of coming here today so that we can introduce you to a person whose heart bleeds for his Indian brethren. Most of us here come from the region which is the home province of Gandhibhai. The place is called Kathiawar. Mr. Gandhi is from a pre-eminent family of Porbandar. His father and uncle were Prime Ministers of the state of Porbandar. His father, in fact, served as Prime Minister in several states. Gandhibhai himself is London-returned. In India, that is considered to be a great distinction. Gandhibhai earned his barrister degree from London. He is a man of progressive ideas. Some of you may have seen in the newspapers how, on the very next day after his arrival in Durban, he refused to take off his turban at the orders of a white magistrate, and preferred to leave the court. For a freshly arrived Indian in this country, this was not an act of ordinary courage. Mr. Gandhi wishes to say a few words to you, as he is upset at the present condition of Indians in this country.*

Tyeb Sheth was next to speak. The way he started off was a little startling.

> *I know very little about this young barrister. He came to me a few days ago rather unexpectedly. I was taken aback to see this young man, all dressed up like an Englishman, walking in quite unabashed and wondered who he could be. Must be an Indian, I thought. After we had talked for a few minutes, all my doubts and suspicions were removed. Mr. Gandhi is a fellow countryman. A few*

minutes with him and I realized that he was no ordinary person but the owner of an admirable personality. Let me also tell you that Mr. Gandhi is here as an advocate for a party which is opposing me in the courts. But all that I know is that this man is an Indian and carries in his heart a deep feeling for the miseries of his fellow Indians here. The pain and the humiliation he had to undergo in the course of his journey to Pretoria he has not kept to himself; rather they have unlocked in his heart a flood of sympathy for his fellow countrymen here. He sees India in every Indian. The pain he has undergone has given birth to a new human being within him who cannot stand slavery of the spirit. I hold this sentiment of his in the highest regard.

When Mohandas stood up to speak, he felt that everything that he had come prepared to say had withered away from his mind. There was no trace of anything. Sweat broke out on his forehead. Even when listening to Tyeb Sheth, his mind had been wandering. He remembered a few things but had missed out others. He thought of the farewell function for High School students, when he had got up to speak on behalf of Class X students. Everything in his mind had been wiped clean. At the Vegetarians' Meet in London, he had taken with him his written speech but had still been unable to deliver it. Someone else had to read it out. He cursed his fate. Whenever he got an opportunity to speak, his brain handed him a shiny, blank slate of frustration.

Suddenly, he heard Tyeb Sheth's voice: 'Where are you, Mr. Gandhi?'

'I was wondering how I should start.'

'Everyone is waiting to hear you,' he said encouragingly.

Mohandas' condition was like that of a participant in a race trying to steady his breath before the start of the race or maybe trying to measure up his spirit against the vast field stretched out before him. The breath was now steady. Only the tension of taking the first leap remained.

He raised his first sentence slowly like an Indian classical singer raising an *alaap*:

Janaab Tyeb Sheth Sahib, today's host Haji Muhammad Sahib and my fellow countrymen. I have been waiting very impatiently to talk to you. I am grateful to Tyeb Sahib for giving me this opportunity. I am grateful to all of you for coming here. I have absolutely no doubt that Tyeb Sahib is a very large-hearted person. Although he knew that I was a lawyer for the party opposing him in the court, he showed a great regard for me by honouring my wish. This shows his sincerity and the generosity of his heart.

By now, Mohandas had regained his confidence. The speech was also catching momentum. He paused a little and then started on his theme.

It has been less than a month since I arrived in this beautiful country. I am wonderstruck at the beauty of this country. Undulating meadows, middling-high hills rising from their edges, trails and tracks leading down from the hilltops … These middling hills do not overawe you like the sky-scraping mountains of India: in fact, they greet you like friends, they talk to you, they lead you by the hand to the tops of the hills, and then, ever so gently, guide you down their slopes. The tribes here remind me of the nomads of Gujarat who lead their flocks of sheep from place to place in search of fodder. Their small desires are never frustrated. That's the reason why they are still alive in every country in one form or another.

Mohandas now felt he was firmly in the saddle and he could now afford to use the spurs.

These people are in their land and in their own country. We Indians have come here from thousands of miles away, crossing sea and land, in search of a living. Some of us reached here, some lost their lives in the watery channels. For their kith and kin in India, they are still alive across the seven seas busy earning their living. No one knows how long they will remain so, though they are never going to return again to them. Who's going to tell them?

Mohandas realized that he was sentimentalizing unnecessarily. He was wandering from the topic of the day. But at least he was able to speak fluently, and people were listening to him intently. He changed the topic.

What I am trying to say is that when we Indians leave home, we have a dream. By the time we arrive, if we are still alive, the stomach and the mind are both empty. A hungry man is like dough: you can give him whatever shape you like. These dark miles are like a bridge between life and death for us. The beauty of the hills, trees and fountains is forever. But when we weigh it against the ever-shortening life, it turns out to be no more than a line drawn on water. People like you came here for a different purpose. You came here at your own expense. But those other people were helpless at home and they are helpless here. They have been brought here like bonded labour and half-slaves. What do they get? Eleven shillings a month. This is the total price of their freedom. But those people still carry love and affection in their hearts, which they have brought with them from their native country like their tattered, old clothing. I experienced that love personally at Maritzburg when the cold of the night was conspiring with the dark to take my life from me.

I too am a girmitiya. *I have a one-year* girmit. *My travelling expenses have been borne by Dada Abdullah. You could have given me a cold shoulder but I sport a tail called 'barrister'. I had the benefit of a starting-line that was much ahead of the others, but, for the whites, we are all coolies, however much we may like to play 'I-big-you-small' amongst ourselves. We have to face this hatred of the whites in our own country, but here it is like a pond in which each one of us is fated to sink up to our necks. We are dirty, we are creatures of filth and we cannot be their equals. Among ourselves, we are nursing our own hatreds.*

Mohandas paused for a while. Everyone was listening to him closely. All their eyes were on him. He looked around and then resumed his talk:

The trader class is better off. There is a saying in the political circles of Britain: 'All is fair in love and war.'

I have heard it said about Indian businessmen that there is no distinction between right and wrong in their business. In fact, wrong is right. For them right is a matter of religion, not of life. But are these two separate things? If so, then religion is bereft of meaning. Life becomes synonymous with wrong. Do the boundaries of right extend only up to the point where it ceases to be profitable to you? Does it cease to be right if it starts causing you loss? There is only one thing I want to communicate to you: a double responsibility rests on you. You can be true to yourselves in a foreign land only when you can take courage in both your hands and change your outlook on right and wrong. The way you acquit yourselves, individually and collectively, will be the touchstone by which the character of the hundreds of millions of Indians living in India will be judged. You are like the bird that may be flying miles away in a remote sky but is firmly and deeply anchored to its own land. Talking of dignity while giving the go-by to truth is like day-dreaming. Money is not the only truth. This applies to all those people who are scattered far and wide in the colonies as businessmen and girmitiyas. *Right behaviour alone will be the criterion for the respect that you seek; otherwise you will continue to be spurned everywhere like animals.*

Everyone was stunned. Mohandas, they felt, had uncovered their true faces and served them on a platter before them.

Mohandas concluded:

I want to put a proposal before you. We should have an organization of Indians which can raise its voice against the difficulties and atrocities faced by Indians here and can make it heard by the authorities concerned. As far as I am concerned, I can assure you that every single minute of my time will be at the service of the organization.

One of the men spoke: 'Each one of us can relate to you a tale of his woes, a tale so horrific that it will open your eyes wide and make your hair stand on end. What you had to undergo was actually ...'

'That is why I have made this proposal.'

Mohandas realized that everyone present was speaking in his own mother tongue. Nobody was following what the other person was saying. At best, everyone was going by guesswork. A few of them knew rudimentary English. They were trying to interpret it to Mohandas. Mohandas was amazed. How on earth did these people run their business: through their mother tongue?

Mohandas said,

> *No language is closer to you than your mother tongue. But since you are in business you must also learn the language of work here. I can start English language classes for you. You must have enough English to be able to understand what the other person is saying and to explain to others what you want to say. If you want to learn individually, I am ready to do that too.*

They all clapped but no one raised a hand.

~

Mohandas set up a free English teaching school and waited for students for several days. The first person turned up after three days. He was a clerk. Mohandas asked him, 'Why do you want to learn English? After all, you are a clerk and must already know English.'

'Yes, I do, but I don't know it as well as my officers. I wish to be able to speak and write English like them so that they look upon me with respect. At the moment, they treat me like dirt.'

'It's not enough to know English.'

'I don't quite understand.'

'You must also try to understand the nature of people around you. Learning about the milieu in which you live is as important as learning the language.'

So he started learning English.

Then there was a barber. He had a saloon of his own. As to everyone else, Mohandas also put the question to him: 'You are a barber. Your job is to cut hair. What's the need for you to learn English?'

'Most of my customers are white. I often fail to communicate properly. The new customers often get irritated rather quickly. They appreciate my work; if they could also appreciate my talk, my business would really look up.'

Mohandas was happy to see the man's devotion to his work. He also started teaching him.

The third student was a small shopkeeper. He had a grocery stall and his ambition was to enlarge his business. He wanted to lead a better and more dignified life. He wanted to acquire the competence to talk to the white customers in their own language.

Mohandas yoked him in too.

Although Mohandas was their teacher, decisions regarding the curriculum, timetable, etc. were in the hands of the students. After his day's work was over, Mohandas went round to their places one after another. Sometimes he would find the barber shaving a customer while two or three waited for their turns. The teacher would wait patiently till the barber signalled to him to go. After all, he couldn't possibly tell the customer to go because he had an English class to attend.

Mohandas would continue on his round. Next he landed at the clerk's place. The clerk still wouldn't be back from his office. The teacher would wait till he was tired of waiting and then left. The shopkeeper's place, it was true, didn't have much of a crowd. In fact, space being in short supply, the teacher would have to take his class standing. If, in the meantime, a customer dropped in, the shopkeeper would desert the class and would get busy selling. If the customer happened to be an important one, he would have to be entertained too. During this period, Mohandas would pace up and down the street. If sometimes there happened to be a rush of customers, the shopkeeper would just signal with a wave of his hand, when Mohandas was still far away, that there would be no class that day.

In the end, Mohandas had to satisfy himself with whatever progress his students were capable of. The barber had started accompanying his snipping with some smattering of English. If he didn't understand what the customer said, he would go 'pardon me, pardon me'. The clerk too had acquired this mantra. The shopkeeper had started maintaining his accounts in English, and sometimes startled his customers by breaking into English. He could also write to his business associates in broken

English. The clerk's was a tale apart. He had started making money by writing English drafts for customers.

~

They had started meeting once every two or three weeks since that meeting at Haji Muhammad Sahib's place. Mohandas was the one to have benefited most from the meetings. He had got to know almost all the Indians in Pretoria personally. He had also established contacts with the *girmitiya*s who lived around the place. They of course at first felt a bit disconcerted when they saw an Indian in English clothes approaching them. Mohandas made a big deal of their discomfiture. Sometimes he also took them to meet the businessmen, even if they didn't like it. There were many among them who had never before seen how businessmen lived. They felt shy and even afraid, but Mohandas would always be by their side. At first, the businessmen too were uncomfortable in their presence: they stank and they scratched. Mohandas was, however, always there to mediate. He constantly repeated a single mantra to them: 'They are our fellow countrymen. They may be poor but love and sacrifice are in their nature. They won't accept anything from you, but when it comes to giving, they will give even their life for you.'

The meeting that day was being held after a whole month. These sessions had no fixed agenda. That day, the topic of railway travel cropped up during the discussion. It was pointed out that it was becoming unsafe and demeaning to undertake a train journey. The natives were beginning to copy the ways of the whites and behaving as if Indians were untouchables.

Someone pointed out: 'Passing in front of a first or second class compartment of a standing train to go to the other side is beginning to be treated as an offence.'

'Yes, the whites think all Indians are thieves and untouchables.'

Mohandas was listening to their talk quietly, but his mind was teeming with questions. 'How do we behave in our own country? Who knows untouchability better than you?' Whenever people talked about untouchability, he always thought of his childhood friend. 'How untouchable was he? Why was he untouchable? What had he done to become untouchable? Can a man choose where to be born?

Mohandas tried to tell himself that it was pointless raising these issues. He thought of his coach travel. Was it any safer than rail travel?

It was Haji Sheth who interrupted his thoughts: 'You are very quiet, Mr. Gandhi?'

Mohandas laughed and said' 'Haji Sahib, I am a bird of passage: here today, gone tomorrow. You are the ones who will stay on here, so it's for you to decide what you want to do. As for me, I think in the past three or four weeks I have gone through whatever I had to.'

'We are ready for anything.'

'Excuse me, Haji Sahib. To be ready for anything means to be ready for any sacrifice you may be called upon to make.'

People started exchanging glances.

Tyeb Sheth spoke: 'We are basically businessmen and are here to do business. We are not in the business of challenging and fighting others. If we want to make some money, we can do it only by keeping others happy.' Hc had figurcd out what Mohandas was driving at.

Mohandas laughed and said: 'In that case, you should have no complaint. You may be pushed out or you may be humiliated, you shouldn't utter a word. Be happy in whatever condition they want to keep you.' He paused a little and then said, 'But make sure you are ready for the day when you are asked to leave Transvaal. Just pick up your things and leave.'

'How can that be?'

'Well, if it cannot be, then make your decision. Do you want to live a life of self-respect or humiliation? A life of self-respect will demand pain; a life of humiliation will certainly help you make money.'

'In the meantime, we can at least write to the railway authorities,' said Mohandas: 'and request them that in view of the sacrifices we have made and services we have rendered, we should be allowed to travel first class, or at least second class. If they concede, it's well and good; if they don't, then we'll see what can do next. Please familiarize yourself with the rules first. It'll be best if we can achieve our goal through paper-work.'

'Yes, we can then have our cake and eat it too! We can avoid offending the authorities and also achieve our goal.'

When everyone was gone, Haji Sheth asked Mohandas: 'What do you think, Gandhibhai? Will the authorities listen to us?'

'Not until you tell them first, either orally or in writing.'

'In that case, please get a draft ready. We are all standing behind you.'

'It'll not do to stand behind me. I am an outsider. I am a rolling stone; I carry no weight. The weight will come from you, from your petition, to be signed by you. You will have to lead.'

That gave Haji Sheth a pause, but he continued: 'That's all right. Not every one of us will sign, but some of us will certainly come forward. Actually, fear rules the heart of everyone.'

'Well, if that is so, they must first get rid of that fear. Fear in a man's life is like salinity in soil. Nothing grows in that soil.'

They walked out together. There was absolute silence all round. When it's winter, the sun goes down early and silence is so thick.

When he arrived home, Mohandas found Matilda waiting for him. Seeing her standing outside the house, he asked: 'Why are you standing outside?'

'My husband's isn't back yet. You too are rather late today.'

'Where do you think your husband might be? I could go and get him.'

'He would be wherever he could sponge a drink off someone, and maybe rolling on the spot.'

'You haven't tried to persuade him to …'

'Can a bleating goat persuade a lion to crawl back into the cave?'

Mohandas said, 'You remember what I told you? Looks like you didn't try the experiment I told you to do. Tell him you have given up eating meat and ask him to give up drinking, then wait and see what happens.'

'How is that possible? That's the one and only thing I like.'

'Your husband could say the same thing. Maybe he also doesn't have any other interest.'

'You mean to say I should give up meat for ever? How will I survive?'

'There are hundreds of other things you could eat. After all, you do make vegetarian food for me. I have no problem surviving.'

'Last time I fell ill, my doctor asked me to give up meat. I didn't do it even at that time.'

'What was the problem?'

'Sores in the intestines,' said Matilda.

'I see ...'

'At that time my husband also tried hard to persuade me. He used to love me a lot. He didn't drink so much then. But when I fell ill, he got a free run of the bar.'

'That means he still loves you a lot. You can certainly wean him away from the bottle. Love makes everything possible.'

'You mean to say … I don't love my husband?'

'Of course, you do.'

'Then ...?'

'The point is how to make your husband feel it. You have already missed one chance. You didn't do what he asked for and he stepped up his drinking. So long as you cannot make him feel your love for him, how would he ever know that you are capable of making sacrifices for his sake?'

Matilda was on the verge of tears. 'Tell me how I can convince him of my love. This home, the children … aren't they enough?'

'They belong to both of you,' said Mohandas. 'How is your stomach now?'

'I still get pain occasionally.'

'If your husband's drinking can make you unhappy, don't you think your stomach aches might be making him unhappy too?'

'I don't quite follow you.'

As Mohandas was about to say something, he saw the husband staggering in.

'Good evening, sir,' said Mohandas.

He just raised his hand. Mohandas said, 'Look, your wife has been walking up and down here waiting for you.'

'You have been waiting for me?' He asked Matilda. 'How's the pain?'

'I am okay.' Matilda wanted to say something more, but words didn't come out.

Mohandas went to his room. His food was on the table, covered.

'Thank you Mr. Gandhi, I think I'll be able to persuade my husband,' said Matilda next morning as she served him breakfast, looking at him with eyes that spoke of gratitude.

She was in a hurry and left after arranging breakfast on the table. As she walked away, she said, 'Today, both of us are going to share your vegetarian food.'

~

Mohandas and Coates used to take their walks together. Mohandas had an early dinner and, unlike Englishmen, no supper. The host's family did have supper, so they started late and went on till late. Mohandas had a rule: a walk after dinner. Coates joined him at home and they together went out for a walk. They had a walk-cum-talk till eight-thirty. At eight-thirty, Coates would take out a watch from the pocket of his robe and start consulting it. A padre, Coates was always dressed in a robe.

'One hour is adequate for a walk. Let's go back. It's almost supper time.'

Mohandas had a craze for walking. Craze may not be the right word, but he really enjoyed walking and it rarely tired him. Mostly they talked about religious matters. Sometimes Mohandas told Coates about Hinduism; at other times, he tried to explain to Mohandas the finer points of Christianity. Mohandas had a good knowledge about Parsees too. He had also read the Quran. He could also talk about other religions. They both listened to each other very carefully. Coates of course listened, but he was a fanatic about his own religion. His sole effort was to set at rest all Mohandas' doubts about his religion. Listening to Mohandas speaking about Buddha, he often said: 'But that's what Christ has also said.'

By the time it was nine, Coates would throw up both his hands and say: 'Enough. No more.'

Mohandas laughed and said: 'We have barely got started.'

Coates would first try to make excuses like: he had supper to get ready or that people would be waiting for him, but when Mohandas remained firm on getting on with the walk, he would get down to the brass tacks: 'Why don't you understand, Mr. Gandhi? It's not the London law or the Indian law that operates here. It's a different law, and they are a different people.'

'But I'm sure you are not one of them.' He would laugh and say.

'Mr. Gandhi, this is no laughing matter. You may land yourself in trouble any time.'

'It will not be the first time. I love landing in trouble and getting out of it. If everyone tried to avoid trouble, trouble would be in trouble, wouldn't it?' He would keep walking

'You know it and yet you pretend not to know it. People like you are not allowed on the streets after nine o'clock.'

'But you are with me—a living pass.'

Coates would throw up his hands. Mohandas would say: 'Do me a favour, will you? Make me a pass. That would mean an end to your worries, uninterrupted walks for me and due regard for these old-fashioned rules.'

'And what should I write in the pass? That you are my domestic servant?'

'I have no problem with that. I would be willing to work for you in return.'

'For God's sake, stop all that. Others may not know you, but I know what you are. Please stop dragging me into sin.'

'What I meant was that you wouldn't then have to speak a lie.'

While walking, Mohandas would often leave the main road and step on to the footpath. Coates had to drag him back on to the road. 'Why don't you walk on the road? Why do you leave the wide road and take to the footpath?' He asked.

'Mr. Coates, you are a padre and yet you seem more scared than me. Tell me what's the difference between the road and the footpath? They are both meant for humans, aren't they?'

'Now I know that you love inviting trouble. No peace without trouble for you, right?'

'How can I assume that I am here to lead a peaceful life? I too am a human being. Doesn't a human being need freedom?' Then he would laugh and say: 'You know, sometimes freedom starts calling out to me. Tell me what I should do. What would you do if your daughter or your mother called out to you?'

Coates would be nonplussed.

Coates was at Mohandas' place at nine. This was the time when he also usually left for work. Coates said, 'Come with me. You have to go with me first.'

'Where?'

'Where I am going'

'Where are you going?'

'Since you have this craze of walking the streets at night, we'll have to do something about it, won't we? Or we'll be behind bars one day. I have a friend, Dr. Krause, who's the State Attorney.'

'Looks like you have got some charges filed against me. Otherwise, what possible connection can there be between my night walks and the State Attorney?'

'No charges yet, but soon there will be. With the kind of lawless behaviour you are engaging in the day is not far when charges will follow you wherever you go.'

At first, Mohandas would try all kinds of excuses. 'I'm not going to lend legitimacy to an unjust law by seeking a pass …'

'You have to come with me. If you are keen to spend time in jail, you can refuse to show the pass. But let me do my duty.'

And Coates forced Mohandas to accompany him.

~

Dr. Krause happened to be in the office when they reached the place. When he learnt that Coates was there to see him, he came out at once. Coates introduced Mohandas: 'My friend Mr. M.K. Gandhi from India. A barrister by profession.'

The word 'barrister' excited his interest. His immediate question was: 'Where did you get your degree?'

'Inner Temple, London.'

Krause raised himself up a little in his chair. Then, controlling his enthusiasm, said, 'In that case, we are both barristers of the same Inn.'

Mohandas got up from his chair and bowed. Krause too got up and shook hands with him. For a moment, when Krause upped himself just a little in his chair, Mohandas wondered how whites scrimped and scraped when it came to sharing their joy and curiosity with nonwhites.

Coates explained: 'I have brought Mr. Gandhi to you for a special reason. He is fond of walking the streets at night. A single man, you know, spends time either reading or walking. If I forbid him, he turns a rebel. 'Not every law needs to be obeyed,' he says. 'Some laws are best honoured in their breach.'

Mohandas added: 'Let you be the judge, Dr. Krause. We can't walk on the roads after nine. You call that a law?'

Dr. Krause let his head hang but said nothing. Mohandas went on: 'Did you find any such anti-liberty laws in London? The British government could have stopped us by clamping down a similar law.'

'It's a pity that people like you need to carry a pass. Actually, there have been attacks on whites by blacks at night. There have been thefts and murders.'

'I am sure they have not gone unpunished. The fact is Indians are very peace-loving people. They are scared even of meeting and corresponding with the authorities.'

'I agree with you. It's not at all fair to tar everyone with the same brush. But, you know, once a law is in place, its enforcement is in the hands of people with little sensitivity. Unwavering like blinkered horses, they keep up their trot as long as the coachman keeps driving them.'

When Coates saw that the matter was dragging on, he intervened: 'Mr. Gandhi is a free thinker. His experiences in this country have been both disgraceful and painful. I want you to issue him a certificate lifting restrictions on his movements at night. Christ has said: Service of man is the service of God.'

Mohandas smiled.

'Why the smile, Mr. Gandhi?'

'I was thinking why they don't think of Christ when they make such laws.'

Coates's face was drained of colour.

Dr. Krause said, 'It's not in my power to issue a pass. As State Attorney, I'll issue you a certificate stating that I am authorizing you to use the streets after 9 pm on my personal responsibility. The police should not cause you any trouble when they see my letter. A pass would anyway not be in keeping with your dignity.'

Handing him the letter, Krause bid goodbye to Mohandas and said, 'Mr. Gandhi, you are always welcome in my house. You can walk in without hesitation anytime you like.'

Mohandas came out with Coates. Krause stood there watching him for some time, then shrugged and went in, muttering to himself: 'Strange!'

~

Whenever Mohandas stepped out of the house, he usually ran into Matilda working outside. On one pretext or the other, she would talk to Mohandas. When Mohandas stepped out that day, Matilda said; 'It's almost evening. You can take my husband with you, if you wish.'

Mohandas felt a bit awkward. 'Thank you,' he said. 'Is your husband at home at this hour?'

Matilda blushed a little. 'Mr. Gandhi, finally it was your idea that worked. I fail to understand why such a simple idea did not occur to me earlier. You were right. My husband does love me a lot.'

'And you too …' Matilda's blush took a deeper colour. Mohandas sighed: 'Every man wants to love his wife. Of course, she has to be able to appreciate his love.' His voice trembled a little but steadied quickly.

'Does that apply only to women?'

'No. it applies to men too. But sometimes women also commit excesses.' He laughed.

Matilda was prompt to ask: 'You never told me much about Mrs. Gandhi.'

Mohandas' face seemed to grow somewhat tender: 'Mrs. Gandhi is a carefree and outspoken lady. She nurses a permanent hostility against reading and writing. She considers anyone who tries to teach her literacy a stupid fool, a tyrant and a wrong-doer. Me, for example.' They both laughed.

'I am sure you are exaggerating a lot.'

'But my wife can outsmart the best of the literate ones. She could steal their ears from right beside their eyes and they wouldn't know a thing.'

'Your ears seem to be safe enough, though,' Matilda said, looking at both his ears.

'A husband's ears are not for stealing; they are for tweaking. Don't you see how long my ears are?'

'I didn't know about this side of yours, that you can be so funny.' Doubled up with laughter, this was all she was barely able to say.

Catching hold of his ears, Mohandas said, 'Making fun of one's wife! And that too in front of another woman who is herself a wife! How can I be guilty of such a crime?' She was now giving peals of laughter. Mohandas' face showed pride: he was able to make a white woman laugh!

When her laughter subsided, she asked: 'What about kids?'

'Three in five or six years. The first one was a still birth. It was a punishment for my sins.' Mohandas noticed Matilda's facial tissues tightening as she heard this. But he was unstoppable. 'We Indians believe in the law of karma. Every action or karma, has a consequence. That was precisely what happened.'

'How?'

'When my father was on deathbed, I was with my wife. Six weeks later, the still birth. Why call it birth? It was birth accompanied by death.' A dark shadow appeared over Matilda's face. Mohandas paused for a moment and then continued: 'The second child came when I was in London.' Mohandas fell silent, so Matilda prompted him again: 'And then?'

'The third one is still a suckling.'

'The second one?'

'Must have started on his first lessons.'

'I'll call my husband. He is in there, drinking.' Matilda quickly added an explanation: 'He has stopped drinking away from home. I too have cut down on my meat-eating and am trying to give it up. He doesn't take more than a peg or two and plans to stop altogether.'

'Let him enjoy his peg,' said Mohandas. 'I'll get going,' and he walked out.

~

VI

Kruger's palace was also in Pretoria. It was more like a big house. It had nothing of the ostentation of a palace. No big lawns, no gardens, no broad avenues running around it. It was a plain residence, maybe slightly more distinguished. Transvaal was basically a Dutch colony. Kruger was its President. In the front courtyard, about a hundred or a hundred and fifty yards long, two lions sat gazing at each other all the time. They did not roar; nor did they keep their mouths open so as to keep their man-eating teeth and prickly tongue in full public view. They had long manes. In the centre of the manes, their peaceful countenances looked like roses. The only difference from a real lion was that a real lion could not possibly sit in the same posture all the twenty-four hours. Otherwise, they were almost real and looked as majestic.

A gold coin showing President Kruger with his bald pate and beard was in currency. Kruger had his own line of thought about Indians. Indians had arrived in Transvaal in 1881, twenty years after they had landed in Natal. It is said that Sheth Abu Bakr Amod of Mauritius was the first one to open a shop in Pretoria. Other Indians followed his example and set up businesses there. Businesses flourished, money multiplied and reputations grew. The white businessmen received a jolt. Jealousies took roots and sparks began to fly. Clouds began to smother the white businessmen's dreams of boundless wealth. The parliament of the province, Volksraad, was an all-white affair. They raised the demand that the Indians must be expelled from Transvaal. Indians were bad-mouthed, and impolite, foul language was used for them. They were denounced as insensitive and cruel to women. They had, of course, all along been considered dirty and uncivilized. In the whole of Transvaal, an air was thus created in which hatred for Indians flourished. Their children were refused admission to schools. If some one spoke for them in the Volksraad, it was taken as speaking against their own side. Hence, everyone spoke for his own side.

When a group of people representing the Indians went to see President Kruger, the soldiers started driving them out. When the group argued with them and beseeched them with folded hands, they were allowed to meet the President's ADC. When the older businessmen narrated this episode, their eyes shone with pride at having met President Kruger. The ADC was a relatively decent man. He told them to form a queue and wait outside. When the President came, they would be allowed to meet him.

The group included some of the big names in the business world of Transvaal. When, after half an hour, Kruger returned, he was accompanied by two army officers. His bald pate shone like a copper plate. They had imagined that he would be carrying a sword, wearing a crown and dressed in expensive clothes. He wore a pair of breeches, shoes and a short jacket.

Kruger's secretary spoke: 'State your grievance. The President is listening.'

After he had heard them out, Kruger told the Indian businessmen: 'You are all sons of Ishmael. It's your duty to serve the children of Jesus. How can the children of Jesus accord you equal status? Be happy with what you have got.' Kruger took the Old Testament literally and had complete faith in it. He took his decisions accordingly.

Kruger departed the way he had come. The soldiers following him kept in step. The businessmen looked at the lions. They seemed to be stirring and opening their mouths. The businessmen cowered in fear.

Whenever Mohandas passed in front of Kruger's palace, he was reminded of stories like these, all passed on by word of mouth. The Kruger coin would start flashing before his eyes. Actually, he loved the road in front of the palace best of all. On one side there was the Kruger palace and directly in front of it stood a church. When the bells of the church tolled, Mohandas had a feeling of entire Pretoria getting up on its feet and looking towards the church. Including the lions. Both caught the attention of the passer-by for their simplicity and majesty.

Mohandas happened to be passing along that stretch of road. Even while watching everything, his mind was still taken up by what he had discussed with Matilda. Should he have told her all those things about Kastur? Why did he do it? How was it possible for an Indian wife to speak English like an English lady? Wasn't he trying to amuse Matilda at Kastur's cost? Even if Matilda had asked a specific question, couldn't he have answered it in some other way?

Wrestling with questions like these he had stepped over from the road to the footpath. The boundary between the road and the footpath had disappeared as he kept forging ahead. He even forgot how Coates kept warning him against walking on the footpath and kept reminding him of the colony law which barred non-whites from the footpath. His mind was lost in the thoughts of Kastur and his kids. He was watching the kids playing; he was thinking of the experimental school for kids in which he had introduced physical education, Gujarati and handicraft. He thoroughly disapproved of English as the medium of education for kids. He had himself studied through the medium of English and what had been the result? Distance from his own people. Once, when Mr. Giles was inspecting the school, he had chosen not to correct the spelling of one of the five words, even at the teacher's prompting, though he would have got full marks if he had. He didn't need to indulge in dishonesty for the sake of one wretched English word. Not really much of a word either, just the wretched word 'kettle'. The teacher had been cross. Every one of his pupils had scored full marks except Mohandas. He was the black mark on his record. English had been Mohandas' biggest weakness. A weakness sometimes works as a chain around your feet and sometimes as a whiplash on your back. He was never able to speak English fluently and, to boot, had to put up with no end of shame on that account. No, this wouldn't do …

Suddenly, he felt himself pushed and went flying like a roasting bean. He could see on one side Kruger's palace, and, on the other, the house of God. He lay wounded in the middle of the road. The palace guards were hitting him mercilessly. They were even more ruthless than the coach leader had been, a sense of authority contributing to the difference. The sense of authority is in itself more dangerous than authority itself. He wanted to tell them that he was carrying a letter from the State Attorney, but they didn't give him chance to utter a word. On whichever side he fell, they started kicking it in. 'You black man, you dare to walk on the footpath,' they kept repeating. 'We'll make a footpath out of you.' Mohandas' tie had unrolled and was now hanging like a long tongue. His jacket was torn at many places. He himself had received many scratches.

Someone cried out: 'Stop! What do you think you are doing?'

It was a white man's voice, so the guards stopped at once. Mohandas had a feeling that Kruger himself had emerged from his palace. There wasn't enough light so he couldn't identify the face. When he sat up, he saw a man approaching him. He helped him get up. Mohandas was bleeding from the mouth.

'Mr. Gandhi!' Someone called out. The voice sounded familiar. 'Mr. Coates!' he exclaimed. He was holding a blood-soaked handkerchief in his hands.

Coates was furious: 'File charges against these guards; I'll be your witness. I have seen everything with my own eyes. These men are uncivilized barbarians. They need lessons in appropriate behaviour. Did they issue a warning before they went for you?'

Mohandas was unable to speak. He shook his head and muttered: 'I didn't hear one.'

'It was wrong to start hitting without advance warning. We are duty-bound to get them punished for this criminal act.'

Mohandas didn't say anything. Coates helped him home. Seeing his condition everyone came out and started protesting loudly: 'How did this happen? Who did this to Mr. Gandhi?'

Mohandas spoke in a subdued voice: 'This had to happen one day. The mistake was not on their part; they were only enforcing the law. I was the one breaking the law. I have been doing so since I arrived here. I'm not quite able to give up this habit of mine, nor am I likely to be able to give it up.' Frequent groans interrupted his speech.

Mr. Coates was in a fury. 'These are tyrants. They must be punished.'

Matilda supported Coates, but Mohandas kept quiet.

Matilda got some warm water in a basin and started cleaning Mohandas' wounds and scratches. She applied whatever remedies were available at home. He felt a little relieved.

Coates was still hanging around. Amid his groans, Mohandas told him: 'Please don't lose your peace of mind over this. We have been born into a country and a community where this has become our destiny. I have seen it happening with others in my own country. The injustice we do to others we consider our right. When it is done to us, we call it injustice. After all, somewhere, sometime, we must pay for our sins.' After a brief silence, he started again: 'These people are uneducated, ignorant and filled with hate. Anyone who is not white is black for them. I was not able to follow your conversation with them; perhaps you were speaking Dutch. But I could get the sense: perhaps the guards were offering an apology. Owning up your mistake is the best penance there is. We don't even do that much.'

'But …'

'You may remember what I had told you earlier: I'll not take recourse to law for the redressal of the wrongs done to me personally. In this case, in fact, they have already apologized.'

Mr. Coates patted him on the back and said: 'Gandhi, only you are capable of this.'

Mohandas lay himself down, his eyes closed and his face showing a sense of relief.

~

Mohandas used to write about everything to Dada Abdullah in great detail. Dada Abdullah greatly enjoyed reading about these matters. If anyone happened to be sitting with him, he also read them out to him while also supplying his own reactions. Marcel Ledue often happened to be the one sitting with him, especially in the evenings when he sat with the nozzle of the chintz-covered pipe in his mouth, raising bubbles in the hookah. The fragrance of the tobacco infused the whole room.

For whatever reason, Ledue always brought them round to Mohandas as the topic of discussion. Though he spoke in jest, what he said always carried a sting: 'Dada Abdullah, you are nonpareil. You hire a barrister as a clerk; then, in compensation, you send him to Johannesburg with full freedom to do what he wants. He is in love with the white colour and there is plenty of it there.'

'No dearth of it here either, is there, Mr. Marcel?'

'Here …?' He would complete the sentence after a pause. 'He can't escape you … his master.'

Dada Abdullah would rejoin: 'These days Gandhibhai is trying to improve his interaction with Christian brothers. He attends their prayer meetings, and he is trying to rebuild the life of his landlady and her husband.'

'Must be white, the landlady?' he would whisper, and then loudly: 'But isn't Gandhibhai a Hindu? I don't quite get this business of trying to improve interaction with Christians.'

'Mr. Marcel, a true believer in Allah keeps his Allah in his heart; he does not wear Him on his sleeve.'

'I have heard Gandhi is an outcaste in his community.' He changed tack.

'Yes, I told you. Hindus consider crossing the seas a sin.'

Changing tack again, Marcel started on Islam and Christianity. 'Islam and Christianity are two sides of the same coin. Both originated and rose to prominence in Arabia. Hinduism, on the other hand, is a religion of idol worshippers.'

'Absolutely right. The mightiest of Muslim emperors, Emperor Akbar, always wore a Virgin Mary charm round his neck and we regard Jesus and Solomon as prophets sent down by Allah.

Mr. Marcel, I hope you will excuse me when I say that the young take a bit longer grasping the essence of religions, especially that of the Muslim religion. No *kaffir* can become a Muslim just by having some water sprinkled on his head. His lips may not move, but a true Mussalman is always saying a prayer in his heart. The four million Hindus who converted to Christianity were all untouchables. Gandhibhai was excommunicated from his caste twice: the first time when he went to London for studies, the second time when he came here to take up employment with me, a Muslim.'

Marcel, interested in prolonging the discussion, said, 'That means he was declared an outcaste. Don't you think, Dada Abdullah, Gandhi is a victim of an extremist and autocratic ideology? He is being tossed from rock to rock by the waves of time again and again. Isn't his fight against this extremism? I think Islam is the place for a rebel like him.'

'What we see is not always what is right,' said Dada Abdullah. 'How can people of a different religion expect a person who does not follow the leaders of his own religion or his caste to follow the discipline of their religion? A rebel is always a rebel.'

Marcel smiled, looked at Dada Abdullah and said: 'You may or may not agree, but Gandhi is cunning and ambitious. If he goes to a church, it's not because of faith but because he wants entry into the European society. Most Hindus would find that entry difficult to manage.'

Dada Abdullah said,: 'That's how some people manage entry into the business world of other communities.'

Marcel's face seemed to grow small. 'What do you mean?' he said.

'Nothing much really. Only the kind of thing man is, he thinks first of his own profit and only next of God's.'

'I understand. You'll never commit yourself about Gandhi. Mohandas is the only Hindu barrister. You are using him to kill two birds. He will work for you, he will set himself up here through you and will stay here as your man. You want to see him in the garb of a rebel.'

'Mr. Marcel, there you are perhaps wrong. No one can earn respect for another person nor can one turn any child into an expert horse rider, unless he has it in him.'

~

Proceedings in the case were about to start. Mohandas was extending the fullest help to Mr. Baker in the preparation of the case. Whenever necessary, he also wrote to Dada Abdullah to check with him. When he got tired of working, he just sat back with his eyes closed. Rajkot and Bombay then began to occupy his thoughts. Had he been able to set up his practice there, he wouldn't have been forced to travel to Natal and Transvaal. Why couldn't he set up practice there? What was the problem? Was the problem with him or with his seniors? Working with Mr. Baker, he was now able to appreciate how a senior is supposed to train a junior. At Bombay, all it involved was to keep your senior in good humour.. Whenever he thought about it, he couldn't help breaking out in laughter.

It was by no means a minor litigation, the Dada Abdullah & Co. case. It involved forty thousand pounds. This was Mohandas' first experience of a case as big as this. The whole case rested on a few IOUs. Some of these IOUs were on stamp paper, some were plain written assurances. The other party refused to acknowledge the IOUs. 'We didn't give these IOUs,' they said. Dada Abdullah had no *prima facie* proof for these claims. Eminent lawyers had been hired by both sides and they were weighing in with complicated legal moves and countermoves. Credibility of the proofs presented by either side was being questioned. Grasping each issue and exposing the credibility claims of the other party—these were murderously difficult tasks. And there was Mr. Baker who would discuss the case for five minutes and spend the rest of the time in expounding the New Testament. That for him was the primary task; legal practice was secondary. Not that Mohandas did not enjoy it, but he could not bear the idea of lagging behind in the job in hand. Concerning religions, his position was that they were all equally good: it depended on each individual which one he found to suit him best. Mr. Coates disagreed. It was impossible to shake his belief that Christianity was the best of all religions. Mr. Baker did not argue the point, but he was also not one to accept defeat. As in the case of religion, so in the case of the lawsuit, he was firm in the belief that a strong foundation was the absolute prerequisite for a strong superstructure.

The fine points of accounting and bookkeeping that Mohandas had picked up from Dada Abdullah and his accountant were now coming in handy for him. Mr. Baker could solve the trickiest of problems without much trouble, but a problem still remained unresolved in his mind: which side was right—Abdullah Sheth or Tyeb Sheth?

Mohandas had just one question for Mr. Baker: 'You know the case inside out. Tell me who is right.' Mr. Baker replied: 'Mr. Gandhi, have you seen a horse coach? If you haven't, go and see one. There are lots of them around here.' He continued: 'A good, running coach is one that has a strong horse, wheels in good condition and an alert coach driver. Whether it is carrying gold or fodder is irrelevant.'

'I don't understand,' said Mohandas.

'Proof is the horse, laws the reins, arguments and counterarguments the wheels and the lawyers that is, you and me, are the coach drivers. The truth according to the law may well be different from the real truth. That is because, according to law, truth is that which is established on the basis of evidence, by the arguments the two sides have used and which is able to win the conviction of the judge.'

Mohandas became restless. Could there be so many truths in a single case? The truth of the plaintiff, the truth of the defendant, the truth of the judge, the lawyer's truth? Isn't there such a thing as the ultimate truth? The truth to be established could well be a fabricated truth, couldn't it? He wanted to ask Mr. Baker this question, but held back. He had a feeling that Mr. Baker's criterion might not be very helpful in getting at the truth. He would have to find it himself. Truth permits no adulteration. You want to find the truth, you have to submerge yourself in it. He devoted himself to uncovering the connotations of each and every word in the documents. He was of course aware that neither reading of documents nor memorizing the laws and giving commentaries on them can reveal the truth. For that, you need a vision. How was he going to find that vision? He wrote to Dada Abdullah to find the answer. He wrote back: 'If you can blend philosophy and practice that is the best solution. If you can't, try to keep them separate. Truth has no colour nor does it have any features which could help you to identify it.'

Mohandas was able to size up the penetrating insight of Dada Abdullah. Though illiterate, he had a keen understanding of human nature and its subtleties. He had left everything to Mohandas' discretion. To be able to get a measure of someone in such a short time, and to place full faith on him, are nothing short of getting a glimpse of the soul of the man, a place which is usually so opaque.

Mohandas' desk displayed the quotation from the late Mr. Pincutt: 'Facts are three-fourths of the law.' Mohandas was looking precisely for these facts. So far, he never had had the feeling that the facts went against his employer, Dada Abdullah. Nor had he any feeling that Dada Abdullah was lying or that his papers were forged. If he was smart enough to get the IOUs, he was smart enough to get the receipts for the goods received by Tyeb Sheth. Tyeb Sheth possibly couldn't be such a simpleton that he would write out all the IOUs asked for but would not demand receipts for payments made or record them in his books. Sometimes, however, there did crop up legal issues when Mohandas felt the law was against Dada Abdullah and then he would start worrying.

Mr. Leonard was considered to be a great lawyer. Mohandas approached him, though he feared that being a novice, he might not get an appointment with him. Moreover, there was the additional burden of being a coloured man. But Mr Leonard gave him a patient hearing and then said, 'Gandhi, if there is one lesson I have learnt in my life it is that if you have the full facts with you, the law is automatically on your side. I'll advise you to study the case very thoroughly once again and then come and see me again.'

Mohandas went through the facts afresh and examined the precedents. He was able to find an instance. Mohandas went to Mr. Leonard again. 'That's it,' said Leonard. 'The battle is won. Just keep track of the judges on the bench.' A pause, and then: 'After all, judges are human too.'

Mohandas continued his own preparation of the case with Mr. Baker. After he had been reassured about Dada Abdullah's side of the case, his thinking about the case was beginning to take a different turn.: 'Is this litigation likely to provide relief to either of the parties? Of course, the lawyers will make their fortunes. The case will move from one court to another, and then to the highest court of the colony. Whatever the final award, will it recompense either of the parties? Both parties are from Kathiawar, and are fellow countrymen. Litigation is a blind knife that slaughters both parties. Sometimes, there is no one left to rejoice at the win or mourn over the loss; and even if someone is left he has no vitality left in him to rejoice or to mourn. Is it not really a slow massacre of humanity carried out legally?

Mohandas had spent the whole night pondering over the case. He had a strange way of working. He would suddenly wake up from deep sleep, work for a time and then go back to deep sleep the very next moment. Kastur too lost no time in falling asleep, while Mohandas would be still awake. Kastur would be fast asleep in no time, causing great irritation to Mohandas. This is ridiculous, he would say, but he would be laughing the very next moment. After all, he too did the same.

Mohandas got up the next morning entirely at ease with himself. He got ready fast and was soon on his way to Tyeb Sheth's house. Now there were two Tyeb Sheths before him: one who had declared war on Dada Abdullah, the other who had called a meeting of the Indians at the request of his representative. All along the way, Mohandas kept up his effort to reconcile the two.

Tyeb Sheth was getting ready to leave for work. When he saw Mohandas, he welcomed him, and wondered what had brought him to his place so early in the day.

'All the paper-work we did with the railways at least yielded some fruit: they have agreed to issue first or second class tickets to persons who look Indian, and sufficiently respectable, from the way they are dressed.'

'So our respectability will be judged by our dress, and the person to decide it will be the booking clerk or the station master. All your learning, and the job you have, are of no …'

'Right. A poor man cannot be respectable, since he doesn't have the right clothes …'

Tyeb Sheth laughed. 'Dear friend, lower your voice. Someone may hear you.' He continued: 'Thanks to you, we have at least been able to secure this much. For years we had been putting up with this disgrace.'

'When the voice is collective, the noise it makes is big. Anyway, I am here today to discuss a specific matter.' Tyeb Sheth was looking intently at him, sure that there was really something special to discuss. The tick-tock of the clock on the wall was getting louder and louder. Mohandas started: 'You remember when I came for the first time; you had described me as an advocate for the opposing party. This was a truth from which there really was no getting away, so all I had then said was I would talk to you on the matter on some other occasion. That occasion has now presented itself.'

Tyeb Sheth arched his eyebrows. He said, 'You are probably talking about the lawsuit pending in the court between us and Dada Abdullah. The case is *sub judice.* It is for the court to pronounce the judgment. Dada Abdullah is a close relative. The wrongdoing was on his part, and he was also the one to start the suit.' His face flushed with anger.

'Do you think that the disposal of the case will be as quick as that? Our scriptures mention an ogress called Sursa. She would go on opening her mouth wider and wider till her victim got into it in its entirety. When she took a breath, it was with such force that it sucked in all the animals, trees and plants in the catchment area. I sometimes feel that this business of litigation is also like the ogress Sursa: when it sucks in its breath, everything at home and outside is sucked into its maw. Do you consider it appropriate that two distinguished trading dynasties from India who have come to this country to do business should return empty-handed losing everything to litigation?'

Tyeb Sheth was not the sort to vent his reaction instantly. He would concentrate on the face of the man sitting in front of him and try to read his thoughts to figure out how sincere the man was. When Tyeb Sheth did not respond, Mohandas took the matter further. 'The question before me is this: you gentlemen make so much money. For whom? I am a very ordinary man; I earn for my family. Perhaps, every man has this desire to keep himself and his family in as much comfort as he can. I am sure you also think likewise. Litigation is like a disease: once it catches you, it doesn't let go of you. Yet no one earns to spend on a disease. If litigation took all, what would be your answer to your kids' questions? Would you be able to prove your innocence to them?'

All that Tyeb Sheth did was to shake his head. After a pause, he said: 'What is it you want?

'Tyeb Sahib, what I do or do not want is immaterial. What is important, and what will eventually come about, is what you two gentlemen want. This maze is of your making. Only you have the map of the route that takes us out of this maze.

'There must be something that you have in mind.'

'I think we should hand over the whole matter to an honest arbiter who has the trust of both of you. His decision would be binding on you both.'

'Will Dada Abdullah agree?'

'I left Durban only after I made sure of this authority from him. I hadn't even met you then. The case is a tricky one. You may have to spend years and years chasing the courts. No one knows which way the horse is going to jump, neither you nor your lawyers. There is this carrot hanging in front of the horse, and both of you are racing in the hope of getting to it first. You are relatives and I cannot help the feeling that both of you have still left in you some of the fellow feeling which makes one feel happy in the other's happiness and sad at the other's misfortune.'

Tyeb Sheth was lost in deep thought. Mohandas had still left a ray of hope in his mind because of his silence. But a fear tagged along too: if he declines, that will end all hopes of any further progress. He told Tyeb Sheth: 'I'm sure you know the white lawyers are stepping up their fees every second day. There are limits to the wealth of even the richest man. Nothing is without a limit. Even the limitless must have a limit. The body atrophies; means shrink; hostilities multiply; tolerance fades into intolerance. Even closed fists cannot prevent time from slipping out grain by grain. Every client rates his own case highly and his lawyer goads him on. He who should have gone empty-handed finds his hands full; he who should have had his hands full finds himself empty-handed. I am sorry to say that the law, and the courts, while they are a great help, are also great hoaxes.'

Tyeb Sheth was fighting a war within himself. From his face one could see that there were a host of Tyeb Sheths inside him, each playing his own tune.

Mohandas then laid another brick: 'Tyeb Sheth, if you feel that I am pleading Dada Abdullah's case, I am obviously wasting your as well as my time. In that case I must reconsider seriously whether I should go on or not. If you feel that making an out-of-court settlement on my advice will make you a laughing-stock, please go on and fight the case. But consider another fact too: just in case the judgment goes against you, will you be able to withstand the shock? Or in case the judgment is in your favour, and Dada Abdullah is unable to stand the shock, will it be a cause for celebration or sorrow for you?'

'What will an arbiter do?'

'Excuse me for saying so, but a law court is an insensitive instrument. Though the judge is a human being, celebration and sorrow are minor considerations for the court. An arbiter, on the other hand, who enjoys the trust of both sides is a friend to both. He is a human being with a profound sensibility. He doesn't go by the law book. His justice is guided by the personal trust of both the parties that he enjoys and the best interests of both that he seeks to serve. Law only serves as an aid to him.'

Agitated, Tyeb Sheth got up and began to pace the room. 'Gandhibhai,' he said: 'I don't know what will be in my best personal interest: to accept your advice or to see the litigation to the end. I can't, however, deny that what you say has weight. Human happiness and sorrow are lost in the jungle of law and documentation. What finally comes out is a cold document which records a win for one party and a defeat for the other. Someone who has the trust of both sides cannot be loveless or heartless. Even if you lose, you will feel that his decision is backed by your own.'

It was for the first time that Mohandas had heard a businessman talk in this vein. He felt that there did exist a minimum honesty on both sides.

Suddenly, Tyeb Sheth said: 'Haji Sheth is a friend of his, and mine too. Ask Dada Abdullah.'

'I give you consent on his behalf.'

Tyeb Sheth smiled and looked at Mohandas: 'Gandhibahi, you are still young and full of beans. In your zest for action, try not to overlook the reality. These matters are not dealt with so simply. Abdullah Sheth is a type apart: suspicious, untrusting of anyone. My advice to you is that before you say anything you may please seek his consent.'

Mohandas saw a glimpse of truth in what he had said. As he got up to go, he said: 'What makes me really happy is that you honoured my word despite the fact that I belong to your opponent's camp. I am really happy. You have strengthened my faith in truth and my confidence in myself.'

As he walked back, Mohandas thought he had been successful in striking a path through two steep and slippery rocks.

Mr. Baker gave Mohandas a patient listening. After a little pause, he said: 'Mr. Gandhi, it wasn't quite correct of you to take such a major decision without consulting Dada Abdullah. From whatever I know of Dada Abdullah, I can tell you that he is not going to like it one bit. It's one of the principles of our profession that decisions such as this one are never taken without consulting the client. Since such decisions can harm our client's interests, they are also unethical.

Mohandas listened to Baker quietly. When he had finished, he rejoined: 'Mr. Baker, so far as professional ethics is concerned, I agree with you. But I have a different point of view. I can't stand the idea of the might of law crushing the spirit of the individual and leaving him incapable of taking independent decisions. There is nothing wrong with taking the help of law, but turning into its slave is wrong. Rules and laws are fine only so long as they aid the mental and intellectual growth of the individual and help him take the right decisions. The moment they start turning you into a mental cripple, it's time to keep them at arm's length. Man too should have a role to play in whether he wins or loses. In any case, eventually it's for you and Dada Abdullah to decide on our final course of action. All that I want to do is a direct experiment with truth and I believe Dada Abdullah will have no difficulty with that. Before I left Durban, I had checked with him about this possibility.'

Mr. Baker said nothing.

~

When Mohandas returned from his walk at night, Mr. Baker was in conversation with his hostess, Matilda. He was delighted to see Baker. Ever since he had received Dada Abdullah's consent for Haji Sheth as the mediator, Mohandas was feeling very pleased about everything. He had tasted success for the first time. He was still wondering how it had all come about. Everyone, from Tyeb Sheth to Mr. Baker, had his doubts about Dada Abdullah's consent. But he had given it.So the first thing he did was to congratulate Mr. Baker: 'Mr. Baker, Dada Abdullah has accepted Haji Sheth as the mediator. I feel that a mediator's decision will be closer to truth and more humane.'

'To some extent, yes. There is one thing, though. Haji Sheth is also a resident of Pretoria and engages in daily interaction with Tyeb Sheth.'

'Mr. Baker, truth and trust place heavy demands on you. If you are facing these from both sides, daily interaction means very little.'

'Mr. Gandhi, that's quite interesting.' Next, he said: 'Let's leave that aside. Actually, I am here for a specific reason. We are going to have a conference at Wellington. I have come here to invite you to go with us.'

'I don't quite understand.'

'Every year, we Protestants meet at some place with the objective of achieving self-enlightenment and self-purification. This time round, we are meeting at Wellington. The meeting will be chaired by Reverend Andrew Murray. He is a respected devotee of our tradition. It's our wish that you should also join us. The convention will last three days. I am really quite anxious about your future. You are gifted with divine inspiration. If you lose your path, it will be a great sin in the eyes of God.'

'For one thing, I am a Hindu. Secondly, I have never participated in such conventions. What will I have to do?'

'Pray. There is only one path that leads you to God: prayer. The power of prayer is far, far superior to the most destructive of powers. Prayer is nothing but the voice of your conscience. God only listens to this voice.' Mr. Baker suddenly remembered something, and said: 'Have you heard of George Molar? He lives in Bristol. For him, prayer is everything. So much so, in fact, that he depends on prayer even for the fulfilment of his day-to-day necessities.'

A host of names filed past Mohandas' consciousness: Narsi Mehta, Mirabai, Sant Sakhubhai, Sant Gyaneshwar, Surdas, Tulsidas, Kabir. He felt he should tell Mr. Baker about them. Devotion and dedication were what made a prayer a prayer. But he did not follow up the matter.

Mr. Baker said: 'You understand what I am saying? I and my friends believe that you should engage with Jesus. I can see Jesus is within you. In the Wellington air, infused with devotion and surrender to God, you will find yourself face-to-face with the boundless mercy of Jesus himself.'

Mohandas had to speak. 'Mr. Baker,' he said: 'The thing I really value most is my inner voice. That alone shows the path I must follow, be it that of religion or action. Still, I'll go with you to Wellington.'

Mr. Baker stood up, gave a hearty handshake to Mohandas and took his leave.

~

Christians do not travel on the day of Sabbath. Sabbath is the seventh day of the week, carrying the memory of the rebirth of Christ. On Sabbath, Christians take a pause in their journey and devote themselves to prayer. The travelling party had found place in a hotel; the only problem was Mohandas. Where would he stay? The hotel owner was adamant that he could not allow a coloured man to stay in his hotel. Mr. Baker was feeling very hurt by this.

'Mr. Gandhi is a member of our party. You cannot discriminate against him,' he said.

'I am sorry. Mr. Gandhi may be anybody, but I cannot go against the rules by putting him up. If I do, it will affect my business.'

'We booked places for the whole party.'

'Under the rules, not outside them.'

'Okay. Then Mr. Gandhi will stay with me in my room.'

Everyone was stunned. Nobody had thought that Mr. Baker would go this far. Mohandas was the only dark-coloured man in a crowd of whites. Whenever Mr. Baker introduced him to any white, he would first give Mr. Baker an astonished look and then, shaking Mohandas' hand, would walk off almost without speaking a word. The people whispered to each other: 'What's come over Mr. Baker? Why is he making so much fuss over a coloured person?' Mohandas was observing the caste system of his country playing out in a different form here.

After Mr. Baker's announcement, all the members of the party made a collective approach to the hotel manager and tried to persuade him to let Mr. Gandhi stay in the hotel and not to hurt Mr. Baker.

'How is that possible? There are others staying in the hotel. What will they say?'

'It's a matter of only one night. We'll be all gone in the morning.'

It was with great difficulty that the manager agreed to let Mohandas stay the night in the hotel.

That however was not the end of the matter. When Mohandas entered the dining hall with others for his dinner, the manager was present again. He extended his arm and stopped Mohandas from entering: 'You cannot go inside.'

'But …'

'No buts. Only whites are allowed in the dining hall. How can they dine with you sitting there?'

Mohandas thought of the Johnston Hotel. Though white, Johnston was a decent man. As Mohandas traced his steps back, he noticed that almost everyone had entered the dining hall. Mr. Baker stood outside. Seeing him standing outside, some members of the party came out of the dining hall. One of them said in a loud voice: 'Mr. Baker, how far will you go for this black man? Isn't it enough for this man that he has been given a room in this hotel? Tell him to go to his room and stop creating problems for us.'

'I am a barrister, and a follower of Jesus. The matter is not as simple as you are making it out to be. It is a question of respect for a man of God. At the same time, it is also a question of the rights of a hotel guest. Everyone staying in the hotel has a right to unrestricted access to the dining hall for his meals.'

It was getting difficult for Mohandas to keep his patience. He said: 'Mr. Baker, please don't put yourself out on my account. I had to face a similar situation in Johnston Hotel. I have no problem with having my dinner in my room. I fully understand my position. I can also see the disgraceful situation in which you find yourself on my account. For me, it's no small consolation that you are doing so much for me.'

Mr. Baker patted him on the shoulder. 'Don't you worry. Truth cannot be suppressed for too long. This too is Jesus' work. There is no disgrace in Jesus' work.'

Mohandas laughed and said: 'The ban on the admission of blacks in your hotels is like the ban on the entry of untouchables to temples in my country.' The thought that kept popping up in Mohandas' mind was: 'Will I ever be able to stand firm like Mr. Baker on the question of admission of untouchables to temples in my own country?'

~

The convention lasted three days. A large number of devout Christians from far-away places attended. They were deeply committed in their efforts to seek self-purification by surrendering the evil in their hearts before the Son of God. Mohandas was profoundly impressed by their faith and their complete surrender before God. When they prayed—'Lord! Deliver us from our sins!' you felt as if they were in direct communication with Jesus. Every moment of their lives they were being delivered from their sins, while in his own religion one's good deeds and bad did not let go of one even after death. Mohandas was really impressed.

Mohandas was introduced to Reverend Murray, who also prayed for him despite his being from another religion. In fact, many others were also praying for him. They were all reciting prayers and singing hymns. It looked as if he was everywhere. Mohandas was enjoying every moment of it.

Every invocation repeated the same thing: Come to Jesus. He is the only Son of God. Only he can deliver you from your sins. Hearing the invocation, he felt that since they were all Christians and already with Jesus, was it possible that the invocation was addressed to him? He was the only non-Christian there. The thing that troubled him most was the concept of confession. Confess everyday and commit fresh sins everyday! He looked for answers to these questions within him but found none.

Mohandas now knew many Christians. They all told him the same thing: 'Mr. Gandhi, you are one of us. You are one of the special favourites of Jesus. It's his grace that has brought you to Wellington and given you the privilege of self-purification. Even the most dedicated Christians are denied this privilege without his grace. You are indeed lucky.'

Mohandas smiled and let it pass. He didn't know what to say. The question that bothered him was: is a religion a dye of some sort that you dip your clothes in, and *presto*! You have a new religion! If so, then a religion is a weak colour indeed! Before you dye anew, you wash and remove the old colour! For three days, he beat around in the morass of questions. These questions related to himself. Was there salvation only for those who believed in Christ? He didn't. Did that mean that his soul would wander around, lost forever? If Christ was the son of God, why weren't the others? If the blood of Christ has washed the whole world of its sins, why is there sin in the world? If a man is not to pay for the sins he has committed, who is? Where do all the sins committed by all the people of the world go?

Mohandas also found himself unable to accept the view that only human beings had souls. He did not of course doubt for a moment that Christ occupied the summit of sacrifice, that he was the foremost propagator of

God's virtues. But he was unable to detect anything in the lives of Christians that he did not also find in the lives of people of other religions—whether from the point of view of philosophy or sacrifice.The sacrifice at Karbala was a unique example too.

Even while at Wellington, Mohandas did not keep these ideas from anyone. Whenever he got an opportunity, he talked to others of the emotionl turmoil that was going on within him. He talked with great humility. Some people listened to him patiently; others, who lacked tolerance, got up and walked away. They also replied to his arguments, but their answers reflected their religious fears and failed to reassure him. This was not because he was a man of great knowledge, but because he argued that there was an ethical aspect of religion which concerned itself with day-to-day behaviour. You could not covert it into a part of your religious ideology and thrust it on people. If you did, you constricted a man's freedom. He also criticized his own religion. It was an imagined idea, not a truth, he said, that the Vedas came out of the lips of Lord Brahma. For if the Vedas could come out of the lips of Brahma, why not the Bible or the Quran? People were startled to hear such arguments from him, but were also reassured by them. A man who criticized his own religion was certain to give up his narrow-minded religion some day and plump for Christianity.

On the way back from the convention, Mr. Baker shot a direct question at Mohandas: 'Mr. Gandhi, what is your decision?'

Though he knew, Mohandas still asked: 'Concerning what?'

'Concerning your conversion to our religious tradition.'

Mohandas had already thought about the answer he was to give. He said: 'Mr. Baker, I am very confused. A whole lot of questions bother me, which I find myself unable to answer. I need light, not only outside but inside too. Can we change our religion like a rented house? Is changing one's religion as simple a matter as shifting to a more expensive house just because you don't like the house you live in? A man or a society has its roots in the faith it professes, and faith has mostly to do with religion. Whatever be the religion, of whatever sort, it is a constantly ongoing and interactive process of experimentation and improvement between the faiths of the individual and the society. There will be new religions and new faiths in future too. People will migrate from one religion to another but old religions will not go away. Hinduism is an example. Instead of calling it the Vedic religion or the Aryan religion, I am calling it by its currently popular name. But no religion in the world is quite free from weaknesses and aspirations.'

Mr. Baker looked at Mohandas, put his hand on his shoulder, and said: 'I understand. Do sort out your questions, but I know that your final decision is going to be in our favour. Our tradition is more scientific and modern.'

Mohandas smiled. He had a feeling people were turning away from him. Only Mr. Baker did not show even the slightest change in his behaviour towards him.

The turbulence continued in Mohandas' mind on the way back from the convention. Mr. Baker had created a strange dilemma for him. He knew that Mr. Baker was a sincere and devout Christian. He genuinely believed that salvation was only possible if one surrendered oneself completely to the mercy of Jesus. Mohandas remembered Raychandbhai. When, on his return from London, he learned for the first time about the death of his dainty doll-like *Ba*, for a time he felt he was losing hold on himself. He had the feeling of a storm closing in on him. That was when Raychandbhai had come to his rescue. Raychandbhai was a connoisseur of pearls, and precious stones. Moreover he was a *shatvadani* (one having the faculty of remembering or attending to a hundred things simultaneously.) He could repeat a hundred things said in different languages before him in the precise order in which they were said, even if he didn't know the languages. On that occasion, he had recited to Mohandas the following lines of Muktanand:

I shall think myself blessed only when I see Him
in every one of my daily acts;
Verily He is the thread
which supports Muktanand's life.

Mohandas could see before his eyes the face of Raychandbhai as he sang the lines. The face was lit up with the glow of pearls as he sang of His glory with his hundred tongues. He was picking out pearls like pebbles with the innocence of a child. Those lines of Muktanand had made a permanent place for themselves in his heart.

On his return from Wellington, Mohandas wrote a letter to Raychandbhai:

Dear Sri Raychandbhai,

On several occasions, after my arrival in South Africa, I thought of writing to you, but ever since my arrival here I have been in and out of so many crises that it is impossible to give you a full account of them. I'll relate them to you if I ever have the occasion to meet you again. This letter, I am writing to you with a rather special motive.

I am currently facing a crisis of faith and existence. Actually, a crisis of faith is itself a crisis of existence. I have just returned from a convention of Protestants at Wellington. I was deeply impressed by the degree of commitment to, and faith in their religion the Christians have. They have an unshakeable belief that, by shedding his blood, Jesus salvaged humanity (which actually means his followers) and rid it of all its sins. Jesus alone is the Son of God. I find this difficult to digest. If Jesus is the Son of God, why not us? If Jesus is God incarnate, why not us? The same God who created Jesus also created us. The sacrifice Jesus made is part of the noble actions he performed. But if God determines our actions, then the actions of a sinner too are determined by Him. Then how can someone else deliver him from his sins? If Jesus alone determines what sin is and what it is not, and if only his religion is the perfect one, are other religions doomed forever? These questions haunt me every moment. There are other questions too: What is religion? What are the measures of the greatness of a religion? If one religion promises you liberation, do others force you into slavery?

Mr. Baker and some other friends of mine who take me to their religious meetings pray for my liberation. Is this not a way of exerting psychological pressure on me? They want me to convert and join their religious tradition. I concede that Christianity has some special features of its own, but having studied and heard so much about religions I don't quite agree that it has anything that my own religion or any other religion, does not. Please show me the way. All these people here are constantly trying to convince me that Jesus alone can get me release from my sins. He may be the Son of God, still how can he alone carry the weight of the myriad of sins being committed every moment of time by such a large human community? The fundamental question of course is why we should not avoid committing sin in the first place? Why should it be necessary to seek the mercy of Jesus for delivering us from our sins?

Yours,

Mohandas

Penning the letter brought some relief to Mohandas. For a long time he sat silently, his eyes closed, conducting an imaginary dialogue with Raychandbhai.

~

VII

Mohandas was caught in a tug of war between two rivals. On the one side was his court case, on the other the conflict raging within him, that is the pressure on him from Mr. Baker and other friends to convert. His priority was of course the court case. He was aware that if he did not save himself from the clutches of the rival he would not be able to do justice to the case of Dada Abdullah and Tyeb Sheth. The letter to Raychandbhai had of course been a relief: he felt he had transferred his responsibility to Raychandbhai. He now felt freer to devote himself to his other responsibility.

~

Haji Sheth never missed a single one of his five *namaz* prayers a day. He was counted among the most devout Muslims there were. He had studied the case closely with the help of Mohandas. If there was anything which he didn't grasp fully, he consulted both the parties. Being a Gujarati himself, he had no problem with the Gujarati language. He listened very carefully to the arguments presented by either side. Before he started his work as the arbitrator, he had got both sides to give him in writing that his decision would be acceptable to them.

The day before he was to give the award, Haji Sheth shut himself up in a room. If one moment he thought of his friendship with Dada Abdullah and the favours he had received from him, the very next moment he would find Tyeb Sheth, with all his honesty and kindnesses, standing and laughing next to him. He would never take a step without consulting Tyeb Sheth. Forty thousand pounds was no mean sum, and that was the sum at stake. It was enough to ruin one and build up the fortunes of the other. That was the dilemma before him. It was not only the loser who would lose the money; Haji Sheth would also lose his friendship forever. He would tell himself: 'I can always get a new friend, but if I lose my honesty, I'll never get it back.' He spent the whole night turning and looking over the documents. His wife kept him company. Every few moments, she would repeat the same thing: 'I told you to keep out of this no-good business; you may not lose your honesty but you are certainly going to lose out in the world. It's all that Hindu's doing: setting friend against friend.'

'No, my dear, honesty is not just for oneself; it also includes your near and dear ones, your friends and your relatives.'

The wife shut herself up or would only say: 'What you say is quite beyond me.'

When it was morning, he said his prayers. 'Dear God, we live in the shadow of thy grace. Do please help me to keep my integrity intact, and let my friends know that I have been honest.'

Haji Sheth's decision came as a bolt from the blue to Tyeb Sheth. Out of the forty thousand pounds in question, he was declared to be under obligation to pay back thirty-seven thousand pounds. The courts too put their seal on the award. Haji Sheth had given his comments on each issue in writing. Tyeb Sheth sat stunned for a long time before saying: 'When my own dearest friend decides to make me bite the dust, who can I trust?'

Thought after thought filled past in his mind. After all, Dada Abdullah was a well-known figure. Was it possible that Haji Sheth felt pressurized? Or was some other kind of pressure brought to bear on him, something that was beyond him? He was feeling guilty even to entertain the thought of pressure. Was Haji Sheth capable of such a thing? Had he ever done such a thing?

The really big question before Tyeb Sheth was: where would he get such a large sum of money? Who would lend him such a huge amount? The news of his bankruptcy would hit the market soon. Was there a trader anywhere who could survive a penalty of thirty-seven thousand pounds? Could even Dada Abdullah have survived it, had the decision gone against him? For a Memon, bankruptcy meant death, that is suicide. In the eyes of his fraternity, his entire family, the whole clan, had been reduced to dirt. No one would like even to look at him. Could there be a more fearful death for a trader's family?

Mohandas could appreciate the situation. If Tyeb Sheth was declared bankrupt, he would not survive. It was not that he didn't want to pay; he could not pay. If he could, he would. Neither of them was lacking in credit. The whole trader community was at their beck and call. This bankruptcy was going to ruin the prestige of the entire Indian business community. He decided to call on Tyeb Sheth.

When Mohandas arrived at his place, Tyeb Sheth first laughed and then said: 'Gandhibhai, does there still remain something to be done? I thought that you had accomplished what you had come here for.'

'No, Tyeb Sheth, there still remains something to be done.'

'What? Is a greater ruin possible? The complainant a brother, the executioner a friend ...! Isn't it interesting?'

'No, Tyeb Sheth, Haji Sheth is a true friend of yours. It was that trust that made this impartial decision possible. If he did not have this trust, he would have wandered from the truth.'

Tyeb Sheth thought for a moment, and then said: 'Maybe what you say is right. When my own trust becomes the excuse for decapitating me and my trust, what remains to be said and what remains to be done?' His face showed bitterness.

'I know that this decision has reduced the earnings of your lifetime to dust. But let me ask you an impertinent question: Had this decision gone against Dada Abdullah, would you still feel the same way about Haji Sheth? Sometimes we are obliged to bend before truths accepting which is the bitterest experience of our lives. You begin to view even your friends differently. You feel relieved shifting your responsibility to others. If he was one of your own, he ceases to be one; if he was not, you blame it on fate. What we fail to take into account are the limits under which the man you hold responsible had to work. Did the man work honestly or was he settling scores? Were you the only one to be hit or did he also get bloodied? It's only when we strain ourselves to seek the truth that we begin to see our own guilt. There are not many people who have the guts to look for their own guilt. But once you are able to see it, there is no peace for you any more.'

'Mr. Gandhi, only a man sitting outside the ring of fire can enjoy the warmth; inside the ring there is only wood, and it is only for burning.'

'But it's not necessary that if there is a fire burning, you rush to warm yourself. I think the decision of Haji Sheth has taken a big weight off your mind. In a sense, this decision has rejoined your relationships broken for years and years. No court could have accomplished this feat. I have come only to tell you that Dada Abdullah will not collect this amount from you in a lump sum.'

'What do you mean?' Tyeb Sheth was taken aback.

'You can repay the amount in easy instalments.'

'I don't believe you! When and how did Dada Abdullah turn into such a generous soul?' Distrust lay thick on his face covering it like a layer of ice.

'Generosity breeds generosity. It was generous of you to accept arbitration. When it was his turn, how could he accept being one down? After all, the same blood runs in his veins too, doesn't it?' Mohandas smiled.

Tyeb Sheth said: 'Mr. Gandhi, although I allowed myself to be persuaded by your arguments, on more than one occasion I later thought of going back on my word. After the decision came, I could not help feeling that, like me, you had glib-talked Hajibhai too into a trap. You of course mind it when you suffer a loss, but it really hurts when you realize that you have been taken for a ride.'

'You are not to blame. One's self-interest often clouds the truth from end to end and one is hard put to find it. Imagination runs riot. When these imaginings clash with reality, trust is the first casualty. If we focused on the truth from the very start, we would never find our path darkened by the shadows of untruth.'

'Exactly what happened with me …'

'Your fears were born out of your sense of insecurity. Imagination still has an anchor of faith of some sort, but fears have their very roots in insecurity and mistrust.'

Tyeb Sheth got up and said: 'Gandhibhai, your talk has a mesmerizing effect on me. I can now see that I was wrong and you and Hajibhai were right. I wanted to acknowledge Dada Abdullah's dues, but was in no position to do it. I simply had no choice.'

Mohandas said: 'It is precisely this thinking that sets you apart from others. In fact, higher.'

'Not at all. It's you who deserve that higher place, not me.'

Mohandas could see that Tyeb Sheth was getting emotional.

~

His errand over, Mohandas was set to go back to Durban, and thence to India.

Mr. Baker congratulated Mohandas on his success: 'Gandhi,' he said: 'you have a Christ in you. Perhaps I too could have done it, but I couldn't because I cared more for my profession. Maybe that's why you kept me out of it.'

Mohandas laughed. 'Of course not, Mr. Baker. You may not have been present physically, but your willed effort was backing me.'

'There is only one regret I have. I wasn't able to recruit you into my religious tradition. But I haven't given up hope.'

'All religious traditions are the same,' Mohandas said: 'only the colours differ. You yourself said that I have a Christ in me. Anyone who has a Christ in him has to mount the cross. It may be a cross of his own making or one supplied by others.'

Mr. Baker embraced him.

~

Matilda felt that the presence of Mohandas in her home gave it an aura. They all felt so close to him that they were beginning to feel that without him the home would cease to be a home. They had all fallen silent, the way everything falls silent just before a storm. Matilda actually said: 'Mr. Gandhi, how will we ever be able to see this home as a home again? It'll be just like a cage with the bird gone.'

'A bird of passage will remain a bird of passage. A man sitting by a river cannot fall in love with a single wave, because the waves keep coming and going. Every traveller has a destination and he has to keep going till he reaches it. Sometimes he may never reach it, but he has to keep going.'

Haji Sheth only said: 'Gandhibhai, by making me the arbiter between Dada Abdullah and Tyeb Sheth you provided me with an opportunity to understand myself. Without this opportunity, I'd perhaps never have understood the difference between duty and honesty.'

Matilda was there with her family. At first, they kept pacing the platform and then came to speak to him: 'Mr. Gandhi, when we got married we made a home. But it was you who spring-cleaned our hearts, and made our home livable at a time when it was falling apart.' The couple's eyes were moist.

Tyeb Sheth had reserved his piece for the very end: 'Gandhibhai, you saved me from going to hell. By arranging the dues to be broken up into instalments, you saved my family from infamy and ruin.'

Mohandas said: 'Tyeb Sheth, you are a Muslim. In your religion God is held to be the true performer. Thank Him, if you must thank someone. The love that lay buried in your hearts, is awake once again.'

Tyeb Sheth took both Mohandas' hands and held them in his own.

~

While travelling to Durban, Mohandas felt as if he was returning to his base port, though he had barely spent any time in Durban. But he was happy. There were two or three reasons for his happiness. If you are lost in a forest of failures and are blessed with even a tiny drop of success, the forest ceases to have any meaning for you, at least for a short time. His biggest success was that he had been able to bridge the ever widening gulf between two families. This was no commonplace success like passing an exam or getting a degree from London. For him, success meant only one thing—anything that showered happiness on others while you were the agent and the cause. Whenever such an event occurred, he thought of his country: Would he ever be able to bridge the gulfs that divided his own people? Would he ever be able to harvest a crop of love? His moment of happiness would begin to fade momentarily. He would begin to see a new India arising on the horizon. Then the thought would occur to him that despite such a close encounter with Christianity he was still standing his ground. And he would see *Ba* standing with him. It was an experience he frequently had while he was in London.

Mohandas' journey to Durban was rather dull. This was exactly the sort of thing that happened with him when he visited Porbandar. Before the visit, he always felt that he was returning home, but on reaching there, everything changed. Durban was even more of an unknown quantity to him. When he thought of the roads of Pretoria, its people, and so on, he felt homesick. Durban had shrunk into Dada Abdullah and into a few of those events which had occurred a year ago.

At Charlestown, when he arrived at the window to buy a first class ticket, the ticket clerk at first extended the ticket towards him without looking at him, but as soon as he saw his face he pulled back his ticket arm and asked: 'Your name?'

'M.K. Gandhi.'

'Please come inside.'

Mohandas went in. He was astonished at the sudden surge of affection for him on the part of railways. The station master's office was right next to the booking office. The station master's eyes were fixed at his face. A black man! Except the colour, the rest of him was exactly like a white man: the manner of speech, dress and so on! There wasn't much he could do about the colour; he had been born with it as his armour. The station master gave him the once-over and signalled to the booking clerk to issue the ticket, who handed him the ticket. The money had already been paid. Mohandas said 'Thanks' and came out.

The station master followed him and said: 'Excuse me, are you the same Mr. Gandhi who had written to the Railways about allowing first class travel facility to the coloureds?'

'Yes, but a few friends in Pretoria were also a party to it.'

'The entire Railway Department now knows your name. But, despite all that, they'll not allow you to travel first.'

'No harm trying, is there? It did at least make the difference that you issued me a first class ticket without much ado. That wasn't the case before, was it?'

The station master was staring at Mohandas' face.

~

At the station, Dada Abdullah was present with his entire retinue to receive him. There were a couple of his business friends too. Only a band was missing. Dada Abdullah's first question to him was: 'How was your journey this time, Gandhibhai?'

'Thank God! Looks like times have changed a lot in the meanwhile.' A brief smile flitted across his face.

'I don't know how to thank you enough. I was thinking Tyeb Sheth might not be able to repay such a large sum and my money was as good as gone.'

'No, that wasn't the case, Abdullah Sheth. Like you, Tyeb Sheth too is a righteous man. There was no malice, only an inability to pay.'

Mohandas could see from Abdullah Sheth's face that he was unable to digest the comparison bit: imagine Tyeb Sheth being compared to him, Dada Abdullah! Since in the meantime Marcel Ledue had also joined them, he gave a different twist to the subject and said: 'You have met Marcel Ledue, haven't you? When you first arrived in Durban, he was there with me to receive you.'

'How can one forget him?' said Mohandas, laughing.

Marcel shook hands with Mohandas warmly and said: 'You are surely a master of some magical tricks. You have tricked Dada Abdullah so completely that he is never tired of singing your praises.'

'I don't think anyone sings your praise if you trick him. What do you think?'

Marcel reddened a little, but Mohandas was quite at ease as he had been all along.

There were two exits from the station. For a moment, Mohandas thought of taking the other one. The most that could happen would be a repeat of what had happened to him when walking the footpath in Pretoria. He was quite used to it now. His body too had grown stronger. Then he thought of Dada Abdullah: it would be wrong to put him in danger. In Pretoria, he had been alone. Nobody could have been caused any trouble, nor given a bad name.

Ledue had branched off and taken the white exit. Though he did not say anything, Mohandas could not help thinking for a moment how Ledue had come with Dada Abdullah and yet gone out alone. The awareness of being a white had him in its grip just as the awareness of being coolies had them.

Dada Abdullah and others had taken the other exit. Marcel Ledue was outside waiting for them. Mohandas said: 'I thought you had taken the other exit home.'

'Dada Abdullah is a friend of long standing, Mr. Gandhi.'

'Of course. I can see that.'

'I don't get you.'

'Not my fault.'

Dada Abdullah chipped in quickly: 'I could never have imagined that the case would be over so quickly and so well. The credit goes to you alone.'

'Nothing would have been possible if you hadn't agreed to arbitration.'

Before Mohandas could say anything more, Marcel butted in: 'But you'd said it was Mr. Baker who was looking after your case?'

The reply came from Mohandas: 'Yes, it was Mr. Baker who was looking after the case. I was only helping him in unravelling the tangled web.'

'The credit actually should go to him.'

Mohandas laughed and said: 'Absolutely right! Thanks for making the correction.'

Dada Abdullah was fuming at the uncalled for interference from Ledue, but he chose to keep quiet. After all, a white was involved. He thought it best to leave the scene.

On the way, Dada Abdullah asked Mohandas: 'How did you manage to persuade Tyeb Sheth? It certainly couldn't have been an easy task.'

'The way I persuaded you,' said Mohandas, 'Tyeb Sheth and Mr. Baker asked me exactly the same question about you. My only answer was that the two of you had respect and affection for each other in your hearts, and neither wanted to be the cause of the other's ruin. The only problem was a misunderstanding which had kept ballooning by default.'

Then, all at once, Mohandas shot a question: 'When is the next Abdullah & Co. ship leaving for India?'

'Why?'

'My work as well as my agreement is over. How long can I continue as a wanderer?'

'What's the hurry? It anyway takes both sides to terminate an agreement.' Dada Abdullah said, laughing.

'It's home and it's where I must settle in a job. You can go gallivanting around the world but only when your mind is away. The moment it's back, you think of home.'

'But you have hardly spent any time in Durban, Gandhibhai.'

'Hospitality for its own sake only helps to make a man lazy.'

'There are a lot of people from Kathiawar in this place. When they get to know that you were here and went back without meeting them, how do you think they will feel?'

'Hardly anyone knows me here, Dada Abdullah. In Pretoria, there were at least a few who were getting to know me. My work over, Pretoria too is history. There is still Durban, but that is only because of you. I did of course get introduced to Marcel Ledue.' Saying this he laughed as if he was talking about a gymnastic doll.

Dada Abdullah came out with a suggestion: 'Why don't you set up practice here? We are here to support you.'

Mohandas recalled his telling Kastur that it was after all only a matter of one year and he would be back in no time at all. He also knew that his brother Lakshmidas would also want him to continue working with Dada Abdullah, if he could. The money was after all being paid to him directly. He also knew that setting up practice in India would require him to put up an entirely fresh effort. He could not however continue to live in a foreign country either.

'Dada Abdullah,' he said, 'if one's luck is what one wants to try, one's own country is the best. It's different for you. You are businessmen. The whole world is your business. We don't have the trick of your trade.'

'That's precisely why we want you to stay, so that you too can learn the trick.' They both laughed.

~

June 25, 1894. At his Clare Road residence, Dada Abdullah had made elaborate arrangements of a farewell to Mohandas. It was a hot topic in the local Gujarati community that Gandhibhai had saved two big Kathiawar traders from total ruin. As a result, almost everyone of the Natal Kathiawari business community was present at the farewell. The invitees, all dressed up, were in a relaxed mood. Parties of course kept taking place every other day, but they were mostly organized on religious or linguistic lines. This was the first one of its type in which people from all communities were participating. Dada Abdullah was taking Mohandas around to introduce him to every single invitee. He was telling them about the miracle Gandhibhai had performed. He does not contest a case legally, he was telling them, he contests it with sincerity and humanity. As a result, there is no injury to truth and no diminution of humanity.

Mohandas said: 'If you couple barristers with goodness, I'll be the loser. It'll be hard for me to become a good barrister.'

Dada Abdullah would continue in his vein: 'Gandhibhai is a magician. I call him the Little Christ.'

'Yes. We heard a lot about him. He did a tremendous job of keeping stalwarts like you and Tyeb Sheth on a tight leash.' That really made Dada Abdullah's day.

Meeting people, talking to them, Mohandas had got quite tired. At the first opportunity, he went and sat down under a tree, with his legs stretched out in the sun. He enjoyed sitting this way during winter days. He closed his eyes and let his body relax.

Coming close, someone called out to him: 'That was indeed great, Gandhibhai. The way you got Dada Abdullah to dance to your tune was nothing short of a miracle.'

His eyes still shut, Mohandas asked: 'In order to get some extra benefit, perhaps?'

'That's for you to tell.'

'It would have been better, wouldn't it, if you too could tell it before you spoke?' He raised his neck and saw it was Ledue.

Mohandas got up. 'You, Mr. Ledue? When did you come?'

'Dada Abdullah was very keen that I should join the farewell. Couldn't refuse him.'

'Dada Abdullah is over there.' Mohandas pointed in the direction. 'I'm taking rest here.'

'I don't understand.'

'Since you said you were a guest of Dada Abdullah, I thought you'd like to meet him.'

'I think you should try to learn how to talk to people like us.'

'That's what I have been doing all along. People talk more or less in the same way everywhere; only their languages differ. Animals of course talk in different ways.'

Mr. Ledue turned on his heels and walked away. Mohandas shut his eyes and lay down again, a mischievous smile playing on his lips.

Whenever Mohandas was agitated, he withdrew gradually from the world outside and tried to hook up with himself. A little later, he would be quite normal. After the departure of Mr. Ledue, he took a while trying to get back to his normal self and then joined the gathering.

Someone was carrying a newspaper. He had not been able to look up the day's paper.

'Could I borrow your newspaper?'

'Certainly.'

Mohandas turned over the pages in a cursory way. Suddenly, his eyes fell on a news item bearing the headline "Indian Franchise". He paused and went through the item from the first to the last word in a hurry. It said that a bill relating to franchise for Indians was under the consideration of Natal parliament. The topic had been dismissed in only a few sentences. Perhaps it was deliberate. The idea could be to carry the news without attracting the attention of the people. Mohandas thought deep and hard about it. Why was the government bringing a bill about Indian franchise before the parliament? It was very unlikely that its aim was to enlarge the scope of the current franchise rights. It must be to prune them further. Mohandas of course didn't have any idea of the current status, but he had a shrewd idea that what was being planned was dangerous.

Mohandas approached a couple of people who were educated and perhaps had some idea about the franchise business. He asked them: 'Have you seen the paper today?'

'Anything special?'

He showed them the news item. It took them a lot of time to get through the item.

'Why don't you tell us what it is all about?' they asked. 'We are not habitual paper readers. Even if we manage to read it, we don't quite get the significance.'

Mohandas read out the news item again and explained its significance. In the meantime, Dada Abdullah had also joined them. He laughed and said: 'Look, the law is beyond us. Talk to us about business, that's what we understand. We merely understand commodity prices the newspapers carry. As for laws, it's for the government to make them and for us to obey them.'

'But the younger generation is well educated. They must be telling you about these things.'

'The younger generation? They aren't the least bit concerned. Why get into trouble by telling us the truth? Most of the educated ones among them are Christians. For them respectability lies in cozying up to white priests and serving them as flunkeys. They think of themselves as part of the white tradition. For them, we are all black Indians.'

Mohandas was amazed. Did one cease to be an Indian just because one had converted to Christianity, he was wondering. If you adopted a foreign religion, were your roots also severed? Had this been the case, all Europeans would have been loyal to the Arab nations, wouldn't they? After all, that's where their religion was born! Are these two things, adopting a foreign religion and patriotism, contradictory or complimentary? Mohandas had raised so many questions to himself that he didn't know what to tell Dada Abdullah.

Someone called out to Dada Abdullah and he left promising to be back soon. Others had already left. Mohandas was unable to decide whether or not to put before them his own fears about the bill. They had got so used to getting their problems sorted out by white lawyers! He knew that white lawyers would never be in a position to appreciate their concerns. So far as he himself was concerned, he was in no mood to get involved in any fresh problem. He simply had to go back to India; the year was on its way out and the family was keenly awaiting his return. He had made a promise to Kastur, and he could imagine the kids' curiosity to see their father. Had he not come here, he would have been so close to his children by now. Now he will have to start all over again to get close to them. A year is not a negligible period of time. Living together changes the whole meaning of life.

The train of his thoughts was suddenly broken. Dada Abdullah had reappeared with two or three traders. Parsi Rustomji was one of them. Mohandas was meeting him after a whole year. Mohandas found him to be a man of a more dignified presence. Abdullah Sheth told Mohandas: 'Explain it to him. He understands politics better than I do.'

Mohandas held out the paper to him. He wanted to get rid of the paper and the specific news item, but, after examining the paper, he too came back with the same thing: 'Please explain it to us. What does this piece of news mean and how is it going to affect us?'

Mohandas was getting deeper into the quagmire. By telling them about that piece of news he had actually stuck his neck out. He said: 'I don't really know what the existing law is or what amendment is now proposed. What however I can figure out is that if this bill turns into law you are in for trouble. It may well prove to be the last nail in the coffin of the independence of Indians here, I mean, if there is any sort of independence that you enjoy.'

Mohandas had actually said all this, a little bit in anger, to shake off the pursuers. But their faces had gone murky. In the meantime, Dada Abdullah had got hold of two more individuals—Adamji Miyakhan and Kolandavellu Pillay. These two were also among the leading businessmen.

Abdullah Sheth said: 'What you say can well be true. There is of course a background to the whole thing.'

Mohandas sounded a bit peeved as he said: 'If you knew the background, why didn't you do anything about it?'

'We didn't know,' said Parsi Rustomji. 'It was only when you told us that the layers started coming off one after another.'

Dada Abdullah continued his revelations: 'Mr. Escombe is a senior and famous Natal lawyer. He takes up most of the cases of Indian businessmen. He is a bit stubborn by nature and hard to budge once he takes up a position. Always ready to pick up an argument.' After a pause, he addressed himself to Adamji: 'Why don't you tell us more about him? You have had more to do with him.'

Adamji Miyakhan had a halting style of speaking. When speaking, he would often halt in the middle as if he had finished whatever he wanted to say. But he would suddenly start speaking again. Often he repeated whole sentences. If he ever said anything for which he thought he deserved applause, he would nod his head vigorously. He picked up the thread from Dada Abdullah and took it forward: 'Mr. Gandhi, this is my first meeting with you but I will not stand on formalities.' Pausing a little, he continued: 'Escombe is a brilliant man. I have never seen such a generous man among the English. There is a running feud between him and the local wharf engineer. There was an electoral contest between the two. The engineer was the official candidate and Mr. Escombe made a shrewd guess that all white votes would go to him. So he called a meeting of his Indian clients and explained his situation to us. On his request, we all went and got our names registered in the Voters' Register. When the time came we all voted *en bloc* for Mr. Escombe, yes, we did.'

'Mr. Escombe won and the engineer lost. The government couldn't digest this. That's the whole story behind this franchise amendment bill,' said Dada Abdullah,

Mr. Pillay elaborated: 'There's always a sword hanging on our heads. Anything we do, the government pricks up its ears and then it tries all it can to divide us. The defeat of their candidate at the polls has made them even angrier with us.'

'If you'll permit me, I want to make a submission to you,' said Adamji Miyakhan with great politeness.

'Of course!'

'Please postpone your plans of departure for the time being and extend your kind services to us at least for a month. We'll also request Dada Abdullah not to let you go and stop you whichever way he can.'

The fear had been lurking in Mohandas' mind and now it was in the open. For a moment, Mohandas thought: 'They too are my fellow countrymen. If I worry so much about my fellow countrymen in India, why not about these people who are stranded in a foreign country without any help? If I can't do anything for them here, what can I possibly do for those in India?'

Abdullah Sheth was not only a businessman; he was a worldly-wise man too. He could guess Mohandas' dilemma. He said: 'What grounds do I have to ask him to stay on? My own work is over. He has a family in Rajkot. How long can he stay here alone? You or me—we are all in the same boat. If we want to do something, it'll have to be a joint effort. He is after all a barrister. He has a position, and there's a fee …'

Mohandas didn't like the last bit. He interrupted: 'On the one hand, you honour me by calling me Gandhibhai; on the other, you talk about my fee. If it's just a matter of one month, I'm ready to stay on. One thing, however, must be made clear. I know barely five or six people here. You'll all have to pitch in, if my stay is to bear any fruit. Otherwise, please let me go.'

'We'll all do as you tell us.'

Mohandas thought for a while and then said: 'I've just told you that I do not want any money for myself, but money will be required for the task we are going to take up. We'll need money for letters, telegrams, paper, printing, running around, for taking delegations, for consultations with lawyers whenever required, for law books, and so on. A legal battle cannot be conducted if you don't know the law. We all have to fight this battle together. Alone, I won't be able to achieve anything.'

'You needn't worry about money the least bit. What are we all here for?' Rustomji said.

Pillay commented: 'It's all the will of God. No one knows what He'll do next.'

Adamji contributed by way of applause: 'Allah! Mysterious are your ways! You sent Gandhibhai to us! We are ever ready. The kindness You have shown will surely see us to our destination. It surely will.'

'Amen!' They all intoned together.

The farewell meeting had turned into a business meeting.

Mohandas was in two minds. On the one hand was his home, on the other, Indian franchise. To have to change your mind after you have made it up once is like having to turn around a galloping horse. To be able to do that, you needed a faithful horse, and a self-respecting rider. The issues were all linked: postponement of his decision to return home; breaking of the promise made to Kastur; delay of a month in his reunion with his children. Mohandas had to explain things to himself, posing as his own teacher.

On the other side, he also had to explain things to those Indians in South Africa who were unmindful of their own condition. He saw the whole of India in them. When he told them to be patient, he felt he was also addressing those who were in Rajkot—Kastur, brother Lakshmidas, Uka and the countless countrymen spread all over the country. He told them:

'If you think you are from a foreign land, the whites too are outsiders. Do not think that because they have power they can do whatever they like. Courage and patience can blunt any sword of tyranny. If there is anyone who has the right to question our presence here, it is the natives. They were born on this soil and this is where they have grown up. But they don't even know what relationship they have with this country and what their rights are. Like people in India, they also live in terror of the whites. That's why I keep telling you not to let your rights out of your sight. The moment you do, the thieves will be at it. When the others who don't know see you, they too will become aware of their rights and responsibilities. Those who think that the whites are the masters of this country and the rest are all slaves are living in ignorance.'

A new dimension was being added to Mohandas' personality as Gandhibhai. Sometimes he felt that this new, emerging face of his might help open new doors of success for him. The seed he sows here would grow into a tree whose branches may spread far and wide, providing shade to all his countrymen, here as much as there.

Mohandas had not been able to sleep the whole night. The trust so many people had placed on him had filled him with anxiety. Would he be able to keep their trust? was also implicit, like the unseen third river, Sarswati, the trust of those people who were absent. They were all passing through a dark tunnel. He himself had forgotten the colour of light. So had everyone else. This was a light whose switch was not in their hands; it was in the hands of those who had seized it. This was the light of their freedom. As a result, the thick dark was their substitute for the light. They were rowing the boats of their lives in the dark. Even the slightest sliver of light could hurt their eyes accustomed to darkness. It was also possible that, dazzled by it, they would even refuse to look at the light. Or, maybe, in a rush to capture the light, they would trample one another down. It was important for him to keep moving forward holding their trust in his tender care like a burning flame. Where there was no trust, there was no harmony. You needed the bridge of harmony to bring the people together. The awakening would follow. An awakening here would mean a rejuvenation there. A revival there would mean a reawakening here. A struggle would be born. This movement would not be something that anyone could keep in his pocket. Nor would it be like a firecracker that burns, flashes and then goes out. There would be Jesus, there would be Buddha, there would be sacrifice and penance in that struggle. Not to kill anyone, but to give everyone life. Mohandas wanted to tell them all these things, but he had a feeling that the ground wasn't ready for them yet.

~

The second reading of the franchise bill was on. The government had by now a shrewd idea that that the Indian community was concerned about the bill. The Indian community had never before been seen in such a state of agitation. It was for the first time that the government had realized that things were on the boil under the calm surface.

One of the things that Gandhibhai had done in the meantime was to effect an entry into the society of Indians born in Natal after 1860. Having acquired English, they thought of themselves as distinct from the illiterate Indians and closer to the whites. Quite a few of the young ones among them had converted to Christianity. Like English, they also considered Christianity to be a gateway to the white community. The leaders of this youth brigade were Mr. Paul, interpreter in the Durban court, and Mr. Subhan Godfrey, Head Master of the Mission School. Students of Mr. Godfrey were spread all over Durban. Though they had converted to Christianity, they revered Godfrey in the tradition of *Gururdevo bhav* (the teacher is God). Their fathers may have been *girmitiya*s, but their English education and religious conversion had filled them with immense self-confidence. Mr. Paul was a functionary of the court and kept the accused informed of the goings-on in the court. So everyone believed that if you could win over Mr. Paul, half your court battle was over. He could play around with law and language to make them mean whatever he wanted them to mean. In any case, interpreters were always moving around with white officers. Anyone who could withstand the airs of the whites was no ordinary man!

Mohandas called a meeting of all of them. He also invited the businessmen. They were the same businessmen who had attended his farewell-meeting.. All the seniors—Sheth Daood Muhammad, Kamruddin Sheth, Adamji Miyakhan, C. Lachhiram, Ranga Swami, Amod Jiva, Parsi Rustomji, Pillay—were present. Employees of some large companies were also present, and so were some clerks from government offices. Some of them were small businessmen who ran stalls or peddled their wares. Seeing so many Indians gathered together gave Mohandas confidence that he might be able to achieve his goal.

Mohandas was asked to speak first. The biggest problem before him was what language to use. After some deliberation, he chose Gujarati. Of course, he also freely incorporated words from English and Hindustani too. He addressed:

My fellow countrymen,

I am overwhelmed by the trust you have shown on me, especially at a crucial time like this when the Natal parliament is going to take some important decisions about us. I have returned from Johannesburg only a few days ago. I was on my way back to my country when I yielded to your persuasion. I can only say that I am ready to put at your service whatever few abilities I have. However, I am running out of time. I have to be back in India in a month.

I see several new faces here. They must be curious to know about me. I am a barrister by trade. I come from Kathiawar but I have been wandering from place to place ever since I returned from London. I arrived here on a year's girmit *to work with Dada Abdullah & Co. The work is over, so is the* girmit. *I was going to return home; in fact, I had been given a farewell too. That farewell function itself turned into a reason for me to stay on. On that very day, the newspapers carried a news item which said that a bill relating to the franchise rights of Indians was before the Natal parliament. If that bill turned into law, the few remaining franchise rights now available to the Indians here would also be taken away. If you have no franchise, you have no citizenship; the two go together. It is grave injustice to deny citizenship rights to anyone who contributes actively to a country's social, economic and political life. We are obliged to live in a state of semi-slavery in our own country too, despite the fact that it is our own. If we raise our voice for our rights in this country, it will also find an echo in our country too.*

You are all contributing to the prosperity of Natal actively. You are creating a dynamic society. Despite that, you are being spurned. India is our own land, but our lives are no better there. What's however happening here is that the rights that had been promised to us or had already been granted to us are being withdrawn. If this bill becomes law, any possibility of your representative ever reaching the Natal parliament will completely disappear. You will not be able to defend your rights outside, while in the parliament there will be no one to raise a voice on your behalf. Do you think that these whites, who hate your colour, your way of living, your way of eating, and who find your bodies smelly—will ever raise a voice on your behalf? For them, you are mere coolies, nothing more.

This is a question of our self-respect and identity. We are face to face with the impending and horrifying danger of slavery; slavery which eventually takes the bread out of our hands. This bill will only darken the colours of that slavery.

You must also understand clearly that the government is not going to like the opposition of this bill by the coolies. It could lead to serious consequences. If you want to fight for your rights, you will also have to be ready to face the terror of the government. Victory will depend on how much of the tyranny you can put up with. You must learn from the trees, which man, in his savagery, severs from the roots but which do not accept defeat. Even if the slightest life is left in it, the plant blossoms again and rises as a new tree. In his arrogance of power, man continues to fell them and, in their humility, they continue to flourish again and again.

I am really happy to see that no one here thinks of himself as an important person or as an unimportant one, as a Hindu or a Muslim or a Christian, or as a Parsi or a Gujarati or a Madrasi … you have dissolved all differences to become one. I wish to see India too becoming one.

One thing however does cause me pain—the absence here of our girmitiya *brethren. Their suffering is greater than ours … their sacrifice too. In the end, they will provide the backbone of this struggle. Are you all ready to take them alongside you? If not, they will hate you more than the whites who find you a smelly lot.*

They all spoke in one voice: 'We are ready.'

To Mohandas, it appeared as if a piece of entire India, complete in itself, had been transported to where he was. His eyes were moist.

When he sat down, Sheth Haji Mohammad addressed the meeting:

We came here to earn our living, but once we were here we fell a victim to slavery. We were slaves at home too, but that was our own country. Here we are like bullocks tethered to an oil-press, going round and round. Gandhibhai has shaken us awake and we now find that the road we have taken is leading us to slavery. Even our rights to live and die are mortgaged with the government. There is only one beacon of light and that is Gandhibhai. Maybe he will lead us to our destination. Amen!

Dada Abdullah had already spoken. He had introduced Gandhi, saying:

When Gandhibhai first came to Durban, I told myself what am I going to do with this Anglo-style Indian? Everything about him except his face looked English. It still does.

Everyone giggled. A thin smile also appeared on Mohandas' face.

Dada Abdullah was carrying on:

I got a glimpse of the real Gandhi inside him on the day of the farewell party. I saw how his heart aches for his fellow countrymen. He knows that love of one's country means sacrifice. We have now to decide whether we are content to hang upside down like bats or we want to walk with our heads high like real men.

On behalf of the new young invitees, it was Godfrey who spoke:

> *Forget your caste and religion. Remember only one thing: our country, our motherland, and her honour.*

At the close, Parsi Rustomji moved a resolution to the effect that the government be asked to stop discussion on the bill immediately, and Gandhibhai be requested to take whatever steps were necessary to get the bill withdrawn.

The bill was passed with unanimous consent. All that had transpired spurred Mohandas into action. His responsibilities had multiplied. Sitting right there, he drafted a telegram to the speaker of the parliament. It said:

> *We, the Indian migrants living in the colony of Natal, are exercised by the franchise bill moved in the parliament and wish to register our opposition to it. We consider it to be an assault on our honour and the honour of our country. We demand that readings of the bill should be stopped forthwith.*

A copy of the same telegram was also dispatched to the Prime Minister of the colony, John Robinson. Although he was an Englishman, Robinson had earned the respect of Indians too. Dada Abdullah proposed that a telegram should also be sent to Mr. Escombe, as they might require his help at some stage. A separate draft was readied for Mr. Escombe, which said:

> *The Indian community lent its support to you against the wharf engineer during the election. The current bill before the parliament seeking abolition of Indian franchise is a consequence of that action.*

A proposal was moved that a copy of these telegrams should also be sent to the newspapers. There were a few voices against this proposal. Indians thought that the white community might react negatively if the matter was pushed too aggressively and they might lose whatever little sympathy the community had towards them.

At first, Mohandas listened to both sides in silence, but, in the end, he had to speak out: 'If it is your intention to discuss all your problems inside closed doors, I am afraid you will end up chasing your own tails. Who is going to be able to understand your troubles and your problems? Your troubles turn into complaints only when they are conveyed to others for a solution or conveyed to those who are in a position to provide those solutions. If you don't do so, the pain inside you will burn through you and will one day reduce you to cinders like lava does.'

Mohandas went on to cite his own example: 'You will probably remember that about a year ago when I had first come to Durban, Dada Abdullah had taken me to show the working of a court. The magistrate asked me to leave my turban outside. I had preferred to leave the court. I wrote to the newspapers about the incident. There were reactions of both types—favourable and unfavourable, but people got to know the name of Gandhi in a single day. A pen is mightier than a sword—it is the cannon of all cannons.'

~

No one had imagined that the speaker of the parliament would respond so quickly—the very next day. It said: 'Reading of the bill is being postponed for two days.' People jumped with unexpected joy. It was for the first time they had realized that their voice could also change things. There were also whispers going around that this might actually be the miracle of Mohandas, the Indian barrister. Mohandas had sent the news to the newspapers. As a result, the newspapers probably thought that Gandhi was no ordinary person. A couple of papers also published short interviews with Gandhi.

The whites too were asking one another: 'Who is this Gandy? What's he doing here?'

One of the newspapers editorialized expressing concern and indignation at the fact that a coloured person could hold up the proceedings of the house. If he could do this he could do anything. With so many white members present in the house, why were the proceedings stopped?

This was the first public victory of the Indians, the credit for which was being handed to Gandhi.

~

Mohandas now desired some durability for this first victory of the Indians. Working against time, he got a seven page petition ready. He also enlisted the help of Mr. Paul in preparing the petition. There were pieces of information which could only be had from white circles or white officials. Only Mr. Paul knew about them. He also had to look up references to certain books which he had studied while in England. Mr. Paul and Mr. Godfrey helped him in locating these books. At least one of the three—Dada Abdullah, Kamrudduin Sheth, and Adamji Miyakhan—was always available and supplied local information. He did not want to have to stop work or for his petition to suffer in any way, on account of lack of information.

Mohandas would occasionally comment: 'Actions always bear fruit. They keep accumulating in your account, and if not immediately, they eventually prove their worth. The problem is that we tend to accept only positive results, rejecting negative ones, but negative results are results too, though they may not be to your liking.'

People listened to his comments very attentively.

Mohandas cited his own example to prove the point: 'I was thrown out of the train at Pietermaritzburg station. At first I thought: let me go back home. It's however only when one falls that one learns to rise again. If I had continued my travel like a parcel on the train, my journey would have been a dull one and I wouldn't be where I am today.'

Dada Abdullah was present and said in a low voice: 'That was my mistake, Gandhibhai.'

'What mistake? Anyway, mistake or not, I got the best of it. If you hadn't made that mistake, I wouldn't have had the beastly experience that I had.'

Dada Abdullah didn't know whether to laugh or cry at what Mohandas said. Mohandas was busy scouring the books for references and underlining them. Simultaneously, he was also working on the draft and replying to people's questions while also making his own comments. He also kept making jokes at his own expense: 'If I could only read what I write, I'd call it a great achievement. There was a time when only God's writing was considered illegible, now there is another one.' He would continue: 'Actually my ambition was to become a doctor, but *Bapu* said: "Why do you wish to commit the sin of killing frogs?" So I could never become a doctor but I did manage to get the handwriting of one.'

Someone would ask: 'But didn't you say your handwriting was next after God's? Now where has this doctor fellow turned up from?'

'You call that writing?' he would say and burst out laughing.

~

The completion of the draft petition saw Mohandas worried on another count: how to send the petition? Such a long petition and such bad handwriting! He asked Dada Abdullah to find four or five young men who knew English and had a good hand.

So Dada Abdullah dispatched his emissaries. Everyone was first tested for penmanship. A tough search produced barely four boys who could be said to have a happy hand. Mohandas got the boys to sit in a row with pen and paper and started dictating. He often had to spell out the words. A whole day went like this, but all the four copies were ready by the evening. Mohandas had to go through each one of them to check for omissions and errors. Now the big challenge was to get them signed or thumb-impressed, by as many Indians as possible in the course of a single night. The copy intended for the Speaker of the parliament had been prepared by a calligrapher by the name of Arthur. Arthur was an Indian, but because of his art he was in demand among the whites too.

When everything was ready, Mohandas called a meeting of all those who were present at the initial meeting at which the decision to send a petition had been taken. Mohandas presented the draft. Since only a few knew English, Mohandas translated the draft into Hindi and Gujarati as he went along. Only after everyone had approved a part he moved to the next part. This naturally took up a lot of time.

The petition was addressed to the Speaker and members of the house.

Honourable Speaker and Members of the Natal legislature,

The signatories to this petition are Indian migrants, subjects of the largest colony of the British queen. Our names are registered in the voters' list of Natal. On this ground, we are entitled to vote in the forthcoming elections to the legislature. A bill to deprive us of this right, the Franchise Amendment Bill, is currently before the House. We are deeply concerned over the fact that, in the event of the bill becoming law, Indians will be deprived of their voting rights. This will naturally raise a question about our citizenship status. We are in sharp disagreement with the contents of this bill. The reasons for bringing this bill before the parliament which are being aired in the newspapers are farthest from reality. We are completely unable to accept that Indians have never used franchise and that they are therefore unfit for voting rights. This proposition flies in the face of history and tradition. Indians knew about the election process long before Anglo-Saxons became familiar with the principle of democratic representation. They have known about it both in theory and in practice. Sir Summerman's book Village and Community *makes a clear mention of the fact that Indian communities have known the principle of representative bodies for a longer time than one can remember. The Indian village panchayat is an example.*

The British member of the parliament, Chisoenstein, once said at a meeting of East India Association that the town municipality system was a gift of the east. In Mysore, there are several public bodies which run on the principle of popular representation.

A five-member committee of Indian traders is currently functioning in Durban and takes all policy decisions. It deserves mention that in 1891, 775 municipalities and 892 local bodies were functioning in India. They all had an elected membership.

In the petition, Mohandas had cited statements by Pincott, Sir Georgewood and Sir Thomas Munro, Governor of Madras, in support of the claim that in intellect and culture the people of India were in no way inferior to the people of Europe. The petition also had quotations from Max Muller, who had written extensively about the greatness of India. Towards the end, it had also been pointed out that quotations from European scholars were being cited as a matter of deliberate strategy so that honourable members might know the truth about India from the lips of the white scholars themselves. In conclusion, a request had been made that, before the Indian subjects of Britain are deprived of their franchise, it would be in the interest of justice to order an inquiry by an independent commission.

People sat stunned into silence by the petition for a while. Everyone watched Gandhibhai's face unblinkingly as if he had performed a miracle with his words. For most of them, it was a first-time realization that their culture, traditions and potential were so rich that even white scholars had sung their praises.

Breaking the silence, Gandhbhai spoke: 'If anyone of you has any suggestions, any additions or subtractions to make, please speak freely.'

Everyone kept quiet. Their faces showed contentment and an initiation of joy. They were Indians. Even the whites, who today look upon them with contempt, have conceded the superiority of their culture. They were amazed that Gandhibhai knew so much! If a mere telegram from him had succeeded in holding up the reading of the bill for two days, how much more could this petition not achieve! For the people sitting in the House, this could be an eye-opener!

Gandhi interfered with their silence by adding: 'Only one thing now remains to be done, and it is the most difficult of all. We have to get the signatures or thumb impressions of as many Indians as possible, especially of those who currently have voting rights.. If we aspire for our rights, sacrifice and suffering are the first conditions.'

Everyone stood up smartly, like a soldier

They all set out on the signature campaign like groups of farmers setting out simultaneously to harvest their crops. It was decided that those who had some mode of transport would aim at the remoter locations while those who didn't would hire one or leg it to more proximate areas. The expense on fares would be shared by everyone.

The roads were dark, but the people were so worked up that darkness and light carried no meaning for them. They woke up the sleeping, gathered them all together, explained the whole thing to them, and gave them Gandhi's message. They told them about Gandhi if they didn't know who he was. In the end, they appealed to them to sign the petition. There were some who were afraid to sign. After all, it was a government measure; how could they oppose it? They had no wish to be sent to the circular jail. The government could even have them thrown into the ocean. They put up all kinds of arguments. Things had to be explained to them again and again and their questions answered. A few came round, some others held on to their fears. Still others argued: 'What can be worse than our present condition? We already think of ourselves as being in a jail. When your country is taken away from you, what remains?' It was the month of June and quite cold. Many of them had set out in great zest without any warm clothing. As they collected thumb impressions, they shivered. When they returned in the morning, they wore despondent looks which said that they had not been able to accomplish the task they had been given. But when the stocktaking was complete, they found that thousands of signatures and thumb impressions had been collected. Mohandas was amazed. Even in his wildest dreams, he could not have imagined that so many signatures would be collected. Considering the very short time in which the work had been done, it appeared to him to be nothing short of a miracle. He could feel a ray of hope breaking. If this enthusiasm could be sustained, they could well achieve their goal.

The next day, the petition with thousands of signatures was submitted to the speaker. After wondering at the size of the petition for a while, the speaker shrugged his shoulders and said: 'What's all this? It would have been sufficient for one man to present the petition. Everything is now in the hands of the House. Its decision will be final.'

Mohandas sent copies of the petition to all the newspapers. Everyone had thought that the white-owned newspapers would take no notice of the petition. They were surprised the next day to find that most of the newspapers had expressed a favourable opinion. It was for the first time that the Indian community had realized that the white press of Natal also took a sympathetic view of their problems.

Most of the people however said: 'Everything depends on who is raising the issue. Had it not been Gandhibhai, who'd have listened to us? For sure, there is something in him that forces the authorities and the press to listen to him.'

Gandhi laughed at their comment and said: 'If I had anything in me, would the coach leader have behaved with me worse than perhaps he behaves with his horses?' Before his eyes Mohandas could see the faces one after another of all those whites who had treated him and spurned him as less than human—the Porbandar agent Lely, the whites who had thrown him out of the train at the Pietermaritzburg station. Can this one small success draw a curtain on the memory of those experiences? He smiled to himself.

~

The petition led to a lot of discussion in the House. Among the members, there were a few who justified the Indian point of view. But when the contest is between a falcon on one side and a sparrow on the other, what chance does the sparrow stand? All the sparrow could do was to flutter its wings and stay still. The Indians however had the satisfaction that their appeal had attracted the attention of the rulers. And it wasn't a passing mention.

The bill was preordained to become law. It did.

The bill's becoming law fell as a hunter's net on defenceless birds. The little hope they had espied had been enveloped by a bigger darkness. You tip an empty large bowl over a small one and it will cover it all even if the latter is full. The bill turning into a law had unmade the very existence of the Indian community. Hit by the hunter's arrow, their soaring hope had plummeted with even greater speed and fallen almost lifeless to the ground.

Not that Mohandas knew nothing about this eventuality. He was well aware of the flip side of every game where the player is out for a duck. The House had spared little time for the bill; even so, the falcon did not have a flawless flight. This was no mean achievement. The whole House now was aware of the Indian community which was slowly gathering strength and whose voice was getting stronger by the day.

Mohandas had made a small beginning. He had struck a small blow at the ice of frozen inactivity. He wanted this ice, in which Indians were frozen upto their neck to break or melt.

~

The bill's becoming law reminded Mohandas of the incident in Transvaal when the whites had made a proposal to their parliament, Volksraad, that the businesses of Indians should be closed down and they should be turned out of the country. In their view, Indians were filthy, uncivilized and barbarous. They beat their wives; they were storehouses of germs; they defecated and urinated everywhere, they slept on bare ground and so on. President Kruger had labelled them 'Sons of Ishmael,' and, as such, fit objects to be governed by the whites. Mohandas did not want a Kruger in Natal and it was to avert this fear that he had mobilized the people. He wanted to save them from the darkness growing within themselves. He wanted to tell them that walking two steps didn't take you to your destination. The destination was often like a mirage in a desert: it moved away just when you thought you were quite close to it.

Mohandas spoke to them all: 'I am an ordinary man. Put on me only as much weight of your trust as I can bear. I may well prove to be the horse that throws off its rider into a ditch.' He continued: 'Success is no kedgeree that you just mix rice and dal in water, simmer for two minutes and, lo and behold, the meal is ready for you to eat and share. Success demands that the spirit of struggle within you be stirred. It causes pain, it chokes you and there isn't a soul around to ask you how you are. You have to stand firm as a rock in the middle of all that pain and pathos, when you are being rocked by wave after wave of misfortune. The House turned down our petition. This is not a reason for despair; indeed, it is a reason for joy. At least, we have left a scratch there, a scratch that we cannot see but they are actually feeling it. Their refusal, this malicious denial, will act as a high-yielding variety of seed for our future struggle. It will make us aware of our rights. It will give us the strength to fight. The parliament belongs to those who cannot stand any talk about our rights. Forget about rights, they cannot even stand the sight of us. But that does not mean that we accept defeat. If win and loss could be settled at the first attempt, living life would not be such a complex affair. Have you ever spared a thought about those people who came here with the idea that they could pluck bread off trees, who thought life would almost be a bed without thorns? They were coaxed and cajoled into coming here. Now they find their labour mortgaged, their lives tethered to the stake of the *girmit,* going round and round it like a beast. They don't even know the meaning of these words. "Right" or "privilege" is far too a difficult a word for them. In fact, even scholars don't understand what it means. They can't rise above their state of slavery, even if they don't know the word for it. So long as they don't break out of this circle of slavery, they won't understand what "a right" means. But when they do, they will know it better than those scholars who know its meaning from books. Do not therefore take this episode to be the end of the affair and despair. If you do, all the roads will be closed to you, and you will keep circling in this wilderness.'

The withered faces showed a gleam for a brief moment.

Mohandas said: 'I am glad to see a gleam on your faces. Each day is the beginning of a new struggle. Each day is the end of a defeat. We must be prepared for both. Our struggle is like no other struggle, and is perhaps unique. We will face countless defeats before we reach the ultimate victory. From the ashes of these defeats will rise, phoenix-like, our victory. We are not armed. We abjure arms. This is the truth about us, and this truth is our strength.'

Mohandas' talk had planted seeds of courage and confidence in people's minds, but Mohandas was a worried man. The reason for his worry was the speech of Natal's prime minister, Sir John Robinson, in the parliament. He had said: 'I don't agree with the arguments of the coolies. Franchise is the legacy of the Caucasian race. It cannot be granted to Indians, who belong to an inferior race.'

The Prime Minister's speech had made Mohandas restless. He wrote to the Prime Minister requesting him for an appointment. It was a pleasant surprise when he received the Prime Minister's message that he would be happy to meet Mohandas and he could come straightaway. It was a good omen, he felt. For a man belonging to the Caucasian race, a prime minister to boot, to give an immediate appointment to a black man, and one who had turned controversial the moment he stepped into the colony, was unbelievable. The moment he received the letter, Mohandas got busy with another petition. He included Dada Abdullah among those who were to go with him. There were four others.

'But we have already submitted a petition,' Dada Abdullah pointed out.

'Whenever approaching a newspaper or a politician, go armed with a document. It is only when pen and paper meet that speech can keep going.'

Quips of this kind were sometimes objects of much merriment among the people.

Sir John Robinson greeted them promptly with: 'Why so late? Why didn't you come early if you had any grouse? What is the sense in submitting a petition after the second reading is over? Neither the House nor the government can now withdraw. I have already recommended to the House that the petition of Indian migrants should be rejected and the bill turned into law.'

Mohandas submitted very politely and respectfully: 'Sir Robinson, most of the Indians in this colony are illiterate. They are not even conscious of their own situation. A few who could understand were either not in Natal or failed to notice the news item because no paper carried a full report on the bill.'

'Only a few technicalities now remain to be completed before the bill turns into law. They too will be completed soon. I am afraid there is nothing that can be done now.'

'Sir John, this is your government and you are of course free to do what you choose. But since in your speech you talked about justice and principles of Christianity, and human virtues, we were inspired to meet you and put our problem before you. However, I do want to say clearly that we are no strangers to democracy, and it is not a divine principle for us. The tradition of democracy in our country goes back to a time when several European countries did not perhaps exist. We have tried to put this in our petition frankly and authoritatively.'

Mohandas was speaking with complete confidence. The remaining five were silent. A mixed expression of fear, hesitation and uncertainty showed in their faces. They could never have imagined that any Indian could engage in such forthright conversation with a prime minister. For them, it was anyway the first, and perhaps the last time to stand face to face with the colony's prime minister, and shake hands with him. This was thrill enough for them. They felt like a mouse who had been asked to carry an elephant: not just a white but a prime minister too! Such a chance had come their way for the first time in life. They could at least make something of what Mohandas was saying, but what Sir John was saying was completely beyond them.

After listening to Mohandas, the Prime Minister was no longer his relaxed former self. 'Mr. Gandhi,' he said: 'what is the point in giving franchise to illiterates, to people who don't even know how many letters there are in the word civilization and what it means? All it would amount to is handing them a weapon with which they would not only cut their own throats but never miss a chance to slash others too. It has happened earlier.' Then, pausing a little and casting a glance at the others present, he continued: 'Of course, there would certainly be a few among them who would use their franchise with discretion and with a sense of responsibility, but such decisions are surely not taken with half-a-dozen people in view.'

Mohandas said: 'Mr. Prime Minister, there is only one request we have to make. Please get this issue examined by an independent commission. We promise full cooperation. To put into effect a law of this kind without proper assessment would only make the already hopeless condition of

Indians worse. The natives will one day surely get their franchise on the strength of numbers or when they become educated, but once the Indians lose their franchise, they will perhaps never get it back. In a democracy, franchise is the only source of strength for the weak and the deprived.'

From his unease, Mohandas had guessed that Sir John was impatient to be rid of them, so he stood up; others followed suit. As he rose, Mohandas said: 'Your Excellency, we are grateful for your patience and goodwill. By giving us a hearing, you have taken a step towards democracy. It is our misfortune that we have not been able to communicate our message to you. But we do not despair. Our voice has reached here today; it might reach even farther tomorrow.'

As they were leaving, Mohandas handed over the petition he had prepared for Sir John. At first Sir John hesitated, then, taking it, handed it to his secretary. The petition contained all that had been said at the meeting. The secretary cast a fleeting glance through the petition, looked wonderingly at Mohandas and smiled.

~

Marcel Ledue had found out that Mohandas had seen the Prime Minister with Dada Abdullah and a few others and that the meeting had been a failure. They had to return empty handed. The same evening, he called on Dada Abdullah. Rarely did Dada Abdullah bring up mention of a subject to someone who was not connected with it.

After talking about shop for a while, Marcel said: 'Why are you giving so much importance to a Hindu? Don't you understand that someone who worships a stone can go to any limit in his flattery of a living being?'

'I don't understand. What are you trying to say?'

'Gandhi is using you. He is trying to use you as a bridge to reach the Prime Minister. A Hindu is clever as a fox. When it serves his purpose, he can worship anyone.'

Dada Abdullah could barely stand it, but out of regard for his white colour, he only said: 'There is nothing of the sort. The issue relates to

Indian franchise. It affects the interests of both Hindus and Muslims. So far as idol worship is concerned, that's a matter of personal faith.'

'Do you think M.K. Gandhi can get you your rights? If a trader like you goes and meets the Prime Minister directly, he will give more importance to what you say. In his eyes, Gandhi is an infamous rolling stone, who is a pain in the government's neck.'

'You may be right, but we have no evidence to support what you say. The question of franchise has absolutely nothing to do with the Hindu-Muslim question.'

'But he wants to turn it into an agitation.'

'How can expression of your views be called an agitation?'

'This is an agitation. By facing off the prime minister, he is setting you up as a target for the government.'

Dada Abdullah thought better of prolonging the argument. Marcel carried on: 'Dada Abdullah, by accepting the tutelage of a Hindu, you have lowered your prestige. It wasn't a right thing to do for you to hold him back.'

Dada Abdullah said: 'I was instrumental in holding him back. I was the one who told him that there was plenty for him to do here and thrust some pounds into his pocket so that he could meet his daily needs. We needed him here. I also consulted Abdul Ghani Sahib. He also thought that Gandhi was a far-sighted man. I think it would be better for us to leave this matter in the hands of the people.' Dada Abdullah's tone had changed.

Marcel could sense that things had gone wrong, so he took his leave, saying: 'Well, I have done my duty. The rest is up to you.'

Dada heard the clip-clop of the horses' hooves as his phaeton left and smiled to himself.

~

VIII

At first Mohandas had thought that he would be able to finish off all the work and set sail for home in a month's time. But though a struggle may be short, its tail is never as short as we tend to think. One end leads on to another and, as it grows, it sets up a fence around you. The more you cut it, the more it grows. Mohandas had always thought that the British are basically fair-minded people. All those who had treated him unfairly he had considered to be exceptions. As the end of the month approached, he found the chains of the struggle tightening on him. He thought of those chains as the agents of his liberation, but the question kept ringing in his ears if he had done the right thing by prolonging his stay. His intellect said 'yes,' but his memories of home told him he was wrong.

Whenever Kastur wanted to call Mohandas, she always came and stood behind the door. She never actually called him by beckoning to him; standing behind the door was her way of beckoning to him and he never failed to respond. He now felt that she had been standing behind the door in his Rajkot room, holding the kids by their fingers, looking unblinkingly towards him, waiting.

Lakshmidas was now providing for two families. Karsan had disappeared from the scene a long time ago. There was a blank space in the picture where he should have been. Sometimes a memory, like a wave, flashed in his mind, but he never appeared in person, nor did his wife and kids. The two of them—Karsan and Mohandas had got married in the same *mandap,* the same day at the same time. This thing never stopped surprising him. More than Karsan, it was Mehtab who occupied his thoughts. They had drunk together and supped together. It was through Karsan that he had got to know Sheikh Mehtab, but Karsan had disappeared and they had been left facing each other.

~

Mohandas was sure that Lakshmibhai would be waiting for him to send money home. Now that his *girmit* was over how would he meet his expenses? Mohandas felt dizzy. He had forfeited the right to stay with Dada Abdullah with the expiry of the *girmit.* It was only his thick skin that was letting him stay there now. No, he must find a place to stay for himself. How long could he stay on like this? If he wanted to carry on as a barrister, he would have to find his own house and his own office. If he wanted to stay on longer, he would also have to take responsibility for the family. He could not go on leading the life of a fugitive, leaving his family to be looked after by Lakshmibhai.

One day Mohandas put it to his friends: 'The way things are going on, there is hardly any chance to reach a conclusion. Whatever hopes we had from the Prime Minister are now also dashed. Had he relented even a little, we could still cherish some hope. If one of you can now take over my responsibility, I can return to India a happy man. One year away from home is one year taken away from your life.' He laughed as he uttered the last sentence.

Adamji Miyakhan took up the clue: 'Had we been capable of anything, would we have waited this long? The way you took on the Prime Minister, could any of us illiterates even think of it?'

Everyone supported Adamji Miyakhan as one man. Mohandas was in a fix. What was he going to do?

Dada Abdullah minced no words. 'Tell us your problem. If it is your family you can get them here whenever you wish.'

Parsi Rustomji joined in: 'I will take full responsibility for the family.'

'I'm sorry. How can anyone else take this responsibility? That would be like a man first agreeing to help a passenger cross a river carrying his luggage, and when midstream, asking to be paid. If I stay here, I also take the responsibility for my family. All of you can certainly help, but only by giving me some work apiece. That should see me through.'

'We should be able to raise enough money for you to devote yourself full time to social service. That should take care of your expenses, and also ensure social work. This too is in a way legal work.'

'I'm sorry, but I don't agree. My work is confined to helping you understand your rights. You don't need a lawyer or a barrister for this work, so where is the question of a fee? Of course, when the need arises, we'll have to raise money for the movement. But using that money for my personal expenses would amount to misappropriation. In such a situation, I'd find myself unable to ask you to contribute even to the movement. It would not only degrade me, it would also bring the movement into disrepute, stripping it of all its effectiveness.'

'We know that you'll never take more than what you need. But we do have a responsibility towards you.'

'Only to see that I don't get corrupted. Human weaknesses are like sparks of fire. They settle down wherever they find a place, and then keep smoldering. The initial enthusiasm too does not last. It's quite possible that during this struggle I may sometimes have to speak to you bluntly. If I accept your hospitality, how will I be able to speak bluntly to you? There will be a clash between the rights of the employee and the position of the employer. All that you may do is to assign me your law-related work, considering that I am a barrister. Of course, a coloured barrister stands nowhere before a white one, so there are dangers in assigning your work to me.'

The matter had ended there. A seed, however, had been sown in Mohandas' mind. On what grounds could these people assign him their work? Would he have to earn his living again by writing drafts, as he had to do in Rajkot? Was he simply not destined to be a barrister? So long as he didn't get himself registered in the Supreme Court, he could not stand up in the court in his gown as a lawyer. If he had to survive, he would have to fight. If he had to fight, he would need a position. A life of dignity was his first condition. The question of survival could not be left to the mercy of others.

~

Mohandas was busy putting his papers in order. The biggest challenge before him now was how to stay on in Natal. Had he been a businessman, all that he would have had to do to get going would have been to arrange for some finance and set up shop. He could only live by the knowledge he had. The only way out therefore was registration.

Dada Abdullah entered the room and announced: 'We have all got together and decided that you will not be allowed to go even if you so want.'

Mohandas raised his head: 'Oh, it's you, Abdullah Sheth.' Then he laughed and said: 'I am the man who failed to keep his word. Such a man has no claim left on the issue for which he had given his word. I had had a good enough farewell party and should have been home by now. But I had to raise that franchise matter and shackle my own feet. Anyway, now that it's done, it's done. There is, however, another matter.'

Dada Abdullah was concerned: 'What matter?'

'If I must stay on, I must do something, and the only thing I can do is practice law. To be able to do that I'll have to get myself registered with the Supreme Court. You can come to my help only after that is done, for it's only then that I'll become entitled to receive a fee for my work.' Laughing, he continued: 'You know when I was at Rajkot, anyone who brought me a client had to be paid the tout's fee. My elder brother was also a lawyer and his partner used to send clients to me. If I refused to pay the tout's fee, my elder brother would be angry with me. His idea was that my earnings went towards meeting the household expenses, and being part of the household, he also enjoyed a share of what I earned. Then why should his partner, who sent the clients, be deprived of his share? Such small earnings I had, and there were so many claimants for a share! I was firm in my opposition to the tout system, and that was one of the reasons why I left the place. I don't know what awaits me here.'

Dada Abdullah held out a sheaf of papers to him and said: 'You needn't worry about that. Twenty of the businessmen have appointed you their legal adviser for one year. Secondly, although it makes me sad, you should be happy to hear it. A two-storied house has been arranged for you in Beach Grove. When you go out and turn left, the first lane is Beach Grove. The house is also called Beach Grove Villa. Right in front is the sea beach and the breeze blows right into the house. Sit in the balcony watching the sea and you will feel the sea waves right within you. I love watching the sea that way. We are just behind you; a little further down the lane is the Attorney General's residence. You can talk to him across the balcony, if you like.'

Mohandas smiled to himself. He didn't say it, but thought to himself: 'The white elephant is going places. What's going to happen to him? Will he perish or prosper?'

Dada Abdullah noticed the change in his expression. 'What are you thinking, Gandhibhai? What's the problem?'

'I was only thinking: the things time can do to you!'

Dada Abdullah turned his face away.

~

Mohandas had sent word home telling them everything. He had a good idea how Kastur and the kids were going to take it, but he had rationalized the whole thing to himself. Maybe it would be taken as a case of broken promises. His first promise was to Kastur; the rest of them had grown out of situations as they had developed. He wanted to justify it as follows: The problem here was not unfamiliar to any individual. There were so many people, there was so much exploitation and so much abuse—how could he possibly ignore it? The fault was of course his—at that as well as this end. It was inevitable that he should fail to keep one of the two promises. There is however a world of difference between going back on promises made to your own people and those made to others. What others, though? They too are my own people, yes, my very own people. The 'I' that I am has grown into a very large 'I'. The I that I was when I was at home was confined to Kastur and the kids; at a pinch, it might include Lakshmibhai. The I that I am now, might grow till it becomes the I of India. He would then start laughing at his own philosophizing: what made him soar so high? Shouldn't there be a limit to one's thinking lest he cross the boundary of logical thought and get bogged down in absurdity? It is indeed a bog, which can swallow logic, illogic, he himself, indeed everything.

Eventually, Mohandas would bring himself back whence he was to make his leap—registration! He would then tell himself: 'Maybe this was what *Ba* meant when she talked about the special quality of an ape. When he perceives danger, an ape does a back flip in mid-flight. Maybe this special quality of the ape has found a niche in man's brain and enables him to do back flips and forward flips at will.'

~

Pietermaritzburg was about eighty miles from Durban. Mohandas had submitted his papers to the Supreme Court for registration. He was the first Indian, in fact, the first coloured person, in the whole of South Africa—to have taken the daring step of seeking registration as an advocate. No sooner however had he submitted the papers than the Natal bar seemed to have been hit by an earthquake. Everywhere, there was only one topic for discussion: a coolie wanting to become a member of the bar.

'They came here as *girmitiya*s and now they want entry in the courts!'

'Want to meddle in intellectual matters now, don't they?'

'It was okay so long as they were confined to indentured labour, but now they want franchise! They have already captured business, now they want to desecrate the temple of law! It is law, not a bullock that anyone can hitch his plough to.'

'You need brains for law, not cow-shit. That's all they fancy—cow-shit. Cow-shit in everything! Thank God, they don't have it for food.'

'Not only stupid, they are impudent too! Thirty-six years ago, in 1857, they slaughtered innocent whites in their country–children, women, officers—mercilessly. Drowned them in rivers, dumped them in wells, strangled them to death! What monsters!'

'They rose in revolt despite the presence of the East India Company's army. Had it not been for a few loyal, understanding and honourable

Indians, they would have swallowed the English alive! Never had such a thing happened in a colony before.'

'We should not overlook the fact that ...'

'I say the natives are any day a far superior lot. They know their limits and mind their own business. They don't go around challenging authority.'

'The Transvaal government permitted one coolie to open a business. Result? There is a whole army of them now. Give them an inch and they will take a mile.'

'They only need a place to live and it becomes their place of business,. They will hawk their goods all over the place and steal the bread of their own benefactor.'

'You just wait and see. Soon all the courts will be full of them. Gandy will be their great ancestor. They will work for the price of a cup of tea and a toast and will take away all the business we worked so hard to build.'

'We will stop his registration,' they said emphatically.

Mohandas was aghast to hear so many reactions. So much hate? Why? Jesus never hated anyone so much! He thought of Mr. Baker. He used to say Jesus mounted the cross while still preaching the lesson of love. These people take pleasure in mounting others on the cross. Well, he thought, if a cross is what he has to mount, that's what he would do.

The Natal Law Society had stood up against Mohandas like one man. There were two pre-conditions that Mohandas had to meet for registration: first, he had to attach testimonials from two European businessmen with the application, and second, the application for registration had to be presented before the court by the Advocate General personally. Mohandas had managed to procure the two testimonials, one of them being from the proprietor of Green Harvey Ekka. Ekka was one of those twenty businessmen who had engaged the services of Mohandas as their legal counsellor. The second condition however sounded to Mohandas impossible, like moving a mountain. Getting the Advocate General to propose registration for a coolie barrister! Especially when the Natal Law Society was geared up to do all it could to stop it! Every single white lawyer was a member of the Law Society.

One day Dada Abdullah himself asked Mohandas: 'When are you going to give us the good news of your becoming an advocate? That day will be the first step towards freedom for Indians.'

Mohandas said: 'Let's enjoy it so long as the hope is alive. I don't think the day will ever come.'

'Why not?' Dada Abdullah sounded worried.

'My application can be taken up for consideration only if the Advocate General agrees to refer it to the court. There isn't half a chance that he will do it, so it is best to forget about the whole thing. Then there is the Natal Law Society which seems to have been hit by a storm. All that we can now ...'

'Is that all?'

'Isn't it enough?'

'Do you know who the Advocate General is?'

'Out of my reach, whoever he may be.'

'In connection with the franchise bill, I had once occasion to mention Mr. Escombe, the man who was the root cause of the bill. He is the Advocate General and a friend of mine. He is very sympathetic towards Indians. You should go and meet him. If you like, I can accompany you.'

'No, that's help enough. Everyone must find his own way to the goal.'

'Allah is all powerful. You are sure to succeed. I am now sure, Gandhibhai, that it was our fate that drew you here, and that you came here only for us. Our blessings cannot go in vain.'

'Abdullahbhai, an adhesive performs a very minor function—sticking together things that have been torn or broken. That's the function that I too perform. The rest is up to you and your people. All that I will be doing is to bring all of you together.'

Dada Abdullah left. Mohandas' face glowed as if light refracted from glass was falling on it.

Escombe had raised hope in Mohandas' breast. At least a way had been found. Maybe the mountain could not be moved, but at least a way to do it was in sight. When Mohandas landed at his place, Escombe was in his study. Seeing his card, Escombe sent for him at once. Mohandas saw an avuncular man: a heavy-set figure and a smiling face. As they shook hands, he remarked: 'Gandy, you registered your presence the moment you landed on Durban coast. What you are now busy doing is causing people no less a problem.' After a pause, he completed his statement: 'Your people need you. They are far too simple, weak and helpless.'

'Thanks for the favourable opinion. You throw a stone into a pond and it causes ripples. Never mind even if the thrower is a small child. The pond takes it all. The stagnation in India was of another kind. In this country, they have turned into a kind of ditch, which presents a more serious problem than stagnant water in a pond. All that I am trying to do is to stir the mud. In the end, of course, it is they who must stir.'

'You are a young barrister. You are self-aware. This self-awareness makes others also conscious of their self. Though I haven't had the chance of meeting you but I have heard about you and I have also sometimes seen you. Tell me what I can do for you.'

'I am a Bar-at-Law. I used to practise at the Bombay High Court. I want to be registered in the Natal Supreme Court. I learn that if my application is presented before the Court by the Advocate General, it could be considered. Natal Law Society is dead set against it.'

Escombe laughed: 'I know. That is one of the duties of the Advocate General. Please let me have all the papers. I'll take a look and if everything is in order. I'll move it before the Court on next Monday.'

'But the Law Society ...?'

'Why do you worry about it? Law and justice are synonymous. If there is no law, there is no justice; and if there is no justice, law becomes meaningless. You must have seen, holding aloft the scales of justice, the blind-folded figure of the goddess of law in the Chief Justice's chamber. Once you enter the portals of a court, individuals and institutions cease to matter.'

Mohandas didn't know how to thank him. He hadn't the slightest expectation that the Advocate General would give him such a patient hearing and would agree to present his candidature before the highest court of the land without demur.

This was nothing short of a miracle to him.

~

The Law Society had nominated one of their senior members to contest Mohandas' application. He also had links with Dada Abdullah. Dada Abdullah told Mohandas: 'Why don't you go and meet the Law Society lawyer? He knows about you.'

Mohandas thought for a while and said: 'I don't think it would be proper for me to see him. It could be taken as an attempt on my part to influence him or to get him to back me. I think it would be wrong both morally and professionally.'

'To tell you the truth, he actually wants to see you. I didn't want to tell you because he had asked me not to.'

'Is it because of your recommendation?'

'No. It's because he wants to understand the case thoroughly.'

When Mohandas went to see him, he took him to a secluded room and put it to him without mincing his words: 'Mr. Gandy, first and foremost, please understand that I am not opposed to you. I have no reason to be. The only thing that worries me is that you may be some colonial-born adventurer or may have links with some extremist group. One reason for this suspicion is that you have not submitted the original certificate. There have been a couple of cases where people have become advocates using someone else's diploma.'

'But this profession here is exclusively white, isn't it?'

The attorney smiled and said: 'Yes, of course, but no one has a monopoly on lying.'

'I thought we were supposed to have it.'

'Not true. Dada Abdullah had also told me about you. Now I learn from you that your father was prime minister of some Indian state. Testimonials from the two European businessmen have no significance for me. What would they know about you? There are people here who have no problem in issuing such testimonials without any knowledge of the person concerned. This is clearly illegal.'

'You are quite right. I am a total stranger here. I am known better in Pretoria, where I worked with Mr. Baker for a year. I had met Dada Abdullah here a year ago and got an opportunity to work on one of his cases with Mr. Baker.'

'Since Dada Abdullah and you come from the same place, and since your father was Prime Minister of the state there, I am sure Mr. Abdullah would be familiar with your family. His testimonial I think would carry more weight. I would then be able to tell the Law Society that keeping Mr. Gandy from becoming an advocate would be difficult.'

Mohandas felt anger rising within him, but he held it back. What the Law Society attorney had said had raised a number of questions in his mind. What did the man want? If he had not enclosed testimonials from the two white businessmen and instead only one from Dada Abdullah, it would have been called a case of Indian intrigue. Conditions not fulfilled, hence application rejected! After all, how could a coloured or coolie businessman be compared with a white one? He tells me now that Dada Abdullah's certificate would work better since he would know my family! What has my registration got to do with my family? Shouldn't he be concerned with my qualifications and my education rather than with who my mother was, what my father did or how my grandfather earned his livelihood? Suppose they got the answers to all these questions, would they then approve my application without satisfying themselves with regard to my qualifications? But Mohandas didn't allow any of these questions to come to his lips. Instead, he put the matter in another way: 'What I can't understand is why the Law Society wants to know all this about me. I doubt that they have the right to ask for all this information.' His voice was getting sharper, but he controlled himself and said: 'If you want a testimonial from Dada Abdullah, I have no objections. But I don't think such a minor change will satisfy the Law Society and it will let me become an advocate. Pardon me for saying so, but I suspect a deeper motive behind this.'

The attorney looked at Mohandas for a brief moment but said nothing.

As he left, Mohandas said: 'I am indeed grateful for the time you allowed me, Mr. Attorney. I however want to make it clear that if I am not allowed to register I will go back to my country, but I will not hesitate to raise my voice.'

The objections that had been raised by Law Society against Mohandas were not only disgraceful but also irrelevant. The first objection was that since Mr. Gandhi had not submitted his degree certificate in the original it was hard to accept his claim. Second, so far only whites had been nominated as advocates in the colony while the applicant was a coloured person. The work of a lawyer required analytical ability and not everyone necessarily possessed this ability. If a coloured Indian was accepted as an advocate, there might soon be a rush for registration, which would not only adversely affect the serious profession of law but would also affect its dignity. It would also contribute to the psychological, economic and social pressures on the local community.

When the objections of the Law Society were presented, Mr. Escombe was not present in the court. The Chief Justice gave a very close hearing to the Society's lawyer and then gave a judgment which took both sides by surprise. Everyone wondered how the Chief Justice could do such a thing.

The judgment said that though it was correct that Mr. Gandhi's application did not carry the degree certificate in the original, an attested copy was enclosed. It would of course have been preferable if the original certificate had been attached. However, even if it was assumed that the attested copy was a false one, surely the applicant could be penalized under the colony laws and his name could be struck off the advocates' list. 'As for the argument put forward by the opposing party's lawyer that only whites have so far been allowed into this profession ... how long is this going to go on? In any case, in the eyes of the law, there is no such distinction between white and black. Everyone must get what he is qualified to get—that is the logical thing to do. It is therefore decided that Mr. Gandhi's name be included in the Advocates' Roll. Mr. Gandhi's application is hereby admitted and he is registered as an advocate under the colony law.'

The judgment was greeted with such stunned silence that for a while one could even have heard the breath come and go, but the breath of the white lawyers, who filled the court, seemed to have stopped. They had come to the court quite assured that a coolie barrister would never become an advocate and that the victory would be theirs. He would be forced to leave the colony. Now that they had heard the judgment, they were wondering how they could best retain some of their dignity in the presence of the coolie barrister.

All of a sudden, the Chief Justice's stentorian voice boomed through the court: 'Mr. Gandy, take off your turban. Once you have become an officer of the court, it becomes your bounden duty to observe the conventions of the court.'

Mohandas raised his head and looked at the Chief Justice. There he was—seated in his full glory on the ornate high chair, but to Mohandas he looked like the magistrate who, a year ago, had issued him the same order in a Durban courtroom. He looked at the Chief Justice once again. Once again, the same idea started flashing in his mind that he should excuse himself and leave the court. For the first time, having won despite the opposition of the Law Society, he had been able to sit erect with dignity. Not just him alone but the entire Indian community, who had so far never had a person in their sights who they could have looked at with pride and said that he was one of theirs. But when this idea flashed in his mind, he felt his spine buckle. He had a split second to make his decision. The Registrar stood waiting to swear him in. He looked towards his friends, who had come with him all the way from Durban. They too looked undecided—would he take off his turban or would he walk out?

Mohandas heard someone whisper: 'He will not take off his turban. He didn't do it in Durban.'

Mohandas' hands rose slowly and went up to the turban. The turban came off, and quite as slowly, landed on the table before him, as if it was made of glass. Dada Abdullah clasped his head in despair. Others also sat stunned. The white lawyers had lost again. They were depending on the so-called stupidity of the coolies, but now they sat with their heads hanging on their chests.

The joy of success seemed to have been wiped off the faces of his companions. When the decision had been announced, it had seemed that they would get up and start dancing with joy. The dance at his victory would have been the first steps of the dance towards the freedom of Indians. Of course, the realization that they were sitting in a courtroom had forced them to keep their feet from skipping and jumping. Had they been white, they might well have overstepped this convention.

When they came out, Dada Abdullah questioned him in a sad voice: 'What did you do, Gandhibhai? You took your turban off at the Chief Justice's bidding?'

Bayat was also with them. In fact, they were all staying at his house. He said: 'We were thinking you would rather walk out of the court than remove your turban. We didn't know that we from Pietermaritzburg were destined to witness such a sight.'

Mohandas listened to them quietly. When they were done, he spoke: 'Do you believe I didn't think of these things? Or that I have forgotten the humiliation I suffered in the Durban courtroom? That insult still runs through my veins like molten lead. My first thought was of course to excuse myself and leave the court. But the two situations were quite different. On the earlier occasion I had gone as a spectator. Today I was taking oath as an officer of the court. Then I was an independent individual; today I was a subordinate of the court. It was now my duty to follow the customs and orders of the court. I think that, in any case, our present situation demands that we ignore the small fights and concentrate on the war.'

Unconvinced, Dada Abdullah said: 'Maybe you are right. Actually, people like us who are used to daily humiliations, tend to become defensively sentimental the moment someone reminds us of our self-respect. On that occasion, when you had refused to take off your turban and preferred to walk out of the court, our chests had swollen with pride. We know very well that had anyone of us been in your place, he would have surrendered to the will of the court on that very day. When you didn't do it, we had felt mighty happy. In the court today, when the decision went in our favour, we felt we had won a big battle, but when you took off your turban at the bidding of the Chief Justice, we felt cheated of our victory.'

'I fully understand your feelings,' said Mohandas: 'but I had only two options: either leave this colony and go home or accept the court's bidding and do my bit in carrying on this struggle. There was a third option too: to live as a parasite on the money collected for the struggle. That option was not acceptable to me.'

It was hard to say whether Mohandas' arguments had convinced them or not.

~

The affair hit the headlines of newspapers the next day. A Coolie is an Advocate! Law Society Protests and Bites the Dust! Chief Justice Brushes aside the Arguments of Law Society Lawyers! White Lawyers Upset! Coolies Celebrate!

Not a single paper mentioned the turban incident.

~

Incidents, in the mean time, had moved at a fast pace. Petition to the Speaker of the parliament, meeting with the Natal Prime Minister, petition to the governor of the colony, Sir Walter Francis Hely-Hutchinson, and his rejection of the petition, fast-paced passage of the franchise bill through the parliament and its immediate dispatch to the Queen for her approval. The Indians would have to organize themselves at every level. The biggest challenge before Mohandas was how to steer this popular struggle to success.

He addressed a meeting of the Indians:

> *It was perhaps a mistake on my part to take on complete trust the fair-mindedness and love of justice of the white society. I believed that if we could*

stir awake their fair-mindedness and their sense of judgment, they would surely try to find a just and logical solution to our problems. It was with this belief that we had presented a petition to the members and the speaker of the parliament.

He reflected for a while and then continued:

It's of course true that our petition reached them late, but we were not to blame for the delay. The Natal government had contrived to get the bill passed on the sly. It's a bit of a mystery how that four-line news item got into the newspapers, which alerted us. Our petitions, however, were consigned to the waste basket. The prime minister offered the delay excuse, while the governor did not consider the petition deserving of any attention. I believe that the bill to deprive Indians of franchise rights was not moved without premeditation ...

Mohandas was silent for a while. Everyone waited eagerly for him to complete his statement with their gaze fixed on his face. Mohandas resumed his speech:

Whenever the party in power takes a decision, it knows well enough who will benefit from the decision and who will be the loser. In my view, petitioning and praying do not produce any effect. They don't lead you anywhere, though, of course, they are the biggest tools of a democracy. By turning a deaf ear to them, the masters only add to your misery. In fact, they take pleasure in adding to the misery of the already miserable and mistreated. My motive in telling you all this is only to tell you not to despair and not to accept defeat. To do so will only mean getting deeper into the trap they have laid for you. I have learnt that the bill has been sent for the approval of the Queen. If it is approved, the Indian immigrants will be forced to live a life worse than that of bonded labour. If you agree, we can take this fight to London. It may just be possible that we get justice there. If we keep sitting here twiddling our thumbs, I am sure we will be inviting a living death for ourselves.

Haji Mohammad Haji Dada, trying to draw Mohandas' attention, said: 'Gandhibhai, the petition that we had sent to the parliament on July 6, 1894, carrying my and my friends' signatures, was presented to the House by Honourable Cambley. That petition carried an excerpt from the declaration made by the Queen in 1858 which said something to the effect that "We find ourselves bound to the citizens of India by the same duties and responsibilities which bind us to our other subjects." I therefore feel that the Queen views all her subjects, be they white or black, as standing on the same footing. She had gone on to say: "It's also our wish that all our subjects should be allowed entry into government jobs impartially on the basis of their education, ability and honesty, and without any discrimination based on considerations of race and religion. Our strength lies in the prosperity of our subjects."'

'We are being deprived of our franchise despite the Queen's declaration,' someone commented.

Haji Mohammad Haji continued: 'A voter parent spends a lot of money educating his son in the hope of making him a public-minded citizen. If, at the end of it, he finds that his son has been deprived of his voting right just because he happens to be the son of a coloured parent, despite the fact that he is better qualified to use his vote than his parent was, would it be called being fair to him? Would it not hurt his self-respect?'

Another gentleman, who had also signed that petition, said: 'Didn't we mention in our first petition, citing historical context, that Indians have had a long-standing affair with democracy, tradition and franchise? We also made it clear that this did not mean that every Indian was fully equipped with this knowledge. In view of this, how can one justify depriving the Indian immigrants of this fundamental right?'

'There must be any number of *girmitiya*s whose children have joined the ranks of free citizens. Why only their children, they themselves may have become free citizens. If franchise is denied to them, the Queen's 1858 declaration will remain nothing more than a joke.'

Mohandas said: 'These are precisely the issues of our struggle, and they will continue to fester till honest solutions are found for them. I therefore wish to make a proposal for your consideration. Lord Rippon is the Minister for Colonies in Her Majesty's Government. We must send a petition to him with at least signatures of ten thousand Indians. They may be *girmitiya*s or free Indian immigrants. I know this is not an easy task, but we must do it with total honesty and commitment. It will be difficult for the British Empire to ignore the strength of ten thousand Indian signatures. Unfortunately, we never learnt to stand united. That's what guaranteed us a slave's destiny. Unity here today can become a stepping stone to unity in India tomorrow. We will have to set out as volunteers, packed lunches in our bags, to collect signatures. Are we ready?'

Every single hand went up. Mohandas felt that every single Indian, from *here* to *there*, was standing in formation. A new chapter had opened. No one knew how it was going to end.

The responsibility for the petition to be sent to Lord Rippon had fallen on Mohandas. He was well aware what it entailed. The task of articulating the voice, suppressed for hundreds of years, of such a large community in the petition was extremely difficult, if not plainly impossible. It was absolutely essential to take that voice to the ears of the Empress and her government. The bill, having been passed by the House, was now with the Governor. It could be sent to London any time now. The petition to be sent to Lord Rippon must reach the Governor before the bill did. And Mohandas had to do it all by himself. There were of course many hands ready to help, but the draft of the petition was his responsibility alone. He had to collect the material—books, figures, facts—without which the draft could not be made ready.

Mohandas collected whatever books he could that very night. He already had a few books, a few more he had to get hold of. Then he dug out some figures. Next he went around collecting information from old and experienced inhabitants of the place; looked up some gazettes; collected information from the Protector's office about Indians who had come on *girmit*s as well about those who had come as travellers. Getting this information out of the Protector's office was nothing short of finding water in a desert. The reputation of Dada Abdullah and his own status as a barrister did help to make the task somewhat easier. Although the Protector had been specifically appointed to gather information about incoming and outgoing Indians and to look after their interests, how effective he was or could be, in performing his duties was a question best left to individual assessment.

The blueprint of the draft to be sent to the Empress that Mohandas had in mind included all those things which highlighted the historical and social background of the Indian community. He knew that another reason why these things had to be brought to the notice of the British government was that if in future the context was the whole of India, these facts could not be denied.

When the parliament had suspended consideration of the bill for two days in response to the telegram from them, the Indians had celebrated it as their victory over the whites. They had then felt as if their goal was almost within reach. But it was nothing of the sort. In their enthusiasm, they had got hundreds of signatures in a single night. What was the fate of that petition? The rubbish bin. Mohandas was worried that if, with the memory of that petition still fresh in their minds, people refused to come forward enthusiastically to sign the Lord Rippon petition, all efforts would be wasted. The weight of the petition would be determined by the ten thousand signatures on it, not by the paper on which it was written.

Another of his worries was that the business community which was helping him had absolutely no idea of the life of the *girmitiya*s. They had only seen it from a distance. They themselves had mostly arrived as travellers. There were a few who had arrived as *girmitiya*s, but when the period of *girmit* was over, they had become free citizens. They were mostly still grappling with the problems of a life of *girmit*. Some young men were in the range of twenty to thirty. They were all Natal born. They worked as lawyers' office assistants, compounders, compositors, clerks and a couple of them were photographers. A few of them were also propertied men. There were twenty-six Indian schools, and two and a half thousand children were studying in them. Mohandas included all these facts in his petition. The petition was not merely a list of demands; it also carried a detailed description of the efforts made by the community.

When Mohandas read out the draft to his friends, it immediately gave rise to a controversy. The reason was that while Mohandas had words of praise for Mr. Cambley and Mr. Don for their support to the bill, he had also challenged their comments running down the *girmitiyas*.

Ahmed Jiwa disagreed with his position. 'They are illiterate, worthless, and poor,' he said: 'it's their destiny that they should slave under the white.'

'And what's ours?' Mohandas asked.

C. Lakshmiram butted in: 'We are two sides of the same coin,' he said: 'we and the *girmitiyas*. Let's beware that we might lose this fight for franchise just because of this emerging conflict between us. If the whites find out that we want the franchise only for those Indians who came to this colony as travellers, they are sure to exploit this division and will turn us down.'

Dada Abdullah and Parsi Rustomji tried to intervene and sort out the issue. 'What do you think, Gandhibhai? Where do you stand on this matter?'

Mohandas did not react immediately. A little later, he asked: 'Does the Natal businessman have it in him to fight this battle all by himself? If he does, does he also hope to win the battle? So many people in India, among them the most distinguished and the most ordinary, have been talking of independence. What has been the outcome? You take a small-bottomed pot and it will take only as much water as its capacity allows. If you need more water, you must either enlarge its bottom or get a big-bottomed pot.'

Adamji Miyakhan said in his usual jocular vein: 'In that case it might be better to go to a riverside or a pond to do the ablutions. And if you need an even bigger bottom, what's wrong with going to the sea itself?'

Everyone laughed. Mohandas didn't like it. He turned serious at once and said: 'More than half the humanity today lives in extreme slavery. If this situation continues, it will probably continue to live the same way even after the chains of slavery are broken—out of sheer habit. When the society finds out that it has in its hands a weapon which can slay the mightiest of the mighty, mankind will be ready to misuse it, and people like you and me will be helping it to misuse the most.'

Mohandas was agitated, so he paused, recovered and then spoke: 'Do excuse me. You and I have so much to gain. Franchise gives you status; it protects your business interests but what are these *girmitiya*s going to gain? Not a shilling is going to be added to their income. For them, the biggest blessing is freedom. You and I cannot understand what freedom means to them. A *girmitiya* slaves away for tens of years, hoping and praying for his liberty, but before he is able to see the sun of freedom rise, he dies. For him, franchise is the only door through which freedom may walk in. He can neither kill nor fight the tyranny unleashed on him. The whole of India is a slave like they are. If you want to fight this war, do not fight it as your personal war. It is quite possible that the flames of this war may reach India tomorrow and you may get the credit for starting it. I wish God wills it that way.' Mohandas fell silent.

'You mean ...?' The words followed after a gap.

'I mean exactly what you have heard. Please don't take me amiss. Knowingly or not, you are putting the *girmitiya*s in the same category as the natives, who are not even aware of their problems. It is true that they are poor and that their way of living leaves much to be desired, but they understand the values of life and they haven't lost their sensitivity. That is why in fact they have come this far to earn a living. Nor do they indulge in behaviour which goes against the values of their culture. Unlike the natives, they are not content with their existing condition. They are dissatisfied and restless. Dissatisfaction is a symbol of man's determination to stand against stagnation and status quo. They are trying constantly to overcome their stagnation and inaction. There are many of you who have overcome that stagnation and are now leading the life of a free citizen. Their struggle is greater than the struggle of those who came here as travellers and then settled down into a stable life. They should be objects of respect and honour, not neglect.'

The same gentleman interjected: 'Our proposal should be a realistic one.'

Adamji Miyakhan elaborated the point: 'Gandhibhai, we must keep it in mind that in the event the Empress expresses an inclination to concede our demands, she should not be put off by an unrealistic proposal on our part. How can a government which is disinclined to confer franchise on competent, reputable, and well known Indians ever agree to confer it on *girmitiya*s, who are lackeys, cooks and coachmen to the whites, who work in their fields growing sugarcane and who lay railway tracks for them?'

Parsi Rustomji intervened: 'We may be able to reclaim our rights piecemeal but reclaiming them at a single stroke may be difficult. Why don't we put it this way: every free Indian should be given franchise? As they earn their freedom, so they will also earn their citizenship rights.'

Mohandas spoke in a slow but leaden voice: 'This is your struggle. If that is what you think, let it be that way. They too will have to fight a battle some day. Whether you agree or not, it is these very people who will one day show themselves to be the ramparts from behind which this whole struggle will be carried on, these very people whom today you want to cut off from your company, labelling them *girmitiya*s. You are of course important in your way, but they are important for one and all. No change is possible without including them. They can cause a flood, and they can also stand as a bulwark against a flood.'

Everyone was looking at Mohandas' face. It bore a shadow of reflection, and it was flushed.

There was a general agreement on Parsi Rustomji's proposal. Mohandas agreed to it arguing that if voting rights are what they were fighting for, they must start by respecting their use in their own affairs. If you are fighting a war, you must be true to it. However, he added the following words to the petition: 'Though franchise may not be granted during the period of the *girmit*, when one is released from the *girmit* and is able to acquire experience and qualifications as a free citizen, to deny him franchise would be plain injustice. Poverty and deprivation are not crimes. Franchise can be taken away only from those who have been convicted as criminals in the eyes of the law. These people are all honest and responsible individuals.'

Mohandas had thus managed to say what he wanted to say, though in a different way. Not many of them could figure it out.

~

Getting ten thousand signatures on the petition was a Herculean task. The responsibility for it had been taken by traders, office clerks, and a few free *girmitiya* hawkers. There were about forty-five thousand people of Indian origin in Natal. There were about as many whites. Mohandas had included this statistic in the petition. The idea therefore was to get the signatures of about one-fourth of the Indian population.

In the meantime, Mohandas had dispatched a letter to the Governor. It said:

> *Your Excellency, we understand that you are likely to forward the franchise amendment bill passed by the parliament recently to the Empress for her approval. The Indians of Natal are in the process of sending a petition in regard to this bill to the Minister of Colonies in Her Majesty's government. This petition should reach Your Excellency shortly. We would be very grateful if the papers relating to the bill are kept in abeyance till such time as the petition reaches Your Excellency. This issue is intimately related to the question of honour, identity and prestige of our country and to the life and death of the Indians living in this colony.*

The campaign had started. The carriages of the businessmen and their horses had already left on the mission. Those without resources were marching on their feet like the infantry. The time allowed was a fortnight. Everyone approached, literate or not, took the sheet in his hands, turned it over once or twice and then asked: 'What does it contain?' Mohandas had made it clear to everyone that getting any signatures or thumb impressions without first explaining the purpose of the petition would be wrong. People also wanted to know how they would gain if they signed and how they would lose if they didn't. Questions like these put the volunteers in a quandary.

They would try saying: 'Franchise is our stepping stone to freedom. If we can secure the right to vote we can raise our voice against repression and exploitation, and make it heard to people in the highest positions.'

'What is this freedom? We have heard only the big shots have it.'

All that they would then be able to say was: 'Gandhibhai says everyone has an equal right to it.'

They sniggered: 'Gandhibhai indeed ...'

The settlements were scattered far and wide. There were large farms and forests which stretched up to the horizon. After walking for miles, they would come across an isolated settlement or two where there were a few Indians. Farms of course had barracks where the *girmitiya*s lived. Those who were not *girmitiya*s mostly lived in clusters, bound together by the similarity of their work and lifestyles. They lived where they worked or contrarily, they worked where they lived.

When the signature parties arrived at the barracks, the farm owners and sirdars were alarmed: 'What do you mean by coming here?'

'What do you mean by "What do you mean?" They are our brothers. Is it a sin to meet them?'

'You can't enter the place without permission.'

The *girmitiya*s were scared. They were afraid even to open their mouths in the presence of the sirdars. But the volunteers did not lose heart. They would manage to meet them on the sly, in ones and twos. A few signed or gave their thumb impressions. Some refused flatly. Their argument was: 'Here we are so far from our homes. Who is going to look after us? If the white masters get to know they will eat us for breakfast.'

'We'll only do what our masters tell us to do.'

A few of them would later turn up secretly and give their thumb impressions. 'We wish things would change,' they would say: 'here as well as at home. May the kingdom of Lord Rama thrive again! At least our next generation may be spared the hardships we are going through.'

Mohandas accompanied one or the other group of volunteers. When he saw the people, his thought was: what sort of country is it that cannot look after its own children? Would India ever change? It must change. A restlessness took hold of him. It only helped to confirm his belief that franchise was the only possible catalyst of change. A cry would rise from his soul: 'Listen, you whites! You have taken everything from these poor souls—their freedom, their home, their country ... at least don't take away their franchise. Who knows one day they may regain their lost lives on the strength of their franchise alone.'

Mohandas tried to explain it to them: 'Franchise is the biggest strength of the poor and the weak. It can change their destiny.' The arguments he offered in support were only heard from his mouth; they were nowhere to be found in books or religions. He said: 'If you keep your feelings bottled up within you, you will suffocate. Nobody will ever come and ask you: "What is eating you?" But if you speak out, they will have to listen. There are things you can share with each other. There are things, however, you must say to those people who simply don't appreciate that you too may have some complaints, some thing to say. For that purpose, you need to have franchise. The man who gets elected with your vote will sit where laws are made, where they playact at giving relief. He will go and tell them what a terrible life you are leading all because you are victims of their neglect. People will then get to know the truth about you. They will know that it is not only their troubles that matter, but that those who are suffering a living death every moment of their lives also have something to say. There will be some among them who have feelings and they will support you. But even if there are none, your voice will carry to your own brethren and will bring you all together.'

They found what Mohandas said so easy to grasp.

Mohandas thought of those fellow countrymen of Kathiawar who led a life worse than these *girmitiya*s. There were so many principalities with princely expenses like those of large states and they could only meet them through exploitation of their subjects, through forced labour and repression. That was the story of the poor all over India; they had to pay for the comforts and luxuries of the princely class. In this country, they did manage to get, one way or another, something to eat, even if not enough. But at what cost? Exiled from home and hearth. Exiled from their country. Homeless and countryless. A foreign land. Whiplashes on their backs! The food did put out the fire in their bellies but it lit another fire in their hearts. Fear enveloped them day and night, like the smoke that enveloped their cubicles and hadn't found an outlet to this day. The morning smoke stayed till the evening; the evening smoke relieved the morning smoke so that it could come and start work the next day. Thatched roofs, mud walls, cubicles sliced from windowless barracks, smoked cobwebs dangling all over the place. Suffocating, damp and stinking. Pots being scrubbed, clothes washed, children urinating, all in a corner of the cubicle, a hole in the wall emptying the sewage into a ditch outside to stay there permanently, breeding mosquitoes and wriggling worms, all of them sharing their lives with them.

What could Mohandas do? For the fruit to ripen, the roots had to be attended to first. Sick roots could hardly be expected to yield any fruit. There was a song of death rising from India which shook him to his innermost self. He wanted to scream: 'Stop! You may die or you may live there, but you will surely be the death of everyone here! The land here doesn't even know their smell; if they die here, they will die strangers to the land. This is their fault: they were born there! They came to this land to escape death, only to find that death was already waiting to greet them here.'

Things were becoming clearer to Mohandas. Everyone, whether he was here or there, was suffering the same fear and the same agony. Those who are here may or may not be aware of the suffering of the people there, but those who are there certainly know nothing of the suffering of the people here. Even so, there is a bond which holds them together. They may have grumbled, they may have been fearful, they may have made excuses, but these people had signed or given their thumb impressions in large numbers. Mohandas found it amazing that in their innermost selves a dim light still burnt like a dying lamp.

The teams returned from their missions and submitted their work for Mohandas' scrutiny. He was astonished. Turning the sheets gleaming with so many signatures and thumb impressions over and over again, he lost the sense of time. He lost the sense of space too, not remembering if he was in India or Natal. Were the signatories Indians or immigrant Natal Indians? Actually, he had blurted out the figure of ten thousand without giving any serious thought to the matter. Later he had regretted the lapse by which he had put his companions to an impossible test. He had also come round to the idea that they would have to make do with whatever number they could muster. But the signatures and thumb impressions before him far exceeded the number that had escaped his lips like a slip of the tongue. What a miracle! But perhaps it was not so much a miracle as an outburst of nonviolent anger in the form of signatures and thumb impressions of various shapes, sizes, and styles.

The signatories too had taken no end of trouble. Everyone had to write, in his own shapeless hand, his name, caste, religion, village of origin, district, passenger number, date of arrival, name of the ship etc. in full detail. Those who gave thumb impressions escaped all this trouble, but they added to the troubles of the literate man in the team, who had to do all the writing. There was at least one such person in each team. If the team included Mohandas, he did all this work.

Most of the signatories were from South India—from places like Madras, Guntur, Malabar, etc. Names of the ships were also misspelt—*Belvadera, Tourro* and even *Sindhian.* Those who had come on ships sailing from Calcutta had place names like Aara, Gajipur, Benares, Gaya, Chhapra, Purulia, etc. after their names. Lucknow also figured at a few places.

Mohandas read each name one after another. As he looked at each signature and each thumb impression, the variety and diversity swept him off his feet. Almost every language figured in the signatures, and the thumb impressions were of so many types! They seemed to bear the faces of the people they belonged to. And the faces represented the common face of the country.

Mohandas' interest in the signatures soon became an object of comments from the people around: 'What's so great in these signatures that you are poring over them as if they were scriptures?' asked one.

Mohandas replied: 'The whole country is represented here. The India which I could not see in India, I can see in these sheets of papers in its entirety, fully alive! But bloodied and violated. It has entered my soul. It is the Mighty One himself ...' A wave of thrill seemed to race through the people present there. Every single word he had spoken had come alive within them.

'There was something in Gandhibhai's words that ...,' said someone.

Mohandas sat with his head bowed.

~

The petition was carted to the Governor's office. The staff of the Governor's office had a hard time grasping what it was and keeping the pages from falling apart. At first, the Governor's secretary had tried his best to turn them down.

'Please name the law which allows you to refuse our petition,' Gandhibhai had to argue. 'This is our appeal. It must reach the Queen, come what may. Please tell us under what provision of the law you are refusing to accept it. We will then send the petition directly to London, mentioning the law. I have already written to His Excellency, the Governor about the petition.'

The Secretary had no reply to Mohandas' questions, so he accepted the petition without further ado. He however looked quite annoyed. He could not understand how a coolie could dare to talk to him in that way?

The petition was put before the Governor. Sixteen pages of writing and hundreds of pages containing signatures of the petitioners.

The Governor asked the ADC: 'What's all this? What's all this rubbish doing here?'

'Your Excellency! A coolie barrister called M.K.Gandhi has submitted this petition against the franchise bill with signatures of ten thousand coolies. This has to be sent to the Colonial Secretary. He has requested that Your Excellency may kindly forward this petition to him along with the Franchise Amendment Bill.'

The Governor was speechless. He looked at his ADC, who stood erect like a statue. The Governor had never seen such a huge petition before.

'Ten thousand signatures and thumb impressions! How is that possible? That is one-fourth of the total coolie population. Is the fellow a magician? I have heard India is full of them. Or maybe he is a madcap. Wasting so much time on this useless exercise!'

'Yes, sir!' said the ADC with a jerk of his head.

The Governor took a deep breath and said: 'What can I possibly do? Let him be a miracle man, if that's what he is. The Prime Minister did indeed write to me about him and I agree with him. These Indians are capable of anything. But, I tell you, all this coolie labour is not going to have any effect on me. Who the hell cares! Gandy is trying to put moral pressure on me.'

He kept looking at the pile of papers before him for sometime. He picked up a few of them and fluttered them in the air. Then he got up and paced up and down the room and started muttering to himself: 'He is a difficult man. How can we possibly give franchise to these illiterate coolies?' He was now looking worried. 'This single coolie is trying to upset the equilibrium of the colony. This cannot be permitted.'

The ADC stood like a statue while the Governor carried on with his soliloquy. From his face, you couldn't figure out if the ADC was listening to what he was saying or not.

~

Sir Pherozeshah Mehta ...! Mohandas suddenly remembered. He had first met him in Rajkot soon after his first experience of humiliation. The slightest humiliation was then sufficient to send Mohandas off balance. Things were different now: they were on quite friendly terms. You wouldn't find Mohandas without there being some humiliation and insult around. On the insistence of his older brother, he had gone to make a recommendation regarding him to the British political agent with whom he had been on friendly terms in London. He of course realized that he could never possibly be on such friendly terms with a white political agent as to make recommendations to him. He may have been a friend in London, but here he was a master. Still, he succumbed to the persistent requests of his brother and went to see him. The moment he heard his brother mentioned, the political agent seemed to go raving mad. The utter lack of consideration with which he got him thrown out of the room by his peon was an insult Mohandas had been unable to accept. It gave him no peace. He spent days and nights thinking about it. He wasn't able to stop himself from threatening legal action against him.

Sir Pherozeshah was then in Rajkot in connection with a court case. Stung by the insult, Mohandas was then hopping around madly like a crazy moth. Yes, he thought, this was the only way to teach the white man a lesson: legal action. He rounded up a lawyer friend and went to see Sir Pherozeshah. He was an elderly man with an imposing presence. That first meeting was firmly imprinted on Mohandas' soul like a mural.

Mohandas told him the whole story, as he listened with his eyes closed. When it ended, he asked: 'What is it you want?'

'I want to avenge my insult. I want to drag him to the court.'

That was his first experience of Sir Pherozeshah's sobriety and simplicity. He said: 'Young man! Such incidents are regular happenings in the lives of lawyers and barristers. Your blood is still running hot and England is still alive within you. You know nothing about British officers. Tell me how many of them you are going to fight. If you want to live in peace, tear up the letter he wrote to you in response to your note. Go and earn your living and live happily. This insult will teach you to exercise self-control. Tolerance might show you another way of dealing with the issues of life. In any case, have you learnt law to defend yourself or to defend others?' And he had laughed like a child.

Mohandas recalled the entire sequence of events. He could now well see how the counsel he had given him was perhaps right. He decided to write a note to

Sir Pherozeshah detailing the conditions in the colony of Natal hoping to attract his attention. Maybe he could show him a way out of the dark. He wrote:

Sir,

A copy of the petition to the British government regarding the Franchise Amendment Bill of Natal Indians has been sent to you under separate cover. Through this letter, I am taking the liberty of informing you regarding the conditions obtaining in the colony. I hope you will take it in that spirit.

Mr. Escombe is the Advocate General of Natal. In his report on the bill, he said that the only purpose of this bill was to prevent the Asians from seeking participation in the government of Natal and to impose restrictions on Indians which would reduce them to a state of humiliation and would render their continued stay in Natal untenable. Not everyone of course wants to drive the Indians out. Certainly not those Indians who are involved in agriculture and work in their farms as girmitiyas. *Such Indians are indispensable to them for their own prosperity, because they work more for less. But the conditions in which these Indians are forced to live are worse than a pigsty. If it had not been for their selfish interests, they would have dispatched these Indians home, packing them like goats and sheep in the holds of ships. Is this the famous British justice under which a lion and a goat are supposed to live happily together in the same stall? If the British government allows this bill to become law, the Natal whites will get what they have always wanted.*

A member of the local parliament thinks that the British government will never allow this bill to become law. Nevertheless, the Indians here are extremely apprehensive. It is absolutely essential that the Empress does not give her approval to the bill.

I am of the view that, in the eyes of Indians, compared to other colonies, Natal is a better place. Indian businessmen lead a relatively more respectable life here. Those Indians who could never dream of owning a piece of land in their own country can, on completion of their girmit *period, become owners of a plot of land in lieu of rent, in case they do not wish to return home. The dream they had in their own country can be fulfilled here. As the end of the* girmit *period approaches, they begin to see a slight hope of freedom and self-sufficiency. This bill will destroy that hope completely. The whites here are seized with the fear that the government of the colony will gradually pass into the hands of Indians. This fear is totally groundless. The Indians are here to earn their living. They have no ambitions of this kind nor will they ever have them. They are simple people, concerned only with minding their own business.*

Yours truly,

Mohandas K. Gandhi

~

During this entire period, Marcel Ledue had been missing. In fact, once or twice, Mohandas had actually said to Dada Abdullah: 'Haven't seen Mr. Ledue for sometime.'

Dada Abdullah laughed: 'The less we see of him, the better. Your name and your deeds cause him to see red.'

'Some people have faces which are like red cloth ...' Mohandas laughed at his own comment.

'If you call yourself the red cloth, what does that make Mr. Ledue?'

'Not my words,' said Mohandas and they both laughed this time.

Then, one day, as Mohandas was coming out of Dada Abdullah's house he saw Marcel going in.

'Running around a lot these days, this fellow Gandhi, isn't he?' Marcel said to Dada Abdullah.

'Why do you say that?'

'I have warned you before. He is going to make you look like enemies in the eyes of the government, and a hostile government is going to ruin all that you have achieved. He has of course nothing to lose. He will cut and run.'

'The government's hostility is inevitable. No government likes people who want to have a say in their own affairs.'

'This is a whim of Gandhi. He wants to play out his fantasies at your cost. He doesn't really want to leave this place and therefore keeps finding new excuses for staying on here.'

'It was actually all of us who got together and stopped him from going.'

'Cleverer than a fox, that's what he is. What he wants done he gets others to ask for instead of asking it himself. He is using you while you think you are using him. It's quite possible that he may cross over to the other side, leaving you high and dry. When he is with you he talks about the Quran; when he is with Christians he starts reading out the Bible. The man has no religion and no honesty.'

Dada Abdullah had this strange capacity: he could laugh even when angry. So he laughed and said: 'Don't you worry yourself, Marcel Sahib. We will sort it out amongst ourselves. You sahibs cannot possibly understand our problems as well as we can.'

'The responsibility for this whole thing will rest on you: you are the one who helped him find his way in. As a friend, I completely disapprove of this.'

Dada Abdullah stood up: 'Please excuse me ...' he said.

Marcel got up, lingered for a minute and then shot out of the room. Dada Abdullah followed him but he had already disappeared.

~

IX

Mohandas was now Gandhibhai in the fullest sense. To get the signatures on the petition against the Franchise Amendment Bill, he had to go from settlement to settlement. He wasn't prepared to see what he saw there. One couldn't of course speak much about how they had lived in their own country, but they had come to a foreign land hoping to improve their living and to live happily ever after. The misery in the foreign land however had turned out to be worse than the misery at home.

During winter nights, the women of the house would sometimes sing songs: it helped you pass the night and also to spare a thought for those who had been forsaken. Mohandas did not always follow the meaning, but the night would drown in the sounds of beating drums and clanging cymbals as if sinking and rising in waves of sorrow.

As the night rolled on, Gandhibhai found himself too sinking and rising in the half-recognized pain. There was one song which he felt was being specially sung for him. The words of the song meant something like the following:

Listen, O Indian!
We have been uprooted from our land,
We shed tears on our fate.
When the ship left Calcutta… and Bombay,
My brother, my sister, my mother, and my home… got left behind.
I remember my land…
I cry.
We simple villagers
Were at the mercy of beastly men.
Brother sold out brother…

Son robbed the mother
For a few grains of wheat
We lost our honour
And turned beggars.

When the music stopped, Mohandas felt as if someone had wrung out his heart. Excruciating pain shot through his heart. He couldn't sleep the whole night. When the direction of the wind was favourable a line or half of a song being sung somewhere far away fell into his ear like a drop of molten lead: 'How do I spend the night in this darkened cell!'

He was thinking: 'These people didn't come here of their own will. Hunger-driven, they ran and ran till they landed here. They didn't see the land, they didn't see the sea; they didn't see who wished them well and who didn't give a damn; they didn't see if it was their own land or a land of strangers; they didn't see the pit. Someone was singing away:

If you raise your head,
You get it on the head;
If you dare to stand,
They kick you to the ground;
They call you an idiot,
They call you a fool,
The rest I just can't get.

'Can such things really happen,' Mohandas wondered. 'Can people live such a life and still sing? Does this song rise from their pain or is it just music?' Those who had come as travellers to this country had very different experiences. The only relationship that existed between them, if there was any at all, was that of master and servant. That was the only relationship they knew and respected. The fact of their being Indians did not establish any kind of relationship between them and that worried Gandhibhai. If this gulf between them was not bridged, he felt, they could forget about any better days to come for themselves and for the country from where they have flown out like so many rivers and rivulets. How can they ever fight back? How can they ever claim their rights?

Mohandas often tried telling others that more than half of their countrymen in the colony were in no position to raise their heads. He would recite the line of the song to them: 'If you raise your head/You get it on the head.' At first, they laughed, but when they saw that Gandhibhai was serious they fell silent too. If ever the *Natal Mercury* came out with something in favour of Indians, Mohandas felt as if someone had wiped a tear from their eyes.

Mohandas told them: 'If ever businessmen are hit on their heads, they won't be able to keep standing like *girmitiya*s do; they will be sprawling all over the place. The whites have sucked the bones dry of the last drop of sap. But the *girmitiya*s will survive and they will think of their country as long as they are alive.'

It made Dada Abdullah uncomfortable to hear Gandhibhai talk like this. He would try to change the topic by saying: 'Why do you worry your head about such useless things? Let everyone live the way he chooses.'

Gandhibhai laughed: 'You are right. I shouldn't have worried my head about the franchise business either. It was basically your problem, but I saw the problems of India reflected in it. Otherwise, wouldn't I have been back home spending time with my family at Rajkot?'

A flustered Abdullah Sheth blurted out: 'That wasn't really what I meant.'

'Whatever you might have meant, the fact is that you are rich, and can afford to buy help. You got me too here on a year's *girmit* to help you. Your work is now over. What am I doing here now? Maybe I am here because so many of these Indian coolies who are here to earn a living have no one to help them. They cannot solve their problems by buying help. In my mind I have a clear picture of the pitiable and inhuman conditions in which they are living. The whole thing is plainly illegal. You cannot see it but I can: creeping and crawling beneath your prosperity are the hapless and helpless slaves, who perhaps shouldn't have come here in the first place. But since they are here, they cannot escape their destiny. I don't know, though, how long they can survive in such conditions, especially when they are without any help.'

Dada Abdullah's face had lost colour. He was nonplussed. All that he could say was: 'I don't know what to say. We have neither wisdom nor ability. None of us, Hindu or Muslim, has ever thought about these questions, nor done anything about them. Call it lack of wisdom or call it the rat race of life. If you are in the rat race, there is no time to think about others.'

Gandhibhai said: 'People like you can take snap decisions in matters where millions are involved and you talk of wisdom and ability in a matter as small as this? I just don't get it. Why don't you say that it just didn't occur to you?'

Dada Abdullah didn't get the point at first, but then said: 'The fact of the matter is that we too came here to earn money in our own way; so did they, in their own way.'

Trying to put the matter off, Mohandas said: 'Fair enough! Daybreak is whenever you wake up ...!'

~

Whenever Gandhibhai looked at the map of South Africa, he thought of his own country. There were Portuguese and French in India as there were in South Africa. The largest part of the country was controlled by the British. The Dutch were gone. There were many similarities between the two countries. People in both countries were mostly agriculturists. The native society in this country was divided into tribes and the chiefs of tribes were the masters. In India, the feudal lords were the masters. The only difference was that the farmers in India were a hard working lot. The land was fertile and produced a variety of crops.

Natal and Transvaal mostly produced corn. Liquor was brewed from corn. Stems of corn were used to make straw beddings the way rice and wheat plant stems were used in India.

Another similarity struck Gandhibhai. Deep down south, India had gold mines. Transvaal too had gold and diamond mines. Till 1840, Johannesburg was a huge grassland. Then the British acquired it from the Dutch. The British were lucky: the mines of Transvaal disgorged gold on a big scale. Johannesburg was gradually turning into an industrial city. Residential areas expanded. That was how Bombay also grew. The rich laid out roads in Johannesburg and lined them with trees transported from far and wide. Wherever they could find a rare plant variety they would bring it and plant it in Johannesburg. Johannesburg was turning into a paradise of trees. Both the trees and the millionaires of Johannesburg were imported from abroad. The grass which once covered it like a single sheet from end to end was no longer to be seen. Mohandas compared it with the big cities of his country. The people in the cities had migrated there on the back of their money power. No *girmit*s for them, and no laws either. It was the labourer who needed a *girmit* and who needed laws. He thought of the Kohinoor diamond produced by the Golconda mines. Transvaal too had its own diamond called Kulinon. A thousand carat diamond named after the owner of the mine.

Different parts of South Africa, like different parts of India, were colonies controlled by different countries. Like Goa in India, the Bay of Delagoa in South Africa was under the control of Portugal. This Bay was the gateway to South Africa, though nothing like a Gateway to South Africa had been built there. Next was Natal, which was under British rule. Then came Transvaal. Transvaal had moved from Dutch to British control. Johannesburg was the capital of Transvaal, as Maritzburg was the capital of Natal. Moving south from Transvaal, you came to Orange Free State, also known as Orangia. The capital of Orangia was Blomfontein. Finally you came to Cape colony. Settled on the coast of Cape of Good Hope, the largest port of South Africa and a beautiful city, Cape Town was its capital city. The friendly Table Mountain was also here.

South Africans believe that nature has been partial to Cape Town. It is twice-blessed, with sea as well as with hills. If you made a list of the favours bestowed by nature on India, you would have a very long list indeed. Cape Town sat in the valley below the Table Mountain, relaxed on the coast but alert, like a pretty child in the lap of its mother.

Mohandas often recalled a poem written by some poetess on the Table Mountain:

Not a mountain but a friend!
Doesn't frighten you with its height,
Doesn't ask to be worshipped.
The old and the young and the kids so small
Run atop you,
Laughing and singing and humming aloud,
Trying to make you laugh,
Filling you up with their echoes.
The houses are like nests on you,
They take everything, from the top to the bottom,
To be their own, their very own.
The sea washes your feet while
Tall trees tower on top like dreams
And tittering flowers fall
Scattering their magical fragrance.

The Table Mountain and the poem transported Mohandas to the Himalayas, though he never had had an occasion to see them. The image of the Himalayas struck awe in him, but it did nothing to reduce the Table Mountain. Its very smallness resisted any attempts at reduction.

Gandhibhai had started seeing Africa in India and India in Africa.

~

Messrs M & M were among the mega-agriculturists of Durban, with acres of farmland under cultivation. The influx of foreign workers had not started yet. The matter was hanging fire between the governments of

India and Natal. M & M were exclusively focused on the cultivation of sugarcane and their new crop was a veritable feast to the eye. Standing on a mound, they could see waves of a green ocean rising at one end and sweeping on endlessly as far as the eye could see. Then they returned and kept returning, wave after wave after wave. The ocean of greenery took the onlookers too in its sweep.

Harvesting time for the sugarcane crop was here, but the native workers were displaying a strange attitude. Those workers who worked at the time of sowing spent the rest of the year in their corrals. They treated work as a relay-race. At any given time, half the workers were at work, the other half at rest, the latter inviting a lot more competition than the former. Work was no marathon race for them where even the slowest makes some progress. Here it was a case of rest-while-you-work.

The M & M crop was such a glorious affair that those uninterested also could not help taking a look. The workers who had worked at the time of sowing the crop had returned to their corrals. The sticks had not yet been passed on to the next group of workers. The tribal chiefs were asking for impossible rates for harvesting the crop. A few were even asking for a share in the crop, an idea the whites found impossible to entertain. So what if they had sown the crop? The whites got so mad that they drove the whole lot away and the news spread to all the tribes. The result was that when any of the company's men approached the tribes again, they too were driven away. Chiefs of the more powerful tribes would even go to the extent of saying: 'If it's your writ outside the tribe, it's ours in the tribe !'

One of the chiefs actually put his life at risk by saying: 'When we enter your areas, we are asked for a pass. How dare you come here without a pass?'

And then there were some tribes whose members had already left to harvest other farms.

Finding all avenues closed, M & M wrote to its directors:

In such a situation, we have no other alternative but to shut down all agriculture. If the tribes carry on their intransigent ways, farming is sure to turn into an economic disaster. Even after such huge investments, we are unable to find people to work in the fields. Economic development of this colony seems impossible in such conditions.

When no alternative arrangements were forthcoming even after a lapse of time, directors of the company issued orders that the entire standing crop be put to the torch. Acres of sugarcane were soon going up in flames. It was a heart-breaking sight. It felt as if these were living people burning. A stunned silence enveloped the entire area. The whites were a dejected lot.

The company then took a decision that as long as imported workers were not in place, it would not burn its fingers in agriculture again. It would not allow itself to be manipulated by the natives.

Gandhibhai knew that events like these were what had pressurized the Natal government to work towards import of labour.

Sir George Gray was the governor of Natal. He was slated to address the Town Council. The Town Council was exclusively a council of white farmers and traders. They had prepared a welcome address for the Governor which also reflected their preoccupation with the question of labour imports to help white planters. Their main grouse was that even a small island like Mauritius was streets ahead of them in the production of tropical crops. They had so much land, so much knowledge and wisdom, but labour shortage had reduced everything to naught.

That was their plaint in the welcome address:

Your Excellency,

Mauritius grows sugarcane on sixty thousand acres of land, and it produces a hundred thousand tonnes of sugar. It employs nearly sixty thousand coolies. Natal is several times the size of Mauritius. We have everything it takes—courage, funds and land. Nature favours us. Our biggest problem is labour. If this problem can be taken care of, we are sure this colony can scale new heights of economic progress in no time.

Your Excellency, the number of native workers in the colony is no more than thirty thousand at the most. This number includes all varieties of workers, not just farmhands. About ten thousand of them are personal servants of the whites. The biggest problem with native workers is absenteeism. The average native worker works only half the year, which means that, of the remaining twenty thousand, ten thousand are unavailable at any time of the year, reducing the effective labour force to about ten thousand. How can one think of economic development in such a situation? It is clear that no economic development would be possible unless we import foreign coolies.

Sir George listened to them very attentively, nodding his head occasionally. When he nodded, it cheered up the white councillors, who thought the desired effect was taking place on the governor. Sometimes, the governor assumed a serious mien, causing the councillors' faces to lose colour. Maybe something they had said did not agree with him.

When the session ended, Sir Gray wound up with a few sentences. The facts presented were disturbing. His government had the issues under consideration and a solution would soon be found. He thanked the members of the Council and sat down. The councillors did not know how to interpret his words.

When Mohandas thought about those days, it filled his mind with wonder. He had studied the records in detail. How the times had changed! In those days, the whites were so keen to bring the coolies into the country; today they just couldn't stand the sight of them. In those days, the white planters were working with a calculated strategy: in a two-pronged effort, they were keeping the Natal government on the one hand and Her Majesty's government in London on the other under constant pressure. Mohandas was amused and said: 'The whites know the technique but lack knowledge of the manner in which pressure needs to be applied. Their technique and our manner could make a truly winning combination.'

The whites did enjoy an advantage: they made frequent trips to London and could present their case to the government there with exaggerated versions of their complaints. They had been so successful in advertising their woes that the Queen's government was beginning to come round to the view that if labour was not imported, the economic structure of the colony would crumble. The fact was that the colony had existed for years and would continue at its snail's pace anyway. The whites however wanted it to trot. They alone knew how fast and for whose benefit.

Eventually the pressure built up to such an extent that the British government became worried that the colony might evaporate. Get the coolies! On February 1856, the Immigration Commissioner had already written to the Undersecretary of the British Government that the Commission saw no reason why Natal planters and residents should be prevented from importing coolies from India.

The Commissioner had in fact moved a step ahead and had also outlined his scheme for the import of labour into Natal: 'It would not be feasible to lift the workers from the ports of Madras and Calcutta. Only the Bombay port could be used for this purpose, despite the fact that our Mauritius experience tells us that lifting workers from the Bombay port entails greater travel expense than the other two ports. It would be difficult to say precisely what the travel expenses to Natal would be like: they could be more or they could be less. The ports of Calcutta and Madras are currently busy catering to the needs of other colonies. The implementation of this scheme would however only be possible after the rules have been framed and the Queen's approval obtained.'

Mohandas laughed. So everything was in place for the wedding except the bridegroom! In other words, the rules and the Queen's approval.

Events were following one another at a quick fire pace. The Colonial Secretary had issued an ordinance regarding the rights of the Natal Governor. Based on the needs and conditions prevailing, a decision had been taken to lay down rules for the import of labour similar to those obtaining in other colonies. Governor Gray had issued a notice to the planters that they should send a detailed requisition setting out their needs so that a consolidated requisition for the whole colony could be dispatched to the Government of India. The white planters were mighty pleased with the speed with which both the governments were proceeding in the matter. They could hardly wait for the coolies to arrive and for the farms to start spewing gold.

Things however had suddenly come to naught. It seemed that the governments of Natal and India had been working to their different plans. In fact, whatever the Natal government proposed, the Indian government disposed. A letter that the Indian government wrote to the Colonial Secretary messed up the whole thing. The letter said:

> *According to the statistics collected from the provinces by the Indian government, the labour requirements of the Bombay Presidency exceed those of any other province. They are so high that it is already running short of labour. The wages too in Bombay are higher than they are in Natal. It's therefore impossible to send workers from Bombay. In any case, the Governor General will not accept for his consideration any proposal in this regard till it is accompanied by definite information relating to the rate of wages and other facilities admissible to the Indian workers.*

The question before the Natal government now was what to do next; how to please the Big Brother?

Sir George Gray had paid careful thought to the arguments put forward at the meeting of the City Council, though his reaction had not been very encouraging. What he had been told about Mauritius had caused him some unhappiness: If a small colony like Mauritius could do so much, why not Natal? Hence, basing itself on the first directive received from the British government, and despite the reluctance of the Indian government, the Natal government drafted an ordinance about the import of coloured labour and sent it directly to London for the approval of the Queen. It now waited hopefully for the approval to arrive and for the ships to start rolling on the waves of the Indian Ocean, depositing loads and loads of workers at their ports. The farms would then start working like automated machines.

When the document from the British government arrived, Sir Gray's secretary came bounding and announced: 'Your Excellency! It looks like Her Majesty's sanction is already here! Everything is now going to be fine.'

Sir Gray signalled to him to open the letter, which he did with extreme caution and decorum lest the Queen's missive might be damaged. Unfolding it, he presented it to His Excellency and stood aside with his hands by his sides.

As Sir Gray's eyes slid down the page, drops of sweat broke out on his forehead. He had now started speaking to himself: 'What on earth are all these people sitting in government good for? Can't even draft a simple ordinance!'

The Queen's government had sent the ordinance back along with a list of errors therein. The most demeaning part of it was that the list included errors of language and grammar. The tone of the letter sounded unnecessarily harsh. It said that the way the letter had been drafted clearly showed that the Natal government had no idea of immigration laws. The Queen had also expressed deep displeasure at the errors in the ordinance. For Sir Gray, it was a matter of shame that the Queen had expressed displeasure at the draft of the ordinance which had his approval. For a long while, he kept pacing the room in distress. Among the errors listed were: the Queen had never before given her consent for so long a *girmit* period as had been asked for to any colony. The second major objection was the lack of any regulations controlling the labour export centres. The third objection was that no attempt had been made to control exploitation of workers in matters of their travel expenses and employment wages beyond saying that the Stipendary Magistrate would have exclusive discretion to alter and modify any condition which he deemed to be inadequate or insufficient.

Enclosed with the letter, as a sample, was a copy of the ordinance which was in force in Mauritius. The letter however did not make a reference to the enclosure. The question now arose: why, in that case, was the ordinance enclosed? No one could quite figure out the reason. It continued to be a subject of lively discussion for many days: Why was a copy of the ordinance in force in Mauritius enclosed? If it had to be enclosed, why was not a reference to it included in the letter? What should be done about it now?

'Let's frame it and hang it on the wall. After all it is from the Queen Empress,' suggested one.

'If we don't make proper use of it, it may be interpreted as an insult to the Queen,' suggested another. Meeting followed meeting. In the end all they could agree on was that since the ordinance had been included, there must be a purpose to it. The Queen's government was not given to purposeless actions. Another meeting was called to discuss what the purpose could have been.

A lot of discussion later, and with a lot of trepidation, it was finally agreed that the indubitable purpose of including a copy of the ordinance in force in Mauritius had to be that the contemplated ordinance for the import of labour in Natal must be modelled on the same pattern. It had taken the Natal government a lot of effort and time to grasp this reason. They had found it hard to accept that the Mauritius government, which had once been a French colony, could draft a better ordinance than them. But now they had no alternative but to admit this fact. Sir Gray too had castigated his government on this count, but he too eventually had to accept it.

The Natal government finally swallowed the Mauritius ordinance like a dose of bitter medicine, modelled its own ordinance on it and dispatched it to the Queen. Its behaviour on this occasion reminded one of the expression on the face of the older brother who had been forced to admit his mistake, after a scolding from the father, in the presence of the younger one. But the eventual result was that, in 1869, the ordinance received the approval of the Queen. The white farmers broke into a dance of joy. For them, the mere approval of the draft seemed equivalent to wealth raining from the sky. Finally, their decision to settle in the colony had been proved to be right.

A copy of the ordinance had been forwarded to the government of India. The white farmers were a little apprehensive about the reaction of the Indian government. Mr. Franklin had been appointed Protector in India immediately after the issuance of the ordinance to look after arrangements for the export of labour and to protect the interests of the workers.

When Mr. Franklin took over as Protector and studied the ordinance, he found a few of the provisions objectionable and wrote about them to the Chief Secretary of Madras. He had made his commentary on the ordinance clause by clause: Clause 5 of Ordinance 14 of 1859 says that a coolie would not be paid less than ten shillings per month as wages. Franklin argued that the ordinance in force in Mauritius provided for wages of ten shillings in the first year, eleven shillings in the second and twelve shillings in the third. He said he had been given to understand that if labour was exported from India to Natal they would have to be paid more than what they got in Mauritius or they would not agree to go to Natal. After all, Natal was an unknown place. About Clause 24, his comment was that in Natal a coolie would be allowed to return home at the end of ten years; this should be changed to five years. He also said that the contract should be between the coolie and the master. The contract should stipulate that the coolie would either be entitled to free food or twelve shillings per year in lieu thereof. The coolie would also be granted by the master a couple of sets of clothes every year. The Natal government had dropped these provisions from their ordinance. Franklin was of the view that it was the Protector's responsibility to protect the interests of the workers and it was for this reason he had taken the liberty to bring these facts to light.

Mohandas did not find in the record any mention of the effect Franklin's efforts had, but it made him happy to learn that there was at least someone who had stood up for the interests of the poor Indians.

~

Dada Abdullah was no longer Gandhibhai's employer. The one-year *girmit* between the two had already come to an end. Gandhibhai now also looked upon his continued stay in Durban in a different light. Whenever he thought about the matter, he saw himself surrounded by all those faces that had been present on the day of his farewell. They had now changed their roles and were present in totally new roles. One moment they were all bidding him farewell; the very next moment they were standing before him as a wall preventing his departure. Something similar had happened to Gandhibhai himself. Instead of going back to his roles of husband, father, brother and friend, he had suddenly turned into a social worker. This sudden switch in his roles never ceased to surprise him. Who was to be held responsible for this switch—time or he himself? Often it is man himself who is responsible but he tries to shift the blame to time or turns himself into a synonym for time.

Mohandas told Dada Abdullah: 'I agreed to stay on, but I am unable to answer the question why. Sometimes I feel that this too is an experiment which, knowingly or not, involves me, my people at home and the people around me here. One party actively involved in this experiment is however completely absent from the scene. I am forced to act both on my own behalf and on behalf of the absent party. The absent party is however very much present in my thoughts and my emotional ties. My wife, my kids and my relatives at home all await my arrival day and night, but they are all present here too as my companions.'

Dada Abdullah's gaze was fixed at Gandhibhai, a look of surprise on his face. He had never seen Gandhibhai so emotional. He spoke a little later: 'It's possible, Gandhibhai, that we lack a real appreciation of your situation, but it's not as if we don't appreciate it at all. We too have all passed through similar situations before arriving where we are today. The only difference is that we are all motivated by our personal interests and personal profit and loss considerations, whereas you have the interests of one and all before you.'

Mohandas had by now pulled himself together. 'Let's forget about that,' Dada Abdullah said, 'that's a tale without end. Tell me what you think we should do.'

'We should have an organization in which we can all work together.'

'Meaning?'

'Meaning we should have an association of all Indians. It should concern itself with only one issue: fighting against excesses and fighting for the welfare of our people.'

You think everyone will support the idea?'

'If they don't, our struggle ends right here.'

Dada Abdullah was stuck with the idea. After a little thought, he added: 'You know Abdullah Haji Adam, don't you? He is also a partner in my firm. He has a deep interest in such matters. Let's talk to him. If he agrees to lead us, perhaps we can make it.'

They both got up and made their way to Haji Abdullah's house.

Abdullah Haji Adam was in the drawing room of his house talking business to some of his employees. Seeing the two of them, he got up to receive them. Gandhibhai had met him before on several occasions and had some idea of what he could achieve. Abdullah Haji Adam too was no less far-sighted. He had a shrewd ability to assess situations and he could now guess that they had something serious to discuss. He disposed of the employees quickly and joined them. Dada Abdullah told him about his discussion with Gandhibhai. Abdullah Haji thought for a minute and then said: 'I completely agree with Gandhibhai. If we cannot all unite, there is simply no point in holding back Gandhibhai.' His face was flushed with the kind of excitement that one might see in the face of someone lost in a jungle who had just discovered his way out.

He continued after a while: 'The white government's policy of colour discrimination means that we have to face a new repressive law every other day. Indian businessmen face the biggest danger as we have investments worth millions at stake. Because of its racist attitude the Indians are soon going to find themselves in a condition worse than the natives.'

'We have to think of others too, not just the businessmen,' said Mohandas. 'The businessmen are not the only Indians here. I keep telling Dada Abdullah that when we construct a building we have to use many things: bricks, cement, lime, stone and so on. Fine deodar wood alone would not do. Only when we all get together shall we able to construct a wall which they will find hard to drill a hole in. If we can't do it that only means that we are already full of holes.'

'Gandhibhai, you need to tell us what we should do. We'll all follow you. If we could do something on our own, wouldn't we have done it already? Allah has probably sent you precisely to help us out.'

All this while, Dada Abdullah said nothing.

The matter of setting up an organization had been left open for discussion and opinion.

~

Marcel Ledue was going round spreading word that Gandhi was an opportunist who had been wandering jobless in India. Dada Abdullah had called him over for a year and now the fellow wanted to boss over everybody. He had his own axe to grind in trying to set up the Indians against the colony's government. The fellow must be sent packing at once or you didn't know what trouble he might land all of them in.

Ledue was doing this on the sly. He felt that Gandhi was trying to challenge the supremacy of the whites and that was something that just would not do. He was most pained when he saw white women going up to Gandhi, talking to him and inviting him. For many people, Gandhi was now turning into a curiosity. Even those who disagreed with him did not want to miss the chance to talk to him, if only to be able to criticize him later. And even while they criticized him, they did not forget to boast that Gandhi had talked to them. This upset Ledue a lot. Why should the whites have anything to do with Gandhi at all?

There were of course people who were fully aware of these activities of Ledue, but they were keeping quiet. No one wanted to take on a white businessman. For all you knew, he could turn out to be the hare's keeper.

In the meantime, Gandhibhai too had been keeping quiet. His wish was to see a flourishing debate on the issue of the new organization. After that day, he himself never went to see either Abdullah Haji Adam or Dada Abdullah. If anyone asked him about it, he told him the reason without mincing words. Despite the various internal differences, one thing had emerged clearly: they could find an identity only if they had an organization. The organization alone would be their voice and a mirror of the others' activities.

~

Another meeting was called at Dada Abdullah & Co. Most of those present were the ones who had been present at Gandhibhai's farewell meeting held at Dada Abdullah's home called Sydenham. Dada Abdullah of course spent most of his time at his West Street home-cum-office, where Mohandas also had his room. Mohandas had also invited some *girmitiya*s from nearby places. *Girmitiya* was written large on their faces. Others didn't even cast a glance in the direction where they sat huddled together in a corner, looking scared. Their presence sat like a dead weight onthe occasion.

There was absolutely no dissent on the need for an organization. People were also agreed that the organization should be completely free and independent of any party. It should not exist under the shadow of any other organization either. They were also of the view that the interests of people in the organization or of people linked to the organization, should not suffer in any way. Off and on, a whispered suggestion for the inclusion of *girmitiya*s in the organization also kept cropping up as an off-key note. The biggest issue however was what to call the organization. Although he was not as yet coming clean on the subject, Mohandas was mentally toying with the name Congress in a light way. The Congress was working for the people in India and all the major leaders and intellectuals of the country were working for it. Gandhibhai had been wondering for sometime whether this organization could also be called Congress. There was no common synonym for the word Congress.

Several names were suggested and noted. In the end, Gandhi was asked for his opinion and he put it forward in clear terms: 'Ever since this question was raised, the name Congress has been buzzing in my ears. I just can't think of any other name. I am aware that the Tories in England detest this name. For them, this name stinks. But it is also true that Congress has sparked off a new life and a new awareness in India. If we turn down this name just because the most important political party of the most powerful colonial nation in the world does not like it, this will be an act of cowardice on our part. There may be many things it doesn't like. It may declare tomorrow that it doesn't like even a nonentity like me. Are we going to be guided in our actions by its likes and dislikes? My advice is that we should select a name for the organization which we can relate to and which can give us inspiration and direction.'

There was silence for a minute.

Abdullah Haji Adam's was the first hand to be raised. Other hands followed one after another.

Then a voice rose slowly: 'Natal Indian Congress ...' Another voice picked it up: 'Zindabad!'

Mohandas stood up and said: 'While we are about it, we should also elect our office bearers. Calling meetings again and again is cumbersome.'

The first name to be proposed was that of Dada Abdullah for President. It was approved unanimously. That set a trend and every name that followed for any office was then approved without any contesting name being proposed. There was no opposition or dissatisfaction. Everything went like a game. The chief among the names were: Haji Mohammad Haji Dada, Ramaswamy Naidu, K.R. Nayanha. Doraiswamy, Pir Mohammad, Mohammad Kasim Jeewa, Parsi Rustomji. There were some from Pietermaritzburg: Amod Bayat, Kamaruddin, etc. When it came to the election of the Honorary Secretary, everyone started shouting 'Gandhibhai, Gandhibhai.' The executive included people from every religion and every caste. There were Hindus, Muslims, Christians, Parsis and others. Abdullah Haji Adam stood like a rock behind them all.

The next morning, newspapers flashed the news about the new party. The white community of Durban was in shock. How on earth had this come about?

Although the Natal Indian Congress had been founded, the question of its goals was still under discussion. Everyone had his own goals to suggest, which mostly had to do with his own interests. This made the discussion quite lively. A few, who belonged to the radical wing, thought that Natal Congress should have no track with the whites. Mohandas considered this kind of approach injurious to the effectiveness of any organization. You may not agree with someone yet have relations with him. How could you have no relations with people who run the state where you live? Why should they listen to you if you have no relationship with them? Adopting an attitude of hostility towards them would create a gulf of arrogance between us. The sea of human relationships is not negotiated in boats: you have to do it in person. This approach would keep all our *girmitiya* brethren out altogether and it is plain that we just cannot fight this war without their help. Mohandas concluded by saying: 'Our aim is not just politics but also to create an atmosphere which is free from hatred and promotes equality and brotherhood.'

It was with great difficulty that the following was added to the list of goals: 'To maintain friendship and goodwill with the European community.'

'Including Marcel Ledue?' joked Dada Abdullah.

Mohandas alone got the joke. He laughed: 'He is your friend. How can we leave him out?'

Seeing the two laugh, others too joined in the laughter.

There were some other goals too. For example: keeping Indians in India informed about the conditions in the colony through newspapers, personal contacts, speeches, etc.; educating the new generation of Indians born in the colony about Indian history and literature; keeping track of the problems faced by Indians settled in Natal and trying to remove them as much as possible; keeping an eye on the conditions of the *girmitiya*s and taking suitable measures for their freedom; helping Indians who were poor and in need of help, and taking suitable measures to improve the material, social and political conditions of immigrant Indians.

It was also decided to give wide publicity to the goals of Natal Congress. This led to the growth of self-confidence among people of Indian origin and a feeling that a community was finally taking shape to which they could turn in their moments of trial and sorrow, and that they were no longer alone.

The day Natal Congress came into existence was August 22, 1894.

The European community was astir. They controlled all the newspapers, which were now all coming out with editorials on the subject. There was a lot of speculation about the nature and implications of the new organization. Apprehensions about these were haunting them like bad dreams. Immediately after the founding of the Natal Congress in 1894, *Times of Natal* came out with a leader with the title "Rami-Sami." Ramis were the north Indians who celebrated Ram and whose names often carried the prefix or suffix. South Indians were all known as Samis. That leader also carried a reference to an article published in *The Times of India* which was favourable to Indians. Gandhi felt distressed as well as angry to read "Rami-Sami" and he wrote a letter to the editor in response, which the editor ignored. Gandhi then wrote a second letter:

Dear Editor,

I find myself obliged to respond to the leading article entitled 'Rami-Sami' published in your esteemed newspaper. Please do not take my letter as a defence of the Times of India *article, because it is not one. Your article, on the other hand, may well be. I have a simple question for you: Don't you think the title of your article, 'Rami-Sami,' is a gratuitous insult to us Indians? In fact, this whole article is bristling with the ill will you bear towards Indians. In your article, you have admitted that India too has its share of cultured and intelligent people. I should perhaps call it very gracious of you to admit it, but I am obliged to think that if it were in your power to do so you would perhaps also strip these cultured and educated people of equal citizenship rights, let alone granting them such rights. Had you been of the view that Indians are stupid barbarians and that on this ground they should be denied equal rights it would still stand to reason, but what grieves one is to note that you are a victim of the unfortunate mentality that takes pleasure in humiliating and mistreating innocent and simple-minded Indians and holds that, even if they are cultured and intelligent, they must be trodden underfoot.*

What you overlook is the fact that the Indians settled in this colony are also descendants of the same Indians whom you, knowingly or not, honour as cultured and intelligent. These Indians also have it in them to become cultured and competent provided they are given an opportunity, much in the same way as the people of East End in London, wallowing in ignorance and vice, had it in them to provide England with a Prime Minister.

I am surprised at how wrong you could be in your interpretation of the petition the Indians sent to Lord Rippon. If able and educated natives are also granted franchise, what possible objection can Indians have? In fact, they will have objection if the opposite happens. All that the Indians want is that no qualified persons should be denied their fundamental rights on grounds of the black colour of their skin. But perhaps all that you care for is the beauty and the colour of one's exterior. Perhaps you don't mind the poison inside if the skin colour is right. Perhaps you are like Pharisee, the Jewish priest, who believed in the prayer that issued from the lips. Perhaps you too do not believe in the prayer issuing from the heart. Is this what you call Christianity? I'm sorry but this is certainly not Christianity. Your accusations against The Times of India *are wrong. Accusations are easy to make but hard to prove.*

At the end of your article, you state that Rami-Sami can be granted all those rights that a citizen can wish for, but they cannot be granted political power.

The Lord said: 'Let all the children come to me.' But the followers of the Lord in this colony are happy to substitute the word 'children' with 'whites.' The Mayor of Durban once organized a fair for children. The surprising thing was that not a single coloured child was present. Was it because they were guilty of being born of coloured parents? May I request you to go back to the New Testament

> *and rewrite 'Rami-Sami' in the light of it? Rethink your leader. If after you have done that you still insist that your article is in keeping with the ideals and traditions set out in the Bible, or that you have nothing whatsoever to do with them, I will gladly withdraw my letter.*
>
> *One more point. I am sorry to say it but it will be a black day for Great Britain and India when you are able to collect large numbers to follow you and your ideals.*
>
> *Yours faithfully,*
>
> *M.K. Gandhi*

Natal Times carried this letter on October 26.

~

Natal Indian Congress was now up and working. As its Honorary Secretary, it was one of Gandhibhai's responsibilities to collect the subscriptions. Of course, he had not been left alone to do all the work; there were many others sharing the responsibilities. A meeting had been called at Congress President Dada Abdullah's place to discuss the issue of subscriptions. There was still enough enthusiasm left in people that they would assemble for a meeting on mere word-of-mouth information. The hall was packed to capacity. Any resolution moved was passed without any discussion or argument. Even a controversial issue like the constitution had a very smooth passage through the meeting. What was tough was to get the subscription money out of people's pockets, though enthusiasm even for this purpose had not yet waned. But you needed money to get money out. The subscription had been fixed at three shillings per month. Not everyone could afford three shillings. The businessmen and the big businessmen of course could, but how could a *girmitiya*? This question tormented Gandhi. It was impossible for a *girmitiya* to pay three shillings. The very people who could have become the backbone of the movement were missing from the scene. Though the question tormented Gandhi, he did not think it proper to raise the question at the meeting.

The question had however been discussed with the members before the meeting. Dada Abdullah had announced that he would pay two pounds per month. A couple of other members followed suit, among them Abdullah Haji Adam. Gandhibhai committed one pound every month, though his financial condition at the time did not quite permit it. A commitment was however was a commitment. Come what might, he would have to part with a pound every month. Many others followed his example and became one-pounders. The ten-shilling tribe was a large one. A few had also made lump sum donations to Congress funds.

As the days passed, people's enthusiasm began to wane. More and more, they began to get busy with their daily business. It was satisfaction enough for them that they now had an organization of their own whose interests were in the safe hands of Gandhibhai. Sometimes Gandhibhai jokingly remarked: 'There are so many of them here concerned about Gandhi's interests that nobody seems to be concerned about him.'

One of Mohandas' clerks was always on his feet chasing the subscriptions, but the money still fell like an occasional drop of manna from heaven. When he called on someone, word would be sent out to him that the person was not in or if he happened to bump into him directly he would be told to come some other time. When the back payments accumulated, it gave people more reason to make excuses. Often Gandhi had to set out himself on a collection drive: a smartly turned out barrister pestering people for pennies. But Gandhi did not take it that way.

Slowly, the situation spun out of control and inflow of money ceased altogether. Party work began to suffer. Whatever could be achieved by using their personal resources, Gandhi and others continued to accomplish, but much more needed to be accomplished. Hence Mohandas had to call a meeting on the issue. Fortunately, those present included some subscription-evaders as well.

Mohandas started on a jocular note:

> *I have called this meeting in the spirit of a housewife nagging her husband when the housekeeping money is exhausted. Right now all of you are the husbands and, being the secretary, I am the housewife.*

Everyone laughed. Gandhibhai then provided the twist:

> *When we met the last time, I was very happy. So were you. Everyone had meant well and everyone had undertaken to pay his subscription. Some of you have done so too. But I know that enthusiasm is not a line etched in stone that it will stay there forever. It is more like a line drawn in water: it stays there only so long as it is wet. No one can see a dried up line. But if you make a commitment, it's not like a line any more. If you make a commitment, it forces you to keep it. Collecting subscriptions, I know, is like drinking water in a leaf: you drink some; you spill some. Maybe you spill more than you drink. It's a pain for you to pay every month; it's a pain for us to collect every month. I therefore suggest that we pay yearly. You might well feel this fellow Gandhi has nothing better to do: he or his man, is at the door everyday, as if you have defaulted on a loan repayment! Now you will have to pay only once a year. So much easier for you to pay only once a year!*

Everyone supported the proposal.

The subscriptions meeting created some signs of activity among the people and they began to take the economic aspect of the problem a little more seriously. The name Natal Congress was also beginning to be recognized. Messages from distant places began to arrive. Those who came voluntarily to seek membership were committed and deposited their subscriptions happily; those who needed persuasion to join often made excuses.

Mohandas wanted the membership of Natal Congress to cover areas outside of Durban and Pietermaritzburg too to include scattered settlements. These settlements were not like villages but more like tribes with their separate corrals. The farms were surrounded by barracks, in which lived the *girmitiya*s. Mohandas was of the view that if things could be explained to them the *girmitiya*s could well agree to support their cause even if they did not become paid members of the Congress.

Thefore, he also took time out to join them. Occasionally, he also dragged Dada Abdullah, Abdullah Haji or Parsi Rustomji along with him. After they had been successful in winning people's confidence, they requested them to become members of the Congress. Becoming members of the Congress filled the people with self-confidence, as they felt they were no longer alone. Sometimes of course they also had to face opposition.

The rules for the payment of subscription were relaxed for the *girmitiya*s. Despite the fear in which they held their masters, Congress membership was becoming a matter of honour and self-respect for them.

~

Mohandas and a few of his friends were on a public awareness campaign in Tongat. It was a fairly large town. Mohandas had been told that the Indians settled there were indifferent towards Congress.

Mohandas arrived at Tongat. His companions went out and collected the local Indians together. Most of them however preferred to stay indoors. The few who came out told him to his face: 'We learn that some barrister from India is here. A few Durbanites have joined him and are trying to incite people against the Natal government. They move around in groups and are trying to spread disaffection.'

Mohandas laughed and said: 'Nothing of the sort. We are not against anyone. All that we are doing is to meet and mix with people so that we Indians get to know each other and develop unity.'

They did not quite understand and their fears persisted.

Mohandas talked to them individually as he went round the settlement. He tried to explain to them what it was like to live with dignity, and how their rights were being ignored. You may do anything about it or not, he told them, but at least you should try to understand your rights. If you don't even know what they were how would you ever secure them?

Sometimes a well-to-do Indian would invite the roving party to his house to a meal and if it was late he would also arrange their night stay. A rich businessman of Tongat once invited Mohandas and his party to dinner. When, after the day's tiring tour of the settlement, the party reached the businessman's house, Mohandas in his usual way proposed that he should become a member of the Natal Congress.

This was a proposal Mohandas made to every one of his hosts. The party would partake of the dinner only after the host accepted the proposal. If the host was very rich, he was also asked for additional financial help. About the Tongat businessman, it had already been decided that considering his economic status he would be asked for six pounds of additional help and this had also been conveyed to the businessman. Before sitting down for dinner, when they asked again, he dug in his heels and said: 'Three pounds is the best I can do. Take it or you can have your dinner and leave.'

Mohandas thought for a minute and chalked out a plan in his mind about how to deal with the matter. First, the way he had said it was derogatory; second, if they consented to accept such a small amount from such a rich person, others would start making excuses even for the payment of subscription money. So Mohandas held his ground. It was midnight and neither the guests nor the hosts had eaten. The hosts could not eat till the guests had eaten first.

Mohandas said: 'Party's need first, ours second.'

The other businessmen from Tongat who were present now started siding with the guests. They tried to explain to the businessman: 'Look, they are not asking money for themselves; they want it for the Indians of this colony.'

'This is arm twisting. How can I pay more than I can afford?'

'But wouldn't you feel bad if your guests left your house without eating their dinner?'

'What has dinner got to do with donation? The two are different things.'

Mohandas' friends were losing patience. They kept on repeating: 'Let's go, Gandhibhai. We are not going to get anything out of him. No donation and no dinner.'

'Be patient!' he advised, 'patience opens all closed doors. If we turn down the dinner invitation, his family will be unhappy, but they have done no wrong. When in public service, we mustn't hurt anyone, and mustn't get hurt either. Service means happiness for all.'

The whole night passed and no one ate. The family was now blaming Mohandas. The birds were astir and their early morning chorus was beginning to drown out the stillness of the night. Their sounds seemed to be coming nearer and nearer every minute. In the businessman's family too, it had been a long night. The eyelids were heavy with sleep. Mohandas' friends were thoroughly bored and wanted to leave, but Mohandas refused to budge.

The first light appeared in the sky. Darkness turned into grey. Light was now gathering speed and it looked it would soon sweep everything out of its way like so much rubbish. Having fought hunger all night, people had drooping faces. The local people were now saying: 'Take whatever the Sheth is willing to give; we'll raise the rest.'

Mohandas replied: 'Raising money is not my only aim. The aim is to make the Sheth understand that the work of Natal Congress is important and that we can go without food for days for its sake. At least I can. Stay hungry, I say, if necessary, but fight for your freedom rather than live in bondage.'

The Sheth listened quietly for a while and then got up suddenly, went indoors and came out bearing six pounds in his hands, which he placed before Mohandas, saying: 'I had thought collecting money in the guise of subscriptions was your only aim. I was wrong. We are ignorant men. We know nothing about what is going on around us. We are just businessmen and know nothing outside of business. It's our only religion. Please come and have your dinner. I have already sinned a lot by keeping you hungry for so long.'

'But it's morning now.'

'Please have your bath and refresh yourselves. If you leave without eating, I'll take it you have not forgiven me.'

Mohandas signalled and everyone agreed. The hunger was by now like slow smouldering fire, on its way out, with no smoke and no flame.

News of the Tongat incident spread all over the north coast areas. Stanger, Church Town, you name it, at every place people knew about what a man called Gandhibhai had been up to at Tongat. Some even called it arm twisting. Arm twisting was not necessarily physical, they said; it could also be psychological. Most people however were with Gandhi. The itinerant parties reached their places to find that people had already made up their minds not to permit a repeat of Tongat in their areas.

From the very beginning, one thing had been bothering Mohandas. It did indeed sound great when it was said that the doors of Natal Congress were open to every such individual who subscribed to its objectives, but how was everyone expected to pay three shillings every month, especially one whose yearly income was eleven pounds? It wasn't enough even to buy two square meals a day for his family, so how could he pay Natal Congress? In other words, only moneyed people would have a place in Natal Congress, and it would always remain so. If a person had no money, there would be no Congress for him and therefore no freedom ever. Even the Congress Committee in India hadn't grasped this basic truth. There too members of Congress were all big and moneyed people. The small fry kept away from Congress sessions, so scared they were.

The first round of the subscription drive had resulted in the enrolment of two hundred and twenty eight members, which was then tom-tommed as a great achievement. One hundred and sixty of them were businessmen, twenty-four or twenty-five were office clerks and the rest included fishermen, barmen, waiters, and hawkers. Most of the hawkers were *girmitiya*s who had been released from their *girmit*s and had now started small businesses of their own. Mohandas had another worry: if some day the business of the businessmen came under threat or if the office clerks found that their jobs were on the line, what would be the fate of Congress? Would they just leave or would they just say 'You can keep the money, but please let us go!' How could a party be run by such people? The Indian Congress had been started by an Englishman called Mr. Hume, a civil servant. He was well-connected with the upper class Indians. The same people continued to be members even today. Mohandas knew that movements were always founded by people from the upper class; later, people from other classes joined in. But here there was still no space for other-class people anywhere, either in India or here. There wasn't anything Mohandas could do about the Indian Congress, but he did want to rescue Natal Congress from such a fate if he could.

~

Among the tales of heroism of Indian businessmen that Mohandas had been told about was this one: in 1890, the Indian businessmen of Transvaal and Orange Free State had been stripped of the right to own properties and other civil rights and had been forced to live in separate settlements like hostages. A committee to protest the treatment had been set up in Durban. It was called the Durban Indian Committee. Haji Mohammad Dada was the President, Abdul Karim Adam the General Secretary. A petition detailing the complaints of Indians had been prepared by Fazal Bhai Wisram of Mumbai and copies of the petition had been sent to the Indian Viceroy and the Natal government. Mr. Wisram had sent the petition directly to the Colonial Secretary in London. The petition included a number of suggestions along with complaints.

Mohandas was astonished to read the petition, which had been made available to him by Abdul Karim Adam. Why was this matter allowed to die a premature death? Why was the matter not taken forward? Had it been given the form of a movement, it would have made some progress, thought Mohandas. That was all that he could do.

He also heard of another episode in the same context. The Colonial Secretary of Natal had forwarded a complaint from the Indian traders to the Protector for inquiry. Haji Mohammad Dada and the other members of the Committee had taken up the matter and written to the Colonial Secretary regretting that the Secretary seemed to have no knowledge about the public status of the Arab traders. They also wrote to the Protector that in their eyes the latter had no *locus standi* in the matter and they considered the Colonial Secretary's step derogatory to their status. They told him that they had nothing to do with his department and the department would also do well to stay away from them.

The Assistant Colonial Secretary, Mr. Bird, was eventually forced to yield to the traders' demands and to concede that, since they had come to the country as travellers, they were outside the jurisdiction of the Protector's department.

While Mohandas did have a word of praise for the traders for their courage, the question that bothered him was this: had they an organization of their own, would they have been content to accept Mr. Bird's assurance that they were outside the Protector's jurisdiction, so much so that they had even let the questions that Mr. Wisram had raised in his petition remain unasked?

Mohandas knew that the traders too were nursing a grievance, but they saw their grievance as distinct from that of the others. Something similar was the case with the lawyers, intellectuals and some people belonging to the feudal order in India. They wanted to prepare their blueprint for freedom under the patronage of the government.

Mohandas raised the question before Haji Adam in an indirect way: 'Didn't people like you, who came to Natal as travellers, have to face a struggle? Did you bring all the wealth of India with you that you could start your business no sooner you had landed on these shores? I doubt it if there were any among you, except maybe a few, who came here with sufficient money to make your rehabilitation a smooth affair.'

'There is actually only one difference, Gandhibhai ...'

'And what is that?'

'I know what you are trying to say. No matter how much a *girmitiya* works, he is allowed to retain only as much as his master permits him to, while we work with dreams of prosperity and no one else has a share in what we earn. Any loss or profit is our own business. A *girmitiya* is neither allowed to dream nor to get the full reward of his labour. The fault is not his; it's the system which is to blame. Daud Mohammad is one of the biggest businessmen here, all thanks to the *girmitiya*s. But he also pays them the same as the whites do. The only difference is that bonds of language and country hold them together and the *girmitiya*s work the skin off their back for him.'

Mohandas laughed and said: 'So that means you exploit them every which way! In the name of language, in the name of country.'

'Yes, you could say that.'

'May I ask you how one man's labour is different from another man's? Maybe your labour brings you ample rewards because your labour is backed by your upper class status and resources. You hold the strings and you can pull them tight or let them loose as you think fit. This is however not a quality that you can attribute to labour. Their labour is mortgaged with the whites; therefore the fruits of their labour also go to them. That's the reason why they starve. They lose out to their hunger. They are of course not a happy lot, but neither are you. In the eyes of the whites, your status is no better than theirs. Can I ask you something?'

'Sure.'

'Suppose some day you need their support, don't you think they too will desert you the way they stand deserted by you now?'

For a moment, Abdullah Adam went into shock.

Seeing his face, Mohandas gave the point a different turn. 'Please do not take me amiss. What I mean to ask is: can't Natal Congress be the bridge between your two classes? If it can't, there is really no point in calling it Congress.

'That's a point we need to ponder.' It was the only response Abdullah could think of.

Gandhibhai thought it best to say nothing. Maybe they are still not ready to face this question, he thought.

Another issue was worrying Natal Congress. While on the issue of *girmitiya*s, they maintained silence, on this other issue they kept pestering

Mohandas. Some Indians had studied or picked up English, had converted to Christianity and were under the influence of Christian fathers. Because of the religious bond, they thought of themselves as honorary whites. They also looked upon other Indians as coolies or blacks. One could not even expect them to warn the fellow Indians about any laws in making that might result in their exploitation and harassment. In fact, they supported such laws. Mohandas was of course pained to hear about such instances, but he was also puzzled. How could an Indian ever think of himself as a non-Indian? It was totally beyond his comprehension.

~

When Mohandas had first arrived in Natal, he had met the court interpreter Mr. Pal and the Protestant Mission teacher Mr. Subhan Godfrey. That was the time he had also met Parsi Rustomji and Adamji Miyakhan. Parsi Rustomji was at the port itself to receive him. That was perhaps June 7, 1893. Mohandas had a vague remembrance of the date. He had found them to be all very decent people. Maybe that was the reason why he remembered them. That was also the reason why he had their support in his opposition to the government's effort to get the franchise amendment bill through the parliament. Godfrey's students too had supported him. His English speaking ability had been of considerable use to the party. Their representatives made up twenty-five per cent of the Working Committee too. But even these Anglophile young men had not been spared by the whites and their laws. They had been tarred with same brush as Indian traders and *girmitiya*s and this had hurt the community deeply.

Actually, things had betrayed the expectations of Natal government. It had not expected that Anglophile Indians would go back to the Indian camp after having travelled with it this far. It now justified its reaction by saying that it always knew that blood was thicker than water, though it had earlier found it more convenient to overlook this piece of wisdom. They had overlooked the possibility that blood could score over religion. And now that it had scored, they started saying that religion and English after all cannot purify blood. 1858 began to haunt them again. These were the very people, they said, who had, some years ago, tortured innocent white women, killed them and their children, drowned them in rivers, forced them to jump into wells and die while the British had left no stone unturned to make them into civilized human beings.

Annoyed by these developments, the Natal government had decided to move an Education Amendment Bill in parliament and this was what was worrying Indians, especially the educated ones among them.

A white member of parliament had only this to say in support of the amendment bill: 'If our children are made to study in the same schools with the children of coloureds and coolies, we won't have to wait long for the day when their children will monopolize all the government jobs and our children will be standing in queues outside the offices. If we want to retain our dignity and purity, let the coolies be treated as coolies. Let them not be given any preferential treatment.'

When the issue came before Mohandas, he had only this to say: 'Education of your children should be your own concern. Do not expect those to have sympathy with you whom you are fighting for your rights. Even if you are somehow able to persuade the government to accept your demands today, it could any day pull the sheet from under your feet and throw you off balance. Hasn't it already withdrawn the franchise?' He paused for a minute and then continued: 'If you consider it fit, let's form a Colonial Born Indian Education Association and run our own schools, but let's not discriminate between children.'

One of them said: 'What difference will that make? Will the government turn the bill down or withdraw it?'

Mohandas laughed and said: 'It will neither turn it down nor withdraw it. You will have to make your own arrangements. The Association will work for the welfare of children. It will help bring together all those Indian young men who have strayed. It will be an open forum for discussion on children's issues. It will run a library for children which will stock textbooks. It will tell them about our country and its people.'

Mohandas noticed that while his proposal was carried there was little enthusiasm for it among the people. The matter of raising a fee for the organization was left to Gandhibhai. A nominal fee was proposed so that even kids with poor parents could also benefit from it.

Gandhibhai now had an additional responsibility. He accepted it with a smile.

~

Mohandas had started his legal practice and was already four months into it. By now he had made his contacts with the young people of the colonial-born generation, using the Natal Congress channel. He had also made inroads into the world of office workers; Indians working in hotels and restaurants were also in contact with him. However, despite a strong desire on his part, contact with *girmitiya*s was minimal. They had all heard of him but very few actually knew him. Meetings with them were few and far-between. Basically, the matter boiled down to this: on the one hand you had a stylish gentleman sahib, and on the other, a low-level, slum-dwelling *girmitiya.* How could the twain meet? Mohandas spent anxious moments wondering at the distance between them despite his keenness to meet them. It seemed to him that somehow they had begun to believe or had been made to believe, that the gulf between the celestial heights in which 'ballister sahib' led his existence and the subterranean depths in which they led theirs was an unbridgeable one. This realization tormented Mohandas no end. Such a long distance already from their homeland … and such a long distance between one Indian and another!

~

One day, a man suddenly appeared before Mohandas while he was getting ready to leave for the court. The man looked as if a typhoon had hit him. A white but filthy-looking turban was tied on his head like a coiled cord. The front teeth had been bashed in and blood was oozing out. The clothes were spattered with blood. His legs shook as if a killer was about to grab him. Hiccups choked his voice.

Gandhibhai asked him: 'Who are you? What do you want? Who has given you these wounds?'

He just stared at him and continued to sob.

He understood neither Hindi nor Gujarati. There was a Tamil clerk working for Gandhi whom everyone called by the name of Ranga, though his real name was something different. Gandhi had guessed that the man knew nothing but Tamil, so he called Ranga over and said: 'I think he understands Tamil. Ask him who he is and why he is crying.'

Amidst hiccups and with a lot of difficulty, he was able to communicate that he was Balasundaram.

Ranga continued questioning him even as he tried to reassure him: 'Balasundaram, you need to worry no more. You have come to the right place. You need fear no one any more. Gandhibhai will do everything to help you.'

People of Mohandas' office also called him Gandhibhai. Whatever Balasundaram was able to tell him, Ranga conveyed to Mohandas in his broken English.

It was for the first time that Mohandas was meeting a *girmitiya* in such a condition. After receiving a lot of reassurance from Ranga, this was what Balasundaram came out with: 'He works as a gardener at a white sahib's house. The sahib is an important man of Durban. He has to do each and every kind of job at his place. At the slightest mistake, the sahib starts raining blows on him. Today, he was a little late in watering the plants, so the sahib beat him up mercilessly.' He again broke into sobs.

Mohandas sat down and closed his eyes, as if looking for a solution within him. His face was flaming red. When he opened his eyes after a while the face was normal and he looked calm. He told Ranga: 'Take him to the doctor. I want a medical statement of his injuries. If you face any problem, just let me know.'

Ranga left with Balasundaram. Mohandas again sat with his eyes closed for some time. His face showed he was lost in deep thought. Ranga was back with the medical certificate in a short while, with Balasundaram following. The thought in Mohandas' mind was: the white man has thrashed us all, not Balasundaram alone. Every moment, somewhere, a white man is thrashing an Indian. Those who have never received a thrashing, cannot understand this pain.

Mohandas saw the certificate, took Balasundaram with him to the courts, and presented him before a magistrate. In a few measured words, he put the case before the magistrate: 'Your honour, my client here is Balasundaram, resident of a southern state in India. He works here as a gardener with a white citizen called Mr. Brown. I hear Mr. Brown is one of the wealthiest persons in Natal. He and the other members of his family make Balasundaram work day and night and often beat him up. Balasundaram thus has to undergo both physical and mental torture. Today, Mr. Brown beat him up black and blue again, and the evidence of his cruelty is before you.' He presented before the judge an affidavit signed by Balasundaram and the medical certificate.

The magistrate was a white man too. He took some time reading the affidavit and even as he did so, cast sidelong glances at Sundaram. Then he muttered: 'Inhuman! How could a civilized man be so inhuman?'

The barrister Mohandas had only one argument to offer: 'If a domestic servant absents himself from duty without leave, one can file a civil case against him in a court and get him a minimal punishment by law. But when a *girmitiya* is guilty of the same misdemeanor, the law is so merciless that nothing short of a criminal case will meet the ends of justice. His condition is worse than that of a slave who is bought like a commodity and who is beyond the protection of law. A white master terrorizes an innocent *girmitiya*. It is true that the man left his country and his kith and kin behind to earn his livelihood here, but it is also true that he had had a greater role to play in bringing about prosperity to this colony than the natives and the whites. Such terrible wounds, both internal and external, have been inflicted on this man that even the law might want to avert its eyes.'

The Magistrate gave urgent orders for summons to be issued to Mr. Brown to be present in the court and offer his defence.

After he had issued the orders, the Magistrate once again glanced at Balasundaram and shook his head as if he had been witness to a crime in which he himself was an accomplice.

The moment he was out of the court premises, Gandhibhai sent Balasundaram for medical attention.

~

Mohandas had been pacing the room for a considerable length of time. With his wounds and injuries, Balasundaram was stuck in his consciousness at such an awkward angle that he was beginning to look like a map extending from India to South Africa on which dripped incessantly the blood of Indian *girmitiya*s. Another question was raising its head in his mind like a snake's hood. Were there no excesses committed in India? Were the whites alone guilty of excesses? At least, they only targeted others; we Indians did not spare even our own people. Could one say everything was hunky-dory in India? Was there no bloodshed? Was there no inequality? Was there no hunger? Would India ever be free of these ills? Questions like these spun like tops in his mind and he stood alone in their midst. Disparate images of tyranny from the two countries spread themselves out before his eyes.

Memories of how Kaba Gandhi's prime ministership had come to an end came flooding to his mind. After the death of his mother, Rupali *Ba*, Thakur Vikmat Singh had ascended the king's throne. His father had already passed away and the queen was ruling the state. It was the queen who had artillery installed at the house of Mohandas' grandfather during his prime ministership. Kaba Gandhi was not so fortunate and he had to give up his position. The issue was the same old one: fight against injustice. Kings, feudal princes, and the wealthy class were not in the habit of putting up with such nonsense. Voices of protest irritated them. King Vikmat Singh's son had drunk himself to death. He had a servant, Lakkhu, who plied him with drink and he was only too happy to oblige. For this crime of his, the king had Lakkhu's nose severed in the public square. The wild screams of Lakkhu, blood streaming from his nose, the nose wriggling on the ground for a few minutes, Lakkhu running from the scene in his condition, arriving on the ramparts of the fort and leaping to his death—Mohandas had seen none of this personally. But when Balasundaram had appeared before him with his bloodied face, Lakkhu had flashed as a reality in his imagination. In a culture in which your nose was synonymous with your honour, you could lose your nose only at the cost of your life, never otherwise. So did Lakkhu. Death is the ultimate limit of your tolerance. Lakkhu had reached that limit.

Kaba Gandhi had tolerated all this, an impotent rage searing his soul. In keeping with the courtly traditions and customs, however, he had tried to convince King Vikmat Singh not to let his love for his son cloud his sense of justice. After the Lakkhu incident, his continuation as Prime Minister became more and more problematic. When the British agent got to know about the incident, he started tightening the screws on the ruler, and Vikmat Singh now asked Kaba to cook up a list of charges against the agent. Kaba Gandhi's spontaneous reaction was: 'That's it. I'll take no more of it.'

First it had been the grandfather, Ota Gandhi, who, trying to escape the wrath of Rupali, had to see his body guard, Makrani, die in the attempt, and now this! What a price you had to pay for taking a stand against injustice, thought Mohandas—and now his father, Kaba Gandhi, was having to deal with the wrath of her son, Vikmat Singh. It had been difficult for Vikmat Singh to be as cruel as his mother. Actually, his father had stated in his will that in times of adversity he should trust only the Gandhi family and no other. The day he had ascended the throne,

Vikmat Singh had sent out search parties in pursuance of his father's advice to look for Kaba Gandhi. Years had passed since the exile of Ota Gandhi when the prime ministership of Porbandar was again returned to his son.

Whenever Mohandas thought of these events in the context of the Balasundaram incident, his reaction was to see tyranny as simply tyranny, not as white or black tyranny. You could not root out tyranny by counter-tyranny or by using weaponry.

When he was a child, the roving bioscope went around the localities playing *The Twelve-ton Washerwoman*. The images of the past were now flashing past his eyes exactly like those bioscope images.

The question was who should bear the blame for Balasundaram? Mr. Brown, or the entire society which, despite being a community of humans, had long been refusing to see a human being as a human being, sometimes in the name of religion, at times in the name of colour and sometimes in the name of caste? It might be a white society or a black one; a European or an Indian: they all looked for an excuse to commit a crime. The blood oozing out from the body of Balasundaram looked to him as the blood of every weak and helpless human being. Who knows how long and where on this earth blood has been shed and will continue to be shed? He thought of Jesus Christ. He thought of Krishna brought down by the hunter's arrow. The blood that was spilled then had not been cleaned up yet. It may be Mohandas himself or it may be Balasundaram: they are as weak and helpless in this foreign land as his grandfather and father were before Rupali *Ba* and Vikmat Singh, or as his friend Uka was before his mother.

Time and time again, Mohandas asked himself if one could not pry loose from the old and ever-expanding chain of suppression and tyranny innocent individuals like Balasundaram. Perhaps not, he felt, since they are perhaps just the right candidates for exploitation for persons in power.

So far as Balasundaram was concerned, Gandhibhai had two ways open to him: either to get his *girmit* cancelled by the Protector or to arrange for another master who would be willing to accept him and treat him like a human being. There was a third way too: get him released from the bloody claws of Mr. Brown permanently. That was Ota Gandhi's way. Ota had himself made good his escape from the killer claws of Rani Rupali *Ba*, never to return. The second way was that of Kaba Gandhi: he had changed masters. He had left Porbandar for Rajkot and had his younger brother take his place there. Still another way was that of Uka. He had stayed the way he was all his life.

Mohandas decided to give Mr. Brown a personal visit and talk it over with him. He would counsel him to stop terrorizing Indians. He had a large contingent of Indian *girmitiya*s backing him; and also a long series of terror episodes.

Mr. Brown lived like an Indian prince. A lot of pomp and show, horse carriages and man servants, cooks and waiters, doormen and lackeys, a small detachment of bodyguards, all raised by dint of money. So raised because they could be so raised; anything that could not be so raised was missing.

At the gates of the villa, Mohandas stood lost in thought for a while. Maybe he was trying to muster enough courage or maybe he was trying to organize his thoughts before the encounter. Actually, you could not quite get your own case ready till you had an image of the opponent's case in your mind. But the opponent was an unknown entity. It took a lot of effort to make it to Mr. Brown's secretary. For a coolie to reach a white sahib was nothing short of climbing up to the seventh heaven. It was quite another matter that Prophet Mohammad's horse had taken him through the seven heavens in a jiffy and was back even before the chain at the front door had come to rest.

Brown's secretary made a thorough interrogation of Gandhibhai. Thick layers of suspicion clouded his eyes. It was after considerable difficulty that he had agreed even to inform Mr. Brown that Mr. M.K. Gandhi was waiting to see him. Mr. Brown too had asked a number of questions: why does he want to see me? How come a coolie became a barrister? What could he possibly want with me? The secretary answered as many questions as he could and offered to go back to get the answers to remaining questions. Mr. Brown disallowed this move.

It was after such detailed investigation that Mohandas was ushered into the presence of Mr. Brown, who then gave him the once-over people generally reserve for a beggar. He was puffing away at a long-stemmed pipe. The smoke rose slowly and then dissolved into the air. As long it remained undissolved, it could be clearly seen rising. His lips were drawn and crooked.

A storm of contempt raging in Brown's eyes, he asked: 'How dare you enter this place?'

Mohandas spoke in a polite tone: 'I am here to talk to you about Mr. Balasundaram.'

'Mister …? The bloody coolie!'

'Mister' is an epithet used with names of males. It does not denote a coolie or a master.'

'A coolie is a coolie. Is it not an epithet in itself? You may go. I have no time for your absurd talk.'

'I am not here to stay nor would I care to. But I'm not going to leave without saying what I'm here to say. Nor would perhaps you be able to leave without listening to me.'

Hearing a coolie talk like this had caused much disorientation in Mr. Brown. Mohandas continued: 'It is not my aim to secure punishment for what you have done. I am here only to explain to you the difficult position you are in. You have inflicted physical torture on an innocent and helpless man. This is an inhuman action and the law does not permit it.'

Mr. Brown's face was flushed bright red. He expelled a flurry of smoke puffs from one corner of his lips like a fish releasing bubbles in water. He hadn't yet asked Mohandas to take a seat. Mohandas stood in a very relaxed manner as if he was in a friend's house. Now he started pacing the room and said: 'I'll be happy if you release Balasundaram from your slavery so that he can go to another master. You will have to give me a letter addressed to the Protector for this to happen'

Mr. Brown laid his pipe down, though the smoke still issued from his mouth. He said: 'That will lead to indiscipline and anarchy among my servants. Every indentured labourer will start looking for a different master.'

'Of course not. You will have to change your attitude towards them. They are here to earn their livelihood, not to pick up quarrels. Indians are anyway peace-loving and tolerant by nature, so long as you do not put their tolerance to an extreme test. If you commit excesses on them, they will have no alternative but to fight back. The court has issued summons against you. Balasundaram is not alone in this fight. We are all with him.'

He looked at Mohandas. His face was stern. It was now Mr. Brown's turn to get up and pace the room. Mohandas' gaze was fixed at Mr. Brown's face. Mr. Brown stopped his pacing and said: 'I agree.'

'Thank you, Mr. Brown …,' said Mohandas, as he got ready to leave. 'Please keep this mind in future too. You may land yourself in trouble some day.'

In a way, the decision had been in Balasundaram's favour, it was a kind of agreement. The agreement had benefited Balasundaram. Some people did raise the point that by helping the white master to escape a jail sentence, Gandhibhai had actually helped him. To such people, Gandhi's reply was: 'There are thousands of our brethren who are working with white masters. Getting a jail sentence for Mr. Brown was a child's play, but saving our brethren from the vengeance of their white masters would have been very tough.'

Those people had no answer to this.

When the victorious Balasundaram approached Gandhibhai after the case, there were more copious tears on his face than on the other day. While his throat was choked, his face was shining with happiness. In his hands, he carried the turban he had been wearing that day. The bloodstains on it had faded and they now looked dark but could be seen distinctly. Seeing him with his turban in his hands, Mohandas couldn't help thinking of the day when the magistrate had asked him to take off his turban in the court. How did the magistrate know that he was not an Arab but a Hindu? To this day, Mohandas didn't have the answer to this riddle. How were the whites able to make such subtle distinctions, he wondered. How hard it had been for him to put up with the magistrate's order to remove his turban!

Mohandas asked Balasundaram: 'Who asked you to come here with your turban off?'

After the case, Balasundaram was now somewhat familiar with Gandhibhai's temperament, so he kept quiet. He had been able to guess that Gandhibhai was not happy with him for taking off his turban. When he asked him a second time, he signalled that it was bad manners to appear before respectable people with your turban on.

Mohandas' voice was shaking when he tried to explain the matter to him: 'It is wrong. Everyone else here is ready to pull our turbans off. If we join them and hand them our turbans on a platter, how helpless and lifeless will our existence be?' Then he told him the entire courtroom story. 'On that occasion, my reaction was that the magistrate wanted to drag the names of my ancestors through mud by ordering my turban off. The turbaned heads of my ancestors were passing before my eyes. Seeing the turban in your hands, I found myself playing the role of the magistrate and you mine. Put the turban on before you come in my presence.'

It was hard to say how much of what Mohandas said went across to Balasundaram, but he shook his head to say 'No.'

'By taking off your turban,' said Mohandas: 'you are not honouring me; in fact you are doing just the opposite: you are dishonouring me. Put it on at once. If you don't, I shall leave the room. This may be the whites' way of doing things, but it's not ours. We are not obliged to follow each and every custom of theirs.'

It was now clear to Balasundaram from Mohandas' attitude and utterances that he had no choice but to put the turban back on. So he started tying it on his head standing right there. As he did so, his eyes were fixed on Mohandas' face, which was now getting back some of its old cheer. The bloodstains on the turban had disappeared for both of them for the time being.

The matter had not ended with Balasundaram's turban. The Chief Justice's chamber too floated into Mohandas' view. He saw himself standing before the

Chief Justice in a barrister's outfit. Despite strong opposition, the Chief Justice had allowed his nomination as an advocate of the court. He must now take his oath as one. The Chief Justice's voice boomed through the court: 'Mr. Gandhi, take off your turban. You are now an officer of the court.'

For a moment, it was the magistrate who Mohandas saw sitting in the Chief Justice's seat, trying to get his revenge. He took off his turban. And immediately a number of questions started raising their heads around him and hissing: Why didn't you take it off on the previous occasion then? Why did you take it off today? That had been Dada Abdullah's question.

Mohandas had a good number of answers, but they were all there to satisfy others. He had to find an answer to satisfy himself. He could think of only one possible answer: so that others could hold on to theirs. That answer was however not yet quite complete.

~

X

The petition had been sent to Lord Rippon. Nothing had moved since then either at this end or the other one. Everyone was happy under the impression that the governor's letter must be with the Queen by now, along with the petition. The government must be giving thought to it. At the level of the Natal government too, there was absolute silence: no information whatsoever. Everyone from the prime minister to the members of parliament seemed to be on holiday. On the franchise front, the silence recalled the silence of the classroom when the teacher napped between lessons. In fact, a nap was what both governments seemed to be in the mood to enjoy while they could. The kids of Congress were on their best behaviour, eagerly waiting to see how the Queen spread her favours. Was it going to be a whipping or a gift? Or maybe nothing at all; the whole thing may be just put off. Deep inside, of course, the anxiety was mounting. If the Queen put her stamp on the bill, it would be worse than a whipping for the Indians.

When their patience started wearing off, the people would put it to Gandhibhai himself: 'What do you think, Gandhibhai? Will the British government accept the bill?'

Mohandas would say: 'Their decision alone will provide the answer. You just have to wait for it. We have done whatever we could do. Now it can go either way.'

'The whites here seem to believe that their view will prevail.'

Mohandas had only one answer: 'They are within their rights to believe that, just as it is the British government's right to accept or reject the bill. How can you be a party to it?'

Mohandas knew that not only in Durban but in the whole colony the whites were determined to strip the Indians of their rights and to send them packing. The whites were making frequent trips to England: that was as much their home as this place was.

When the whites came back from England, they would be carrying bagsful of news from 'the horse's mouth' to rile the Indians. When a planter called Wilson returned from England, he told everyone that the Queen was not at all in favour of coolies continuing in Natal, except the *girmitiya*s. Others could leave. Once the *girmit* is over, their right of residence will also stand cancelled.

Indians would react to such talk in one of the two ways: either they would feel very bitter but be unable to give voice to their disappointment, or they would fear that they may be someday simply packed in ships and sent home. They were anyway suspicious and docile by nature. How could any courage or confidence survive a journey to such faraway land? Losing sleep was no longer just an idiom with them: it was their reality. By the time they discovered the unsubstantiated character of one rumour, another came rolling down, like a rock down a hillside, and then they lay buried under its rubble for some time. When you are weak and also scared, the strong man does not need to resort to action to take advantage; plain talk is enough.

Fears had been planted in the minds of Indians. Now they were taking roots. Mohandas could see that their will was weakening. So he called a meeting of his associates, in which it was decided that a letter be sent to the members of both parliaments. Some people opposed this move. They argued that the result would be a veritable death in life.

Mohandas laughed to hear the argument. 'Sure,' he said: 'if you are happy with your life now, there is hardly any point in carrying on with this theatre.' Then, turning serious, he explained: 'Look, the aim of all our drafting and dispatching is to protect our rights. We are asking them not to take away the rights we already have. If this little request annoys someone, so be it. We cannot let our boat sink in midstream for fear of annoying him. We must do all we can to save it.'

'And what good will that do?'

Mohandas enjoyed the cut and thrust of such debate. 'If by good you mean instantaneous gain, you must understand that the gains of a struggle take time to materialize. You add salt to something and you can just about taste it. It's not like milk which will turn a bucketful of water white. Struggle gives you courage. It helps you understand your situation and it tells others that you too have a voice.'

Mohandas' explanations did produce an effect on the people, and when once affected, the people stood their ground.

When there was a consensus, Gandhibhai himself was asked to get ready the draft of the letter to be sent to the members of the parliaments. It took him two-three days to get the draft ready. It was then read out to the members of the committee. The letter started on a dramatic note:

Dear Sirs,

It was my desire to keep this letter anonymous, but it is not possible to say serious things in an anonymous letter. An anonymous letter is anyway a sign of cowardice. I want to make it quite clear at the very start that I have no selfish motive in sending this letter. I am not seeking any personal popularity. I have only one objective in sending this letter: to promote goodwill among Europeans and Indians, to bring the two together and to serve the country of my birth. The only way of achieving this objective is to make an appeal to the representatives of the people and to prepare public opinion in its favour. If the two communities are able to live together in peace, the credit will certainly go to you. If they are not, pardon me for saying so, the responsibility for the failure too will be laid at your door. Edwin Arnold, in his 'Song of the Celestial' says that the choice of the wise is also the choice of the people. Common people always emulate the conduct of the select few.

In this colony, Indians are looked down on. They are objects of derision. The reason is hatred. And the reason for hatred is colour. There is no getting away from colour. It's idle even to entertain the idea that one can get rid of colour. One can change one's thinking, but one can't change one's skin. So the only way out is for the coloured to depart the land as soon as possible. Had there been any other reason for the hatred, one could have hoped that removing that reason could help us secure the rights that are rightfully ours. There are about forty thousand Indians in this colony. It is impossible to send them all out. The most you can do is to stop any further immigration. The problem before you therefore is how to manage the Indians: by terrorizing over them or by taking a sympathetic view of their problems?

It was a long letter. Mohandas paused and scrutinized the faces around him. They were all eager faces. He continued reading:

Permit me first of all to say a few words about the girmitiyas. *You call them coolies, but they are here on a* girmit. *They may be domestic servants, attendants, farm labourers, railway workers or whatever—their introduction here has been beneficial for the colony. No one here doubts for a moment that they had a crucial role to play in turning Natal into the garden of Africa. Take them off your sugarcane farms and see the result! The natives are no substitutes for them. If they could be substitutes, you would not have imported these people here as* girmitiyas *from a distant land. In his election meeting, one of the members of your parliament, Mr. Galland, had himself admitted as much. The Indian coolie turned out to be precisely the kind of worker the industries of this colony stood in need of. Had they not been imported, the European population in Durban would not have reached even half its present strength. Where you have twenty labourers working today, you would not have had even five. The price of the land would have been three to four hundred per cent down on what it is today. Even the natives address Indians coolies disdainfully. Despite the invaluable help and cooperation received from them, their desire to settle in the colony is ungratefully rejected.*

Mohandas also made a reference to a letter published in *Natal Mercury* of August 11, 1884 from one Mr. Johnston, which said:

This multi-ethnic and multi-religious Indian race has helped in laying the foundation of and in developing British, Portuguese, and East African trade along the coast. Introducing these simple, altruistic, frugal, hard-working, proficient and intelligent Indians in central Africa will aid its development. We will be hard put to find telegraph workers, smalltime grocers, skilled craftsmen, cooks, low level employees, scribes, railway workers, etc. If we want to be able to run our industries in this tropical country in an organized manner, we cannot do without them.

He paused again to scrutinize the faces. The level of eagerness had not reduced, though he could detect signs of fatigue setting in. He increased his pace of reading:

Newspaper commentaries indicate that those Indians who are erroneously called Arabs have proved themselves to be successful businessmen. Thanks to their simple living, these small businessmen are always able to score over their white peers. This cannot be a valid reason for expelling them from this country. Do you think the civilized society in this country will stand for such autocratic behaviour? How can they ever compete with you? They are simple and straightforward people, not barbarians, as your newspapers like to call them. The reasons for their success are: no drinking, keeping off all vice and self discipline. And no dishonesty. They know how to be content with a small profit margin.

The fatigue was now showing. Yawns were getting larger. Mohandas stopped reading and said: 'Looks like you are getting tired. I am testing your patience a bit too much, I think. But in a matter like this, it is just not possible for me to move a step without your advice.' And he started reading again.

In the matter of cleanliness, despite the pain it causes me, I have to accept the accusation you make. These people are unable to maintain cleanliness. But much of what is said against them on this count is motivated partially by hatred. While it is true that they don't come up to our expectations in this regard, they cannot be bundled out of the colony simply on this ground. They are so poor; how

> *can we expect them to be clean? But despite their degrading poverty, they are not lawless. They are a disciplined lot. I should like to quote a Natal scholar on the subject. He says: 'We must concede that Indians are an orderly and law abiding community. They are second to none in their respect for constitutional authority. Indian labourers are not only preferable but in fact represent the most responsible and useful constituent of the colony's citizenry. Their continued stay in the colony is an essential prerequisite for its prosperity.'*

Mohandas did not read any further. He had taken care to omit those portions which he thought would be beyond the grasp of ordinary folk. The cultural and social history of India, details of the contradictions between the treatment meted out to Indians, and the British traditions, etc. were some such topics.

When Gandhibhai finished reading, there was silence for a time. It took awhile for everyone to realize that the reading was over. It also took them some time to emerge from the silence within. Then a single voice was heard, but it felt as if it came from the throat of every man present in the room: 'No one thought or said anything like this about us ever before.' Like spilled water, the words spread to all corners of the room.

~

It was during the days when all kinds of rumours were being spread about the franchise bill that a white trader returned from London. His family lived in London while he looked after his business in Durban. He used to visit London at least once a year, sometimes even twice. When this time he returned from London, something happened that seemed to send the white community into shocked silence. The rumour mills suddenly stopped grinding. The big boasts that were made earlier were no longer repeated. Supervision of the *girmitiya*s was becoming stricter and discipline too was being enforced more strictly. They were now not being permitted even to leave their barracks. Work over, they had to remain holed up in their hovels. Supervisors went around the settlements, most of them

Indians. The white masters were of the view that Indians were good at roughing up their fellow countrymen. An English dog barks to see another dog; an Indian bristles to see another Indian. The *girmitiya*s got one set of uniforms every year; the supervisors got two. A bait's worth of difference was all there was. They had a smattering of English. A kick in the pants from the master was like a prescription drug for them. The master might not be anywhere around, but his all-seeing eye could spell disaster. It could pop up anywhere and not spare even a supervisor. So the Indian supervisors did their muscle work with all sincerity.

Mohandas was worried about this sudden change in the attitude of white masters towards *girmitiya*s. What could have brought about this change, he wondered. Was there a fresh decree from Her Majesty or had the whites made up their minds to use the slow-poison method: if you can't throw the Indians out, use slow poison and see them dissolve like salt in water. When Mohandas failed to find any clue to the change, he wrote a letter to Sir Pherozeshah.

> *The government won't let on. Papers say that the Queen has turned down the amendment to the franchise bill passed by Natal government. The whites have turned enemies of Indians. Silently, the level of torture and harassment of Indians is rising. Please let me know what the real situation is.*

Slowly, a fresh round of rumours started. People started saying that the Englishman who had returned from England had informed the local whites that Her Majesty's government was not in favour of the amendment bill. The bigger ones among the employers had got together and decided that news of this development should not be allowed to leak to Gandhi and his coolie community. In the meantime, screws on the community must be tightened so hard that more than half of them should run away of their own accord. If they didn't run away, they should be reduced to a miserable state so that they couldn't survive in the colony. Some people disagreed with this proposal. They instead wanted some rumours to be spread so that the reactions of coolies could be fathomed and their thinking ascertained. The whites eventually tried both methods. They did spread some light rumours but kept the truth well-hidden. However, the truth could not be kept hidden for too long. The pressure on the tightly held-down lid began to grow too much and leakage started. Coolies were alerted. Dissatisfaction against the Queen among the whites started growing. 'It's supposed to be our government,' they said: 'and we have no voice! Does she think she can run a government with the support of these illiterate, uneducated, and filthy barbarians?'

Reactions of this kind began to stir a new sign of life among Indians. Gandhibhai started receiving congratulatory messages.People walked up to Gandhi and said: 'If you hadn't been around, we would have been flattened into dust. It was your support that kept us going.'

~

Membership of Natal Congress started soaring. The enthusiasm was however confined to the traders or to those who were somewhat educated. The *girmitiya*s were mostly unaffected by this development. All that they had grasped was that the 'ballister' from Bombay had carried tales to the Queen and the Queen had tweaked the ears of the government. That knowledge was enough for the *girmitiya*s. The pain of slavery was still there, but, with this bit of happiness, the tragedy had subsided a little. For once, it was both win and loss, not just loss and loss.

Finally, day came when a notice from Her Majesty's government also reached Mohandas. By then everyone already knew. The notice said: 'Her Majesty's government is not in favour of colour discrimination in franchise. Her Majesty is therefore pleased to withhold her approval to the Franchise Amendment Bill.'

The pleasure in fact belonged to the Indians. Celebrations continued through the night. People queued up to congratulate Gandhibhai, which did embarrass him a little. 'How can I claim the credit for all of it?' he kept repeating. 'It was a popular decision and it had everyone's dedicated support.' But no one was prepared to listen. On the other hand, darkness had descended in the white areas of Natal and Transvaal. They were beginning to believe that this man called M.K. Gandhi was using magic. Newspapers published cartoons with the caption "Gandhi: The Black Magician." Gandhi's immediate reaction was that the papers were trying to fish in troubled waters. If their trick worked, the *girmitiya*s would be the worst victims of the ensuing conflagration; the businessmen would be able to save themselves one way or the other. So Gandhibhai quickly got a statement ready and got it signed and approved by prominent Indians. It said: 'The objective of the Indian community is to raise the feeling of brotherhood with the white community.'

The whites ridiculed the statement: 'Feeling of brotherhood between the ruler and the ruled? What nonsense! Queen's kindness seems to have turned their heads. Let the coolies not forget that the Queen belongs to us ...'

'Gandhi is an enemy of the whites and the white government.'

The whites had started sharpening their main weapon–colour discrimination. This alone was their answer to the increasing political power of Indians. They could hardly wait to prune this so-called power and cut the Indians down to size. But the biggest cause of worry was the coolie barrister. He had started haunting them in their dreams and they were now certain that he was the main road block in the path of their progress. The white planters felt that they were listening to their own funeral music played by their own orchestra.

Sanderson was one of the biggest planters of Natal. A party was on at his bungalow. In addition to thousands of acres of agricultural farms, he also had extensive property in the cities. He owned a fleet of ships which transported goods to and from Lanka. The party had been organized so that people could have a free exchange of views on the new situation. Only select people had been invited. They were the top people from their respective areas. Drinks were served and guests got into a jolly mood. Talk veered round to the bodies of Indian women, which seemed to be little more than tasty meat for them. As soon as coolies were mentioned, their knives and forks came into action. Knives sliced, forks pierced and morsels of meat disappeared into their mouths. One of the planters was however glum and concentrated only on drinks. When someone mentioned the amendment bill and commented that Her Majesty's government had not done the right thing by rejecting it, he ignited like a bomb and screamed: 'You are the ones responsible. You are the ones who imported these detestable creatures into this colony. And now that they are multiplying like pigs, you whimper and whine!'

One of the senior planters tried to explain the situation: 'It's true that we got these coolies into Natal. But have you ever paused to think who helped us grow the tropical crops? Do you think we whites could have worked the fields in this hot and cold climate? Do you think the native *kaffir*s, with their women and their chiefs hogging all their time, could have provided a solution? Don't you know that M & M had set on fire hundreds of acres of ripe sugarcane crop because the tribe chieftain tried to take advantage of their situation? It was only after the coolies arrived that these *kaffir*s came to their senses. That's the reason they too cannot stand the coolies.'

'So what? Who doesn't like to fish in trouble waters?'

Another drunk white joined in: 'When we needed them, we used them. That doesn't mean that they turn the whole Natal into a pigsty, shit all over the place, and then grumble.'

'Mind what you say. And mind your language! You too are equally responsible. Had the coolies not been imported from India, we couldn't have continued living here. Not all whites are rich. Not all of them can walk into big stores and buy cartloads of goods. There are the poor amongst us whose daily needs are supplied by these hawkers with their baskets balanced on their shoulders and selling their goods at cheap rates. If vegetable prices are low today, it's because of them.'

'But don't these activities affect our business? Earlier, we had the monopoly of these fields; now the coolies are everywhere. I tell you the enemy is within us and we are helping it thrive. But what is most surprising is that some of our own people have started speaking the coolie barrister's language!'

The man who had been targeted responded very patiently: 'The problem with people like you is that you are living in terror of that man. Ever since the Franchise Amendment Bill was returned, he has been haunting you in your dreams.' After a pause, he added: 'Take it easy. For me, he is just another man, with no special status. In fact, he is a blot on humanity.'

'Let's stop bickering, shall we? We are here to discuss seriously the difficult problem that faces us, not to discuss some worthless people.'

Sanderson tried to bring about a compromise. 'I think,' he said, 'the planters did no wrong by importing coolies. That was the need of the time. That was a time when the whole of Natal could not muster up ten thousand native workers. Imagine! Acres and acres of land and barely ten thousand workers! And some workers—working only when they felt like it! Was it possible for you to work your farms with such workers? Today, we have sixty thousand workers doing every kind of job on the farms.'

'Coolie labourers, yes. Others, no.'

This last statement saw most people rising vociferously in support, some of them actually dancing. The orchestra music rose in crescendo. They shouted: 'Long live the Queen!'

When they started dinner, sense had already deserted them. One of them hollered: 'Gandhi, the coolie.'

Another screamed: 'Hang him from a tree.'

Then they all chorused: 'Gandhi, the coolie! Hang him from a tree!'

One of them got up and mimed the act of hanging from a tree. His shadow fell on the wall, where it looked as if he was hanging himself.

~

As his reputation grew, Mohandas got busier at work. His clientele increased. He now also had some white friends. Most of those who approached him professionally were either Muslims or Christians. Hindus were generally very poor and included few businessmen. However, whenever need arose, it was Mohandas on call. Muslims were mostly businessmen and were members of the Natal Congress.

He now needed someone he could trust to look after his expanding activities. He thought of his elder brother, Lakshmidas, but promptly rejected the idea reproaching himself even for entertaining the idea. How could it be possible? Who would look after the affairs at home? In fact, the very idea that he should order his brother, who had always been his guide, here to look after his affairs was absurd. The next name he thought of was Sheikh Mehtab. He had stood by him as a friend all his childhood days; let him do it again. It had been ages since he had seen him. Mohandas often felt so lonely after work. The family had not been able to join him yet. Somehow, he was now fixated on Sheikh Mehtab. A whole era flashed before his eyes, as his face broke into a smile. What a wonderful thing is childhood! That was a time when he couldn't take a single step alone; now there was nothing but to walk alone.

Thinking of Sheikh Mehtab, he couldn't help thinking of his home and the people at Rajkot, Kastur, the kids, Sheikh Mehtab and *Ba*. *Ba*, who was no more, but whose touch he could feel on every part of his body! It was as if all these people had been hiding in some corner and had spilled out at the very mention of Sheikh Mehtab to announce their presence. How close, yet how far! Finally, he wrote to Sheikh Mehtab:

> *Sheikhbhai, if you came over, you could help me out in my work. It would also help me pass my lonely hours. I also want to call Kastur and the kids, but I must get a good idea of the circumstances developing here before I do that.*

Gandhibhai went personally to the ship to receive Sheikh Mehtab. He found him completely changed. He himself had changed but perhaps not quite as much. Sheikh Mehtab had put on weight and his hair had receded like a losing army. The body was no longer as taut and age was beginning to show. His eyes however frolicked about quite freely and were never still. The clue to the roving eye seemed to lie in the hairline and the advancing age.

The memories of Rajkot seemed to keep holding them together. The whole city seemed to come alive between them. Mohandas kept staring at Sheikh Mehtab for a long, long while. Kastur, his elder brother, his sister-in-law, Hari, Mani, all the relatives who held him close seemed to come alive in his face. It was as if his face had become transparent glass.

Thinking of that event in his childhood brought shivers to Gandhibhai. When he was going to look up Tulsi uncle to seek his permission to go to London that night, he had been lost in thoughts of Sheikh Mehtab. He had had a quarrel with him earlier in the day. The issue must have been some trivial one. They hardly ever needed an issue to start a fight. That day it must have been his farewell blues. He couldn't imagine how Sheikh Mehtab would live without him, though, in actuality, just the opposite was the case. Lost in thought, he had collided with an oncoming vehicle. He had hardly recovered from the collision when, near the house he was visiting for an evening of devotional music, he stumbled over a stone and fell. *Ba* had become very upset. He too had become apprehensive that he might not be able to go to Porbandar and his departure to London might have to be postponed. He had however made it to Porbandar. In London too, he had not been able to put Sheikh Mehtab out of his mind. He seemed to occupy an angle of his mind where he could be seen from any corner. Mohandas sometimes reprimanded himself for the infatuation. But Mehtab encouraged Mohandas, and there he was again, smiling. The devil!

Mohandas smiled to himself.

A little later, when they settled down a bit, this was the first question that he asked Sheikh Mehtab: 'You remember how you teased me at school—sometimes threatening to set the boys at me, sometimes protecting me against them, sometimes encouraging me to eat meat and sometimes threatening to report the sin? You didn't allow me peace even in London. Anyway, I'm glad we have finally left those adolescent days behind.'

Sheikh Mehtab gave a loud laugh: 'If you had, why would I need to be here today? But if that's the way you feel, I have no problem. But, tell me, we are now going to stay together, aren't we?' His eyes twinkled with mischief.

Mohandas laughed. 'We are no longer kids. Come on, forget the childhood days and get a move on. All right?'

'Isn't childhood a part of life? Can you ever forget it? Had you been able to forget it, would you have remembered me today? Try however hard you may, you can never forget your kid days. They are always there, right in front of you, at every turn of life.'

'I should have known I can't beat you as a lawyer. You would never miss a chance to hit back. But don't forget we have our own kids now.'

'But the kid that was in us is still within us. Even as we talk of being fathers, we are holding him by the hand.'

'Touché! You win and I lose, okay? I sent for you because I needed help. There is no one here I can turn to.'

'But let me also make one thing clear to you: the Sheikh Mehtab standing before you and the Sheikh Mehtab of old are not very different creatures. The old Mehtab still thrives within me and so do those bonds. We are not snakes that we may shed our skins and make ourselves new altogether. So long as we live, those bonds live too.'

Mohandas looked at him and gave him a Gandhibhai smile. Mehtab hadn't yet noticed the difference between the two.

~

Gandhibhai was living at Beach Grove, in a double-storeyed house. Sheikh Mehtab too had made himself comfortable in the house. Lawrence, Gandhibhai's clerk, also lived in the house. In fact, any member of Gandhibhai's staff who was without a place to live would come and make himself comfortable there. There was an Indian cook who cooked vegetarian meals for all of them. Lawrence too was Indian. He had converted after coming to Natal, but despite his conversion his identity remained unchanged: he looked a coolie every inch. Mohandas had hired him personally and now he was a regular member of Mohandas' household.

Lawrence's job was to look after Mohandas' court affairs: maintaining files, getting case papers ready, keeping track of court dates, timely filing of papers in the courts, keeping in touch with the clients, informing them of the court dates and so on. Sheikh Mehtab was charged with book keeping and accounts. Correspondence with clients was also his charge. He sometimes also engaged Mohandas in political discussions, from which it was clear that though he knew little about Natal politics, he was desirous of a full stake in political matters. Mohandas tried to tell him that he should get a good understanding of the issues involved before opening his mouth on the subject, but, Mehtab being Mehtab, the counsel had no effect on him. Though he was unable to say it openly, his feeling clearly was that, though Gandhibhai might well have become a barrister and might even have made a name for himself in Natal, it did not change his status as his protégé.

Sheikh was also a bit of a bully and very status conscious. He believed that a clerk should be treated as a clerk, a servant as a servant, and so on. The democratic style of Gandhibhai was not at all to his liking. That only gave them ideas, he thought. Both Lawrence and the cook called Gandhibhai by his name, even in the presence of clients. Lawrence even called Sheikh Mehtab Sheikhbhai, which made him squirm with discomfiture.

On several occasions, Sheikh Mehtab actually warned Mohandas: 'I say you must keep Lawrence in his place. Don't give him so much importance. He doesn't deserve the trust and the respect that you shower on him.'

Gandhibhai normally ignored the warning, but when it was repeated time and again, he brushed it off with: 'Look, I know you are not happy with him. He is actually very hard-working and sincere. He has never given me an opportunity to find fault with him or to pull him up. Nor do I wish to hurt anyone's self-respect by my behaviour.'

Lawrence too ignored Sheikh's behaviour. Often when Gandhibhai was not around, Sheikh made caustic comments to him: 'You think Gandhibhai cannot function without you? I have only to tell him and he would throw you out the next moment. He has been my friend since childhood.'

Lawrence replied very coolly: 'You needn't worry on my account. I'll leave the day Gandhibhai wants me to.'

Sheikh felt that he was a victim of deliberate neglect from Lawrence and that he was always trying to slight him. So he carried larger-than-life tales to Gandhibhai, so much so that sometimes Gandhibhai found himself having second thoughts. He had to remind himself that despite all his shortcomings Lawrence was a decent man. His behaviour with people in Durban was decent too. Finding his complaint ignored left Sheikh Mehtab very bitter.

Then on one occasion, Sheikh Mehtab brought up a financial matter. He knew that that was one matter Mohandas never compromised on. His claim was that Lawrence fiddled with money; it was his major weakness. As ill luck would have it, Lawrence also turned up at the spot. Mohandas had not quite recovered from the shock yet and he blurted out: 'Lawrence, I learn you are doing things you shouldn't be doing. Your behaviour with Sheikh Mehtab also needs to improve. You are slipping.'

There was a glint in the eyes of Sheikh Mehtab.

It was an unexpected blow to Lawrence. He stood stunned for a while and then walked out without a word. He might have been a clerk but his mind was quite uncluttered. One who works in a law court knows only too well which side his bread is buttered. When he walked out without a word, Gandhibhai knew he had goofed. He had hurt Lawrence's self-respect by talking to him the way he had done.

When he returned from the court that evening, Gandhibhai went to Lawrence's room to ask for his forgiveness. The room was empty. Lawrence had left with his things. There was no trace of him anywhere.

As he plodded back from the room, Gandhibhai knew what had actually transpired.

He called the cook and checked: 'Did Lawrence leave a message?'

'He is gone,' said the cook. 'He said he had lost your trust and so there was no way he could stay here any more. He also said that he had never complained to you about Sheikh Mehtab because he knew he was your friend. What you did wasn't right, he said.'

Mohandas returned to his room without a word and sat in darkness for a while. When he got up, he muttered to himself: 'I should have turned on the light. When it is dark, you need it all the more, don't you?'

He lighted the lamp. It then struck him that it was Lawrence who every evening lighted the lamp in his room and office when he returned from the court.

~

XI

When even after the year's *girmit* was over and Mohandas failed to return home, a fresh round of speculations and worries started at Rajkot. Gandhibhai too was conscious of this fact. It also worried him to think that he might have been wrong in his decision not to return home. But he had been unable to find any reason which would convince him that he was actually wrong. The strongest reason perhaps was that he had failed to keep his promise to Kastur. But he had not done it for personal reasons. The interest and the entreaties of an entire community were at stake. A tragedy involving such large number of people certainly weighed more than the failure to keep a promise to one person. Or did it? That was the big question.

He often had the feeling that Kastur was demanding to know when the promised year would end.

Mohandas still didn't have an answer to that question.

It came as a big shock to Kastur to learn that Mohandas had chosen to get Sheikh Mehtab over to Durban. So Sheikh turned out to be dearer to him than his near ones, didn't he? What did he see in Sheikh that he found missing in her? Sheikh had left, and had left a number of questions for her to ponder. The questions leapt up like flames in her mind, often singeing and scorching her. Mohandas' promise that he would be back in a year surged again and again like a wave and washed over her, leaving her wondering if it was because of Sheikh Mehtab that he had broken it. If that was the case, why had he assumed the responsibilities of a married life? Or was it that he had been left with no choice? Was it solely a decision of *Ba* and *Bapu*?

Hari often asked about his father, which always set her on edge. He had spent some time with his father unlike Mani, who was still young.

When Hari asked, she would get irritated and ask 'Why do you keep going *Bapu-Bapu*? What does he care for you?'

'Do you think he doesn't care for us?'

'No, he doesn't,' was her angry answer.

Hari would be in tears. The question kept bothering him: Why did *Ba* say a thing like that? After all, he is my father, isn't he?

Such were the issues bothering Mohandas, the most important one being that of ethics, of a broken promise, of failed responsibilities. He had failed in India, and that was the real issue. It was not for lack of trying. How long could he continue to live off his brother? For years, he and his family had been dependent on him. For years, he had listened to the barbs of Kastur. Perhaps he wouldn't have regretted it so much, had he not been in possession of a barrister degree from London. He could then have been open to any kind of job. He had been doing 'any kind of job' even with a barrister degree, except a barrister's job. He had lost *Ba* in his pursuit of the bar-at-law dream. In the end, neither *Ba* had been around to see him earn his bar-at-law degree, nor had he been around to see *Ba* go. In the meantime, his elder brother's expectations from him went soaring. He had had no expectations from Karsan. He was happy if Karsan was able to support himself. Mohandas was the hub of all his expectations: 'When he comes back from London, all our troubles will be over. We will move into a castle.' An ordinary man couldn't even dream of living in a castle. When a man starts building castles in the air, he finds even his lowly accommodation taken from him. A bird in hand is always better than two in the bush. Had *Ba* been alive, would she also have had the same expectations from him? If she had, she would also have reached the same conclusions about him, that he was a fool and knew nothing of the ways of the world. Maybe she would be right. Maybe making money was not his forté. You needed to be a lot smarter to do that. Kastur however had never spoken a word about this. She either didn't know how important money was, or maybe she could make do with whatever she had. Like the kids, she also has a share in whatever was handed out at home. But what about my share, Mohandas thought and laughed: My share is whatever I am: ragged, half-done and often mistaken.

Sheikh Mehtab was like a bitter pill for her. She tried again and again to swallow it, but every time it came popping out. His relationship with Mehtab, their partnership in joy and in sorrow, antedated Kastur. Even after Kastur, he had been the bridge between her and him—the messenger. Hadn't he been around, who would have conveyed his messages to Kastur and brought their tidings to him? He had tried really hard to get Kastur to learn to read and write but it hadn't worked. They had both been to blame. Had she become literate, Sheikh would have been sent out of the way a long time ago, particularly since others too at home too found the relationship rather odd. They didn't realize that an elder brother could hardly substitute for a friend for the kind of services that the latter provided.

She cannot be faulted for wanting him back at home, but who does he go back to? To those touts who made a draftsman out of him? To those men who were his brother's friends yet who sought their cut in his clients' fees? And his brother found nothing wrong in it! The work he did here earned him respect. People sought him out to provide him briefs. A will for life was stirring in those who had been half-dead. A desire for an independent identity was taking root.

'No, Kastur, not now. I can't come now.

Shekh Mehtab is here. Lawrence has left.'

Had the two been able to get on with each other, success would have had a new face.

'It was my fault. I let things go out of control.

Kastur! You are still to learn how the making of one leads to the unmaking of another.'

~

The Balasundaram case had planted the name of Gandhibhai in the hearts of the *girmitiya*s like a seed of a new crop. The protection of law had been secured for an Indian worker without spending a penny. The credit for this achievement was being given to Gandhibhai. It was not as if the law had not been approached earlier. The *girmitiya*s did knock on the doors of the court, but they returned literally empty-handed, stripped of all their earnings. In fact, their condition became much worse, as the master's stick was now constantly shadowing them. The stick also acquired a greater sting. The wooden sticks of earlier days were replaced, post-return, by iron rods. This event had however lit a tiny flicker of hope in the terrorized hearts. The 'Bombay Ballister' was nothing short of a talisman, which put them beyond all fear. Actually, though, fear did survive. To give themselves courage, they now used his name as they used the name of *Bajarang Bali*. When Hindus recited this god's name, no ghosts and demons dared to come near. These people had to face these spirits everyday, so The Name helped. When troubles multiplied, they chanted the mantra over and over again, remembering Gandhibhai.

In their eyes, Mr. Brown was no less powerful than Ravana himself. 'Only *Bajarang Bali* or Gandhibhai could have rescued Balasundaram' from his barracks. Mohandas was now both hero and friend to them, a friend they had never set eyes on. As time passed and they got to know that Gandhibhai actually lived like Englishmen, dressed in their style and spoke their language, they didn't know what to think. What sort of Hanuman was this? How could they ever approach him? There were a few of them who had seen him and they thought times had changed. In these times, if you wanted to take on the enemy, you had to live like him and talk like him. Only then would the enemy realize that there was finally someone who lived the way he himself did and could well take him on. Hanuman was living in the times of bears and demons, so he had to assume that form. This kind of explanation made sense to them. Balasundaram had appeared before him in tattered clothes, neither speaking nor understanding his language, yet Gandhibhai had been able to uncover his real thoughts. 'Won't he be able to discern ours? Why not?' This thought redoubled their faith and gave them courage.

~

The Government of Natal had not been able to reconcile itself to the rejection of the Franchise Amendment Bill. Like a smitten snake, it was readying itself for a counter-attack. The Indian community now looked to it like a jinn growing larger and larger limbs everyday, which could swallow the entire white community in its ever-expanding mouth any day. The mouth was what they hated most: the coolie barrister M.K. Gandhi.

There had been a series of meetings. Having suffered a loss of face in the matter of the franchise bill, they were now targeting the *girmitiya* law. There was however no unanimity among the white planters on this issue. Those opposing the move argued that securing an amendment to the girmitiya law would not be a cakewalk. 'After all,' they argued, 'it was on our request that the Queen had granted her approval to the law in the first place.'

The yea-sayers were however in no mood to backtrack. 'Doesn't the colonial government have the right to amend a law that has gone wrong?' they argued.

'No one is denying that right. But it is not only the Natal government that is involved; there is another government to consider. Can you subordinate its rights to your own?'

'What do you mean?'

'Look, you young people are a hot-blooded lot. Once you set your mind on something, you just keep going till you get it. At the moment you are only thinking of your own profit. Nothing wrong with that, but you must also consider the legality and illegality of your course of action. To us, the legal side of the matter is clear as the day. You cannot always have everything your own way.'

Mr. Wilson, the speaker of these words, was one of those planters who had worked actively in formulating the labour import scheme. Another planter, who had also been associated with the project, expressed his support for Wilson by nodding vigorously.

A young planter however refused to be cowed down and spoke in a raised voice: 'How much longer shall we carry on the burden of your mistakes? We are not responsible for what you did or why you did it.'

The assent-nodding planter now spoke: 'In 1860, when this was all barren land, the only workers were the *kaffir*s. Actually, they were less of workers and more of blackmailers. It was impossible to grow sugarcane. That was when the Natal government took up the matter of labour import with the government of India. The Government of India was quite unwilling. It was only after the British government intervened that it agreed to send its workers here on a five-year *girmit.* At the end of the *girmit* period, the workers were free either to go back to India at their master's expense or to acquire a piece of land equivalent in value to the expense and settle down here.'

The first young planter retorted vehemently: 'If the Government of India does not agree, we will simply throw these damned coolies out of Natal before they complete their five years. This way they won't be able to complete their *girmit* and won't be entitled to buy land and settle here.'

Everyone was silent for a while. Then a middle-aged sort of planter spoke: 'Not possible. You may be able to force out ten or twenty or hundred, what difference would that make? There are sixty thousand coolies in the colony. And if you use force, will the Indian government remain a passive spectator?'

The senior planters were beginning to get the upper hand. Another one of them said: 'suppose you succeed in throwing them out. What will happen to the thousands of acres of land under cultivation? What will happen to our sugar production? To the tropical crops? The *kaffir*s have learnt nothing in these thirty-five years. Most of the vegetables we consume today are the ones the coolies have brought with them from India. They are the ones who have worked hard, and worked competently, to grow them in this land.'

'There is only one way out. Let us send them back as soon as they complete the period of their *girmit*.'

'But if they refuse to go and demand land in lieu of the travel expense home, we will be under legal obligation to meet their demand.'

People sobered up as they realized the gravity of the problem. One of the young ones made a suggestion: 'Why don't we issue a fresh *girmit* at the end of two years, accompanied by a raise in salary. Poor and greedy, these people will find the temptation irresistible. The conditions attached to the five-year *girmit* will thus become infructuous.'

No meeting-point between the two classes of people was in sight. The young ones wanted just this: the coolies should continue to stay on *girmit* but should not be allowed the right to settle. The senior planters called it their wilfulness. They argued that their actions must conform to the existing rules. They also argued that the British government would certainly not want to displease the government of a large colony like India for the sake of a small colony like Natal.

The young planters raised another objection: 'What is so special about these coolies that the Indian government will favour them in preference to the whites? The government of India shares religion, race and colour with us.' Another white added: 'but that coolie barrister of yours says we share our race with them. In his letter sent to the members of parliament, he has used every possible argument to establish this point.'

'Poor barrister.'

After hours of argument, it was agreed that an *ex parte* cancellation of the five-year *girmit* was not possible; nor was it possible to evict the coolies forcibly from the colony. They could think of only one way out of this impasse: a law must be legislated with such stringent conditions that the *girmitiya*s and other Indians would find them impossible to fulfil and would be obliged to leave the colony. This way, the whites could have their cake and eat it too. Finally, they all agreed to pressurize the government to impose a poll tax of twenty-five pounds a year on those coolies who decided to settle in Natal. Those failing to pay this tax would not enjoy the benefits of the *girmit* conditions and would not be permitted to settle in the colony.

One of the planters opposed this move: 'This is completely unrealistic,' he said. 'You cannot expect labourers getting a monthly salary of fifteen shillings to pay twenty-five pounds in tax.'

'That's their problem,' said another and laughed.

The Natal government had been smarting under the humiliation of the franchise bill rejection and was keen on a healing package, which would include a rap in the knuckles for the Indians. It quickly grabbed the proposal for a poll tax. The problem however was the consent of the Indian government. The agreement with the Indian government related only to the *girmit*. There was no scope for a poll tax in it.

The Indian viceroy at the time was Lord Elgin. On top of being Governor General of the largest British colony, Elgin was also a stubborn man. The Natal government was well aware of these facts. It also knew that Lord Elgin prided himself on being the greatest protector of India and Indian interests. After a lot of deliberation, the Natal government decided to send two representatives to meet Lord Elgin and to soften him up in its favour. The problem was who to send. The first consideration was that at least one of them must be eminent enough to be able to talk to Lord Elgin on terms of equality. Second, the members must have the necessary behavioural and conversational skills to be able to bring Lord Elgin round to their point of view. They must also be fully conversant with his temperament and attitudes. The name of Sir Henry Binns was suggested from various sources. He was among the top diplomats of the colony, who stood out especially for two reasons: first, he was a big businessman himself and was well aware of the problems of businessmen;second, he had a good standing in politics and diplomacy. He had led a number of delegations sent out by the British government.

When the proposal was put to Sir Henry, his first reaction was to try and wriggle out of it: 'I am an old man. I can't stand long sea voyages. It would be better if you find a younger man.'

Mr. Mason was the Protector. He was quite familiar with the problems of the *girmitiya*s and also knew what the white businessmen really wanted. He was young and quite close to Sir Henry. Extremely fond of travel and sight-seeing, a visit to India was one of his cherished dreams. Actually, every white man looked upon a visit to India as an achievement. So when Mason was asked he not only jumped at the offer but also took it upon himself to persuade Sir Henry.

To Sir Henry, he said: 'Sir, I'll take care of all your comforts. You have only to tell me what to do and I'll do it. The matter concerns the white community, which wants to be relieved of the burden of the coolies. There is no one else but you who can do it for them.'

Repeated entreaties from Mr. Mason finally persuaded Sir Henry to lead the delegation. This was indeed happy news for Natal government. It knew well that once Sir Henry undertook to do something he saw to it that it was done. He had pulled many chestnuts out of the fire for the British government, chestnuts which the British government had given up for loss. Sir Henry devoted himself first to a detailed study of the situation and then to a thorough understanding of the political views of the Natal government. Next he addressed himself to the wishes of the bureaucracy. He examined the likely consequences of the decision on the local population and tried to delve into the thinking of the British government on the issue. Only after he had made a thorough assessment of all these points did he formulate his own arguments. Sir Henry was neither a solicitor nor a barrister. He had however made a detailed study of British laws and colonial practices and customs. He was quite definite on one point: Indians should not be permitted to settle down in other colonies. Work over, they should go home, be they *girmitiya*s or travellers. When a lawyer personally subscribes to an argument, you can be sure that half the case is won for the client. He was quite convinced that it was the whites who had developed the colony and brought it to a stage where it could call itself a colony of the British Empire. How could anyone else be allowed to take it over? The first right of course belonged to the natives, but were they bothered at all?

They were getting enough to justify the little they did for the land. The Indians of course worked, but they were paid for it. He thought the Indians were not fit to be free citizens. As slaves, though, they were fine. He believed that Indians were fundamentally uncivilized barbarians, quite unused to the manners of a cultured society. They were carriers of diseases and instruments of infection.

Mr. Mason represented the views of the white businessmen, whose basic fear was that the Indian businessmen would one day take away all their business: working with small margins, selling in big quantities, hawking their goods from door to door, even doling out goods on credit. The white businessman, big or small, always sold cash. Most worrying was the fact that they had even devised ways of importing goods from India and they had absolute monopoly over those goods. It sent a shooting pain through white businessmen's hearts to realize that they could do nothing in the matter. Their view was that if the Indian businessmen had to sell Indian goods they must procure them through the white traders. Mr. Mason always wore a pathetic look, which evoked sympathy in the listener's heart. He was particularly bitter towards Indians. This fact was universally known and served as an additional qualification for him to be made a member of the delegation.

Sir Henry and Mr. Mason got off at the Bombay port after a long journey by sea. After a couple of days' rest at Bombay, an assortment of trains and other means of transportation took them to Delhi. Though Delhi was not the capital yet, but it was fast becoming the centre of activities. Lord Elgin loved Delhi and that was where the two were going to see him. The long journey had tired them out completely, even more than the sea voyage. After another couple of days' rest, word was sent to Lord Elgin that a delegation of the Natal government, under the leadership of Sir Henry Binns, was desirous of meeting the Governor General.

Sir Henry was quite sure that they would be called in as soon as Lord Elgin was informed of their arrival, but that was not to be. A day passed, another day passed and then almost a whole week was gone.

Not a word from the Governor General. There was one development, though: they were given the status of guests of the Indian government. Now, if you are in love, you may not mind waiting, but this was a different kind of waiting, which produced uncertainty. Not that there was anything lacking by way of comforts. They were being looked after most generously. Every small detail was taken care of. A flunkey of the Indian government was always in attendance. The best delicacies were served to them. They were taken on sight-seeing trips. Often, Sir Henry found it difficult to negotiate steps, so Mr. Mason was always with him. Whenever required, he lent a hand.

It was evening. Sir Henry and Mr. Mason were sitting around on the lawns, glasses in hand. Each day was passed waiting for the next one, hoping it would bring about the desired rendezvous. Sir Henry had always called him Lord Elgin, but now he had given up that appellation in favour of Governor General. In an attempt to lighten the mood, Mr. Mason laughed and said: 'I would say our wait was not entirely wasted. We at least got to know the people of this land.'

Sir Henry didn't speak a word. So Mr. Mason continued: 'A beautiful country. Nice people.'

Sir Henry only nodded his head.

Mason now put it directly: 'Don't you think the people here are a better lot than the Indians in Natal?'

After a long pause, Sir Henry took a sip and commented: 'In their place, these people would have been the same too. It makes a lot of difference whether you are in your own country or in another one. We have been here only a few days. It's not for us to say how good or how bad they are.'

Finally, the day arrived when Sir Henry and Mr. Mason were to be presented before Lord Elgin. Mr. Mason had never had the occasion to meet such a great dignitary before, so he was a bit nervous. The tales of Lord Elgin's bullying and brash behaviour that he had heard had made the situation worse. He nursed many apprehensions. You never knew when the old man might decide to get rough and end their long journey in failure. Sir Henry, however, was quite unperturbed.

~

The procedure for the meeting was marked with extreme formality. Sir Henry led the delegation, flanked by two white officers. Mr. Mason followed after him, while the rear was brought up by two of the Viceroy's bodyguards. Painstaking efforts were evident in the attempt to keep the three rows equi-distant. More than once, Mr. Mason found his feet knocking together but he promptly recovered his balance. Sir Henry was unaffected and walked, pipe in hand, as if he was a contestant in a game going forward to meet his opponent. Of course, he took care to conform strictly to the footwork protocol appropriate to a Governor General: short, soundless steps.

The six-man, three-row procession had to negotiate a rather lengthy route to reach the Viceroy's chamber: long corridors, vast courtyards and many rooms. Mr. Mason's glances often slipped to take in the splendour of the place. Perhaps it was for the first time he was seeing so much of it. Natal too had its share of impressive buildings, but this was a thing apart. The chamber which actually contained Lord Elgin was of course expensively done up, but its size too did full honour to the eminence of the position he occupied. Ivory chairs covered in gold foil ranged along the walls. Lord Elgin himself occupied a high and glittering chair. Mr. Mason stole a glance or two, but stolen glances were just not adequate to size up a hall so big and with so much to admire. It had taken them full eleven minutes to take their positions in front of the Governor General.

The place where they were positioned was directly below a giant candelabrum. Light did not explode from this candelabrum; rather, it stole out in different shapes and shades. When his eyes first fell on the candelabrum and its variegated light emissions, Mr. Mason stopped short. His legs began to give way beneath him. Suppose this candelabrum were to fall down, would they survive? Struggling hard to stand clear of it, he discovered that there was no way he could avoid standing at the designated place. Fear was stamped on his face. Sir Henry, in the meanwhile, had stopped smoking the pipe and now carried it in his hand. He was absolutely normal and at peace with himself.

The Viceroy's face glistened like an orb. His ADC stood unmoving like a stone statue behind him. His eyes, though, were fixed at Mr. Mason, who too was conscious of it.

Sir Henry and Mr. Mason were presented to the Governor General with a formal announcement. Next, Sir Henry took a few steps forward and presented his credentials. The Viceroy took the letter and handed it over to his ADC. As he took the letter, he raised himself slightly in his chair. Later, a personal letter from the Governor of Natal was also delivered to him, which his secretary quickly opened and presented to him. He glanced at it and said: 'Please convey my thanks to him and give him my good wishes.'

Sir Henry introduced Mr. Mason as a member of the delegation and said a few words of appreciation for him: 'Mr. Mason is a dedicated Englishman.' Lord Elgin smiled and shook hands with him.

Then Lord Elgin turned towards Sir Henry.'I hope you had a pleasant journey,' he said.

'Yes. Thanks. Your good wishes made sure of that.'

Next he asked Sir Henry a personal question: 'How are you keeping?'

'Quite well, by God's grace.'

Lord Elgin smiled and said: 'That seems quite obvious.' Sir Henry too smiled. Lord Elgin continued: 'I am glad of the great contribution Indian labourers are making to the wealth and prosperity of your colony.'

Mr. Mason gave a start. His face dropped. The lower lip dipped a little. The smile on Sir Henry's face stretched longer than normal. He made sure to tag 'Your Excellency' after every sentence of his.

'Beyond a doubt, Your Excellency. They have been a blessing for Natal.'

Mr. Mason was finding Sir Henry's parroting of Lord Elgin too much to bear. Layer after layer of colour was draining from his face.

Allowing a little pause and keeping up his smile, Sir Henry launched on his presentation: 'Your Excellency, it's a great honour for us to be hosted by you in this beautiful historic city of this great nation. We are indeed grateful to you for this honour. It gives us great pleasure to see the people of this great colony living in great happiness under your protection and praying for a long and happy life for the Queen Empress.'

Lord Elgin merely issued a smile.

Sir Henry continued: 'The planters of Natal are indeed quite pleased with the work of the workers who have been sent there.' He paused a little and then said: 'Mr. Mason is the other member of this delegation. He is an Englishman, but he lives in Natal and is looking after the interests of the coolies there quite well.'

Mr. Mason's face brightened with joy, but he was curious to know what Sir Henry was going to say next.

Sir Henry said: 'The problem of Natal includes the problem of the *kaffir*s. They are quite undeveloped. Indian coolies are hard-working and forward looking and the natives are quite peeved with them. If the influx of Indian labourers continues, tensions between the natives and Indians will only get worse and the whole colony may be engulfed in a crisis.'

Only when the sentence was complete did Mr. Mason breathe a sigh of relief. Then he nodded to give his assent.

Lord Elgin looked at them both quizzically and said: 'Is that so? In that case we will certainly not allow our labourers to go to Natal. We do not wish the peace of your colony to be disturbed on account of our people.'

Lines of worry appeared on Mr. Mason's face. He sat up straight.

Like the skilled conversationalist that he was, Sir Henry gave a smile and said: 'Maybe I failed to convey what I really wanted to say. In fact, what I wanted to say was something totally different.' Allowing the sentence to peter out, he looked at Mr. Mason from the corner of his eye as if asking: 'What do you say now?'

Resuming, he completed the sentence: 'No one doubts for a moment that it was because of them that large scale farming in Natal became possible and sugar production soared.'

'What do you want then?'

'Our request is that on completion of the five-year agreement, every coolie must go back to his country. The problem arises when they go on settling in Natal.'

Lord Elgin's face flushed red. Sir Henry at once knew that he had committed a faux pas. He tried to backtrack. It was said about Sir Henry that he had an ape's intellect, that is that he was a nimble backtracker. He was still thinking of the best way of doing it when Lord Elgin swivelled his cannon to face him directly: 'Do excuse me, Sir Henry. This is not an issue on which we can hold a discussion. Our two countries have been tied for the last couple of decades by a contract—a contract between two governments. Do I believe that your government is seeking an *ex parte* annulment of the contract?'

Both of them were struck dumb. What was wrong with Lord Elgin? Their distress could be seen on their faces, though Sir Henry was quick to get over it. Mr. Mason was still struggling with the question: Why would the Viceroy, himself a white man, deal with other white men so?

Sir Henry gave a quick twist to the matter: 'Your Excellency, we are not in the least opposed to Indian workers or businessmen. They are the main pillars of our economic system. The white planters are greatly impressed by their methods of work and their integrity. Our problem is a different one and we don't know who else we can take it to if not you. It was not our intention to bring any personalities into this discussion, but we have no choice. A barrister called M.K. Gandhi has arrived from India. While the coolies are simple and hard-working people, this coolie barrister is out to misguide them and spread disaffection among them. He incites them to create disturbances. He writes in the newspapers against the government and the white planters. He even went to the extent of writing to Her Majesty's government against the colonial government, spreading infamy and distorting facts. Indian coolies and businessmen are being misled by him.'

Lord Elgin was listening closely to Sir Henry. The new twist provided by Sir Henry had pleased Mr. Mason and he was eager to make a contribution. On two or three occasions he even made an effort, but words got stuck somewhere between the throat and the lips. Sir Henry was keeping an eye out for Mr. Mason, expecting him to elaborate a point or two. But he was also aware of the butterflies in his stomach and felt apprehensive that he might make a faux pas, the responsibility for which would fall on Sir Henry. Still, he kept quiet and willed Mr. Mason to speak, which he eventually had to do. 'Your Excellency,' Mr. Mason said, 'These coolies are filthy and dirty. They are sick and diseased. They are storehouses of infections and they mistreat their women.' He got so excited that his voice broke. He looked at Sir Henry.

Lord Elgin had a fixed look in his eyes as he said: 'If you dislike them so much why do you wish them to come to your country and do your farming for you? We had been opposed to the export of labour from the very beginning. I wish to make it quite clear that there is no question of any amendment in the agreement that our two governments have signed. As far as this Indian barrister called M.K. Gandhi is concerned, he cannot be such an important man that two governments would modify their contract for fear of him. As for what he writes, every subject of Her Majesty's government has the right to express himself in writing.'

Sir Henry realized that things had been messed up. He quickly got into the damage-control mode: 'I'm sorry things took this unfortunate turn. Actually, Mr. Mason is an emotional and sensitive person and cannot see his people suffering. The Natal government has no desire for any amendment in the contract signed by the two governments. We respect the agreement as much as the Indian government does. What we do desire is that these people should also feel some loyalty to the colony which gives them their livelihood. They must also think of themselves as a part of Natal just as much as they think of themselves as a part of India.'

'What would you have them do to show their loyalty to Natal?'

'Pay the government something as poll tax in case they want to settle down in Natal after their term of agreement is over.'

'How much?'

'Twenty-five pounds per person per year.'

For the first time, the Viceroy's secretary put in a word: 'Which means a family of four has to pay a hundred pounds as Poll Tax ...?'

The Viceroy asked a different question: 'How much do you think a labourer makes in a year?'

Mr. Mason got excited again: 'Your Excellency, they are thieves. They steal money.'

'What else do you expect them to do when they have to pay a Poll Tax of twenty-five pounds per year? What this means is that you are trying to legalize thievery by imposing this heavy tax.'

'Your Excellency, what I wanted to say was that if they want to live in Natal they have to find some way of making money. It's their problem.'

Sir Henry signalled to Mr. Mason with his eyes to stay quiet.

'So, Mr. Mason, your government wants twenty-five pounds per person as Poll Tax! No matter how he gets it or where he gets it. I don't think your proposal will be acceptable to the Indian government. It will not allow its subjects, who are making such significant contribution to the economic progress of your colony, to be subjected to such exploitation.'

Sir Henry saw things slipping out of control. Quickly, he backtracked again: 'Your Excellency is absolutely right. It's not our aim at all to harass those people. All we want is that they must pay something for gaining permanent citizenship of Natal. They must feel they too are contributing a part of their earnings for the progress of Natal.'

Lord Elgin reflected for a moment and then said: 'Even if they pay a pound or two, all their savings will be gone. Twenty-five pounds is however ridiculous. You must simply forget about that proposal.'

Lord Elgin stood up. Others too got up. Sir Henry bowed a little and shook hands, as he said: 'We will await Your Excellency's verdict.'

Lord Elgin didn't respond to the point but asked: 'Have you been around Delhi? There is so much to see.'

'Thanks, Your Excellency. We have been to a number of places.'

Lord Elgin turned and walked away. The duo went back the way they had come.

As they trudged back, Mr. Mason happened to look up and saw the candelabrum spinning. Then he saw it coming slowly down. The light it emitted was going full blast but outside its centre of existence. The centre was unable to hold. Mr. Mason drew back with a jerk. The retinue accompanying him looked at him startled but did not let anything on.

Outside, by the steps, the coach had drawn up. Descending the series of steps took them some time. At the bottom of the steps, Sir Henry looked back and for a moment the steps looked to him like ascending waves of a sea. Or they could have been a path hewn out of the side of a mountain. For a moment, he couldn't take his eyes off the concatenated series of climbing steps.

Mr. Mason always followed Sir Henry into the coach, but this time he got into the coach first. When it occurred to him, he scrambled to get down. Sir Henry smiled and waved him back into the coach, saying 'That's all right.' The half-risen Mason slumped back into his seat. The coach started and for a long time the hoof-beats were the only sounds to be heard. A heavy stillness reigned inside the coach, rendered heavier by the clip-clop of the horses' hooves. The buildings formed a crescent around them and the coach was passing through the centre of it. The building too resounded with the sound of hoof-beats.

Mr. Mason was the one to break the ice. 'His Excellency does not seem favourably disposed. It's possible the coolie barrister has written to him too. The fellow is more of a draftsman than a barrister.'

The coach had emerged from the crescent. The concentrated clip-clop of the hooves was getting diffused.

Sir Henry smiled: 'Here's a Viceroy running a huge colony of the Queen's empire and you think he is guided in his decisions by the scribbling of a coolie barrister? Britishers are born rulers, you know.'

'What do you think, Sir Henry? Will the Viceroy favour us?'

Sir Henry did not seem to hear. His gaze was fixed somewhere outside. Mason was about to repeat himself but stopped. The coach had travelled some distance. Without looking at Mason, Sir Henry said: 'It looks like you did not pay close attention to what the Viceroy said. I'm not so pessimistic.'

'What makes you say that?'

'Do you see my grey hair and the wrinkles on my face?'

Mason didn't speak another word. They spent the whole day going round Delhi. Sir Henry was quite relaxed, laughing and chatting all the time. Tension however sat like a stone slab on Mason's chest. Sir Henry chirruped: 'Look, Mason! Look outside. How pretty! Don't sit there all shrivelled up. Come on outside. See how beautiful it is.'

But every time Sir Henry said something, Mason just repeated his pet theme: 'If the Indian government doesn't agree, what are we going to do? The coolies will cover the whole of Natal like weed.'

'Mr. Mason, when you are travelling, keep yourself light,' said Sir Henry, 'shed all unnecessary baggage or you won't be able to finish your journey. And you will gain weight. You are a guest of the Governor General of India. Enjoy the hospitality. Such a beautiful country! A silver bird, if not a golden one! Have you ever seen a bird like this one?'

Mason only laughed. 'No point in wasting time here. I don't expect anything.'

Sir Henry's gaze was fixed at New Delhi, which was coming up: the tall trees, the deep blue Yamuna, its deep and sedate waters, the buildings rising and sprawling and the huge lawns. Sir Henry tore his eyes away from all these and said: 'Leaving this place without waiting for the Viceroy's verdict will amount to contempt. He is the Queen's representative—the Viceroy! India is the brightest jewel in the British crown. The whole of the British Empire is shining in its glory!'

Then he patted his shoulders softly and said: 'Be brave! Don't lose heart.'

The main worry of Mr. Mason was however Gandhi. He was under the impression that Gandhi must be a well-known figure in India as he was in Natal. He wanted to collect as much information about him as was possible. Anyone he met, he never failed to ask: 'Do you know Mr. M.K. Gandhi?'

He hadn't come across a single person who knew Gandhi.

Their steward was an Englishman called Canning. He was incomparable when it came to attending to white guests. There were hardly any non-white guests who stayed in that guest house, in fact almost none. Mr. Mason called Canning over and said: 'Canning, I want you do something for me.'

Canning knew that they were guests of the Governor General. He bowed and said: 'At your command, sir.'

'There is a coolie barrister in Natal called M.K. Gandhi.'

Canning expressed surprise: 'A coolie and a barrister, sir?'

'Indians who go to Natal are called coolies.'

It was all Canning could do to stop himself from bursting into laughter.

'I want full information about the man. Where does he come from? Why is he in Natal? Is he an enemy of the British government?'

'Who is Gandhi? Where does he come from? In such a big country as this, it is impossible to find out all this about one man, sir. Either I should have his address, or he should be a famous person like Sir Pherozeshah.'

Disappointment showed on Mason's face. How could a man, unknown even to a steward, become such an important figure in Natal? How could a mere coolie get a bill sent to her by the Government of Natal disapproved by the Queen? Mr. Mason kept repeating this to himself for a long time.

Sir Henry laughed at such preoccupations of Mr. Mason. 'Young men are rather quick to lose patience,' he said. 'You know I think you are more worried about Gandhi than about Natal and the problems of the white people there.'

'You know what? He is nobody in this country. A complete non-identity. And he is an active politician there, always pulling at the reins of Her Majesty's government. The Chief Justice of Natal honoured his word. The attorney of the Natal Law Society, Mr. Green, could do nothing. Who knows whether he is a genuine bar-at-law or not? The man doesn't have his certificate in the original. The Chief Justice overlooked the rules and enrolled him as an advocate. Maybe one could trust him if he were a white man, but how could the Chief Justice place trust on a coolie? They are liars, they are cheats ... they are everything.'

'Mason, don't get worked up unnecessarily. I know that Justice Rege is also a bar-at-law from the Inner Temple. Every student of the Inner Temple has a record of all graduates of the institution, including the dates and other details of graduation. We are not here to discuss the conduct of the Chief Justice of Natal.'

'But we must do something when we are back.'

'Exactly what?'

'We must show him his place before he can interfere in our politics. We must break his legs before he can ride roughshod on us.'

'I sometimes feel you want him to ride roughshod on you. He occupies your brain more than Jesus does. The more you discuss him, the more importance he gets.'

'What do you advise we should do, then?'

'You know what the words "to wait" mean? That's what you need to do.'

On the third day, they received a message from the Viceroy's secretary. The secretary wanted to see them. Mason was quite agitated as they went to see him. Sir Henry too was agitated: he was wondering why it was the secretary and not the Viceroy himself who was going to meet them. They fidgeted all the way as they rode in the coach.

Mason had decided that things were going to sour. He didn't however express himself as Sir Henry always contradicted him. He had also decided that there was a lot of scope for improvement in Sir Henry's knowledge about Natal. That was the reason for the lack of seriousness on his part. Still, he couldn't contain himself and blurted out the question: 'Can our government go ahead with the Poll Tax even if the Viceroy disagrees?'

This time, all that Sir Henry did was to squeeze his shoulder a little.

They found the secretary examining the India-Natal contract papers when they arrived in his room. He got up from his seat to shake hands with them and then moved over to a sofa.

'His Excellency would have liked to talk to you in person, but he is very busy. He has given a lot of thought to your proposal. After wide-ranging consultations, he has reached the conclusion that if you wish to impose a symbolic Poll Tax the proposal could be considered.'

They looked at each other. The light in each one's eye could be seen reflected in the other's. The secretary continued: 'His Excellency does not at all relish the idea of using the poll tax as a weapon to drive the Indians back to India.' He paused and tried to read their faces and then continued: 'He also wishes the Natal government to legislate a provision that no *girmitiya* will incur criminal liability even if he wishes to remain in Natal but is unable to pay the Poll Tax.'

The life that the first proposal had breathed into the duo was quickly sucked out by the second one. The light of their eyes dimmed. The pupils darkened. The secretary wasn't allowing them to put in a word edgeways. He even went on to specify a ceiling on the amount of Poll Tax on behalf of the Viceroy: 'The Poll Tax will in no case exceed three pounds per person per year.' He sealed it with: 'The Viceroy feels that even this small tax will be beyond their capacity to pay. He however agrees with Sir Henry's point that an Indian who wishes to make Natal his home must make his contribution to its development.'

Back in their guest rooms, Sir Henry and Mr. Mason couldn't decide whether they should be happy or sorry at the decision of the Viceroy. The decision was certainly not in Natal's favour. The amount of poll tax fixed was so low that every coolie would be able to raise it. The only saving grace was they could go back to their people in Natal with their face more or less intact.

When the delegation arrived back in Natal, they found the people quite agitated. By now even the common people knew that a delegation was in India trying to get approval for a Poll Tax for Indians. The agitated people were arguing that any change in the contract already agreed upon would be immoral. They included some white people too.

Articles by M.K. Gandhi were a regular feature in the local newspapers. The Natal government regularly sent cuttings of the articles to the Indian Viceroy. Its selfish motivation in doing so was to insinuate in Lord Elgin's mind an unfavourable opinion about Gandhi and the Natal Congress, thus facilitating acceptance of its anti-Indian proposals. Lord Elgin kept himself informed of the developments in Natal. By now he was convinced that Natal Indians were in no position to pay any Poll Tax. The mention of M.K. Gandhi by Sir Henry had raised his interest in the man. He read his articles very carefully and every article helped him to know him better. When discussing the poll tax affair with the Member (Home), he had actually brought up a reference to Gandhi and said: 'Whatever else may or may not be true, one thing is sure: Gandhi knows the problems of the Indians well. I feel it would be quite wrong to impose a Poll Tax on labourers who earn twelve or thirteen pounds in a whole year. Natal government is doing it to drive them out of the colony.'

The Member (Home) thought that a Poll Tax would give Indians a moral right to settle in the colony.

'But how much?'

'Five pounds.'

'No, three at the most.'

'Will they agree?'

'They will have to. They cannot violate the contract *ex parte*.'

They had then decided that the Governor General would get the secretary to communicate the decision to the delegation instead of doing it himself.

And that was what had hurt Sir Henry the most.

In Natal, when Gandhi found out that the Indian Governor General had agreed to a three-pound poll tax, he was greatly exercised. How could an official, sitting half way across the world, strike a deal about further impoverishment of the already poverty-ridden Indians? It may well be that these men are capable of deciding where and when the sun would rise or set, but this was a matter which involved human lives. Mohandas wrote in an article: 'By agreeing to a three-pound Poll Tax, the Indian government has stabbed those poor Indians in the back who took its word when they came to this colony to work under a five-year agreement. The Indian government is supposed to be their patron and protector. The Indian government assumed that mantle and is now murdering their interests. The Viceroy's action is inhuman. The saddest part of it is that the Viceroy has sacrificed the interests of the poor Indians so that white men can prosper.'

This statement of Gandhi was immediately conveyed to the Governor General.

~

XII

Gandhi's sensitivity was increasing day by day. Deeply entangled in the affairs of Natal, he wasn't able to shake off Rajkot either. Several questions about himself pursued him relentlessly and gave him no peace: Why am I here? Am I trying to run away from my responsibilities at home? Thoughts like these closed in on him and surrounded him like a threatening crowd. There were the goings-on in Kathiawar, his elder brother's expectations from him, his failure to measure up to them, Kastur's intransigence, the oppressive burden of relationships. It was not as if he couldn't have established himself there, but he felt living there was like living under a dome of multi-coloured glass where the colours of the glass determined his vision. There were walls all around him, but these were not brick and mortar walls: they were walls of relationships, relationships which were being redefined and reconstituted every minute. As far as his vision extended, all he could see were relationships like clothes hung out to dry on a clothesline. He however knew quite well that if he was going to understand these obstacles, the path also lay through the obstacles.

It was true that like so many others he too had come here to earn a living, even if his contract was only for a year. That was what he had told Kastur too when bidding her goodbye. The year was now over and he was still here, like a *girmitiya* released from his *girmit*. Whatever had happened to the family which, despite its absence, he saw every day at bedtime in full strength? Where had it disappeared? There was this other family that was slowly emerging from the horizon, like land emerging at the end of a sea journey. He had no memories of this new family. The only family he had ever thought of was the family left behind a year ago at Rajkot. That had been the only centre of his attraction. All that had changed now. How had this come about? Had there been another India, a small, destitute India growing like a foetus within him of which he had been completely unaware? When was it conceived? When did it start growing? He was sure it had been there within him even when he was in India. It must have come with him. Off and on, he had encountered it there: sometimes as Uka, sometimes as petitioners in *Bapu*'s court and sometimes as a legacy of the heart-rending stories *Ba* used to tell him. India was much too large. He was in need of a smaller India which could lead him to the larger India. Sometimes he heard whispers in his ears: Tell me: what makes India? Does India make India or do Indians make India? The question startled him. What a question!

He suddenly found Balasundaram standing before him. 'You, Balasundaram?' He keeps cropping up before me, thought Mohandas, sometimes in reality, at times in the abstract. It has been a long time since Balasundaram's case was disposed of, but he still carries his wounds. India and Balasundaram. Balasundaram and India ...

'How come you are still carrying your wounds, Balasundaram?'

He laughed to hear the question, perhaps for the first time in his presence. 'When did we not have the wounds? We had them since the days of our forefathers. They may sometimes become visible, but look inside us and they are always there. They are like ulcers: when they are painful, the pain never stops.'

Gandhi looked inside him: he too had wounds. All of India, he felt, had wounds.

For the first time, there was something within him, he felt, which hurt.

'You, Dada Abdullah? You are a great name, and the things you say? One never knows about them, does one? Bitter like neem one moment and sweet as syrup the next.'

'Dada Abdullah, you lived like a *Nabob* in Nagpur. What brought you to this far away land?

'I know. You did tell me. You are a businessman. A businessman goes where his business takes him. Right?

'But when I arrived here first, you called me a white elephant. When did I change colour? From a white elephant, when did I become a mule elephant?

'You say you live in fear. Why do you live in fear? Don't you think we live in fear when we choose to? When we choose not to live in fear, we could be lions!

'Quite right! When you didn't know me, you took a small man like me to be an elephant. But I chose not to be afraid. I could not have lived with you if I had chosen to be afraid. One can die afraid, one cannot live afraid.

'I was not afraid because I had got to know fear. Fear faces you at every turn in your life. You fear the law; you fear the king; you fear the police, and you are running from fear. Fear keeps driving you. If you stop, it stops too. It looks you in the eye and asks you: "Afraid, aren't you?"

'It's true that your fear is an import from Orange Free State. You fear that you too may be asked to leave the country. But you believe, don't you, that a businessman is a constant traveller, like the sun and the moon? How will a frightened businessman ever find his destination?

'A businessman is by definition one who goes where business takes him. He must go wherever it rains profit.' Gandhibhai laughed aloud.

He stopped laughing and looked around. Dada Abdullah was nowhere to be seen.

~

'You, Mr. Baker? But I had left you in Pretoria. It's more than a year now. Happy days, they were.'

'So, what's your decision, Gandhi? Coates, Miss Harris, Miss Gabb—all your friends prayed for you day and night. Lord Jesus, take this our new friend in your shelter. Forgive his sins. But why am I telling you this. You have yourself read Jesus and understood him well.'

'Mr. Baker, prayer also cleanses the self. You may pray for anyone, but it works for you too. I know about all those prayers you are telling me about. The love you have for me and the purity of your souls has been an experience for me.'

He laughed and continued: 'By praying for my forgiveness without first learning about my vices and my sins, you have put Jesus too in a difficult position.'

'I don't think I know what you mean.'

'How can anyone else know what sins I have committed and what mistakes I have made? I must face the consequences myself. Jesus laid down his life for truth. Can an ordinary mortal match that sacrifice? That's why Jesus is the Son of God. But why should he bear my sins? Why should someone else be the sinner for my sins? And how can someone else pay for my sins without first becoming the sinner for those sins? I would never, never wish someone else to take upon himself the burden of my sins, Mr. Baker, especially a noble soul like Jesus. In fact, I'd rather wish that I commit no sins, that even the thought of a sin would not enter my mind. The mind is after all like fallow land: you reap what you sow. In our scripture, Gita, it is said: "Surrender all thy good deeds and bad, sins as well virtues, to me and free yourself from all desire".'

'No, Gandhi, that's not possible. As long as man lives, there will be sin and man can never free himself from all desire.'

The word 'impossible' kept ringing in Mohandas' ears for a long time. Is it not possible to replace 'impossible' by 'possible'? 'I want to fight the impossible with the possible—for myself, for my country, for every creature on this earth? Will you pray for my success, Mr. Baker?'

~

'When you left you'd said you'd be back in no time at all.'

'I'm sorry I couldn't keep my word. I admit my guilt.' He muttered the words without looking at Kastur.

Kastur laughed. Mohandas raised his head and looked at her. Her face gave away nothing. Only her laughter was a puzzle for him.

'Why did you laugh?'

'They say "laugh while you can" for crying when it starts, never stops.'

Mohandas wondered if Kastur was laughing at him. But he had no answer to this question.

Kastur said: 'Your wife, your kids, your brother, who is like father to you, ...?'

Mohandas cut her short: 'They all have their place. But this responsibility is not mine alone. All of you must help me fulfil it.'

'You needed Mehtab Bhai. You got him over.'

'Kastur, I seek your cooperation. I am joined to you all—to God, to you, to the kids. And you are all joined to me. But there are thousands of Indians here who have no one to call their own. They must all join up with one another. One man speaks the vow, but everyone affirms it and assures cooperation.'

'I have limited understanding. I only know that all my joys and all my sorrows are centred on you. So long as these kids do not grow up, their joys and their sorrows too will revolve around you.'

'My sorrows are my strength. You never understood it. Perhaps I am to blame. For both of us, our bodies were the streams in which we loved lo lose ourselves. Of course, I cannot escape blame by holding you responsible. Nor can you. But I want to stay away now.'

'Stay away from me?'

'No, not from you, but from the stream which is constantly flowing within us. When that stream is in flood, it sweeps everyone off their feet. The flood sometimes started at this end, sometimes at the other end. Perhaps neither of us could escape the flood. Kastur, are you listening? Oh, you are already off!' The children followed her in a line.

Mohandas was dozing. Things were getting all muddled up.

~

Mohandas had joined the battle for franchise no sooner he had returned from Pretoria. It was a new battle. He had no idea who his foot soldiers were, nor where the battlefield was where the battle was to be fought. Perhaps that is the way every battle starts—in ignorance. He was slowly getting to know his soldiers, getting them to know one another and trying to find the common ground with them, irrespective of whether they were with him or against him. He believed that those against you were also partners in your battle. They might be Indian or British, businessmen or *girmitiya*s. People were getting to know him too. Anyone who had a problem came running to him. The queue of people was getting longer and longer. He was running around all day and burnt midnight oil. He went to bed late at night and queues started forming early next morning. Sheikh Mehtab slept till late. There would be knocks and noises galore, but they made no difference to his late sleeping.

~

Mr. Spencer Walton was the head of South African General Mission. Mohandas had struck up a good relationship with him. On his return from Pretoria, he had not been able to forget Mr. Baker and his other friends there. His meeting with Mr. Walton had stirred up within him the curiosities that had been with him while he was in Pretoria. Mr. and Mrs. Walton were both very humble people, and like all humble people they were also very affectionate. Their manner was very proselytizing: they would have their say and avoided controversy. Argument was not their way. Their life was an open book. Anyone who wanted could read it. 'That's the way we are,' they seemed to say, 'the rest is up to you.'

Though Mohandas belonged to a different religion, the Waltons extended to him the same warm welcome that they extended to their co-religionists. Mohandas' way of thinking was also different. He had made it clear to them in the very beginning that he did not think that Jesus was the only son of God. We are all His sons and daughters, he said. Anyone who was born on this earth was His child.

Mr. Walton had listened to him carefully without disagreeing. All he had said at the end was: 'That's also a way of looking at it. But the greatness of Jesus was exceptional.'

'No question about that, of course. But what I say does not in any way take away from the greatness of Jesus. No matter who the father is, a man is not great unless his own actions and his own sacrifice make him so.'

Walton would only give his head a shake and keep his mouth shut.

You would never find Mrs. Walton unoccupied. She was always busy doing something or the other. She could never let a comment like this pass without a rejoinder. 'The love of Jesus is universal. There is room for everyone in it. Come and seek shelter in it and you will feel the touch of his love.'

Gandhi replied: 'Mrs. Walton, love is like a stream in which anyone who is willing can take a dip. One doesn't need to enlist to feel its touch.' Laughing, he continued: 'When I found shelter in you, I also found love.'

Mrs. Walton was a good-looking lady. Her face was like a beautiful calligraphic rendering of lines from a sacred scripture. She laughed and said: 'No, Mr. Gandy, no. There is no shelter like Jesus.'

Gandhibhai laughed.

The difference of opinion between Gandhi and the Walton couple had not hardened into ideological extremism. In fact, they enjoyed each other's company. In this respect, Walton was almost like Mr. Baker's twin. Meeting the two had given Mohandas an opportunity to develop a deep understanding of the Christian religion and had also satisfied his craving for knowledge about other religions.

Mohandas had a standing invitation to Sunday lunch at the Waltons' and he took full advantage of it. Naturally, he was not at home on Sundays and Sheikh Mehtab took full advantage of that. If someone came looking for Gandhibhai, he would let him have it: 'It's Sunday today, do you know that? On Sundays, Gandhibhai is not to be found at home. His Sundays are busier than his other days. No chance of meeting him on Sundays, OK? What makes you think Gandhi will see you, anyway, with a face like that?' The poor fellow could do nothing but beat a hasty retreat.

~

Gandhi happened to be reading Arnold's *Light of Asia* in those days, a book which he found very engrossing. Walton and Mohandas had an agreement between them to let the other know if one of them came across an interesting work. On a Sunday lunch, Gandhi mentioned *Light of Asia.*

'Who is the author?' asked Walton.

'Arnold.'

'I don't think I have.'

'You must read it. You will then see the extent of Buddha's love. It is not confined to human beings only; it covers all life, including animals and even plants. Rabbits ran up his shoulders; deer grazed around him unafraid of him. Did that happen with Jesus too?'

He paused and then said: 'Not that I know of.'

Mrs. Walton was busy doing something. She looked up startled. Mr. Walton signalled her to say nothing and instead turned to Gandhi: 'Let's go and have lunch.'

They both moved to the table. There was always special vegetarian food for Mohandas. The kids always livened up when they saw Gandhi. They had struck up a good friendship. The younger son, Albert, who was five or six years old, was particularly fond of Gandhi. He called him 'Gandhiboy'.

Albert was served meat. Gandhibhai had apple and other fruits on his plate. Gandhibhai laughed and said: 'You know, Albert, an apple equals two chickens. When a chicken goes into your stomach, it goes cock-a-doodle-do! The apple, on the other hand, is disposed of quietly.'

Albert looked at his mother. He stopped eating meat and instead picked up fruit pieces from Gandhiboy's plate. Mrs. Walton was taken aback. She didn't know what to do. Albert said: 'I'll also eat vegetarian meals like Gandhiboy.'

Mr. Walton was eating silently. Mrs. Walton was trying to explain to Albert that vegetarian food was nothing but grass. Eating only vegetarian food would ruin his health. For strength, you needed to eat meat. If you didn't eat meat, you finished up last in life.

Albert was adamant. When Mohandas saw the matter getting out of hand, he tried to persuade Albert: 'Albert, you must do as your Mom says. Good boys always do what their Moms say.'

But he would not relent. 'Look, how strong is Gandhiboy! You know how much he can walk? He is not afraid of anyone! I want to be like Gandhiboy.'

There was a rush of blood to Mrs. Walton's face. Mr. Walton still said nothing and concentrated on eating. Albert refused to budge. The meal ended in complete silence that day.

When it was next Sunday, Mohandas couldn't decide if he should go or not. Finally, he decided that it would hurt Waltons' feelings if he didn't. He himself would consider it as intolerance. When he reached there, they had finished eating. Mr. Walton had gone out after his meal, which was rather rare because he always had some rest after his meal. Mrs. Walton was at home. At the sight of Mohandas, she said: 'Walton waited for you at lunch as usual.'

Mohandas looked at the watch and said: 'I'm sorry, I was held up. I have come to apologize for not being able to come on time. I'm indeed sorry that Mr. Walton had to wait for me.'

Mrs. Walton kept quiet. Mohandas too had nothing to say. After a while, Mrs. Walton spoke: 'Mr. Gandhi, there's something I wanted to tell you.'

'Sure. Please go ahead.'

'Please don't take it amiss. Unless it was absolutely necessary, I wouldn't have said it. Albert is still a child. He is not your age. Some of the things you say may have the wrong influence on him. Since that day, he has been causing problems at meal times, demanding vegetarian food. I cannot see him like this. If he doesn't eat meat, he will grow up an abnormal person.'

Tears had welled up in her eyes. Her beautiful face was getting disfigured. Gandhi could never stand disfigurement of beauty.

'I agree with you,' said Mohandas. 'A good mother needs to worry about her kids' health. I am a father too. What I eat or don't eat has an effect on my kids. It's natural. I know that your entire family loves me. I shouldn't be returning that love with problems for you. I think I should stop my Sunday lunches here. Please be sure, this will have no effect on our friendship. I do hope you'll not take me amiss.'

Mrs. Walton smiled a little, saying nothing. Hard to say if Mohandas saw the smile or not. He talked shop for a while, but when he left, Mrs. Walton came to the door to say goodbye. Ordinarily, it was Walton who did.

Mrs. Walton spoke in a low voice: 'God bless you, Mr. Gandy.'

~

In South Africa, January is pretty hot.

It was two o'clock in the morning. The streets were deserted. People lay fast asleep in their homes. Bullver Road was quite busy during the day, but at night the silence was so thick that the clatter of police boots and the clip-clop of the horses pulling the coaches of the whites returning from their clubs sounded like they were trying to escape the tight grip of the prevailing silence. A few people were clustered under a tree, waiting for the dawn to break. Occasionally, they dozed off. They must have been about eighteen or nineteen in number. Their shoulder-borne carriers, laden with fresh fruit and vegetables, lay nearby. They were waiting for the darkness to lift a little so that they could continue their trip to the local market. Suddenly, three or four policemen on beat appeared, all of them natives led by a white. They approached the sleepy, tired bunch and demanded sharply: 'What are you doing sitting here at this hour?'

Fear was the axis around which all British colonies moved. The instrument of fear was the police. When the police spoke, people trembled in their shoes. These were former *girmitiya*s, who were now free citizens engaged in vegetable and fruit business.

'Where are your passes?' The policeman's voice cracked like a whip.

They all looked at each other.

'Don't you know that it is a crime for a coolie to be on the streets after nine at night till six in the morning without a pass?'

'No, sir.'

The policemen's eyes lit up like the eyes of a predator when it sees its prey.

'Come with us to the police station.'

They looked at one another once again, but this time they were only looking at the fear in the eyes of one another. One of the younger men, trying to shake off his fear, dared to speak up: 'When the day breaks, we'll go with you wherever you wish. In the dark of the night, we won't.'

The white lifted his baton and pushed it hard in the young man's stomach throwing him backward. 'You dare to speak in my presence?' he said and spat out a stinking abuse in his own tongue.

They were now shaking with fear. There were two women among them, who were trying hard to disappear into the tree. Unfortunately, there was no hollow in the tree. The police suddenly started swinging their batons. All of them had to pick up their shoulder-carriers and march single file after the police to the police station. The fear of the baton was forcing them to run. The heavy weights they carried were causing them to sag and heave. Even as they walked, they were trying to explain: 'We were going to the market to sell the things. It is still some time before morning, so we thought we would rest our limbs a little. But, we promise, it won't happen again.'

'Which market?' One of the native policemen asked in his own language. The Indians acquired a smattering of the language over the years.

'The one near the Gray Street, under the big mosque. There is a fruit and vegetable market there.'

'Where are you coming from?'

'From Bel Air.'

'Why are you moving around without a pass? You think you own this colony? Is there no law in this land? You coolies think you run this place?' and he let them have another of his choicest abuses.

At the police station, the shoulder-carriers were taken away from them and they were all thrown into an airless cell where some natives were already incarcerated. The natives seemed quite at ease, as if it was their own home. The coolies huddled together in a corner, squatting on the ground. The two women were crying themselves hoarse. Being in custody was for them a matter of shame and utter disgrace.

Next morning at nine, they were presented before a magistrate, a white man called Dillon.

'What were you doing at the place so early in the morning?'

The interpreter explained the question to them.

A lawyer was representing them. He said: 'These people were going from Bel Air to the fruit and vegetable market near Gray Street to sell their goods. It was still some way to daybreak, so they sat down under a tree on Gray Street to rest themselves. They always start their trip at night so that they can be at the market when it opens and they can get a good price for their goods and the customer can also get fresh fruit and vegetables. They are not on the streets loafing and loitering but to serve the people of the colony. Hauling them into custody is sheer persecution.'

The accused were standing huddled so close to one another that it looked as if they were afraid that if they separated they would be killed on the spot. Dillon looked at them and ordered: 'Let them be released at once.'

The wilted faces of the group suddenly brightened up like long-dry plants receiving a dose of water. Their circle of happiness slowly grew larger and larger till all of them were inside it. Their shoulder-carriers lay outside in a scattered heap. Fruits and vegetables rolled all over the place. Their fresh merchandise now looked so stale. Their faces dropped as they saw the state of the goods. The joy of release turned into sorrow when they thought of the next meal for their family. They gathered up the fruits and vegetables in their shoulder-carriers, and sat there grieving for some time as if mourning the death of a near and dear one.

When Gandhibhai was told about the incident, his comment was: 'What better reward can this government give to honest and hard working people!'

That day, Gandhibhai's mind could not help harking back again and again to the incident that had happened with Lachman Roberts and Samuel Richards. The two were simple, civilized Christian young men. Educated and always well-dressed, they spoke fluent English. One was teacher in a school, the other was preparing for the civil services examination under Gandhibhai's guidance. They were out on a post-dinner stroll on the streets. They were aware that coolies were not allowed on the streets after nine without a pass, but they did not think of themselves as coolies. When the policeman asked them to show their passes, they responded in a tone of authority: 'Passes are for coolies.'

'And who may you be?'

'Do we look like coolies to you?'

'No, you look like British royalty.'

'We are Christians and we are educated.'

No one however paid any attention to their nonsense. They were hauled up before Mr. Waller, the magistrate. That day, for the first time after his return from Pretoria, Mohandas was reminded of the occasion when he had to seek a letter of permission from the Attorney General through one of his friends to escape harassment. He always had to carry that letter on his person, the reason why he had been able to keep the police at arm's length.

The police officer asked one of them: 'Your name?

'Samuel Richards.'

The sergeant laughed to hear the name.

'How long since you had this name?'

'Almost eighteen months. Since I converted.'

'What did your parents do?'

'They were *girmitiyas*.'

'Caste?'

'Dhobi.'

'So you didn't like your family name.' He paused a little and then continued: 'Did you inform the police that you assumed a Christian name to get rid of your Indian name and religion?'

'No, sir.'

The officer uttered a drawn-out 'H'mmmmm.'

It was Lachman Roberts' turn next.

'Your father?'

'*Girmitiya*.' Lachman made no attempt to hide anything.

'Did you think if you changed your name the police would spread out a red carpet for you?'

'My face and my personality should be enough to ensure that.' Roberts was very fair and had an imposing personality.

Bail was granted to Roberts but denied to Richards. As he left, Roberts assured Richards that he would get him released too with Gandhibhai's help.

The white sergeant gave a big grin to hear Gandhibhai's name. Waller paid little attention to the threat, but turned to the sergeant and asked: 'Who is this Gandy?'

M.K. Gandhi was now a name known to everyone, white and non-white alike.

Gandhi represented the two young men in court. Speaking fearlessly, Gandhi said: 'As long as I was conscious of how people might take what I said, I was shy in speaking. Once I shed that fear, there was nothing to hold me back.' He put forward his arguments before the court without mincing words.

'Milord! I am not aware of any law which decrees that non-whites, especially Indians, should be kept tethered at night so that they are not let loose on the streets and bite the whites, that in case they escape into the streets they should be shot at sight or should be locked up in government stables. The Indians are humans too, and they have a right to live like humans belonging to other races. The fact that they are black, or that they come from non-European countries, does not deprive them of the right to be treated as humans. When God made man and gave him limbs, nose, face, looks, brain and body, there existed no distinction of colour or country; so who is man now to put conditions on the free existence of men and impose discriminatory rules on them? Have these two young men, who stand before you as the accused, lost their right to be treated as humans just because they were born to *girmitiya* parents and because the white masters don't like their colour and their country? They are educated, they are cultured and they are respectable citizens of this colony. Their conduct is proof that no criminal or illegal acts can be held against them. Roberts is known well to the police. The court had at one time issued orders that he should be issued a pass so that he can use the streets after nine. Had he not fallen sick, he would have secured this permission from the Mayor. He was arrested without being given an opportunity to be heard. This is clearly a violation of his rights as a citizen. A country which cannot ensure the rights of the common man cannot be considered a politically aware nation. Sometimes, civil rights of some citizens are suspended because a threat to peace is apprehended from them. These citizens present no such threat; in fact, love for peace and patience run in their blood. They are no professional criminals.'

The magistrate was listening to Gandhi very attentively. Gandhi looked at him and continued: 'Milord! I don't think it should be necessary for Richards to present himself before the Mayor to get him to certify that he is a good and peace-loving citizen. Roberts had made an application to this effect before the Mayor, but he was denied a certificate on the ground that no teacher or clerk had to this day been accused of being a danger to society. Is Roberts to be blamed for the denial of the certificate to him? It is my appeal to the court that, when pronouncing a verdict in such cases, care should be taken to see that colour considerations do not stand in the way of the divine ordinance which guarantees equality to all human beings. Justice is the birthright of every individual; it is for you to deliver it.'

The magistrate rose from his seat and announced unexpectedly: 'The accused are discharged with honour.' Everyone was stunned.

Mohandas looked at the duo. He could see tears in their eyes. Perhaps tears of joy.

The magistrate's decision had taken the white community by surprise. The newspapers were full of it. The decision was condemned as being in violation of the colony laws. It was called an assault on the rights of white citizens by a white magistrate. It was argued that the verdict would create the impression that the Natal law was biased against the non-whites and that the whites used the law to tyrannize over them. The white community was up in arms. If the courts allowed themselves to be pressurized by the coolie barrister to side with the coolies, it saw no other choice for itself but to challenge the decision. It could not stand aside and see someone who belonged to the dust beneath their feet being raised above their heads.

There had been another incident before the Richards-Roberts episode. Superintendent Pillai of the Eddington Coolie Depot ran a very busy establishment. It was Pillai's custom never to carry the day's work over to the next day. That day, when he left the office it was quite late. Next to his office was a school. A teacher who worked in the school was also late to leave that day. The two set out together on foot and took the Albert Road, which housed mostly very rich people. Pillai was a very simple and god-fearing man.

Suddenly the voice of a policeman rang out: 'Who goes there?'

Pillai had a pass issued by the Mayor's office. He took it out fearlessly and showed it to the policeman. The policeman muttered to himself: 'Coolies strolling on Albert Road at night!'

Pillai didn't quite get him. He asked: 'You said something?'

The white policeman must have mistaken his intentions because he grabbed him by the throat and threw him backwards. Pillai was puzzled. Trying to steady himself, he asked: 'Why are you behaving with me like that? What did I do?'

The policeman now pushed him with full force: 'Get lost, you bastard coolie! Or I will throw you into a cell.'

The teacher stood hiding behind a tree, shaking in his boots. He could neither flee nor stay where he was.

Pillai was almost in tears. An impotent rage was spreading through his body. That rage also perked up his brain and he did some quick thinking. He knew that if he stayed on at the spot, things might get worse. As he left, the teacher also sneaked out of hiding and joined him. The policeman had missed him, but he was so scared that he kept looking over his shoulders to check if someone was following him. Pillai, his teeth clenched in anger, was quite unaware of the teacher. He was so upset that he couldn't sleep that night. He spent the night tossing in bed and thinking.

The next day, he headed to the courts and filed a complaint against the police in Captain Lucas' court. Ever since the Balasundaram case, *girmitiya*s too were finding themselves mustering enough courage to demand justice for them.

The police argued in their defence that Pillai was blowing the case out of all proportions. Under M.K. Gandhi's influence, he was trying to vilify the Natal Police Department. Pillai was to blame as he had refused to produce the pass when asked to do so. The policemen only did his duty by administering a rebuke to him. Pillai was making this an excuse for harassing the police.

Captain Lucas asked: 'Can anyone believe that a coolie, when asked to show his pass by a policeman, would refuse to show it? How many cases have been witnessed so far where a coolie has refused to show his pass to a policeman?'

The police had no satisfactory answer to this question. The court imposed a pound fine on the policeman.

Instances of this kind were serving to confirm the white community in its belief that the courts were siding with the coolies and ignoring the interests of their own kind under the influence of M.K. Gandhi.

The police department was peeved at the attitude of the courts towards the police. The policemen too were also annoyed. They took the verdicts in these two cases to be an insult to their honour and as obstructions placed in the path of the performance of their duties. The Police Superintendent even went to the extent of issuing a statement to the press: 'We are puzzled. Strange things are happening. First, a white cop is fined. He is accused of dragging a coolie by the scruff of his neck. Actually, it was the coolie who was to blame. He did have a pass but he refused to show it to the policeman. One lad was nabbed walking the streets at night; another one flouted the orders of the magistrate. What's more, he lied to the court that he couldn't get his pass made because he was sick. The entire colony knows and appreciates the civilized ways of the Durban police. No Arabs and respectable people have ever complained about being stopped or harassed by the police. The policemen are not clairvoyants that they should be able to tell whether or not someone has a pass just by reading his face. The coolies are trying to escape the clutches of the law by changing their names and religion and then walking to the streets at night, without so much as a word to the police. If the courts accept this practice as legitimate, coolies all over the colony will start the same practice.'

When Mohandas' attention was drawn to the Police Superintendent's statement, he felt worried. Was it proper for a police officer of the rank of a Superintendent to issue statements to the press on a small matter like this? Would the police now make it a practice to issue statements about accused persons absolved by the courts merely because they happen to be children of *girmitiya* parents? He himself was on a one-year *girmit*. Of course, things had also happened to him and more could happen in the future. But was the attitude of the police justified? How was it going to affect the upcoming generations? Will the seed of hatred that was being sown now yield a fruit of love in the future?

Gandhibhai felt that the incident was going to involve him more and more. If he did not protest this statement, he would also become a part of this unseemly politics. He wrote a reply to the Police Superintendent's statement and sent it to *Natal Mercury*. In it, he said:

> *What is the crime of these two boys, Richards and Roberts? Is it that they are sons of* girmitiyas? *Should it matter to a society that takes pride in merit-based evaluation of individuals? Did not the same society confer the status*

of a great poet on the son of a leather worker? Why, then, such hullabaloo over the change of religion and name by a boy? Is it because some police officials want to justify or cover up the unwarranted arrest and humiliation of an innocent lad by one of their men? One of the boys could well have used his looks and his skin colour to disguise his nationality and parentage, but he didn't do so. Why, then, does the Police Superintendent assume that he had changed his religion and name in order to escape the clutches of the law? The way the lad had answered the questions of the police frankly and fearlessly, it was obvious that that he was not at all ashamed of his name, religion or actions. It is also important to mention here that the Police Superintendent was so impressed by the frankness of the young man on the occasion that he actually told him: 'Young man! If everyone followed your example, the police would be saved a lot of trouble.' If changing one's religion is not illegal, why should changing one's name be so? Didn't Mr. Culeus become Haji Abdullah? General Babe assume a Muslim name after conversion to Islam? Did anyone ever point a finger at him? But if an Indian assumes a Christian name and adopts European clothing, it becomes a crime inviting punishment. I believe that the two boys are honest Christians, if it is at all possible to say who is and who is not a true Christian. Like other Indians, and like people of other religions living in this colony, they too should get the benefit of the doubt.

Mohandas also commented on what the Police Superintendent had to say in reference to Arabs:

The Police Superintendent writes that the police treat the Arabs and other respectable people in a civilized way. Didn't the two educated young men fall in the category of civilized non-whites for him?

Gandhibhai's letter evoked strong reactions among people. Blacks and whites alike reacted with sympathy towards the two young men. One newspaper wrote: 'We are surprised to see the Police Superintendent trying to present his constables as angels. There is actually no need for the

Police Superintendent to react in print to every case, especially when he knows that his entire case is as strong as a house of cards.'

Another newspaper wrote: 'The Police Superintendent had absolutely no right to use impolite words when talking to the young men.'

The reactions should have pleased Gandhibhai. After all, the purpose of writing the letter was to expose the attitude of the police and the truth regarding the incident. But instead Gandihbhai was uncomfortable. He wondered if he had done some injustice by writing the letter. Since the two boys had been acquitted, where was the need for him to pursue the matter further? The Police Superintendent was not a bad person. Had he not been basically a good-hearted man, he would not have responded spontaneously to the lad's statements by saying that if everyone followed his example, the problems of the police would be greatly reduced. How could a man who could burst involuntarily into praise for a coloured man be a bad person at heart? The same sincerity which impelled him to praise the young man must have inspired him to speak for his subordinates too. Every good officer has a duty to protect the honour of his subordinates. The fault lay with the particular policeman.

Ideas were swarming in Mohandas' head. It wasn't enough to win the case: what was required was to reduce the gulf between Indians, particularly *girmitiya*s, and the police. If even the slightest room could be created in the policemen's hearts for the *girmitiya*s, the daily excesses committed on them could be significantly reduced. On the other hand, if the police got annoyed, they would not let go any opportunity to harass and humiliate the *girmitiya*s, with or without reason. In fact, from *girmitiya*s today, they could move on to others tomorrow.

The Central Police Station was on Mohandas' way to the courts. The Police Superintendent had his office at the Police Station. On that day, Mohandas stopped over at the Police Station on his way to the courts. The entire police staff was present, but no one at first recognized him. Then someone must have identified him as the coolie barrister who had defended the two boys and had subsequently written a letter to the newspaper attacking their officer. Once the word spread, the attitude of every policemen present changed. Time to get our own back! Sidelong glances, knowing smiles, sly signals, making faces—the full repertoire was on display.

Gandhibhai spoke without a trace of hesitation: 'I am M.K. Gandhi. I'm here to meet your Captain and you all.'

One of them asked dryly: 'What for?'

'To make friends.'

'Were you the one to write to the newspaper?'

'Yes, it was my letter.'

'And still you are here?'

'In your line of duty you keep ticking off people and warning them. Can't I, as a barrister, do my own duty? And we can both be wrong at times.'

The person talking to him was a white and had two stars on his shoulders.

Gandhibhai laughed: 'I know that you are annoyed with me. But neither I nor my clients are unhappy with you. You did your duty, I did mine.'

As he made to say something, the Police Superintendent arrived in his motorcar.

'Hello, Gandhi,' he greeted him.

'Good morning, Mr. Alexander.'

'A new case?'

'No, the same old one. I came here you to meet you and your friends here. May I have a few minutes with you? I have had a chance to talk to others.'

Alexander thought for a minute and then said: 'Well, all right. You may come in.'

Gandhibhai followed him into his office. It was simply and unostentatiously furnished. Right above his chair there was a cross on the wall. Alexander looked at the cross and crossed himself. Gandhi did the same. Alexander swivelled on his heels and, facing Gandhi, waved him to a seat and asked: 'What can I do for you?'

'Before I come to that, let me tell you something I remembered. When I was in Pretoria, Mr. Baker, Dada Abdullah's solicitor, took me with him to a prayer everyday. We all prayed together. It was there that I realized that if you pray with a true heart, hatred and ill-will can be turned into love and goodwill.'

Alexander fixed a steady gaze at him and said: 'I don't think I quite understand.'

'Actually, it's quite simple. Don't you think if we dedicate whatever it is we do, good or bad, to God, it is equivalent to prayer? I do my duty, you do yours. We catch the wrong-doers and try to get them punished. Sometimes, an innocent person may also be judged a criminal and may get punished. As a lawyer, I try to save the innocents and to get them justice. Sometimes, even a criminal is saved while an innocent person isn't. In truth, though, it is only God who knows who is a criminal and how much of a criminal? As far as we are concerned, we keep creating new and arbitrary definitions of who is a sinner and who isn't, and keep changing them. We really have no standards. There is really only one way out: do your duty with a pure heart and surrender it to God. Lord! I did what had to be done and I did it with a pure heart! Now you decide whether it was right or wrong. That's what a prayer is.'

Alexander said nothing.

Gandhibhai paused a little and then said: 'I came here only to tell you that the Indians settled here are weak and helpless. They get punished when they sin; they also get punished when they don't. My mother used to sing a song which went as follows: *A man of God is one who can feel the pain of others*. These people should not be objects of our hatred and anger; they should be instruments of our prayers. When I went with Mr. Baker into the prayer room for the first time, everyone present there joined in a prayer for me: "Lord! As you have guided us and showed us the true path, as you have shown mercy on us, so must you guide this brother of ours and save him from the path of evil and adversity." I felt then as if it was my mother singing.'

Alexander spoke for the first time: 'I read your letter in *Natal Mercury*.'

'I am sure you did. Do you think I shouldn't have written it? I felt that the statement you issued would only deepen the fear in their minds of annoying you and I thought with my letter the fear might be lessened a little. Fear, you know, acts like slow poison. Do believe me when I say those people are not really as bad as they are made out to be.'

'Was what the boys said true?'

'You were satisfied that it was, weren't you? Truth is its own guarantee; it does not need proof. When you face the truth, you know it is the truth. There are of course some weak and diffident characters who want to speak the truth but end up speaking falsehood because of the fear within them.'

'What is it you want, Mr. Gandhi?'

'Sympathy and goodwill for an uprooted, transplanted, weak and frightened lot of human beings. It is easy to punish them, but only you and your police can help restore their shaken hearts and shattered faith.'

Mohandas waited for a moment for him to respond. Then he got up and took his leave: 'I'm sorry I took so much of your time. As I said, our deeds are our prayers. How effective our prayers are will depend on how honest our deeds were.'

At first, Alexander did not get up. Then he rose slowly. Without a word, he extended his hand. Gandhibhai took it in both his hands and gave it a light shake before walking out.

Even after he had walked out, the Police Superintendent kept standing as if mesmerized.

~

Natal Indian Congress was now a functioning body, although it was still known only to those who were its members. Others knew little about it. Mohandas was not in favour of this kind of freemasonry. Nor was he in favour of undue self-advertisement of the Congress and its activities. The public relations activity of the Congress was carried out in a door-to-door fashion in the manner of the missionaries. The way it carried on its work was also unique. Its workers would first listen to people's complaints, report them to Gandhibhai and would then convey whatever assistance was available to the needy persons. Everything was done on a voluntary basis. Mohandas was the kingpin of the whole activity. Other people were also of course involved but everyone looked to Gandhibhai for guidance. Mohandas tried to tell them in no uncertain terms: 'Look, I don't count. Everything depends on you. Please take your own decisions. Don't come running to me.'

But they had developed dependence on him. Whatever they did had to be communicated to Mohandas; so too whatever they didn't, and so also whatever they couldn't. Mohandas was thus becoming a cure-all medicine.

~

It was the middle of 1895. A case was in progress in the court of Captain Lucas, the designated court for cases pertaining to Indian coolies. Punnuswami and three of his companions were charged with assault on Murugaswami Pillai. Mohammad Ibrahim Asgar, aka Asgara, was the witness. Asgara had been a member of the Natal Congress. Its members were worried that if Congress appeared to be working against the interests of *girmitiya*s, it would be difficult to persuade them to join it.

Mohammad Kamruddin Moosa was an office bearer of the Congress. The accused were in his office to meet him. Asgara lived somewhere close to Moosa's office. Dada Abdullah and Dawood Mohammad were also present. Asgara was summoned to the office in the presence of them all. Asgara was accompanied by two of his hangers-on. The presence of hangers-on was a matter of prestige for persons like him. A clerk storekeeper by the name of Rangaswami Padaychi, who was also a Vice-President of the Congress, was also present. When Asgara appeared before the panel, it was Padaychi who asked him questions; the rest all remained silent. Padaychi asked: 'Are you thinking of appearing as a witness for Pillay?'

'I have received the summons all right.'

'But what have you decided?'

Asgara kept quiet.

Actually, it was Kamruddin who had him summoned but he wasn't speaking now. Everyone sitting there listened to what the two said, but no one tried either to stop Padaychi or to interrogate Asgara. Asgara left the place without answering the question.

When Asgara was summoned to the court, he told the magistrate that he had seen Murugaswami Pillai and Punnuswami engaged in abusive verbal exchange in the street. He also said that he had been summoned by Kamruddin Sahib and that Dada Abdullah and Dawood Mohammad had also been present. Padaychi had asked him some questions, in the presence of all these people, which he felt were intended to dissuade him from giving evidence in the case. He had also threatened him. Padaychi, he said, was a Vice President of Natal Congress and an influential man of Durban. He could always get what he wanted.

Twice during his disposition, Lucas repeated: 'Natal Congress! Natal Congress!' Finally, he said: 'What has Natal Congress to do with this business?'

Lucas was an army man. He knew as much about law as an army man normally did. He got so irritated by the repeated mention of Natal Congress that, without thinking and without bothering about the law, he handed out conviction to all the four accused. He could not, of course, write that the Natal Congress was behind all this mischief, or that its objective was to spread discontent and disaffection in the colony, or that it was out to incite a rebellion against Her Majesty's government, but in some devious way he had managed to mention its name in his judgment.

Mohandas had been in Durban for barely two days when he had run into Captain Lucas, a meeting Captain Lucas had not allowed himself to forget. The mere sight of Mohandas was enough for Captain Lucas to be reminded of the scene when, defying his admonition, Mohandas had walked out of his court, his turban still intact on his head, and he had been left staring after him. Never had a thing of this kind happened to him before. Imagine a magistrate issuing an order and a mere coolie, no matter in what position, refusing to stand by it! The fellow had actually thrown the order back into his face. Mohandas was now also present in court in the Asgara case.

All the four accused had gone on appeal to the Supreme Court against Captain Lucas' verdict. Their plea was that the court's decision was based on a statement for which no proof had been presented. Another Police Magistrate, Mr. Waller, had summoned Padaychi. Now, though Asgara did mention Padaychi in his statement, he had never been summoned as a witness. When Captain Lucas got to know that Waller had summoned him to his court and that he was thus interfering with a case already settled by him, he again got the entire case transferred back to his court. Waller was informed that the case had been recalled and the case file sent to the 'Clerk of Peace,' is that the case had been filed for review. This decision of Captain Lucas caught Padaychi on the wrong foot. He approached Mohandas with folded hands and requested him to take up his case.

'Why do you want me as your lawyer?' Mohandas asked.

'Lucas is strict and is also sore with Congress. He is sure to hand me severe punishment.'

'If your purpose in hiring me is to escape punishment, let me make it clear that it will only make your situation worse. Mr. Lucas is essentially a good man, though of course he is quick to lose his temper. Especially when he sees I am around.'

'What do you suggest?'

'Get Mr. Miller as your lawyer. I'll do whatever I can to help.'

So Mr. Miller appeared in the court for Padaychi. Mr. Coddler was the official prosecutor. Mohandas was also present in the court, busy taking notes and assisting Mr. Miller whenever required. Lucas had an eye out for him. The presence of Mohandas in the court did not go down well with him. Somewhere at the back of his mind was the feeling of insult that Mohandas, a mere coolie, had caused him by defying his orders. Had Mohandas been actually arguing the case, he was sure he could have found an occasion or two to show him his place, but, though present in the court, the fellow was trying to pose as if he had nothing to do with the case.

For two days, Lucas watched and suffered. On the third day, watching Mohandas sitting in a corner and taking notes, he couldn't contain himself any more. He looked at Mr. Miller and asked: 'What is Mr. M.K. Gandhi doing here without his gown on? Is he your clerk? I'm surprised that an English-qualified barrister does not feel ashamed doing such a thing? If he wanted to appear in the case as a lawyer he should have been wearing his gown. Obviously there is something the matter that he can neither come out in the open nor can keep himself completely hidden?'

'Do you have any objection to Mr. Gandhi working as my clerk?' There was a touch of bitterness to Mr. Miller's otherwise courtly modesty.

Lucas looked at Gandhi and said: 'I know it only too well!'

Mohandas kept quiet. The next day, a respected paper like *Natal Mercury* came out with the following comment: 'What gave Mr. Lucas the right, either as a magistrate, or as a retired army officer, or as a cultured citizen, to put such a humiliating question and to make such a humiliating comment aimed at Mr. M.K. Gandhi? Why didn't Mr. Gandhi ask Mr. Lucas on the spot to explain what gave him the right to interfere in his work? For the sake of the prestige and honour of his profession, he must take up this question to the highest quarters.'

Lucas' behaviour had made the Asgara-Padaychi case a hot topic in the newspapers and all eyes were now on the court proceedings. Everyone now awaited the final outcome. Almost all the newspapers sided with Mohandas. But when Asgara's statement appeared, the tables were turned. The whites reacted with concern and consternation at the mention of Natal Indian Congress. It was almost an emergency situation.

The *Natal Advertiser* wrote: 'It appears that a big political organization of Indians, with roots in India and England, is operating in the colony.'

Another newspaper wrote: 'News of the existence of Natal Indian Congress is an alarming development. The government must immediately learn its lessons and lose no time in finding out how the future of the colony will be affected as the influence and power of the Congress grow.'

All kinds of charges were being made against the Congress. Each paper was coming out with its own inventions. Everything rested on conjecture. In its September 24, 1995 issue, the *Natal Witness* came out with a malicious charge against Indians and included the Natal Congress among its targets. It said that false affidavits, amounting to contempt of court, are submitted in the colony courts where Indian lawsuits are decided. It is now clear, it said, that lying and deception are not just individual traits of Indians, which they have developed into a fine art, but are 'institutionalized' characteristics. The branches of this institution cover the entire colony. The government must try and find out what the real intentions of this Congress are. Careful investigation may indeed reveal that some smart Indians are busy creating unrest by spreading word among the natives that while they (the Indians) live in this colony as free citizens, the nativesthemselves lead a life of slaves.

Mohandas was trying to study this demand for Congress' blood closely. The controversy had put the wind up the Indian business community. The government could adopt a hard attitude and think up a hundred ways of making their life difficult. The smaller businessmen were particularly worried. The government could ask the City Council to cancel their licences. The Protector had any number of small privileges which it could use to harass them. The white masters could start a fresh round of repression which could send them scurrying for cover. Most *girmitiya*s were however quite ignorant about thc dclicatc situation.

Gandhi was trying constantly to reassure them that there was actually nothing to worry about. There was nothing in the objectives and provisions of the Natal Congress that could harm the interests of the government. Newspaper reports should start worrying the government only when it finds something objectionable in Congress' goals and rules. He also tried explaining to them that he had avoided responding to the defamatory remarks made by Captain Lucas in court and it was only Mr. Miller who had responded as he had thought fit. The newspapers too had commented on Mr. Lucas' remarks, but Gandhi had also not acted on the suggestions made by the newspapers that he should take the matter up to the highest quarters of the government.

But the pressure on Gandhi went on increasing. He was finally forced to respond to the ridiculous charges that were being levelled at him and the Congress. Through the pages of *Natal Advertiser*, he said: 'If it didn't involve the issue of contempt of court, I would have commented on the question whether or not the sub judice matter has anything to do with Natal Congress. So long as the verdict on the case is not delivered, I would prefer to keep my mouth shut on the matter. But as to the other charge against Congress that it operates as a secret society, I am obliged to respond emphatically. In fact, this matter had been made sufficiently clear at the time when the Congress was in the process of formation. If I am not wrong, you (the *Advertiser*) had yourself published this declaration in your esteemed pages. There cannot be any question of the Congress functioning as a secret society. Very recently, Congress had in fact invited to its fortnightly meetings all those European friends who sympathize with its programmes and are desirous of attending its panel discussions.'

Natal Advertiser however continued its tirade. The clarifications issued by Gandhi made no impression on it. It replied by saying: 'Whatever one might say, and whatever might have been written at the time of its founding, the fact is that no one could predict at the time what the shape and character of Congress were going to be. The most objectionable thing is that the organization has functioned as an undercover organization for so long.'

When the issue did not stop snowballing, the *Natal Mercury* came out with an editorial in favour of Mohandas. It said that it was a case of a mountain being made out of a molehill. The founding of the Congress was common knowledge. The Natal newspapers had covered the event quite extensively. Congress had been carrying out its functions without making a hullabaloo about it. That did not make it a secret society engaged in unlawful activities. As long as it was not established that the Indians were indulging in antinational or subversive activities, they had every right to a political organization.

Making a wry comment on all this journalistic hyperactivity, someone called Cape Argus commented: 'If Indians wish to confine all their activity to the political arena, they have a right to do so. The allegation made by the magistrate is now working in favour of the Congress.'

Gandhi was feeling relieved that the controversy was coming to an end when the debate flared up again. *Natal Mercury* published an article signed 'H' giving rise to hot speculation about the identity of the author. Could he be an Indian? Almost around the same time, the *Times Magazine* published an interview with a journalist called R.H. Tatham. The interview contained almost the same material that was in the article by 'H.' The possibility was also not ruled out that H might be an Indian and Tatham might have picked up points for his interview from the article. In any case, it was kite-flying of a sort. It said that M.K. Gandhi, the General Secretary of Congress, was paid three hundred rupees a month. Another, even more interesting point it made was its reference to an interpreter in the magistrate's court, who was supposed to have played an important role in the founding of the Congress and also written its constitution. The report on the franchise bill that had been sent to the Queen was also attributed to him. The appointment of Mohandas as the General Secretary was also said to be a result of his bidding.

Gandhibhai was at his wit's end. Who could be behind the kite-flying and what could be his motive? Who was the interpreter referred to? Was he an Indian or some other? The possibility had also been hinted at that behind all this might be a French trader called Marcel Ledue, a regular visitor to Dada Abdullah and a Gandhi-basher. Mohandas however did not react to the suggestion. For sometime, Mohandas maintained a neutral stance towards the swelling tide of rumours, but when they looked like assuming alarming proportions, he was forced to break his silence.

On September 25, 1895, Mohandas wrote in the *Natal Mercury* that the person to bring Natal Congress into existence was Abdullah Haji Adam and no one else, and that he had himself been present at the meeting from the start to the end. No bureaucrat had been present at the meeting. Regarding the salary supposedly drawn by him as General Secretary, he made it clear that he didn't get a penny from the Congress. Some Indian businessmen paid him for looking after their legal affairs and that was the source of his livelihood. He had concluded by saying that there was nothing confidential in Congress affairs.

By the time Gandhi had replied to one allegation, another one would be ready. A new allegation had now sprung into life: A war on the government was being planned under the leadership of M.K. Gandhi. The *girmitiya*s were being incited to fight for their demands. Gandhi extorted money from traders and labourers promising to seek relief for them but spent the money on himself.

What worried Gandhi most was the conspiracy that was going on in secret to destroy Natal Congress by giving it a bad name. He was observing the developments closely and patiently.

Captain Lucas in the meantime had revived the Asgara file and dates for hearings were being announced at a fast pace. Indians were greatly upset. The Congress had had several meetings on the subject. A meeting was called at Rustomji Parsi's home three days after Mohandas' statement appeared in *Natal Mercury*. Rustomji's home on Field Street was large and very impressive. He was Vice-President of the Congress and enjoyed participating in its activities. He had a good standing in the Indian community. Mohandas was asked to address the meeting. He confined himself to the topic of Congress only. Starting without the slightest hesitation, he said:

'Congress is now a household word. Every one of us now owes it to himself to pay his subscription on time. We need at least of four thousand pounds to make our party strong. If every businessman agrees to pay five shillings on every hundred pounds of his sales, we can raise the requisite amount. I am thinking of making a trip to India by the year-end and I'll be trying to get some barristers over.'

The magistrate's attitude in the Asgara-Padaychi case was very discouraging, but it had its good side too: it had shocked the people out of their complacency and had served as a wake-up call. There was therefore unanimous support for Mohandas' proposal. They resolved not to allow Congress to be weakened and to raise whatever amount was needed in whatever way they could.

What had however surprised people was that, amidst all the allegations directed at him, Mohandas had maintained perfect equanimity.

~

October 2. Mohandas' birthday. That was the day when Captain Lucas delivered the judgment after an eleven-day long hearing. The judgment read: 'Asgara was pressurized by the organization. He had been a member of the organization called Natal Indian Congress. He was called to Mr. Moosa Haji Adam's office, where other leading members of the Congress were also present. It goes without saying that this organization was founded for the realization of certain political objectives. The evidence gathered during the hearings establishes that this organization has been trying to extend its influence with the intention of murdering justice. I can say without the slightest hesitation that Natal Indian Congress is an insidious and pernicious organization, which presents a standing threat to the citizens of this colony, be they white or black. The accused may well have been used by this organization as a weapon, but this does not reduce his culpability. The accused is sentenced to six months' hard labour.'

The judgment left Padaychi rooted to the spot.

Captain Lucas's judgment opened the floodgates of newspaper attacks on Mohandas, but Mohandas was totally unaffected. He argued that if the good or bad effects of an action which a member of an organization performed in his individual capacity were to be routinely transferred to the organization, no organization in the world would ever be able to claim to be clean and blameless.

Natal Witness and *South Africa Telegraph* went even further and said: 'Attorney Gandhi seems disappointed with Captain Lucas' judgment. It would be in his interest, while of course it would be good riddance for this colony, if Gandhi were to extort whatever money he wishes to extort from the Indian community and leave for his own country, or Guyana or England.'

South Africa Telegraph in fact had included the entire Indian community in its attack: 'Everyone knows that Indians represent a greater danger than the natives. When you have such a dangerous group of people in your midst, it becomes the responsibility of every member of the community to find a solution to the danger so that incidents such as those that happen regularly in India can be avoided here.'

On October 6, 1895, H came out with another article in *Natal Mercury*. It said: 'Taking advantage of his privileged position, Gandhi conveys confidential information regarding matters of public interest to Congress. Gandhi is a professional agitator, who is misleading the common people by calling himself the General Secretary of Indian National Congress.' He went on to invite the white community to 'upset Gandhi's apple cart' and prevent him from going around enlarging his area of influence. How was it possible, he went on to ask, if not for his influence, that communities which were at each other's throats in their own country, and in places as far apart as Mumbai and Mauritius, were working together so enthusiastically in this country?

Referring to a specific meeting of the Congress, H said: 'Gandhi has promised the Indians that he would bring three barristers from India.' He said he had evidence to prove his claims and he was ready to present it to the government.

Mohandas found himself in a delicate situation. He was totally at a loss. If the mud-slinging at Congress was allowed to go unchallenged, the very existence of the organization would be in jeopardy. But he was also aware that the Padayachi case was in appeal and making any comments on the case might invite trouble. He was in constant consultation with his colleagues. While he had a lot of support from them, no one was prepared to take any concrete steps. Everyone said the same thing: 'We have complete trust in you. We'll support any step you take.'

This single sentence raised his responsibility manifold.

Finally, and after a lot of deliberation, Gandhi decided to make the British government a party to the affair. He prepared a draft letter for the Colonial Secretary, in which he made the following points:

1. *There was never a formal decision to summon Asgara; nor was any official advisory issued to him. The magistrate's accusations against the Congress had no basis at all. The questions that the magistrate asked after the arguments were over had no legal standing.*
2. *During the questioning, it had become clear that there was no meeting of the Congress during that week. Some Congressmen were certainly present in Moosa Haji Adam's office on August 12, 1895 and Asgara was indeed asked a few questions about the case. Linking this incident with the case, the magistrate drew certain conclusions of his own and decided that a meeting of the Congress had been held in Moosa's office. Meetings of the Congress are always held in the Congress office. Copies of all notices issued for Congress meetings had been presented to the court during the hearing.*
3. *No evidence presented in the court was of a nature to prove that there was a well thought out conspiracy behind the whole affair.*

Mohandas concluded the letter by reaffirming that the aim of the organization was to build goodwill between the two communities and to help the government, while also seeking its help, in resolving the problems of the Indian community. It had no intention whatsoever of creating problems for the government, nor any rules which would do so. If the government agrees with us that the case has nothing to do with the Congress, it should issue a statement and put an end to the controversy. If it doesn't, it should order a *de novo* inquiry into the whole affair.

What ultimately happened was something quite different. Before the letter could be sent to the Colonial Secretary, the Supreme Court issued its judgment. Mr. Viewmount was the officiating Chief Justice. He had paid close attention to the appeal. His verdict was: 'the charge remains totally unproven. It is unfortunate that the able magistrate allowed himself to be carried away by some ideas which had not even the remotest connection with the issues at hand.' The verdict also discharged Padaychi. Walter Rege was the Chief Justice. When the full bench judgment came, it carried the following sentence from him: 'The magistrate's decision has many infirmities, which are a symptom of legal disability.'

For the first time, *Cape Town Times* wrote in its editorial: 'We must now accept the Indian community as a political force. To ignore its existence will be the greatest mistake we can commit. The followers of Gandhi have been fully successful in establishing themselves as a political entity to reckon with. An experienced politician, we are sure, will not commit an error in this regard.'

Within one year, the membership of the Congress had reached two hundred and twenty eight. Among new members were those who worked in banana plantations. For them, the annual fee was five shillings.

Mohandas felt his dream was coming true.

~

XIII

Gandhibhai lived in Beach Grove. His home was neatly maintained but was completely unostentatious. It was a two-storey house with an iron gate at the entrance. The entry was through a smaller gate inside the larger one. A balcony looked out on the Bay of Durban. When Gandhibhai returned from the court, he always spent sometime sitting in the balcony. Breezes from the sea came in scampering like small kids and went scampering back after touching him gently. He would feel rejuvenated in every part of the body. The winds suffused him with their kindliness and child-like transparency. The ships on the far-away horizon looked to him like large birds that had chosen to swim rather than fly.

The living rooms were upstairs while services like drawing room, kitchen, baths, etc. were on the ground floor. A set of parallel bars had been installed in the courtyard for exercise. The drawing room had wall-to-wall carpets, sofas, and two *chaises longues* on the arms of which one could drape one's legs to relax. A cloth-covered large table sat in the middle of the room. A revolving bookrack held Gandhi's favourite books: books by Tolstoy, Blavatsky and Edward Maitland; books on Christianity, Hinduism, Quran and other religions; lives of some national leaders and so on. The dining room contained a large oval table with eight chairs around it. Sometimes, two or three rounds had to be gone through at table before everyone in the house was fed. Two of the five rooms on the upper floor were provided with wardrobes. The beds were all hardboard, with no thick mattresses or springs. Everyone, including Mohandas, slept in these beds.

Dada Abdullah & Co. had its office where Beach Grove Lane joined West Street. Its entire business was transacted from this office at 427 West Street. The building belonged to one W.G. Baker and had been rented by

Dada Abdullah & Co. Dada Abdullah had his drawing room in this villa, though his residence, Sydenham, was on Claire Road. Mohandas had lived for a year in this villa. Next to Dada Abdullah & Co. were the offices of Harvey Greenacre & Co., which was one of the leading European firms in South Africa. Harvey Greenacre had also hired Mohandas as its legal adviser. For a European company to hire a coolie barrister as its legal adviser was worrying enough for whites. The owner of the company, Mr. Benjamin Greenacre, was one of the first mayors Durban had. A few years later, his son, Walter Greenacre, also became Mayor. The most interesting thing about these premises was a colourful and pretty stone at the centre of the building which carried the company's name: HARVEY GREENACRE & COMPANY. Since nameplates of this kind were still not in popular currency, it was something of a curiosity in those days. The offices of the company were furnished in the British style. The Greenacre family had its living quarters on the upper floor while the ground floor was office space. The Reception Office was also on the ground floor. That's where Mohandas could sometimes be found working.

Gandhi's office was barely a stone's throw from West Street. A number of clerks worked in the office, two of whom looked after Congress affairs like collecting subscriptions, conducting correspondence, keeping records, contacting members and maintaining accounts.

Joseph was in charge of the Congress office. Son of *girmitiya* parents, he was the first Christian to become a member of the Congress. Although still a lad, he had earned Gandhi's respect for his sincerity and hard work. Gandhi was later to help him to go to London for further studies. Even after he returned from London with a law degree, he continued his affiliation with the Congress. Although he was the quiet type, he sang beautifully. When he sang, even whites felt captivated. For Joseph, it was Gandhi, Gandhi everywhere.

The Gandhi home was a centre of all kinds of Durban activities. Indian businessmen often gathered there. The whites who came were also not small in number. Gandhi's areas of work included the social, the political and the legal. Anyone in need headed to Gandhi's door. So much so, indeed, that Gandhi found no time to look after domestic matters. Sometimes even daily needs went unattended. The stream of visitors started early in the morning and continued till late at night. Fortunately, Gandhi ran a simple household, providing just the basics: vegetarian food, hard beds; a blanket in winter, a thin sheet rest of the time. Whites were warmly welcomed but no exceptions were made as far as household rules were concerned. There was absolutely no embarrassment involved.

Mohandas was like a boatman rowing several boats together. There were eddies and whirlpools, rocks and hard places, flows and ebbs. There were the Congress, the colonial government, the white community, the natives, the *girmitiya*s, and, last, the fourth estate, that is the press.

One of the things that Mohandas could never get out of his mind was the intense misery of *girmitiya* lives. Their spirits had been completely crushed. Those who were responsible for crushing their spirits then charged them with having no spirit and no strength of character. On the very day he was recruited, a *girmitiya* also entered into a *girmit* with death. To honour that *girmit*, the *girmitiya* had to live a silent tragedy, a tragedy that produced no echo and had no name. It existed only in experience. No one knew about it and no one told them how to get rid of it.

Mohandas decided to study Indentured Law. If a way out had to be found, the problem had to be taken head on. The most dangerous clause was Clause 101, which sought to choke even the cry of the victim. If a *girmitiya* absented himself from duty without permission in order to file a complaint against the master, he could be prosecuted and, if found guilty, could be sentenced up to two pounds in fine or two months of simple imprisonment or hard labour. If a *girmitiya* absented himself from work for twenty-five days in a year, his *girmit* period was extended by fifty days. At the end of the five-year *girmit*, a fifty-day extension felt impossible to live through. Because of reasons such as these, many weak and sick workers were unable to complete their *girmit* all their lives and met their end while still waiting for release. Their wages were docked even for sickness, five pence per day during the first two years and six pence in the remaining three. In cases of excessive absenteeism, the worker, male or female, could be sent to jail, in fact, were actually sent to jail.

Children and women were worse off. A law had been passed in 1891, Clause 25 of which said that women and underage labourers would be required to work according to their capacity. Some examples of the kind of work they could do were also cited, like cutting sugarcane, carrying sugarcane bundles, loading them on to trolleys, drawing water, cutting grass, etc. But these rules were observed more in their breach. Women were made to carry large bundles tottering under their weight. If they objected, they were charged with stealing and their wages were docked. Abusing, slapping and hitting were normal day to day activities. If some employers were found wanting in this respect because of their decency, this was attributed to their incompetence and timidity.

The most outrageous of all things was the man-woman ratio of a hundred to forty. The women in question were not necessarily wives of the coolies. The system of distributing women among men was an invention of the masters and was prevalent all over Natal. After separating the married couples, the remaining women and girls were allotted to single men by the sirdars and overseers. Sometimes, even married women did not escape this distribution system. At least three but not more than five men shared one woman. Which men would share which woman was also a decision of the master's men. The masters defended the system by arguing that a woman worker among four or five men made for a stable working environment. Women *girmitiya*s were therefore called Coolie Marys.

Marriages performed in the Indian way had to be recognized by the Protector's office after they had been registered. Although Indentured Law did not permit husband, wife and children to be separated from each other, but once they were in the hands of the masters, Indentured Law turned into the Master's Own Law. Husband, wife and children could be disposed as the Master wished. The work to be done by them also depended on the Master's whims. The result was that most of the *girmitiya*s were victims of sexual diseases. Child mortality was so high that no one could say whose child would be the next one to die. Mothers worked in open fields from four in the morning till night carrying their children with them. Some children died of exposure to cold, other fell victims to heat. One day, a crying mother took her sick child to the sirdar and said: 'Please save my child. He needs medicine.'

The sirdar laughed: 'Go back to work! And let me know when you are done. I'll get you the child's death certificate.'

For them, a good quality horse meant more money than a *girmitiya*. If the animal fell sick, doctors would queue up with medicines. If a *girmitiya* died, even the master's certificate was hard to get.

~

To Mohandas, Indentured Law was more like a butcher's manual. He started collecting more information about the Law. A few cases came to his notice. The persons involved were all *girmitiya*s, but a law meant for them was of no help at all. Gandhibhai got their files dug out from the registry.

Mr. Dillon was the magistrate dealing with cases of transgression of Indentured Law. The case of a beggar was before him. In 1895, a young Indian had been charged with creating nuisance by begging while being physically completely fit.

'Why do you beg?' asked Mr. Dillon.

The man stood silent though the interpreter had translated the question to him.

'Can you hear?' asked the magistrate.

'Yes, sir, I can hear but I cannot see,' said the young man.

The magistrate was shocked. He asked: 'Are you blind from birth?'

'Had I been blind from birth, who would have allowed me to come here? I would have been better off in my own country, where helping a blind man is considered an act of piety.'

'How then did you become blind?'

After a brief silence, he wiped his blind eyes and said: 'I was working on a *girmit* on a white man's farm. Once there was fire at the farm. He asked me to put it out. I was alone. He was very frightened and was egging me on to put the fire out. The fire was big with the flames touching the sky. Whenever I pulled back, the master poked me and hit me and I kept doing whatever I could to extinguish the fire. At the end, I fell down unconscious. When I regained consciousness, I could see nothing. I had become blind. I pleaded with him, begged him but he did nothing to get me any treatment, nor did he pay me fare to go back home. On the contrary, he dismissed me from work without paying any compensation. Cancelling my *girmit* as a one-sided decision, he left me to roam the streets. I couldn't go back to my country, no one gave me work here, so what choice did I have except to beg alms? The rich can get away with any thing; the poor have to pay even if they do nothing.'

Mr. Dillon acquitted him. He wrote in his judgment that *ex parte* cancellation of an agreement, without payment of compensation, was an inhuman act. However, since there was no claim for compensation, the court could do nothing to help the complainant.

Mohandas opened the next file. It involved a coolie waiter.

This coolie waiter worked in Royal Hotel. The event had taken place in May that year. Mr. F.A. Johnson (Junior) asked the waiter to get a tray from the kitchen. Johnson Junior was Manager of the hotel. The coolie waiter was called Rahmat.

Rahmat went into the kitchen, but he couldn't see any tray there. He spent some time looking for the tray. Johnson Junior got mad at the delay The moment the coolie got back to report that he couldn't find a tray, Johnson fell on him. He twisted his arm and kept hitting him till blood spurted from his nose and mouth. His turban got soaked and his jacket was streaked with blood. The case went to court and there were witnesses. Barman Brown appeared for Johnson. Johnson admitted twisting Rahmat's arm but denied that he had hit him or injured him in any way. It was idle to expect that any one in an all-white hotel would appear for Rahmat and nobody did.

Mohandas was astounded to read the judgment. The magistrate had said that the case had been blown out all proportions. The complainant had hit his nose against the wall during the scuffle, which had caused the blood. The bloodied turban was a result of this. Actually, said the magistrate, the complainant had preserved every drop of his blood carefully in his turban so that he could file a case against Johnson.

The judgment concluded by saying that Mr. F.A. Johnson (Junior) was legally guilty of scuffling with Rahmat and was therefore fined a penny.

At a loss for words, Mohandas could only think to himself: So what this means is that this waiter called Rahmat was such a smart fellow that he knew in advance that Johnson was going to hit him; that, according to the magistrate, he was going to hit his nose against the wall, and that he would then use this incident to trap Johnson in a case. It was for this purpose that he had collected every drop of blood in his turban. Wonder why such a smart fellow had to become a *girmitiya*!

Look hard though he did, he couldn't find the answer to this question in the file.

The third file was for the month of June.

This case had also been filed in the court of Mr. Dillon. A *girmitiya* was accused of refusing to work. He had been in jail for two years on this charge. Every time he came out of jail after completing his sentence, he was asked to go to work and he would refuse. Once again, he was sent to jail for violating the conditions of the agreement.

Mr. Dillon asked him: 'Why don't you want to go to work? If you are willing to go to work, you'll be discharged.'

With folded hands, the man said: 'Please sentence me to death, but don't ask me to go back to that man. He is a butcher.'

'Why didn't you complain to the Protector?' Mr. Dillon asked.

'I did. Not once, but time and again. No one came to check and no one replied to my complaint. So I ran away. I am happier in your jail than I was in his.'

The file did not record what Mr. Dillon said in response. It only recorded the judgment.

The judgment said: 'This is a case which makes me rebel against my position. There are people who don't want to go to work because of fear of torture! What greater proof for this can you find than that a coolie finds it better to spend his life in jail than to go back to work with his master! But my hands are tied by law. I am constrained to work within the boundaries set by law. The accused is given a thirty-day notice to go back to work.'

A snippet from *Natal Mercury* was also pinned to the file. Mohandas read it out of curiosity. *Natal Mercury* had this to say: 'Something is surely wrong somewhere. This matter calls for a sound investigation. It is quite easy to say that if a coolie is mistreated, he should seek redress in a court of law. But for a coolie to prove that he was actually mistreated is almost impossible. It is actually for the Protector to make the investigation and to find a way of helping the coolie.'

On that day, Mohandas wrote in his diary:

> *These are the reasons why suicides among girmitiya*s *are rising day after day. One thousand and eighty persons killed themselves last year.*

Mohandas was very agitated the whole day. Many faces, known and unknown, passed before his eyes. He felt as if he was seeing a ship breaking on the shore and disintegrating into pieces.

~

When Sir Henry Binns and Mr. Mason returned from India, people got to know that the Indian Viceroy had no objection to a Poll Tax. The Indian community felt let down by the Indian government. They cried out in pain. They had been expecting the Indian government to rescue them from this misfortune and to abolish the *girmit* law so that they could earn their living in peace. They were hoping they would be able to leave their dark cells for open spaces under the wide sky, that they too would have a place and an individuality of their own, and that they would be treated on a par with others. Earlier, their hopes had been dashed by the Franchise Amendment Bill; the remaining hope would now be dashed by the forthcoming Immigration Amendment Bill. Though no formal agreement had been signed between the delegation and Lord Elgin, he had given a partial nod to their proposal.

After the delegation had left India, Lord Elgin wrote to the Secretary of State, Mr. Fowler, that the best way of ensuring that Indians went back to India at the end of their *girmit* period was to impose a tax on them. Fowler grasped the intention quickly: it was to expel a class of Her Majesty's subjects. Fowler passed on Lord Elgin's letter to the Colonial Secretary, Lord Ripon. He wrote to Lord Ripon:

> *If a tax is imposed on those who choose to settle down in the colony at the end of the agreement period, there is every likelihood that even those who came to the colony as travellers at their own expense may also be included in the tax net.*

Lord Ripon replied:

> *This amounts to a fine on the coolies. It violates the conditions of the voluntary agreement signed with them.*
>
> After he had received Lord Ripon's reply, Fowler wrote to Lord Elgin about the suggested tax:
>
> *This is like locking the stable door after the horse has bolted. Moreover, though the Government of India has accepted the tax in principle, it is yet to make a formal proposal.*

A formal proposal was sent to London on September 17, 1894. The first new condition was that if a labourer did not sign a new agreement at the end of the five-year term, he would have to go back to India. The travel expenses would be borne by the master.

The second condition was that a labourer desirous of staying on in the colony even after his initial agreement period was over could do so by renewing his *girmit* every two years. He could also change his master. At every successive two-year renewal, the wages would go up by sixteen, seventeen, eighteen, nineteen and twenty shillings per month. Twenty shillings would be the ceiling.

If some labourer did not wish to leave the colony, he would not be sued under criminal law.

The proposal to reduce the number of women per hundred men from forty to thirty was rejected on the ground that the existing average of women to hundred men among labourers is already forty-five. Reducing it to forty would be an injustice to women.

After Lord Elgin's letter was received, the Natal government got an Amendment to 1891 Indian Immigration Bill ready and gazetted it in April, 1895.

The bill had been tabled in May. The Indian community was greatly concerned about the bill and Gandhibhai now had the responsibility to find an antidote to the bill. He was continually in touch with members of the party. The newspapers were continuously fanning the fire of these concerns.

Natal Mercury showed the greatest interest in Indian affairs. It wrote: 'The free Indians are the villains of the piece. They are the ones spreading discontent among the *girmitiya* Indians.' Another newspaper had this take on the affair: 'If the tax system is to be made really effective, every single Indian child should be made to pay tax. Only then there would be some control on the exploding Indian population.'

The Indians were of course beginning to feel the growing pressure of these changing conditions and of the anti-Indian laws. Mohandas too was under pressure. More than the Franchise Amendment Bill, the new bill was helping to stimulate anti-Indian sentiment. The whites were now openly airing their concern about the ill effects this 'filthy race of people' was likely to have on the colony. Some even went around expressing themselves on the utter futility of parliamentary bills in such matters, for you never knew what the London government had in mind. It could be something quite different from what they did. *Natal Witness* wrote: 'No tax is going to help reduce the number of Indians. If the Indian worker makes up his mind to stay on, he will have no problem arranging the tax.'

The attitude of the newspapers had added to Gandhibhai's worries. He decided to prepare a draft of a letter addressed to the Speaker and members of the parliament.

Mohandas wrote:

> *The 1891 Indian Immigration Law Amendment Bill is unjust and illogical. The proposal to impose a three-pound tax on girmitiyas desirous of settling down in the colony at the end of their girmit period violates the spirit of the original bill. This amendment is not comparable to any of the laws in this regard which are in existence in other colonies.*

He stopped for a while and then started again:

> *Supposing we take the average age of those Indians who came to Natal originally as twenty-five years. This means that by the time they are released from the* girmit, *the best years of their lives would have been spent in slavery. If he returned to his country now, he would be a total stranger in his own land. People who sit in positions of power cannot imagine what it means to become a stranger in this way. It is nothing but sheer foolishness to force a person to return to his country after spending ten years in a foreign land. By this time all his ties at home would have been severed; neither would he have collected enough money during this period to be able to live off its interest. The world of business would anyway be closed to him.*

A girmitiya *earns a total of seventy-eight pounds in a ten year period. He spends about thirty pounds of it on necessities. Even if he is somehow able to save fifty pounds, he will earn just about enough interest for bare survival in a poor country like India. As a result, he will probably be driven back to this place as a* girmitiya *again, which means he spends his entire life as a slave. Of course, if he has his family too with him in Natal, he won't be able to save even fifty pounds.*

So far as the three-pound tax is concerned, this clause is sure to lead to widespread discontent and harassment. One wonders why the most useful segment of Her Majesty's subjects is being specially picked out for this tax.

It is sheer injustice and deceit to place these abjectly poor and helpless people in the category of voluntary signatories to the agreement, guided by free volition. They are men without choice, otherwise who would sign a contract for one's own ruin? Out of sheer helplessness that they might sign even more stringent conditions than the ones laid out here.

When the draft was ready, Mohandas read it twice or thrice. Then he sat still for a long time with his eyes closed.

~

People had hoped that, as on the previous occasion, the reading of the bill would be stopped on receipt of their letter. What however happened was just the opposite. The letter was not even acknowledged. Mohandas waited for the Speaker's action. When nothing moved, he decided to write to Chamberlain. The letter was a long one, but its substance was that if the bill was passed with the new clauses incorporated in it, a *girmitiya* wishing to settle in the colony at the end of his *girmit* period would be condemned to a life time of *girmitiya* slavery. Was the fair-minded British government ready and willing to put its stamp of approval on a law which would ensure lifelong slavery for a section of its defenceless subjects? Was the imposition of a three-pound tax on the colony's Indians, who had helped to make this colony green and prosperous, evidence of British love of justice and fair play? In a way, law of this kind only meant turning the five-year *girmit* into a contract for lifelong slavery. If this bill could not be described as being opposed to humanity, he didn't know what law could ever be described in those terms.

The letter concluded by requesting that, if the colony found itself unable to adjust to Indians, the import of labour from India should be stopped forthwith. 'We Indians find ourselves obliged to oppose this bill tooth and nail. The benefits of this law will all go to one side only, the side that already has full control over wealth and power in this country. They neither need these benefits nor should they be granted to them.'

Mohandas had put in everything he had trying to get the letter ready on time. In his heart of hearts, however, he knew that there wasn't going to be a repeat of all that had happened the last time.

The whites too were in a quandary. Their position was somewhat like that of a child who wants to have his cake and keep it too. Newspapers like *Capital* showed that they knew the situation well when they wrote: 'Citizens of Natal both want to enjoy the services of the coolies and also cannot stand their presence in Natal. When they don't leave the colony at the end of their *girmit* period, our citizens get provoked. But they also get worried that when they go away they will also take their services with them. So they get annoyed with them, but they also know that they are not going to go away either.'

On May 18, *Natal Advertiser* wrote: 'If coolies are to be taxed, why not those other subjects of Her Majesty who have not the remotest connection with the European races? Taxing the coolies while permitting other strangers to settle in the colony goes against the much-vaunted principle of equality by which Her Majesty's government swears.'

Such human concerns however carried no value for the Natal government and for its white citizens. In fact, on September 14, *Natal Mercury* published a long poem mocking at the situation of the coolies:

Ha, Ha, Ha, Ho!
Rami-Sami have to go!
Long did they make us suffer,
Much did they make us pay,
Now that the time is here
Let them go! Let them go!

The Natal pariliament had turned a deaf ear to the cry of the *girmtiya*s. Across seven seas, in London, Lord Chamberlain sat on a red-velvet seat, with two roaring lions pressed under his armpits. The cry that was raised in Natal was smothered in its own domes; it was idle to expect that it would reach London.

~

The last three years had seen Gandhibhai's work grow so enormously that he now had no time even for himself. But every now and then he was reminded of the promise that he had once made and that now stood waiting hesitantly in Rajkot, hoping that some day it might be heard. Sometimes, when he was by himself, his own words resounded in his head: 'Don't worry, Kastur! What's one year? Don't worry, I'll be back in no time at all.' But three years had gone by! Three home visits had become due, and he hadn't been home even once! It pained him to think of this. But, of course, he wanted to go. Of course, he wanted to give up his commitments, but the commitments didn't give him up. Though his practice as a lawyer was now flourishing, it was actually the other commitment which he had made, knowingly or unknowingly, out of his own will, that was really holding him up. With his legal practice now on the upswing, the chances of his being able to get his family over to Durban were also getting brighter. And as the chances got brighter, his unfulfilled promise was getting back at him with increasing vehemence. Mohandas knew what was happening. He was also aware that for the first time he was being useful to the society and his existence now mattered to others too.

The problem before him was to find someone who could devote some of his time to party work while he was away in India. There were now some among the businessmen who were ready to be trusted with any responsibility. A related problem was that the person to be picked must be proficient in English. After a lot of deliberation, Mohandas settled on two names: Adamji Miyakhan and Parsi Rustomji.

Haji Adam was the President of the Congress. Gandhibhai approached him and said laughing: 'I have come to you with my leave application.'

Abdullah Haji was puzzled: 'I don't get it,' he said.

'It's three years now since I left home. I came here for a year which has dragged to three. My promises lie waiting for me at home.'

'And what will happen to the movement? None of us is competent enough to take up an issue for discussion verbally or in writing.'

'That's not true. You have so many dedicated workers that there should be no trouble at all. And I am going to work for Congress even while I am in India. I will try to mobilize public opinion against the three-pound tax in India. We won't be able to achieve our goal unless we do it. I am going only for six months. I'll return with my family.'

Abdullah Haji Adam breathed easy. 'But who'll look after your work while you are away? As you know, I am an illiterate.'

'You needn't worry, I have thought it out. Adamji Miyakhan or Parsi Rustomji—whosoever you prefer will shoulder the responsibility. I have talked to Parsi Rustomji and he feels that Adamji Miyakhan would be the right person. I too agree with him.'

When this matter was presented to the Executive Committee of the Congress and Adamji Miyakhan's name was proposed for Secretary, everyone was caught unawares. 'What? Gandhibhai quitting the position? Why?' So many questions were raised that Abdullah Haji had to stand up and proffer an explanation: 'Gandhibhai is going to do Congress work in India too. It is the Indian government that has sanctioned the three-pound tax. It is necessary that public opinion should be created in India against this decision. There is no one else except Gandhibhai who can do it. The Indian people must know what calamity their brethren across the seven seas are facing. If we can expect any help from any quarter, it is India. Moreover, Gandhibhai has been away from home for three years now and his family is impatient for his return. Is it right for us to expect Gandhibhai to work for us while we don't spare a thought for his family?'

Gandhibhai was listening to Abdullah Haji quietly. In the end, he himself made the proposal that Adamji Miyakhan would look after the work of General Secretary.

The proposal was accepted unanimously. Another proposal came from the Chair: 'Mr. M.K.Gandhi is deputed as a representative of Natal Indian Congress to visit India. A sum of seventy-five pounds is sanctioned for his travel and living expenses.'

Mohandas wanted to oppose the latter part of the proposal, but no one would listen. They all raised hands and gave the proposal unanimous approval. The Chair declared the meeting closed.

Gandhibhai was scheduled to leave for India on June 5, 1896 on *S.S. Pongola.* The Indian community's disappointment at his leaving was quite evident. They were worried if some adversity befell them while he was away, how would they face it? The Gujaratis and the Tamils organized a joint farewell function for him on June 4. Dada Abdullah presided over the function, while Lawrence, who had rejoined Gandhi, acted as the interpreter. When Dada Abdullah got up to speak, he had a lump in his throat. He said:

> *It is hard for me imagine Durban without Gandhibhai. For the last three years, it's not Gandhibhai who has been with me; it's me who has been with Gandhibhai. So long as he is here, I mean he is with us; I want to be with him all the time. We think we are businessmen, we earn a lot of money and we can buy whatever we wish and we can gift away whatever we wish to. Gandhibhai however came here empty-handed and with empty pockets, but ever since he came here he has done nothing but give, give, give to us. We are now fakirs in his presence; so much so indeed*

that today we have nothing to give to him. Giving is not all about money; when you decide to give, you can give so much that is priceless that no money can equal it. Gandhbhai is here before you. As he leaves for home today, he has promised us that when our call goes out to him, he will not decline. We have been responsible for his going back on his promise to his family: he had promised to return in a year; he is going back after three years. For us, it's enough that he'd return ...

Words failed Dada Abdullah and he could not go on.

A citation was then read out in Hindi, Urdu and Tamil. It described how Gandhi had awakened them from their slumber, how he had given a voice to them, who had been dumb, and how he had given a face to those who had faces but no features. It then went on to detail his achievements during the last couple of years. In the end, he was presented a gold medal. Mohandas examined it and then put it on the table before him. Then he stood up to speak. He spoke in a firm voice. Without responding to anyone in particular he said whatever he had to say:

What makes me happy most of all is that Indians of all classes and communities are now coming together irrespective of the differences that separate them. They are now all keen to bond together. I regret that I shall not be able to speak in Tamil. It is my deepest desire, however, that, whether or not you understand the languages used, please come to party meetings in large numbers. Language is not everything: it is our hearts that have to meet. That's what will give us strength. If we think that we can make the Congress strong just by talking, we are mistaken; we can make it strong only through sacrifice and action. These have no language of their own. It's my appeal to you to raise the current capital of one hundred and ninety-four pounds of the Congress to a thousand pounds by the time I return from India. You can do this only if you all work together.

The Tamils also organized an independent function. Gandhi had carved for himself a special place in their hearts after what he had done for Balasundaram.

For the Natal press, functions of this kind were a curiosity. People in South Africa often went abroad and also came back, but functions of this kind were seen for the first time. Newspapers labelled them as unique expressions of friendship and affection.

A *Natal Advertiser* reporter came to interview Mohandas the same evening. Answering a question, Mohandas told him fearlessly: 'The aim of Congress is to ensure that the promises made in the 1894 declaration are honoured ...' He continued: 'The political objective of Congress will be met the day Indians in Natal are given the same respect that they get in India.'

This statement had alarmed the white community, but Indians felt relieved. They were delighted that, even as he was leaving, Gandhibhai had spoken out their deepest wish fearlessly.

Someone raised the fear that the Natal government might not permit Gandhibhai to return. What then?

Their faces fell and a stunned silence enveloped them all. Their inner voice however assured them that he would return.

Gandhibhai too heard the question. He just smiled.

~

Twenty-four days later, *S.S. Pongola* docked in Calcutta harbour. The voyage had been very uncomfortable for Gandhi. Using soap with the salty sea water had produced rash on his body and he was feeling itchy all over. Scratching was not pleasant and produced a burning sensation. From Calcutta, he immediately caught a train for Bombay. The journey was a long one and the itching gave him no peace. When the train stopped at Allahabad, thinking that it was an important station and the train would certainly make a longish halt, he came out of the station and looked for a medical store. Though there were shops right outside the station, he took some time locating a medical store. The shopkeeper was sleeping behind the counter and had to be woken up. He took his own time waking up and then finding the medicine, muttering all the time: 'Couldn't you have gone to another store?'

By the time Gandhi reached the station running with the medicine, the train had left. It was just as well he had informed the station master, who had even held up the train for a minute, for when the station master saw that Gandhi wasn't back, he got his things removed from the train and kept them with him before letting the train go. Though the train had left, getting reunited with his things fully intact was a great relief to Gandhi. The next train was on the following day, and Gandhi had no choice but to wait for it. What he was now wondering was how best to utilize the time that had been made available to him by the rash medicine.

Pioneer was considered to be a leading newspaper of the north. Mohandas had heard about it. George McClone Chesney was the editor. Let me start my campaign with *Pioneer*, said Gandhi to himself.

Stepping out of the station, Gandhi checked with a ticket-checker: 'Can you tell me where the *Pioneer* offices are?'

'Chatham Lines. You can hire an *ekka,* if you like or foot it via Hewett Road.'

Mohandas decided to foot it. Luckily for him, Mr. Chesney was in office when he reached there. Mohandas sent in a note: 'I have come from South Africa and am on my way to Bombay. Unfortunately, I have missed my train here. I am staying at Kellner's Hotel. I wish to talk to you about immigrant Indians in South Africa.'

Mohandas was expecting *Pioneer* to be unsympathetic towards Indians. He had however decided that, without bothering about who was in favour and who was not, he had to put forward the tale of Indians' woes in South Africa before everyone. He simply had to convey their cry of help to them.

Mr. Chesney reacted to the note by stepping out of his office, shaking hands with Gandhi with 'Hello, Mr. Gandhi. You're welcome' and ushering him into his office. He was a fairly senior journalist.

'Tell me what I can do for you.'

'Only this: Just listen to me, if you have the time.'

'Sure. Please go ahead.'

'I am in India only for six months. I have come here to convey to Indian intellectuals and journalists like you the sorry state of affairs of Indians settled in South Africa. Their life is a living death. They want help in coming out of their miserable state from anyone and everyone who has, or can have, even the slightest sympathy with their situation. I have brought with me cuttings of the letters that I wrote to the newspapers there; also copies of the correspondence I have carried on with the governments of Natal and Britain in this regard. The Natal government, with due approval of the government of India, is going to impose a three-pound tax on those poor and helpless people. How can a person who earns thirteen pounds in a year pay a tax of three pounds per person in the family? Four members in the family, which I believe is the smallest family size, mean twelve pounds in tax! The threat of depriving Indians of franchise rights is of course already there.'

Mr. Chesney was paying close attention to what Gandhi was saying, while also simultaneously turning over the pages of Gandhi's file. He was also taking notes intermittently.

Gandhibhai also spoke about those *girmitiya*s who had been victims of white planters' violence. He was also carrying the files of those court cases. At times, Chesney stopped reading and started listening carefully to what Gandhi was saying. Whenever he was speaking of a particularly brutal and inhuman incident, Chesney grimaced and his head started shaking.

When Mohandas had finished, he got up, and so did Mr. Chesney. Shaking hands, Chesney said: 'We'll be pleased to publish anything you write for our newspaper.' After a pause, he said: 'It may not be possible for me to support all the demands of Natal Indians. I have some obligations: we have also to think of the viewpoints of our colonial governments. We cannot oppose them indiscriminately. Nevertheless, we'll do whatever is possible.'

'Mr. Chesney, I'm deeply obliged. The support you have promised is enough to assure me. I only wish you to make a study of the whole situation and, if possible, discuss it in your paper. We only want justice, not power.'

When Mohandas came out, his face bore a look of satisfaction. What he liked most was that his campaign had started in Allahabad. Securing an assurance from a senior journalist like Chesney was the first feather in his cap.

From the *Pioneer* offices you could take a road directly to *Sangam*. He however decided against walking and instead approached a *tongawallah*. 'Can you take me to *Sangam*?' he asked. He was looking forward to a *tonga*–ride.

The *tonga* started its jolly ride. Mohandas was all eyes as they dug into the surrounding scenery. A city so old, and the roads so wide! The bungalows occupied acres of land. It was green as far as eyes could see. Field after field sported a flourishing crop. A strange mix of tradition and modernity!

The *tongawallah* pointed in the distance: 'There! That's the *Sangam*. Then he bowed his head in the direction and it seemed was reciting a mantra.'

The *tongawallah* was now in full flow, speaking in Awadhi: 'Here, this is the fort. The Akshaya Vat is here. They say when the Big Flood comes everything in the world goes down in it except this tree.' Mohandas could make out a little but not much of what he was saying. What was uppermost in his mind was how cheerful the man was! Had he been without work, he too would be a *girmitiya* today in some colony or the other and wouldn't then be chattering away like this. Mohandas was particularly impressed by the fact that the fellow was singing away praises of the *Sangam* even as he drove the *tonga*. What a pleasure it is to sing the songs of your soil! What songs can they sing who have nothing left but sorrows to sing of? Mohandas was back with *girmitiya*s again in their land.

Mohandas' *tonga* came to a halt just below the fort walls. The expanse of water covered a great distance. The Yamuna flowing in from the west looked profoundly grave. Mohandas muttered to himself: 'When the moment of surrender comes, all one's frivolity and lightheartedness does turn into grave sobriety.'

For a while, Mohandas sat in the *tonga,* watching the scene of confluence. The *tongawallah* said: 'Sursati disappeared.'

At first, Mohandas didn't get it. Then he remembered that this was supposed to be a confluence of three rivers. Ganga came prancing and dancing; Yamuna flowed in quietly, but Sursati, that is Sarswati, disappeared underground. Gandhi smiled: 'Confluence or merging, always needs sacrifice on the part of someone or the other.'

Mohandas got off the tonga and paid him off. Then he strolled to the point from where he could make out the lines of confluence quite clearly: On one side was Ganga: bright and light; on the other Yamuna: dark and coloured. That's real convergence: to flow into each other and yet preserve your colour and identity. On the other bank, he could see small villages looking down into the water, like small kids. Mohandas was captivated. Waves rose and fell and broke in his mind and, for a while, he was a river. 'Why can't we too converge like these streams?' he asked himself. 'You must find the answer yourself; no river will find it for you,' was the answer he got.

'Would you like to visit Akshay Vat, Babu?' It was a holy man asking.

'I have no wish to become *akshaya* (immortal). Only a vat (banyan tree) can be *akshaya*,' he said, laughing.

As he was preparing to leave *Sangam*, he remembered that he hadn't performed *aachman* (a self-purifying ritual every Hindu is supposed to do). He went back and performed *aachman*, sprinkling water all around him. Whenever *Ba* went to a river, she always performed *aachman.* Flowing water, she used to say, was holy; by touching it you acquire some of that holiness. Whoever touches a river becomes a river for a moment; it suffuses him with its holy flow. Mohandas had a feeling that *Ba* too was a *Sangam.*

When he returned to the hotel, he was at peace with himself. He was still thinking of the line of confluence. This line joins us all together, he thought. Memories connect persons settled in colonies far apart. Yamuna, calm and measured in its flow, kept coming back to him.

Gandhibhai left Allahabad charged with energy. *Sangam* stayed with him for many, many days. The assurance he had received from Mr. Chesney was indicative to him of a success the like of which he hadn't come across before. It had given him a purchase. Now he could write for an important paper like *The Pioneer.* While still at the *Sangam*, an idea had occurred to him to write a four-pager on behalf of the Indians settled in Africa with the title, "A Call to all Indians". He would have to make sure that it reached all those people who considered it their duty to join up with them in their hour of adversity.

Mohandas continued on his way to Rajkot, without stopping over in Bombay. Rajkot was beckoning to him continually. When he suddenly landed at home, everyone was taken aback. They knew he was coming but no one had any idea that he would spring up so suddenly.

He saw Lakshmibhai first, who was speechless with surprise. He took a few minutes to assure himself that it was indeed Mohaniya who stood before him. When assured, he embraced him hard as if, with Mohaniya in his embrace, he had everything in the world he could want. He had gone away and now he was so close to him ... so close that he could touch him, feel him and embrace him. But his voice was still caught in his throat. He wanted to ask him: 'When did you come? How was the journey?' But these questions kept circling in his head, humming like a bee that had lost its way. And then suddenly there sprang to him a question, quite separate from others, like a snake sticking up its hood in a rustle of dry leaves: Was he back for good? But the words did not come out.

Kastur stood behind the door, absolutely calm and waiting. He was probably stuck a bit too hard in her large eyes.

Mohandas called out to her softly as he entered the room, a touch of impatience raising his voice a little. This was of course against his true nature.

Kastur came out of the shadows and stood before him. 'So, you are here!' she sputtered, surprise and acceptance blended in her looks. The heart was like a sea rocked by waves.

'You are still unsure?' Mohandas laughed.

'Unsure I never was, but it took a while to muster belief.'

'As long as I was away, you complained why I wasn't here; now that I'm here, you complain why I am. Right?'

Kastur was leaving, but that brought her up short and she turned her large eyes at him. The eyes that had once waited for her were now filled with pain, and the pain was quickly giving way to revolt. That is the problem with transparent eyes: you can conceal nothing. There was still the same fight in those eyes that Mohandas had left behind when he had left, spilling out like foam on sea waves.

Mohandas covered her eyes with his palms.

'Where are the kids?' he asked.

'Will you know them?'

'No one knows the kids but their mother,' Mohandas laughed. 'Even the father knows them only through her.'

The kids were peeping out at him from corners of the room. Harilal was growing up and one could clearly see emerging in his eyes a glimpse of his father. Now he was looking hard at his father, as if to give a deeper tinge to that glimpse. That was a signal to Manilal that *Bapu* was here. Mohandas called them to him. They approached him gingerly. He took both of them in his arms, Harilal on one knee, Mani on the other.

'You know *Bapu*?'

Hari was quiet, but the answer was in his eyes.

Ba looked at Mohandas and said: 'That's your *Bapu*. He has come back after three years.'

They moved a bit closer to him.

The kids had gone to bed. Mohandas and Kastur were still awake.

'I want to confess before you that I couldn't keep my word. I am sorry. People there were facing a calamity. They have developed so much regard for me. They don't move a step without asking me.'

Kastur said nothing.

'That was what kept me so long.'

'What happens next?'

'I have many things to do while I am here. I'll have to travel to many places. Then we'll all go back together and stay together.'

'Do you still ...?'

'No. Now I have a legal practice. I have a house of my own. The Indians are fighting repression. They live a life worse than animals. You will see for yourself.'

'We all ...?'

'You'll all stay with me and we'll work for their freedom'

'Sheikh Mehtab?'

'He doesn't stay with me any more. That was a mistake on my part.'

Gandhibhai had a feeling that Kastur sighed with relief. Her eyes were closed. Slowly, Mohandas moved to enclose her in his arms.

As soon as Mohandas reached Rajkot, he buried himself in the papers he had brought with him. When they saw him lost in his work Kastur and the kids withdrew. *Bapu* was still nowhere near them. Kastur even nagged him once or twice: 'You are here, but still not quite here. Half the time you are with the people of Natal; the other half you try to be with us but it looks like they don't let you go.'

Mohandas laughed off: 'Not at all. It's just that I must finish all this work in six months and be back in Natal.'

Kastur didn't smile. Only the left corner of her lips dipped a little.

~

Mohandas was obsessed with his mission. The Natal Congress, representative body of thousands of Indians, had entrusted him with the task of conveying the piteous cry of Her Majesty's suffering Indian subjects to the people of India. Newspaper clippings and files containing his correspondence with the governments that he had brought with him lay around him at all times. He would be studying them, taking notes and getting the draft of *An Appeal to the Indian Public from Indians settled in South Africa* ready. He wanted to finish the work as quickly as the work was large.

He started the draft by introducing Natal first, although it was not going to make much of a difference. He wrote:

'Natal is a British colony like India. Its administration is autonomous and it has a parliament of its own which consists of thirty-seven elected members. The Upper House has twelve members appointed by the Governor. The Governor is a representative of the Queen. There is also a cabinet on the British pattern. Sir Robinson is currently the Prime Minister ...'

In the second paragraph he went on to speak of a few more things about Natal like the ratio of Indians in the local population. 'From the viewpoint of the population of Indians, Natal is the most important colony of the British. There are about four hundred thousand natives, about fifty thousand whites and fifty-one thousand Indians. Sixteen thousand of the Indians are *girmitiya*s. About thirty thousand Indians are released *girmitiya*s, who have settled down in the colony. They work as domestic helps, small farmers, fruit and vegetable hawkers, gardeners, goldsmiths, technicians, handicraftsmen, shopkeepers, teachers, photographers, etc. There are five thousand Indians who travelled here on their own and started new businesses with their own investment. The *girmitiya*s are imported via the ports of Calcutta and Madras. Those who come via Madras speak Tamil and those who come via Calcutta speak Hindi. Most of the *girmitiya*s are Hindus, though Muslims are also in substantial numbers. There is however no caste feeling among them.'

Gandhibhai also gave a description of Zululand (annexed to Natal after the Anglo-Zulu war of 1879-1887) in his appeal. He pointed out that the Zulus were the real natives of the place. The administration of Zululand was with the Governor rather than the Natal government and that was the reason why it was called Crown Colony. The Governor was the real representative of the Crown. A new town of Melmoth was established in 1880, in which Indians had also bought property worth two thousand pounds. Later, when the towns of Eshowe and Nondveni were settled, Indians were refused permission to buy properties and only whites were allowed in. Indians appealed to the Governor, who refused to intervene. The matter is currently before Lord Chamberlain in London. The laws governing the gold mines of Zululand also make buying and storing gold by Indians an offence punishable by law.

About Transvaal, he wrote: 'It is a republic under Dutch control. The Dutch here are also called Boers. Their parliament is called Volksraad, which has a Speaker. Then there is the executive. Whites number one lakh ninteen thousnd and two hundred twentyeight natives six lakh fifty three thousand and sixty two while the number of Indians is only five thousand. Indians are confined to Johannesburg and Pretoria only. Two thousand of them are hawkers and fifteen hundred work in hotels and private homes. Till 1885, Indians were doing business independently, but that year the Volksraad took away that right and, on top of that, imposed a three-pound tax on them.'

Mohandas wanted to give a complete picture of South Africa in his appeal to the Indian public so that it could have some idea of the place and the condition of Indians there. About Cape Town, he wrote: 'Cape Town is situated on the Cape of Good Hope and is an autonomous colony like Natal. It has a population of eighteen lakh, with four lakh whites and ten thousand Indians. The Indians are either traders or hawkers or plain labourers. Getting a business licence is extremely difficult for them, while the whites can have one delivered to their homes. One Ismail Suleman set up a store in the city of East Geequaland but he was never granted a licence. A couple of traders who had been granted licences were also stripped of them.

Mohandas went on to mention Orange Free State, a free republic, with its capital at Bloemfontein. Population: two lakh seventy thousand and five hundred; whites: seventy thousand and seven hundred sixteen; natives and coloureds: one lakh ninteen thousand. Indians can be counted on your fingertips, all doing small jobs. In 1890, it had three Indian stores with a total worth of about £ 9000. They were all handed a one-year notice and forced to leave. There was of course no question of compensation of any sort. This state has a law which is called Coloured Flood Blocker, Coloured meaning Indians. No Indian is allowed to stay in the state for more than two months. Owning property, farms or business is of course a pipedream. Even if one somehow manages to get the President's special permission, he has to pay a ten-pound annual Poll Tax. The first violation of the Flood Blocker legislation invites a fine of twenty-five pounds or a three-year jail. On each successive violation of the law, the fine amount is doubled.

There are two or three other states but none of them has an Indian population of more than a hundred or so, all of them labourers or bearers. Business licences are denied to them everywhere, though there is no such law. In one of the states, an Indian had managed to secure a business licence from the court. The law there is now being rewritten to deny the courts jurisdiction over Indian cases.

Mohandas was aware that Indians might not be interested in such geographical descriptions, but he also knew that without knowledge of the overall picture it would be difficult to grasp the local situation.

Only after he had written all this, did Gandhibhai come to the real issue, which was the pitiable condition of the *girmitiya*s and other Indians. He wanted to highlight this part of his appeal, while also keeping it short. He knew that not many people would have real concern for those helpless and homeless people. Unless he was able to arouse their maximum concern by using the minimum of words, it would be difficult to stir the conscience of a people well settled in their homes in their own country. The Indians could be said to be, and not to be, curious to learn about those people: they were curious because, after all, they too were Indians. But that wasn't enough. Therefore, he hoped that at least those who read the appeal would understand. He started enumerating the grievances:

The first grievance was franchise. Under a royal decree of 1850, as subjects of the British kingdom, Indians settled in South Africa had franchise till 1893. On November 25, 1894, Natal parliament, through an amendment of the relevant law, took away from the Asian community the right even to register their names in the voters' list. The reason offered was that Asians, more specifically Indians, were unfit to exercise franchise. Only those whose names already figured in the voters' list were allowed to retain franchise. The parliament did not consider it necessary to pay heed to the petitions made by the Indian community. In the end, a petition signed by ten thousand Indians was sent to the Colonial Secretary of the British government. The result was that the British government withheld its permission to the bill passed by the Natal parliament and it had to withdraw the bill. The Natal government now brought out another bill in its place. This bill sought to declare as unfit to register as voters subjects of those countries where elected bodies did not exist. Once again, protests started. Another petition was sent to the parliament which labelled the bill 'an instrument of torture'. The parliament was unmoved. Then a letter was sent to Lord Chamberlain. It was learnt unofficially that the government was considering the grievance, but the reality was something different. Natal government had obtained the consent of Lord Chamberlain to the bill before it was presented to the parliament.

Gandhibhai wrote:

> *Indians settled in South Africa cannot be compared with Indians at home. Political harassment also exists in India, but in South Africa, all laws are based on colour discrimination. It is their colour alone which has pushed Indians into the untouchable category.*

The second grievance concerned the immigration of Indians, that is about the *girmit* system. While writing this, the faces of Balasundaram, Roberts, Pillai and others flashed before his eyes. When they were *girmitiya*s, they were forced to lead a life worse than that of animals. He wrote:

> *I wish I were a painter! I cannot draw in words a portrait of their faces and the conditions in which they live.*

Gandhibhai conceded defeat at this point and, shaking off the slough of sentiment, he chose to describe the objective situation literally.

> *The Attorney General of Natal argues that Indian coolies came to this country to sell their labour for the development of local industry. There was never any intention of integrating them with the South African society, though that is what is happening now.*
>
> *In 1891, a list of demands signed by Haji Mohammad Haji Dada on behalf of the Indian Committee was sent to the government. It demanded that the Protector should be familiar with Tamil and Hindi languages. If possible, the Protector should be an Indian. We still hold to the latter demand.*
>
> *Till 1894, the Indian labourer came to Natal on a five-year contract. The contract provided for free travel to Natal and free food for him and his family, and a monthly salary of ten shillings with a one shilling increment every year. At the completion of five years he was released from the contract and was given the option of returning to India with free passage.*
>
> *In 1893, Natal government sent a delegation to India consisting of Sir Henry Binns and the Protector, Mr. Mason, with the aim of securing the Indian government's consent for a modification in the original contract. The result was the new law in 1895, which ensures that an Indian labourer would now remain a* girmitiya *all his life instead of five years. He would of course get a salary of twenty shillings in his ninth year. If he doesn't renew his contract for two years thereafter, he will have to go back to his country. If he chooses to settle down in Natal, he will have to pay an annual poll tax at the rate of three pounds per person in the family. The Indian Viceroy gave his consent to this bill very regretfully. The regret was momentary; the harassment would last a life time. The Viceroy did lay down two conditions: His consent was subject to the approval of the British government and there would be no penal action on the labourer if he chose not to return.*

Mohandas also raised the subject of the increasing incidence of suicide among *girmitiya*s. His heart and his eyes were full while writing on the subject:

> *These people went there to make a living. What they got was death by suicide. The ever-increasing rate of suicide among the coolies not only raises doubts about*

how they are treated by their masters, it also puts a question mark on their behaviour. Some of the prisoners have actually said in their statements before the court that they would prefer to kill themselves rather than go back to their masters.

The third grievance: Gandhibhai was reminded of the Pretoria incident when he had to get a letter from the Attorney General to venture on the streets after nine. The Durban police had subjected two Indian youth to humiliation merely because they were on the roads after 9 p.m. Mohandas made Law 15 of 1869 the subject of his complaint and entitled it "Curfew". He wrote:

A coloured person cannot stir out on the streets after nine in the evening. He needs a licence, if he wishes to do so; otherwise he needs to submit a justification. There are frequent instances of respectable Indians, teachers and others, who needed to be out on the streets after nine and were thrown into cells. This law is based on colour discrimination and is a tyrannical law.

The fourth and final grievance related to the licence law.

You need a licence when you have violated a contract or committed some bad behaviour. But it is used in this country to harass the Indian community and to tyrannize over them.

After he had got the draft ready, Mohandas attached copies of petitions sent to the government and newspaper clippings and sent the whole thing for printing.

~

The plague had broken out in Bombay. Rajkot too was slowly falling into its clutches. Fear and terror reigned everywhere. Rumours were thick and fast. Everyone had a story to tell: X locality got it today; in Y locality so many dead. People were living in fear of death, which they had cast over their heads like the roof of a tent. The roof was getting ever larger. You never knew when death might sneak in like a rat and disappear with you in its mouth.

Mohandas wrote to the state government:

> *I have come here from South Africa, but I want to help the people here in their hour of adversity. I offer my services to the government to use in whatever way it thinks fit to prevent the spread of the plague.*

Mohandas already had a reputation and people knew a lot about him. Some knew of him from earlier days as the younger son of the famed Prime Minister of the state of Rajkot, Kaba Gandhi. The state government had constituted a committee to take measures for the control of the plague and it now nominated Gandhibhai as a member.

At the very first meeting, Mohandas said: 'If we want to fight the plague, cleaning of homes and cities must be our first priority. Without cutting off the root, we cannot expect the branches of this tree to dry up.'

All the members agreed with his suggestion.

It was decided to carry out a door-to-door survey of the toilets first. This was taken by people as an invasion of their privacy. What, however, they saw horrified them. Ordinary people had generally no toilet facilities at all in their homes. The few who did had no objection to an inspection, though they did feel embarrassed. But the better-off people had serious objections. Most homes had a latrine, which was used for urination as well for defecation. A two-storied house they saw had a pipe leading to the ground which carried the waste. The room stank so much that they found it impossible to stand there. Mohandas was amazed that people actually lived and slept in the midst of such a terrible stink.

He made a suggestion: 'You could use a bucket. It will help suppress the stink.'

He was told to mind his own business.

Another person in the same family said: 'We are not asking you to clean it up. It's our family affair. We'll live as we choose.'

'Insanitation is what is causing the plague.'

'We'll cross the bridge when we come to it. Why are you worried?'

All the committee's suggestions went down the drain.

Temples were the worst offenders. Left-over food from religious feasts and the leaf-plates in which it was eaten were piled up in corners. Kites and crows were hovering overhead all the time. To look at the temple premises you would think they hadn't been cleaned since the temple was built. The stink was all-pervasive and unbearable. Mohandas was perplexed: Hinduism was such a big champion of purity and cleanliness and here it was the biggest culprit.

He announced that a physical and moral cleansing of all the Hindu religious places was called for. People laughed at him, or just shook their heads and kept quiet.

Mohandas proposed in the Committee that it should also visit Dalit homes as they were in greater need of their counsel.

The Committee members were annoyed. 'It would be a waste of time. When the rich and the well-off cannot maintain their toilets, what do you expect from the poor Dalits?'

At such moments, Mohandas thought of his childhood friend Uka. Where could he be? Mohandas looked for him but it appeared he had left the place. How neatly dressed he used to be! How methodical in his work! How many times he had tried to persuade him to go with him to his home, but he had always been ready with an excuse.

Mohandas tried to persuade them gently: 'Look, they are an essential part of our community. Maybe, they can do without us, but we can't do without them. If their houses are filthier than ours, we'll have to counsel them; if they are cleaner, we must learn from them.'

He was reminded how the businessmen in Natal also thought of the *girmitiya*s in similar terms.

The Committee members put their foot down. Mohandas, however, stood his ground. Politely but firmly, he said: 'I think it is absolutely essential that we call on them. If you don't wish to join me, fine. I'll go alone.'

When he got up to go, another member joined him. The rest of them snickered. When Mohandas came out with the other member, he was marvelling at his good luck.

Their cluster of houses was called the Bhangi Tola. His friend Uka also came from the same class of people. A couple of them knew Mohandas and spread word that the younger son of the old Diwanji had come. The people were filled with excitement.

'Son of Diwanji visiting our home! May God give him our years too! What luck!' they whispered among themselves.

Mohandas went among them and caressed their kids. He asked them how they were, and then told them about the plague. 'We want to see your toilets ...,' he said, and then realized that maybe he should not have.

'Toilets?' one of them said. 'What toilets? It's the big people who have them. The open fields are our toilets, though, of course, we do service yours.'

Mohandas felt as if someone had rejected his profferred hand. He laughed it off and asked: 'Can we see your houses?'

'If you enter our homes you will have to go back and have a purificatory bath while we'll acquire demerit.'

Gandhibhai responded with a smile: 'If you can acquire it, you can also lose it. Don't you acquire it when you come to our homes?'

Mohandas and the other member entered their homes. They were cabin type mud houses. No windows or skylights. Gandhi wondered for a moment how they could possibly be living in such houses. They were however clean, neat, washed and painted. The door step had been swept; the utensils cleaned and shining. The walls and the courtyard had been washed neatly with yellow clay and cow dung.

'It's better to live in these small houses than in dirty ones,' remarked Gandhi to his companion. 'They will never catch the plague.'

On his way back, Mohandas wondered: 'What irony! Neither our temples nor our homes are clean, yet we claim to be purer and higher than them. They have pure hearts and clean homes, yet they are the dalits and the hated ones!'

~

Gandhi's *An Appeal to the Indian Public* came out as a pamphlet. He had written it in English on purpose. He wanted the English bureaucrats also to read it and get an idea of what was happening to the Indians in South Africa and how they were spending their lives. The pamphlet had a green cover and came to be known as the *Green Pamphlet.* The cover carried the title and other details. The main title "The Grievances of the British Indians in South Africa" was in five lines. "of" and "in" were in small type but figured singly in the second and the fourth lines respectively. A vertical line followed. The last three lines carried the subtitle: "An Appeal to the Public" Another vertical line, followed by the size of the print order; then the name of the press, that is the press line.

Right at the bottom was the year: 1896.

An Appeal to the Indian Public was to be distributed in thousands. Mohandas had used various sources to collect addresses of people. Sending the *Green Pamphlet* by post was not a simple job. He didn't have enough money to hire people for the work, so he collected neighbourhood kids. Mohandas had a collection of stamps. He promised the collection to the kids if they helped him make packets and write addresses on them.

The kids jumped in. Mohandas was also keen to see how the kids would respond to demands for voluntary work.

The kids put in two or three hours every day. Mohandas also worked with them and kept up their spirits. He told them about a far away country, thousands of miles across the seas, called South Africa. The country had a large number of Indian labourers and businessmen. The labourers lived a life which was worse than that of slaves. They had children who could not go to school. Mohandas' story raised the kids' interest and they wanted to hear more and more of it.

Amidst all this interest, enthusiasm and labour, the big job was finished in no time. There were onlookers who wondered at Mohandas' magical capacity to get so much work out of the kids, wrapping up so big a job in such a short time.

Mohandas was delighted. His experiment had worked. He had seen selfless dedication in the kids. No money, no prizes, just stamps! The profound impression the creativity of the kids made on him was to last with him for a long time.

But sending the pamphlet by post was not going to be enough; he would have to make personal contacts too. So he decided to visit Bombay. Most of the intellectuals and political bigwigs were concentrated in Bombay and they ruled the roost in the whole country.

Physically, Mohandas was certainly in Rajkot but his spirit was taken up by his work, to which he devoted his days and his nights: how to communicate the message of Indians in South Africa to the Indians here. He was keeping so busy that even his meetings with Lakshmibhai were limited to once or twice a week. His only topic of discussion with visitors who came to see him was also the suffering of Indians in South Africa. Any other topic occurred only in passing. Everyone said that Kaba Gandhi's younger son had been adopted by South Africa. He was here only on a visit. The South Africans now formed his real family: the one that was here was a mere shadow of a family.

When he was told what was being said about him, he would laugh and say: 'It's your deeds that make your family; the deeds that you do for others.'

To anyone who could read, he passed on a copy: 'Be the voice of a helpless people, if you can. Tell everyone about them.'

Harilal acted as his assistant. He collected the kids and ran errands. Anything that he could do for *Bapu* would never be left undone. He was very active in distributing the pamphlet too.

Kastur too pitched in. She listened carefully to him and told the ladies who came to visit her about what was keeping Hari's father so busy. She arranged refreshments for the people who happened to be working with Mohandas. But she also didn't let the opportunity pass for a barb or two: 'You could have done this work staying there too, couldn't you?'

Mohandas knew the consequences of challenging Kastur, so, unless it became absolutely necessary, he kept his mouth shut. Comments like this, he would either ignore or laugh off. But whenever he had the opportunity, he also tried to explain: 'When you are there, you'll see it for yourself. You'll see how helpless and how deprived those people are. I know you'll forget everything and go all out to help them and share their sorrows.'

Kastur would say: 'I'm not like you ...' and Mohandas knew that the target was his last sentence.

Kastur didn't let on her reaction when he decided to visit Bombay. 'Do as you please. Home or abroad—for me, it's all the same.' Mohandas had guessed, so kept quiet. He actually wanted to organize a public meeting in Bombay, which would not be possible if he didn't go there personally. He had tried to explain to Kastur that only part of the work he had to do had been accomplished so far—that of getting the pamphlet ready and distributed. It was the spoken word that produced the greater effect. Kastur listened, gave her head a jerk and stomped off.

Bombay was the ideal location for a public meeting for more than one reason. The echo of a meeting there travelled to all parts of the country. The whole of India heard it and knew. Justice Ranade was an influential personality and he was interested in matters of this type. Mohandas went up to him directly as he landed in Bombay. Meeting such important people was not easy, but it looked it wasn't so difficult either.

Justice Ranade stood up to shake hands with him: 'Mr. Gandhi, I know you have come from South Africa. I have heard a lot about you. Tell me what I can do for you.'

Mohandas had already sent him a copy of the *Green Pamphlet*. He also had some copies with him. He again presented him a copy and said: 'I have attempted a description of the social, political, constitutional and economic aspects of the situation obtaining in South Africa to the best of my ability. The government there is nothing like the government in this country. They are using Indians to enrich themselves while pushing them deeper and deeper into the abyss of poverty and slavery. They come out with new laws everyday and every law is another step towards depriving the Indians of the smallest liberties they are left with. Indians there are now looking very eagerly towards intellectuals and freedom-lovers in this country to take at least some action towards getting them a release from their chains of slavery and towards pulling them out from their quagmire. His Excellency, the Viceroy, has, on the contrary, responded by giving his approval to a three-pound Poll Tax to be imposed on them. They were hoping that the Viceroy would help in restoring their freedom; he has responded by tying another hefty knot in their rope of slavery. People who earn eleven shillings a month can neither return home nor survive there. The government also cannot bear the sight of Indian businessmen. Its complaint against them is that they sell their goods cheap, that they hawk their goods, that they live in small houses and that they are not dressed stylishly in neat and clean clothes. It cannot tolerate the way Indians behave and the way they look. When the situation is so bad, I think people like you can do a lot to extricate these poor, defenceless people from the boiling cauldron of hate. Please don't leave them to die bit by bit at the mercy of the authorities of a strange land.'

Mohandas felt he had overdone it. He shouldn't have talked in such an emotional manner before a man so distinguished. As he realized it, Mohandas clammed up. Justice Ranade had been listening to him with his eyes closed. When he stopped speaking, Justice Ranade opened his eyes and looked at him.

'Mr. Gandhi, I don't think I can help you, although I agree with everything you have said. I think it would be better if you met Justice Badruddin Tyebji, though he may not be of much help either. The only person who can help you is Sir Pherozeshah Mehta.'

As Mohandas left, Justice Ranade said: 'I wish you a great success, Mr. Gandhi.'

Mohandas thought it best to meet Justice Badruddin Tyebji. He had been President of the Congress before he became a judge, the first Muslim to be elected President. His name reminded Mohandas of the Tyebji in Pretoria, though the two did not share any similarity at all.

Justice Tyebji sent for him at once and Mohandas narrated his piece again: 'Natal has fifty-one thousand Indians, five thousand of them businessmen. They are mostly Muslims but are known as Arabs. This saves them from being addressed as coolies and raises their prestige level. Most of them are also small businessmen. There are sixteen thousand *girmitiya*s and thirty thousand lapsed *girmitiya*s. The whites number only forty thousand. These forty thousand whites keep four hundred thousand natives and fifty-one thousand Indians firmly under their heels. I envisage that in the days to come the laws are going to be harder and more humiliating for Indians.'

Mohandas' tale produced lines of worry on Justice Tyebji's face. He pondered for a while and then said: 'Justice Ranade and I can give you the same advice. Our positions do not permit us to participate in such activities directly, but our sympathies are with you. The right man for you to approach is Sir Pherozeshah. He alone can help you.'

Mohandas was quite familiar with Sir Pherozeshah's name. He had also nursed a desire to meet him but had never been able to muster enough courage. He pondered the Ranade-Tyebji advice for a couple of days and then decided to take it. Maybe Sir Pherozeshah's considerable influence over the people of Bombay was just the thing that might work for him.

He was able to land an appointment with Sir Pherozeshah without much delay, but he was so much in awe of his reputation that he couldn't decide how he should approach him and with what words. Finally, he decided that the best way to honour his enormous reputation would be to approach him with his own lack of one and then wait for the results. Bombayites called him 'the uncrowned king of Bombay' and 'the Bombay Lion'. Why 'the Bombay Lion?' Was this an honourable title to give a human being? Maybe this was their way of honouring someone who was dear to them. But if someone was a lion, how on earth did one approach him?

When Mohandas was face to face with Sir Pherozeshah, he did not feel as if he was facing an emperor or a lion, or that either his imperiousness or his ferociousness was weighing him down or making him shake in his boots. He sat in his chamber surrounded by his friends and supporters. Special among them were Mr. Wacha and Mr. Cama. Mohandas had heard of Wacha. One of his friends, Veerchand Gandhi, had once told him that Wacha was the right-hand man of Sir Pherozeshah. And this right-hand man had everything on his fingertips.

When he was ushered into the presence of Sir Pherozeshah, Mohandas submitted: 'I am Mohandas Karamchand Gandhi. I was asked by Justice Ranade and Justice Tyebji to see you.'

Sir Pherozeshah replied: 'Do you think I'd have refused to see you if you had come to me on your own? I have heard of the good work you are doing in South Africa.'

How did he know so much about a man in the street like me, Gandhi wondered.

'What can I do for you?'

Mohandas had rehearsed his piece repeatedly. He put forward his case in measured words: 'You know that Natal is a colony of the British Empire. When the English wanted to grow tropical crops in Natal but did not receive support from native labour, they started import of Indian labour with the cooperation of the Indian government. It is only because of the hard work of the Indian workers and their skills that the local planters are a prosperous lot today. The worker, however, who made this miracle possible, is being exploited more and more every day. The worker is a coolie by definition, but even Indian businessmen and barristers are described as coolies. As British citizens, Indians had always enjoyed voting rights in Natal, but they have now been withdrawn on the ground that India does not have elected representative bodies. Finally, a three-pound Poll Tax is being imposed on every person who wants to settle down in Natal at the end of his *girmit* period. A delegation sent by the Natal government has already secured the approval of our Viceroy, Lord Elgin. The only option the *girmitiya*s now have is to come back to India at the end of their *girmit* period, but they have nothing left here to come back to: even their relatives and their local ties have all disappeared ...'

Sir Pherozeshah interrupted him to say: 'I do have some idea of the situation, Gandhi. I'll do whatever I can to help you.'

Everyone present was now looking at Gandhi's face, which had the glow of a last-minute winner's face. To receive an assurance of help from Sir Pherozeshah was nothing short of a miracle.

Sir Pherozeshah continued: 'I'll arrange a public meeting for you. Put your case before the public. I'll be present too.'

He looked at his secretary, Mr. Munshi, and said: 'Get a date and make all necessary arrangements for a public meeting.'

Sir Pherozeshah then got busy. Mohandas came out with Mr. Munshi. September 26 was fixed as the date for the meeting.

Mohandas could now think only one thing: Strange are the ways of the world! It calls this man an emperor, a lion, and much else! A simple, straight man and so many strange names!

~

When Mohandas had left for London, he did not call on his sister, Raliyat, and his brother-in-law, Vrindavan Das, though they were living in Bombay. Now he thought of them. 'Why didn't you call on them?' he asked himself and recalled the incident. Was it only because his brother-in-law had refused to give him back the money he had left with him? After all, he too was a victim of kinship. True, the money was Mohandas' and had been left with him only for safekeeping, but how could he have violated the community diktat? Shame! Such a small matter! He had heard that Vrindavan Das was ill, so he made a beeline for their place. He found that Vrindavan Das was in a bad shape. Raliyat herself was too weak to look after her husband all the twenty-four hours. Financially, they were in no position to hire a nurse or a servant. It didn't take Mohandas a minute to make up his mind: they both must go with him to Rajkot, where he would tend his brother-in-law and try and save his life. He got them packed, sent for a victoria and announced: 'We're going to Rajkot!'

Somehow Mohandas and the coachman managed to lift Vrindavan Das into the coach. He was in no condition to walk to the coach himself. At the station, the coolies helped take him to the platform. The train was unbelievably crowded. Mohandas had to beg and cajole fellow passengers to get seats for his sister and brother-in-law, while he himself travelled standing all the way. Reaching Rajkot was quite a struggle. Fears of an untoward happening on the way kept troubling the minds of both brother and sister, though neither of them spoke a word.

When they were home, Mohandas accommodated his sister and brother-in-law in his own room, which had to be vacated by Kastur and the kids. Both Kastur and his brother tried to hint to Mohandas to accommodate them in some other room, but he argued: 'He needs looking after all the twenty-four hours; you can't do it if you worry about your own comfort. Raliyat is also not in a condition to keep a twenty-four hour vigil. If he is in my room, it'll be easier to look after him. I am in no position to take a risk.'

He heard it said under the breath: 'Why don't you also go with him to the other room? Better than pushing out three or four persons with all their things.'

'That also counts as service,' said Mohandas.

Mohandas was by his brother-in-law's side all the twenty-four hours. While he looked after him, he also carried on his own work when time permitted. He kept awake nights so that medicines could be administered in a timely manner. Whenever required, he also pressed his hands and legs to relieve pain. Kastur and the kids were in the next room, but they always met in Vrindavan Das' room. That was how that room was now beginning to be referred to. Mohandas had never been able to forget that he had left his father's side for pleasure and his father had not survived it. This idea possessed him especially when he saw Kastur. Suppose, he thought, I leave him even for a minute, and something happens to him, it would be an injury on top of an injury, which would fester all the lifelong. The guilt of father's death was like acrid smoke choking him from within. In his service to Vrindvan Das, Mohandas saw himself as making amends for the sin he had committed. The deep satisfaction that he was deriving from this service could well give one the impression that this was his sole preoccupation. But inside him, there was an unbroken chain of prayer: 'Dear God! Give me strength enough to serve him and relieve his pain. Give me his pain, if that is what it takes.'

All his prayers could not save Vrindavan Das. His only satisfaction was that he had spared no effort. He felt his soul cleansed, purified and refreshed by this feeling of satisfaction in him. He wished that he could have gained the same sense of satisfaction by tending to his sick father. The devil of sensuous desire in him had then desecrated his worship at the altar of filial devotion. This time he had not allowed it anywhere near him. This had been a joyous experience which he was never likely to forget.

With a heavy heart, he tried to console the weeping Raliyat: 'All man can do is to serve and pray. I am now sure that if one can do this much with a pure heart, he has done his duty. The satisfaction that one has done one's duty is one that stays with you all your life. In the end, one is left only with either satisfaction or the lack of it: you are now beyond all that.'

His face showed as if he was addressing all this to himself.

~

The last rites of Vrindavan Das were over.

Mohandas left for Bombay, entirely at peace with himself. Though the demanding duties during his brother-in-law's illness had sapped his body, internally he felt quite fresh and light. Having performed one duty successfully, he was now ready to take on another. The uninterrupted service that he had been able to render Vrindavan Das had brought him a new kind of joy. He now wanted to spread that joy all across the world.

Landing in Bombay, he made a beeline to Sir Pherozeshah Mehta's place. A big challenge awaited him. The moment he set eyes on him, Sir Pherozeshah remarked: 'You look very tired.'

Mohandas gave a wan smile. He didn't want his joy to lessen by setting an explanation to it.

Sir Pherozeshah asked: 'Is your speech ready?'

Mohandas stuttered: 'I haven't exactly written it down.'

'That won't do, Gandhi! Not with me!' Sir Pherozeshah shook his head and said: 'The reporting in Bombay is not quite up to scratch. You must write down whatever you want to say. It must be ready and printed by morning tomorrow.'

It was five in the evening. He had to write the speech, revise it and get it printed by morning. How was that possible? The anxiety inside showed on his face.

Without raising his head, Sir Pherozeshah said: 'There will be someone at your place to collect the manuscript of your speech at eleven tonight. I'm sure it'll be ready by then.'

'I'll try my best.' He tried his best to hide the nervousness in his words.

'I know you can do it.' Sir Pherozeshah said as he placed a soft hand on Mohandas' shoulder. Mohandas felt a current of selfconfidence race through his body.

As soon as he was back in his room, Mohandas got down to the business of getting his speech ready. He spent a long time wrestling with the problem of a good beginning to the speech. Many sheets of paper were sacrificed in the process. The pristine fear raised its head again: Would he be able face such a large gathering? Would he be able to read confidently and without goofing? He tried repeatedly to brush aside the fear, telling himself that he couldn't possibly escape his responsibility of getting the script ready by citing the fear that he might not be able to read it! Especially now when such a towering personality was backing him.

No sooner had he given the last touches to his speech, there was a knock at the door. It was exactly eleven at night. Opening the door, he found a man with a note from Mr. Munshi. The note said: 'Please let the bearer of this note have the script of your speech. It must be printed during the night. Sir P.S. wants to see it first thing in the morning.' Sir Pherozeshah wrote his name with a P. Gathering the sheets together, Mohandas stuffed them into an envelope and handed it over to the messenger. Then he went to bed, but there was no sleep for him that night. What if Sir Pherozeshah didn't approve of the speech? What if they were unable to decipher his handwriting? What if the meeting was cancelled or if he had to speak extempore? Or maybe Sir Pherozeshah stopped him halfway ... It was indeed a night full of fears.

Even as he was getting ready next morning, some printed copies of his speech were delivered to him. He gave it a cursory glance. It was neatly printed and seemed to be error-free.

'Has Sir Pherozeshah seen it?' he asked the messenger.

'Yes. It was he who asked it to be delivered to you.'

'He approved?'

'I can't say, but Sir P.S. didn't approve, he would have returned it straight away.'

It was for the first time that Mohandas learnt that his staff referred to him as Sir P.S.

Mohandas sighed with relief. He felt he had been to a lion's den and back. A lion? Again? He smiled and gave the speech a slow once over. The printed speech felt better than the original.

The meeting was held in Sir Fromji Cowasji Jehangir Institute Hall, with Sir Pherozeshah presiding. The hall was packed to capacity. Sweat had broken out on Mohandas' forehead. He hadn't the slightest idea that it would be such a large gathering. The meeting began with an introduction to Mohandas. Next, he was requested to speak. Mohandas tore himself from the chair and took the rostrum in a single movement. There was applause. When he started speaking, he could feel that his voice was not carrying. The fatigue had finally set in and lay heavy on his chest. Only a few could hear what he was saying.

Sir Pherozeshah tried to boost his morale: 'Very good. Make it a bit louder.'

Mohandas forced out a few sentences at a louder pitch, but the voice was falling. Keshav Rao Deshpande, one of the admirers of Sir Pherozeshah, was watching and sized up the situation. He walked up and took the speech from Mohandas and started reading it. He had a deep, bass voice. But the audience wanted to hear Mr. Wacha. It shouted: 'Call Mr. Wacha. We want him to read it out.'

Sir Pherozeshah looked at Wacha. As Wacha got up, there was a round of applause. He too had a baritone voice; in addition, the tone of his voice rose and fell like a musical melody. He knew where emphasis had to be laid, where a pause was intended and where a longer pause was in order. Wacha brought his full range of oratorical skills to bear upon Mohandas' speech. Mohandas sat reviewing in his mind all the occasions in the past when speech had failed him and he had to resume his seat without delivering. This was his first speech before a distinguished Indian audience. Had his speech not been written down, what could Deshpande or Wacha have done? Every now and then, his eyes sought out Sir Pherozeshah, whose eyes spoke admiration. There was disappointment too, but it was also accompanied by satisfaction.

Words escaped Wacha's lips like tiny birds and flew straight into the listeners' hearts. Whenever it came to descriptions of the excesses committed on Indians in South Africa, the humiliations heaped on them and the injustices and iniquities they had to undergo, the audience cried 'Shame! Shame!' The groundswell of sympathy rising in the hall again and again pulled Mohandas back from the state of self-absorption in which he sat lost. Wacha was now reading the concluding portion of the speech: 'We are under siege in South Africa. This is our youth and it is all hatred and adversity. We believe we have the right to request you for protection. We have narrated our tale of woe to you. If the yoke of tyranny and torture that presses us down is not lifted, you will also not be able to escape your share of culpability. It's your responsibility too, of people freer than us and like elder brothers to us. Those who watch their fellow countrymen being swallowed in the quicksand of tyranny in a foreign land and do nothing, they too belong to the category of our tormentors. We sincerely believe that the cry rising from our tormented hearts will reach your ears and will not go unheeded.'

The speech was peppered with factual details and was long. Mr. Wacha's delivery had made tolerable a speech which would otherwise have left the audience completely bored. Mr. Wacha's oratorical skills had the whole audience hanging on to every word that escaped his lips. When Gandhi's speech and Mr. Wacha's delivery ended, the hall broke out in loud applause. The dikes of people's emotions had been breached by the heart-rending tale of the suffering of their brethren settled in South Africa.

Sir Pherozeshah stood up next. It was as if the level of the entire hall went up an inch. Suddenly, there was complete silence. Sir Pherozeshah said: 'Gandhi was very tired. He had been awake all night. His speech was every bit as factual as it was moving. We cannot turn away from our responsibility. For the present, we express our sympathy and solidarity with all our brothers on whose behalf Gandhi's speech was read out before you by Mr. Wacha. We stand by them in this hour of their suffering.'

Several founder-members of the Indian National Congress were present at the meeting: Jhaverilal Yagnik, Mohammad Yasin, Mr. Chambers (Editor of *Champion*) and others. They all lent their support to Sir Pherozeshah's proposal. The audience at large also expressed its support through a standing applause.

The newspapers next morning reported the proceedings of the meeting in full detail. An account of the meeting and a summary of the resolution passed had already been telegraphed to London by the Presidency Association.

Though Sir Pherozeshah had lauded his speech as 'very moving,' Mohandas was aware that the credit for the Bombay public meeting did not go to him. Had Keshav Deshpande and Wacha not come to his help, the meeting would have sunk without a trace. But despite this realization, Mohandas was happy with what had been achieved at the meeting. He had absolutely no doubt that, thanks to Sir Pherozeshah, he had won his first victory in the most dynamic and aware coastal city of the country. He had climbed the highest Himalayan peak of politics in this city, a peak so high that its height could only be guessed. There was before him now a deep ocean, each of whose waves could rise to the height of the same Himalayan peak. Like the height of the peak, the depth of the ocean too was only a matter for conjecture. Mohandas was conscious that his journey would remain incomplete until he got a measure of the ocean too.

Mohandas left for Pune. The tallest lighthouse of India was to be found there—Bal Gangadhar Tilak. Immeasurable and unfathomable like the ocean. When Mohandas entered his home, Tilak was seated on the floor with a low table in front of him, writing. Cropped hair covered the head like closely mowed grass. You could see just enough of it to be sure it was there. He wore a short-sleeved undershirt styled as a shirt. Mohandas felt totally at ease in his presence. Touching his feet, he withdrew to a side. Tilak lifted his head and looked at him.

He introduced himself: 'I am M.K. Gandhi from South Africa.'

'I know.'

Mohandas was taken by surprise. Tilak had read his predicament just by looking at his face.

'I am also a journalist. I read about your meeting at Bombay. I appreciate the work you are doing. Be not afraid to speak.'

It looked to Mohandas as if a Wise Man had been waiting for him to offer him his blessings.

'I'll try,' said Mohandas. 'I have come to India with the objective of putting before my (and theirs) fellow countrymen the torture and the suffering that Indians are undergoing in their struggle to survive in South Africa. I want to secure the support of all the parties for this cause. If this cannot be done, it will become very hard for the Indians living there to survive. They are sure to be crushed out of existence.'

'I understand. Your efforts to secure a consensus of all parties on this issue are not unjustified. There really cannot be two opinions in this matter. However, you know that I and Ranade have our separate ways. If you want to hold a public meeting in Pune you will have to find a person who doesn't take sides between us. He should actually be politically neutral. If you can get such a person to preside over the meeting, both Ranade's Public Society and our Deccan Society can share the same platform. I am keen to help your cause. You are free to see me whenever you wish.'

Mohandas was overwhelmed by Tilak's response. It also gave him courage to put forward his own problem: 'I am new to this city. Finding a neutral person acceptable to all will be a problem for me.'

Tilak was quiet for a minute and then said: 'Prof. Bhandarkar has withdrawn himself from all public affairs. Go and meet him and then come back and tell me.' After a pause he continued: 'You may also see Gopal Krishna Gokhale. He is a professor at Fergusson College.'

The roadblocks are taking care of themselves, thought Mohandas.

Mohandas decided on the spot to call on Gokhale. He had already met Ranade in Bombay. When he arrived at Ferguson College, he ran into Gokhale in the college grounds. A buttoned-up black jacket, a turban and a scarf round his neck. Mohandas touched his feet and introduced himself: 'I am Mohandas Karamchand Gandhi. I have come from South Africa.'

Gokhale looked at him and smiled. 'I know you. I was waiting for you.'

Mohandas was surprised. They had never met before, so how did he know him? However, he said nothing. Gokhale put his hand on his shoulder as if he was an old acquaintance.

'I know you are Gandhi,' he said smilingly. 'Let's go and sit in the office. The work you are doing is important. You are destined for even greater things.' Though he wanted to ask how he knew him, Mohandas could not bring the question to his lips.

Gokhale gave him a tour of the college on his way to his office. Mohandas was feeling recharged by Gokhale's touch. He was feeling completely refreshed now, like *Ba* did after *Chaturmas.* She never touched food till she saw the sun, even if it took the sun four days to show itself. The children got worried but she was smiling: 'The sun has to show itself, if not today, then tomorrow for sure. Why do you worry?'

Mohandas told him about Africa and then about the meeting at Bombay.

'Do you have a copy of your Bombay speech?' Gokhale asked.

Mohandas offered him a copy of the *Green Pamphlet* and his Bombay speech.

Gokhale turned them over and said: 'So, this is your *Green Pamphlet*? I'll read it later. Let me just go through your speech.'

When he had finished reading, he thought for a while and then said: 'I agree with Tilak. You must go and see Bhandarkar. I am sure he will help you. If he presides, everyone will participate.'

When he came out, Mohandas was feeling so refreshed as if he just had had a dip in the cool waters of the Ganga. All the fatigue was gone. The cool waters were quite a different experience from the vastness of the Himalayas and the profound depth of the ocean.

~

Dr. R.G. Bhandarkar sat on a swing in the verandah of his home, reading a book. A pile of books lay by his side. As the swing moved, the books also too seemed to move with it. He was so absorbed in reading that Mohandas felt entranced to see his concentration. It would, he felt, not be proper to interrupt the quest of this untiring seeker of knowledge. He even thought of going back, when there were footsteps from inside the house. Bhandarkar's concentration broke and he looked around and saw Mohandas.

In a fatherly tone, he inquired: 'When did you come?'

'Just arrived.'

'Do sit down. Why are you standing?'

So full of loving familiarity was his way of speaking that Mohandas stood wondering for a while. He continued: 'Pull up that small seat and draw it closer to me.'

Mohandas could see no seat, so he kept standing. Dr. Bhandarkar got the message. Pointing in another direction, he said: 'There! It's some distance away. I hope you didn't mind. You are a young man, so I took the liberty.'

Mohandas got the seat and pulled up close to him. Dispensing with any introductory remarks, he handed his *Green Pamphlet* to him and said: 'This pamphlet is the distress call of the Indian migrants in South Africa to their fellow countrymen in India.'

'Yes, I know. I have already received it in post. How did you find my address?'

'I collected the addresses of intellectuals and thinking politicians from various institutions. I am happy that I found your address among them. I want to organize a public meeting in Pune on this subject. How can I expect the people in this country to respond to their call unless I present before them the true picture of the sufferings of their brethren who are fighting a war for their identity and their rights in a far away country? I learn that there are two leading societies here, but they will consent to come to a common platform only if the meeting is presided over by someone who is acceptable to both of them.'

'Absolutely correct,' he said, 'there is no other way of getting them together.'

It was getting to be evening. He put down the book. Birds were getting noisier and noisier, as they returned to their nests. Mohandas looked up at the sky, which was getting red in some places while in others mud-coloured clouds still wandered about. It was a picture of sadness.

He mustered some courage and said: 'No one other than you has the respect of both the groups. I have talked to Tilak Maharaj as well as Prof. Gokhale.'

'You must have found out that I do not take part in politics, but I won't refuse you. Seeing your purpose and your devotion to the cause I have no choice but to accept. I will attend your meeting. It was thoughtful of you to have talked to both Tilak and Gokhale before coming to me. Go and tell them that I have agreed to preside over the public meeting. Find out about the time from them. I'll be there whenever they choose. There is no need to bother about my convenience about time.'

As Mohandas bent forward to touch his feet, Dr. Bhandarkar lovingly held both his hands in his own. To Mohandas, it felt as if it was *Bapu* standing before him.

~

Madras was Mohandas' third stopover. The land of Balasundaram washed by the blue waters of the ocean and covered by tall coconut trees. The roving Balasundaram tale had already made it to his land, like a cry of pain. People were curious to know about this saviour in a faraway land who had taken under his wings a completely friendless and clueless man, who had no one to call his own anywhere. This man had nothing but the sky above him and the strange land beneath him. Land is the same everywhere, but the way people treat you makes it a stranger to you. This was precisely what had happened to this man. Balasundaram was there among the strangest of the strange. The Balasundaram incident had set up a link between Mohandas and Madras which would never break, nor ever catch a snag. Gandhibhai, the Gandhibhai of Balasundaram fame, is landing in Madras—this news had fired people with enthusiasm.

Mohandas had absolutely no idea that people in Madras would be so crazy about him. They carried him on their shoulders: 'What great luck! A man, who knew the pain of one of our own people in a far, faraway land, is amidst us!' It was not only people belonging to Balasundaram's class who displayed this enthusiasm; even politicians, journalists and lawyers and others in senior positions, who wouldn't even look at people like Balasundaram inside the country, were overflowing with it. In Bombay, Mohandas had to run around for this little job. In Pune, he had to hunt for a person to preside over the meeting who would have the nod of the two opposing parties. Here, success was leading the way like a friend. Things were taking care of themselves. Everyone he met was already waiting to lend support to the fulfilment of his cause.

Parameshvaran Pillay, editor of *The Madras Standard*, already knew a lot about Gandhi's mission and what he did not know he now found out in great depth by meeting Gandhi personally. Mohandas visited him in his office and briefed him in finest detail about the issues involved, while Pillay put before him his own programme of action. The first thing that Pillay did was to start a page in his newspaper about the problems of Indians in South Africa. In a way, it was Mohandas' page. G. Subrahmaniam, editor of *The Hindu*, had also started devoting himself with all his energy to an understanding of the problems of Indians in South Africa. A number of jurists had also joined Mohandas.

The day finally came when an appeal from M.K. Gandhi, a barrister from South Africa, for a public meeting, sponsored by Madras Mahajan Sabha and signed by forty dignitaries, appeared in all the newspapers of Madras Presidency. The signatories included such leading personalities as Sir Ramaswami Mudaliar. The appeal announced that the meeting would be addressed by an intellectual who has been fighting for the rights of poor Indian workers and businessmen in South Africa. The meeting was to be presided over by Anand Charlu, who was one of the founders of the Congress.

A lot was said by way of introduction to Mohandas. His own speech was a rambling one in which he mentioned a great many incidents, cited examples, raised legal issues and gave a detailed description of the various ways in which the whites ill-treated Indians. The most surprising thing was that though he spoke in English, everyone, whether or not he knew English, listened with rapt attention.

Mohandas told them: 'There is an association of traders from Madras in South Africa. They have their own building and a shopping complex in Durban. Their shops are called 'coolie shops' and their masters 'the coolie masters'. The white staff of the railways and the tram company treats the coolies like animals. Even neatly dressed Madrasis are not allowed on the footpaths. Those Madrasis who nevertheless use the footpaths are constantly afraid of the moment when they might have to face humiliation.'

'In the eyes of the whites, we are dirty, filthy, deserving to be ill-treated and abused, storehouses of vices, rice-eaters, oily, smelly, spending our lives in tatters, vermin, and what not. In their textbooks, Indians are called earthworms and Asians are said to belong to uncivilized races of the world. Do you know what their biggest regret is?'

'No,' everyone screamed. 'Tell us.'

Mohandas' face flamed red. 'That they cannot shoot Indians down like rabbits,' he said.

'In Transvaal, Indians are not permitted to use the coaches, nor allowed to stay or eat in the hotels. In the Dundee village of Natal, an Indian store was set on fire by the whites.'

Mohandas also told them in detail about the plot to ensure lifelong slavery for the *girmitiya*s on payment of a twenty-shilling tax. He also mentioned the law which sought to include coloured domestic servants in the category of *kaffir*s (natives) by registering them officially, while, in reality, the *kaffir*s never did an iota of work while the Indian servants never got a moment to themselves.

Gandhibhai made special mention of one incident in his speech. 'An Indian bought a second-class ticket and got on to a train at Charlestown. On the way, he was abused as 'Sami' and thrown out of the train. Exactly the same thing had happened with me within a week of my arriving in Durban. Muslims in South Africa are all known as Arabs, be they Indian Muslims or non-Indian Muslims. He was therefore in the category of Arabs, which was a different category from Indians. He went and sat down in some other compartment. He was again thrown out at Pietermaritzburg, the place where I had also been once thrown out of a first class compartment with all my luggage, despite the fact that no fellow passengers had raised any objection to his presence in the compartment.

Once again he had to go to another compartment. The chain of humiliations had however still not ended. A white member of the railway staff escorted two white passengers into the compartment and exclaimed: 'I'm sorry, there is a Sami sitting here. If you find him smelly, I'll find some other seats for you.' Thankfully, those passengers did not propose that he be thrown out again, or, he would have been another M.K. Gandhi spending his night shivering in the cold.

He laughed a little before asking seriously again: 'Tell me, is this not beastly behaviour? The matter went to court and the Indian got a compensation of ten pounds. But was ten pounds an adequate compensation for the terrible humiliation he had undergone?'

He read out the comment *Natal Mercury* had to make on the episode, protesting the incident: 'Our people are forgetting that Indians too are British subjects. Our Queen is their Queen too. Why should we use insulting epithets to denigrate them? The white community never has a good word for them, and there is no end to the stream of insults ...'

Everyone in the audience, whether or not he understood what Mohandas had said, was shaken. Their faces were red with fury.

In his speech, Mohandas also listed the demands of the Indians. He gave an account of the correspondence with Lord Chamberlain and of the talks that had been held. He described the positive and friendly attitude the Indians had taken. He cited favourable as well as unfavourable comments from the press. He also explained that the reason why the whites nursed such ill-feelings towards the Indians was that they didn't know enough about them. He mentioned the *Green Pamphlet*, which he had offered as the distress call of the South African Indians.

The concluding words of his speech touched the heart:

> *Friends! The people of Bombay gave their verdict with words. We have no hesitation in admitting that we are most of us young men, relatively fresh and inexperienced. We think we have a birthright to claim from you, you who are all our seniors and relatively more free, a birthright to appeal to you for*

help and protection. We are groaning with intolerable pain under the weight of torture and tyranny. Does our cry reach your ears? Whips of tyranny are being rained on us day and night. Please forgive me if I say that, to some extent, you too are responsible for it.

The speech ended. The applause was as loud and as prolonged as the patience and the interest with which the audience had heard him had been great and intense. Mohandas kept wondering how his speech in English had made such an impact on an audience which was mostly made up of illiterate persons. How did they get the sense of it? Does language really cease to matter when love prevails? Mohandas was reminded of the episode in the Ramayana where the rocks that Nal and Neel had dropped into the ocean to construct a bridge had started floating instead of sinking. For most of the listeners too, Mohandas' English words were like those rocks, which, instead of sinking, were floating on the surface and forming a bridge between the two. Possibly, this is what makes this land so special. A voice suddenly rose: 'We protest the excesses and atrocities being committed on Indians in South Africa. We will retaliate!'

This was one resolution which had burst forth from the hearts of the audience like a fountain. Mohandas accepted it gratefully. It took him some time to size up the scale of the success that he had achieved.

Mohandas was so overwhelmed with his success that he got a thank-you message inserted in *The Hindu* of October 27, 1896: 'When the news of this meeting, overflowing with love and sympathy, reaches those heart-broken, desperate and harassed Indians in South Africa, they will dance with joy. Their broken hearts will be welded together again. They will know that their brethren in India haven't forsaken them. For a moment, the sorrows of their hearts will be washed away by love and joy. The goodwill you have shown towards them will break out of the dark clouds of adversity and tyranny like a ray of hope and will show them the way to the future.'

There was a run on the *Green Pamphlet* at the meeting. Those who could read it, as well as those who couldn't, made sure of a copy. They wanted to preserve the word images of Gandhi's 'holy voice'. Mohandas was forced to say: 'I'll never be able to forget this festival of emotions. I promise those who haven't got a copy of the pamphlet that I will get it reprinted and send copies to the secretary of the Mahajan Sabha. Please collect it from him, but only a single copy and only those who didn't get a copy today.'

The venue reverberated with wild applause. A few days later, when Mohandas left for Calcutta, a huge crowd gathered at the station to bid him farewell.

~

It was now going to be a month since Mohandas had left Rajkot. His leaving Rajkot so soon after his brother-in-law's painful death had not been well-received by the family. In fact, it had been hard to take. Everyone, and not just Raliyat (or sister Goki), aimed his or her barbs at Kastur, who mostly took them in silence. Sometimes, however, when her tolerance gave way, she couldn't help a riposte: 'He is not just my husband; he is also something to you. Why didn't you stop him? It's not as if I sent him out or that he is out doing something for me. Year after year I have watched him leave home again and again and never said a word. How much would the kids love to have their father with them! So why pick on me?'

After the kids had gone to bed at night and sleep evaded Kastur, she let her mind roam: He belongs to everyone; he belongs to people living half way across the world; the only ones he doesn't belong to are her and the kids. He cannot bear to see the suffering of others, except hers and the kids. She had been the only grass widow in the family. Soon after marriage, he had left for England. That wasn't so bad as it was, after all, a question of his career. When he returned, he was running between Rajkot and Bombay. That too was okay, as he had to settle down. When he returned finally to Rajkot, we were all happy that we would be a family again. But then he went overseas again. For one year, he said, but returned after three. And when he did come back he had with him so much baggage of other people's sufferings that the suffering of his own people was no more than a few specks of dust in the folds of his baggage, unseen, unnoticed.

His brother-in-law died in full bloom of his youth; he brushed aside the sorrow of his death as so much fungus. Suppose she were to die tomorrow? Well, one would have to live out one's allotted destiny, wouldn't one?

She dozed off. Suddenly, she felt Mohandas was calling her out softly, standing next to her. She woke up with a start, but lay herself down again. What a fool she was! Mohandas, here? As she turned on her aside, a couple of tears stole out of her eyes into the pillow.

Mohandas was still nowhere near the end of his journey: Calcutta lay ahead and it was a long way off. He couldn't help thinking that Madras and Calcutta had been the two ports which had exported Indians, so maybe the people of Calcutta would probably show more or less the same sentiment that had been so prominent in the people of Madras. They too would probably cry out in sympathy to hear the distress call of their brethren. Waves of goodwill and sympathy rising from these two places would certainly touch the hearts of those Indians who were struggling to survive in the ocean of misery and would give them comfort. It might prove the straw that they can clutch at, and, who knows, might even save them.

But when he landed in Calcutta, it didn't take him long to realize that Calcutta was a different proposition from Madras. Calcutta was not going to fall as easily as Madras. For one thing, he knew little about Calcutta. The faces, the land, and the people—everything was strange. From the railway station, he went straight to the Great Eastern Hotel. He had heard of the place and knew that it admitted Indians. That's why probably it is called 'Eastern,' he thought. And because it accommodated both whites and non-whites, it was also called 'Great'. The thought brought an invisible smile to his face.

Getting a room was no problem. He deposited his things in the room and went down to the lounge and sat there wondering where to start and whom to meet. He had heard that Surendranath Banerji was the Sir Pherozeshah Mehta of Calcutta—its uncrowned king.

An Englishman strolled in and sat down at his table. Mohandas raised his head and looked at him.

'May I sit here?'

'Of course!'

Mohandas introduced himself. He responded: 'I have heard of you. I am Ellerthorpe. I represent *The Telegraph* and am on the look-out for a prey.'

'A prey?' Mohandas didn't get it.

'Precisely. It is a reporter's job to be on the lookout for a prey, a prey that will make a story. You could be one.'

Mohandas laughed out loud. 'You seem to be a true-blue reporter.'

'I am at the Bengal Club. If you have no problem, we could go and talk there.'

'Sure. I have no problem,' said Mohandas.

Ellerthorpe was so absorbed in talking to Mohandas that he headed straight for the lounge, which was a large and magnificent place. But he had to pull up suddenly, which also applied brakes to Mohandas' legs. The Manager stood barring the door. He pointed to a sign. Ellerthorpe now noticed the sign. Mohandas had already noticed it.

'Let's find another place,' said Mohandas.

Ellerthorpe went red with embarrassment. 'Do excuse me, Mr. Gandhi. I didn't know colour of skin mattered so much here. I never noticed this sign, or I would never have brought you to this place.'

'Actually, I should have known. But, never mind, I'm quite used to such happenings. Pardon me for saying so, but the colour white breeds discrimination wherever it goes. I no longer bother about such insults, as I know that nothing more than arrogance of skin-colour is what lies behind it. But skin is nothing more than a covering and its colour means nothing. Here today, gone tomorrow.'

'Let's go to my room.'

Mohandas considered it for a while. If he refused, Ellerthorpe might be offended.

'Okay. Let's go,' he said. But then he paused. 'But'.

'It's my room. As long as I am in it, it belongs to me.'

Mohandas went along. It took them a few minutes to get back to normal. It felt as if they had passed through a tunnel covered with cobwebs and the cobwebs were clinging to them. Mohandas had already rid himself of them. He started on an account of the reasons which had brought him to India and then never looked back. He told him what had brought him to Calcutta and what had transpired at the meetings at Bombay, Pune and Madras.

'Have you met Surendranath Banerji? He can work wonders here.'

'Surendranath Banerji?' repeated Mohandas and the matter ended.

~

Mohandas found Surendranath Banerji surrounded by his admirers and supporters, like Sir Pherozeshah. It would be a problem to have his ear to himself. You told him something and he shot back at once, sparing you the trouble to rephrase or reformulate your idea. When it was Mohandas' turn, he presented his case and handed him the *Green Pamphlet*. He kept turning its pages. People around him also continued their babble in Bangla. When you don't know a language, it sounds like babble. Sense alone makes sense. Mohandas was quite ill at ease: this was not something he had bargained for. Nor could he raise his voice to a man of such distinction.

Every now and then, Mr. Banerji would also issue a hint: 'Make it brief.'

Mohandas raced through his presentation. Finally, Mr. Banerji made his response: 'Well, Gandhi, I don't think people here would be interested much. We Bengalis have so many problems of our own. Until we tackle them, we can hardly spare a thought for others. But no harm trying. Get the princes to take interest, if you can. Meet the representatives of the British India Association. Raja Sir Pyarimohan Mukherji and Maharaja Jatindranath Tagore are interested in public affairs. They are liberal-minded men. See them and seek their help.'

Mohandas had of course realized as soon as he arrived in Calcutta that things were not going to work as smoothly here as they had in Bombay, Pune and Madras. If Surendranath Banerji himself was non-committal, who else would come forward? Still, it didn't take him long to decide that he had to meet both the Raja and the Maharaja. He knew that meeting Rajas and Maharajas was no child's play. But he was lucky again. Both of them agreed to see him.

Both of them also talked in the same style and also made the same excuses.

'Yes?'

'I am Mohandas Karamchand Gandhi from South Africa.' And, as usual, he dived headlong into the main issue.

Both of them periodically broke into yawns. Mohandas wondered if all Rajas and Maharajas were like these two. This was his first encounter with the species. The couple of princelings he had met earlier had been of the local variety. These two sported the British stiff upper lip. Actually, they were titled princes, a shade different from the state princes.

Both of them had the same thing to say, maybe with different choice of words: 'Arranging a public meeting in Calcutta is not easy. If there is anyone who can do it, it is Surendranath Banerji.'

Having failed in his mission, Mohandas sat dejected in his room. Would he go back empty-handed from a location which had witnessed shipload after shipload of workers being dispatched to South Africa? He thought of Madras, where it was the newspapers that had come to his rescue: *Madras Standard* and *The Hindu*. There was the *Amrit Bazar Patrika* here. He got up and made for its office. That was his only hope now.

He approached the editor. A few minutes into conversation with him and Mohandas realized that the editor thought of him as a usurer on his collection round. He moved on to another paper, *Bangabashi*. After making him wait first, the editor, listening to him with only half an ear, burst out: 'Can't you see how busy I am? There are dozens of people like you coming in everyday. How on earth do you think I would be able to get the paper out on time, if I were to listen to them all? Enough! Now get going!'

Mohandas tried to recall if he ever had had such an experience in Natal. Then he smiled and muttered to himself: 'But this is my country. These are my people.'

Mohandas was finding himself forced to return empty-handed. But he didn't want that workers in South Africa should feel that their fellow countrymen thought of their sufferings as worse than objects intended for the garbage bin. He decided to make a last-ditch effort and landed at the office of *The Statesman*. If unsuccessful again, he decided, he would go back. The editor was Paul Knight, a true-blue Englishman. There was another English paper too: *Englishman*. The editor was Mr. Saunders.

Paul Knight gave him a patient hearing. At the end of the meeting, when Mohandas stood up to leave, Knight got up and shook hands and said: 'I'll see what I can do.' Mohandas wanted to say: 'You'll see, but I have seen,' but he came out without a word. There was now nothing for him to do but go back. But instead he found himself in Mr. Saunders' office.

He could judge from Mr. Saunders' talk that he empathized with the South African Indians. He questioned Mohandas very closely. Anyone else in Mohandas' place would have seen safety in escape, but Mohandas had an answer to every one of Saunders' questions. Even the stiff interrogation did not make the slightest dent in Mohandas' determination. He laid bare the truth about both parties to the dispute before Saunders.

As Mohandas made to leave, Saunders stood up and said: 'Gandhi, I'm impressed with your devotion to truth and your passion for freedom. You have been completely even-handed. If you had so wished, you could have painted the whites black.'

'Those who seek justice for themselves need to be just to others, Mr. Saunders! We crave justice; how can we expect to get it if we inflict injustice on others?'

Saunders' attitude had filled Mohandas with hope. From what Saunders said, he inferred that the public meeting could well be held on the coming Friday. He also mentioned this in a letter to a friend. He was excited and happy. It looked as if his dream was going to come true. He would now be able to tell the people of this city too about the adversity-hit Indians in South Africa. After all, the first ever ship to leave for Natal had set sail from this city.

The meeting was scheduled for November 13. On November 11, Mohandas sat in his room preparing himself for the meeting when a telegram was delivered to him. It had been sent by Dada Abdullah to his Bombay office, which had redirected it to him. The telegram read: 'Send Mohanlal Gandhi stop road enforcing Indians to locations.'

Mohandas read the telegram again and again. He couldn't make out what 'road' stood for. How could a road force Indians to reserved locations? His own name was written wrong: Mohanlal instead of Mohandas. But it was 'road' which puzzled him most. Was it a code or a sign which he didn't know about? Mohandas recalled that the Cape parliament had passed a law authorizing the local East London Council to frame laws and bye-laws to dispatch Indians into locations that had been especially reserved for them, thus in effect banning them from the city footpaths.

After a lot of thought, Mohandas reached the conclusion that it must be the East London Municipality which was enforcing the new laws and forcing the Indians to confine themselves to the locations that had been reserved for them, though the whole issue was supposed to be under the consideration of Chamberlain. 'Road', after a lot of brainwork, he interpreted to be 'Raat,' which was the name for the Cape government in their language.

This context made the matter very serious indeed. Mohandas was left with no choice except to go back. He had anyway given them word that when he was called he would return immediately. The time had now come for him to return. He went to Saunders and explained the whole matter to him. Saunders grasped the situation quickly. Mohandas issued a written statement explaining the situation in which he was being forced to return to Natal. He expressed his regrets over the fact he had not been able to bring home to Calcuttans the tragic tale of Indians settled in South Africa.

~

XIV

Mohandas instructed the agent of Dada Abdullah & Co. in Bombay telegraphically that accommodation for him and his family should be booked on the first available ship leaving for Natal.

Dada Abdullah had recently purchased a new ship called *Courland* and he wanted Gandhibhai and his family to travel by that ship to give it an auspicious launch. Their travel would be free.

Mohandas thought it best to accept the free passage offered by Dada Abdullah. Engaging in any kind of negotiations would have meant creating doubts about their ever reaching Natal. Natal Congress had given him seventy-five pounds, which he had finished a long time ago. The forty pounds he had brought with him were also almost finished: the few left would see him through the journey.

Mohandas took the next train to Rajkot. There were many loose ends to tie up there. He hadn't even made a start on a number of things he had to do. The most important ones were to sell the idea to brother Lakshmidas and to get Kastur's consent to go with him. Then Kastur and the kids had to be fitted out for South Africa. Mohandas knew that Lakshmidas would not be happy with the idea of his taking his family with him, but he had no choice.

Fitting them out for South Africa was a big problem. They would have to follow the local style in clothing. The clothes Kastur and the kids wore in Rajkot would just not do. Their clothes would have to be a compromise between the modern and the Indian. Kastur would simply not wear any clothing that revealed even the slightest of skin. Nor would it be possible for them to set foot in that modern land in the traditional Kathiawari business family ensemble. The biggest problem was going to be Kastur. It was impossible to get her to do anything unless she wished it.

All that Mohandas wanted was that when his family landed there, they should not look old-fashioned and indecent.

Mohandas decided to check with Kastur. 'We must leave immediately for Natal,' he told her. 'I want you and the kids to be dressed suitably in clothes which are not old-fashioned.'

'What's wrong with these clothes? You don't expect us to be suited and booted like yourself, do you?'

Mohandas laughed: 'Of course not. Nor did I ask you to get into suit and boots. What I think is that the Parsi dress is both Indian and looks modern too. It also looks pretty decent.'

'You mean our dresses look indecent?'

'Not at all. But it would certainly look awkward if I wore the western dress and you wore this kind of stuff.'

She didn't deny it, but stayed silent.

Her not denying it, Mohandas took as acceptance. So he went out and got Parsi saris and blouses for Kastur and Parsi jackets, trousers and caps for the kids. Socks and shoes were mandatory. Parsi women too wore them. So Kastur also got shoes. But how would a person who had never put her foot inside a shoe ever walk in them? The real problem was the proper fit. For both Kastur and the kids, the western types of shoes were nothing short of punishment. The shoes pinched. The kids somehow managed to walk in them, though there was no fluency in the walk. But Kastur hit a real roadblock. She felt as if she was being asked to walk a rope and that each of her upright moments was her last. Her feet sweated so much that the socks were soaked. Blisters covered her feet where the shoes had pinched them.

Mohandas couldn't help feeling that by imposing western shoes and socks on them he had exceeded the limits, but bare feet wouldn't do, would they? Kastur might well be thinking that, he being the lord and the master, they had to submit to his will. Parsi clothes had transformed the lot completely. From Gujarati baniyas, they had turned into Parsis. Mohandas was conscious how they went along quietly with whatever he told them: both Kastur and the kids. He felt it especially strongly when he told them to start using knives and forks. Kastur resisted, but the kids picked them up. At first, of course, they too felt eating with knife and fork was punishment. For all their questions, Mohandas had only one answer: modernity. Eating with your hands was a sign of backwardness and rusticity. It was the same story as with the Parsi dress. It was not as if Mohandas didn't know how they felt, or that they were finding it difficult to swallow all this. But at the time modernity was his obsession.

For the kids, this was their first journey by a ship. The sight of an endless expanse of water all around them at first made them nervous. What would happen if the ship were to go down? There wasn't even a tree around whose branches you could hold on to. Mohandas laughed and told them: 'No trees in an ocean and, no, ships do not go down everyday.'

Their nervousness lasted a day or two; later it turned into fun. Since the ship belonged to their father's friend, they had the freedom of the ship. Along with Kastur and their kids, Mohandas had also brought along his sister Goki's son, Gokaldas. He was the oldest among the kids. Mohandas had taken over responsibility for him after his father's death. The kids enjoyed the sea breeze the way they enjoyed a light shower and the accompanying cool wind during summers at home. It was Kastur who was having a hard time. The various prohibitions she observed in respect of food and drink, the use of utensils, etc. kept her from enjoying anything. Mohandas tried to make her see reason: 'Look, Kastur, you can't go on like this. You are giving up a small world for a big one. In this big world, you'll come across people of all kinds. There will be Gujaratis, Madrasis, whites as well as natives. You'll have to meet them and mix with them. If you don't do it, your life will be impossible. We are going there to fight for the rights of our fellow Indians. When you are fighting a war, your action is your religion. You have a role in that war.'

Kastur always reacted strongly: 'You keep that role. I don't need one.'

Mohandas didn't give up. He told her tales of people's woes. Kastur had a tender heart and a mild nature. Tales of other people's woes melted her heart and she was often overcome with emotion.

Being the oldest among the kids, Gokaldas was always followed around by the other kids and he acted as their supervisor. At meal times, everyone came together. Mohandas told them how to use knives and forks, when to cross them and when to place them parallel to each other and how to eat soundlessly. They were served only vegetarian food, which was prepared quite separately from the other food. Kastur kept a close eye on the proceedings lest the illegitimate pollute the legitimate food.

~

When *Courland* had set sail, another ship, *Naderi*, had also followed it. *Naderi* also belonged to Dada Abdullah & Co. and it was also going to Natal. The journey was quite an uncomplicated one. The ships were to reach Natal in eighteen days. Fourteen days had passed eventlessly. When *Courland* was four days from Natal, a storm broke over the sea accompanied by hail. December is a summer month in South Africa and rain is always a possibility. Hail wasn't totally unexpected either. But this hailstorm was so fierce that the passengers were completely at a loss. The hailstones were big and could well cause damage. If they were to hit someone, he was sure to get injured. There were sure to be fireworks, if they hit your head. The hailstones hitting the ship sounded like an artillery barrage. The kids were cowering in corners. Kastur was ruing the day she decided to leave the safety of her home to come to this hell. Would she ever see her home again?

The storm and the fright it produced achieved one thing: it made all the faces look alike, wiping out all differences. No one was a Hindu, or a Christian or a Parsi any more: they had all merged into a great One, even if they bore different names. Everyone was calling out to that One. Mohandas was amazed to see how differences of faith vanished in the face of danger. Fear of death knew no colour or religion. Fear was a mountain which crushed everything beneath it. There were vows being taken: 'Never will I tell a lie again!' 'Never will I cause hurt to anyone.' 'Never will I be dishonest again.' 'Never will I be unjust to anyone!' 'Never will I forsake you again!' Near and dear ones were being remembered: father, kids, brother, mother ...

The Captain was going round trying to reassure people: 'Don't be frightened. There's nothing to worry. The storm is receding. The ship is fully equipped to face such emergencies; the storm can do no damage to it. Have faith; faith is what will see you through.' But the passengers were agitated and the Captain's talk had no impact. The only faith they had was in God. They heard weird sounds. The ship would start tossing suddenly and it appeared it would capsize any moment. At times, it felt as if it had hit a rock and was about to go down. A cry started at one end of the ship and by the time it reached the other end the whole ship had sent up a big wail.

The ship was unsteady for about twenty-four hours. People kept up their train of vows. Then there was an assembly for prayer. One could see in their eyes an ardent desire to live but lost hope dogged their steps. Prayer provided the only consolation. The Captain also joined the prayer assembly. It looked as if he too was now waiting for the Great Boatman to come to his rescue. As he genuflected, his eyes were turned to the sky. After disappointment all round, this was the only recourse left for him: prayer!

The sun came out, brightening up the faces of the passengers. The brightness of life and hope dimmed the shine of God and prayer. Fear of death disappeared. Life was spreading its light everywhere up to the horizon and beyond, like the ocean itself. Food and drink, song and dance everywhere. Mohandas saw and wondered if the prayer had been an illusion. The reality was the food and the drink, the song and the dance.

When the storm was at its peak, Gandhibhai had been going round, supporting himself against the walls, encouraging them to keep up their spirits. Now that things were back to normal, people had begun to think something was wrong with this man. He must be either sick of life or had faced some tragedy in his life. Otherwise, why would a man go around during a storm asking others to keep their chin up instead of saving his own life? At the time, they all wanted him to sit beside them; now they were wondering why this man was not afraid of death. Mohandas had been busy at the time getting the latest report on weather from the Captain's cabin and relaying it to the passengers. When the weather started improving, the withered faces of the passengers began to revive; when it worsened, they were downcast. Gandhi would then ask them not to be afraid. Fear, he told them, was death. At the time, his talk seemed to make sense to them. Now they were laughing at each one of the things he had said.

Courland dropped anchor at the Durban port on December 18, 1896. *Naderi*, which was following behind, also did the same a little later. Altogether, there were about eight hundred passengers in the two ships, all of them Indians. Each one of them was to be medically examined. One could see land coming up at a distance. The passengers were impatient to touch land after a lapse of eighteen days and were relieved that the ship had survived a watery grave. Everyone was packed and ready for disembarkation.

Hari, the younger one, asked: '*Bapu*! Why aren't we getting off?'

Mohandas explained: 'The Health Department people will be here first and they will examine everyone. Only then will the steps be lowered for us to get down.'

'Why will they examine us?'

'To see if any one of us is carrying an infectious disease. If anyone is, he will not be allowed to get down. He will be separated from all others.'

'Why will he be separated?'

'So that others do not catch the germs of the disease.'

While he was explaining all this to the kids, the thought was constantly haunting his mind that at the time they had left India the plague had broken out in Bombay. The local authorities could well make it an excuse for not letting the Indian passengers disembark.

Courland and *Naderi* had both put up the yellow flags. They would be taken down only after the Health Department's clearance and disembarkation certificate had been received. Visitors would also be allowed on board only after that had happened. Currently, the situation however was that neither the Health Department inspectors were to be seen anywhere nor were there any signs of the yellow flags lowering.

Finally, the doctor showed up. The faces of the passengers lit up as if a release order for prisoners had been received. He examined the passengers cursorily and slapped five-day quarantine on all of them. No one could leave the ship or come on board for five days. Mohandas had been correct in his conjecture. The doctor said that germs of the plague were active for twenty-three days. They had passed eighteen days in the sea; five remained.

The passengers felt their release order had been held up and their prison sentence extended by five days at the last moment. They unpacked again and, dejected and disappointed, looked for their old stations again. For eighteen days, they had seen the whole world float on the waves of the ocean. The storm had only shattered their will, but the quarantine order had broken them completely. The rope had snapped when the ledge was only a hand away.

~

The day *Naderi* and *Courland* entered the port, *Natal Advertiser* published a notice signed by Captain Sparks, a commissioned officer in the British army. The notice read: 'Every citizen of Durban is requested to attend a meeting on Monday, January 4, at Victoria Café to join in a collective effort to block the Asian passengers from disembarking.'

The meeting was eventually held on January 4, not at Victoria Café but in the Town Hall. There was no notice to this effect, though, nor any correction of the earlier notice. Nearly two thousand whites attended the meeting, all of them young and most of them technicians.

Captain Sparks presided over the meeting. The meeting started by providing some background information: The Tongat Sugar Company wanted to import different categories of technicians from India, which would render the native technicians jobless. The Board had approved the proposal, but when there was a protest, the Board withdrew its permission. Nevertheless, this coolie called Gandhi was now here with two shiploads of technicians and the ships were waiting offshore for the quarantine period to be over. The technicians were going to be allowed permanent residence in the country. Everyone knew that these people were only too happy to work even if oil-soaked bread was all they were given to eat.

A series of incendiary speeches followed. One of the whites declaimed: 'This coolie called Gandhi has dragged the name of our country through mud in India.' A wire dispatched by Reuters about Gandhi's *Green Pamphlet* was published in the Natal papers on September 14, which said that Gandhi had been spreading the canard in India that Indians were mistreated in Natal. Justice was denied to them. The blood of every Natalese has since been on the boil. Respectable gentlemen in this country have no peace.

Dr. Mackenjie, who had been deputed to examine the passengers aboard *Courland* and *Naderi*, had also been invited to address the meeting. He started with the name 'Gandhi' and stopped. A big roar went up. Abuses were hurled at the name. Dr. Mackenjie nodded his head in approval and raised both his hands in a posture of blessing. When the noise subsided a little, he continued: 'This man came to Natal from India and settled down in Durban, where he was welcomed with open arms. As much respect and honour was given to this coolie as could possibly be given to an outsider in Natal. He took the fullest advantage of our hospitality and gentlemanliness and extracted whatever he could from us. And what does he give us in return? Abuses, accusations and allegations that we mistreat Indians and rob them of their possessions!'

A voice from the rear said: 'He is a starving coolie. Who would rob a starving coolie?'

Everyone laughed ho-ho at the joke.

Dr. Mackenjie continued: 'This man called Gandhi has dragged our honour through mud and slush in India. He has made our name black and dirty like the colour of his own skin.' There was prolonged applause.

Dr. Mackenjie resumed: 'I'm amazed that these dirty, filthy and honourless wimps aspire for franchise! It was with great difficulty that our government succeeded in taking franchise away from these people and now they want to enter our parliament and rule over us Europeans! They dream of making laws that will govern us! They want to run the government while we work in the kitchen! We know that Indians form the largest group among the Asians. Our government had decided that if these people behaved themselves, they would be treated decently. But if they choose to take advantage of our decency by consorting with a nefarious character like Gandhi, they are going to receive the same treatment that we are soon going to hand to Gandhi.'

Though Mackenjie was taking a lot of their time, people were enjoying his speech. They cried themselves hoarse in applause and started dancing. When the meeting place became little quiet, a resolution was moved: 'It is high time that Natal government imposed a total ban on the landing of any Asians, especially Indians, at the Port of Natal.' It said further that the passengers hiding in the *Courland* and *Naderi* should be immediately ordered back to India.

They all stood up and, singing and dancing in the style of the natives, expressed their support for the resolution.

The meeting was over.

~

The issue however was not over. In fact, it was leaving a trail behind. Captain Sparks called another meeting in the Town Hall on January 7. This time, the tempers ran higher. Captain Willie was the first one to speak: 'The government agrees with our resolution, but it wants the freedom to pursue these goals in its own way.'

Dr. Mackenjie was more aggressive this time, with Sparks merely presiding over the meeting. He said: 'The fit place for these ugly and ill-mannered Indians to go is the bottom of the Indian Ocean. That's where they should be buried right away.'

The audience burst out laughing.

Mr. Walker said: 'Escombe has assured us that the government is with us. We should therefore not do anything which will restrict the government's ability to act. We have however told the government that if it doesn't act, we'll be forced to act ourselves.' There was applause at every point which was made to insult and denigrate Indians.

Someone raised his voice to suggest: 'Let the quarantine period be extended indefinitely. They should neither be able to disembark nor go back.'

Another voice supported the idea: 'That's it. That's what must be done.'

A sailor stood up and said: 'I'm ready to part with a month's salary as reward to anyone who goes and puts a bullet into Gandhi.'

Other also joined in: 'Me too. Put a bullet into a passenger aboard the ship and collect a month's salary from us.'

'Parliament must be reconvened immediately to extend the quarantine period.'

Dr. Mackenjie laughed and said: 'There are some elderly women among us, though.' Then he went on to suggest: 'The government should close down the port. That will make it easier to deal with the passengers, especially with the villain of the piece. When we are at the port, everyone must follow the leader. Understand? You must do only what "he" tells you to do.'

The organizing committee of the protest had distributed a list containing the names of those people who had volunteered to stop the passengers from disembarking. Their occupation, names, etc. were all recorded in the list.

Sparks stood up last. He put what he had to say in a few, carefully chosen words: 'We request those traders and trading establishments whose employees are attending this meeting not to interfere in our activities. If they do so, we'll know whose side they are on. This could create a problem for them.'

'We'll boycott them,' someone shouted.

'Yes, we will. Yes, we will,' everyone chorused.

~

Mohandas was being kept informed about the goings-on onshore by Dada Abdullah & Co. The whites were adamant that the ships carrying

Indians should be sent back at once. News of various meetings being held onshore was being transmitted to the ship. Dada Abdullah & Co. was being threatened with reprisals in case the ships were not sent back. But the company men remained firm, which led to a reconsideration of the earlier message. They were told that the company would be compensated for the loss incurred in sending the ships back. But, Abdullah Haji Karim, who was looking after the company's affairs at the time, was unbending. His word was final, he said. He was also the one sending messages to Mohandas.

It was with his help that one day Mansukhlal Naazar came aboard ship to see Mohandas. Boarding a ship in quarantine took a lot of courage and pulling of wires. He told Mohandas: 'Indians too are greatly agitated. It's with some difficulty that they are being held back. There is a war going on out there. On one side are a handful of Indians and a few of their English supporters. Harry Escombe is attending meetings on the other side. But our lawyer, Mr. Laughton, has come down heavily on the whites for their shameful behaviour.'

Mohandas now had a shrewd idea why the two Indian ships had been sent into quarantine using the plague as the excuse. The real reasons were the hatred for the Indians in the government and a desire to punish them and to harass and insult them.

The threats of the whites were unceasing: 'Indians! Go back! Or get ready to die by drowning.'

While the threats continued, the mediators were active too. The message they brought was: 'Go back and you will be reimbursed your fares. Refuse and you die.'

Mohandas was worried that the passengers might not be able to stand the pressure and crack. He visited each passenger individually and told them: 'Look, they can neither send us back, nor can they sink the ship. We must remain steadfast at our respective stations like soldiers. The victory shall be ours. You are not here to take away any one else's share: you are not here to cause pain to anyone; so there is no question of backing down or going back.'

The same issues agitated the passengers of *Naderi*. Mohandas had been trying to keep up their spirits by sending them messages at regular intervals. He told them: 'You may have left home to come here, or you may be returning from leave, your journey will be complete only when you step on to the land of Natal.'

All the indoor games available on board had been made available to the passengers. Those who didn't know how to play were being instructed in their use. The idea was to keep them entertained so that depression did not set in.

Mohandas also knew that he was the target of the agitators' fury. This worried Kastur and the kids. Mohandas himself was not so worried, but he had to make extra effort to assure Kastur and the kids. He knew that in situations like these, the family was worried more about its selfish interests.

Worrying about the self, or being happy about the self, both caused problems.

Meetings were a daily occurrence. New plans were formulated. Causes and consequences of events already past were scrutinized closely. People offered suggestions. A couple of them even suggested: 'What's the point in dying like this, out of hunger and thirst? Let's go back. If we survive, we'll be able to do something or the other and get something to eat.'

'At least we'll die in our own land,' was another suggestion.

Mohandas explained it to them: 'If that was what you thought, why on earth did you come here in the first place? You couldn't earn a living there, so you made for this place. Where are you heading next? India is not waiting with an offer of a job for you. When you left home, you left an empty pot behind. Will it give you enough to eat and to feed others? Determination, don't lose your determination. That's the only thing that will see you through. Never, never lose it.'

It was Christmas time. *Courland* had been decked up for the celebration, but the Indians weren't exactly excited. The Captain had invited all the saloon travellers. Mohandas, Kastur and the kids were his special invitees. As they feasted, the people all worried about what awaited them. Would they ever reach their destination or would they be required to go back? Mohandas was asked to speak a few words on the occasion.

Mohandas started with the sentence: 'This is no occasion for a speech. My heart is not in the festivities of Christmas; it is in Durban, where an imaginary battle is being fought without an enemy and without enmity. I have no hesitation whatsoever in admitting that it is I who am their target and not anyone of you. I have been informed that there are certain allegations against me. For example that in India I vilified the Natal whites and made unjustified allegations against them. I am also being accused of bringing two shiploads of technicians with me with the intention of displacing the white workers from their jobs.'

'I am fully conscious of my responsibilities. If you are facing adversity today, it is because of me. Dada Abdullah & Co. is in trouble because of me. The passengers of both the ships are feeling insecure and in serious danger. My own family is paying for placing their trust on me.'

'I cannot go around asking everyone to believe me that when I boarded this ship I didn't know a single face on this ship. I didn't know where these people came from and where they were headed. As for vilifying the white people of Natal, all I did I in India was to tell the people about the problems that were being faced by the Indians of Natal. I did not speak a word against the whites. I have proof which will show what I said in India. I haven't the slightest hesitation in admitting that I opposed the culture which sought to turn humans into animals and to discriminate between one human and another. This culture is a product of the white community of Natal and it is we who are living its consequences. My heart and mind were feeling the pressure of this culture, so when I found myself among my own people I couldn't help telling them about it.'

Everyone, including the Captain, was listening to him attentively. They all understood him in the sense in which he wanted to be understood, meaning that western civilization was not the same as eastern civilization.

Western civilization was founded on power and pressure, be it political power or economic power.

The Captain put a direct question to Mohandas: 'Suppose the whites were to translate their threats into action, how would you face them with your principle of non-violence?'

'I'll pray to God to give me strength to put up with their excesses and to forgive them for their actions. I have no grudge against them; it is they who have one against us. Therefore the question of my seeking to punish them, or to make accusations against them, does not arise at all. Nor shall I ever use the force of law against them. I only regret that they are humans yet do not understand the misfortunes that can befall humans. Whatever they are saying today they hold as true because they lack understanding. That cannot be a reason for me to nurse hatred against them and thus to defile my own mind.'

The Captain gave a smile which showed his distrust. Mohandas didn't miss the smile.

On one point, there was general agreement. They had earned the right to disembark on the land of Natal after a long journey and they were not about to give it up. This was conveyed to the agitationists, who naturally felt even more enraged.

Kastur was worried about their fate after disembarkation. There were the small kids to think of. Why punish the innocent kids? But Mohandas was unflinching. Kastur tried to explain it to him, but he only said: 'Forget about yourself and forget about me. If so many are to be killed, we can hardly think of our own survival.'

She found herself all alone. Everything she said to Mohandas got her only one answer: 'Now that you have chosen to be with me, you will have to face whatever is to happen. You all go wherever I go. Okay?'

Sometimes Kastur felt that she should get the people all together and tell them that one could not win a war so far from home. But where were the people? They were now all followers of Gandhibhai! Like a ship-bound bird, she fluttered her wings and stayed put, for where was the way for her to go?

At last, the ten-day quarantine passed. Both the ships lowered their yellow flags and started their approach to the shore. It was now twenty-seven days since the voyage had started. The process of disinfecting was carried out on a daily basis. Bleaching powder was used liberally. Even mail was not allowed on board. The passengers' clothes and beddings had been incinerated. The ships were without food and water. Repeated messages were being dispatched to the government, which seemed to be in hibernation. The Natal Indians were doing the best they could, but they couldn't go beyond a point. The government was siding with those people who believed that the proper place for the coolies was in the Indian Ocean and that was where they should be provided permanent homes.

On January 13, a government steamer called *Church Garden* steered close to the ships and, twenty minutes later, issued a command asking them to enter the harbour. The owners of the ships had not been intimated of this development and they were still waiting for official orders. At around quarter to one in the afternoon, *Courland* was pulled in with the help of *Richard King*, and was stationed near *Buoypul*. Mr. Escombe appeared with the ship's Captain on the ship and told the assembled passengers: 'Each one of you must consider you as safe here as you feel in your village in India. The Natal government undertakes to provide you complete security.'

At three o'clock, the Captain announced that the passengers were now free to disembark. The joy of the passengers knew no bounds. For so many days they had been so close to the shore yet so far.

Demonstrators had started to assemble on the streets. A bugle call had gone out at ten to assemble the faithful. Shopkeepers had downed their shutters. Office workers had left their offices. By eleven, there was a good gathering at the harbour. By twelve, Alexandra Square had filled up to capacity with railway workers, technicians, printing press workers, shop assistants, tailors, masons, some ordinary people and a few natives, about thirty-three hundred in all and all whites. This motley crowd was led by two whites with the names Spred Brough and Vincent. The demonstrators had been told that they would be led by a native midget. When this midget marched, everyone clapped and laughed. When the whites made a display of stick-fighting amongst themselves, the midget danced like a clockwork toy. Various kinds of entertainment shows had been arranged to hold the natives' interest.

The passengers aboard the ship were nervous. The demonstration by the whites could take an unpredictable turn any moment. It could well turn violent. There was no sign of any official security arrangements. Captain Milne of the *Courland* had positioned his ship ahead of *Naderi* and had ordered the sailors' red Union Jack to be hoisted on the midship flagstaff. The staff had been ordered not to allow the demonstrators aboard the ship under any circumstances. If they defied all requests and forced their way aboard the ship, the Union Jack was to be taken down and handed over to them. After this signal of surrender, no English demonstrator would probably dare to harass any passenger.

Police Superintendent Alexander had in the meantime evacuated Alexandra Square of all the demonstrators. Riding horseback, he was supervising all the arrangements personally. All eyes were set on *Courland.* People stood forming a long line from the south to the far north. They intermittently broke into slogans and then fell silent. Their slogan shouting was fiercely aggressive and put the wind up the passengers. Mohandas and a few of his companions stood on the deck taking in the scene. The Captain had put a telescope at their disposal. Mohandas had a look on his face which could be described more carefree than troubled. His companions too were maintaining their untroubled aspect. As *Courland* approached the shore, commotion began. People started running up and down, shouting slogans. They had again entered Alexandra Square. In a sing-song rhythm, they sang the lines:

Bring Gandhi ashore.
Let us spit at his face.
Teach black Gandhi a lesson.
Sink the whole lot into the Indian Ocean.

Dr. Mackenjie seemed to have taken personal responsibility for making speeches that would keep people's anger at a high pitch. He was saying: 'If this scum from the stinking sewers of India is imported in our midst and if we are forced to live in its company, the British government will find it difficult to continue its rule in this country.' There was loud clapping. He continued: 'Gandhi is a close friend of mine. You believe it, don't you?' There was laughter. When the laughter subsided, he said: 'He is hiding like a rat in one of these two ships, isn't he?'

'Yes, he is. Fish him out.'

Dr. Mackenjie continued: 'We have to attend to him, don't we?'

'Yes, we do. We must.'

'He is very tired after a long journey. A good hiding will fix his fatigue, won't it?' A long spell of clapping welcomed the suggestion.

'He wants to become a martyr, but we won't let him become one. He must stay alive so that we can spit on his face. If we grant him martyrdom, we will miss this chance. If I had been in his place, and if I were to be spat on, I would have preferred to hang myself than live a life of such disgrace.'

All this was being said in the presence of Mr. Escombe.

Finally, Escombe assured them that he would call a special session of the parliament to consider the issue in full detail. After this assurance, the crowd started scattering. The passengers now started leaving the ship in small groups in boats and landing ashore. Everyone was nervous and alert, although now peace reigned all around.

Mohandas was still on the ship and was watching the passengers being ferried ashore safely. He was happy to see their safe landing.

Captain Milne approached Mohandas and, placing his hand on his shoulder, took him aside. Now Kastur and the kids were almost by themselves on the deck. They were puzzled to see the Captain take Mohandas aside. Worries flooded their minds. Listening to rumours all the time, their minds had become so used to bad news that any good news was beyond their comprehension. After all, so many of the passengers were allowed to disembark, why not them? So far, the Captain had not stopped anyone, nor taken anyone aside to speak to him, then why only him? Especially when the ship belonged to a friend of his.

Captain Milne said: 'Mr. Gandhi, the Captain of Water Police is here with a message from Mr. Escombe ...'

'Anything special?'

'He says the white people are very agitated and they want your life. He therefore wants that you should leave ship only after dark. Port Superintendent Mr. Tatum will escort you home under his personal supervision.'

Mohandas considered the proposal for a while. Should he, or shouldn't he, accept Escombe's proposal? Would it not amount to cowardice? But then there are the kids to think of. He decided to accept the proposal. 'If he wants it that way, let's do it that way,' he said.

He got back to Kastur and the kids and told them in no uncertain terms that the city was tense and anything could happen. They might have to stay aboard for a few more days. For Kastur and the kids, to hear those words was to see the sun go down in mid-day and the darkness to take over. The kids were sick of living with water around them all the time. They had seen all the others leave. To see them leave, they felt as if they had committed some crime and their punishment was that they could not step on land. They so much wanted to be on land, to play, to walk, to touch. Kastur had only one thing to say: 'A creature of water needs water to survive, so a creature of land must have land to survive.'

A little later, Mr. Laughton, lawyer to Dada Abdullah & Co. appeared on the scene. He had been busy trying to get the two ships released risking the displeasure of the whites. He spoke to the Captain: 'I am here to take Mr. Gandhi and his family with me.'

The Captain told him that Mr. Escombe had advised them not to disembark before sundown as the city was tense and Gandhi's life could be in danger.

'I am the company's lawyer. You are under no obligation to accept Mr. Escombe's advice.'

'You can sort it out with Mr. Gandhi.'

Mr. Laughton approached Gandhi. 'I am Laughton, Dada Abdullah & Co.'s attorney,' he introduced himself.

'I know. I also know that you support Indians.'

'I suggest that Mrs. Gandhi and the children should leave in the car for Mr. Rustomji Parsi's house. You will go with me on foot. I do not wish that a man like you should steal into the city like a thief. No one will dare to lift a finger against you. The city is quite peaceful now. The demonstrators have left. I hope you are not afraid. Please remember that I'm with you.'

Mohandas looked at Laughton's face. 'Afraid?' he asked himself. 'Am I afraid? If I am, I must rid myself of this fear.' To Laughton, he said: 'Fine. I am ready to leave with you.'

The kids, who were listening, jumped with joy. So, Kastur and the kids were dispatched in the car to Parsi Rustomji's house. It was around five in the evening. Laughton and Gandhi got down at Eddington. Rustomji's house was about two miles from the place, about an hour's distance on foot. They got on to a boat and went as far as Cottage Creek, where some people saw them disembarking. They had to walk as far West Street, going via Customs House, but the people who saw them getting down started screaming 'Gandhi! Gandhi!'

Hearing the shouts, a crowd of people converged on the place like a swarm of locusts as if they had been hiding somewhere close by like guerilla warriors. Mr. Laughton now looked worried. He apprehended a swelling crowd might pose a serious danger to Gandhi's life. He therefore hailed a rickshaw at the Smith Street crossing. Mohandas was at first not ready to use the rickshaw, but when, after a lot of persuasion from Mr. Laughton, he agreed to sit in it, the rikshawpuller, seeing the gathering crowd, became nervous. A few of the young men approached him and threatened him: 'Take Gandhi on your rickshaw and we will see to it that you never pull a rickshaw again.'

The rickshawallah looked at the two of them, shouted 'Khaa!' and sped off. The rickshawpuller was a native. In his language, 'Khaa!' meant 'No!'

The crowd went on swelling. The two were now surrounded on all sides. Every step forward was an effort. They were being pushed and jostled. A giant of a man stepped forward from the crowd, dragged Laughton away and shouted: 'You are playing bodyguard to this man, are you?'

Mohandas could not hear Laughton's response in the din.

Mohandas was now by himself. He couldn't see Laughton anywhere. He closed his eyes and reflected for a while. He couldn't run away from the situation. If he tried running, the crowd would chase him like wild wolves. He therefore decided to stand fast on the spot. The crowd was now pelting him with stones. In fact, they started throwing at him whatever they could lay their hands on: brick halves, rotten eggs, rotting fish, mud ... One of the boys stepped forward and knocked off his turban. His head was now bare and became the target of the blows of anyone who cared to land one. Others started kicking and punching him. Anyone who succeeded in landing a kick or a punch on him immediately started a celebration, commemorating the blow with an impromptu dance, as if he had performed a noble deed. Mohandas was now feeling dizzy. He got hold of the railing of a house nearby and tried to recover his breath. It was however difficult to escape the flood of blows being rained on him by so many of them simultaneously. Some had chosen to play the role of mere onlookers of an amusing spectacle, as if a dangerous animal was being baited and hunted.

Sarah, wife of Police Superintendent Alexander, happened to be passing that way when she heard the crowd screaming 'Thrash the fellow! Thrash Gandhi!' She knew Gandhi. She immediately made her way into the crowd and pushed herself in, although the crowd was now hysterical and out of control. She was carrying an umbrella, which she now blew open as a shield, positioning herself between the mob and the injured Gandhi. The mob held for a minute, then rushed again, with Sarah doing everything she could to save Gandhi with her umbrella.

'Fold the umbrella!' the mob shouted.

Cracking her voice as a whip, Sarah lashed out at the crowd: 'The umbrella will stay where it is till you stop your attack on Mr. Gandhi.'

That brought the mob up short. A white lady and wife of the Police Superintendent at that! Attacking Mohandas in the face of her resistance could mean a possible injury to her. But still they tried and managed to steal a punch or two on Mohandas, though it was generally an oblique blow and lacked real punch.

Mr. Alexander had in the meantime been informed of the attack on Mr. Gandhi by a violent white mob with Mrs. Alexander also caught in the fracas. Alexander promptly dispatched his men who threw a protective ring around Gandhi and Sarah and escorted them to the police station, with a mob screaming 'Gandhi is a traitor! It's a sin to let Gandhi live!' on their tail.

The Borough police station was on the way, the place where Mohandas had met Mr. Alexander the first time. Alexander stood outside the station waiting. The police had stopped the mob short of the station.

Alexander told Mohandas: 'It would be better for you if you spend the night at the police station. The mob is agitated and could cause you harm.'

'Thanks, Mr. Alexander. But for Mrs. Alexander, I wouldn't be alive today. No body can say what would have happened if you hadn't sent your men in time to extricate me from the mob. But it would send out a wrong signal for me to stay at the police station. Please let me go. The courage shown by Mrs. Alexander has set an example for me. I'm sure once they realize the error of their ways, the people will be pacified. I have absolute faith in their judgment.'

'Where do you wish to go?'

'To my friend Parsi Rustomji's house. That's where my family is at the moment.'

'Fine. I'll have you dropped there.'

Mohandas had bruises all over his body. Dr. Dadibarjor, *Courland*'s official physician, was already at Rustomji's house and he attended to Mohandas' injuries. Although it was still painful to walk, Mohandas was feeling better.

Everyone was worried. Kastur, whose very first visit to this strange and faraway land had seen such extraordinary things happen, was holding herself somehow responsible. Inability to share her feelings with anyone was making her restless. The kids were extremely scared. They couldn't quite grasp how their father had got so many injuries that he couldn't get up without Gokaldas's help. Gokaldas was of course the oldest of the kids. Mohandas could not help thinking of the time when Kaba Gandhi was ill and he was about the same age as Gokaldas was now.

News soon arrived that the whites had surrounded Rustomji's house. It was now getting darker by the minute. The crowd stood chanting: 'We want Gandhi! or we will burn the house down. Rustomji was quite unruffled. His face did not show the slightest sign of fear or anxiety. Alexander was standing with the crowd. He had guessed that as soon as the mob got to know that Gandhi was in Rustomji's villa, it would try to lay siege to it, so he had arrived there with his contingent and had infiltrated the crowd. His detectives were all over the place.

Alexander had his own style of controlling a mob. He stood in the middle of the crowd shouting the same slogans as the others. Occasionally, he would stop shouting slogans and announce: 'Here comes Gandhi now!' People would start looking towards him. Seeing no Gandhi, they would look at him and he would say: 'Oh! It's me!' and would start going 'Tra-la-la,'Tra-la-la'. The boys too would then start 'Tra-la-la, Tra-la-la'. When Alexander raised the tempo of his dance, so did the boys. Gandhi slipped from their minds for a while. Now and again, Alexander would make faces at someone in the crowd. He was thus entertaining them, sometimes mimicking them and making them laugh even as he shouted slogans with them. But he knew that if he didn't find a way out soon, the crowd could attack the house and it would then be difficult for him to control the situation.

He now sent one of his detectives into the house with the message: 'If you want to save the house and property of your friend from destruction, please leave the house from the back door in a soldier's disguise. Things may soon go out of control and many lives may be lost. This is now the only way out. Please hurry.'

Since the afternoon, Mohandas had encountered many contradictory situations. Mr. Laughton had advised him to go with him on foot as it did not become him to leave like a thief. Mohandas had followed Laughton's advice and his body had become a collection of injuries. Now a Police Superintendent was advising him to leave in disguise or everything would be lost. All these recommendations were driving holes in his courage. He assessed the situation and accepted Alexander's advice, but found himself facing a number of questions within. Had he accepted this advice out of fear, or out of a concern for his friend's house and property? He couldn't say. Earlier, he had agreed to walk out with Laughton and face the crowd lest he look like a thief; now he was being forced to leave in disguise very much like a thief! He couldn't help laughing at himself.

An Indian soldier lent him his uniform, which he put on. A Madrasi turban on his head (Balasundaram had taught him how to tie one), with a helmet on top. Two detectives accompanied him and they filed out of the rear entrance. They passed through a number of lanes to arrive at a shop. Leaving the shop from the rear, they negotiated their way through the crowd to arrive at the corner of a lane. A car stood there ready to take Mohandas away. From the end of the road, where it stood, the car took a circuitous route to arrive at the same police station where only a short while ago Alexander had proposed Gandhi to take shelter for the night. Mohandas laughed and followed the soldiers quietly.

When Mohandas was putting on his disguise, Alexander was busy singing with the crowd: 'We'll hang him from the sour apple tree!' The crowd was quite carefree. When the Police Captain was with them, nothing could stop them, they thought. After all, it was a question of white solidarity. But Alexander's eyes were searching the scene ceaselessly. One of the two detectives caught his eye and signalled to show that the task had been accomplished.

Alexander stopped singing, climbed on to something and addressed the singing and dancing crowd: 'What is it you want?'

They all cried in unison: 'We want Gandhi!'

'What are you going to do with him?'

'We will hang him from the sour apple tree. Or we will burn him to cinders.'

'If he doesn't come out.'

'... we'll burn the house down!'

'Gandhi and Rustomji Parsi have their wives and their kids too in the house. They have done you no harm. Won't you disgrace yourself killing innocents?'

'The responsibility will be yours. We don't wish to harm anyone. We only want Gandhi. If you don't hand us Gandhi, others are bound to get caught up in the crossfire. You can't hold us responsible for that.'

Alexander laughed and said: 'The game is over. The bird has flown. Now everyone can go home.'

Everyone shouted in unison: 'We want Gandhi.'

Some of them thought Alexander was joking and that this was the latest prank in his series of pranks that had included singing and dancing. Others told him pointblank: 'You are lying.'

'Fine,' said Alexander, 'If you don't trust me, send two of your men with me. They can search the place. If you find Gandhi, you can take him away and do whatever you wish with him. If you don't find him, you must leave this place. I do not want Rustomji's property damaged and his family hurt in any way just because of one man.'

The crowd agreed to send two of their leaders with the Police Captain. They searched the whole house thoroughly, including cupboards, large boxes, bathrooms, and so on. Gandhi was nowhere to be found. They couldn't figure out where he could have gone. He had entered the house before their eyes and now he was nowhere. They went up and down and right and left and finally came out dejected.

'Gandhi has fled,' they announced to the crowd.

A roar went up, and then another, till the roar lost steam and people started slipping away in ones and twos. If Gandhi himself had left, what was the point in their staying on?

They held Alexander responsible for the fiasco. 'It's the Police Superintendent's trick,' they said.

'If he didn't have a hand in it, would he tell us? He sang and danced with us, but he also made sure that Gandhi escaped.'

'When he received the signal, he stopped singing and dancing and went back to being a Police Superintendent.' Everyone was expressing his opinion.

'We were going to hang Gandhi from the sour apple tree. Instead, Gandhi has left us hanging upside down.'

They laughed, but it was a sheepish laugh.

~

News of the incident reached Chamberlain in London. From Colonial Secretary, Chamberlain had now become Home Secretary. He immediately sent a telegram to the government of Natal: those who had attacked must be immediately arrested and prosecuted. The news spread throughout Natal like wild fire. The British government, which ruled the world, was so solicitous about a coolie! Down with the British government!

As soon as he received the telegram, Escombe sent for Gandhi. It was January 20. Escombe was unusually polite. He stood up to receive Gandhi, offered him a seat close to him and said: 'Even a scratch on you is a matter of shame and sorrow for me. You accepted Mr. Laughton's advice and you had to go through all this. It was of course your privilege to accept the advice you thought best. If you had followed my advice, perhaps we could have avoided the unfortunate incident. I now have only one request to make of you. Please help us identify those who attacked you so that we can get them punished. Lord Chamberlain also desires that the rioters and the attackers should be penalized.'

The Congress had also been pressing Mohandas to file a complaint against the attackers. If they were allowed to go scot-free, such elements would only feel encouraged and they would step up their attacks on us, it said. Life for Indians would become that much more difficult. Mohandas had listened to all such talk quietly, without even once opening his mouth. But now he had to respond to Escombe.

'I am not in favour of any prosecutions. It's not that I won't be able to identify at least a few of them, but I am not interested in getting anyone punished. What would that get me? It'll only intensify the feeling of revenge, which will mean more harm coming my way. In fact, I don't consider the attackers responsible at all for the attack.'

Escombe looked surprised, but he said nothing. Mohandas continued: 'They had been told that I vilified the Natal whites in India; that I had given speeches against them. It's no surprise that they took those things to be true and got annoyed and angry. Please excuse me if I say that the really responsible people are their leaders, the newspapers and you. You could have explained the facts to them, but you instead took the Reuter message to be true and took it for granted that Gandhi had spoken ill of you in India. I'm sure that when they get to know the truth, they will be ashamed at the way they behaved.'

There was an obvious look of relief on Escombe's face. He asked: 'Can you give it to me in writing? I'm answerable to my seniors, you know. You can consult Mr. Laughton, if you so wish. All that I can say now is that if you forgive them, it will be easier for me to restore peace and, of course, your prestige will be enhanced. Your reaction will come as a complete surprise to them.'

The injuries still hurt Mohandas. He smiled and said: 'Thank you for the suggestion, but I have no need to consult anyone. I had made up my mind even before I came here that I was not going to press charges against anyone. They were only doing what they had been told.'

Escombe looked at him as if he was setting eyes on Mohandas for the first time.

Mohandas took a sheet of paper from Escombe and wrote:

I wish the misbehaviour of some people towards me last Wednesday to be ignored. A misunderstanding was created among the Europeans here by the things I said to my people in India about the sufferings of Asians in this country. The incidents on Wednesday were a direct result of this misunderstanding. The people present at the time of the incidents are only as much to blame as others who were not. The Water Police had advised me to step out of the ship only after dark and in the supervision of the Port Superintendent. However, I accepted the advice of Mr. Laughton and, on my own responsibility, chose to go on foot. I also did not inform the Water Police of my decision.

Mohandas read what he had written and handed over the sheet to Mr. Escombe. Though his hands held the paper, Escombe's eyes were on Mohandas' face, which looked to him like the face of a small child. As Mohandas got up to leave, he stood up to shake hands with him and his eyes followed him long after he had left the room.

~

Mohandas had to spend three nights in the Borough Police Station. His family was at Rustomji Parsi's place. Durban, in the meantime, had returned almost to normal. The Police Superintendent of course had a role to play in this but the local newspapers had also made their contribution.

The *Natal Advertiser* reporter was on the ship as soon as the yellow flag had been lowered. The first thing he did was to corner Mohandas: 'You vilified Natal whites in India and dragged their reputation in mud?'

Mohandas had been eating something. He did not stop and said quite firmly: 'Totally wrong.'

'How do we know you are speaking the truth?'

'That is up to you. Truth is the hardest to accept. You may not accept it today, but tomorrow you will. I am in no hurry either.'

'Do you have any proof?'

'Neither do they. I don't have to give any proof, but, for peace and tranquility in Durban, I am ready to give you proof.'

Mohandas thought of Sir Pherozeshah. His advice to get the speech written and printed now seemed steeped in foresight. Had he not insisted on getting the speech written, Mohandas would have had no proof today whatsoever. 'All the speeches that I delivered at Bombay, Pune and Madras are available in the written form, and I can let you have copies,' he said.

'And the much talked-about *Green Pamphlet*?'

'That too ...'

Mohandas handed over copies of all the speeches and documents to the *Natal Advertiser* reporter and told him: 'If you still cannot bring out the truth, I can only sympathize with you.'

'Why do you want to settle Indians here? What was the necessity of bringing with you two shiploads of them?'

Mohandas laughed: 'Why didn't you ask the disembarking Indians whether they were here out of their own will or whether they had been brought here?' he said. 'I didn't know a single one of them before I got on to the ship. It was only after I was on the ship that I learnt that many of them were actually residents of Natal and many were going on to Transvaal, which offers better job opportunities than does Natal.'

The reporter sat a little confused for some time and then got up and left. A couple of days later the newspapers carried the message: 'Gandhi was blameless. Great injustice was done to him by the people of Natal by attacking him without first finding out the truth. Despite this, Gandhi flatly refused to take the government's advice to him to press charges against the attackers.'

For a long time after the incident, whites averted their eyes whenever they passed Gandhi on the road.

~

Mohandas' successful escape from the jaws of death had proved beneficial not only for his reputation but also for his profession as a lawyer. People had started looking on Indians with a new sense of respect. They had begun to feel that Indians too could stand up for truth and self-respect when situation demanded it. With the number of cases coming his way increasing, his load of work also went up. The most important of his preoccupations was of course his social work. This had another aspect too. When a person begins to show some spine, and when it begins to appear that he is beginning to develop awareness of his identity, he is promptly labelled as subversive by the authority. The authority prefers to deal with bowed necks, stooped shoulders and dragging feet. Soon after the incident, the government moved two bills in quick succession in the House. One of them affected the Indian traders directly, the second related to the immigration of Indians. The two bills had considerably increased the volume of Mohandas' work, though no bill had so far been able to put into effect any colour-based discrimination against Indians.

Another achievement during Mohandas' absence had been the raising of a one-thousand-pound fund by Adamji Khan. The whites were quite upset by this development. After the failed demonstration against the Indian passengers aboard the two ships, and the attack on Mohandas, the fund went up to five thousand pounds. The Congress Party had bought some property with this money. A regular source of income had also been arranged. A result of all this was that the availability of time with Mohandas was now somewhat like availability of food with a poor man or visibility of the sun during the rainy season. The most affected were Kastur and the kids. He had no time when they could see him or talk to him. Strangers in a foreign land, they didn't know how else to spend their time.

Children's education was another major concern. Gokaldas was the oldest of the kids: must have been ten or eleven. Hari was nine, Mani five. Had he so wished, he could have got them admission in a European school, but that would have meant incurring obligation of the whites. It was also not certain if white children would allow them into the school. If Indians were having a hard time surviving in a large country, anything could happen in a small school. These schools anyway had no Indian kids. There were, of course, some Mission Schools, but Christianity had such a strong presence in these schools that Mohandas did not think it proper to send his kids to them. The medium of education in those schools was English; some may have been imparting a little of inadequate Tamil or Hindi, if at all. Mohandas was of the opinion that a wrong initiation into the world of language could cripple a kid permanently. Finally, after a lot of deliberation, Mohandas decided to educate the children himself.

Mohandas failed to maintain regularity in his instruction. If he got involved in some other activity, children's education was the first casualty. The kids would be waiting for *Bapu* to turn up and start teaching, but he would go missing. As a result, the kids could neither study nor go out to play. This made Kastur real mad. She knew the misfortune of those who could not study. And she made it a point to make it known.

'If you had no arrangement for the kids' education, why did you drag all of us here? They were at least getting some education at home. What are they getting here? Education too is gone. Father's care was never on the cards, neither then, nor now. Of course, once in twenty-four hours, they are granted a glimpse of the father.'

Mohandas tried hard to explain: 'It's not that I don't care for my kids' education, but I am helpless. I'm sure something will turn up soon.'

'Like hell something will turn up soon. Where do you have the time for the kids in the midst of your busy schedule? Millstones round your neck, that's what we are.'

'Of course not. I must first do what I'm staying here for, mustn't I? And I do do other things too, don't I?'

'Enough! If you had to do what you were staying here for, why didn't you let us be where we were? We didn't ask to be carried here like bundles to be deposited in your warehouse.'

Mohandas had no choice but to shut up. He had finally concluded that the best way of dealing with Kastur's annoyance was by keeping his mouth shut. The hope to win a slanging match with Kastur with your next riposte was like a gambler's hope to win the stakes with his next bet—prelude to an endless chain of losses. He kept up the accompaniment for some length, but eventually abandoned his instrument and stood aside. A little later, Kastur had to cease her aria too.

Eventually, a good teacher to teach Gujarati was found, but English remained a problem. Mohandas put out an ad in the papers: 'Wanted a teacher to teach English to three Indian kids.' The word 'Indian' was a deliberate choice. The ad produced results and a lady to teach English was found at seven pounds a month. She started her English classes, while Mohandas taught the remaining subjects himself whenever he found time. The kids' Gujarati improved largely as a result of its use with *Ba* and *Bapu* in day to day conversation, but English continued to be a problem. Sometimes Mohandas wondered if it would not be better to send the kids back to Rajkot, but then he thought that it was wrong to separate the kids from the parents during their growing days. Moreover, they had anyway been living separately so far. Gokaldas had of course been separated from his parents by fate.

Many questions about the education of children bothered Mohandas. Should he give them school education or should he teach them at home? Will home education develop the necessary discipline in them? He thought of his own childhood. When his father was ill, he still had to attend games classes compulsorily. Once he had to pay a fine on that account, though it was not his fault. He hadn't lied. He could see in his mind's eye, clear as a picture: Mohan standing like a criminal before Principal Jimmy. But, despite all that, Mohandas thought that home education would be the best for his kids. School would give them a coolie complex. The white kids would make their lives miserable.

His friends often asked him: 'What was the harm if the kids got some formal education?' What right did he have to stand in the way of their education? How would the kids make a career without degrees? He did not think the objections had any merit. For him the major question was: 'What should be the objectives of children's education? Should it be self-respect and independence, or degrees and career? He was inclined to accept the first alternative. The pinch of slavery which he sometimes felt within him, the pinch against which he had to put up a constant struggle, was a result of the education that he had received in that kind of ambience. He wanted to spare his kids that kind of mentality. Education without self-respect and independence, or no education—they were both the same to him: little more than lumps of earth, producing clockwork dollies that need winding up before they can use their own legs. He found it hard to explain this to others. These were things one could not point out to others as proofs, as one could point out a tower or a river. Mohandas kept quoting these arguments to himself. At times he felt he was losing the argument; at other times he seemed to be coming out on top.

~

That day, Mohandas was at home, sitting alone in the balcony of his Beach Grove villa, when he noticed that a man had been walking up and down in front of the house for quite some time. He was walking with a limp and his hands seemed to have no fingers.

Mohandas called him and asked him: 'What's the problem? Why are you pacing up and down here?'

He said nothing. Mohandas asked him again.

'I have leprosy. Everyone avoids me. No one is willing to treat me. I don't know what to do and where to go. My master removed me from his service even before the *girmit* had run out. No one is ready to listen to me.' His tears had dried up.

Mohandas offered him a seat and arranged for some medicines. He dressed his wounds and arranged a meal for him.

He said: 'Where do I go? I have no one to go to. The ones I can go to won't even look at me.'

Mohandas offered him some living space in his own house. When he returned from the court, the first thing he did was to attend to his wounds and saw to it that he was properly fed. Though Kastur was not happy with this decision of Mohandas and often spoke harshly, everyone got his meals on time in her dispensation.

Though his health improved, the leprosy showed no signs of diminishing. His body gave out a kind of foul smell. Kastur was worried about the kids since the disease was contagious. When her worry mounted, she could not help speaking out: 'Finding time for the kids' studies is a problem for you, but let anyone catch you miss a session with his wounds! That's something you never forget.'

Mohandas said: 'He is a fellow countryman. He has no one here to call his own.'

'Neither do we. The one we had has already deserted us for others. What did we get by coming here?'

It was not as if Mohandas had no appreciation of Kastur's suffering. But the question that bothered him was that of his fellow countrymen who were being forced to lead a hellish life in a strange and unfamiliar land. No one knew anyone. When you are in a foreign land, even the slightest hint of recognition in the other's eye gives you strength. If you are in trouble or in pain, that hint becomes your blessing and cure. After all, trouble and pain could come to anyone unannounced and anyone in pain had the first claim on our service. Mohandas was however becoming conscious that he might not be able to entertain his guest much longer. Questions concerning him that he saw floating in the eyes of Kastur and the kids were becoming too probing to ignore. He was beginning to realize that a man's will power too could be pushed into a corner.

One day, Mohandas sent for the ambulance and took the man to a hospital. This hospital treated *girmitiya*s. When Mohandas rose to leave, the man's sunken eyes turned moist. He couldn't utter a word, but he raised and folded the stumps that were his hands. All Mohandas could do was to pat him on the shoulders and walk out silently. All the night, and for many days to follow, his stump-like hands, shorn of fingers, kept swimming before his eyes. Behind those joined stumps, the shadow of a question grew larger and larger: 'Would you, Mohandas, have walked out of your responsibility leaving one of your near relatives in this condition?' This question kept cropping up before him in different forms in different contexts, but every time it remained unanswered.

Sometimes, an unsteady answer did rise to the surface: 'Mohandas, only service to others can get you relief.' Service, he felt, was beckoning to him.

When he thought of service, memories of *Bapu* flooded his mind. How pleasurable were those moments! He thought of Principal Jimmy: an immaculately white man with a shining, ruddy face! How petty had the punishment given to him by Principal Jimmy seemed to him when he thought of those pleasurable moments of service? Only one memory stuck out like a sore thumb. *Ba* told him stories of ancient saints who strayed from the path of virtue and had to undergo penance. He too had strayed like the saints. The penance: he lost his first child. That pain refused to go. The service he had rendered to Vrindaban Das had helped him in his penance too. He remembers how all his evil emotions—envy, jealousy, anger and whatever else he had—had resolved themselves in those moments of service.

The moments of service spent with the helpless victim of leprosy—how pleasurable they were! The sweet fragrance of service suppressed the foul odour of his wounds. Kastur had never been able to understand this pleasure; but then she had not been able to understand him either.

The music of service constantly plucked at Mohandas' heartstrings. One day, he made it to Dr. Booth's, who was the Director of St. Adams Mission Hospital. A kindly soul overflowing with a sense of service to humanity. Mohandas told him: 'I have sinned twice by breaking my vow of service. The first time, I left my ill father's bedside to seek pleasure in my wife's arms, and my father died. The second time, I brought a leper home to tend to him and then broke my vow again by getting him admitted to hospital. The word service keeps echoing in my ears all the time. I want to listen to it and to redeem myself of the sin of breaking my vow of service.'

Dr. Booth looked at Mohandas and discovered a strange glow of penance on his face. He asked: 'What do you want of me, Mr. Gandhi? I am with you.'

'You would probably know my friend Rustomji Parsi. He has a religious endowment, what you could call a Trust. I have talked to him.

The Trust runs a library, and also helps needy people. When I suggested to him that the Trust could also run a hospital, he was delighted and said: "Gandhibhai, you can do whatever you wish. There is no greater service than service of the sick. Service to the ailing humanity is service to God." So we have set up a hospital. I want you to come and take a look at it.'

Dr. Booth joined Mohandas and looked at the hospital. He was very pleased to see the equipment that had been collected for the treatment of patients. He had not expected anyone who was not a doctor to be able to collect such equipment on his own. Medicines were arranged with the help of Dr. Booth and the hospital started functioning.

Dr. Booth devoted his morning hours to the hospital and because of him the number of patients visiting the hospital shot up very quickly. The way Dr. Booth examined his patients, it felt as if he was caressing a child, so soft was his touch. The way he treated his patients, they felt the disease would never visit them again. Treating patients was an addiction with Dr. Booth. He would go anywhere, any time, to see a patient.

Mohandas often visited the hospital. One day he spoke to the doctor: 'Doctor, as a child I so much wanted to be a doctor, but my father refused as my medical education would have involved dissecting frogs and other animals and that would have meant violence. So my wish remained unfulfilled. Could I work as a male nurse with you? That way, I'd be able to do what I wanted to—to serve, to do penance and to fulfil my dreams. Unfortunately, however, I can only spare little time.'

Dr. Booth laughed: 'You should have been a doctor. A desire to serve others is an essential prerequisite for a doctor. But you had this hospital opened—that itself is service enough.'

'The credit for that goes to Rustomji. All I can offer is this body of mine ...'

'How much time can you spare?'

'A couple of hours everyday.'

'Good. Please come in the morning and help prepare medicines for the patients. There is another important task to do—that of an interpreter. I don't understand the language of these people, which creates a problem for the patients. You could be the solution. Nurses are of course required all the twenty-four hours. It should be gratifying for you to perform such important work as nursing for a couple of hours.'

Mohandas' work as a lawyer was done mostly in his chamber. Court visits were rarely required. Most of his cases were truth based, requiring no deceit or dissimulation. Mohandas had brought Mr. Rahim Karim Khan with him from London and he worked as his assistant. He looked after all the court work in his absence. Mohandas now left his chamber in his charge and turned himself into Dr. Booth's assistant. He would leave home early on foot and was in the hospital at the appointed time. The *girmitiya* labourers started queuing up quite early. Mohandas worked like a machine. He listened to the patients' complaints, explained them to Dr. Booth, prepared medicines according to his prescriptions, explained their usage to the patients, kept the accounts and completed all this work in a space of two hours. The majority of patients were Telugu, Tamil or Hindi speaking. Mohandas just about managed Telugu and Tamil. He was discovering a new truth about life: 'What great relief it can be for a man in trouble to be barely understood! You figure out the pain a man has and you are his brother!' Mohandas had begun to realize that there was no stronger foundation for friendship than adversity.

The hospital was more than an institution for Mohandas. It was an instrument of change within him. The change was no delusion. It was more like a lapse of consciousness. This lapse was causing a lot of damage within him. When he saw the condition in which the patients turned up at the hospital, his eyes turned to look within himself. Were they very different from him? How different were they? Were not the body, the bones, flesh, marrow, breath, feelings good and bad, the same? Weren't the differences confined to the skin, to the food they ate and the ways they lived? Mohandas could not find any differences between him and the *girmitiya*s, except in clothes. Everything else was the same.

These questions started following him home. Mohandas had spent a lot of care doing up his home. It was for the first time he had the opportunity to use his own money to decorate his home. His life was now on track for an easy and comfortable living and he began to get an uncomfortable feeling of getting trapped in a spider web growing all around him.

Mohandas scrutinized his expenses on clothing. Getting his clothes laundered in the laundry everyday was a huge waste. Those people perhaps couldn't afford to get their clothes washed even once a week, but for him two or three dozen shirt and collar sets also proved insufficient. Maybe a shirt could last three days, but the collar had to be changed everyday. That must stop right away. Higher income should not mean higher waste. 'Why don't you wash your own clothes?' Mohandas thought, 'Working with your own hands doesn't make you good or bad; maybe it makes you good, but certainly never bad.Wash your own clothes.'

But how?

Mohandas went out and bought a book and made a deep study. He also read it out to Kastur. It told you how to iron the clothes and stiffen them with starch, and so on. He was going to have to take a lot of battering internally in his drive to wear home-washed clothes. The fear of getting isolated in the bar was causing him concern. These little experiences not only battered you internally, they also set you on a different trajectory from the others. His first experiment was with the collar. He washed it, applied starch to stiffen it, and then used a coal-fired iron to press it. This was his first venture in the laundry business. He had no idea how hot the iron needed to be. Apprehensive of burning the collar, he used an iron much below the required degree of heat. The result, therefore, despite the very conscientious ironing effort, was an extra stiff collar. He thought of washing the collar again and applying a hotter iron, but dismissed the thought out of hand and wore the collar to the court. He could himself feel his neck jutting out of the stiff collar like a gargoyle.

One of the white lawyers stopped him on the way and asked: 'You didn't, by any chance, leave your collar in a flour bin, did you?'

Another lawyer commented: 'Your collar seems to be no less miraculous than your Indian folktales. It sheds flour.'

Mohandas knew what they were driving at. Lack of experience had resulted in over-application of starch. But, without batting an eyelid, he retorted: 'This is my first experience of washing and starching the collar myself. That's what is causing it to shed powder. But it doesn't bother or embarrass me. In fact I am happy that it is causing mirth to you.'

'Is the city running short of laundries that you had to take the trouble yourself?'

'No, no, there are laundries aplenty. The point is that what you spend on washing a collar costs you more than the collar itself. And you not only spend on the laundry but are also at the mercy of the launderers. This way, you can get rid of both the nuisances. If you want to be free, reduce your dependence on others, that's the motto. The less you depend on others, the more independent you become.'

Everyone around gave a big laugh. One white whispered to the other: 'That must take the prize for the century's stupidest remark.'

Another one remarked: 'They are born eccentrics anyway. You can take a horse to water, but can't make him drink. You can never teach them cleanliness.'

Mohandas sat silently. Perhaps he didn't hear what was said. But the rest of them had smiles on their faces.

~

The Indian community was witnessing some improvement in its condition. A new look of respect for Indians could be seen in some white faces. The community was seeking help from all quarters to improve its status and Mohandas had an important role to play in this effort. During his trip to India, Mohandas had made every category of people, from the common man to top leaders, aware of the situation of Indians in Natal. England held sway over both the colonies—India as well as Natal. London called the tunes to which the colonies danced. Naturally everyone had to keep his lines with London open. A committee of Indian National Congress, called the British Committee, was functioning in London. Though Natal Congress had nothing to do with the British Committee, Mohandas maintained contact with the Committee. Every week a letter went to Dadabhai Naoroji. Sir William Bederburn was the Chairman of the British Committee. Whenever it was felt that it might be necessary to send copies of the letter to others as well, a sum of ten pounds was also remitted so that the British Committee did not have to bear the expense.

At first, the idea was to send the money also to Sir Pherozeshah. He could send it to Sir Bederburn, if he saw it fit. Dadabhai Naoroji's reaction was quite contrary to expectations. He returned the money post-haste with the comment that the money as well as the letters, reports etc. should be sent only to Sir Bederburn. He assured them however that he would do everything possible to help the cause of South Africa's immigrant Indians. The regular exchange of letters between Dadabhai Naoroji and Mohandas also continued uninterrupted. It was Dadabhai'scustom to reply to letters by return post, at least an acknowledgement in case the letter didn't require a reply. Usually, though, he tagged on a couple of sentences by way of encouragement. Nor were the letters replied to by his assistant or his secretary. He would write them personally, with a copy going into records.

Mohandas carried out extensive correspondence. He also wrote to people belonging to other parties keeping them updated about the situation of Indians. And he kept Dadabhai informed about the people he wrote to. Leading ones among these were Sir Bhuncharji Bhavnagari and Sir W.W. Hater. Sir Bhuncharji was also a Member of Parliament. He sent in his suggestions regularly. Sir William Wilson Hater was among those who, although they were English, kept up an active involvement with the problems of Indians. He was editor of the Indian section of *The Times.* When he was first sent a letter about the problems of Indians, he showed tremendous interest in them. He wrote to various people to lend their support to the Indians of South Africa. Whenever any important issue cropped up, he did not hesitate to write to Mohandas. Each one of his letters had this refrain: 'You are conducting your campaign with courage and in a peaceful and gentlemanly way. I have never seen you getting excited or angry. I feel that this is a remarkable quality. My sympathies are with you, both in private and in public. It will always be my effort to secure justice for your cause. You should not budge an inch from the positions you take, since your demands are quite just. No right-thinking person should ever ask for any amendment in them.'

As long as Sir William lived, he did not budge an inch from his position.

The way it had sent Mohandas to India, Natal Congress had also sent Mansukhlal Naazar to London to secure support for Indians from various political parties and to enlighten the British about the condition of Indians in South Africa. He had met Hunter, Sir Bhuncharji and a host of retired members of the administrative services. As a result, people from different spheres of life got to know about the problems of South African Indians and the issue rose to the top of their agenda.

While colonial Indians thus awakened to their rights, there was an awakening among the whites too. This awakening was connected to the awakening taking place among colonial Indians. The impending changes were turning into a real cause of fear.

~

XV

Mohandas was fighting on two fronts. There was another battle he was fighting about which no one else knew. It was a battle within, an entirely personal battle. All his own. There was another character in it—a woman, but she didn't know that anyone was fighting with her, or that she was the cause of an inner battle within someone. That woman was Kastur. Mohandas had surrendered himself to her from the very first day of their marriage. He could never put her out of his mind. It was her magnetic attraction that had drawn him away from his father's sick bed. When he had regained his senses, it was too late and there had been nothing left for him to do except regret or penance. He had taken it as his own weakness, though Kastur too had been singed. He had always felt that his wife was an organic part of his pursuit of truth and love. His love for her was reinventing itself after their arrival in South Africa. He was himself a witness to it. How had it come about? Why? A scrutiny was on within him. As far as he could recall, Raychandbhai's had been an important role in shaping his life and personality. In this context, he could never forget an incident that had taken place in his life.

Mohandas was singing high praises of Mrs. Gladstone, wife of the British Prime Minister, in the presence of Raychandbhai. She insisted on preparing tea for her husband even in the House of Commons. This action of hers had bowled Mohandas completely over. Raychandbhai listened to him patiently before finally asking with a smile: 'Tell me, Mohandas, which of the two you value more: the love of Mrs. Gladstone for her husband or her devoted service to him independent of her relation to him?'

It looked from Mohandas' expression that he was struggling to uncover the significance of the question, so Raychandbhai explained: 'Let me put it another way. Suppose, it was his sister, or a devoted servant, who was serving Mr. Gladstone with the same devotion that Mrs. Gladstone displayed, serving him tea personally in the House of Commons. So far as devotion is concerned, a servant's devotion would also be of the same order as Mrs. Gladstone's. Would you then praise the servant's services in the same way as you are now doing for Mrs. Gladstone?'

Raychandbhai got up to leave as he had an appointment to keep. Mohandas followed suit.

Since that day, Mohandas had been thinking about these two situations. Was there a necessary relationship between devoted service and the husband-wife relationship? Which was more important: service or relationship? Though, at the time, what Raychandbhai had said had sounded strange to him, but he had left behind a smoldering question. The point about the servant upset him particularly.

What was the difference between the spirits of service that the two displayed: the servant and the wife? Wasn't the servant's spirit more significant? Husband and wife were joined by a lasting and an inviolable bond of love, and a spirit of service was implicit in love. Mutual surrender and unification of souls—that was the basis of conjugal love. There was no such relationship with a servant. His devotion to his work might be counted as a virtue in a servant, but devotion to his master was neither necessary nor feasible. The seed planted by Raychandbhai in his mind had now burgeoned into a tree. It had virtually become an essential part of his existence. When the branches of the tree shook, Mohandas grew restless. He felt so agitated that no matter what he was doing his mind could think of nothing else. Ever so slowly, he was gravitating towards the conclusion that service and conjugal life were two things apart. Possibly, they led you in two different directions.

Mohandas wasn't happy with the current status of his conjugal life. The question 'What should be the ideal form of conjugal relationship?' loomed like a rock before him. He was also aware that a discussion on this issue had the potential of turning this very personal of issues into a joke. He often asked himself: 'Isn't my union with my wife motivated by lust? If you are a slave to lust, does unification have any meaning?' As lust overcame him, image after image passed before his eyes and he felt being pushed towards a cage. Kastur was not an active partner; no woman is, at least in the beginning. She never played the coquette. Mohandas was active and sometimes he also had to beat a retreat. Possibly, no great purpose inspired him then. Why great, there wasn't a purpose at all. At one time, there was the purpose of service to his father, which too he had failed.

Mohandas was trying to sort himself out. It wasn't as if he didn't know that if he set out on this path he would not only be declaring a war on himself, he would also be making other too, willy-nilly, a part of his war. He removed his bed to another room and stopped sleeping with his wife. He kept busy at work till he was dead tired. He would not go near his bed till he was sure that he would fall dead asleep the moment he hit the bed.

But success eluded him again and again. He lost. Why did he lose?

~

Kastur's fight was at another level. She was puzzled by Mohandas' behaviour. For a time, she kept looking for the key, but when the distance between them went on increasing, she ventured to ask: 'Will you tell me what it's all about? I'm with you all the way, but what accounts for this behaviour of yours: sleeping away from me, returning late at night all done in, and so on? Am I the reason for this behaviour or is there some one else?'

Mohandas thought for a minute and said: 'No, not you. Actually it's me. I wanted to tell you myself, but I have been so busy. There just was no time.'

'I knew that I couldn't be the reason. But then I thought if it's happening to me, I must be in it somewhere.'

'I am happy with the kids we have.'

She looked at him puzzled: 'Did I ever say I wasn't?'

'Sex between husband and wife should be only for the sake of procreation, not pleasure. Otherwise, how would man be different from an animal?'

Kastur couldn't help laughing: 'Did I ever say anything different?'

Mohandas was in free flow now: 'Animals have no sense of time or occasion. Lust also makes us animal. We have now reached a stage when we must learn to differentiate between desire and determination. We must come out of our animal existence. Only determination can help us do it.'

'I know nothing about determination and I don't understand it. All I know is that you draw away, or draw up close, as fancy takes you. I have no role to play. This is perhaps for the first time that we are living together like this. The last time it was in Bombay, but those were hard days and we spent our entire time moving house.'

'That wasn't what I meant, Kastur.'

'I know very well what you meant. You have a tailor's style of sewing up decisions. What a tailor does is to stitch clothes and others have to wear them. Never mind if they are tight or loose. You take decisions and I have to wear them. As for the determination that you are talking about, tell me, does it or does it not require trust, especially with you at the one end and your wife at the other?'

'I don't blame you, Kastur ...' said Mohandas in a hurt tone. 'Losing to yourself again and again can break you. After all, how long can you go on losing to your own lusts?'

Kastur found it all very strange. She had never seen Mohandas get so emotional, not even when *Bapu* had died. 'Doesn't God's will mean anything to you?' she asked.

Mohandas found that his own weaknesses sometimes stood as rocks before him. He tried to dislodge them, but they didn't move an inch. If they are weaknesses, how come they are so hard to move, he wondered.

Kastur continued: 'We are husband and wife, right? Partners in each other's joys and sorrows, victories and defeats? If each one of us labelled the other as the cause of his or her defeat and barricaded ourselves in our respective strongholds, what sort of husband-wife pair would we be? Doesn't what you call determination turn into an ever-tightening noose round the neck of our freedom of behaviour? Is it not like getting tethered to a stake?'

'I have also tried to pacify myself with arguments such as these, but, at the end of the day, they all seem to be excuses only for one thing: how to satisfy your lust.'

'What lust? Whose lust? Have you ever thought of a woman whose husband had always to stay away from home, or who remained so absorbed in his own world of ideas or actions that the wife was as good as there and not there. If there were kids, the father always thought of them as fruits of his lust and nothing else. What's your purpose in telling me all this? You want me to make myself cease to be? Sometimes one does cease to be, but that's usually because of the other. If you were to find a live snake in your path, how would you deal with it? Would you just stand there full of determination?'

'If we didn't know that a bite of the snake meant sure death, neither our determination nor our escape would have any meaning.'

'I have never heard anyone dying of the bite of what you are referring to as a snake. Whatever God has endowed us with, He has given us as a resource for living. If you feel safe living away from me, do so by all means. But remember one thing: I am not the cause of any of your fears and apprehensions.'

She felt, once again, that her husband had travelled far, far away from her.

Mohandas spent a long time thinking about all that had been said. The lines of Nishkulanand kept coming back to him, as they had done so frequently: 'Renunciation won't last without detachment ...'

Renunciation? Renunciation of what? Of his wife or of his lust? Renounce your companion? What sort of principle is this? Kastur is his truth. How can he renounce her? But what about his lust? His lust is an obstacle to truth hanging like a curtain between them.

'No,' he muttered to himself, 'I'll not accept defeat.'

~

The control of the gold mines of Transvaal was in the hands of the British. These British owners of gold mines had been trying to seize control of Johannesburg in the manner in which East India Company had seized control of Indian princes and their princedoms. They figured that President Kruger would not get to know about their conspiracy, and by the time he did, they would have established their hold on Transvaal. He would then be left with no choice except to eat the humble pie. The same subterfuges the British had used in India before 1857 to usurp control of the states, they were now trying in Transvaal. Both Transvaal and Cape Town were Boer kingdoms under the suzerainty of the Dutch.

Kruger however knew of each and every move of the British. The British had led a very secret and silent move against Johannesburg, but the moment the forces of the British traders advanced on Transvaal they came under heavy fire. The mine owners had no idea that such a welcome awaited them in Transvaal. They had been congratulating themselves on their clever strategy: a panther-like movement and Johannesburg would be in their clutches. Once in their grip, there would be nothing for it to do except stay out.

Kruger kept tightening the screws till the mine owners lay down their arms. Their soldiers had been killed and wounded in large numbers. Kruger was not only a general; he was also a skilled diplomat. He released the soldiers but arrested the leaders of the mine owners. Her Majesty's government was badly shaken. Traders of an empire in which the sun never set had been taken prisoner! Kruger's strategy was clear: only make moves which you can sustain.

The Queen's vazirs were on their knees, begging. Kruger knew that the matter wasn't going to end there. The leader of the mine owners, Johnson, was not likely to forget the humiliation in a hurry. Still, he accepted the entreaties of the Queen's ministers and let the mine owners go.

The white traders of Natal had ensured that Indian traders never moved out of the margins where they had been pushed. They were not even allowed to buy a piece of land: Rule There made sure of that. The British traders of course had no dearth of men or money. Many

British lawyers and traders were also ready to take up arms on the side of the British, if need arose. The British soon regrouped and consolidated their resources and declared war. This time round, the war was between the Queen's forces on one side and Kruger's forces on the other.

Indians now found themselves in a difficult position. What should they do? Who should they support? Or should they stay neutral? Many of Mohandas' fellow white lawyers had already joined the war effort. Indians were being subjected to sarcastic comments. Anyone with an opinion, or without one, felt free to let them have it. Mohandas had to put up with a lot of them during the court hours:

'When these coolies want to make money, they think of South Africa. But when South Africa faces a problem, they look the other way.'

'They are like corpses on the nation's shoulders, that is what they are! If you carry them you die of the weight; if you don't, the smell kills you.'

'They are termites eating into the vitals of the nation. An empty shell of a nation is what we will be left with by the time they are done.'

'The country may be surrounded by enemies, but you can hear them fiddling. No donations, no help of any kind!',

'On the contrary, we will have to protect them too!'

It pained Mohandas to listen to the comments. He found himself caught in a cleft stick. He had always thought of the Boers as a proud and brave race, but other Indians did not share his perception. Nor could they afford to, since the nation was now their destiny. One word from them in favour of the Boers and the Indian traders could find their establishments wiped out at one stroke.

An association of Gujarati traders was already functioning consisting of some very experienced traders. It was a different kind of association from the Natal Congress. There was no written constitution. It was called the British Indian Association. A meeting of the Association had been called to consider the Boer War, where people expressed their opinions freely and frankly. Mohandas too was invited.

The majority view was something like this: 'Both the British and the Boers have exploited and harassed us. The situation in this regard is no better in Natal and Cape Town than it was in Transvaal. In all the colonies, our condition is worse than that of slaves. But how can we disregard the fact that a small nation of Boers has taken on a mighty power like Britain? Why should we allow ourselves to become instruments of its destruction? Moreover, if the Boers win the war, they are sure to get back at us.'

Mohandas could well understand their sentiments, but he was also making his own assessment of the situation. He was inclined to think that they should be guided by reason rather than by emotion at a juncture like this. He stood up and voiced his disagreement with the general view: 'We must remember,' he said, 'that whatever situation we find ourselves in today in this country, whether good or bad, is wholly due to the fact that we are subjects of the British Empire.

Time and again, whenever we have sent petitions to the British Indian government, we have stressed the fact that we are its subjects and we therefore expect it to protect our rights. We have said that we are proud of being British subjects. Our rulers too have been assuring us of their protection in that capacity. How many of those assurances have actually been fulfilled is another matter. What we however know for sure is that if our rights can be protected at all, only the British government can do it. Would it be right for us to hail the British government as the protector of our rights on the hand, to declare ourselves to be proud of being its subjects, and, on the other, stand as silent witnesses to its destruction? All because they do not treat us right? We too are guilty of worse than misbehaviour with certain sections of our society in our own country because we think of them as our subjects. I'm afraid the line of thought we are following will land us in difficulties. Actually, we now have an opportunity to prove all the allegations made against us false. If we miss this opportunity, the fault will be ours entirely. Whatever course of action we follow in this country will have its repercussions in the politics of India.'

The audience was amazed to hear Mohandas. Was this Mohandas speaking, they wondered. One of them got up and asked: 'But, Gandhbhai, you are fighting against the British, aren't you?'

'Yes, for our rights. And it's for our rights that we are also with them. We are not powerful enough to secure our rights on our own. If we don't take this opportunity to prove the accusations that are constantly thrown at us to be unfounded, we'll forever be branded as liars and traitors. In that event our lives in this country will become that much more difficult. If we want freedom, we must support the British government in its hour of difficulty. I admit that justice is on the side of Boers, but because we are British subjects our loyalty lies with them. We know that if the Boers win, our lives will become more difficult, but when a soldier joins battle he does not make calculations of victory and defeat, or of life and death. Not even for a moment. At this moment, we are all soldiers.'

Tension was apparent in the faces of many in the audience following Mohandas' speech. A couple of them stood up and protested: 'Let there not be any divorce between our words and our deeds. That will be our undoing. Is it right that we should fight against them here and fight with them on thc front?'

Another one raised a query: 'If the Boers win, will the fact that we did not support the British carry any weight with them?'

'A ruler understands the pain of another ruler, a subject that of another subject. As subjects, we are giving importance to the injustice done to the Boers despite the fact that we are not their subjects, nor do we know them. If the Boers win, they will probably be better at understanding the pain of another ruler. But I still think that we should do what it is right for us to do.'

'But what is it that we can do? We have never handled a weapon before. How can we help them?'

'True. If they want us to march in step with them to the front, they will be disappointed.'

'The whites will use us as coolies, to transport their material.'

'Is it necessary that they will accept our offer of help?'

'These points are all well taken,' said Mohandas, 'but they do not justify any negligence on our part. Let's make an honest effort and God will be with us. Let's not bother about respectable and less respectable varieties of labour. There is no place for such distinctions when the aim is service.'

Mohandas' arguments succeeded in converting dissent into slow assent. In the end, a draft of a letter was arrived at by unanimous consent. It said: 'Many of us are trained as nurses. We can attend to the sick and the injured. We also carry certificates of good health. As subjects of the British Empire, we are ready to offer all cooperation that we are capable of giving.'

As they trudged back from the meeting, their pulses raced at the thought of the kind of service the British government might choose for them.

The proposal from the Indian community offering assistance in the war effort was placed before a high-powered committee. Dr. Booth and Mr. Escombe were also members of the committee. One of the members took a look at the proposal and commented: 'Coolies in a battlefield! Do they have any idea what war is? The first gunshot they hear might ...,' Even before the sentence was completed, everyone burst out laughing.

Another one said: 'They are not made for facing dangers. Selfish cowards! Making money is all they are good for.'

'But when it comes to their selfish interests, they go to any extent.'

Dr. Booth sat listening quietly for some time, but finally he had to intervene: 'I don't agree,' he said. 'I know these people. When they undertake a responsibility, they see it through. I have trained them myself.'

Mr. Laughton also intervened: 'Their courage is well known. The stories don't need retelling.'

Escombe said: 'The proposal they have sent shows great humanity. We should not try to belittle it.'

The final decision was a foregone conclusion, but the language had acquired some decorum. It said: 'Thank you for your proposal.

We regret that we cannot use your services at the present juncture, but when we are in a position to do so, we will certainly get in touch with you again.'

The letter thus shoved the matter under the carpet, good and proper.

The Boer army was on the march and unstoppable. As it crossed new landmarks, worries mounted. What would happen when they reached Durban? More and more soldiers were getting killed and injured. The problem of looking after injured soldiers was assuming serious proportions. The British army was the worse affected.

Mohandas told the British India Association: 'Though the British government has rejected our offer of help once, we should repeat the offer since they are truly in need of help now.'

So the BIA repeated the offer. It said: 'Our earlier offer of help stands. If we can extend any aid to the injured soldiers, we will be happy to do so.'

After the letter had been dispatched, Mohandas met the Bishop of Natal with a letter from Dr. Booth. He explained the whole matter to the Bishop. He explained that an offer had already been sent, that the aim of the BIA was only to attend to the wounded soldiers and to do its duty by the British government by extending its cooperation to it in its moment of difficulty, that the medical contingent would include people of all religions like Hindus, Muslims, Parsis, Christians, etc., that they had all undergone formal training in first aid and were ready and waiting to receive the orders, and so on. The padre gave a patient listening to Mohandas and said: 'Service blesses both: for the giver it is the grace of God, for the receiver it is the nectar itself. I'll do all I can to help you.'

The war flared up further. Pressure on the British forces was mounting. The number of wounded soldiers kept going up. A letter from the Bishop of Natal had also reached the authorities. There was a detachment of British Ambulance Services in the battle zone but it confined its services to white soldiers only. In the end, an invitation from the government did land up in the office of the British India Association. Mohandas looked upon it as another opportunity to serve humanity. The scope of his service to humanity had now extended from his father and brother-in-law to the country and the world.

He sat there for a long while with his eyes closed.

~

The ambulance contingent consisted of eleven hundred young men. It included lawyers and accountants. Some of them were manual workers like masons, carpenters, technicians, among others. Three hundred of them were free citizens, the rest *girmitiya*s. There were Hindus, Muslims, Tamils, Gujaratis, Christians, Parsis, in fact, representatives from almost every section of the society. Traders were not directly involved. As for *girmitiya*s, who would normally not be allowed to take off from work even for their own death, they had been released from slavery for a few days to serve in the cause of national security.

Dr. Booth led the contingent personally. The contingent was fully equipped and rearing to go. It was being provided the rations by the army but they were not enough to cover its needs. That was where the Indian traders played an important role. Indirectly, they had come to assume an important responsibility by pooling together their resources to supply provisions to the contingent. The *girmitiya*s were; in fact, ready to work even if they had to go without food, for they had convinced themselves that working for the ambulance team was a pious act. If they were happy despite the conditions, it was because this single fact weighed the most with them.

Initially only free Indians and *girmitiya*s released from their contracts were permitted to enrol in the contingent. When permission was sought again to include *girmitiya*s, it was denied on the ground that as the *girmitiya*s were unclean themselves, they could not be trusted to clean others. Mohandas had raised serious objection to this argument. Service to others runs in the blood of Indians, he had argued and the government had finally come round.

When the eleven-hundred strong contingent set out for Transvaal, the hearts of the members were jumping for joy. For the first time in their lives, they had been invited to perform a respectable duty. Their enthusiasm for the work of service they were going to do had lent a spring to their step. There was admiration for them in the eyes of the persons who had come to see them off. For the first time in their lives, the *girmitiya*s were seeing a sense of respect and admiration for them in the eyes of people who normally had nothing but kicks and blows to give them. There were some white masters among those who had gathered there to bid them farewell. There were many who had brought sweets for them. Escombe, who was the head of the European Voluntary Force, had sent his greetings.

The Durban papers were astonished that a force had been raised in such a short a time to attend to the wounded and the sick by people who had always been considered to be sick and lazy. One of the papers published a poem in praise of them by an Englishman:

We are sons of this Empire.
We will lay down our lives
To save the honour of the Queen!

Discrimination had also followed the Indian contingent into the battlefield. It was not allowed to enter the fire zone. Government ambulances transported the sick and the wounded to the place where it was stationed and it took over from there. The European ambulances had a deeper access to the battle zone, though both contingents were temporary formations. This discrimination pained Mohandas and his friends and they raised the issue with the authorities off and on. What was the fear behind the denial of permission to the Indian ambulance corps to enter the battle zone, they asked. Did they fear that the corps would not be able to perform its duties effectively, or would take to its heels at the sound of firing? But while they asked these questions, they also continued to perform their duties with absolute sincerity. It was indeed no small wonder that the European ambulance team had been working in tandem with the Indian team without any sense of discrimination. One reason for this might have been that the Indian ambulance corps was led by Dr. Booth. Mohandas was number two in the team.

Dr. Booth had great affection for the Indian volunteers. Many of these volunteers had been trained by Dr. Booth himself. No wonder the enthusiasm of the Indian team knew no bounds.

Ladysmith was a dangerous battle area where a fierce battle was raging. The forces were being led by General White. The number of wounded was showing a constant rise. General Buller pulled some wires and obtained permission for the Indian contingent to visit Ladysmith. It was a remote place and the base hospitals were at considerable distances from the battle areas, ranging from seven to twenty-five miles. There were no roads to speak of. Transporting the wounded to the base hospitals was an uphill task for the Indian ambulance corps.

Mohandas deployed all members of his team in the task of transporting the wounded soldiers to the hospitals. They had to walk eight to ten miles carrying the patients; sometimes even twenty-five miles.

Dressed in the army uniform, Gandhibhai lifted the stretcher from the front while others took it up from the side or the rear. Periodically, Gandhi would also check the condition of the patient. Sometimes the condition of the patient did not allow speedy movement, while slow walk proved very tiring. But the bearers switched hands and kept up their walk. They started at eight in the morning and were required to reach the base hospital before five in the evening. A white injured officer always complained and protested more than the others. Sometimes the volunteers ran out of water but they would still not cease their march.

The British had suffered considerable loss of lives and material at the defeat of Spion Kop. There were a very large number of wounded soldiers and evacuating them from the battle zone presented serious problems. British officers finally had to lift their embargo on the entry of the ambulance corps in the firing zone. General Buller called Mohandas and told him that they were free to enter the firing zone.

'Thanks, General Buller,' said Mohandas.

'I didn't want your men to come to any harm. Even now, if your men are unwilling, we will not force them to go to the forward areas. We are aware that they have no experience of operating in battle zones.'

'When it is a matter of doing his duty, an Indian doesn't think twice about his own life. You can rest assured that none of my volunteers will evade his duty for fear of his life.' Mohandas said.

General Buller stood up, shook his hand and said: 'I can see that for myself. I don't for a moment doubt what you have said.'

There was a change in the attitude of everyone towards the Indian volunteers, especially the *girmitiya*s, be it the white soldier or his officer or volunteers of the European Ambulance Corps, their faces now showed a certain respect and their behaviour was touched with politeness. The attitude of disrespect and disregard was being replaced by an attitude of friendliness. Members of the Indian corps were feeling greatly enthused by this change. They were beginning to look upon dangers as part of their duties. Mohandas often exhorted them: 'The mightiest rock of danger will dissolve like salt in the contact of selfless service.'

~

It was pitch dark. Flashes of artillery fire occasionally lit up the battlefield. Torches in hand, members of the Indian ambulance teams were going around looking for the injured and the wounded. The artillery fire inspired majesty and awe as it found its targets. Flashes of fire blinded the eyes while the roar of the guns deafened the ears. One of the teams heard someone groaning. It stopped and tried to locate the direction from where the groan had come. A big soldier lay soaked in blood and crying in pain. The pain was intolerable and he was flailing his head from side to side. The team picked him up promptly, placed him on the stretcher and attended to his wounds in the light of torches and shell fire. After a preliminary dressing of the wounds with the help of whatever limited material they carried in their First Aid Box, they made double-quick time to the Base Hospital. The patient had already lost a lot of blood and was losing consciousness fast.

One of the ambulance men said: 'Looks like enemy personnel to me!'

Mohandas turned towards him and said: 'Our vow is to protect the wounded and provide relief to the sick. He may be enemy personnel, but he is a soldier. And he has been wounded in battle. Relief to every wounded soldier—that is our duty.'

No one spoke after this. Rotating hands and shoulders, the volunteers kept up their silent trot. They walked so fast that they were at the base hospital in less than the average time.

Dawn was breaking, spilling red over the eastern sky. When the volunteers of the Indian Ambulance Corps appeared at the hospital, only emergency staff was on duty. Mohandas informed the nurse on duty that a soldier in a serious condition was waiting and needed urgent attention. The moment the doctor and the nurse set eyes on the soldier, a storm hit the hospital. The doctor, an army man, promptly saluted the wounded soldier, who was of course in no condition to return the salute. Suddenly, a host of other doctors also appeared from nowhere on the scene. It was for the first that the ambulance men had seen so much fuss being made over a wounded soldier. They were truly curious to know who the great man could be.

As Mohandas stepped out of the hospital with his men after handing over their charge, the Officer Commanding of the hospital came up and stood before him. Mohandas looked at him with scant interest. 'Thank you, Mr. Gandy. The life of General Woodgate is a precious one for us. We are indeed grateful to the Indian ambulance team for getting him to the hospital alive and in a reasonably good condition.'

Mohandas had heard of General Woodgate; today he had also got to see him in person. But what a state he was in! He closed his eyes and muttered to himself: 'Thank you, God, for rescuing us from the slough of hostility.'

~

In addition to the English population, Ladysmith also had a few Indians, some of whom were traders. The rest were *girmitiya*s, railway workers and flunkeys in the attendance of white sahibs.

The war had taken a serious turn. The number of the dead and the wounded kept on rising. It was now clear that civilian help had to be called for. The Commanding Officer carried out allotment of work to civilians. There was a *girmitiya* called Prabhu Singh, whom the English called Coolie Prabhu Singh. There was a hillock just outside Ladysmith standing on which one could see the entire expanse of the battleground. Boers had put up a pom-pom, quick-firing two-pounder cannon, on top of the hillock. Shells from pom-pom took a couple of minutes to reach the target. If they received timely warning, people could make it to their safe havens in good time. The two-pounder had already caused a lot of damage. Many buildings had been levelled and not a few lives lost.

Prabhu Singh had been posted on a tree. He kept himself well-hidden in the leaves even as his eyes were fixed on the cannon. The moment a spark flew off the muzzle of the cannon, he would sound the gong. People ran to their shelters the moment they heard the gong.

Prabhu Singh carried out his duty with extraordinary sincerity and unfailing regularity. He never failed in his performance. If ever anyone failed to reach the shelter, he was blown to bits and Coolie Prabhu Singh always felt he had been slow in sounding the gong. His attempt was to see that the spark and the gong went off together. He had fine-tuned his eye-hand coordination to such a degree that he worked as an automaton. He knew that he faced the maximum danger: a single hit on the tree would have flattened the tree along with him. But he had cast that idea out of his mind completely, as if neither the cannon, nor his life, held any significance for him.

The news of Prabhu Singh's bravery reached the ears of the Indian Viceroy, Lord Curzon. He called a meeting of his officers, who advised him against giving any importance to a coolie, since it would pose a problem for the government of the South African colony.

Lord Curzon was however of the view that honouring an Indian citizen, a British subject, who had saved the lives of so many other British subjects, at grave peril to his own life, would only strengthen the loyalty of Indians towards the British government. So he sent a Kashmiri robe and a testimonial of bravery to Prabhu Singh. The Mayor of Durban was entrusted the responsibility of presenting these to Prabhu Singh at a well-publicized public function honouring him on behalf of the Government of India. Accordingly, a function was organized in the City Hall of Durban. This was the first time an Indian was honoured in a hall where entry of Indians without permission had been previously prohibited.

At the function, with many invited Indians and whites watching, the robe was placed on Prabhu Singh's shoulders and the letter from Lord Curzon was read out.

The next winter, Prabhu Singh recycled the robe into dresses for his kids.

~

The war was over by 1900, though sporadic guerilla fighting continued. Three towns including Ladysmith and Kimberlane had been liberated. Lord Kitchner had conquered all territories up to Transvaal and Orange Free State. The war had ended in the defeat of the Boers.

Whites were fighting whites in the Boer War. They had thought that Indians would be enjoying the spectacle from their ringside seat, but Mohandas frustrated their expectations by putting on the non-combatant's uniform and taking to the battle with his ambulance unit. Transporting a wounded soldier on a stretcher, or dressing his wounds, Gandhi kept grappling with the question 'Why? Why are these people bent on killing each other? Does this give any pleasure to them? After all, they both belong to the same race. Is it possible that it is their colonial self-interests which have set one against the other? Is a colony higher than man and his existence? What is more important: power for the sake of power or survival of man? Has power ever allowed anyone to survive? Power is not forever, neither are those who live by or for it.'

When he saw blood oozing out of soldiers' wounds, he sometimes felt as it was he himself who was bleeding; he felt as if it was he himself, along with all those boiling in the cauldron of hatred who lay bloodied on the stretchers. But none of them was in a position to escape the war, was he? Could they just drop the war and run? Everyone was the solitary warrior of his war, except that, for ordinary people like us, war was not a matter of killing people, but a struggle for existence, a struggle which might at times make it necessary for us to die, not by a weapon, but by determination, so that others may live. Killing was not war. It was not only the dead who lost the war, the killer too might. Forgiveness, goodwill, freedom from the fear of death—these were the points of war where nobody killed and nobody died!

Suddenly, there was a groan. Mohandas ran but found no one. He was puzzled: could it be it was he himself?

There was another war in the Beach Grove Villa. No violence, but the spirit sometimes became violent. The actors often forgot that the violence of spirit could also kill and maim. The pain of the bloodied soldiers was pain of the body, but the pain of the spirit crackled like a charge set to detonate any moment. Kastur was so close to Mohandas, yet the feeling never left him that a crackling charge connected the two of them.

Transporting wounded soldiers day and night, Mohandas' own wounds were beginning to reopen. When he was in London, memories of home melted away in the twangs of the violin. Then the violin itself faded away, although it still swung from the peg in his London room. Sometimes he felt it was he himself swinging from the peg. Memories persisted. He felt slowly rocked by them like a boat on water. Memories might get old, but when they revived, they were fresh as new and young as ever. After he had arrived in Natal, he had handed them all over to the Durban Indians, bartering them for their joys and sorrows. Now he had a family with him, he had extensive company, but nothing was the same. The family had expanded and there was more depth to it. The arena of war had reverted from the outside to the inside. Wherever there were two individuals, a personal war was inevitable, whatever its form.

Kastur was stuck in a time warp—with not an inch of progress to show. He couldn't blame her either. She too must have had her dreams—of a home, a husband, kids and some quality time. Hadn't he had dreams of things he hadn't had? And now he had them. Then what was the problem with Kastur's idea that, though they were together now, the wife was still without a husband and the kids still without a full-time father? Where exactly did the problem lay?

Kastur had brought with her her baggage of religion and rituals, something Mohandas had not been able to identify with. He had his own baggage with which Kastur had no identification. She had absolutely no idea of the relationship her husband had with the local people and society, or of the responsibilities he carried. She wasn't even aware that her husband had renounced his caste loyalty towards the Vaishnav sect. He now had a new religion which was part and parcel of his philosophy of action. Mohandas still had no idea how practical that philosophy was, but for him a number of personal relationships which are generally considered god-given had already snapped. He also expected the same of Kastur—that she should accept as her own all those who did not understand the language of ritual, nor could speak that language, people whose language had only a single dimension, the dimension of life. Even caste meant nothing for them. For Kastur, that meant everything.

Kastur was uncontrollable: 'If you think that Kastur knows nothing, that she is carrying with her the burden of her bonds from whom she will not separate, why complain?'

'Why don't you try?'

'What you say and what you do are two different things. What is this if not violence? Kastur's Jain upbringing had instilled in her strong and singular notions of violence, non-violence and forgiveness.'

The very idea that he could be guilty of violence shook Mohandas. 'Violence? I am committing violence?'

'Yes, you are! The one who commits violence does not realize it. Ask the one it is committed on.'

The war within Mohandas intensified; the war outside lost its significance. He could feel the heavy shelling within him. He could detonate any moment!

~

If it was Mohandas' home, it was home to everyone. Welcome, one and all! Young and old, workers, traders, whites and blacks—there was room for everyone. It was rarely the case that Mohandas would be at home and would not have visitors. Kastur and the kids waited and watched. Their share in the life of Mohandas was as his relatives, but that did not give them a proportionate share of his time. It gave them a share when guests had to be entertained, or when household work had to be done. Hari was no longer a child, neither was Gokal, even Mani was beginning to figure out things. Among all of them, it was Hari who always wanted to be with Mohandas and partake of his time, though he had a sense that *Bapu* was carrying on his shoulders a burden of work that was heavier than a mountain and more extensive than the ocean. Still, he just couldn't give up the desire of his company. Sometimes, when he would go out for a walk with *Bapu*, Harilal looked around him with pride, feeling on top of the world as its most important person, with everyone's eyes on him. After coming here, Harilal had taken leave of all the Kathiawari knowledge he had acquired back home—Kathiawari numerals, multiplication tables, alphabet and so on. During the walk, Mohandas would try to re-educate him in all those things. Kastur and Manilal didn't have this kind of opportunity. Manilal was still too young, while Kastur was too busy in house work. Gokaldas still managed to snatch a few moments of walk with

Mohandas. Harilal however pined for the company of his father and when he got it he inwardly enjoyed it to the hilt.

Mohandas' associates also lived in Beach Grove Villa. Attending to their needs was part of Gandhi and Kastur's duties. Their meals, their sleeping accommodation, their waking-hour needs were all attended to by the Gandhi couple. Their rooms were all provided with chamber pots for urination at night. The bathroom was at some distance, and not everyone could access it at night. Winters were particularly difficult. Mohandas himself undertook the task of cleaning the chamber pots. Kastur didn't like it one bit. She was of the view that everyone should undertake to clean his own pot.

Mohandas would argue that, for one thing, those people were our guests, and, for another, the work was only part of the vow of service.

'A guest is someone who stays for a day or two ...'

Mohandas did not like arguing about such matters, so he did not take the discussion any further.

Mohandas had a clerk working for him. He had been an untouchable Hindu before converting to Christianity. Conversion meant his untouchability was gone. One day when Mohandas was busy he asked Kastur to clean up the pot in his room.

Kastur ignored the instruction. A little later, when Mohandas saw the pot still lying uncleaned, he reacted by first moving to clean it himself, then stopped and asked Kastur:

'You didn't empty the pot?'

'No,' said Kastur, without raising her head from her work.

'Why not?'

'My religious convictions do not permit it.'

'Service to others is a part of religion.'

'Yes, but one is free to choose how much service one wants to do.'

'If you want to stay with me you'll have to do more.' Mohandas' voice grew sterner.

'What do you take me for?'

'You are my wife ...'

'Wife or a *girmitiya*? You will fight for *girmitiya*s all over the place.' Kastir's voice sank.

Kastur's retort sounded like defiance to Mohandas. She seemed to be insulting Uka as *Ba* had done. But *Ba's* was a different case altogether. Kastur had fallen silent.

Strain showed on Mohandas' forehead. The usually soft eyes looked hard. Raising his voice even higher, Mohandas said: 'I have made it clear to you that if you want to stay with me you will have to accept service as your duty and no discrimination! The vow I have taken will be yours too. Only then can we share our joys together.'

Hari was watching. He made a move towards the pot. Mohandas stopped him. 'No, not you. Your *Ba* must do it.'

Hari stopped, his eyes overflowing. Mohandas made another attempt to control his rage. 'How many times must I tell you to do your duty happily, no matter how unpleasant?'

'I too have a right to decide on the duties. You want me to do unpleasant work and to do it smiling? I am your wife but I also have my independence.'

'There is no independence apart from your actions; your actions will determine whether you have independence or not. Arrogance and hatred do not lead you to independence; they are a recipe for your slavery.'

'I have told you; I will not clean the pot.'

'You will have to do it.'

'Why don't you do it?'

'I do it everyday. If you want to live in this house you will have to do it.'

'You will throw me out of the house just for this?'

'Not for this, but for the malice in you, for being stubborn.'

'Am I the only one being stubborn?'

'Is that your final decision?' Mohandas had had enough.

Hari looked harried and troubled. He wanted to say something but couldn't bring himself to utter it.

'For the last time, you will stay in this house only if you clean the pot.'

'You will throw me out?'

'Yes!'

'Try.' Kastur flared up.

Mohandas had lost control of himself. In two long strides, he was beside Kastur. He took her by the hand and dragged her to the door. Mani woke up and started crying. Kastur said: 'Listen to what I have to say before you do it.'

Mohandas stopped short. Kastur said: 'You are my husband. I left home and travelled across the seven seas to this foreign land only for your sake. I don't know anyone here and I have no relations or parents. You are mad with anger and out of your senses. Did you for a moment consider where I could go in this foreign country? What are the people going to say? That you threw out your wife like all other Indians do. You are going to prove the whites right who say the Indians mistreat their women.'

Mohandas' hands dropped. He took a couple of steps back. The kids stood cowering. Hari looked confused. He had never seen his father in this form before. Something was breaking within him like a glass-framed picture. Two of the kids went and stood by their mother.

Mani asked: 'Why is *Bapu* throwing you out?'

She spoke in a low voice: 'After all he is also human.'

'I'm so scared,' said Mani. Hari was weeping profusely, but kept silent. The face reflected helplessness mixed with anger.

Mohandas walked out.

He returned a little later, in his usual outfit—trousers with suspenders and a shining pair of shoes—he came and stood by Kastur. Placing a hand on Kastur's shoulder, he said: 'You and the kids saved me today from turning into a beast. I am sorry for the way I behaved.'

Kastur said nothing. She only looked at him. A couple of tears escaped the eyes. Pulling herself together, she said: 'It matters little what happens to me. I was alone there; I am alone here. But think of the kids. They came all the way looking for their father.'

She could not continue. Mohandas stroked her on the shoulder and walked out. The kids snuggled up closer to their mother.

~

Mohandas recalled the incident when members of his ambulance team had been trying put a wounded soldier on the stretcher to take him to the hospital. Gunpowder smoke enveloped the whole area. Even in his wounded condition, the soldier had been trying to free himself from their captivity and escape. Shelling and firing was intense. Shots would whiz past their ears and shoulders, but the volunteers had got used to them in the eight or ten days they had been there.

It was with great difficulty that they had been able to hold him down on the stretcher and now they were moving fast to reach safely. Mohandas was moving with them. When, in the shelter of a mound, they were trying to clean and dress his wounds, the soldier jumped out of the stretcher and ran shouting: 'Our freedom is in danger. The British will make slaves of us all.' His legs were bleeding profusely. He was speaking a mixture of Dutch and English.

'He is a Boer,' said one of the volunteers.

Mohandas, silent at first, said 'Makes no difference,' and continued to dress his wounds.

After the dressing was over, the volunteers asked: 'Where are we going to take him?'

'To hand him over to some Boer officer.'

They had walked off to do that at a fast trot.

Mohandas was thinking: 'Love of freedom is not the trait of a weak person. Only he who can fight for it can love freedom.'

Intermittently, Mohandas found himself lost to the world and someone would ask: 'Hello! Where are you? Can we have you back?'

'I was thinking. Freedom is not necessarily a man's virtue or a woman's. Whenever we try to suppress it, it turns into a revolt. We can understand the importance of our freedom only when we respect the freedom of others. If we fail to do so, we demean our own freedom.'

Kastur wasn't around to hear what he said.

~

Mohandas' third son, Ramdas was born in Durban. This was Kastur's fourth pregnancy. The first one had miscarried in Porbandar and had left Mohandas feeling guilty and answerable to his lost child. Kastur had said nothing. This time, felt Mohandas, he had fallen a victim to his weakness again. Kastur had cautioned him, but at that time hers had sounded like alien voice which he had never heard before. Later, it came back to him: it had been his own voice: 'Kastur, I'm quite happy with the kids we have. The union of husband and wife should only be for procreation, or how's a human being different from an animal?' 'Different?' he repeated now.

Mohandas always had this feeling that his weaknesses on the one hand, and his logic of self-control on the other, always kept putting him to test again and again. And, again and again, he kept losing to them. Were these losses going to lay the foundation of his final victory?

For now, however, he had accepted his defeat.

Kastur was all by herself. There had been so many people at Rajkot. Never for a moment had she felt alone. She had had two kids, but was she ever made aware of how they grew up or who brought them up? Every moment there was someone or the other looking after them. The first thing her brother-in-law did after returning from court was to ask for the kids. Kastur had felt particularly enervated during this pregnancy. This made Mohandas worry all the more in his already stressed condition. He tried to keep her company as much he could. He had to do two things simultaneously: negate his own self and his own feelings and present a polite and easy front to Kastur. Tending to Kastur took him back to his *Bapu* days; the next milestone had been Vrindavan Das; third was the *girmitiya* with whom the chapter of his service had remained incomplete. If that was atonement, this was duty.

Whenever he tended to Kastur, helping her get up or bathe or wash, he had the feeling that within him was a dutiful and faithful Shravan Kumar, who was a Shravan Kumar not to his parents alone but to everyone else too.

~

Kastur's pregnancy had reached full term. Mohandas tried to be at home as much as he could, though Kastur was under the care of doctors. At Rajkot, all this work had been the charge of women of the family and midwives. Being looked after by white women gave a strange feeling to Kastur. Sometimes, she would tell Mohandas: 'The things I have to go through! All because of you!' Mohandas gave a laugh, but inwardly he winced.

Mohandas was busy working when he heard Kastur groan. He ran to her side and found her in extreme pain. So intense was the pain that it wasn't possible to leave her alone to go and call the doctor. Mohandas couldn't think of anything else and set about preparing for the delivery. He had been reading a number of books on account of Kastur's weakness and indisposition. He had also been preparing himself for the delivery in a limited way. He had this idea lurking somewhere in his mind that though the husband might not be able to do much, he could at least be of some help at the time of delivery. He also wished to make an experiment in this regard, though he knew that Kastur would never consent to it.

Mohandas took out the rubber gloves from his first-aid box, boiled the knife, put gauze and cotton on the ready, got some hot water and was set to conduct the delivery. Kastur resisted fiercely and continuously: 'I'd rather die than have you do it.' Mohandas tried to explain it to her again and again: 'Look, I can't possibly leave you alone in this condition to go and fetch the doctor. Never mind whether the doctor is a male or a female; you will be less comfortable with him or her than with me. We are after all husband and wife and have been together in all sorts of situations. That's the way you must think to rid yourself of your shyness. The baby is not going to wait for the doctor, nor for your religious scruples and your shyness. Keep calm and think only of the guest who is about to arrive.'

The pain was at its peak. Kastur was bathed in sweat. Mohandas stroked her stomach gently. Exerting slow pressure, he was trying to coax the baby downward. Kastur was in a terrible condition with all the pain and the shame.

Mohandas' hands of course lacked the experienced touch of a midwife or nurse, but they were soothing and felt familiar. Mohandas was completely engrossed in his work. Kastur tightened her fists and pushed gently. The moment the baby emerged, Kastur felt as if a steep climb was suddenly over. Mohandas wiped the sweat off his forehead with his sleeve. He cleaned and wiped the baby and, wrapping it up in cloth, put it beside Kastur. Kastur couldn't help smiling. She took Mohandas' hand and placed it on her forehead. All his wiping and cleaning had made both the mother and the baby look fresh and glowing.

Mohandas laughed and said: 'So there. What do you think of my midwifery skills?'

Kastur was focused on the baby. This one looked more handsome than his predecessors.

Having delivered the child, Mohandas felt fatigue overcoming him. Kastur was naturally tired too. The baby's eyes were still closed. Even after he had exited into the open world outside, it seemed as if he was still enclosed in his old world. Soft as fine cotton wool, his bright pink skin looked as if even a mild touch would see it come off like a layer of dust.

Mohandas stepped up closer to the child and examined it carefully. He might have hurt the child with his rough, inexperienced touch. The child looked clean and contented. Mohandas retreated and sprawled himself on the easy chair. He didn't want to leave the room as Kastur might still need him for something.

~

The war within Mohandas was still on. Kastur and the newborn of course occupied centre stage of his concerns but that had not meant the end of the war. He was growing progressively disinterested in the war, but bullets and killings were the reality of the time, death from wounds being the culmination of it all. Bullets, violence, wounds, blood, the denuded country behind, the sky, the stars—they were all units of a larger reality, but they were all unattached units, unrelated to one another. The only human truth was the one that was unfolding in the battlefield in its undiminished ferocity, rushing forward like a current with uncontrollable force. Lives were singing the song of death. Mohandas was beginning to look at death as a new beginning. He often thought he was engaged in a direct dialogue with death. 'I am Death,' she was telling him, 'Why are you so keen to befriend me? Once I pick on someone, I never let him go back whole.' The lust for power, with a skull for a begging bowl, was going round, filling its empty bowl with the blood of soldiers. The sole question that buzzed in Mohandas' head was: 'Isn't there a way of overcoming this lust? Are all lusts unconquerable?'

Mohandas thought he heard the baby stir. He got up and checked. Kastur had dozed off. The baby was sleeping too. He was equally responsible for bringing the baby into this world, maybe more than equally. How different were the two lusts! This lust gave birth to new life; it created a new world. Was there no way we could synthesize the two lusts and create a new desire which did not lead to murder and bloodshed, hatred and the murderous reign of death, and the purposeless hunger for power?

Kastur was awake and asking softly for water. Mohandas made himself busy with heating some water.

~

The end of the Boer War came as a signal to Mohandas that his work had ended too. It was seven years since he had landed here first. It never ceased surprising Mohandas that someone who had come here for one year had lasted seven. The family too had been here for quite some time now. Kastur was worried about the children's education. On occasion, she got quite agitated and then it was hard to stop her: 'I know that I am your wife and therefore tied to you, but what crime have the kids committed that you are making their lives the guinea pigs of your experiments? You can be a Gandhibhai to all and sundry; why can't you be a father to your own kids?'

Mohandas often tried to explain: 'Try to understand. Learning a few words of English is not all there is to education. The real education is character, control over self, sacrifice, satisfaction and freedom from desire.'

'Don't give me all that. I know enough about you and your self-control.'

'The Indian schools here are not yet up to the mark. I don't think they can teach much to our children. If we send them to English schools, they will perhaps soon forget what *Ba* and *Bapu* mean.'

'Then let's go back to Rajkot. If you don't want to come, at least let us go.'

That would put Mohandas in a fix. Why couldn't she understand that studies were not all that mattered? There was a churning going on within Mohandas in relation to both what Kastur said and his own responsibilities in the matter. Sometimes he felt that he had had enough and it was time he went back. There was slavery in India too. People were getting used to the yokes round their necks and losing their sense of identity. A role was awaiting him there. Now that there was nothing more left for him to do here, what was the point in holding on to the stall when he had nothing to sell? People were beginning to know and respect one another; schools and libraries had started functioning; a small hospital was also in place. Indians were also beginning to participate in Natalese festivals. A printing press was functioning. People were beginning to appreciate the importance of education. All the stretcher-carrying in the Boer War had given them a separate identity. Couldn't one say something had been achieved?

But how could he leave without the consent of all those friends with whom he had worked shoulder to shoulder to realize the dream of freedom for Indians? That dream was now casting its shadow across the seas to India, like a magic lantern: the projector stood by you but the faces flickered on the screen far away.

One day, Mohandas called all his friends home. They were the usual crowd who anyway kept calling, but on that day a special invitation had been sent out. Sending for someone was not Gandhi's style: he considered it very autocratic. If he had business with anyone, he would call on him himself; so everyone wondered what Gandhibhai could want with them. Must be a special occasion, they thought.

Mohandas came to the point directly, without bothering with an introduction: 'It is with a special purpose that I have given you the trouble of coming here. I came to this country on a one-year *girmit* from Dada Abdullah. That was seven years ago. A relationship came to be established between you and me such that you wouldn't let me go and I wouldn't go. The love that you splurged on me gave an edge to such meagre abilities as I possessed. It was only as a result of this that we were able to achieve whatever little we did. I think my work is now over. My stay in Natal has given me a dream for India and has helped me to prepare a blueprint of that dream. Whenever I fought against the government here standing by your side, I always had a feeling that I was also fighting for India, though I was well aware that we were thousands of miles from India. I think that all that man can do is to dream and sometimes try to fulfil those dreams. But the essential thing is the capacity to dream.' Mohandas stopped. With his eyes closed, he reflected for a moment.

He resumed and said: 'You know very well the experiences that we had to go through when I landed on the shores of Durban with my family. Well, that is all over now. You have now before you a fairly clear picture of your future programme. Living with you, I have learnt the lessons of freedom and of service to others; I have learnt to set aside my personal interests so that I can join my interests with the interests of others. This has been my school: a school is where you learn things. I now want to apply what I have learnt in this school to my country, working with my people. A new dawn is taking place there. As in this country, the Congress is leading a new awakening in that country too. If I can plant some of the seeds of your experience in their soil, it is possible that a new crop of freedom will grow there from your experiences, just as they have led to a flourishing crop here. But it will be ungrateful of me to leave without your permission.'

They all heard him with full attention, but not a word seemed to have entered their heads.

Dada Abdullah's unflinching gaze was fixed at Mohandas' face. It was Rustomji who spoke: 'What's this you are saying, Gandhibhai? We saw a light. The light showed us the way. We took a few steps on our path and now the light says: "Well, I have shown you the way and my duty is over." There may be a ditch or a well ahead. How shall we ever see it without a light?'

Mohandas laughed and said: 'There are all of you. There is Mansukhlal Naazar, R.K. Khan and so many young barristers. Rahim Karim Khan here can beat the best of persons in the field of law. In the circumstances, by asking for permission to return to my country, I hope I am doing no wrong ...'

Complete silence prevailed for a while, with everyone staring at Mohandas.

Dada Abdullah broke the ice: 'Fine. If Gandhibhai wants to go back, let him do so. But we have a condition. Should a situation arise which requires his presence, Gandhibhai will not disappoint us. It should not happen so that the house is reduced to cinders and Gandhibhai doesn't even hear about it.'

After a few moments' silence, Gandhibhai gave his consent.

With heavy hearts, all others too joined in the consent. Gandhibhai set about making his preparations to return.

~

XVI

Marcel Ledue had been missing from Durban. Then one day he suddenly appeared from nowhere and made his first appearance at Dada Abdullah's place. Dada Abdullah had almost lost track of him completely and hadn't even cared to find out if he was in Durban at all. The moment he saw him, Dada Abdullah exclaimed: 'Oh, it's you! Where have you been all this time?'

'I was travelling through Europe. What a beautiful place is Europe! People living in countries like this one can have no idea of its beauty. Its beaches are covered more with beautiful girls than by sand. That is why your Gandhi too likes Europe.' He laughed and then asked: 'So, how is your coolie barrister, ah…, what's his name, yes, M.K. Gandy,' mispronouncing the name deliberately.

He continued, 'Though you helped to sort out the case, I'm still doubtful if the man knows even the ABC of law.'

A thin film of irritation appeared on Dada Abdullah's face, but he still held his ground: 'No, it's not quite like that. The case was of course sorted out, but Gandhibhai also taught us Indians how to fight for our rights.'

'Oh, no, please don't say that,' Ledue drawled.

'Oh, yes.' Dada drawled in the same style.

Ledue made a long face and asked: 'Where is he now?'

'He is returning to India. There is a farewell function on October 15.'

'Don't give him a swollen head. All he has achieved is to give you Indians a bad name in the eyes of the authorities forever. The authorities think that you are a burden on the government. You are parasites.'

Dada Abdullah knew Ledue was crossing the limits, but he still observed the respect due to him as a member of the sahib class and said: 'Mr. Ledue, we traders used to believe that we had a role to play in transforming the economic picture of South Africa, but Gandhibhai helped us to break free of that illusion and made us realize that it is indeed the Indian labourers who are behind the prosperity of this colony. Hadn't they been around we traders would have deserted this colony long ago.'

Ledue was shocked and surprised to hear this. 'It looks like he has succeeded in brainwashing you all. You are far, far superior to those dirty coolies inhabiting the barracks.'

'Come on, let's forget about it. Let's change the topic.'

But Ledue wasn't ready to change the topic. He said: 'But why is he going back? He can have everything he wants here.'

'That's his personal decision. You also went back, didn't you? Did anyone ask you?'

'Maybe he didn't get here all that he wanted.'

Dada Abdullah was reluctant to continue the conversation. He stood up and said: 'Please excuse me. I have arrangements for Gandhibhai's farewell to look after.'

Though unwilling, Ledue had to get up too. As Dada Abdullah walked into the house, he extended an invitation to Ledue: 'You must come to the function, Mr. Ledue.'

~

Most of the arrangements had been made by Parsi Rustomji. The invitations were printed on his letterhead and bore his signatures. The invitees had been requested to attend a farewell function for Mr. M.K. Gandhi at 8.00 pm on October 15, to be held at Congress Hall, Gray Street.

Rustomji was also the secretary of the committee set up to prepare a citation for the occasion.

The function was attended, in addition to Indians, by a large number of whites. Ledue was also present. He went around telling people: 'Good riddance of bad rubbish. The coolies will be rudderless without him.'

He told this to the whites or to people who he thought were opposed to Gandhibhai. Nobody, however, reacted. Mostly they just about gave a smile, with everyone using his own special angle of lip configuration.

The citation was read out by Abdul Qadir:

On this occasion of your farewell, we, the citizens of Natal, present this letter of appreciation to you on behalf of all the Indians here. We are deeply obliged and full of gratitude for the tireless services you have rendered us with always a smile on your face even in the most difficult of circumstances. We do not have adequate words to express our appreciation but assure you that this letter carries our deepest feelings. The sacrifices you have made for your fellow countrymen settled here in these seven years, from the day you set foot in this colony to this day, have been unparalleled.

Your character is virtually an object lesson in sacrifice. We assure you we will follow the rich traditions you have founded here as the ideal of all our activities. We hope that, after you have fulfilled your family responsibilities, you will come back to us and join us again in our struggle for freedom.

We wish you success. We pray to God never to cease his shower of grace on you.

We remain,
Forever yours,
Abdul Qadir and others

A hypnotic silence reigned all round for a few moments after the citation had been read out. Then, slowly, people began emerging out of the hypnotic curtain.

Most of the invitees had brought with them presents according to their capacity and their affection. Abdul Qadir was the first one to present his gift to Mohandas. It was a diamond pin. As he took it, Mohandas looked quite unwilling. A dilemma seemed to be writ large on his face. Next, the secretary of the Citation Committee, Parsi Rustomji, presented a gold necklace, a *savaran* purse and seven gold coins. As Mohandas took the gifts, he placed them on the table in front of him, though Kastur sat right next to him. She looked amazed. A happy smile plastered her face as she saw each gift. On behalf of Dada Abdullah & Co., Mr. Joseph stood up with a gold watch and wanted to tie it on Mohandas' wrist, but Mohandas took it from him very gently and placed it on the table along with all other items. Next a diamond ring was presented to him on behalf of the Indian community of Natal. As he took these gifts, Mohandas' face showed neither happiness nor any tension. All one could see on his face was a feeling of detachment and indifference. His kids were also present; Harilal being the eldest of them was struggling hard to make sense of this detachment and indifference of his father. A heavy necklace of gold was next presented on behalf of Gujarati Hindus. Mohandas mechanically added it to the heap of gifts.

A few *girmitiya*s made their way hesitantly to the dais with flower garlands in their hands. Seeing them approach, Mohandas extended his neck towards them. Their faces were wreathed in smiles instantly. Everyone watched in wonderment.

When Mohandas stood up to speak, he stood silently for a while, his eyes closed. His heart was full.

Mohandas spoke in Gujarati. Off and on, he also broke into Hindi.

'I had asked my friends and associates' permission to go back to India. I told them that my country needed my services. There is a new wave rising in India. You have enough educated people in this country. You have people like Rahim Karim Khan and Mansukhlal Naazar. Many young people have returned from London having passed their Bar-at-Law degree. My friends gave me permission but also put a condition. If they call me sometime within the next year, I will have to come back. A bond of affection ties me to you. How could I possibly refuse? I am reminded of a devotional song of Meera: "I am thy servant of love." The bond that holds me to you is too strong to break, even if I tried to break it. *Vox populi, vox dei:* Voice of people is the voice of God.'

'You have given me so much love. You have given me so many gifts. You have said so many nice things about me. All this has given me a swollen head. I am now finding it difficult to express my gratitude. In fact, I just can't understand what I have done to deserve so much.

Whatever was done was actually done by Natal Congress. Some six or seven years ago, we together founded Natal Congress. If it continues to do well, the way it has been doing so far, the fog that hides us from one another will lift one day and we shall all be able to recognize one another.'

Ledue could not make out what all the fuss was about. He got up, and, muttering to himself, left the venue: 'What is the great achievement of this man? Why all this drama? Sheer stupidity!'

The rest of them were all trying to make sense of Mohandas' speech by checking with one another.

The newspapers next morning were all full of reports of M.K. Gandhi's farewell function. For once, Mohandas was completely indifferent. Normally, he read newspapers like textbooks and then collected snippets, but on that day he just turned them over and put them aside. He had had a restless night. He couldn't decide what he was going to do with so many valuable gifts. He had been given many presents when he had left for India the first time, but they were not such precious gifts. He had felt distressed on that occasion too, but the farewell function this time had been like a forceful current sweeping everyone off their feet. He did not want to be swept off his.

Memories of the previous farewell organized at the Claire Road residence of Dada Abdullah kept returning to him. He had been asked to stay on in connection with the franchise amendment bill. Dada Abdullah had raised the issue of his fees in case he chose to stay on. At that time, he had asked: Does service crave a fee? Then what are all these precious gifts if not a fee? So many people leave the colonies to go back home, hardly seen off by anyone even at the port. They still manage somehow to reach home sooner or later. To be sure, some of the presents are from his clients. They are like his wages, with no favours involved. The whole attitude is quite different. But these gifts have been given by ordinary members of society, people with whom he had shared a struggle. Service has no fee. That precisely is the difference between a client and a companion of your struggle.

There was a gold necklace worth fifty guineas. It had been presented to Kastur. The question that bothered Mohandas was: Why such an expensive gift for Kastur? Was it because he had joined them in helping others? Mohandas was pacing the room ceaselessly, unable to find a way out, as if the walls had expanded to cover all doors. He found that ignoring these questions was as difficult as living with those gifts under the same roof. Keeping those gifts would mean accepting a fee for the service he had performed. What lessons would his kids draw from the episode? Help but charge a fee! Service would become a smoke-screen for making money. Rates of service would be fixed. The greater the service, the higher the fee!

Tired, Mohandas sat himself down. Then he got up and opened all the boxes and cupboards in the house. Is there a single piece of valuable jewellery in this house? Do the precious gifts have a single companion here? How will they survive without company? Everyone needs company—be it a man or a jewel. Without a companion, a jewel here would be like a drop of excreta in a vessel full of milk. When it comes to it, one can sleep on a bed of thorns, but one cannot feast on money earned by selling one's ideals. The awful smell the feast would give! How keen is his family to wear the gold necklace and the diamond ring! Let someone ask: Where did you get the jewels? Did you earn them? You never had any money! Do you have any explanation other than that you sold the merit capital you earned by helping others? What good are gifts which seek to put a price on a man's honesty, gifts which first put you to test and then show you up as a man of no substance at all?

The next day, Mohandas got all his family together. The kids were the first to report as Kastur was busy. Mohandas said: 'I have spent a sleepless night. I cannot decide what I should do with all this jewellery received in gifts. If someone asks me where I got all this, what will I say? Let the kids be the judges. I believe that we cannot keep these pieces. They have been given to us in lieu of the service we performed, but I am not ready to sell my service. I think I should hand them back to the Indian society here. They belong to it. Render unto God what belongs to Him.'

The kids looked at one another. Of course, only Hari and Mani got some sense of what was going on; Ramdas was still too young. Hari spoke on behalf of the kids: 'Do as you think fit.'

For the first time ever, Mohandas embraced his kids and asked them: 'Will you help me persuade your mother?'

'Sure. What's *Ba* going to do with jewellery? She never wears any,' said Mani.

'Maybe she wants to keep it for us,' said Harilal after a pause. 'But we don't want any.'

'What do we do with the jewellery then?'

Kastur walked in after her chores were over. Mohandas said: 'I was telling the kids what I have been trying to tell you. This precious jewellery is of no use to us. What shall we do with it? That was what I told the kids and they agreed with me.'

'I know that you don't need this jewellery; neither do the kids. I also know that you won't ever let me wear it either. This house runs on your whims. Not a leaf can stir unless you want it. Let someone go against your wishes and she will find herself in the streets. But soon I'll have daughters-in-law. What are they going to wear? What do we have to give them? I will never allow these pieces, given to us with so much love and affection, to be returned.'

'As for the daughters-in-law, we'll cross that bridge when we come to it. Should we buy ourselves a headache by keeping the jewellery and worrying about its safe-keeping, losing our sleep in the process? Should we allow our greed a free rein? Listen to me, Kastur, these gifts and presents make you greedier than the things you earn, because they come free. We must try to escape their evil influence. When even the kids are ready, why do you feel so attached to them?'

'Kids? Same kids! Dancing to their father's tune all the time! And you? You are always making a big deal of respecting other people's feelings. Do you think the people gave you these presents without any feelings?'

'Look, Kastur! It's not as if the kids are going to get married next week or next month. I don't want them to get married at an early age like we did and go through all that we had to go through. When they grow up, they will earn for themselves and shoulder their own responsibilities. Neither do I wish for daughters-in-law whose idea of supreme pleasure in life is jewellery. And if they do want jewellery, I will still be around. Do you think I'll refuse if you ask me for it?'

'I know you only too well now, so don't provoke me. There is much more to you than appears on the surface. You took all my jewellery; did I say a word? If I were greedy for jewellery, would I give it to you like that? You were going to England for higher studies, so I thought: What the heck! Won't I get all the jewellery I want once you get back? But did you ever ask? I know you'll never let me live in peace. All you care for is your own peace, and your name. But I won't allow my daughters-in-law to go bare-limbed. You want to turn my kids into hermits with tongs and loin cloth. What do you expect if you won't even allow them good education? Who are you to return the necklace that was presented to me, I ask you?'

'Did we get it in lieu of the service that I did, or what you did?'

'Maybe we got it for your service, but don't I have a hand in the service that you do? Day and night, I work my back off, for whom, may I ask? Any Tom, Dick and Harry that you pick up in the streets you bring them home and dump them on me and I must play the maid for every one of them. I have shed tears of blood … doesn't any of this count as my service? Do I do all this for myself? At home, I had to put up with that Sheikh Mehtab fellow; here it is every Tom, Dick and Harry, in-caste or out-caste.'

Mohandas spoke peaceably: 'I don't deny what you say. But I'm sorry I can't change my decision. I can't understand why a small thing like this, which even Hari, Mani and Ramdas can grasp, is so difficult for you to grasp. I don't want to lose the respect of my kids, and my own respect, by keeping these pieces.'

Kastur went without food that day. She felt she had been conned for a second time by her own husband.

~

Marcel Ledue had been on a back-biting spree ever since he had come back, spreading all kinds of canards about Mohandas. After the presentation of valuable gifts to Mohandas, it had become impossible for him to hold back his urge altogether and he was now going round inflicting himself on anyone who would listen to him. Since Dada Abdullah was out of town, he called on Qadir Sahib and told him: 'Look, you have no idea of the kind of person Gandy is … he has the knack of getting people over to his side. Did you ever pay any thought to why he has created this drama of departure? Because he knows that you will again try and stop him from going. The last time he went, he was back in six months. He simply loves the educated, white gentry of this place. What has India to offer in comparison? You just wait and see—he will be back in no time at all. The last time the gifts he got weren't so precious; this time he got more precious ones; the next time when he goes back, he'll get even more precious gifts.'

Qadir was a short-tempered man, but was careful when speaking to whites. Even so, he offered quite firmly: 'No, Mr. Ledue, you have been misinformed. He came back the last time only because we called him back telegraphically. If he comes back again in future, it will be only if we call him.'

'Oh no. For Dada Abdullah actually Gandy is God himself and it is he who goes all out to do all this for him. Had you presented such valuable gifts to the Governor of Natal, all your problems could have been taken care of at one stroke. You are pouring all this precious stuff into a bottomless pit.'

Qadir retorted: 'Mr. Ledue, it would be better for you to keep out of this issue altogether. You won't be able to appreciate what Gandhibhai has done for us. You belong to the ruling class. You have no idea of our sufferings, or of what Gandhbhai has done for their mitigation. He doesn't crave a penny of anyone's money. He has been very, very careful with each penny of Congress that he has spent.'

'He hates the whites.'

'You are wrong, Mr. Ledue. If he hated the whites, he wouldn't have put at risk his own life and the life of his friends during the Boer War.'

'You are very simple people. He is too clever for you. He can think today what you'll think a year hence.'

At this point, Adamji Miyakhan also dropped in. He laughed and said: 'Hello, Mr. Leidu.'

'Not Leidu. I'm Mr. Ledue.'

'But you too call Mr. Gandhi, Gandy, Gaindi, and God knows what else. We are illiterate people, knowing nothing about your language and its pronunciation. So if it comes out as Leidu Sahib, please don't be offended.'

Ledue said nothing, while Adamji Miyakhan continued: 'Leidu Sahib,' Ledue frowned at him, but Miya Khan ignored his reaction and carried on: 'Gandhibhai is our saviour precisely because he can think a year ahead. We can't even think a moment ahead. Take your own example. You could tell that Gandhibhai can think a year ahead; we couldn't even make out that you were here to speak ill of Gandhibhai.'

Qadirbhai smiled to himself. Ledue said: 'Gandy is a great magician. He has cast a spell on all your intellects. It is worming its way through your brains. Hell with Gandhi.'

'You are right,' said Miyakhan in a low voice. Ledue felt encouraged and said: 'Gandy is nothing before the Government of Natal. An insect, that's what he is—an insect.'

~

Mohandas was conscious that Kastur was unhappy with his decision. For him, however, the only important question was this: Was there, or wasn't there, a relationship between service and the gifts they had received. If there wasn't a relationship, what was the point of Kastur's annoyance? Giving up the jewellery was a problem for Kastur, while keeping them was one for Mohandas. Each one had his/her arguments. Mohandas' argument was: people also sometimes give you flowers as a gift. They carry their feelings and their love for you. But do we keep the flowers? The beauty, the softness, the love, the respect—they all come together to make them priceless for you, but don't they all find their way to the garbage bin after a brief while? Diamonds and jewels, gold and silver are valuable items, so we keep them with care, although from the point of view of love and respect there is no difference between them and the flowers.

Mohandas decided that while Kastur's unhappiness was his too, his regret was that her happiness could not become his.

Mohandas decided to set up a trust to manage the wealth.

The night was no longer young. Beach Grove Villa was enveloped in total silence. The agitated face of Kastur flashed before Mohandas' eyes again and again, hurting him every time it did. Mohandas felt sad to realize that he was making her unhappy by forcing his will on her, but, even after having examined the issue from every possible point of view; he had been unable to find any logical argument in favour of keeping the gifts with him. The cask of jewellery looked to him like a snake pit with the snakes crawling over one another. Kastur was sleeping in another room. The children too were asleep. The only satisfaction he had was that the kids were on his side. How he wished Kastur too were!

Mohandas pulled his chair close to the table and started writing a letter to Parsi Rustomji.

Having given a lot of thought to the matter, I have decided to hand over the gifts I have received to the African Bank Corporation. More than the gifts, I value the love which has inspired those gifts. I am therefore instructing the Bank that the jewels listed in the accompanying list may be handed over to the Natal Indian Congress and a receipt obtained from the President or the Secretary/Secretaries. I list below the conditions under which the jewels are to be handed over to the Congress:

1. *An Emergency Fund to be constituted from the jewellery/proceeds of the sale of the jewellery. The Emergency Fund to be used only in the event of the Congress running out of funds and assets barring the two properties in its possession.*
2. *In the event of the Congress using the jewellery/proceeds of the jewellery for purposes other than the one specified above, or purposes which in my view are not beneficial, I reserve the right to withdraw any single piece of jewellery/all the pieces of jewellery at will.*

I will consider it an honour if, before the jewellery is used for a specific purpose, I am consulted with respect to whether or not the specific purpose in view falls under the definition of an 'emergency purpose'. However, the Congress is free to use the Fund in accordance with the purposes defined above without the need to consult me.

At the end of the letter he wrote:

I am taking this step in full possession of my senses and with a sense of prayer. I can neither use these gifts for my personal benefit, nor for the benefit of my family. In fact, they are so sacred for me that I cannot even sell them; neither can I allow my heirs to do so. If there are any other possibilities, it is not possible to say anything about them at the present juncture.

Taking into account all these conditions and possibilities, I find that the only choice I am presently left with is to dedicate these symbols of love my friends have honoured me with, to a noble and holy cause. These gifts have actually been given in honour of the principles the Congress stands for. It is only appropriate that they should go back to the Congress.

As he finished the letter, Mohandas felt the tension within him releasing through the pores of his body. He lay down on the bed. This was his third sleepless night. In a few moments, he was fast asleep.

~

XVII

No matter how fast a ship may be cruising on the sea, you always feel as if it is stationary, or floating slowly like a duck. Seated on the deck, Mohandas was watching the vastness and the majestically slow movement of the infinite ocean. Scenes from the Boer War passed through his mind. At times, he felt those scenes would any time start enacting themselves on the waves of the sea. Wars had strange histories. India had suffered many wars, but what were their consequences? Massacres! Victory for one and defeat for another! Humiliation! Overthrow of one power and founding of another! The riddle that Mohandas couldn't solve was: Why does man nurse the illusion of superiority of his race over that of another's? Why does this animal mentality rule man's world? Man is endowed with a sensitive heart and he is an evolved species: he should be characterized by love, not by violence and bloodshed. Why does he turn into an animal and try to establish his supremacy in his society?

He often thought of the two lions seated outside the Kruger's palace. Lions everywhere are shown in a roaring posture, be they stone or clay. But those two lions were peace personified. If the lions could be so peaceable, why do we humans become so agitated, restless and bloodthirsty? Kruger was supposed to be an icon of bravery. When Chamberlain asked him, he forgave the rebellious goldmine owners. But the same Kruger had dismissed the Indians traders so contemptuously telling them: 'You are the sons of Ishmael. Slavery is your birthright.' All because the Bible says that when he was thirteen years old Ishmael had participated in the Divine Massacre. The Zulu king, Dingaan, was one of the victims of that massacre. Once, when the British requested him to grant recognition to the English language, Kruger had said: 'This is my country. It will follow my law and my language. Those who accept these conditions can stay. Those who have problems with my law can leave.' But the Boer War had brought him down too. It was a blessing that the English only punished him with exile. Why is it that, though ourselves human, we see other humans as beasts brought to the altar for sacrifice? Mohandas saw the map of his country emerge before his eyes. 'No,' he said to himself, 'I'll never let such a thing happen in my country … Never!'

Occasionally, the ship's hooter let out a blast as if some ferocious beast was being slaughtered. Some other sounds too distracted his attention. Sometimes it was a splash, as if someone hit water. It would be a boat passing. At the beginning of the voyage, the kids were scared by the hooter's blast, but it was their second voyage and they soon got used to it. Mohandas liked to take the kids with him to the deck. Sometimes, when he sat on the deck with Kastur, he found himself left alone, lost in thought. It was as if history abducted him, took him on a trip of its vast kingdom and gave him a few dips in the sea of future possibilities.

Mohandas thought of Bombay. He had seen some of his worst days there. His daily trudge to the court and his daily empty-handed trudge back. Repeat the next day. He seemed to be on an endless road to poverty, a meaningless trip to nowhere. His efforts to earn a livelihood showed the agility of a hobbled horse. But today he was returning from abroad as a successful barrister. His country was dreaming of freedom; it wanted to open its eyes, stand up, and light up its world by becoming its own morning sun. Mohandas too had a dream of the freedom of his country. There were some people who were busy trying to see their country awake. Again, there were some who were quite content to see it remain asleep.

'No,' muttered Mohandas, 'She must wake up.'

'What did you say?' asked Kastur.

'Nothing,' said Mohandas, 'How big is our country! How far away were we from her! We are getting closer to her now.'

'Hard to say anything about you. Who can say when you will choose to be far away and when to be close to whom?'

Mohandas laughed like a child. 'Yes,' he said, 'you could say that.'

'All our life, we lived in Rajkot. We could well have lived on there. We were living there anyway. Couldn't we have spent this time also there? How much did we not go through during these years—from the day we got off the ship to the day we got back on again! That day, when we got off the ship at the port of Durban, the thought in my mind was: Did I come here to lose you? Was it here that I was to lose my destiny?'

His answer to this question was another question: 'Didn't you like it there?'

'Like it? What was there to like? Black people … yellow people … the boundary wall of the Beach Grove house … it reminded me of Porbandar, but everything was so foreign, so strange. My biggest occupation was just to wait and wait, and wait for you. Fortunately, I had a long practice in it. And when you came, there would be half a dozen people with you, who made themselves comfortable in the house. Then I had to feed them, and also to clean their waste. If I didn't do it, I would incur your wrath. If you had thrown me out that day, where would have I gone?'

'Good and bad, pleasant and unpleasant … they are all in the mind, Kastur.'

'Not for everyone … especially not for someone who has to suffer the worst … certainly not for her.'

'Kastur, we must try and forget the bad memories just as much as we forget the good. If you remember the bad as bad, it makes your life that much harder to live.'

'Yes, a noble thought, for others to follow.'

'I am speaking of myself too. Didn't you see? Had it not been true, would the Indians here be able to live through such a horrendous life? Whatever I had read in the Gita, I learnt from them in practice.'

Kastur stared at her husband. It happens sometimes—someone says something and it leaves you staring at him wide-eyed.

Just then the hooter went off and the kids started clapping. They both looked at the kids at the same time. There were other people around, but they felt they were a family again, just because they looked together! The youngest one was fast asleep!

The ship was heading to Mauritius and was going to cast anchor there that day. Mohandas still remembered Durban as a flat green plain where spring was always camping in its full glory. It hadn't however been so glorious that he could forget all the pain and the hurt. In the last seven years the network of his relations had spread so far and wide that seeking an exit had been a labourious exercise. The question of identity agitated the Indians there. There were debates and discussions at Congress meetings. There were agreements and disagreements. The insults and tyrannies inflicted on them by the whites were subjected to condemnation and excoriation. Blood-spattered fellow countrymen roamed the streets. Though on the ship, Mohandas was still in their midst and they were all harboured within him. Kastur and the kids looked to be circling around this central ring. To Mohandas, Kastur sometimes looked silent like the earth and at other times raging like the waves. The children were like flowers in bloom sending out signals of lasting innocence.

Mohandas thought of the Beach Grove Villa: the peddlers on the beach, the lazing ships and then their house. All those people who had been living with them must now be looking for places to live.

Kastur asked: 'What's keeping you so quiet?' and interrupted his stream of thought.

'It's been only a few days since we left Durban, but it feels as if it has been ages. People there have learnt the lessons of peace and service from their own struggles. Service is what you do with peace, to find peace and to give peace. Selfishness and agitation are like splashes of filth on a clean and holy set of clothes. How quick are these people to forgive the tormenting whites!'

'Why don't they fight?'

'We do. So what do we get?' said Mohandas, laughing. 'Unhappiness … agitation … anger.'

'That's a different kind of fighting.'

'And the most malice-free and safe. Isn't it?'

'I'm talking about fighting oppression and tyranny.'

'In other words, you are talking of the fight between the weak the strong. The weapons are not yet ready which will help the weak beat the strong. If the weak fight back using the weapons of the strong, they can never hope to beat them, for they are their practised and familiar weapons. But those weapons will be ready one day, and they will be stronger than the conventional weapons the strong have been using to crush the weak. The day the weak and the harassed understand this, they will win the day.'

'Does anyone ever understand what you think and what you do?'

'One day, they will. When the time comes, they will. You will lead that war.'

'Me?'

'Yes. Why not? Our war will be one without bloodshed, without hatred and malice. It will be a war of service and truth.'

~

The ship was called *S. S. Naushera.* It cast anchor a long way from the shore. They could see the Port Louis harbour and the city from a distance. Both the sea and the city seemed absorbed in a dialogue with themselves. The buildings in Mauritius seemed quite different in shape and size from those in Durban.

Mohandas asked the captain; 'Why have we stopped so far from the shore?'

Mohandas always got very friendly with ship captains. He sometimes even helped out the captains in maintenance work. The captain was T.P. Gurchi.

'Mauritius has the plague,' he said.

'I have lived through the scare of the plague in Durban four years ago. Our two ships had to be in quarantine for twenty-three in place of the regulated eighteen days. When we left Bombay, Bombay had the plague. We got punished for it when we reached Durban.'

The Captain laughed.

Mohandas said, also laughing: 'Is it possible that *Naushera* may also be quarantined like the mother of a newborn?'

'It's all for the good of the passengers, Mr. Gandhi,' said the Captain.

'Yes, and sometimes the motives for doing good to the passengers can also be different.'

'Though there is no plague in South Africa, *Naushera* will anyway be disinfected,' informed the Captain.

Like India, Mauritius too had the plague every year. Thousands lost their lives to it. Whole families were wiped out. Mass burials had to be resorted to.

The Health Department officials let *Naushera* go after disinfection. The process took four days. *Naushera* entered the harbour on October 29. All this time, no one found out that a man called M.K. Gandhi was aboard the ship. Some six days later, on November 4, *Planters and Commercial Gazette*, *The Standard*, *Journale de Maris* and some other papers published a small note which said that a famous advocate named M.K. Gandhi was on his way from Natal to Bombay. Mr. Gandhi was known for leading a struggle for the rights of Indians settled in South Africa.

The French papers added a couple of more lines: 'Mr. Gandhi will be in Mauritius for a few days. The Indian community looks forward to welcome Mr. Gandhi to Mauritius.'

The Indian community was indeed delighted with the news. The news however had reached only the English and French knowing Indians and whites. A few businessmen also heard of it. Most of them were barely literate but still subscribed to English and French papers for business reasons and had the papers read out to them. The readers made a few extra bucks this way.

Gandhibhai knew no one on the island, though the name of Mauritius was always on his lips. Mauritius was always mentioned whenever the Indian struggle for equal rights was discussed, especially in letters. The *girmit* laws of Natal had been prepared with the Mauritius law as the model. When Mohandas got off the ship, he was told that *Naushera* would raise anchor on November 8. The passengers were free to go as they wanted till that time. The question before the Gandhi family was where to go. There was no one they knew.

The sea of Mauritius was like a bovine on one side, so placid that a child could keep teasing it and it wouldn't turn a hair. On the other side, it raged with such fury that it could overturn a ship. In some places, the sea was deep blue, in others, it looked blackish. The soil too had seemed to them to be similar to the soil of eastern India.

A man came aboard asking for Mohandas. Someone from the crew directed him to his cabin. The man introduced himself very politely: 'I am Ahmed Ghulam Mohmmad. We have dealings with Dada Abdullah & Co. I came to know about your visit, and am here with the request that you may kindly agree to come with me to my humble place and allow us the pleasure of being your host.'

'What?' Mohandas was taken by surprise.

'As a proof I have this letter, which will show how close we are to Dada Abdullah. I am also aware that your family is travelling with you. We have arranged suitable accommodation for you.'

Mohandas turned down the invitation at first, but Ghulam Mohmmad persisted and he had to agree.

Waiting outside for the guests was Ahmed Ghulam Mohmmad's coach, pulled by two dark brown horses of fine species, alert and energetic, ears cocked high and absolutely fit. They wore leather pads above the hooves and on the knees. The coach glistened with spit and polish. Mohandas was in his European outfit.

On the road, the coach was flanked on both sides with expanses of thriving sugarcane. The leaves were dark green, so dark that a little black seems to be mixed in it.

Mohandas asked: 'These fields belong to you?'

'To the whites. The Indians put in the labour. The whites contribute the capital, the labourers the sweat.'

'Do Indians have a role in politics, or is it the same as in Natal?'

The kids were enjoying themselves. Along with Kastur, they had their attention fixed on the expanse of green in the fields outside. Snatches of their conversation sometimes flew up and caught the ears of Kastur and the kids.

Kastur shifted her attention from the fields and spoke in Gujarati: 'Why do you talk about Natal? All that you did there was to turn everyone into your replica. Someone hits you, and you tell them to lie down at his feet and say: Come, please hit me a bit more.' And she again went back to the kids.

She was holding Devdas in her lap and showing him the birds in the sky. He looked all right, but it was hard to say if he got what he was supposed to see. Of course, he was sure to get it one day, thanks to his mother.

Mohandas replied in Gujarati: 'There is more than one way to fight.'

Then he turned to Ghulam Mohammad and repeated his question.

Ghulam Mohammad set out to explain: 'There is a storm right now. Mr. Bruce is the Governor. A few months ago, the Duke and Duchess of York were visiting. The Indians went all out to welcome them. Two of them, Dr. Nalletambi and Ibrahim Aticha, made very special efforts, so the Governor nominated Dr. Nalletambi to the Council and appointed Aticha as a member of the New Basein and Rosehill municipalities. Aticha knows neither English nor French. The rumour is that this was done on directions from above. The Board Chairman and two white members resigned on this issue. The Governor accepted their resignations and replaced them with three officials. The Governor holds Indians in high regard.'

Mohandas listened in silence. The kids were silent too. For a short while, the coach cruised under the cover of silence. One could of course hear the clip-clop of the horses' hooves running parallel to the road.

Suddenly, the children cried out: 'Look, what a big hole!'

'A volcano. Still spews lava at times. I took this detour to show it to you,' said Ahmed. The kids didn't quite get it.

'Live or dead?' asked Mohandas.

The question passed over Ghulam Mohmmad's head.

Mohandas kept looking at the volcano. A volcano comes alive only occasionally. When it does, it spews fire. The sea has tides. When there is a tide, you feel as if the sea is standing on its heels. The two have different tempers.

By the next day, almost everyone in the city of Port Louis knew that an Indian barrister by the name of Gandhi was in town and that he had been fighting for the rights of Indians in Natal. This was enough to fill the Indians with excitement.

Whenever Mohandas went out, it was in Ghulam Mohammad's coach so that everyone knew. People lined up on both sides of the road and watched him intently. Some old-fashioned people greeted him with 'Ram-Ram,' a style which still survived there. Those who could meet him went up to him, shook hands and exchanged a few words with him.

Mr. H. Burtin was an attorney-at-law. When he found out, he too came to see Mohandas. He talked for a while about the political situation in Natal. Mohandas told him about the travails he had to go through in getting himself registered as an attorney.

Mr. Burtin laughed and said: 'I can well understand. Fortunately, we don't have such problems. There are still some French traditions left.' He talked shop for a bit more and then said: 'I want to take you to the Supreme Court. It will be a pleasure to introduce you to the members of the bar.'

Mohandas looked at Mr. Burtin in surprise: 'Who would know me here? But, if you insist, I will go with you.'

Mr. Burtin took him to the bar common room first and introduced him to the members. Mohandas noticed that there was no Indian among them.

Mr. Burtin briefed him about the past Chief Justices and their dates, the date when the court buildings were constructed, the grasp the different judges had on the cases, judges whose decisions were still cited as models, and so on. Some of the lawyers Mohandas met had actually heard of him and were also familiar with his work. As soon as they were introduced, they would ask: 'The same Gandhi who is leading the agitation for Indians' franchise and poll tax in Natal?'

They would then start questioning him about the situation in Natal. Gandhi replied to their questions with great patience. The English lawyers were the most vocal; the French were indifferent. Occasionally, the English lawyers would get excited and start bad-mouthing Indians. Mohandas disposed of their questions in a sentence or two.

A couple of the lawyers also quizzed him on the Pietermaritzburg incident. Gandhi said: 'That was like a strenuous exercise for the mind and the heart. Many stiff joints became loose.'

They all laughed.

One day, a businessman came to see him, a south Indian. He wanted Mohandas and his family to accept his hospitality. He had heard of the Balasundaram episode.

Mohandas tried to fob him off with an excuse: 'The ship is leaving on November 8. There are only two or three days left, but I'll come and see you.'

But he was insistent on their staying with him. 'Please don't disappoint us,' he said, 'Please come with me. You saved the life of a brother in a foreign land. Don't you consider us fit enough even to entertain you?'

Mohandas had to consent. The man owned huge property in Mauritius and wielded considerable influence in the Indian community. The horses of his coach were milk white. The children loved them. While at his home, Mohandas had an unending stream of visitors. The kids enjoyed their stay.

Naushera was supposed to set sail on November 8. On November 7, a notice in the newspapers informed them that it would now leave on November 12. Scheduled to sail via Colombo, it would now sail directly to Bombay. Kastur was all packed and ready a day in advance; now she had to unpack all over again. The kids went all limp. They were so impatient to reach home. Gokal was thinking of his *Ba* all the time. Hari and Mani were looking forward to be with their *Tauji* (father's elder brother). Everyone had his own memories of Rajkot, which had now come alive. Ramdas and Devdas of course had no memories yet.

On November 7, a white official from the Governor's House made his appearance. He was carrying an invitation with Governor Bruce's signature. It said: 'On the occasion of the sixtieth birthday of His Majesty the King, on Saturday, November 9, you are invited to dinner at my residence, Re Duit. It will give me great pleasure to welcome you on the occasion.'

Mohandas had had no occasion to meet Sir Charles Bruce before, nor did he know of him. All that he knew about him was what his host, Ghulam Mohmmad, had told him. He had also discovered that Sir Charles Bruce had acquired knowledge of Sanskrit at the King's College and had translated the Sanskrit text, *Nala Damayanti*, into English. Mohandas was surprised to find his name included among the official invitees. After all, he was a passenger in transit. A transit passenger has no permanence and no significance.

A carriage arrived from the Governor's House punctually to escort Mohandas, with an official in attendance. When he reached the Governor's House, Mohandas was received by the Governor's secretary. Mr. Bruce was with the guests inside the house. There was a large lawn in the rear of the house. The grounds of the house extended as far as eyes could see. It was the start of the summer, so people were enjoying being in the open.

As soon as news of Gandhi's arrival was whispered into his ears, Sir Bruce turned around and approached Mohandas. Stepping up to Mohandas, he then shook hands with him very warmly and said: 'Welcome Mr. Gandhi. You are our honoured guest.'

Mohandas thanked him, saying 'Long live the King! I am extremely grateful to you for inviting me on this happy occasion. The Indian citizenry of this island is a great admirer of Your Excellency and places its deepest trust on you.'

Mr. Bruce replied: 'Thank you, Mr. Gandhi. I have been reading about you in the newspapers. I greatly admire your courage, your judgment and your love for your country. When I got to know you were in Mauritius, it made me very happy. I was keen not to miss this opportunity of meeting you. It's my wish that you should stay for a day in the Governor's House as my guest.'

Mohandas promptly said: 'I greatly respect your knowledge of Sanskrit. It's an indication of your love for the east.'

'My knowledge of Sanskrit has given me a new way of looking at life. The respect of man for man and equal regard for life and death—these are unique features. Please come, let me introduce you to the dignitaries of this place.'

There were quite a few of them. When people got to know about Gandhi being present at the dinner, they all gravitated towards him. He was introduced to the Chief Justice. Mr. Burtin was present too. He also talked to French and English businessmen. Mohandas could understand French but couldn't speak it. There were a few Indian businessmen too, but he had already met them at Ghulam Mohammad's.

Gazing at the large expanse of the Governor's House compound, Mohandas reflected on the expansive lifestyle of the British. Maybe that was the reason they expanded from one corner of the globe to the other. He was full of praise for Governor Bruce for having respect enough for Indians to invite them to parties like this. But he wondered if Mr. Bruce ever found out about thousands of those poor and hapless Indians who slave throughout their lives so that Mauritius can flourish and stay green. For 'these' people to see 'those' people must be as hard as it is for us to see those innumerable hardworking fishes in the sea without getting into water.

He went and sat down on the round marble bench in the rear of the house. A silver sheet of moonlight covered the entire area. The guests were still busy drinking.

Another notice appeared in the morning papers on November 12. It said that for some unavoidable reasons, the departure of *Naushera* was being postponed. It would now depart instead on November 14 for Bombay.

The kids were getting upset by the repeated postponements. Spending a few days with a Tamil family had of course been a change. Of all the south Indian preparations, Mohandas had taken a fancy to *idli:* vegetarian, non-fried and delicious.

The postponement of *Naushera*'s departure was countered by Ghulam Mohammad Azam & Co. and a few other Tamil traders by organizing a special dinner in honour of Mohandas in the Roshcoast Building. Actually, this dinner had been repeatedly postponed, once because Mohandas had accepted Mr. Bruce's hospitality. Earlier, it had to be postponed because he chose to be the guest of a Tamil family. When people came to invite him for this dinner, Mohandas joked: 'Had the ship sailed on November 8, I'd have missed this dinner. I must be grateful to the ship's captain for postponing the departure again and again till I caught this dinner.'

~

On his arrival at Roshcoast, Mohandas found people waiting for him. They all stood up as he had arrived. Mohandas shook hands with everyone. The dinner was a western style occasion and Mohandas felt a little out of place. Kastur and the kids had stayed back at home. The dinner started with toasts to the health of everyone from the King Emperor down to Sir Bruce, though Gandhibhai drank a different toast from the others. The Chief Guest of the evening was Mr. M.K. Gandhi and a toast was also drunk to the good health and pleasant journey of the Gandhi family. In the end, Mohandas was requested to speak.

Mohnadas' speech was a short one. 'My landing here was an accident,' he said. 'I am grateful to Sir Charles for having invited me on the occasion of His Majesty's birthday. I am also grateful to you for this dinner. This island is like a lighthouse for Indians travelling to South Africa. Its beauty is indeed spellbinding. I haven't been able to meet many people during my visit here, so it would not be appropriate for me to make any comments on the situation here. However, I would like to make a point or two, points that I also make to my friends in Natal. You have to be alert to your rights. You must see to it that your children are well-educated. It is education alone which takes man as raw material and chisels a fine individual out of it. Truthfulness and honesty are the furnaces which produce a golden man. Indians and Asians will become deserving of respect only after they have established their credibility in this land. My best wishes are with you for you success and progress.'

Reports of this celebratory dinner kept appearing in the local papers for many days following. Every paper had its own take on it. One paper said that Gandhi incited the Indians to participate in politics. Another one said that Gandhi asked the Indians to get their children western education. A couple of papers even reported that Gandhi extended his good wishes to a local Indian candidate for the chairmanship of the local municipality and thus took part in a political propaganda war.

The ship did not leave even on the 14th. It finally left on the 15th evening at 5.00 pm. A good number of Indians were at hand to bid farewell to Gandhi and his family.

Mohandas laughed and said: 'Four years ago, we were quarantined in Durban. At Mauritius, we escaped quarantine but had to spend a fortnight flailing our wings in the dock like birds in captivity.' The Captain laughed off the comment.

When the ship was about to raise anchor, the last hooter had sounded and Mohandas was about to step aboard, the Tamil host approached him with folded hands and said: 'You dedicated yourself to the cause of freedom of Indians in Natal and in South Africa. Now we also need a Gandhi who can show us the way.'

Mohandas put his hand on his shoulder and said: 'Wait. You must wait. Someone is sure to come along.'

Emotions ran high with many of the people present there.

~

XVIII

Bombay looked exactly the same as Mohandas had left it years ago except that the crowds had grown a bit bigger. There was more motor traffic on the roads. Bombay was anyway the first city to have automobiles. More traffic obviously meant the number of automobiles must also have gone up.

It was only after landing in Bombay that Mohandas found out that the Congress was going to have a session in Calcutta in December. The session was to be presided over by Dinshaw Wacha. Mohandas had already met him. The last time when Mohandas had been unable to read out his address at the public meeting, it was Dinshaw Wacha who had come to his rescue. That was when he had discovered the oratorical skills of Dinshaw Wacha. He was also the right-hand man of Sir Pherozeshah Mehta. Mohandas also recalled that had it not been for Gokhale, his resolution would have remained a dead word. He recalled all these incidents precisely in the order in which they had occurred.

All the way to Rajkot, Mohandas kept thinking that a better opportunity would be hard to come by. If he could raise the issue of South Africa at the huge gathering, the impact would be awesome. But November was almost gone, and the time left was barely enough. Kastur was eyeing his ominous silence and knew that something was cooking in his mind. In the end, she spoke out: 'You haven't spoken a word to me or to the kids ever since we left Bombay.'

Coming out of his shell, Mohandas looked at Kastur and said: 'I have been thinking about the Congress session which is going to be held very soon in Calcutta. I will have to leave soon after I drop you at Rajkot. This is an excellent opportunity to raise the issue of South African Indians. All the top leaders of the country will be present.'

'May I ask why you came back to India at all? You didn't really want come back home, did you? You came here to continue the same work here. Dump us at Rajkot and bye-bye.'

Mohandas looked at her: 'Try to understand. Their lives are utterly devastated. We are much better off.'

'They are surviving, aren't they? So where is the devastation? We too are barely surviving.'

'You haven't seen the real India. Those people don't even own clay vessels; metal is a pipe dream. I have seen people go to bed hungry.'

'But for socializing you pick out men of gold and silver, don't you?'

'So that I can help those who don't even have bread. Those gold and silver people didn't even have an idea that their own brethren were living next to them in such a state, despite the fact that it was in them that their true strength lay.'

The kids were barely able to sit upright because of sleep. Gokal saw and heard everything but didn't speak a word. He was the only kid awake and looking out of the window. Coal dust, blowing in with the wind, settled on their clothes, making all of them look the same colour.

'For the first time in years, for the first time after our marriage, we had something resembling a family life, with a home and a kitchen, but could it hold you? Could it ever become a true home? Your true home has always been the world outside. If you have to go, you will go, and let anyone stop you! When we were here before, it was your brother we had to live on, and we are back to him again. Let's count our blessings and thank you for the days you could spare for us.' Her voice trembled as she spoke. Perhaps the train was switching lines.

Mohandas looked out of the window. He saw a tree start racing the train. It stopped after a short while and another tree took its place. This went on till his eyes caught the wires alongside the track. The wires kept rising higher and higher till suddenly they got a jolt, as if someone pulled them all down at one go.

Ramdas, who could speak now, asked: '*Bapu*, how far is Rajkot?'

'Still a long way off, son.'

'A very long way off,' said Kastur. 'To your father, every place is a long way off except that black hole of a country.'

Like the kids, Mohandas kept his eyes fixed on the game of trees and pillars being played outside the window. The pillars were of course few and far between. Often, they disappeared altogether.

Dropping his family at home, Mohandas left at once. His elder brother was unbelieving. He tried to persuade Mohandas: 'Take a few days off. What's the big rush? You owe something to us too, don't you?'

'I owe everything to you. But there are people to whom no one owes anything. In any case, I have come back for good and will be here all the time.'

'As you wish. You can see for yourself—see the condition the house is in.'

Mohandas said nothing, but inwardly a question raised its head: 'Which house? Is this house the only house in this condition? Is there nothing outside this house?'

No one could stop Mohandas and he left. The sun had set again for Kastur. The kids got busy with their play. Harilal didn't like his *Bapu* leaving. Having lived so long in his company, he was now greedy for more.

Mohandas found himself on the same train by which Sir Pherozeshah Mehta was travelling to Calcutta with his party. Sir Pherozeshah always travelled in a saloon car. After all, he was not only a *sher* ('lion'); he was also a *shah* ('king'). He always travelled with the full paraphernalia of a king and an army of courtiers and attendants.

~

Mohandas had obtained an appointment with Sir Pherozeshah. Those desirous of an appointment were told in advance about the stations at which they would enter and leave the saloon. Mohandas too had been accordingly informed. Mohandas was in considerable tension. For one thing, Sir Pherozeshah was a man of few words; for another, till you met him, you were ordinarily anyway in tension. The hardest part was that he allowed you only a few minutes to say your part and immediately pronounced his judgment in a few sentences. And then you were out. When you were out, you kicked yourself for not having said this thing or that thing which should have been more effective.

Sitting in his compartment, Mohandas wrestled with the problem of how to present the situation in South Africa in the fewest possible words so that everything became self-evident. The train occasionally disappeared completely for him till he became conscious of it, and then it would be back. The rest of the time it was his impatience to meet Sir Pherozeshah, the condition of Indians in South Africa and things like that occupied his mind.

The train stopped. Mohandas rushed out of the compartment and dashed to the saloon. It was a small station. An attendant stood at the door of the saloon. Mohandas quickly told him his name. He turned back for a moment, picked up the signal from inside and Mohandas was in the saloon. The man coming out looked sad and sullen. The saloon was in semi-darkness. The window glasses were curtained. Sir Pherozeshah was sprawled on the chair in a half-reclined position. On his one side sat Dinshaw Wacha, on the other side Cheemanlal Setalvad. The trio was deep in discussion on some topic.

Sir Pherozeshah was saying: 'No, that's not possible. Whatever we get will be British largesse. We must trust their sense of fair play. They are a brave and large-hearted nation.'

Wacha said in measured tones: 'I agree with you, but if you want to extract its essence, even a chameli flower has to be squeezed, what to speak of almonds.'

Even before his sentence was complete, Setalvad butted in: 'The constitutional method of achieving our goals is the safest way of struggle.'

Mohandas stood silently, waiting to be addressed. Suddenly, Sir Pherozeshah noticed him and said: 'Hello, Gandhi! How are you? When did you get back?'

Even before Mohandas could respond, and without even listening to what he had to say, Sir Pherozeshah continued: 'I'm sorry, Gandhi. There's nothing we can do for you. We are slaves in our own country. What rights do we enjoy ourselves? So long as we don't have autonomy ourselves, what can we possibly give to other colonies? The most we can do is to pass a resolution to show our solidarity with them.'

When Sir Pherozeshah said his first sentence, Mohandas felt as if a strong gust of wind had hit him, hurling him back. He hadn't even opened his mouth yet. He hadn't even written the exam yet and the result had been announced. Setalvad was playing the yes-man to the hilt, while Wacha had only one word floating in his eyes for Mohandas: 'Poor man!'

Mohandas tried to say something, but Sir Pherozeshah raised his hand shutting Mohandas up. Who could dare to speak in the presence of the uncrowned king of Congress? Mohandas drew whatever satisfaction he could from the fact that at least a reference would be made to his plaint in the court of the king, that is a resolution would be passed at the session of Congress! The train was still in motion and just would not stop. Mohandas was already outside Sir Phrozeshah's saloon and waiting for it to stop.

The saloon door opened and he heard Dinshaw Wacha call out to him: 'Gandhi, let me see the draft before you present the resolution.'

'Yes, sir.'

The train stopped and Mohandas stepped out quickly. A man stood outside, dripping sweat. There was complete silence at the station. Mohandas ran to his compartment. The moment he stepped in, the train started. A question troubled his mind: Will the Congress ever be able to identify itself with the dreams and sorrows of the people of this country, if this is the way it functions?

The train had picked up speed.

~

A crowd of thousands had gathered at the Calcutta station to receive the Congress president. Members of the reception committee ran here and there busily. Carriages and coaches, decked out in full glory, stood waiting. Bands played music. The Bengali gentlefolk had turned out in their traditional festive finery: pleated dhoti-kurta and a shawl draped on the shoulder, shiny pump shoes or *Shantipuri* slippers.

The place where the president was supposed to stay presented a unique sight. The President's camp was a visual delight. The full range of artistic skills of Bengal seemed to have been exploited in getting it ready and doing it up. For the ordinary man, even access to it was a trying proposition, but still people managed to reach there, some to gawk and some to keep an appointment. Volunteers ringed the place. The president was ushered into his camp with full honours. Each one of the top leaders had a camp to himself. Volunteers were on duty at each of the camps. Mohandas waited till each of the top leaders was in his camp and the volunteers got some relief. Then he caught hold of one of the volunteers and, introducing himself, asked where he was supposed to stay.

The volunteer replied in Bengali: 'Why are you asking me?'

The irritation he showed made Mohandas wonder what mistake he had made. The volunteer fled on the double perhaps to escape being buttonholed again.

Mohandas caught sight of another volunteer and asked him: 'Could you tell me where the delegates are supposed to stay?'

The volunteer said nothing but signalled that Mohandas should follow him. It looked as if he had taken a vow of silence or the volunteers had been forbidden to speak. Mohandas did as he was told. The volunteer kept up his wordless walk for a while till they came to the Ripon College gate. The gate had a board carrying the college name. The volunteer entered the gate and Mohandas followed him in. The volunteer pointed out a building to him and quickly turned on his heels as if to escape being spotted. Mohandas was left staring after him. He wanted to thank him, but he had made good his escape as if successfully evading an impending disaster. Mohandas couldn't help breaking into laughter. Anyway, he had found his destination and that was what mattered.

Most of the delegates had been put up in the same building. Mohandas too was given a place in one of the rooms. Later, he found out to his amazement that Tilak Maharaj was also staying in the same building. A top leader like Tilak Maharaj in this place! But he felt good. He hadn't forgotten that it was Tilak Maharaj who had made his Pune public meeting possible.

Tilak's court ran without a break. There was however a difference between the courts of Sir Pheroze and Tilak Maharaj. Sir Pheroze's was a royal court controlled strictly by formal conventions. Tilak's was an open house. Even if Tilak was sleeping, visitors waiting for him would gather outside and kept up a regular racket chatting. The editor of *Amrit Bazar Patrika,* Babu Motilal, was a close friend of Tilak. The place was always ringing with his laughter. When he spoke, his voice carried to the other end of the building. When Tilak was turbanless, he kept stroking his cropped pate. In between, he wielded a nutcracker with which he cracked betel nuts, disposing of the output into his mouth.

Tilak had a single-point agenda: 'If you want freedom, oppose every excess of the white man. Never forget the excesses; like beads in a prayer string, count and recount them in your head. Do not nurse hatred, but let anger grow within you. When your anger is affirmative, it becomes your strength.'

Every morning, Mohandas got up, got ready, paid his respects to Tilak Maharaj from a distance and walked out. Never did he once meet him in person, though during his last interaction with him he had helped him out. Things of course had not progressed much beyond that point. He did not think it proper to trouble him further. It also did not help that he belonged to the radical group in the Congress, while the party was dominated by conservatives.

The volunteers in the Ripon College camp ignored everyone except Tilak Maharaj. If you asked one of them something, he would pose as if the matter had nothing whatsoever to do with him and would pass the buck to another volunteer. The second one passed it on to the third one, the third to the fourth and so it went on. Eventually the chain—from asking to grasping to turning it into action—grew so long that the end point would be impossible to locate. The volunteers would frequently get into altercations. One would tell the other: 'When you were asked, why didn't you do it?' The other would retort: 'You were the one asked first. It was your duty.'

Mohandas was completely foxed by these strange goings-on. An organization as big as this running without any discipline and self-restraint! The country may not be free but here everyone was free! But this freedom had never heard of discipline. Could there be freedom without discipline? Mohandas started cultivating the volunteers. He didn't of course make any direct criticism, but told them about South Africa. In that land, he told them, everyone worked with everyone else. Even the richest man was open to the meanest work. There was no squabbling at work. Use your body and your mind for work, not your tongue. The tongue is for tasting—tasty food or tasty talk. But craving for tasty food often makes a man dishonest; craving for tasty talk makes him foul-mouthed. Such men only waste their time. There is no place for either of them when your aim is to serve. Nor is there any room for a proxy in service. If you wish to serve, you must do it yourself. For service, commitment comes first, experience second and skill last. Indians in South Africa have now begun to appreciate this.

They listened to Gandhi very attentively. A few also laughed at him behind his back. 'This is India, Mr. Gandhi!' they said. It was a rare person who tried to put the ideas into practice. So no material difference ever showed up in the situation. Mohandas knew this, but still kept up his efforts.

Two separate kitchens were being run for the delegates, at opposite corners of the camp. When Mohandas discovered this, he asked: 'Why two separate kitchens?'

'Tamils are rather finicky about purity; hence a separate kitchen for them.'

'You mean others are not pure enough?'

'Well, our Tamil brothers asked for a separate kitchen.'

'This is caste discrimination. Caste and religion have to do with your actions, not with hatred and touchability. The Congress belongs to everyone equally.'

They had no answer to this, though one of them tried to answer it by asking Mohandas: 'Are you a Hindu?'

'Couldn't you make out from what I said that I was a Hindu?'

They all dispersed.

Mohandas went around the toilets and was horrified to see the condition of the toilets. His head was ready to burst with the stink that emanated from the toilets. He came back and checked with a volunteer: 'Aren't there any arrangements for the cleaning of the toilets?'

'Not my business. Ask the *bhangi*.'

'Can't we be our own *bhangi*s?'

The volunteer sniggered. A couple of other volunteers also landed on the scene.

Mohandas asked: 'Is it possible to arrange for a broom and a bucket?'

They looked at him with surprise and sniffed as if they were standing next to the stinking mess.

One of them asked: 'Why?'

'We create the mess. Why can't we clean it?'

Their look of surprise gave way to another expression which said that this suited and booted person was either off his rocker or maybe belonged to the lowest caste and was dressed in borrowed plumes. Ignoring what Mohandas said, they slipped away one by one.

With great difficulty, Mohandas was able to locate a broom and a bucket. Then he tied a piece of cloth across his face and entered a toilet. He felt he would throw up. In Beach Grove, he had only cleaned the urine pots, and Kastur couldn't stand it at all. Mohandas got bucketsful of water and started flushing out the excreta. The stink had got into his head and he could barely contain himself. The stinking mess was stuck to the floor and he was trying to clean it with the broom, rubbing it hard on the floor.

The volunteers, standing at a distance, laughed.

Mohandas came out and said: 'Please don't worry. I have cleaned this toilet for my own use. How can we ever learn the major task of serving others until we first learn to serve our own selves? What I have done today for myself I will do tomorrow for others.' His voice was quite indistinct because of the cloth tied to his face.

'For others?' One of them wanted to say something, but Mohandas interrupted him. 'It needs preparation before you can serve others,' he said.

There were holes all around. Mohandas looked at the stinking toilets and then at the holes. He looked next at the yawning gap between the delegates and the volunteers and then at the noble Congress which was going to have its session in two days.

Everyone is happy in his own way wherever he is, Mohandas felt. A long sigh and he got busy with his work again.

Several times that night, he had a feeling it was raining outside. He would hear the sound of a stream of water falling strongly, then thinning out and finally stopping completely. This happened several times during the night. Every time it brought him awake and he would start thinking about the events of the day. He couldn't believe that he had been able to do what he had done. The excrement sticking to the toilet pits! The stink like a gush of steam rising from the sea! He will have to do all this here. Someone will have to clean up this hellish mess of centuries. Who will do it? He felt his stomach coming up to his mouth again and he pulled himself up: Wrong! This is wrong! You are shrinking from service! You are showing disgust with service!

He turned over and started on another journey. Natal to Rajkot, Rajkot to Calcutta and then this foul storm of stink! The scene of farewell was still fresh in his mind. His wife and kids were still at Rajkot. That end of the memory was tied to his innermost being. He felt it tugging at him repeatedly. The things Kastur had said were rolling over and over again in his mind. He tore himself away from them to fly back to the present. It was not sweet music, but it was there—an echo that kept billowing up again and again.

When he woke up in the morning another blast of foul smell laid siege of him. Small heaps of excrement lined the ground along side the verandah, with the moisture still not quite gone. People had been relieving themselves right outside their rooms throughout the night, as if it was a phase in their sleeping process. He recalled what Kastur had told him: Can't these people go out in the open? How he wished she could see this sight! But going out in the open was not exactly a solution. In Natal, he had seen the ditches behind the *girmitiya* barracks, the foul smell from which enveloped their whole existence. Their whole lives were spent in a haze of stink. They slept, awoke, sat and ate in that haze. It was not for nothing that the whites called them all sorts of names. Mohandas felt a lump in his throat. Two different types of stink were now challenging him. Such a large country and every house a hellhole!

The night volunteers were going off duty. He called them and showed them the sight: 'Do you see this?'

'Of course.'

'Why didn't you stop them?'

'How can you stop someone from attending to nature's call?'

'What I mean is stop them from using the verandah for this purpose. They could have gone round the corner or something. Can't this be cleaned up?'

They came up with the same old answer: 'Not our job.'

'What is your job?'

'To look after the delegates, to get the list of the day's programmes to them, to cater to their needs, to get them any special information they might ask for and so on.' This was said with great defiance.

'And to keep their surroundings as filthy as possible,' Mohandas said, laughing. Then he made a request: 'If you will please pour the water, I will clean it up.'

They took to their heels as if being chased by a ghost.

Once again, Mohandas took up the broom and started cleaning the place with bucketsful of water.

The delegates were worried. They expressed shock to each other at the kinds of people that were gaining entry to the Congress sessions.

'I hear he comes from South Africa.'

'When they go to South Africa, do they lose all sense of what's pure and what's impure, what your religion allows and what it doesn't?'

'The man must have been one of "them" in the last birth.'

'If he was not, he will be in the next.'

'Actually, some people adopt such low tricks to pressurize others.'

That night, Mohandas was not woken up by any untoward noises.

~

Mohandas had made rounds of all Congress offices and camps the very next day after his reaching Calcutta. There was a lot of activity: people coming, going, meeting, talking about the session plans, writing notes about their needs and handing them to the Congress offices, nursing the egos of the seniors and the juniors going round registering their attendance at the doorsteps of the seniors.

Two of the secretaries, Bhupendranath Basu and Ghoshalbabu, were looking after the session's work. Mohandas went up to Bhupendrababu and introduced himself: 'I am here as a delegate. My name is M.K. Gandhi. Please assign some work to me. I have nothing to do.'

Bhupendra Babu gave him the once-over and then went back to his work, dismissing Mohandas with: 'I have no work for you. Go and see Ghoshalbabu. He may have something.'

Mohandas saw a man surrounded by many volunteers. He approached him:

Although a Congress secretary, Ghoshalbabu lived in great splendour. He was always dressed immaculately mostly in western clothes. He first gave Mohandas a visual examination to see how much of him was genuine stuff and how much phony. Then he announced: 'I can assign some clerical work to you, if you like.'

'There is no work that I won't do, from cleaning to the most responsible.'

Pressing his lips together in the style of an Englishman, Ghoshalbabu said: 'Bravo! That's the spirit!' Then he turned to the volunteers and said: 'Did you all hear what this young man said? He is London trained and he is ready to do whatever he is asked to.'

Turning to Mohandas, he said: 'You see that pile of letters? Take that seat and start working. There are hundreds of people here to see me everyday. Where do I find the time to reply to these letters? Nor can I find a clerk to entrust the work to. Read all the letters carefully and send acknowledgements. If you find something special in any letter, check with me; if there is something very special just give the letter to me.'

Mohandas was happy that a stranger could be considered worthy of so much trust.

Mohandas went through the letters like a breeze. A fleeting glimpse and he could tell which letter pertained to which subject. He sorted them out in different piles. The few that needed Ghoshalbabu's attention he handed over to him. The letters had all been taken care of in a couple of hours, with short replies to them ready for dispatch. Ghoshalbabu was delighted.

A loquacious person, it was hard for Ghoshalbabu to keep quiet. He kept up a regular conversation:

'Where do you come from?'

'Kathiawar. I have returned from South Africa after many years.'

'What did you do there?'

'I was a barrister. I also worked for Natal Congress. We had founded a Congress there.'

Ghoshalbabu looked up, startled. 'Why didn't you tell me all this before? I am sorry I made you work like a clerk.'

'So, what's wrong with that? Compared to you, I'm only a beginner. You have grayed in the service of the Congress. You are my senior anyway and I am nothing but a raw youngster. By giving me work to do, you did me a favour. I wanted to work for the Congress and you gave me an opportunity.'

Ghoshalbabu couldn't have been more pleased. 'Honestly speaking, that's the spirit. The young men today are strangers to that spirit. I have been with the Congress ever since it was formed. Along with Mr. Hume, I had a contribution to make to the founding of the Congress.'

When he went to have lunch, Ghoshalbabu insisted on taking Mohandas also with him. 'Our friendship begins today,' he said.

Ghoshalbabu always enjoyed a siesta after lunch. When he was ready to go back to work afterwards, he called out to his manservant a few times but he had apparently taken off. When Mohandas saw it was getting late and Ghoshalbabu getting worried, he said: 'Tell me what you want. I'll do it for you.'

'Irresponsible chap! It's time to go to the office and he is nowhere to be seen. People must be waiting for me. And there is a pile of work waiting to be done. If the fellow had to go, he should have at least taken out a fresh shirt for me and helped me put it on.'

'Tell me where you keep the shirts. I'll help you put it on.'

'How do I know where he keeps the shirts? They could possibly be in that drawer.'

Mohandas took out a shirt. Thc collar was just as stiff as hc uscd to wear in London. In Natal, he had used starch to make it stiffer and had to put up with his friends' ridicule for the effort. But now he was an expert both in washing and ironing shirts. He smiled to himself.

He took out the shirt and fixed the buttons in place. As Ghoshalbabu put it on, he said: 'You see, Gandhi, a Congress secretary has no time even to put on his shirt and button it. Tell me, what can the poor man do?'

It was all Gandhi could do to keep himself from bursting out laughing. His laughter would have caused pain to Ghoshalbabu. If not pain, anger. Anger would have spoiled his image. Mohandas was of course happy that he had got to know a man so busy and so senior that he had worked with Mr. Hume. But questions never allowed him any peace. The one that was bothering him now was: Is ostentation so necessary? Sir Pherozeshah Mehta was such a distinguished patriot, but he needed such an expensive saloon for his travel!

Such questions always brought him up short.

~

Whenever he had the time, Mohandas set out to meet the leaders. He told them the sad story of Indians in South Africa. At times, he had the feeling that he was turning into a storyteller. Then he reminded himself that one could not experience the pain of others without experiencing it oneself, nor could the other understand your sorrow unless you told him about it. You had to keep at it hoping one day something would give. When Mohandas returned to his room at night, questions would start chasing him again. So many of the top leaders in attendance, yet time flowed past like so much dirty water in the drain. Why didn't someone do something about it? If you weren't ready to make sacrifices yourself, how could you expect anyone else to listen to lessons in sacrifice? You couldn't erect a building on the foundation of sand! The top leaders towered so high that they were barely visible from below. Everything seemed pointless and purposeless. English was the only language used, so dialogue moved in a closed circle. The language in which one laughed and cried could be used only for laughing and crying. Nobody was interested in the work he was doing while everyone worried about what the other person was doing. And everyone boasted of the great job he would have done had he only been doing what the other man was doing.

Taking stock of the day's work, all that Mohandas got was a big zero. Then he told himself that maybe, given the conditions, no one could do any better. Was it not enough that they had organized a session as big as this? Why entertain negative thoughts? When it will be our turn to do something, what will we aim at?

Slowly, Mohandas was overcome with sleep. He felt the stink rising again and people fleeing with their noses covered. He saw himself standing with a broom in his hand. Slowly, the foul smell began to give way to a fine strain of fragrance. Where was the fragrance coming from? Mohandas was now wide awake.

~

It was the opening day of the Congress session.

A huge stage had been erected. All the top leaders were seated on the stage, most of them in western dresses. There were a few exceptions like Tilak Maharaj and Surendra Nath Banerji, who were in Indian clothes. Most of the leaders from Bengal and Maharashtra could be recognized by their regional outfits. The volunteers, in glittering uniforms, ringed the stage like guards in a king's court. Mohandas had never seen so many top leaders sitting together on a stage, nor had he ever witnessed a political party's session staged with so much pomp and show. Sessions of Natal Congress were held in people's homes in the beginning; later, they were held on Pine Street, where Natal Congress had got its own hall. Mohandas was overcome with emotion.

Another question now raised its head in Mohandas' mind: 'Where are you in this gigantic show?'

He couldn't help laughing at the question. Then, addressing himself, he said: 'Doesn't the thought signify impatience? After all, what has been your contribution to this effort? There is still a long way to travel for you. These people here, sitting on the stage, have performed a long and arduous journey to get where they are today. Their position wasn't exactly gifted to them.'

The President started on his speech. It was a veritable tome. Reading out the speech was like an innate skill. Listening to it was a test of the listeners' patience. The President read out a few sentences here and a few sentences there and left the remainder to be read out by the others. A tremendous applause followed.

Dinshaw Wacha, the President, sat down, smiling. Mohandas couldn't make out if the applause was for his reading out only a few sentences, or for leaving out so much.

The first session was declared closed after the President's speech and the applause. Thousands of people emptied on to the streets at the end of the session, like pigeons escaping from a dovecote. Most of the Bengalis were dressed in their formal ceremonial clothes. A few also wore necktie and jacket. Some Gujaratis sported a *pheta.* Delegates from the north wore variegated dresses: some wore kurta and dhoti, others *achkan* and pajamas and a few wore suits. Suits were of course not in significant currency. Only those who were fully westernized wore them.

Gokhale came down from the stage and beckoned to Gandhi. Mohandas had met him before. Parting the crowds, he reached Gokhale. 'Follow me,' said Gokhale.

Mohandas followed. On the way, Gokhale said: 'The Subjects Committee is meeting. You are one of the speakers.'

'I know nothing about it,' said Gandhi.

'Don't worry about that. Come with me. If you don't do it, who else is going to raise your issue?'

'My thought, precisely.'

'If Sir Pherozeshah Mehta has told you to, you must make sure you are there.'

Mohandas took a seat some distance from Gokhale behind him. Like a child attending a fair for the first time, he was filled with curiosity for everything. Everybody who mounted the stage delivered a long speech. At the end of it, he moved a short resolution running into a few lines and everyone okayed it by raising hands. Very few resolutions were followed by any discussion. Everything seemed planned and pre-arranged. English was being used the way a boatman uses a pole to push his boat forward in the river. Every resolution was backed by some prominent leader or the other. When the resolution had been read out, the leader would nod his head and the resolution was through. Mohandas had begun to wonder if in the roar of so many top guns, the whistle of his piffling air gun would make any sound at all. As the proceedings progressed, Mohandas' heart started racing. He found himself in a position similar to the one in which he had once found himself in the Vegetarians' Conference in London. This, despite the fact that the agenda of the meeting made no reference to his resolution.

The agenda was moving fast towards conclusion. Items were being disposed of at a lightning speed. Twice or thrice, Mohandas, half rising in his seat, tried to catch Sir Pherozeshah's eye but was unsuccessful. A voice came from one corner: 'Hurry up!' Another voice from another direction said: 'Do you intend to spend the night here?'

'Are we going to have dinner after dinner time is over?' People had started walking out.

Mohandas dragged his chair to where Gokhale was sitting. Gokhale had already seen the resolution.

'Please do something,' said Mohandas in a trembling voice.

'I remember it,' said Gokhale in a low voice. 'I won't let it go by default.'

Sir Pherozeshah, pushing back his chair, said: 'Good! That's that!'

'No,' said Gokhale, 'The South Africa resolution is still to be taken up. Gandhi has come here all the way only for that purpose.'

'Have you seen it? I haven't,' said Sir Pherozeshah.

'Absolutely. A very well thought out piece.'

Sir Pherozeshah gave his neck a slight angle and said: 'Then get on with it.'

As Mohandas stood up to present his resolution, his legs were shaking beneath him.

'Mr. President, my resolution reads as follows: This grand session of the Indian Congress expresses its sympathy with the struggle for existence being carried out by Indians settled in South Africa. While drawing the attention of His Excellency, the Viceroy, towards the anti-Indian laws in force there, it expresses hope and confidence that His Excellency would extend meaningful help in the evolution of a fair and just decision in matters relating to questions of respect and dignity of the British Indians settled in Transvaal and New Orange State, which await the consideration of the Colonial Secretary of His Majesty's Government.'

Prof. Gokhale stood up and said: 'I second this resolution.'

Dinshaw Wacha looked at Mohandas and said: 'You have five minutes to speak on the resolution.'

Mohandas had in the meantime prepared his speech with great care. He had also decided to himself that he would not read his speech, but would speak extempore. But now he found that the resolution had been accepted on Gokhale's assurance that he had seen the resolution. No one had made any effort to find out what the subject of the resolution was or what its background was. Mohandas had lost all his enthusiasm on this account. If everything was to be decided without the need for any background knowledge, what was the point in even reading out the resolution? Still, he decided to speak. He felt however that the oratorical skills he had cultivated in South Africa were taking leave of him in the towering presence of these leaders.

Wacha called out: 'Yes, Mr. Gandhi?'

Mohandas organized himself and started on his speech:

'Our grievances are of two types: the first has to do with the general anti-Indian attitudes of the European colonialists; the second is related to the oppressive anti-Indian policies of the four British colonies of South Africa. For example, every Indian, no matter what his profession, is addressed by the humiliating epithet of coolie, is not admitted to hotels and is, in general, treated with contempt everywhere. The immigration rules of these colonies force the Indian immigrants to fill the immigration forms only in a European language, or they cannot enter the colony. Grant of a business licence under the Dealers' Act depends on the sweet will of the authorities and no appeals are entertained. These issues are currently under the consideration of Mr. Chamberlain. The session this evening started with a song, which went like this:

With the love of your country in your hearts
With knowledge capital in your minds

With the strength that lies in unity
Go abroad, my countrymen …

This is a call from the Indians settled in South Africa. If you can take a lesson from the lines of this song and come to their help, maybe we can find a solution to their problems …'

A bell sounded. Mohandas noted that three minutes were over. He looked at the chairman and went back to his seat. Others had spoken for half an hour or three quarters of an hour and the bell had not sounded. For Mohandas, it had sounded after three minutes.

Gokhale spoke: 'You can take a couple of minutes more, if you like. You have been given five minutes.'

Mohandas didn't hear what Gokhale had said. If they were going to accept what he had asked for, he thought, it would be like hitting in the dark. You may hit your object, or you may hit the wall, or maybe something else.

Mohandas heard the bell ringing throughout the night. He felt he wanted to say something but he wasn't being allowed to. All the *girmitiya*s collected there, all the Indian businessmen were pushing him forward, asking him to go forward and speak: 'Speak! Speak!'but the bell was unrelenting was ringing … ringing … and not letting him speak.

Mohandas woke up. It was dark all round. Deep inside, someone was telling him: 'Did you hear the voices? Did you notice how many voices your voice represents? If you let your voice be stopped, all the voices will be stopped. Don't let your voice be stopped.'

Mohandas closed his eyes and sat still. He never found out when the morning broke.

The session ended. The participants started leaving. Some had already returned. Mohandas had decided to stay on in Calcutta for a month. The purpose was to make the people and institutions of Bengal aware of the situation of Indians settled in South Africa. People in London who sympathized with the Indians of South Africa always wrote to him to start a movement in India, to wake up India. If possible, take a delegation and meet the Viceroy. Strengthen our hands, they said. Only then will we get justice. Mohandas had said in his address that he wanted to hold meetings all over the country. The people of Natal did not want money. They had enough of it. They wanted support and sympathy. And they wanted this message to be conveyed to everyone in India.

Since it was not possible for Mohandas to stay for a whole month in a hotel, he had brought an introductory letter for India Club, where he got a place as soon as the Congress session ended.

This was also the time when Lord Curzon held his famous durbar. This was not the sort of durbar where a common man presented his petition to the King for redressal of injustice. Rather it was a display of one's power and wealth and a means of impressing people of one's superiority. Only kings, princes, very senior officials and wealthy citizens had access to the durbar. Expensive gifts were offered to the Viceroy. Grand sessions of the Congress differed in this respect that no gifts were offered and the top leaders had the freedom to speak their minds. Otherwise they too were no better than the durbar princes. Many members of the India Club, mostly kings and princes, had been nominated to the durbar. When these gentlemen appeared at the India Club, they were dressed in their traditional attire: Bengali kurta, dhoti, shawl, etc. Of course, they wore expensive dresses, customized and full of glitter. But when they went to the durbar, they wore dresses which looked like an attendant's livery: turbans, trousers, jackets and shining shoes with bands of gold or silver thread running through them. Our kings and princes had the same status as their attendants, except that their turbans, their gem-and diamond-studded feminine style jewellery, the plumes on their turbans and the swords set them apart. There was no difference in the smartness with which they attended to their masters. In South Africa, there were no such durbars, nor did the native tribal chiefs wear such fancy dresses. It was their colour that distinguished them.

Mohandas inquired of one of the durbar kings: 'You normally wear dhoti, kurta and shawl and look quite decent in them. Don't you feel awkward wearing the dress of jokers and attendants to the durbar?'

He replied: 'No one can appreciate the sorrow and the humiliation that one undergoes better than oneself. Only we know the humiliation that we have to undergo. In exchange, of course, we are able to earn a few pardons and a few titles.'

'But why do you need turbans, trousers, jackets, etc. for that purpose?'

'Don't you notice any difference between us and the cooks and attendants? Though we have our own attendants, we are worse off than the Viceroy's attendants.' The durbar prince laughed a pained laugh and continued: 'If we ever made the mistake of going to the durbar in our day-to-day clothes, our kingdoms and principalities may be confiscated and we may be reduced to beggars.'

'I would in fact say that you should attend the durbar in clothes which would tell the real story about the way the ordinary people in this country live. How I wish I were in your position.' Mohandas laughed.

The durbar prince said: 'Don't forget that we have to live our lives with these people. And, you know of course that no barber can muster the courage to hold up the mirror to the king to show him the spots on his face. In fact, this is the only occasion when we can display our loyalty and have a few words with the Viceroy. Otherwise, years pass before we can set eyes on him. Our requests for an appointment simply go unanswered. Mine is a rather small state, but even those with large states suffer a similar fate.'

Mohandas noticed a passing shade of shame on his face.

He did not think it proper to continue with the topic. He simply shook hands with him and went off for a stroll. The pitiable condition of a prince occupied his thoughts. He was unable to decide whether to treat him as an object of sympathy or of hatred.

~

When Gokhale asked, Mohandas accepted his invitation and went to stay with him. Mohandas had his own style of working. He would do all his work with his own hands and when the work was over he went and spent some time with Gokhale discussing current affairs. Then he set out on his day's mission. Gokhale took every care to see that no inconvenience was caused to Mohandas. Mohandas had minimized his needs to the barest. Simple food and a strict timetable. Gokhale's life too was transparent. There was no topic that he could not discuss with Mohandas. It was at Gokhale's place that Mohandas had met P.C. Ray. In those days, P.C. Ray lived close to Gokhale. Once Gokhale told Mohandas, introducing P.C. Ray: 'Mr. Ray has a salary of eight hundred rupees per month. He spends forty rupees on himself and the rest on social service. He never got married and perhaps has no intention to get married either. He fears if he gets married, his salary will no longer be his own.' They both laughed.

'Congratulations, Mr. Ray,' Mohandas found himself saying: 'Service and marriage, science and marriage, wanderlust and marriage, self-denial and marriage ... they simply don't go together, or hardly at all. Service demands loyalty to one person; marriage demands it too: everyone demands loyalty.'

When Mohandas had said it, he suddenly looked around. Then he laughed to himself. 'How one can get deluded!' he said to himself. 'Kastur is in Rajkot.'

Gokhale wouldn't allow even a single minute of his to be wasted. The work he did was his, but it had to be done to help others. Everything he did was for the country's freedom, or for its welfare. He spoke nothing but the truth, and eschewed nothing but falsehood. His constant refrain was: freedom for the country first, everything else second! He considered Justice Ranade to be his guru. Justice Ranade was not only a judge; he was also an economist, a social reformer, a historian and much else. When Gokhale started on his eulogy of Ranade, it was hard to stop him. Mohandas then concentrated on his eyes where he felt he could see waves of the purest water rise and fall. He had seen such pure innocence in the eyes of *Ba*, his mother. The eyes of *Bapu*, his father, on the other hand, were like the reflection in the clear water of a pond of a tree standing by its side. Mohandas had never been able to understand if what was reflected was his position, or the fact that he was a male. He could feel the same reflection stirring within him. He was however sure of one thing: what the reflection showed was certainly not position or power.

One day, Mohandas queried Gokhale about his use of a horse carriage for transport.

'Do you find it completely impossible to travel by a tram? Is it somehow degrading for an important leader like you to use the tram?'

Gokhale had a transparent face. It showed his feelings as clearly as a cinema screen shows moving pictures. A thin film of distress now covered his face. 'Gandhi,' he said, 'I'm sorry that even you could not gauge the reason. You know that the allowance I get as a Council member, I do not spend on myself. I am very envious of the carefree way in which you can use the tram. The day you reach the level of fame in which I find myself today, you will also find it impossible to travel by tram. If not impossible, it will certainly be very difficult. We should not assume that people who occupy important positions in public life do whatever they do for their comfort and to show off their importance. I admire your simplicity. I too try to live as simply as possible. But there are some expenses which one simply cannot avoid.'

'You don't even go for walks. Could that be the reason for your ill health?'

'Have you ever seen me avoiding walks when I have the time to do so?'

Mohandas felt further discussion would only add to his distress, so he took his leave. On the way, he kept wondering if he was satisfied by the answers he had received.

~

Mohandas legged it all over Calcutta. He knocked on the door of everyone who he got to know had the slightest interest in South Africa or could do something to help. Babu Kalicharan Banerji, Justice Mitra, Sir Gurudas Banerji, Raja Sir Pyare Mohan Mukherji—there was no one he had not called on several times. He would wait for them and the moment he got an opportunity, he put forward his case like a missionary. Some supported him; some just heard him out and then showed him the door. Mohandas nevertheless thanked them before he left. In either case, he felt he had made some progress towards his goal. Even if someone refused to do anything and sent him packing, he still had the satisfaction that he had at least conveyed his message to him which would act like a dormant seed and which, who knew, may actually burst forth one day.

He recalled that the last time too he had to return empty handed from Calcutta.

People often asked him about the Kali temple: Did you do obeisance at the Kali temple?

He hadn't. People said: 'Kali temple is an awakened place. It was with the goddess's grace that Ramakrishna became a *paramhansa* (enlightened). Narendra turned into Vivekananda. You cannot succeed in your mission until you pay your obeisance to the goddess.'

Kalicharan Banerji was a Christian, but he worked devotedly for the Congress. He too had asked Mohandas about Kali temple and they had talked about sin and godliness. It was on his recommendation that Mohandas decided to visit the Kali temple. Justice Mitra also lived in the same area. He first called on Justice Mitra. A depressing session later, he moved on to the Kali temple.

Flocks of sheep blocked the way to the temple. Mohandas had to pick his path through the bleating sheeps very carefully. The sheeps were marked with different colours as if in an attempt to paint them. Mohandas touched one of the sheep. Its skin shivered as if it was detached from the body. Rows of beggars lined the path to the temple. As they begged, they produced a great variety of sounds from their throats. The women among them had tonsured heads.Wrapped in a single piece of cloth, some of them were so old that you couldn't see their face for the wrinkles. Some of the men among them were almost naked. Mohandas felt that here was another herd of bleating sheep. He couldn't however touch any of them to see if their skin was also detached from their bodies. People gave them alms as they passed them on their way to or from the temple.

They are buying merit by throwing coins at them, thought Mohandas. He felt disgusted and had an impulse to snatch away the money from them and throw it into the river. When they try to find it again, they would at least be putting in some labour. The alms would then turn into earned income and they would probably be saved from the sin of beggary.

It looked to him as if he was being pushed back by the crowds that were pushing forward to the temple.

A little way up, a man sat on the verandah of his house. Though a householder, he had all the trappings of a holy man. 'Where are you headed, son?'

'To the temple.'

'Sit down.'

Mohandas sat down and asked: 'Where are all these sheep going?'

'To be sacrificed.'

'Is this animal sacrifice a religion?'

'Who would call it religion?'

'You are a religious man. Why don't you speak out against it?'

'Not my job. My job is to worship God.'

'Is this the only place where your job can be carried on? Isn't there any other place?'

'All places are the same to me. People too are like flocks of sheep. They go wherever the shepherd drives them. That's not the job of us holy men.'

Mohandas wanted to say that you yourself are the shepherd driving this flock, but he bid farewell to him with folded hands and headed towards the temple. The courtyard of the temple was sticky all over and one could see bloodstains which had grown black with age. Moving up, he could see what looked like a river of blood. He felt the blood rising and entering his brain. He gave his head a shake. The sheep that had been blocking his path now seemed to him to be swimming in the stream of blood and casting helpless looks all around them. Suddenly, everyone seemed to him to be sinking in the river of blood one after another and bleating like sheep.

The devotees were collecting the *prasad*. Mohandas made a quick about turn and started walking back. The flood of blood was following him. The sheep were lost in the flood; only their bleating could be heard.

Mohandas had a feeling that the bleating was gradually taking over the whole country. Everything else had perished; only the bleating remained.

Mohandas wanted to meet Vivekananda, so he took the road to his house, but the sun, he felt, was too strong. Your journey may be a short one, but if the road is not tree lined, the destination is hard to reach. Mohandas' journey was a long one and he needed shade to refresh himself.

He met Niveditabehn on the way. The way she was turned out, all pomp and expensive finery, he felt the sun was getting stronger. His road would now be more difficult and he had a long way to go. He thought it best to go back and quickly retraced his steps.

~

Mohandas was travelling third class. The sentence that his host had spoken, that sacrificial sheep know no sorrow or pain, kept coming back to him. The sound of drums and the incantation of holy mantras kill their consciousness. The fatigue of the journey and the acid-like sentence of his host were making him restless. Was this the reason that bands accompanied soldiers leaving for the battlefield? Are these soldiers too like sacrificial sheep? Do they also lose their consciousness and feeling? Scenes of the Boer War passed before his eyes one after another.

He had deliberately chosen a passenger train and bought a third class ticket. The compartment was so crowded that one had to stretch one's neck high above the others, like fish raising their gills above water, to take a breath. Filth was everywhere, like an institutionalized custom. Here too there was a flock of sheep and he was a part of the flock. Necks shaking and ears covered, the passengers waited patiently for the next station. Mohandas recalled the Pietermaritzburg station where the white conductor was asking him to join the *kaffir*s travelling in the wagon and he was adamant that he wouldn't. He would only travel first class. Eventually he neither travelled first, nor wagon. Instead, he spent the whole night shivering on the platform. Today he was travelling wagon out of his own will. He had been a barrister then, and so he was now. But it was dissent then, while it was assent now. And there was the desire to get to know your own people. A deliberate snub to the culture of the saloon! The right to travel first was the cause of a struggle there; here, travelling third was a means of getting to know. The situation had upset him so much there; it was a welcome thing here.

Mohandas got down at Banaras. Travellers ...! The very word caused him to laugh out loud. Here the word was applied to pilgrimage seekers, persons out on a hunt for merit or virtue. In Natal, the word described persons who crossed the seven seas at their own expense to set up a business there. How do words change their meanings with change of place! Same word, different meanings! Hadn't the word 'Mohandas' too changed its meaning? He couldn't help smiling to himself.

When the train steamed into Banaras, it was morning. Chanting *Har Har Mahadev*! or *Baba Vishvanath ki Jai*, throngs of travellers rushed out of the train. Mohandas had a Gujarati dress on. Standing by the side of the road like a Gujarati villager, he was wondering where he should go. Suddenly, a number of *panda*s surrounded him, each one shouting into his ears: 'Where are you from?' What are the names of your father and grandfather?' Each one carried a register in his hands. One of the *panda*s looked relatively clean to Mohandas. He was looking at him all right but was not asking any questions like the others. Mohandas went with him quietly.

He took Mohandas to his house. There was a cow tethered to a stake in the courtyard. Living quarters were upstairs. Mohandas had made it clear to the *panda* that he won't pay more than a rupee and a quarter as the priest's fee. The man said: 'The fee is not important when your aim is to serve others. For me every client of mine, whether poor or rich, is equally important. The fee depends on the client's faith and the ability to pay. Neither your faith nor your ability to pay is something that I can do anything about.'

Mohandas looked at him. This was something new to him. A merchant of religion was expounding his own version of service. Mohandas felt he had been handed a new and strange line of experience.

The ritual was performed strictly according to rules, without cutting corners. It ended at noon. Mohandas had nursed a desire to visit the Kashi Vishvanath temple ever since the days of *Ba*, who often expressed a wish to visit the place. Before he went to Natal, when he was practising at Bombay, he had also attended a lecture on 'Travelling to Kashi' in the Prarthana Samaj Hall. That had whetted his appetite for a visit to Vishvanath. He entered the lane leading to the temple. Immediately he felt something giving way within him. He felt the milk of desire within him being diluted by the water of distaste. The lane was so narrow and so filthy that entrance was an ordeal. You could slip and fall at any step, so Mohandas was being extra careful. The shopkeepers and the visitors were speaking to each other so loudly that you had a feeling there was a fight on. Flies buzzed around you as if you were an old acquaintance of theirs. Or maybe you were a heap of garbage.

Entering the temple, the first sight he saw was women sitting on the floor with their eyes closed, looking completely oblivious to the world outside. Mohandas thought that if that were true, that would be their own achievement, not something the temple could take credit for. The temple itself had everything that could distract your attention. Mohandas' hand automatically shot up to cover his nose: something was rotting somewhere. Whenever he went to the palace with *Ba,* he used to feel the same smell. He looked around. A pile of flowers was rotting in a corner. Why did they allow fragrant things like flowers to rot? Wouldn't god Vishvanath, for the pleasure of whose nostrils the flowers were presented to him, feel displeased to receive the smell of the rotting flowers? Or, could it be that that the rotting smell too had become part of the ritual?

The floor was quality marble studded with gold and silver coins faded and slippery with age and, in places, with mere hollows where the coins might have been prised out. One of the *panda*s was explaining that the solid silver doors of the sanctum sanctorum had been donated by Ahlya Bai, but the doors were singularly devoid of any sheen. There was no room for beauty in devotional ritual, thought Mohandas. Some devotee had added premium to the monetary value of the floor by getting coins stuck into it, but in the process had smashed beauty to smithereens.

Mohandas had heard of Gyanwapi (lake of knowledge). It was considered the done thing to follow up a visit to Vishvanath by a call on Gyanwapi. Mohandas looked for knowledge and for god, but, finding neither, checked with a sweet-seller: 'I can neither see knowledge nor god anywhere. What I can see is garbage.' The man grinned at him.

A priest was esconced in the temple, glorying in his priestliness. Mohandas struggled with the dilemma for a moment: to give or not to give? Why reward filth in the name of God? Still, he took out a pie and extended it to him. Anything more than a pie would be honouring sheer laziness. There were three pies to a pice.

The priest hurled the pie away: 'You insult me. You will go to hell.'

Mohandas enjoyed his reaction. Assuming a serious mien, he said: 'Please do not worry about me. If hell is my destiny, that's where I'll go; if it's heaven, I'll go to heaven. A man of knowledge like you should not get into this question at all. As for the pie, it's not at all a burden for me. If you wish, you can still have it, or I'll take it with me.'

'Get lost. I can do without your pie, you evil man! You rogue!' He let him have a string of abuses.

Mohandas picked up the pie and said, laughing: 'Sir, you have lost a pie and I have found one.'

As he was about to walk away, the priest said: 'Come on! Give it to me! I am not an evil man like you. If I do not accept your gift, evil may befall you.'

Mohandas put the pie on his extended hand, took a long sigh, and said: 'Some religion!'

~

Anne Beasant was head of the Theosophical Society. Mohandas asked his way to her place. She was recovering from an illness and was very weak, but still entertained him. For him, it was partial compensation for his inability to see Vivekananda at Calcutta. Mohandas introduced himself, paid her his respects and said: 'I had been told that you are not well. I only wanted to pay my respects. You have done me a great favour by seeing me despite your illness. I won't cause you any more strain. Please allow me to leave! My respects, again!'

He remembered that Vivekananda had also been ill.

~

Mohandas had been on the go ever since he had returned from South Africa. First he went to the Calcutta session of the Congress as the spokesman of South African Indians. Then he went to Banaras as a traveller. Next he visited Agra, Jaipur, Palanpur, etc. as a tourist. These places were actually en route to Rajkot, which was now going to be his resting place. That's where Kastur was, and his kids, and his elder brother and his family. Also the memories of *Ba* and *Bapu*. He couldn't help thinking that, like a 'bird living on a ship,' it was his destiny to return to Rajkot again and again after every little trip out.

He still remembered Kewalram Dave. It was his father, Bhavji Dave, who had encouraged him to go to London. Kewalram Dave was a well known lawyer. Once, of course, he had almost thwarted Mohandas' London dream by calling it an expensive proposition.

Everyone now was of the opinion that Mohandas should settle down at Rajkot as a lawyer. Kastur had expressed herself only once: 'Since you are now back home, what's wrong with working here? How long will you play the peripatetic mendicant? Let your eldest brother also feel a bit more relaxed that there is someone to share his responsibilities, now that your middle brother has chosen to settle at Porbandar.'

Gokhale however wanted him to establish himself as a lawyer at Bombay and to work shoulder to shoulder with him in the public sphere. Public sphere meant only one thing to him: Congress. Mohandas too was inclined to agree with him, but his old experience deterred him. Even after South Africa, he didn't have the self-confidence that he would be able secure work as a lawyer in Bombay.

He spent a lot of time struggling with the dilemma: Where to start his work? Should he honour the wishes of his family or should he respect the word of Gokhale? Kastur and the kids were not at all ready to leave Rajkot. Eventually, the scales tilted towards home. He decided to stay and start his practice at Rajkot. Kewalram Dave gave him his first three cases. Mohandas had lost touch with Indian law during these seven years. He was naturally apprehensive that the old story may repeat itself again. He might be left gaping while the judge waited for him to say something. Kewalram had helped him prepare the cases. From his South African experience, Mohandas had at least learnt that law, no matter which country it might be, had to do with justice, and justice had to do with people. Before he had left for South Africa, he had studied Indian law and commentaries thereon, which had helped him a lot. The result was that he won all the three cases in a row.

That sent Mohandas' self-confidence soaring. Since he had started contributing to household expenses, the family also started developing confidence in him. Everyone began to feel assured that he would now be more of a home bird and take more interest in family affairs. His own apprehensions and disappointments were also beginning to fade slowly and a desire to settle down at Rajkot and establish himself professionally was beginning to take root in him.

Then Kewalram appeared one day. After talking shop for a while, he came to the point: 'Mohan,' he said, 'The proper place for you is Bombay. You have no future in Rajkot. We wish to see you as a top lawyer.'

Mohandas was a little surprised. When they had met first, Kewalram had encouraged him to settle at Rajkot. So much so that he had even passed on his own case to him. Now that he had made a good start and had even made up his mind to settle down at Rajkot, why was he singing a different tune? He said nothing, but wondered if he was beginning to see him as a professional rival. He hadn't been able to put Gokhale's offer out of his mind even for a second. He always had the feeling that a bigger destiny awaited him. A bigger horizon, a greater calling! Mohandas found himself unable to concentrate on his work.

One night, he announced to Kastur: 'I am going to Bombay. That's where I propose to start my practice.'

'Bombay?' Kastur was aghast. Everything seemed quite normal till a little while ago. What had gone wrong suddenly?

'They need me there. Gokhaleji also wants it that way. He has always helped me and shown me the way.'

'I know nothing about who showed you the way and who didn't. But I know that our needs are no longer your needs. How long are you going to lead a nomadic life? Rajkot is home. Things are also looking better than they did the last time; you have already won so many cases. If you go and settle down in Bombay, what's going to happen to me and the kids? Are we always going to be dependent on others? The kids are in the school-going age; they too need their father to be with them.'

'Didn't I take care of your needs when I was in Natal?'

'You did, but only as much as you could from that distance. The kids certainly didn't have the benefit of your proximity and your love. You always lived with your *Ba* and *Bapu* and enjoyed their care, so you won't understand what they have been missing.'

Though heavy at heart, Kastur did not allow a single tear to escape her eyes. She continued in a low voice: 'You will never know the pain of a child whose father lives away from him and who is forced into the shelter of some other.'

Mohandas was quiet for a moment. He looked at the kids. He felt they were looking at him even as they slept and all those questions were floating out of their eyes like musical waves and coming towards him.

Lakshmidas did not like Mohandas' decision. He was getting on in age, there was a large family to look after, and he alone had the responsibility of maintaining the sanctity of familial relationships. When Mohandas returned, the hope awakened that he would share the responsibilities and he would be able to relax a little. Mohandas' *ex parte* decision had left him in the lurch. He had however decided not to question his decision. He couldn't of course say anything to Kastur and the kids: it was none of their fault and they hadn't been a party to the decision. Actually, it wasn't exactly Mohaniya's fault either. All that he could be accused of was taking an arbitrary decision.

Mohandas took a snap decision to take his family with him. His elder brother had no chance to express an opinion.

He was to receive some payments from Natal. He stayed at Rajkot till the money was received and left for Bombay immediately after.

Kastur commented: 'You stayed on at Rajkot not because of us, but because of the money, didn't you?'

When Kastur left, the remaining household had to reorient themselves to a life without her, but, even in her absence, the illusion of her presence occasionally didn't let go of them.

~

Mohanda's legal chamber was in the Fort area but his home was in Girgaon. A new struggle to start a fresh life in the same Bombay which had once turned him back with an admission of failure was now on. But he was not without hope this time around. His experiences of Natal now topped his previous disappointments. Even Kastur and the kids were finding life in Bombay a thrill. Kastur had assumed that she and the kids would probably have to continue to live at Rajkot but Mohandas' decision to bring them all to Bombay had filled them with a new spirit.

One day, all of a sudden, Manilal started running fever. He had had an attack of smallpox only a short while ago. He was still weak and occasionally still coughed. When he got fever, everyone had a scare. They were still new to the place and hardly knew anyone. They didn't know what to do and who to ask for help. Fever kept mounting. At night, Manilal went into delirium. He started talking of Natal: 'There is a ship in the ocean. Let's go home.' Sometimes, he would say: 'Books … Let me have my books. I must study … When's *Bapu* coming back? It's morning.'

A doctor was called. He announced his judgment: 'The child's life is in danger. It's typhoid with pneumonia. He's getting weaker everyday. He must have egg and chicken soup. His body must get back some strength, or it will find it hard to fight typhoid and pneumonia.'

Manilal was all of ten years old and in a state of semi-consciousness. Mohandas wanted to ask him if he would be ready to take egg and chicken soup, but a ten-year old in such a state could hardly be expected to express an opinion. So Mohandas decided for him: 'Doctor, we are vegetarians. He can neither have egg, nor chicken soup.'

'In that case, you could give him milk, but it will provide very little strength. I am a regular visitor to many Hindu homes, and, in a situation like this, no one has ever turned down my advice. I would advise you to think of the child and forget about other things.'

Mohandas listened to the doctor very carefully. When he had finished, he told him: 'You are right. That's the correct thing for a doctor to say. Had Manilal been an adult, I'd have sought his opinion and followed it. But since, the conditions are such that I must take the decision for him, I have no choice but to say that I am not in favour of following your recommendation. I believe that occasions like this represent the true test of a man's beliefs and his patience. It's not possible for me to give him egg or chicken soup. I'm ready to risk his life for it. I'll now turn to nature cure. My only request to you is that you may please make a regular examination of his pulse, lungs, etc.'

The doctor agreed to the request. He called every two or three days, did a thorough check-up, warned Mohandas about the patient's condition and called it quits. He did not mention treatment, nor did Mohandas ask him about it.

The fever went up to 104 degrees. The delirium worsened. Kastur was worried, but was in no position to say anything. All she did was to pray to Krishna, her god. Mohandas was getting nervous. He would be blamed for sacrificing his child's life for the sake of his obstinate beliefs. Was it for this that you took your kids to Bombay, his elder brother would probably ask. Should he get a second opinion? Should he consult a *vaid* (an Indian physician)? Who knows his medicine might work? What right did he have to inflict his beliefs on his child? An unceasing train of thoughts, both good and bad, ran through his mind. Then he would tell himself: 'I'm only doing to him what I'd have done with myself, or with Kastur. How can I overlook my beliefs? How can I not trust my beliefs?'

Intermittently, Kastur asked: 'Will my son be safe?'

'Have faith in God!' was all he could say. Kastur fell silent, continuing her prayers. A little later, she would ask again: 'He will be all right, won't he?'

Placing a hand on her shoulder, Mohandas would say: 'God will certainly respond to your prayers. After all, all that the doctors do is to experiment with the patient's lives. That is exactly what I am also doing. But my experiment is backed by my faith and beliefs. Both our prayers are behind him. Life is solely in the hands of God. We must continue to do what we are doing. That's the only way our faith will be vindicated.'

Kastur wanted to cry out: 'My child!'

Then she stopped herself. She told herself that whatever was happening was right. How could her child eat meat? When he had regained consciousness briefly, Mohandas had asked him: 'Mani, the doctor says if you have egg and chicken soup, you will be fine quickly. If you want, you can have it.'

'No, *Bapu*. I don't want it. If I am to get well I must get well your way.'

That gave Kastur some relief. She gained confidence that her husband's services would not be in vain.

Kastur had dozed off. Mohandas was with Mani whose body sizzled with fever but he had no sign of sweat. As Mohandas sat with his eyes closed for a few minutes, he felt someone whispering in his ears: 'The cure lies in water.' He got up instantly, soaked a bed sheet in water, squeezed the extra water out and wrapped Mani in it. Then he covered him in a couple of blankets and placed a wet towel on his forehead.

Then he woke up Kastur: 'I am very tired. Could you go and sit by his side for a bit?'

She woke up with a start. 'Is Mani okay?' she asked.

'Yes, he is fine. I have given him a strong dose. Don't get upset. I'll be back shortly.'

Mohandas walked out in the direction of Chowpatty. The evening hum of Chowpatty had died down quite some time ago and it was quiet all round except for an odd figure or two. They must have been either tired souls like him out in search of some fresh air, or needy victims of misfortune looking for some relief, or maybe plain latenighters. When the occasional lamp-post loomed up in front, it restored their faces on their shoulders and they had an identity. The lamp-post gone, their faces too disappeared and all you could see was flat faces floating in darkness. Mohandas was lost in thoughts. He was enveloped in an armour-like prayer: 'God! This is a time of trial for me. I surrender this child into your protection.' Slowly he found himself sucked into a recitation of the name of Ram and he lost sense of space and time. His breathing slowed down, with no movement or irregularity in it. When he reached Chowpatty, the sea breeze woke him up and he returned to his self. He could now feel his pulse returning and his breath reviving. His mind was absolutely calm. He headed home.

The moment he stepped into the house, he heard Manilal's voice: '*Bapu*, are you back?'

'Yes, son. How are you now?'

'Take me out of this furnace, *Bapu*. I am burning.'

'Are you sweating?'

'I am soaked.'

Mohandas placed a hand on his forehead. Beads of sweat like little droplets of rain water had sprouted on his forehead. The fever was sliding. Mohandas closed his eyes and sat still for a while. A little later, he said; 'Mani, wait a little longer; the fever is coming down.'

'No, *Bapu*. I am burning. Please take me out of this furnace. If you like, you can wrap me up again later, but I can't stand it now.'

Mohandas started caressing his body. Mani could feel the fever subsiding. Mohandas removed the blankets. The bed sheet was dry and crisp. Mohandas now looked like a child, without a care in the world. He lay down by the child's side and told Kastur to go and rest. He would stay by Mani's side.

A little later, Mani was sleeping soundly, one of his hands resting on *Bapu*'s chest.

~

The house at Girgaon was fine except that it did not get any sun at all. There was barely enough light and the place was damp. The kids fell sick regularly. Mohandas was desperate to find a new place and spent whole days looking for one. He wanted a place at Bandra or Santa Cruz. He located one at Bandra, but it was next to a slaughter house where whole carcasses of goats were strung out on display. He liked the house but the public display of flesh and violence was more than he could stand. Though he couldn't prevent the display, he also could not have remained a passive spectator. A few other houses that he had been able to locate were too far from the beach. Porbandar had been on the beach; Beach Grove had been a pebble's throw from the sea.

For him, the breezes from the sea had been like neighbourhood kids, streaming into the house at all hours of day and night, screaming, shouting and full of beans, fresh from a dip in the sea. At Porbandar, they lost their sea-character by the time they reached the house, but at Durban, the breeze rising from the sea had their first resting place at Beach Grove Villa.

After a lot of house-hunting, Mohandas found a bungalow at Santa Cruz which fitted the bill from every point of view—clean, green and well-maintained. Though it was not even a patch on the Beach Grove Villa, it was open and quite airy. Mohandas paid his last respects to the Girgaon house and took residence in the Santa Cruz house.

From Santa Cruz, Mohandas took a train to Churchgate. He had secured a first class season ticket for this purpose. Few people travelled first in those days, especially Indians. Whenever Mohandas stepped into a first class compartment, he was reminded of the Pietermaritzburg incident. One never knew when Pietermaritzburg might visit him in this land. The thought brought a smile to his face. What a piece of work is human mind, he thought. How it could transplant a scene from one locale to a totally different one! He often found himself alone in the first class compartment. That filled him with a sense of being a person apart and his face glowed with the realization of his special status. But the question soon started troubling him whether it was indeed a matter of happiness to be different from others. On some occasions, when he got delayed and the train left without him, or when he wanted to be with others, he walked all the way to Bandra and caught a train to Churchgate from there. Even as he sat in the first class, he often thought of the third class compartments: passengers packed like sardines in filth. He thought of the top notch lawyers of Bombay who set out for the High Court in their carriages, decked out in full glory. Perhaps the pomp and the show were intended to add to their professional status. Most of the clients too made a beeline for them while one could also see a glimmer of respect for them in the eyes of the judges.

Gokhale was delighted to have Mohandas in Bombay. Mohandas had now become a factor in his plans for the future. He had already visited Mohandas in his chamber a couple of times and this had raised Mohanadas's status in the eyes of the bar. For Mohandas, events like these– Gokhale calling on him and holding consultations, etc.—were the stuff of dreams, which were now turning into reality. Gokhale talked to him about national politics, introduced him to his friends and laid out before him the vision for the future. Professionally too, Mohandas was doing well and he was beginning to look forward to a steady career. South African clients were also beginning to approach him and he was now earning a regular income. Of course, the case that would give him a big name had still not come his way. But he was at the High Court every morning, consulting the library, listening to arguments, taking notes and poring over tomes of law.

Mohandas was beginning to think that the time to play the second fiddle was coming to an end for him. The time when his name and his work would be noticed by everyone was going to be here soon.

~

Mohandas sat in his chamber when a telegram was handed to him, causing him to sit up. His apprehensions had mostly to do with his elder brother, Lakshmidas. He was getting on in age and had been the sole provider of the family since *Bapu*'s death. The telegram was however from South Africa. He opened the telegram. His fears had come true.

Chamberlain arriving. Come immediately.

The hope of a stable life that had barely surfaced had been shattered. He had been wrong to think that the ship of his life had cast anchor in the harbour. He was still in transit. He forced himself to concentrate and saw passing before his eyes all those faces which would be waiting for him there, faces which had etched on them the promise he had made to them. Sometimes you found yourself perched on a ledge of stability so that the slightest movement on your part changed your entire perspective and you began to wonder why you ever made that move. Mohandas strove to free himself from that state of mind and told himself that there was no way for him except to go.

He did not consult anyone and sent his reply: 'Send money. Will start as soon as money is received.'

Kastur once again found her universe rocked by an unexpected storm, but said nothing. She thought to herself: the happiness I had taken to be a lasting one has turned out to be a mere shadow. Uncertain joys only end in sorrow. If I couldn't hold my husband, what is the chance that I would be able to hold my children? Come the time, and everyone will take wings. Everything is more fleeting than water and more crumbly than mercury. Hold it as much as you would like, water will join the waves, no matter how measly the waves. So many were the thoughts that passed through her mind!

Mohandas surrendered his chamber but retained the house. His elder brother wrote to him: 'I am still around. Must you leave the family at Bombay unattended?'

Mohandas wrote back: 'I know you are still very much around. Whenever they wish to do so, they will join you. They must learn to live independently, or how would they make any progress?'

Lakshmidas didn't reply to the letter, nor did he write again for a long time.

~

Once again, Mohandas was on his way to South Africa. This time, three or four young men were accompanying him, among them Maganlal Gandhi. Mohandas remembered his father. Whenever he could, his father put young boys to work. So much so that when he gave up his prime ministership of Porbandar, he got his younger brother to take his place. Mohandas also wanted the young men of his clan to see the world and learn new things. There were worlds outside their world. They would learn to be independent only when they stepped out of their homes. Anyone who was willing to take on this challenge accompanied Mohandas. In fact, Harilal too was keen to go …

For the first time, leaving home gave Mohandas a sense of getting uprooted. All that he had built up at Bombay rose like a picture before his eyes and then shattered like glass. Incomplete faces of Kastur, Hari, Mani, Ramdas, Devdas and others looked at him from the pieces of glass and he struggled to put the pieces together again to make wholes. The sense of a joint struggle through the choppy waters of life had come undone again. A new period of uncertainty was beginning. What awaited him at the other end he knew well; what he was not being able to assess correctly was what he going to lose at this end. He knew it was ridiculous to look for permanence in a world so full of uncertainties and impermanence. Whatever was happening was also becoming history. The only permanent thing was the truth that your experience yielded and the faith and the trust with which you regarded it.

Mohandas' eyes were focused on the sea as wave followed wave. Slicing the waves right through the middle, the ship thrust its way forward. Though sliced so deeply, the waves still managed to come together, embrace each other and be level again, seamless and quite undisturbed. Full of mischief as they were, the waves were also so forgiving and so magnanimous.

Mohandas was mesmerized. He felt the sea making its way deep into his heart and a new prospect opening up before him. What that new prospect was, was still not clear to him. It was nevertheless a prospect and that was all it was for the present.

~

Chamberlain had already landed in South Africa. Everything was in full readiness. An Indian delegation was supposed to meet Chamberlain and Mohandas was a member. He was also supposed to get the petition ready. Mohandas had prepared himself for any eventuality. He often thought of the injured soldiers of the Boer War, who, despite the injuries, never turned away from war. Their thoughts turned towards home only when the war returned to the barracks. Lying alone in their beds, they were tortured by memories of home. Watching over them, Mohandas always thought that their minds were as active when they were lying in their beds as when they were fighting in the battlefield.

And then he thought of himself too as a soldier in a battle.

Chamberlain was taken to be an Indian sympathizer. It was due to his efforts that the Queen had withheld her consent to the franchise amendment bill. The white community had taken this as undue interference in the affairs of the colony and a humiliation of the entire community. But this time around the Indians sensed a change in the attitude of Chamberlain. Problems of the Indian community seemed to have no place in his list of priorities. His first priority was raising a sum of three hundred and fifty lakh pounds from South Africa, which only the whites were supposed to contribute. His attention was therefore wholly focused on the whites and their problems. The Boer War had created a fissure between the Boers and the whites. The whites too were divided right down the middle. To repair this division was one of the priorities for Chamberlain.

He started with Durban. The Indian delegation also got a chance to see him. He gave the delegation a very patient hearing, never interrupting and never asking a question. When the delegates had finished, he said: 'I'll talk to the Natal government, though I don't think a law that has been passed and is already in implementation will be easy to amend. It may not even be desirable.' He went on to clarify: 'You know the British government believes in justice and fair play. It does not believe in interfering in the affairs of its autonomous colonies. Still, I'll see what I can do. After all, you have to shape your future living with them.'

Mohandas almost blurted out but didn't: 'And what about them? Don't they have to live with us? Don't they have any duty in the matter?'

Chamberlain's response poured cold water on the aspirations of the delegation. A clear picture was now beginning to emerge. Mohandas realized that the whole battle would now have to be started afresh. In a way, Chamberlain's reply could not be faulted on any count. He had said whatever he had to say with absolute clarity and complete decency. He had made it clear that they had the power and they intended to use it. And they were using it.

Mohandas explained the ropes to all and sundry, which had left them all worried. If Chamberlain wasn't going to listen to them, who would?

Chamberlain's next stop was Transvaal. Mohandas had still not lost confidence in Chamberlain, so he decided to go to Transvaal to see Chamberlain again and to explain the situation of Indians to him. He was sure Chamberlain would listen to him, though he hadn't yet been able to forget all that he had had to go through during his first visit to Pretoria. Like a fearful picture, it was firmly inscribed on his mind's plate. Nor did he want to ever forget it. He believed that whatever else your humiliation did or did not do to you, it at least kept you firmly rooted to the ground beneath your feet and did not let you lose sight of the realities of the situation. Respect, honour, etc. on the other hand could produce illusions.

Though Transvaal was now a British colony, restrictions had gone up manifold. You required a permit to enter the colony. There were no exceptions, but Indians were taken up for special treatment. After the Boer War, the economic condition of Transvaal had deteriorated fast. Food and clothing were scarce. Shops had downed their shutters. The whites had little problem getting the entry permits. Every port had an entry permit office for the whites. Asians however were dealt with by a special office for this purpose and the process of securing a permit was a lengthy one for them. This was despite the fact that most of the employees in the special office were of Indian origin. Their attitude however was even more dictatorial and dismissive than that of the whites. The problem before Mohandas was that if he went through the entire rigmarole of the application process, Chamberlain would be gone from Transvaal by the time he received the permit.

Mohandas thought of a way out. He approached Mr. Alexander. The Alexander couple had proved to be his saviours during the Field Street attack on him. When he entered Mr. Alexander's office, he found Alexander busy working. His eyes went to the cross on the wall behind Alexander's desk. His hands automatically went up to his chest and drew a cross.

Alexander got up to see Mohandas and said: 'When did you get back from India, Mr. Gandhi?'

'Only a couple of days ago.'

'Welcome. Looks like you didn't need our services this time.'

'You wouldn't be sitting here in your office if I did, would you?' They both laughed.

Mohandas said: 'I won't take too much of your time. I am here on a special business. I have to go to Transvaal to present a petition to Mr. Chamberlain on behalf of the Indian community. People are waiting for me there. You know that I have lived for a year in Transvaal. It is clearly impossible to get an entry permit from the Asiatic Department in such a short time, but I can get one here. I need you help.'

Alexander picked up his hat and said: 'Let's go.'

At the Permit Office, he said: 'Mr. Gandhi is a friend of mine. He has lived in Transvaal before. Please issue him an entry permit.'

The Permit Officer promptly issued the permit.

There was half an hour to go before the train left. Mohandas picked up his luggage and started for Transvaal.

Transvaal was completely deserted as if marauding forces had just passed through the place. Shops and markets were closed. There was anyway no point in keeping shops with empty shelves open. The situation in Pretoria was even worse.

The Asiatic Department was supposed to cater to Asians, but for Indians it was a veritable morass of problems. The officials were themselves the biggest problems.

When Mohandas went to the Asiatic Department to report his entry, the officials were taken by surprise. They of course didn't have the courage to ask him directly, but they would ask every Indian they saw in the office how Gandhi had managed entry into Transvaal.

When the Indian replied how he was supposed to know they flew into a rage as if it was the duty of every Indian to keep track of every other Indian, especially Gandhi.

In the end, they sent a telegram to Durban: 'Gandhi in Transvaal. Was entry permitted by Durban?'

They received a one-word reply: 'Yes.'

When they got to know that Gandhi had an entry permit, all their preparations to take him into custody came to naught. Mohandas' first thought on learning of this was: If, by some chance, the reply had been 'No,' in place of 'Yes,' he would be rotting in jail today. An invisible smile played on his face at the thought, invisible also to himself.

The next day, a verbal message was delivered to him that he should go and see the Chief of the Asiatic Department. There was nothing in writing: no order, no seal. The Chief was from Ceylon. The Indian delegation was supposed to meet him first. When Mohandas arrived at his office, he found Tyeb Sheth already present. He was the leader of the Indian delegation.

In Mohandas' presence, one of the officials asked Tyeb Haji Khan: 'Who is this man? What's he doing here?'

'He is our adviser. He has come from Natal on our invitation.'

'And what are we supposed to be doing here? You think we are incapable of protecting your interests? What would an outsider know about the conditions here?'

'Mr. Gandhi is one of us. He speaks our language and is well-versed with our problems. He has lived here. You represent the authority.'

After a lot of discussion with Tyeb Haji Khan, Mohandas was taken to the Chief.

The Chief frowned at him and asked: 'What are you doing here?'

'I am here on my fellow countrymen's request.'

'To do what?'

'Helping them with my advice and counsel.'

His face flushed with anger, the Chief said: 'You have no right to be in Transvaal.'

Mohandas wanted to speak, but he didn't let him. He continued: 'I know what you are going to say: that you have an entry permit. That was issued by mistake. You are not an Indian immigrant. Go back at once. You cannot meet Mr. Chamberlain. The responsibility of protecting the Indians lies with me and my department. Who are you to butt in here? Get lost.'

He also detained the delegation and came down so heavily on the members that they were unnerved. 'Send this man packing at once, or I will have each one of you in jail.'

They all trooped back, feeling deeply humiliated. Mohandas alone appeared calm.

This was not the first time Mohandas had been humiliated. He had suffered humiliation in all its shades and colours. This particular instance had however affected him deeply. Even so, there was a point at which this chain of humiliations always came unstuck, and this was the point where he decided that his first priority was the achievement of his goal; the business of humiliation could be taken care of later. After every such humiliating event, Mohandas asked himself the question: 'Did you learn anything from this event? Extricate yourself from this morass of insult, humiliation, respect ...; stand away from it; only then will you learn anything. If you don't, you will only get deeper and deeper into this morass.'

At the end of each episode of humiliation, he had to prepare himself afresh, much as a horse has to be refreshed at the end of a long journey over treacherous territory. Like the previous episodes, he had added this episode too like one more page to his book of experience and had then turned it over.

The same evening, he received a sealed cover from the Asiatic Department. It said: 'You have already seen Mr. Chamberlain in Durban. Your name is therefore being deleted from the list of delegates.'

When the message was read out to the delegates, they were thunderstruck. Tyeb Sheth announced his decision straightaway: 'We are not going to see Mr. Chamberlain. If we are going to be stripped of our brain and our voice, what can we possibly think and say?'

Mohandas closed his eyes. When he reopened them, he said: 'To do so would be to invite disaster for the Indian community. Chamberlain is no ordinary official. He is the representative of the British crown. To treat him this way would be to seal the fate of India forever. It will be taken for granted that you neither have any grievance, nor any submission to make. In any case, you are not required to speak much in his presence; all that you have to do is to submit the petition, which is ready. It does not make too much of a difference whether it is presented by you or by me. Our goal is to make our grievance known to him in writing. Where does he have the time to listen to our long tale of woe?' He continued after a short pause: 'Silent work is the need of the hour. We must set aside all talk of humiliation and self-respect for the present.'

Tyeb Sheth was still very agitated. 'By humiliating you, hasn't he humiliated the whole of the Indian community? How can we overlook the fact that you are our sole representative?'

'That's fine, but remember that we may have to be ready to put up with the humiliation of the entire community in order that we can achieve our goal. Only those communities have made any progress in history which have put up with the severest humiliation and most extreme tyranny but have never lost sight of their goal. We too will put up with all that comes our way.'

'No, not us. Why should we put up with every insult the government heaps on us? '

'It's no use acting on angry impulse. We too have our limitations. I suggest you take Mr. George Godfrey with you. He is an Indian, also a barrister and sets great score for Indian interests.'

Mohandas had a feeling that their faces now showed, in addition to their helplessness, a shadow of consent.

The moment the delegation entered the hall, Mr. Chamberlain greeted the members with: 'Well, gentlemen, it's not much use, is it, listening to the same person again and again? Why don't you go on ahead and say whatever you wish to say?'

Tyebji looked at Godfrey, who nodded back: I know who he is talking about!

Mr. Chamberlain continued: 'I have already met Mr. Gandhi in Durban. My purpose now is to find out about Transvaal, not Durban.'

When the delegation later told Mohandas about this, he laughed and said: 'Chamberlain was merely repeating what the Asiatic Department had coached him to say. They don't know that I have spent time in Transvaal. If I didn't know about Transvaal, would you have invited me here? Anyway, there's little point speculating about these things. The fact is that the local whites are scared to come within a mile of Gandhi and his name.'

'Just as well,' he said a little later, laughing. 'If they touched me, I might also turn white in my thoughts.'

It was now clear that the whites were influencing Chamberlain. Word had spread that Chamberlain had refused to see Gandhi. Last time, Chamberlain had refused approval to the Franchise Amendment Bill under the influence of the same Gandhi. Times were certainly changing. The true Gandhi was being unmasked.

Some of his own people also wouldn't miss the opportunity of taking a swipe at Gandhi: 'An ambulance team indeed! Helping the British at the front, he said. So what did you get out of it, mate!'

'Did you take Chamberlain to be a kid who would fall for the guiles of Gandhi?'

Gandhi would normally pay no attention to such talk, but now he felt that allowing confusion to persist in the matter could harm his interests as well as those of the community. He therefore issued an explanation: 'Taking part in the Boer War was not wrong. We only did what was our duty. We have duties as human beings, and we have special duties during times of crisis. The Boer War demanded both kinds of duties from us. We therefore do not ask for any return for the duties we performed. I only know that only good can come out of good. Whatever has happened has happened. We must now get ready for what is to come next.'

Everyone nodded his approval with a heavy heart.

~

Having handed the gift of a humiliating rejection to Mohandas, Chamberlain headed back to London. Mohandas too was through with his business. The only issue that now remained to be decided before Mohandas was whether he should return to India or stay on and carry the Indian struggle forward. The treatment that Chamberlain had meted out to him stood as a challenge before him. Should he accept the challenge or swallow the insult quietly? Mohandas was struggling with these questions day and night. He also sought the counsel of some of his friends. There was also the question of Kastur and the kids who were stuck half way in Bombay, which was neither home nor abroad.

At a meeting, Mohandas put his dilemma before his friends: 'The job for which you had invited me here has lost its relevance. Chamberlain wasn't here to listen to us; nor did he have anything to give us. He has gone back, and so must I. However, I'm facing a dilemma: should I stay on, or should I go back? I have no intention of staying and working in Natal, at least for the present. I can only consider Transvaal. If I decide to stay here, I'll simply have to forget about returning to India. The only way I can hope to deal with the Asiatic Department is by registering myself with the Supreme Court of Transvaal. If we don't do it, the Asiatic Department will one day have all the Indians out of Transvaal. Chamberlain refusing to see me, the local authorities throwing insults at me—these are all a prelude to the kind of treatment that the Indian community is going to receive at their hands in coming days. Compared to what awaits the Indian community, the insults I received would count as nothing.'

In one voice, everyone present said, 'We all wish that, like Natal, Transvaal too should have a Gandhi of its own.'

Mohandas said nothing. He wanted a little more time to consider the whole matter. In fact, he was apprehensive that, as had happened in Natal, the Transvaal Law Society would do everything to prevent his registration, and he wanted to be assured of his registration first.

As it turned out, his registration was such a smooth affair that it took Mohandas himself by complete surprise.

The registration business taken care of, Mohandas started the process of settling down in Transvaal. Using an agent's services, he got a chamber allotted to him and rented a house in Albemerry Street. The house was flanked on both sides by roads. The house, No. 14, stood like an island between the two roads, which joined the main road right in front of the house.

Although Mohandas had a house in Johannesburg, the house at Santa Cruz always clouded his thoughts like as an ever-present worry. The kids were by themselves in Bombay, while he was by himself in this metro city of Transvaal. He often found his vow of service to humanity riddled with holes of concerns of security, future, stability, etc. Suppose something untoward happens someday, who or what would take care of it? Thoughts like these had kept haunting him even while he sat in his Bombay chamber.

One day, he sat alone in his Johannesburg chamber. When you are alone, you sometimes find your thoughts losing focus while sometimes they focus wonderfully. Anyway, it was just then that a man walked in. Handsome, smooth-tongued and well dressed. He started talking to Mohandas like an old acquaintance. 'Mr. Gandhi,' he said, 'In America, insurance is very popular with people belonging to your class and status. I think you too should get yourself insured. After all, life is so uncertain. Insurance is your battle against accidental death. Actually, in America, insurance is treated as a religious ritual. In fact, in your country too people are now being insured. Why don't you also take out a small policy? If the insured survives, he gets the benefit of it; if he doesn't, his children enjoy the fruits.'

People like him also often waylaid him in Natal but he always managed to give them the slip. If you were committed to serve humanity in the name of God, how could you entertain such total lack of faith in life? There was no way he could reconcile the two positions. However, this man had Mohandas so completely in the grip of his glib talk that he couldn't find a way out. His description of the transience of life was so convincing that one was led to believe that he had already unravelled the mysteries of life. For the first time, Mohandas found himself haunted by a fear: if something happened to him, what would be the fate of his kids? If he got himself insured, they'd at least get a lump sum of money. Kastur was already penniless. She had sacrificed all her jewellery for his London training and he had not been able to recoup even a penny worth of it. This meant that the entire responsibility would once again revert to his elder brother. In addition, who knew how much longer he had to live? All his life, he had discharged the responsibilities of a father towards Mohandas, and even now, he was discharging them towards his kids.

The man was watching Mohandas' face very closely and trying to read each one of his emotions. When he saw an opening, he immediately latched on to it: 'Do not waste any more thought on it. You simply cannot predict the years life has in store for you: if you are lucky, you may live to be a hundred; if you are not, you may not see tomorrow. Your life may be called meaningful only judging by what you leave behind for the next generation; it may be your name, your money or your work. You have of course still a long life ahead of you. May you live to be a thousand!'

Doubts, uncertainties, apprehensions—they had all cast their shadows on Mohandas' mind. Soon, the shadows grew so long that his mind ceased functioning as an independent entity and the man's talks grew to fill all of it. Fear of death replaced the trust he had always placed in life. Mohandas lost the battle.

In his current sojourn of South Africa, Mohandas was no longer his older self. He was a divided soul, torn between services to humanity in the name of God on the one hand and a lack of certainty about life on the other. He didn't know how long he might be required to stay in South Africa. He might or might not be able to return home. It might be the evening of his life before he could think of going back. What would happen then? Wouldn't it be better if he had his wife and kids with him and worked for their happiness? Worked harder for them and made more money for their needs? If he were able to do all this, would he still need to have insurance? Even supposing he were to die now, would his elder brother refuse to look after his widow? He was sure his brother would not deny him this. Then again, where was the certainty that he would be dead soon? Life and death were not in his hands, nor, for that matter, in the hands of his elder brother. They were in His hands, you understand, 'HIS' hands!

It was for the first time that Mohandas was finding himself facing a dilemma of this sort. At times, death seemed to be gaining the upper hand; at other times, it was life which, tied to the string of hope, seemed to soar high in the sky like a kite. A strange game of hide and seek seemed to be in progress. When the dark shadow of death deepened, hope seemed to be on its last legs; when life spread its light, fear of death scampered away like a dog with its tail between its legs.

Slow realization started to dawn on Mohandas that by accepting insurance he had allowed himself to be carried away by his fear of death. He had betrayed his own faith in the divine power. He had impugned the courage and confidence of his wife and his kids. He had given a vote of no confidence on their capacity to shape their own destinies. So what if I died? Heavens would not fall. Myriads of people die in this world everyday. God has given the capacity for self-preservation to everyone. Adversity befalls everyone, and as the seed of adversity grows, the capacity for self-preservation too grows to cover the growing plant like an ever-expanding shrub. The greater the adversity, the greater the capacity to face it, and the greater the determination to protect oneself against it.

The storm of false arguments raging in his mind in defence of insurance had allowed him no space to take a stand against them. Fear of death and worries about the security of his kids had beaten him back from his declared stand. He had already paid the first instalment of the premium. This was his third defeat, he felt. The first time he had lost against meat; the second time, it was theft, and now it was against fears of insecurity. Surely, there was someone behind these defeats. Who was it? Was it possible that it was he himself? Why should he blame anyone else?

~

It was the left wing of his 14, Albmerry Street house that received the first rays of the morning sun. Rising early was one of Mohandas' oldest habits. It took him about thirty-five minutes to get ready: fifteen minutes for the customary activities and twenty minutes for bathing and getting into his clothes. *Shloka*s from the Gita were written on the bathroom walls. Whenever he read any new *shloka*s, he wrote them up on the walls. He would read and recite them as he took his bath. When he came out of the bathroom, a rising sun like a happily laughing child, causing him to bow his head in reverence, would greet him.

Surya-Namaskar (Greeting the Sun) was his favourite Yoga exercise.

Every little incident turned a teacher for Mohandas. One day, some members of the local chapter of the Theosophical Society approached him and said: 'Please help us to read the Gita and the other texts.'

Mohandas was in a fix. 'Look,' he told them, 'I know very little Sanskrit. The few Hindu texts I have read only in translation. I won't be of much help to you.'

'Do you believe in reincarnation?' One of them asked.

'Yes, I do.'

'That means you have the necessary instincts. I've heard instincts go a long way. You must help us.'

There was no way out for Mohandas. After a lot of deliberation, he started reading *Rajayoga*, Vivekananda's commentary on the Gita. Mohandas had been unable to meet him when he was in Calcutta, but had been able to secure a copy of his commentary. He went on to read Patanjali's *Yogasutra.* Some of these books, Mohandas always carried with him. His daily routine now underwent some changes. After his morning bath and *Surya Namaskar,* he sat in the balcony of his house and studied for an hour. As he went deeper and deeper into the Gita, he found himself coming under its spell. He had thirteen of its chapters by heart.

It was a new experience for Mohandas. The Gita, he discovered, was to human beings what the stars were to sea voyagers and desert travellers, lighting up their paths at night.

Mohandas felt himself spellbound by words like *aparigraha* (non-possession). Question followed question and then followed the answers. What did equity mean? How could you be equitable in your treatment of the wicked, the abusive and the narrow-minded? How was non-possession possible? How do you non-possess what you already possess? Was your own body someone else's property? Don't all those books stuffed in the cupboards belong to me? Should I destroy them or give them away? But wouldn't giving them away mean creating chains for others? What about wife and kids? Why so much affection for them? Should I give everything up and follow God? Didn't serving human beings amount to serving God?

The study of the Gita was throwing up questions, which bothered Mohandas day and night. The answer that seemed to emerge was: You can find Him only if you give up everything else, that is *aparigraha.* But wouldn't finding Him negate the very idea of non-possession? Obviously, non-possession could not cover everything. Non-possession too must be a means to bigger end? What could possibly be a bigger end than Him?

Mohandas thought of a word from English jurisprudence: the word 'trustee'.

'Trustee.'

He repeated the word. 'Trustee.'

He felt a ray of light breaking out. Enlightenment was spreading. Thinking was opening new doors. 'Non-possession' and 'equity' (equality) were beginning to become visible like shiny stones at the bottom of a transparent stream. They seemed to be calling out to him: 'Discriminate, change and alter your behaviour! You can renounce everything and yet possess them; you can possess everything and yet renounce them. Everything belongs to you, yet nothing is yours! Everything belongs to everyone, and what belongs to everyone belongs to you!' 'Non-possession,' 'equity,' 'trustee'—Mohandas had the feeling that he had found the truth. Archimedes-like, he rushed to his table and wrote in his diary:

The Gita *is an endless stream. If you take a dip, you never go unrewarded.*

Then he dashed off a letter to his friend, Rewashankar, in Bombay:

> *I committed a great sin. I no longer want the insurance. Please terminate the policy. Get back whatever money you can; forget it if you can't. He who created my wife, my kids and me will also provide for us. Neither insurance, nor anything else will make a whit of a difference. I do not wish a relationship of distrust with my God.*

The next letter was to his elder brother Lakshmidas. Tears welled up in his eyes as he wrote. Truth stood bare before his eyes. He thought of all the things his father-like brother had done for him and his family. Yet he wrote:

> *A new light has dawned on me. What we call our own in a boost to our ego has nothing in it that is truly ours. Of course, we earn, but only that part of what we earn is truly ours, which is required to meet our needs. In a sense, we are its trustees. To consume all that we earn within our own family is to betray God's generosity. It is a betrayal of His authority. So far, I have been sending you my earnings so that you could take care of my*

family. Never did I pay a penny to any one else. I shared whatever I earned with my own people and we partook of it all together. I will no longer be able to do so. I do not have any claim on what I earn. My claim is limited only to what is required to meet my needs. The rest belongs to the whole community. Let everyone earn, but let everyone keep only what his body and his stomach need. Let the rest be shared by everyone. If you do not give up, how will you ever get anything?

A ray of light seemed to be guiding his pen as it moved from word to every word.

~

The main reason why Mohandas had settled in Transvaal was the Asiatic Department. The problems of Asians were mounting. Entry permits for Transvaal were selling at a hundred pounds apiece. Whether or not eligible for entry, one could pay one's way in with a hundred pounds, while eligible and needy people were left high and dry. People approached Mohandas and requested him to do something about it since there was no one else who could.

A dash of realism was now beginning to colour Mohandas' concern for the Asians.

Mohandas went about collecting evidence. He came across a number of Asians for whom entry into Transvaal was a basic need, but since they were unable to raise a hundred pounds entry was denied to them. At the same time, there were people whose eligibility was doubtful easily got entry.

Mohandas took all the evidence to the Police Commissioner, who was also a white.

'I am M.K. Gandhi, barrister. I was a legal practitioner in Natal, but I am practising here now. I need your assistance concerning the Asiatic Department.'

'Sure. What can I do for you?'

'The Asiatic Department is riddled with corruption. Eligible people are being denied entry into Transvaal while all rules are being waived for people who can part with a hundred pounds.'

The Commissioner was no pushover. 'They are all your people manning the department, aren't they?' he retorted.

'The question is not whose people they are, but what attitude they take towards the different people they deal with and how honest they are in their dealings. What is a person who cannot part with a hundred pounds supposed to do? They got mad with me because I had been issued the permit by the Asiatic Department of Natal, denying them their share and their influence.'

'Do you have any evidence to prove your allegations?'

Mohandas had collected evidence from diverse sources, which he now placed before the Commissioner. The Commissioner studied the evidence in depth and raised some questions. He was finally convinced that there was no element of misrepresentation or fraud in the evidence presented by Mohandas.

'You know,' he said, 'The jury consists of only whites. A white jury rarely hands out punishment to officers. Still, I'll see what I can do. To let the guilty off without taking any action against them would also be a betrayal of my responsibilities. I'll make sure that they are at least arrested.'

The two officers with the maximum evidence against them were both whites. After completing the necessary preliminaries, the Commissioner got warrants issued against them. People knew that Mohandas was in regular communication with the Police Commissioner. They also knew that no newcomer to Johannesburg had any chance of getting close to the Commissioner. The two white officers had their own network of spies, which was keeping a close watch on the activities of Mohandas and the Commissioner. When hand-stitching, a tailor always puts on a thimble on his finger, which serves two purposes: it helps to pull the needle out when the cloth happens to be coarse, and of course it protects the finger. The two officers were also doing the same: they were protecting themselves and were keeping a watch on the activities of Mohandas and the Commissioner.

Many Chinese and Indians were also in the meantime working actively to get the two officers arrested. In fact, if they had not been stalking them silently, the officers might well have flown the coop. One of them actually managed to flee, while the other went and quietly settled down in another colony. However, the Commissioner had got him arrested and extradited to Transvaal.

The arrest of the two officers caused a flutter in the dovecotes of the Asiatic Department. The very name of Gandhi was giving nightmares to the employees of the office. A coolie versus two white officers! Could there be anything more absurd?

The two officers were prosecuted. There was hearing after hearing. Witnesses came forward with evidence without fear or favour. But eventually the Police Commissioner's experience prevailed. Both officers were acquitted. The one who was absconding hadn't even been booked under a specific statute. In fact, his flight from justice had been sought to be justified.

Shaking his hand, the Police Commissioner told Gandhi: 'I'm sorry that we failed, Mr. Gandy. But I'm happy we did our duty.'

Mohandas was serious: 'It's a wonder, Mr. Commissioner, that with so much evidence at our disposal, we could not prove the guilt of the accused.'

'The law is not an infallible test of guilt or innocence; nor is it like a mathematical proof. Those who interpret the law in favour of, or against, a human being, are also human beings, and every human being has his prejudices and pre-conceived notions.'

'But, Mr. Commissioner, where the law refuses to listen, it is the collective voice of the people that forces it to listen. If the good deeds that people do cannot be missed, the bad deeds are even harder to miss.'

The Commissioner didn't say anything beyond: 'Let's wait and see.'

A few days later, the Commissioner sent for Mohandas. When Mohandas arrived, he stood up to greet him. 'Mr. Gandy,' he said, 'your efforts have not been wasted and your faith has been vindicated.'

Mohandas was puzzled.

The Commissioner continued: 'The evidence was so incontrovertible that, though the jury had overlooked it, the government couldn't bring itself to do it. Removing the blindfold on its eyes, the law looked at the colour of the accused, while the government only looked at the file. The faces were missing in the file.'

'I don't quite get it ,' said Mohandas.

'They have been paid off and sent packing. When you go to the Asiatic Department now, you'll find that your voice will be heard.'

Mohandas closed his eyes for a moment as if prying within him: Who was behind all this?

~

Mohandas' work was growing by the day. Ever since the two white officials of the Asiatic Department had been dismissed, clients had begun thronging his office. He had to work till late at night. He now had four clerks working for him, who also lived with him at his house in the Beach Grove Villa style. As a result, they were more like members of the family than clerks of the office. The typing work itself was so enormous that they were hard put to cope with it, even though two of them did nothing but type. They made so many errors in typing that Mohandas often found himself going crazy. The staff he had in Natal had eventually been trained, but here everyone was a novice. Difficulties in obtaining entry permits meant the Natal staff could not be imported here, though had Mohandas made a personal approach to the Asiatic Department they could well have obliged him. But Mohandas wasn't ready to take on any obligation for personal benefit. Pay a bribe or pull strings—what was the difference?

Mohandas wanted to hire a white man or woman for the work, but the difficulty was: would any white person like to work with a coloured man?

Mohandas visited a typing school. 'I am an attorney and I want to hire a European steno,' he said. 'Can you help me?'

'Would you hire a girl?'

Mohandas liked the idea. 'I have no problem. But would she care to work for a coloured Indian?'

'You need have no worry on that score.'

Mohandas left. The next day, a white girl visited him.

'Your name?' Mohandas asked.

'Miss Dick. I am Scottish.' She volunteered her nationality.

Mohandas repeated the same question to her: 'Would you mind working for an Indian?'

She gave a smile. 'What difference does that make to me? I only want some respectable enough job.'

'What salary do you expect?'

She replied with another question: 'Would seventeen pounds be asking for too much?'

'No, provided I am happy with your work.'

Next he asked: 'When would you like to start work?'

'I'm ready to start now.'

Mohandas looked at her. He was impressed with her replies. Straight away, he assigned work to her.

Mohandas' law practice was now several times more than what it had been in Bombay. In fact, he was now so well established that that had he so wanted he could have carried on his practice both in Transvaal and Natal. His house was now home to several people. Sometimes, when alone, Mohandas couldn't help thinking that the people to whom the house truly belonged, the people for whom it was really meant, were themselves thousands of miles away. For what fault of theirs? He couldn't personally go to Bombay to bring them over, as the situation here was changing every minute. Kastur had never undertaken such a long journey alone. Though Hari was now a grown up boy, undertaking such a long voyage with four kids was nothing short of a trial by fire.

It worried Mohandas to think of Kastur having to wind up things at home all by herself while looking after four kids, in case he asked her to come over. He had of course a number of friends, who were always ready to lend a hand. The longer he continued to put off Kastur's travel, the greater was the pressure on him to act. Finally, he selected Rewashankarbhai for the job. He sent a message to Kastur through him asking her to wrap up things at home and head for Natal with the kids. It was not possible for him to come personally to fetch them. He had a big house and it felt desolate without them. There was no reason for her to worry. Thousands of illiterate Indians, without any acquaintances and without anyone to help them, made it to Natal every year. He would be waiting for them. She should also let his elder brother in Rajkot know about it.

When Kastur heard the message, she lost her cool. 'What does he take us for? It has been barely a year when he took us and dumped us at Durban. Now comes another fiat: "Move." At whose word? At the word of a man who doesn't know his own mind? If that was what he wanted, why couldn't he take us with him? It has after all only been a few days since he left. What does he think: Is it a child's play to travel with four kids? Tell him, we are not coming.'

Rewashankar and other friends tried a lot of persuasion: 'Don't take it in that spirit. He has called you. You must go. Once you get on to the ship, it is smooth sailing till Durban. Gandhibhai has made all the necessary arrangements.'

The night before she was to leave, Kastur could not sleep a wink. What was she destined to suffer this time round? What God-forsaken places was she doomed to? At Rajkot, she at least knew where she was. Travelling across the seas without a male escort was not a joke. 'We may all drown, or we may survive, who knows? It all happened the last time we went, didn't it? May God shower His blessings on the Captain's wife, who came to our rescue, otherwise who knows where I would be today?'

Hari didn't want to go. He wanted to continue his studies here.

'Of course, he doesn't have to bother about these things. He is a man after all, isn't he? There was Ram, who travelled across seven seas to bring Sita home! The times have flipped, haven't they?'

The ship was cruising nicely. But thoughts coursed through Kastur's mind: Hari is sixteen now, but how many days has he spent with his father? Son and father have been running a sort of relay race: the son comes running and touches him and he takes off; or he comes running and touches and the son takes off! Now that it was time that he stayed with his father and acquired some knowledge, he takes off for Rajkot to stay with the elder brother! Now that I can be with my husband, I have to leave the son behind. The last time I went how scared I was to see water all around! He made me sit on the deck all the time and drove the fear of water out of me. I must thank him for it today. The kids too are not scared any more. For Devdas, of course, it is the first time, but the way he races across the deck, you would think he has always lived on a ship. His father used to ask him: Have you seen Fear? If you haven't, how can you have it? What are you afraid of anyway—the sea? Or the sky? Or maybe the fellow passengers? If you fear them, they'll fear you. If you start fearing, everything will turn into a fear—the sky, the sea of course, even this ship which is taking you across. So long as you don't fear them, they are your friends, indeed your brothers. Gokal was also with us. He was the first one to lose his fear, and then he would guard over the other kids. He died young. Sister Raliyat was heartbroken. But who can question Death?

Her thoughts were like birds frisking about from place to place leaving her breathless as she tried to keep them in check.

Suddenly, a man came running: 'Your child has injured himself.'

Kastur ran in panic. O God! What a disaster! Ramdas was howling. A few sailors had appeared on the scene and one of them, a white, had Ramdas in his arms. Ramdas was finding it difficult to move his arm. Swelling was increasing by the minute. The white sailor, who was actually the ship's doctor, took Ramdas with him and laid him on a bed in a cabin. 'Mrs. Gandy,' he said, 'Since we cannot get a specialist doctor on the ship, we can rig up a splinter bandage to hold his hand in place which will enable him to make it to Durban, if it's okay with you?'

Kastur had no choice but to agree. The doctor got a splinter ready and put Ramdas' hand in a sling.

Kastur was finding it hard to control her emotions. Her thoughts kept returning to Mohandas. Sitting there nice and comfortable, while his son is crying here in pain. All that he craves is applause and a ring of admirers, people who should follow him around chanting 'Gandhibhai, Gandhibhai'. He needs no wife, no kids. Crazy of us to rise at a single call from him and race across the seas to do his bidding. Would he have responded to my call in the same way? It was a man's world all right.

She spent the whole night with Ramdas in her lap. The sounds from the ship sounded like the End of the World, with mighty banks crashing into the waves.

They disembarked at the port of Delagoa where they were supposed to take a train for Johannesburg. Vasudevbhai, who knew Mohandas very well, was travelling with them. They got first class tickets and took their seats on the train. Manilal was insistent that he wanted the window seat. Everyone tried to deter him but he wouldn't budge. Then the windowpane fell and caught Mani's thumb crushing it badly. He cried out loudly. The ship at least had a doctor. Here there was only Kastur and the fellow traveller, Vasudevbhai. The best they could manage was a bandage of wet cloth. Kastur had somehow accepted Ramdas's injury but she was finding it difficult to accept Mani's. It was the last straw. She felt broken. She could neither cry nor keep her tears in check. Vasudevbhai was quite unperturbed.

At Johannesburg, they hired a coach. There was no one at the station to receive them. Kastur had now arrived at a philosophical stage where it mattered little to her whether they reached their destination or not. Who was bothered anyway? If your own husband didn't care, who else would?

Kastur was attired in a sari, which she wore in the Parsi style. That was the style Mohandas had preferred for her and the kids the last time. He had found it to be more modern than the Kathiawari village style.

When they arrived home, Mohandas was startled to see Ramdas' arm in a sling and Mani's bandaged thumb. 'What's all this?' he demanded.

Kastur broke into sobs.

Mohandas first tested Ramdas' arm. Next he removed the bandage from Mani's thumb and held it. Mani screamed. 'Couldn't you even look after the kids?' he blurted out.

All that Kastur had thought she would say, and the way she would say it, meeting after such a long gap, vanished in a flash. She had been afraid she might lose control of her emotions. But this one sentence had made a clean sweep of everything. Vasudevbhai, who had been witness to everything, gave a detailed narration. Mohandas now realized that he had been rash to put the blame on Kastur.

Kastur had only said: 'Some reward! You yourself didn't take the trouble of coming even to Delagoa. You think looking after three kids was a joke? Did you expect them to sit still like adults and wait on my pleasure?'

Mohandas could not say anything after this.

Mohandas put a paste of wet clay on Mani's thumb and bandaged it. He washed Ramdas' wound with potassium permanganate and tied a clay bandage around it. The bandages were removed after four days. Mani's wound was healing and Ramdas' bone was joining up.

~

XIX

When Mohandas arrived in Durban to see Chamberlain, he was introduced to Madanjit, a young man bubbling with enthusiasm, who ran a printing press called International. Madanjit was a hard-working man and had worked as a journalist in India. It was only much later that Mohandas found out that his printing press had been running at a loss. Madanjit tried to convince Mohandas that the kind of work he was engaged in required a newspaper, even if it was a weekly, through which he could establish a dialogue with Indians spread all over Natal and South Africa.

Mohandas listened to him in silence.

Madanjit was saying: 'Through a newspaper, the Indians here will be able to see a portrait of themselves. Moreover, it will give them an identity. So long as their aspirations, needs and grievances are not talked about, how will they ever get to know about one another and about the problems being faced by them at different places? Shared sorrows and troubles bond people together faster than anything else. The printing press is already available; you will only need to spend on paper, and there will be a few overheads.'

Mohandas too had been feeling the need for a newspaper. Every time he wanted to say something, he had to run to the English newspapers. These newspapers were of course honest enough to publish whatever was sent to them, but the average educated Indian had no access to them. As a result, his message at best reached a few educated people, if at all. The whites were anyway not interested in news about Indians.

So Mohandas agreed to the proposal. It made him happy to think that he would now have his own newspaper in addition to his own opinions. He decided to call the newspaper *Indian Opinion.* Plans to bring out the paper in four languages—Hindi, Tamil, English and Gujarati—were quickly given final shape. Since the printing press was in Durban, it was decided to publish the paper from Durban. After making a quick estimate, he also handed over money for the initial expenses to Madanjit. Mansukhlal Naazar was appointed editor and Mohandas himself shifted his residence to Johannesburg.

The problems of South African Indians were so complex that, despite being a journalist, Madanjit found himself quite unable to do justice to them in his coverage. As a result, that responsibility too soon fell on the shoulders of Mohandas. The expenses too kept mounting. His idea that after the initial investment the rest would be plain sailing turned out to be an illusion. It soon became clear to him that it would be difficult to sustain *Indian Opinion* without external financial assistance. Currently, it had only one source of finance and that was his own earnings. Whatever he could save from his income he ploughed into *Indian Opinion.* Several new avenues of expenditure had opened up.

His biggest challenge was collecting material for all the four editions. It also meant extra expenditure. His legal practice and social work had demands of their own. In the end, Mohandas had to shut down the Hindi and Tamil editions. The material for the English and Gujarati editions had also to be selected carefully with an eye on the maximum possible dispersal of news to Indians. While it was necessary to educate the Indians, it was also important that the news and the demands should also reach the whites. It was necessary for *Indian Opinion* to become an instrument for the removal of misunderstandings between the two communities. The fight for justice and against injustice had to continue unabated.

Mohandas was turning into a successful journalist. He was getting to know his own community while also keeping an eye open for India. It was important to keep the Indians in South Africa informed about the developments taking place in India. Events in India were actually helping Mohandas prepare himself psychologically for the future. He could feel the restlessness of India within himself. It really got him quite agitated but he made sure that he never spoke a word about it.

One day, Miss Dick came up to him with a complaint. She laughed even as she complained: 'Gandhibhai,' she said, 'you hired me for office work and all that I find myself doing is newspaper work.'

Mohandas never let pass the chance of a joke. 'Complaining already?' he said, 'work is work. It has no colour, caste, or creed. There is nothing like white work or black work, Hindu work or Christian work. There is a lot of work awaiting you about which you know nothing yet. And no one is going to help you out with it.'

Miss Dick just laughed.

What was special about Miss Dick was her capacity for work. Mohandas had in fact on some occasions to pause and think twice about assigning more work to her. After all, how much work could you burden her with?

Among Mohandas' acquaintances was one Mr. Ritch, a Theosophist. He was one of those Theosophists Mohandas had met when he came to Johannesburg. It was on his insistence that Mohandas had started teaching the Gita. This had brought him in close contact with all the local Theosophists. He of course never became a Theosophist himself, much in the same way as he never accepted Christianity. What Mohandas particularly liked about Theosophists was that their way of life, their eating habits, etc. were very similar to those of the Hindus. One day, Mohandas asked Mr. Ritch: 'Would you like to work with me, Mr. Ritch? The *Indian Opinion* and my law practice will both benefit greatly from your experience.'

Mr. Ritch worked as a Manager in a commercial firm. He however readily accepted Mohandas' offer and resigned his job to join Gandhi. He became the source of a lot of new information about the whites for Mohandas. He was also very helpful in collecting material for the *Indian Opinion.* That also offered Miss Dick some relief.

Miss Dick was now more like a sister or a daughter to Mohandas than a steno. She never gave Mohandas a reason for complaint. She now also maintained the accounts and handled the cash. Whenever Mohandas needed any money, he would approach her. She also now felt quite free with

Mohandas and he soon became her confidant even in personal matters. She would tell him freely about her male friends: who she had been with, what they told her, and so on. There was nothing that she kept from Mohandas and he listened to her talk with the greatest interest questioning her on various points, even cracking jokes and making suggestions.

Miss Dick's boyfriend was Macdonald. She told Mohandas everything about him quite openly. On occasion, she took time off from her work to go on a date with him. Mohandas never stopped her, no matter how urgently he required her for work. At times, he even teased her.

'Miss Dick, have you ever paused to think how I feel when you go on a date with Mac?'

She laughed and said: 'I'd surely convey it to Mac, though I can always tell a lover from a friend.'

'You mean Mac is a friend …'

'Oh, no.'

'All right, all right, I'll content myself with the status of a friend.'

Mohandas knew that the speed with which Dick and Mac were moving towards each other, he might soon have to say goodbye to Dick. The increase in the pressure of work had made him worried. If he was unable to find a steno with Dick's intelligence and capacity for work, how would his office function? He quietly started his search for another steno who could work as responsibly as Miss Dick. He was sure he only wanted a woman, because he believed that women were more responsible and took greater interest in their work.

One day, Miss Dick appeared and put it before him: 'Gandhibhai,' she said, 'I and Mac have decided to get married. We seek your blessings.'

Mohandas laughed and said: 'What will become of me?'

'I'll pray to God that Mrs. Gandhi joins you soon.'

They both laughed.

Mohandas was present at the wedding of Dick. After the ceremonies were over, Mohandas shook hands with Mac and said: 'Do you know how one feels when he sees his treasure being stolen from right under his nose?'

Mac laughed and said: 'He can never forget the thief. And the thief can never forget the generous owner.'

Dick intervened: 'The treasure also keeps returning to the owner.'

Mohandas took their hands in his and kissed them. 'God bless you, my children,' he said.

Though Dick said she would keep visiting him, Mohandas knew how difficult it was for a married girl to keep that promise.

When Mohandas was by himself, he thought of Dick. He thought of how Dick would have done this or not done that. Sometimes he actually called out to Dick out of sheer habit. It was only then he realized that Dick was elsewhere—with Mac.

Mohandas had spoken to many people about his need for a new steno, but none had been forthcoming.

There was a gentleman Mohandas knew called Kallenbach, a German. A tall young man with excellent physique, handsome and sociable. An architect by profession. Some of the biggest European companies were among his clients and he was sought out by them exclusively for their design work. They also liked their buildings to be constructed under his personal supervision. As a result, Kallenbach enjoyed an excellent relationship with Zulu and Dutch masons and labourers. As for his personal life, he lived like a prince and enjoyed the good things of life. He had his daily shave while still in bed and a barber was in attendance. He had a razor for every day of the week. Mohandas often joked with him: 'You should have a razor for every day of the month, or maybe you should get three hundred and sixty-five razors on the first day of the year.'

Kallenbach would laugh and say: 'That is what exactly I should have done if we did not count our days on a weekly basis.'

~

Work was piling up on Mohandas' table. He would take on any work that any one failed to complete, or expressed his inability to perform, and then find that he had no time to do it. Actually, this had been his habit even during the time Dick was around, but in those days Dick would lend him a hand, or he would give her a dictation. The work of *Indian Opinion* was also lagging behind. Important letters were not being dispatched. His work and his troubles were growing by the day. Earlier, he was able to spend some time with friends like Kallenbach, but now all his time was taken up by office work. The four clerks were also hard at it all day, but the work didn't seem to diminish at all.

One day, when Kallenbach came to see him, he was accompanied by a pretty young girl. Mohandas was so completely absorbed in his work that he did not notice them enter his office and take seats. It was unprecedented that he should not get up to receive Kallenbach.

Kallenbach laughed and said: 'Gandhibhai, do you remember me?'

Mohandas tried damage-control. 'I'm so sorry,' he said, 'Ever since Dick left, work never seems to end and I have to do all of it. You aren't much help either.'

'Well, that's why I am here. This is Sonja Sleshin. She teaches in a High School. She will work with you.'

'But I need a steno, not a teacher.'

'Actually, you need both. Look, I can't be with you all the time. Sonja can. She is a bit outspoken, though. You'll have to be careful. You make a mistake, and you'll hear from her on the spot.'

'Will Sonja care to work for a non-white?'

Sonja spoke out: 'What has white and non-white got to do with work? Work, no matter for whom it is done, is a matter of honour ...'

'Mr. Gandhi,' Kallenbach completed.

Mohandas looked at Sonja closely and then asked Kallenbach: 'And the salary?'

'That's for you two to decide.'

Sonja said: 'Kallenbach tells me that you are a decent man and a good friend and that you are always ready to help the needy. I am not here to make money. I only need six pounds to survive.'

'Dick collected seventeen and a half. How will you ever survive on six?'

'Leave that to me.'

'When would you like to start work?'

'We don't need to fix a date and a time to start work. I believe in starting work whenever there is work to do. Actually, my work started the moment Kallenbach brought me to you. You have only to tell me what the work is and how I am supposed to do it.'

Mohandas was awestruck. Not even Dick had ever talked like this. The only time Sonja Sleshin took was the time spent in explaining the nature of work to her. Once she got started, it was as if a machine had been turned on. She never got tired, and she never stopped. She stopped only when the table had been cleaned out. She typed faster than Dick, and flawlessly. Mohandas was amazed and delighted too.

Dick was now also slowly receding from his memory.

~

The Indian immigrants were known as coolies in all the colonies and Natal and Transvaal were no exceptions. In India, the term denoted a porter and was a significantly more respectable designation. But in this country every Indian was a coolie and quite outside the mainstream of citizens. Coolies were clustered in Coolie Locations, which were outside the city of Transvaal; much in the same way as in Indian cities the untouchables were located outside the city limits. The coolies were not allowed to live anywhere other than the Coolie Location. The times when they could visit other parts of the city were also fixed. Plots in the Coolie Location were leased out for a hundred years minus one. The location was chock full of Indians with the population growing every year. The area of the location had remained unchanged and would always remain unchanged. The municipality took care of the cleaning of the latrines but nothing else. There were no sanitation facilities, no roads and no lighting. Since the City Council didn't give a damn about the inhabitants of the Location, who would bother about the civic facilities? Filth reigned everywhere, bringing the inhabitants of the location a bad name. They wallow in filth, they are carriers of infection—

they were responsible for all the ills. Instead of getting the place cleaned, the prevailing filth was cited as the reason for not undertaking any cleaning. No one was ready to venture into the middle of the filthy lot! Taking advantage of this argument, the City Council was seeking the removal of the Coolie Location from its existing site. And that was what finally happened. Taking recourse to the very filth for which it was itself responsible, the City Council approved a proposal to remove the Coolie Location from its present site.

The inhabitants of the Location however had ownership rights on their sites. It would be impossible to remove them without granting them compensation. The inhabitants had the right to accept or reject the terms offered by the municipality. In the meantime, a tribunal had been appointed to go into the issue. The City Council was insistent that the coolies should be made to vacate the Location. The problem before the inhabitants was where to relocate. The compensation that was being contemplated would not be enough to pay even for a thatched roof.

Two of the inhabitants of the Location were Jayram and Badri. They knew practically everyone in the Location, both good people and bad. Everyone could depend on them in their hour of need. Under their leadership, the inhabitants decided that they would hire Gandhibhai as their lawyer and contest the case. Originally, both of them were *girmitiyas'* but they had both been released from their contract.

They went and told Mohandas the whole story, showed him all the documents, and said: 'Please accept the brief and help us tide over the crisis.'

Mohandas gave his consent readily.

They told him that they were poor people but would be ready to pay his fees if he told them how much.

Mohandas laughed and said: 'No fees.'

They entreated him to name some figure, to which Mohandas said: 'If you win the case, which I expect you will, I'll accept whatever the court determines as the fee.'

'And if we lose?'

'If you lose, ten pounds for each claim, which will include the expenses. Half of the fee you give me will go towards building a hospital or setting up an organization to help the poor.'

They looked at him in utter disbelief. First, it was an expression of distrust, but soon it turned into a wave of surprise and happiness.

Mohandas however didn't say a word.

In all, Mohandas had seventy cases in hand. The seventy complainants had formed an association, which monitored the cases and arranged the cases to be argued in the court. A majority of them were either *girmitiya*s or lapsed *girmitiya*s. They either belonged to Bihar and its neighbouring regions or the south of India. Badri was a very sensitive person and he did all the leg-work involved on behalf of everyone. During this period, he became very close to Mohandas. For him, every word of Mohandas was gospel.

Badri had left some of his money with Mohandas to keep. There were many others too who deposited their money with Mohandas. Johannesburg had a vegetarian restaurant, but, most people being non-vegetarians, the enterprise was running at a loss. For Mohandas, any work associated with vegetarianism was part of a mission. He often missed meals at home to eat at the restaurant. The restaurant was run by a German. When the accumulating losses mounted beyond his capacity, he closed the restaurant down. The Theosophists were all vegetarians. The closure of the restaurant created a problem for them. One of them was a lady. Though she was an artist, the problem being faced by her fellow Theosophists led her to open a small vegetarian restaurant. She had a good number of friends, who all ate at her restaurant. Slowly but steadily, the lady was enlarging the scope of her activities. She rented a number of large rooms and added a hotel to her restaurant. Her demand for capital grew and the amount of work began to spin out of her control.

She approached Gandhibhai and said: 'Gandhibhai, please help. You had been helping the German too. Where will I find a greater supporter of vegetarianism here?'

Mohandas examined her accounts. When he had satisfied himself that there was no hanky-panky, he called Badri and said: 'Look, Badribhai, I have some money of yours with me. The lady who runs the vegetarian hotel is in need of money. If you agree, can I loan some of your money to her to help with her hotel business?'

'Gandhibhai, you can do whatever you think fit. I only know you. I know nothing about any hotel business.'

Mohandas had all the seventy clients chasing him all the time. He had to try and grasp the intricacies of each case individually. Badri and Jayram were always around to help him. Each case had its own weak points. In some cases, even the documentation was not complete. Collecting all the documents was not an easy job. The clients themselves washed their hands of the problem by saying plainly: 'We have handed you whatever we had. The rest is all up to you.'

Blind faith of this kind put Mohandas under an obligation to live up to the expectations of his clients. He knew what it would mean for them if he lost the cases. An additional problem was that each client would approach him individually to ask: 'We'll win, won't we?'

Some of them broke into sobs as they said: 'What'll happen to us if we lose?'

Mohandas had to work at several fronts at the same time: Completing the documentation, keeping up the clients' spirits, preparing each case individually, and so on. Whatever time was left was given to *Indian Opinion* and the other cases that he was handling.

Many hearings and long arguments later, the decision was announced. It took Mohandas completely by surprise. He had won all the cases except one. The court had also awarded him handsome fees. He had in fact to send sixteen hundred pounds out of those fees to *Indian Opinion* right away.

Sonja teased: '*Indian Opinion* is very dear to you, isn't it Gandhibhai?'

Mohandas got her thrust. He laughed and said: '*Indian Opinion* is to me in public life what you are to me here.'

That took Sonja by surprise.

Mohandas explained: '*Indian Opinion* helps me in my public life the same way you help me here.'

'I don't get it.'

'Journalism, you know, can be a very potent force. It has a big role to play in any social transformation, provided, of course, it aims solely at service of the people. This proviso is necessary because a pen that goes astray can destroy everything like an uncontrolled rush of water.'

Sonja worked for Mohandas with single-minded devotion. Mohandas never had to use his pen on documents typed by her. On many occasions, Mohandas joked with her: 'You must forgive me, Sonja. I was wrong when I told you then that I didn't need a teacher. Now I think a teacher was exactly what I needed.'

She reparteed: 'Gandhibhai, you are so good in fooling people to work their backs off for you. You did that to Dick first and now you are doing it to me. And tell me who can write English like you here?'

'Well, if that's the way you feel, you must put in only as much work as you think proper.'

'Oh, come on. Don't pull a long face like a child. You know, we don't work for you; we work for the spirit behind your work. Who would like to work for a crusty and tactless man like you?' She smiled.

Sonja Sleshin loved to crack jokes. She could be naughty and wilful, but she was always and absolutely free of malice. She never smoked; nor did she drink like most white women.

Mohandas of course hated smoking and drinking. Sonja also knew that he was never soft on weaknesses of character. One day, Sonja finished her work early. She didn't know how to keep herself busy. Sitting idle was a punishment for her. So she borrowed a cigarette from a colleague, lighted it and slumped into a chair in front of Gandhibhai. Gandhibhai was busy doing a letter for *Indian Opinion*. Everyone was a little surprised at Sonja's behaviour since everyone knew the consequences of defying Gandhibhai's known likes and dislikes. Sonja took a long puff and blew the smoke at Gandhibhai's face. Everyone went pale with shock. Gandhibhai continued to work unperturbed. She took a second pull and again blew the smoke at his face. Then she repeated it a third time. Gandhibhai got up and, right before everyone's eyes, slapped Sonja hard a couple of times. Sonja wasn't quite prepared for this. At first she was startled; then, her hand covering her cheek, she said in a teary voice: 'I was only trying to find out how angry Gandhibhai can get, or does he get angry at all?'

Mohandas looked at her and went back to his work.

That day, Mohandas wrote in his diary:

Sonja has the forgiving nature of a child. And me—the arrogance of a street male.

~

The tribunal had confirmed the ownership rights of sixty-nine out of seventy residents of the Coolie Location. They could not be evicted without compensation. The Municipality paid compensation and thus acquired the ownership rights of a substantial portion of the Location. The tribunal's verdict however included an additional condition, viz. that alternative living arrangements for the dispossessed residents would be the responsibility of the Municipality. Since alternative living arrangements were not easy to come by, eviction of the residents was getting postponed. In the meantime, garbage and filth was piling up. From owners, residents of the location had turned into tenants and as tenants; their responsibility had reduced to zero. The City Council was now the owner, and as the owner, the responsibility of maintaining cleanliness and hygiene rested with it. Earlier, the residents were the owners and, as such, at least part of the responsibility lay with them, which was also gone now. Now they spent their time wailing about the Council's responsibility, and their worries about their own and their families' health ended with their wails, as if that also ended all their responsibility.

Then one day, black plague broke out in the colony. Black plague is much more dangerous than bubonic plague. Also called pneumonic plague, it directly targets the lungs. The outbreak of the plague had actually started in the gold mines of Johannesburg and not in the colony. The mines were surrounded by colonies of workers, mostly blacks. The responsibility for cleanliness and hygiene in the colonies rested however with the white mine owners. These mine owners treated the workers like slaves, irrespective of whether they were blacks or coolies, who did not need any cleanliness or hygiene. The mines also had some *girmitiya* workers. Some twenty-odd of them had fallen prey to the plague one after another in a short span of two or three days. Unable to think of anything else, they made a beeline for the coolie colonies, expecting to be with their own kith and kin during their last days, who would at least perform their last rites. They were of course in no state to ask: who would perform the last rites of those who looked after them? Their arrival in the colony started a stampede. Who was going to shelter the victims of plague, and black plague at that? But nor could they drive their own kith and kin away.

Madanjit happened to be in the area at the time. He was going around selling subscriptions of *Indian Opinion.* He saw the black storm rising and was shaken to his bones. Everyone was in panic. He didn't know what to do; then he remembered Gandhibhai. All that he had with him at the time was a pencil stub. With it, he scribbled a note on a scrap of paper: 'Plague breaks out here. High fever and racking cough is making people miserable. We must do something to stop the outbreak or this entire Coolie Location and the nearby colonies will all turn into a cremation ground. Come immediately.' He sent a man to Gandhibhai with the slip.

Madanjit was going round trying to keep up the spirits of the people. 'Don't worry,' he would tell them, 'everything would be fine once Gandhibhai is here.'

The major problem was where to house the twenty-three patients who had arrived. No one was ready even to touch them. They had arrived with the hope that they would be granted life, but were seeing the shadows of death getting longer and longer. In their situation, loss of hope could be a greater killer than the disease itself. One could find ways of escaping a disease but loss of hope was like a quicksand which pulled you down and kept pulling till it swallowed you. Madanjit could fathom their psychology. He took his courage in both hands, broke open the locks of an empty house and moved the patients into the building. He sent Gandhibhai a message telling him what he had done: 'Take care of the fallout. I had no other choice.'

The moment Gandhibhai got the message he requisitioned a colleague's bicycle and set off at a flying speed. He also got intimation sent to the Town Clerk about the conditions which had necessitated breaking into a locked house. He did not wish that to blow up into an issue by itself.

All the four clerks working in Mohandas' office were Indians: Kalyandas, Manaklal, Gunwantari Desai and another one. Kalyandas had been entrusted to Mohandas' care by his father. He was a family man. Mohandas had sent for all the four but was in a fix whether or not to put Kalyandas on nursing duty. If something went wrong how would he face Kalyan's family?

He called Kalyandas and said: 'Look, Kalyan, though I have sent for you, I am in a fix. For one thing, you are a married man; for another, you were entrusted to my care by your father. I am unable to decide whether or not to put you on nursing duties for these patients.'

He replied: 'You are also like a father to me. Maybe the other three were not entrusted to your care by their fathers, but they too have parents like I do. If you can put them on nursing duty, why not me? Joy and sorrow are the same for everyone except that one may cry while the other one may take them in silence.'

Mohandas then called all the four and told them: 'Although officially you are my clerks, your sacrifice has made you my companions. You are more than my sons to me. Go and serve these unfortunate people. God bless you.'

Manaklal was still unmarried. 'We'll go where you go,' he said.

Mohandas' eyes were moist, but the heat rising from the groans of the sick dried them very quickly.

It took a while for Dr. William Godfrey to be informed, but he managed to reach the Coolie Location by the evening. The following night was a dreadful one. Dr. Godfrey, Mohandas and Madanjit—all the three kept a nightlong vigil tending the patients. Some groaned, some were hysteric with high fever and some were sure that they were dying. In his life, Mohandas had tended all manners of patients, but this was the first time he was seeing patients going through such terrible agony. He was on his feet the whole night, administering medicines, helping with toilet, cleaning beds. The effort, as far as possible, was to divert the patients' attention from their misery and to keep them entertained. Everyone also had an eye on the sky outside. They were waiting anxiously for the night to pass and the dawn to break. Sickness is such a dead weight at night. The presence of Dr. Godfrey was so reassuring for everyone—at least they had a doctor with them. The presence of a doctor gives even a dying person courage to take a last stand against death.

The night passed somehow. They had brought the patients out of the jaws of death. Another day had begun. Everyone was awestruck by the courage and the perseverance displayed by the four young men.

The next day, the Town Clerk also appeared, but he did not have adequate resources to fight the menace. He was profuse in his thanks to Mohandas and Madanjit for bringing a difficult situation under control. He got a large warehouse opened and handed it over to Mohandas. The warehouse had been out of use for a long time and had never been opened. Dust and refuse seemed to be its natural state. Moving the patients here was like inviting expeditious death for them. The Town Clerk's men were in no position to undertake its cleaning. Mohandas considered his options carefully. Night had passed. Keeping twenty-three patients in the small house might mean losing some lives. So he gathered up his four companions and plunged into the task of cleaning the warehouse, while Dr. Godfrey and Madanjit took care of the patients. When Mohandas finally emerged from the warehouse, his frock coat and silken hat were plastered with dust. At any other time, his ghostly appearance would have caused a lot of amusement. Now the question was where and how to place the patients, whose bodies were racked with pain. Dr. Godfrey had vetoed the idea of placing them on the floor. They had begged and borrowed some rags which had seen them through the night, using them both as mattresses and covers. Mohandas could think of only one way out: he dispatched Madanjit and his friends to the homes of his clients, irrespective of the fact that they had been sleepless and foodless for the past twenty-four hours.

The warehouse had a new look at the end of the two-hour exercise. By evening, it was beginning to look like a respectable hospital ward. In the meantime, the Municipality had also dispatched a nurse, some medicines and some basic equipment. The Johannesburg businessmen had provided beds and bedding and also arranged for meals. Though Mohandas had got the warehouse cleaned, he had not been able to do anything about its haunted-house look. It was such a huge warehouse with twenty-odd beds in it!

The nurse was a kind-hearted lady. She had brought a bottle of brandy with her and was administering a dose to each one of the patients, while also taking one herself. Her duty was only to give medicine to the patients and she was performing this duty with all sincerity. She had been warned to avoid touching the patients as far as possible.

She also asked Mohandas to take a dose. 'It'll help you avoid the infection,' she said.

Mohandas replied: 'Thanks, Sister, but I don't think brandy will help. The true saviour is God, though brandy may run away with the credit.' Overnight, Mohandas had grown a stubble and his face looked dry, but he was still quite alert.

The patients showed no improvement. Mohandas took Dr. Godfrey aside and spoke to him. 'Doctor', he said, 'the situation is bad. I don't think we can save the patients. If you agree, I can try my treatment on those three patients who refused brandy.'

'What treatment?'

'Naturopathy. If nothing else, it might give them some relief. The end may be a little less painful.'

Godfrey thought for a minute and then said: 'Mr. Gandhi, I know nothing about this treatment. I have no way of telling how successful it will be. If you want to try it, I have no objection. You are perhaps the best well-wisher they have here.'

Mohandas got clay poultices ready, spread them on strips of jute and covered the heads and chests of the patients with them.

The patients were in terrible pain. Their bodies were burning with fever.

Mohandas changed the poultices on those three every fifteen minutes. The poultice that was shed would be warm and without its cold touch. Dr. Godfrey, at one point, threw a hint that the chill of the cold clay could make the disease worse. Mohandas however continued changing the poultices and said: 'Doctor, I have now left everything to God. I am only doing what He is directing me to do. I don't know if He wants me to be His excuse for their deaths, or His instrument for keeping them alive.'

Godfrey moved on to other patients, his face lined with worry and discomfort.

The dead were being taken out of the warehouse. When the doctor declared someone dead, they felt as if one more challenge had been lost. The doctor's person seemed to shrink a bit. Madanbhai was dead tired: he had been at work since before anyone else had arrived on the spot.

One of Mohandas' patients too expired. Mohandas was by his side at the time. He only exclaimed 'Hey Ram' and the words were lost within him. He stood there wordless for a moment, his eyes closed. Whenever a patient died, those were the only words he said before continuing with his work. This time he lingered a little longer.

The other two patients were beginning to look better: the shadow of death was receding from their faces. Consciousness was returning. The fever was subsiding. The skin still burnt. Cough still racked their frames. Godfrey returned every now and then to take stock. Silently, he was amazed at their recovery.

Mohandas had increased the interval between the changes of poultices. The task of wetting and kneading the clay had been given to Manaklal. As he kneaded the clay, he picked out the stones and pebbles. When Mohandas spread the clay on the jute strips, he also tested the mix for smoothness. It would not do to have any pebbles in the mix.

By the next evening, the warehouse was without its occupants except those two patients. The rest of the patients had joined their Maker. Mohandas told Dr. Godfrey and Madanbhai: 'I think our task here is over. I will anyway stay on to look after these two patients, so you can go and take some rest. You have been awake tending the patients for forty-eight hours now.'

Madanjit was dead tired but he still didn't want to go. He had to be removed forcibly. Godfrey did not want to miss the miracle that Mohandas was unfolding at the site.

There wasn't now a soul left in the warehouse, but the presence of those patients could still be felt. They were gone; they were still around. Their voices had been silenced but their groans still echoed. Often a groan would be missed, but you saw the vacated beds and the groans came back.

Godfrey examined those two patients. The fever was gone. The lungs were relaxed. Cough still recurred but abated quickly. Life was trickling back bit by bit, like water in a sand-filled drain.

Godfrey clasped Mohandas' hands and said: 'Gandhibhai, you extracted life from clay to bring these dead bodies to life! What are you?'

Mohandas laughed a tired laugh. 'Nothing, Doctor, nothing. Neither I, nor the clay, amount to anything. Faith is everything.'

Having sent the two surviving patients to their homes, Mohandas was returning home on a bicycle. His legs still moved fast, except when he thought of the nurse. Then his legs started going limp. What a spring she had in her feet! The way she ran up and down administering medicines to the patients, it looked as if they were all her near relatives. No whites vs. blacks for her! She used brandy like nectar, the drink that made you immortal. Every few minutes she took a swig and gave it to the patients too. When the doctor or Mohandas asked her not to touch the patients, she would say: 'Don't worry at all. I have brandy with me. A complete disinfectant.' She had even had the doctor take a swig. Madanjit and the others had refused, taking their clue from Mohandas. Those three patients hadn't taken it either.

She tried to reason with Gandhi again and again: 'Look, Gandhibhai, we are at risk. Anything can happen here. Brandy can be a great help.'

Gandhbhai patted her on the shoulder and said: 'Sister, your true strength lies in your service. Have faith in your service.' He had never challenged her faith in the brandy.

It was the afternoon of the next day. The nurse had been running around as usual. Then all of a sudden she started shivering with cold. Dr. Godfrey noticed and ran to her. Mohandas too went post-haste. Her body was burning with fever. The fever had come like a horse—galloping!

She groaned: 'Doctor, I have the plague. I am going to die.'

'Come on. Don't entertain such thoughts. Nothing wrong with you, just fatigue. You'll be all right.'

Suddenly, she was convulsed with cough. She was trying to say something. When Mohandas put his hand on her forehead, she opened her eyes. Mohandas looked at Godfrey. He shook his head. Mohandas tried to remove his hand, but she put her hand on his. It was burning hot.

Mohandas called out: 'Sister!'

She could not speak distinctly. In her broken words, she said: 'Gandhibhai, I'm so happy I had the chance to join you in God's work. Pray for me. Jesus will accept your prayer. Let my folk know. May God bless you!'

The bottle of brandy was still attached to her belt, but now it fell and broke. The brandy in it spread out in a circle.

Godfrey covered her body with a sheet; 'She had the speediest end of all.'

Only one word had escaped Mohandas' lips: 'Ram'. Godfrey was an Indian and knew what Ram meant. As he pronounced the word, Godfrey also crossed himself.

The Coolie Location was put under guard. No one was permitted to enter it; only Mohandas and his companion had been issued entry passes. The Municipal authorities had been greatly impressed by the attitude displayed by the Indians during the plague because of which a large number of white lives had been saved. Coolies and *kaffir*s had taken the brunt of the attack. Despite this, the authorities had taken certain decisions which had created serious problems of the Location for coolies. They were being asked to vacate the Location and move thirteen miles out of Johannesburg. The administration had set up tents in the new location to accommodate them. This was such a huge calamity for those helpless folk that they didn't know how to cope with it. Three weeks after their departure, the Location would be consigned to flames. Like birds in a forest on fire, the coolies were beating their wings in vain. Where could they go? What could they do? Who was bothered about their resettlement?

They were all so poor that everything they earned was spent on necessities, or in repaying debts. If someone was able to save some money, he would bury it underground, where its value would remain static—neither going up nor down. Of course, there were more chances of it going down. Yet, they had more faith in that money than in God. Come adversity, and it would be the money that would come to their help. Leaving the Location meant losing the money. Even if you took it out of the ground, where would you hide it in the forest? After all, the tents were not going to belong to them. They hadn't heard of banks, nor did they know how money was deposited in them. Hence, they were adamant on not leaving the Location. It was death either way! If they died at their own place, they would at least die with peace and contentment in their hearts.

Here was another problem for Mohandas. The authorities were insistent that if the residents did not vacate their houses, they would be forcibly evicted and the houses would be incinerated. They believed that if the residents were not evacuated to another place, more local people would fall victims to the plague. Mohandas now started visiting each and every house personally and trying to convince the people to leave: 'I understand your pain and agony. I also understand that it is no easy thing to dismantle with your own hands the house that was your dream and that you built facing so many difficulties. But an even greater misfortune is to see your own children die before your own eyes. We have seen with our own eyes people dying terrible deaths due to Black Plague. Give up your attachment to this place. Once you have been in the other place for a few days you will begin to think of it as your own. Think of your life, think of your children—don't think of the place. When you left your home to travel across seven seas to come here you didn't think of the place. Why didn't you? Because your survival was more important. Because you thought if you survived, giving up home would also become meaningful. If you sought hunger and death, you could have had it right there. After all, they are the same everywhere; then why did you come here?'

What Mohandas said made sense to them. It made them unhappy. They were transported to their villages or cities and found themselves standing at the doorsteps of their homes. The entire scene flashed before their moist and trembling eyes.

But they still had one apprehension: What will happen to our savings? Who will protect them there? We'll be ruined.

'Don't worry about your savings. We'll make some arrangement.'

The reassurance did not quite bring cheer to their faces but they did look a bit reassured.

Those with savings to excavate kept digging all night. Some had buried silver and copper coins while some had buried notes in a clay pot. In some cases, the notes had their corners eaten by moths. The coins had turned black. Only a rare coolie had a gold coin. Coins and notes had piled up in Mohandas' office. It was getting difficult to keep track of each individual's portion. All the four assistants and Sonja were engaged in the task.

They counted out each one's share and entered it into the records. Five or six people worked through the day to prepare the registers for the people of the Coolie Location. At the end, the collection amounted to sixty thousand pounds. It was an amount that could not be kept in the office: it wouldn't be proper. The bank wasn't ready to accept sixty thousand pounds in coins and moth-eaten notes. The biggest objection of course was to handling money from a plague-infected area. Nobody was ready to touch it. Mohandas first got the money disinfected in everyone's presence. It was only after a lot of persuasion on the Bank Manager's part that the bank staff agreed to keep the money in the bank.

There were some among the residents who had forgotten where they had buried their money. In some cases, the person who had buried the money was no more. All they knew was there was money buried somewhere in the premises. They approached Mohandas with their tale of woe: 'The land has swallowed our money. Please come and help. If you only touch the land, Mother Earth will let us have our money back.'

There were others who said: 'Wealth is never constant. If one is not fated to have any, his wealth will escape like water to the next man.'

Mohandas tried the same line of reasoning with everyone: 'Look, you earned that money with your own hands. You still have your hands; only the money is gone. So what? You'll earn it again. But don't let the land have it now. Put it in a bank.'

But he knew that what he was saying sounded good only as consolation. Those who had lost the money were not really getting consoled.

The residents were taken by a special train to Klipspruit Farm, thirteen miles outside Johannesburg. They had been given provisions by the Municipality, but it was hard for them to forget all that they had to leave behind. Only till yesterday, they had been property owners and today they had been reduced to a nomadic existence. Seated in the train, they could only see their houses and the Coolie Location spreading out all around them, though they were getting left behind every minute.

The tent-covered farm looked like an army camp. Looking at it, Mohandas was reminded of the Boer War camps. The displaced and hapless residents of the Coolie Location were cooking their evening meal. As they cooked, their hearts cried. Some of them fed the kids but went to bed themselves without eating. It went on like this for a couple of days. But, though one might somehow fight flood waters, fires of hunger are hard to fight. Even though unwilling to eat, they had to eat something.

There was a deathly quiet for a couple of days. It cast its shadow even on the voices of children. Mohandas visited them frequently and talked to them, inquiring if they were facing any problems. His visits gave them strength.

'All the problems are over forever, Gandhibhai,' they said: 'Piece by piece we had got our home up, and, at one stroke, it's all gone. There will never be another home for us.'

Time respects neither joy nor sorrow. Bit by bit, their sorrow too dissolved and they regained patience. Ever so slowly, the sound of songs began to be heard again. Every once in a while, a smile began to dance on their lips.

What Mohandas had told them had stayed with them: 'Brick and mortar do not make a home; it's your thinking that makes one. There have been kings and emperors who left their homes to live in the forests, and their homes turned into forests while the forests turned into homes.'

The hearts of the residents of the Klipspruit Farm tents were still stuck in the Location. The Location would be burnt to cinders in three weeks' time. Or maybe not! They just wanted it vacated, and we have vacated it. Well, at least the house we built with our own hands will escape destruction. Who knows, someday we might still get them back?

It didn't take three weeks. One day they learnt that the entire Location had actually been burnt down the day after they left it. They felt as if they themselves had been set fire to. Their dream of returning to their homes one day had been reduced to ashes.

A burning smell hung over the place. A few dogs sniffed around. And there were the earth and the sky, stunned into silence. Air hung like water in a still pond. The burnt-out Location was above one and below the other, but didn't exist itself.

They picked up some ash, smeared it on their foreheads and went back.

~

Ever since Kastur and the kids had joined him, the house was beginning to feel like a home to Mohandas. Mainly because of the kids. They were playing all day. As in the Beachgrove Villa, the responsibility of running the household was entirely on Kastur once again. Ever since their arrival, Mohandas now spent almost as much time at home as outside, though sometimes it was more outside. Even when he was at home, though, he never seemed to be without the outsiders.

When the plague was at its height, Kastur and the kids were worried sick. All sorts of news kept coming in. So many dead! There were rumours galore. Once, the rumours didn't spare even Mohandas. The nurse's death gave credence to the rumour. At one point, the rumour was that everyone working with the Sister had joined her. There was no one Kastur could ask to go and find out the truth for her. She was anyway new to Johannesburg. Most of the residents of Albmerry Street were whites, who didn't like talking to the coloureds. Even if they sometimes agreed, language created an obstruction. Kastur was reminded of Durban. There

Mohandas had only received threats to his life, but here she felt as if her tongue had been lobbed off. She prayed to God: Only you can save us, God! At Durban, she at least had so many friends she could call on; here, it was a barren scene.

The kids were in a fright. Sonja was the only one who showed full self-assurance. She constantly said that Gandhibhai and his companions would remain unscathed. She was with them regularly and looked after them the best she could in view of the communication problems. Sometimes, communication indeed became a real struggle.

When Kastur became extremely nervous, Sonja made a great effort and, in broken language, told her: 'Don't worry about Gandhibhai. He is fine and nothing is going to happen to him.'

When Kastur failed to make any sense of what Sonja said, she would get irritated and mutter to herself: 'God knows what the wretched woman is saying. "Gandhibhai," "Gandhibhai," all the time!' That was the only word she could make out in her whole sentence.

Sonja read the reaction on her face and laughed like mad.

When Mohandas was told all this on his return he laughed and said: 'Don't ever trust a rumour. It's an elder sister to a lie, and an undesirable extension of imagination. If you trust it, you push yourself into the abyss of doubts and fears. And once in that abyss, only God can save you.'

Kastur said nothing. She looked glum.

The plague incident had made Gandhi's name known to the poorest of the poor Indian living in Johannesburg. They had escaped with their life and the money in the bank was also growing steadily like a child. Even the whites were beginning to acknowledge him. However slightly, they were beginning to feel a little obliged to him for their lives. They were beginning to feel that to acknowledge the coolie barrister was turning into a moral obligation for them. Word had spread everywhere that had Gandhi not stood as a wall between them and the plague, death would have been knocking at their doors too.

~

Mohandas often went to the vegetarian restaurant for his evening meal. The restaurant was like a club for him. He had met many important people there.

Mohandas sat alone. The waiter arrived with a card on a plate. It said: 'May I see you?'

Mohandas asked: 'Where is this gentleman?'

The waiter pointed out: 'Over there.' Mohandas got up and went up to his table and introduced himself: 'I am M.K. Gandhi. Please come and sit with me.'

'I am Polak. Sub-editor of *The Critic*.'

'Pleased to meet you.'

Polak joined him at his table. He said: 'I read your article on the plague in the newspaper. You were absolutely right in holding the Municipality squarely responsible for the outbreak. It was callous on their part. I have been waiting to meet you since that very day.'

Mohandas was listening to him very carefully. He laughed and said: 'I'm surprised that you had to go through so much formality to meet a common man like me. I am really the man on the street.'

'I'm a great admirer of your policy of fighting against evil.'

'Mr. Polak, that is not a policy with me; it's my faith. It is what causes me to fight. It is also what causes me to be beaten up at times.' He laughed.

'I'm impressed with the experiment you carried out with clay in order to save the life of the patients. Did it really happen? Is it possible at all?'

'You can find out only if you come and live with me. Unless you work in the laboratory, you cannot find out the truth or otherwise of the results.'

'I do wish to join your laboratory.'

Mohandas laughed: 'I'm my own laboratory. I carry it with me wherever I go.'

'I am also quite mobile.'

Mohandas laughed out loud and said: 'A mobile laboratory is fine, but mobile minds are not. Whatever may be the fate of mobile laboratories, mobile minds will certainly invite doubts on their very existence. '

It was Polak's turn to laugh this time.

'Now we are friends. Nothing like laughter to join hearts, wouldn't you say?'

Not only his face, Polak's entire personality seemed to have undergone a transformation as a result of his meeting with Mohandas.

~

Mohandas was in no doubt that he had annoyed his elder brother with his letter. He had received a letter from him after a long time in which he had expressed his annoyance quite unreservedly:

> *The theory that you have advanced in defence of your unwillingness to send money home is a load of rubbish. You call it enlightenment! Do you claim to be wiser than our father? He looked after the entire family all his life. As the younger brother, it is your duty to defer to you elder brother and to serve him in every way…*

Mohandas reflected on his letter for a few days and then sent a reply:

> *Our fellow countrymen are also part of our family. We also have a duty towards them. They are part of our greater family. As members of this greater family, you, I and everyone else are duty-bound to share in their joys and their sorrows, to serve them, to help them financially and to make them stakeholders in our wealth and property.*

That letter silenced the elder brother for good. He stopped writing letters. Whenever Mohandas thought of him, his unhappy and angry face flashed before his eyes. Kastur and the kids had lived as his dependents. The kids still recalled him with affection. Kastur was deferential towards him and held Mohandas squarely responsible for all that had happened.

Mohandas was unhappy on both these counts. His brother was of course miles away and it was just not possible to make him understand.

Nothing like a face-to-face when you have to explain your point of view to someone; letters are such a poor substitute. The expressions that your face carries are missing from the words, since words just cannot be the face you have. But he did try to make Kastur understand. He told her: 'You also misunderstand me, like elder brother. How can I dissociate myself from these Indians settled so far away from home? They are a part of the sensibility which I have inherited from my traditions. You throw a pebble in a pond and it creates a ring of water which grows larger and larger till it encompasses the entire pond. The ring itself loses its existence; it becomes a part of an even larger ring. I, my brother, you, the kids—everyone is a part of that larger ring. How can we think of anyone as independent of that ring?'

'Look, I'm a poor uneducated woman. All these highfalutin ideas are beyond me. What however I don't understand is that if even I can understand what elder brother is saying, how come you don't understand it? You are such a wise man.'

Mohandas shook his head and said: 'You will soon also understand what I am saying; just give it some time.' He continued: 'Do you think I feel happy to cause hurt to my elder brother? But if I didn't carry out my duty here, my unhappiness would have been many times what I have caused my elder brother. There isn't the slightest fall in my regard for my elder brother.'

'What does one do with mere regard? You know your brother doesn't need your money. He needs respect and your goodwill for his family. Your letter has violated his trust in you.'

'I know, but one has to sacrifice minor interests for the sake of a higher good. When a bride enters a new family, she has to merge her old interests with the new ones that she assumes. When you sacrifice your family to dedicate yourself to the society at large, something similar takes place.'

'Don't thrust similarities on things that are quite dissimilar. You know your brother is not well.'

'I know. I also know that I am also the reason for that.'

'Well, then?'

'There is nothing I can do for him except pray.' Mohandas got up and went outside.

~

For Mohandas, *Indian Opinion* had been like a dream come true. As his struggle intensified, Mohandas was getting confirmed in his belief that the shape of the struggle would remain ill-defined so long as a medium of inter-communication between the different sections of the Indian community was not firmly in place. Mohandas lived in Johannesburg but his heart was in Natal—running the press. The material was sent from Transvaal to be printed in Natal. It was not enough to send the material; even more important was the money. Mohandas contributed seventy-five pounds. The question troubling Mohandas now was whether he should continue running the paper or close it down. There wasn't the slightest doubt that *Indian Opinion* had started an awakening in the Indian community. It had given a direction to the thinking and expression of the Indian community and made them ready to join the struggle. Mohandas did not want such a potent medium of awakening to fold up for lack of finance.

Mohandas thought of Albert West. Mr. West was a partner in a private printing press. He was a regular visitor to the vegetarian restaurant and sometimes sat with Mohandas. After dinner, they would go out walking. Like Polak, West too had read Mohandas' article on the plague in which he had held the Municipality responsible for the outbreak. Not exactly an article, it was actually more in the nature of a letter to the editor. The letter had really upset Mr. West. How inhuman we could get, he thought.

Since Mohandas was engaged in relief work those days, he had stopped his evening meals. With people dying in large numbers like rats, eating a full stomach and belching somehow felt obscene to Mohandas. Even otherwise, a light stomach always helped in keeping awake and working through the nights. That was also a principle of naturopathy. Always keep the stomach light at night. In fact, he even had his lunch early. After disposing of his work, he had an early lunch and then he cycled off to the camp.

Every day, Mr. West checked with the restaurant manager: 'Has Mr. Gandhi been here? Where is he?'

'He is busy in relief work for the plague victims. He has stopped meeting people. He doesn't want to infect people.'

News of plague deaths was streaming in regularly. There had been several deaths in a span of mere two days. Mohandas' self-imposed quarantine had lasted for about a month. During that month one hundred and thirteen people had died in Transvaal. The number of whites was the smallest among them—twenty-five.

Lying in bed, Mr. West suddenly had a sort of apparition: Mohandas has high fever. He can't walk, has red eyes, and is breathless with coughing. But he is still at it, attending to the patients. He goes from patient to patient, tells each one of them: 'Give me your pain'. And the patient starts recovering. Mohandas gets worse. The fever rises further. Cough is tearing his chest out.

Mr. West sat up. It was the time before dawn. Sweat broke out on his whole body. He had a drink of water and went back to bed but couldn't sleep. He got out of bed and made it to Mohandas' house quite early. It was quite a distance. He knocked at the door. Mohandas was ready to leave home. He opened the door himself. The moment Mr. West saw him, he exclaimed: 'Thank God!' and stood for some time, holding Mohandas' hand in his. Then he spoke: 'Didn't see you for so long. I was so full of apprehensions. That's why I am here so early. Thought couldn't miss you at this hour. So happy to see you hale and hearty. Jesus loves you. I am here to seek a favour: I am ready to work for you. I'll do whatever work you assign to me. It'll make me so happy to be able to serve the patients. You know that there is no one who will miss me.'

Mohandas laughed and said: 'We will miss you. Don't you want us to miss you?' He continued: 'I won't have you work with the patients. There aren't very many patients left anyway. In fact, we may all be relieved in a day or two. But I had been thinking for some time of requesting you to do something else for us. I just didn't get round to telling you about it.'

'Go right ahead.'

'Would it be possible for you to go to Durban and take over *Indian Opinion* there? It would be a big weight off my chest if you could.'

'Give me some time. You know I also run a press here, with a partner, of course. We'll talk about it when we are out for a walk this evening.'

Everything was settled during the walk, even the salary: ten pounds a month. A share in the profits, if there were any.

Mr. West left for Durban the very next day. Mohandas was happy for *Indian Opinion* that it had now got Mr. West. As usual, he went into a reverie. A whole reel of film started unwinding. But he also had a great quality: he knew how to rewind the reel quickly.

The very first report from Mr. West on *Indian Opinion* shook Mohandas up. It said: 'It's a losing game you have inducted me in. It's a dead loss. The accounts are in a bad shape. There are unrealized debts which need to be realized at the earliest. A complete overhaul is what is needed. But you needn't worry. Loss or profit, now that I'm here I'll see to everything.'

Mohandas left for Durban at once. He couldn't stand the idea of losing *Indian Opinion*, no matter what. It was a pillar of his whole programme. It was his only means of a dialogue with his fellow countrymen living in South Africa and with those members of the white community who had any wish to understand the problems of the Indians. All through the journey, Mohandas kept thinking of how credulous he had been to trust everything Madanjit had told him. Was such credulousness justified in a man who was engaged in public service? If it were a personal business, it would not matter whether you earned a profit or incurred a loss: that was your personal matter. But where interests of others were also involved, it was a sin to be careless. Mohandas was full of regret for his irresponsible conduct. It was not enough to have aspirations and perseverance; you also needed to have commensurate standards of behaviour. Mohandas was inconsolable and full of remorse.

There was a part of Mohandas which insisted on holding Madanjit exclusively responsible for the situation. But there was another part of him which stood firm confronting his own arguments: How about you? Are you blameless? Is not your inaction responsible? When he thought of Naazar, he again found himself in the dock. Naazar was only supposed to concern himself with editing. Management was your responsibility. By leaving it in the hands of Madanjit, you brought about this situation.

In the end, Mohandas had to confess that he had been guilty on all counts.

Polak had come to the station to see Mohandas off. He was working as Mohandas' articled junior. He studied law at night while working in the office during the day. He was also living with Mohandas. A Jew by religion and ethnicity, he had the complete confidence of his senior and was an efficient worker.

When the train was steaming out, Polak handed Mohandas a book and said: 'Here is a book that I'm sure you will love to read. Yours is a long, twenty-four hour journey. This will keep you engaged.'

As the train caught speed, Mohandas sat for a while with his eyes closed. Diverse expressions passed through his face. After sitting in that position for a while, Mohandas came out of his reverie and opened the book Polak had handed him. The book was called *Unto this Last*. He glanced through the whole book cursorily and decided that it deserved a reading. He had never read Ruskin before, though he had heard a lot about him. Focusing his attention, Mohandas started reading. He had hardly started on it when he found himself completely absorbed in the book. He lost track of everything—of his own self, the train and the journey. He would now sit up straight, now rest his back against the seat and now lie on his back. For full twenty-four hours, Mohandas didn't so much as sleep a wink or doze off for a second. He felt that the book was on a rampage inside him—destroying everything that had been there and turning him upside down. Outwardly, the book looked like any other. Its white pages had a lot of writing on it, but this was writing that grabbed you by the scruff of your neck and every word in it tore into your brain. He felt that words, which normally held their peace and shifted the burden of getting at their meaning onto the reader, couldn't in this case stop jabbering away.

They ran a riot. They forced you to stop doing whatever you were doing and to concentrate on them and them alone. They joined themselves one to the other like flowers in a garland. And in a short while they had turned themselves into a forceful current which swept him along with it. There was a flood of ideas bursting forth from the words.

When he had finished reading the book, he sat there for some time, still lost in it. He felt he needed a new type of discipline in himself to internalize fully such iconoclastic thoughts. It would only create indigestion in him if he tore into this feast of mouth-watering dishes like a starving man. He felt that the soil within him was turning fertile and new seedlings were bursting open every minute. Mohandas was no writer, and he felt that it would take a writer to give words to the internal contradictions and shades of meaning that lay hidden within man. An understanding of those meanings would also depend on the concerns that motivated the reader.

'... In the good of all lies the good of the individual. The aim of man's life is to do well to one and all. Be it a barber or a lawyer, the value of their labour is the same. Everyone has a right to earn a living. The life of a stone-breaker is as important as the life of an artist ...'

Pronouncements like these were constantly reverberating in the mind of Mohandas. The first truth, he felt, was the universal truth. In his world lay buried all the truths.

When Mohandas got off the train at Durban, he felt that the man who got off the train at Durban was not the same man who had got on at Johannesburg.

Mr. West was present at the station to receive Gandhi. Mohandas was still under the influence of the book. A few formal exchanges and he was back to the book: 'Have you read Ruskin's *Unto this Last*?'

Mr. West thought for a minute and then said: 'Yes, but it was a long time ago.'

Mohandas laughed. 'With such books it makes no difference when one reads it. You may read it now or you may have read it a long time ago, you can never forget such books.'

Mr. West only laughed.

Till they arrived at Rustomji's place, Mohandas kept on talking about the book without a break. Mr. West responded with an occasional 'H'm' or 'Yes.' Once at Rustomji's place, Mr. West wanted to talk about the sad financial state of *Indian Opinion.* Mohandas promptly affirmed: 'Exactly. What else have I been trying to tell you all this while? I have been trying to tell you that for one who has read *Unto this Last* such things do not matter at all. It is not a problem at all for him.'

Mr. West stared at him. Then he laughed and said: 'Looks like you are lost in a dream.'

'There is no life without a dream. You wouldn't know how long I have been dreaming this dream. I have a cousin who lives in Tongat. Once I paid him a visit. He runs a store and behind the store he has a one-acre farm. It has some fruit trees in it—so beautiful that they defy description. The land is so fertile that you could raise a variety of stuff in it. My brothers are wasting their time running the store. So much natural beauty and so much work to do—and they hire workers to work for them! Why don't they work themselves? If they worked themselves, the place would be in a much better shape than it is now. When I was there, I saw this dream of a farm where everyone worked and everyone's work was valued the same. That was the very dream that Ruskin brought alive before my eyes.'

'I don't quite get it,' interrupted Mr. West.

'When I came to South Africa, I had a dream—a dream of communal living; a dream of a place where we would learn to live together and where everyone would be equal. When I got a house at Beach Grove, I tried to give a practical shape to my dream of communal living on a small scale by living with my colleagues in the same house. My cook, my office colleagues, a couple of friends—we all lived together. We had all kinds of experiences, some sweet, some not so sweet. We tried to forget the not-so-sweet experiences. The sweet experiences we did not try to compare with the not-so-sweet ones, but rather we cherished them on their own. Most of all, I find my inspiration in the life of the Trappists of Marian Hill near Pine

Town. They have voluntarily embraced poverty. Ignoring the differences of colour, creed and race, they have all joined their hearts together. Neither language nor ethnicity separates them. They work with their own hands, they cook and eat in communal kitchens and they consider this to be their only religion and their only duty. Purity and dedication—they have it all.'

Mr. West laughed and said: 'You are not thinking of setting up a Gandhi Settlement on the lines of the Trappist Settlement, are you?'

'Will you help me, if I am? It will be home to everybody. I believe that the highest goal of man is to reach God, whatever be our concept of Him, whatever be the form we give to Him. The whole world of action—religious, political or social—is geared towards the same goal. In our country, we used to have the *tapovans,* little forest settlements where the guru instructed his disciples in tradition. He taught them about life, duty, truth, untruth and so on. Even a king's son would go there and live the life allowed by the guru, like a farmer's son. Thus he learnt to surrender his ego to the society. Then the guru told them: "Go forth into the society and turn loose whatever you have learnt!" To beg for a living was not to turn into a parasite; rather, it was to join your ego with the ego of that other man who had no means and who had no other option but to beg. This is the way to grasp the significance of communal living and the prevalent misconceptions about it. What *Unto this Last* has done is to validate my dream.'

As Mohandas spoke, Mr. West's unblinking eyes were fixed on his face. He could see a new horizon rising in his eyes and a new light shining. Mohandas was actually talking to himself. Words flowed from his lips in a continuous stream: 'Our traditions are falling apart. Our values cannot hold together. Truth cannot retain its integrity. The glory of man is in decline. Men enjoy causing pain to others.' Mohandas closed his eyes for a second and then continued: 'Mr. West, how will we ever be able to protect these without faith in truth and non-violence? Is it possible to have a social and political life without self-sacrifice and renunciation? Do not think of politics as a milch cow that you can milk with both your hands. Don't you think service and action should form the backbone of political life? How will the walls that divide us ever come down unless we learn to appreciate the dignity of labour. Labour is what gives you the supreme education. Our environment will never return to normal till we learn to work with our own hands, to protect the cow, and to put it to its proper uses. For all this, you need a disease-free body and a perversion-free mind. How do we achieve this? Only through work, dedication and a voluntary acceptance of a life of labour.'

Mr. West was awestruck. He had never heard Mohandas speaking like this. It appeared to him that Mohandas was wandering in a land where dreams were strewn all over the place. Like a child he was gathering them in his bag and handing them out to others.

All of a sudden, Mohandas addressed himself to Mr. West: 'Will you help me, Mr. West?'

Mr. West wasn't quite ready for such a question. Unthinkingly, he blurted out an answer: 'Sure.'

He was mesmerized.

~

When Mr. West had landed in Durban suddenly, he was only carrying a letter from Gandhibhai for Madanjit. It said:

> *Seeing the problems of* Indian Opinion, *Mr. West is coming to you as a new associate and a friend. Please extend him your fullest help and cooperation.*

Madanjit sat for while nursing the letter in his hands. Then he asked Mr. West: 'How are you going to help me?'

Mr. West wasn't ready for this question. Still, he laughed and said: 'Please do not worry yourself on my account. I'll help you anyway you want. Our effort should be to see that *Indian Opinion* continues to be published and doesn't lose money. Gandhibhai is worried about the financial health of the paper.'

'Why doesn't he shut it down then?'

'Shutting it down is not the solution. This is the only medium available for communicating with the Indians and for conveying their grievances to the whites.'

Madanjit got all worked up. It was with great difficulty that he could be persuaded to show the account books. Naazar also didn't like the idea, but he kept quiet as the matter fell outside his field of responsibility.

Mohandas explained his new scheme to Madanjit. He wanted all workers of *Indian Opinion* to live together and lead a communal life. Everyone would be paid three pounds per month for his expenses.

That was enough to annoy Madanjit. 'Foolish idea!' was his instant reaction. Mohandas said nothing.

Madanjit tried for some time to recover his balance. When he couldn't control himself, he continued: 'I know how I set up this press. Door to door! I went from door to door to raise subscriptions for this paper! I risked my life for this! Everything I had, I put into it. If the workers get to know, they will lock out the place. Why should they give up their families to live with you here? I am telling you today that if you try to run the press in such a high-handed manner, it will become impossible for you to bring out the paper. My press will be ruined. Gandhibhai, you are a great man, but please spare us. Do not turn us into your laboratory. This is the only means of livelihood I have.'

Mohandas listened to him peacefully. Then he adopted a conciliatory attitude and said: 'It's quite possible that what you are saying is right, but what's the harm in giving it a try? The idea of *Indian Opinion* was also yours, but we all got together to bring it out. Why don't we also ask the others?'

Madanjit was quiet. He didn't know what to say.

Mohandas reflected on Madanjit's behaviour for a long time. He could see that his proposal had hurt Madanjit and that it was natural for him to react in this way. Instead of continuing with him further, therefore, Gandhi talked to Mr. West and Maganlal Gandhi. Maganlal worked for *Indian Opinion.* He used to run a personal business on the side. Mohandas explained the whole project to him.

Maganlal was not only his nephew but also a faithful follower and a disciple. He had come to Durban with Mohandas. He promptly gave his consent to Mohandas' idea.

Machineman Govindasamy also followed suit.

Mr. West sometimes teased Mohandas: 'Gandhibhai, when you call the tune, no one has any choice but to dance to it. You never give them any choice, do you?'

Gandhibhai laughed.

The rest of the workers refused to move out to another place to live, but they agreed that they would go wherever the press was relocated. That put paid to the remaining hopes of Madanjit.

The collective decision shattered Madanjit. Although he was keeping quiet, he wanted to shout out loud that Gandhibhai had ruined his plans and destroyed everything.

But he knew that no one would be listening.

~

The dream of Mohandas had taken flight like a kite, with Mohandas chasing it with the string in his hands. The dream was still either in his eyes or stuck in the sky. He was busy finding ways and means of bringing it down to earth. He advertised in the papers and talked to people looking for a place where there would be fruit trees and a spring of water, where the land would be generous and return four-fold whatever was sown in it. He was told about a twenty-acre plot. Without telling anyone, Mohandas took West with him and went off to see the place. It was about two and a half miles from the Phoenix station in the sun-lit valley of Pijeng river. This was the northernmost tip of Zululand. Orange and apple trees, waterfalls—Mohandas' heart danced with joy. It wasn't exactly like Marian Hill where the Trappists lived, but it was in no way inferior in beauty. Mohandas stared at the scene captivated. He felt his dream coming down from the sky to the earth and emerging from his eyes to assume a concrete shape.

Next to it was an eighty-acre plot thickly populated with trees. To Mohandas, the place looked like a *tapovan* waiting to receive him. He bought it up too. The whole deal cost him a thousand pounds. Mohandas' joy knew no bounds. Occasionally, he thought of Johannesburg, but what he was witnessing here was a dream transforming into reality. How could he leave it behind? The happiest thing was that the money he had been earning was being put to a worthy cause. He was trying to reach out to Ruskin's soul and it was coming closer and closer to him. He also thought of Polak, the man who had introduced him to this god.

The big question before Gandhibhai now was: How should he name it? A monastery? A *tapovan*? An ashram? All these names had specific connotations linking them to Hindu culture. He wanted a name which would be linked to the soil, a name which would awaken the locals' latent feeling of identity.

Someone muttered: 'Phoenix'.

He jumped for joy. 'Yes, Phoenix! Absolutely right! Native to the soil! The phoenix dies again and again but rises again from its ashes. It never dies. This name complements our aims. This name will never die. The local people will always keep it alive. How important it is that your principles, your values and your identity should stay alive! Time and again, they are trampled upon, but every time they spring back to life like grass in spring.'

A board was put up. It said: 'Phoenix Cooperative.'

A hundred acres of Phoenix spread out before Mohandas without a soul to live in it! The dream that was descending from the sky was suspended in mid-air. There were only three of them: Maganlal, Machineman Govindasamy and West with Mohandas himself completing the foursome. Three or four men and a hundred acres of land! A hundred acres of broken land, overgrown with tall and short grass, infested with insects, a veritable snake pit, teeming with challenges to life—that was the cooperative.

This was the place where a farm was to be set up, a press started and a human settlement established. The million-dollar question was: How was all this going to be accomplished?

~

October 1904. Mohandas kept going off and on to Johannesburg. Whatever money he earned there he spent on Phoenix, whose needs now topped his own and his family's needs. Some of the land was flat and even. Mohandas announced the construction of 'Phoenix Settlement.'

Parsi Rustomji was a ready partner of Gandhibhai in all such adventures. He got some steel girders and corrugated sheets from his godown sent. Gandhi was still in contact with some masons and carpenters who had worked with him during the Boer War. When they got to know that Gandhibhai was getting the Phoenix settlement constructed they all started trickling in. With their help, Gandhi first started the construction of a shed for the press. The racket that the construction work made day and night sounded like music to Gandhi' ears—an odd music of creation, with rhythm and refrain. Tents had been fixed all around for workers to live in, but they never reminded Mohandas of the battlefield. Maganlal, Govinda and West also lent a hand with the work. Gandhi kept shuttling between Johannesburg and Durban and did his full share of work. His style of living was also the same as that of the others.

Construction was catching speed, but a great scare had been created by snakes. They had the knack of appearing anywhere, anytime, and when they did, people took to their heels at great speed.

Mohandas always asked them: 'You share King Parikshit's traditional enmity with snakes, do you?'

Not everyone got the reference to Parikshit, but they got his drift and answered: 'Of course not.'

'Well, if you are sure that you have done nothing wrong to the snakes, and if you nurse no hostility towards them, then why do you entertain the fear that they will bite you and thus promote hostility?'

That cut no ice with the people. Gandhi laughed and said: 'I know that you are not going to bite the snakes and they are not going to bite you. They are of course not going to bite me as I treat them as my friends, and so do they treat me.' Sometime a whole colony of snakes would pass by him and he would go on walking fearlessly.

On one issue, everyone disagreed with him politely. Gandhi wanted clay huts to be put up for housing, using locally available materials. In his view, that would be environment-friendly. The houses would be cool and airy. However, no one supported the idea. They argued that it was fine that they should work with their hands and that the homes should meet only the basic needs with no allowance for comfort and luxury, but that should not mean making any compromise with security and safety.

Mohandas tried to tell them: 'Look, it's not the house which provides you security; it's your own mind, it's your own fixity of purpose. You may have a fortress for a house but if you stay cowering inside it, the house is not going to make you fearless.'

But despite his arguments, his proposal was turned down unanimously. Mohandas laughed and said: 'Everytime you do whatever I say. Let me do what you say just this once?'

That made everyone happy.

Every problem presented a challenge. A big one was transporting the printing press from Durban to Phoenix. The distance was at least fourteen or fifteen miles. The road was in a bad shape. Two or three rivers would have to be crossed. There were no bridges across them. Madanjit had withdrawn his support completely. The move was being labelled as Mohandas' 'Daulatabad Adventure'. Some thought of it as Mohandas' whim. The vilification campaign was being orchestrated mainly by Madanjit.

Among the problems to be sorted out were: Who'll travel to Phoenix Settlement to get the printing done? How'll the expenses of the press be met? Will the newspaper be able to raise enough money to meet all expenses?

But nothing deterred Mohandas. He hired several large farm wagons. Each wagon was pulled by sixteen bulls. The machines were dismantled and loaded on the wagons. Mohandas walked with the wagons all the way. Crossing rivers and drains, the wagons trundled into Phoenix by the evening, leaving everyone astonished. 'The man is a magician,' commented some: 'otherwise how could such heavy machines be transported so quickly over such a distance?' Whatever, the man's magic worked.

That problem was over, but now another one loomed up. How to set up the machines?

Mohandas wanted the press to be run manually. Mr. West was totally opposed to the idea. He argued that manual operation would waste time, delay the work and the paper would not be able to meet the publication deadline.

'We can raise the number of workers. That would mean more employment for people.'

'Look, men can't be machines. Men will get fatigued, will need to eat and meet their daily needs, and might fall sick...'

The discussion continued for a few days. In the end, Mohandas had to yield. An oil engine had to be purchased. But Mohandas also bought a manual printing machine, a treadle press.

'Machines are machines,' he argued. 'They are fine so long as they are running, but when they stop running, they do so without letting you know the reason. The poor human, on the other hand, works so long as he can, but when he stops working he tells you why.'

The announcement that the first Phoenix issue of *Indian Opinion* was going to hit the stands had been made. Everyone was excited and busy doing something or the other: folding paper, stacking it nicely, trimming irregular sheets, and so on. Mohandas was however full of apprehension.

There could be a last-minute hitch. So Mohandas reduced the pages of the paper to a single foolscap page. His thinking behind doing so was that in case of any trouble, the treadle machine could be pressed into service.

It was the night of long knives. The paper had been cut to the size and stacked. The time came to start printing. Mr. West went with the engineer and pressed the button. The engine, like a laggard horse, stood unmoved. The engineer had been sent by the company to see to it that the machine is handed over in a working condition.

Mr. West looked at the engineer and asked: 'Why isn't the engine running?'

'It has to run. Let me see what is wrong.'

He got busy tightening the nuts and bolts. West also joined him. West was the most anxious of all. No engine would mean no paper! Mohandas sat at a distance and looked on unperturbed. Time was running out. Light from the paraffin lamp streamed out of the shed.

A few attempts later, the engineered reported to West: 'Hard to say what the problem is. We'll have to wait till morning.'

'But the paper has to be in the stands by that time.'

'I'm helpless. A machine is a machine. Only a thorough check will reveal where the problem lies.'

'But …'

'I'm off to bed. Nothing more can be done at the moment.' And he marched off to bed before Mr. West could complete his sentence.

Mr. West's main worry was how to report this to Gandhibhai without losing face. He went up to Gandhibhai and, with his eyes brimming over and his voice trembling, said: 'Gandhibhai, the engine refuses to start. We have very little chance to get the paper out in the morning.'

Gandhibhai laughed like a child. 'Kids, kings and women are known to be hard to persuade; we should now add machines to this list. In fact, you can persuade almost anyone to see reason, but a machine can neither be persuaded nor wheedled into doing your bidding. So it's no use shedding tears. We have to find some other way which would stop the wilfulness of the machine and at the same time let us have what we seek. Actually the machine has its wilful way only where man stops using his hands and beomes a slave to machines. What do you feel about the treadle machine? I have a feeling it won't misbehave.'

Mr. West looked at Gandhi. There was no sign of any malicious pleasure on his face. It looked totally innocent.

'We'll need eight people to run it. Where do we get them? Four in each shift. Our men are dead tired.'

Mohandas laughed and said: 'Don't give up, Mr. West. A man's courage is his greatest asset, greater than any machine. In the absence of courage, even the most efficient machine is reduced to mere fuel. Why don't we wake up our construction workers, the masons and the carpenters? I'm sure they will be ready to help.'

'They have worked throughout the day. I don't have the heart to wake them up.'

'Leave that to me. No one understands the need of the moment better than a human being, and that is what I rely on most. Anyone who wants to fly high has to think of the time when he may come down crashing.'

As Mr. West considered the importance of what Gandhi had been saying, Gandhi himself was busy examining the treadle. Mr. West didn't know what response to make to Mohandas' remarks. He had managed a press, but he had never faced a situation when the engine might have failed to start and the print order not executed on time. And a new engine at that! He was wondering if Gandhibhai had some sort of premonition that the engine would not work, because if he didn't, why had he arranged for a treadle machine? Maybe he was planning for the possible crash landing. West was truly amazed. So negative in his thoughts on the one hand and so positive on the other at the same time! So distrustful of machines and so trustful of his hands!

Mohandas woke up his workers. 'Wake up, brothers! Our engine has failed. We need help.'

They were right there, sleeping in the shed. Everyone got up pronto. It was a little past midnight. 'If it wasn't a fight against time,' said Gandhibhai, 'I wouldn't have bothered you at this inconvenient hour.'

'Gandhibhai, if we can't help you in your hour of need, what's the point of our existence? We are not machines that we accept the feed and then ditch you in return. We are human beings with real limbs and a stomach. We need to have work, and we also need to have food.'

Another one said: 'Gandhibhai, you go and take rest. Turning a wheel is child's play for us. The wheel turns us and we turn the wheel. Actually, we are old friends.'

Mr. West was amazed. London did not have this custom that you got up at the middle of the night and plunged into work. He was witnessing a completely new dimension of the life of workers; something which he had never imagined was even possible. Gandhibhai too started pushing the wheel. In sheer joy, West started singing even as he fed the paper in the machine. His song meant something like: 'We are so happy! Our sheep have started giving milk.'

As one man got tired, another took over at the wheel. A third one took over from him. The wheel went on turning till seven in the morning. By then everyone was dead tired, though work still remained to be completed. As they saw someone growing tired, Mohandas or West promptly relieved him themselves.

Mohandas told West: 'Go and get the engineer up. He is sleeping and so is his engine. If he gets up, maybe his engine will get up too.'

West went up to him and said: 'Please wake up, sir. You have slept all night, while we have been awake all night. Actually, it should have been vice versa.'

The engineer got up. West didn't like waking him up: in the western culture, it is considered improper to wake up a sleeping person. The engineer got up and walked straight to the engine.

Mohandas intercepted him: 'Wouldn't it be better if you performed your ablutions first?'

The engineer ignored him and kept walking. Either he was offended by Mr. West's remark, or maybe he realized that it must have been some very urgent business indeed to keep them awake all night.

The engine sprang to life the moment the engineer touched it, leaving everyone at a loss to grasp for a moment what had really happened. When they finally grasped it, they started dancing with joy. Everyone was wondering why their night-long efforts had failed to make it budge an inch while it had sputtered to life after the night-long watch had taken its toll with them.

Mohandas offered a salute to the engine. 'Mr. Engine, sir, we are grateful to you for helping us finish our work by getting the machines started at this time. Otherwise, the possibility of all our night labour going to waste could not be ruled out. Is it possible that the sincere and hard labour that we put in really melted your iron heart?' Everyone had a good laugh.

The newspaper was on the stands at the appointed time, sending everyone's spirits soaring high.

'There is nothing that Gandhibhai cannot do.' This sentence was now beginning to drop more frequently from people's lips.

Though the newspaper had made it to the stands, the problem of Phoenix was still unresolved. Efforts to settle people in Phoenix were on. Even those people who owed their entry into Natal to Mohandas had cried off. The few who had joined had been granted an acre or two of land each and asked to farm the land or get a house constructed. Everyone had to help himself.

A few houses were under construction—some of them flat-roofed. You could sleep on the roof during summer days. The ground crawled with snakes, poisonous spiders and insects of all descriptions. Although they had not caused any mishap so far, even the thought of the menagerie was enough to banish sleep. Since the work of construction was on, masons, carpenters and others had to live on location. They worked all day, cooked and had their meals in the evening, had song and dance sessions and then went off to sleep on the floor of the shed. The scared lot always wondered why *they* were not scared.

~

Work was piling up in Johannesburg. Polak, Sonja and the office clerks tried their best to dispose of whatever work they could, but there was a lot of work which could not have been disposed of in the absence of Mohandas. Mohandas was busy trying to fashion the Phoenix Settlement so that its residents would become self-dependent, help bring out the newspaper and make the Settlement as a whole an autonomous entity. This was not work that could be completed in a hurry. It needed time. But when Mohandas was reassured that *Indian Opinion* would not cease publication in his absence, he decided to return to Johannesburg, entrusting Maganlal with the duty of keeping the flock together at Phoenix. Mr. West was entrusted with *Indian Opinion*. Naazar hadn't consented to leave Durban for Phoenix. He edited *Indian Opinion* from Durban itself.

Before leaving for Johannesburg, Mohandas called Maganlal and said: 'You must promise to me that you will never leave Phoenix. You will live and die here. Everyone else may leave Phoenix, but you won't ever! This campaign for self-dependence must never end. Look at these people: they work with their hands and they cook and eat themselves. They may be slaves in the society, but, as individuals, their minds are free.'

Maganlal touched his feet and said: 'You are my teacher and patron. I give you word that I shall never leave Phoenix.'

Mr. West was also present there. He asked Mohandas: 'Why did you get Maganlal to make this promise? Is that not also a sort of bondage or slavery?'

'No, it's not. Slavery is violence. This is voluntary. Fine if you do it; fine, if you don't.'

'Did you not apply pressure on him?'

'Moral, not physical. There are pressures and pressures. Religion, parents and your kids—they all apply pressures that you have to put up with. Of course, there is nothing anyone can do if you don't. In fact, sometimes, even good intentions and a sense of responsibility can also apply pressure. I know Maganlal. He is the only person capable of shouldering this responsibility. That was the reason I got him to give me an undertaking. But, if he doesn't wish it, he is of course free to go.'

'By asking for an undertaking you have tied him hand and feet.'

'No, I have released him from the tyranny of alternatives. Unless you harness it, you can't even canalize the energy of a horse. Bondages too can be good or bad, you know.'

Mr. West did not take the issue any further. He had another issue bothering him: Why didn't Gandhibhai ask him?

It took Sonja and Polak several days before they could relax after the return of Mohandas. When the pressure of work eased a little and Gandhibhai could spare time from work, he asked Polak: 'Do you know how Phoenix was set up?'

Polak laughed and said: 'Gandhibhai, you are an unpredictable man. You went to Durban to check on the working of *Indian Opinion* and ended up raising Phoenix Settlement.'

'You are the one responsible.'

'Me?' Polak was taken aback.

'Yes, you. There'd have been no Phoenix, had you not given me *Unto this Last* to read. When I read that book, I knew that I had found the key to my dream: the dream of equality. The same labour for everyone, the same kind of work, the same food, the same living and, of course, the same payment ...' and he laughed. Then he continued: 'Everyone at Phoenix is engaged in bringing out the paper. Someone runs the machine, someone folds the paper and someone feeds it into the machine. When everyone works, there is economy. Whatever is thus saved is used for the good of everyone. Everyone has a share in the profits and everyone—machineman, compositor, editor—has the same share. Everyone helps in farming, growing vegetables, baking bread and there is no envy and no jealousy:

only competition—competition to see who can grow more and who can work more. Sometimes I wonder if that can happen some day in India too.'

Polak jumped for joy. 'Gandhibhai, you were so quick to grasp the essence of *Unto this Last.* All I did was to read it over and over again. Can I also join Phoenix? I also dreamed like Ruskin and you. I also had a dream of an ideal society, but you beat me to it.'

'Those who want such a society created will always beat others. I am a simple *girmitiya* worker.'

'You haven't answered my question.'

'But, at the moment, it's all a big mess in Phoenix. No comforts and no facilities. If you want a drink of water, you have to dig your own well—that's the situation that you'll have to face. You whites are really not used to that kind of a situation.'

'All that you need to get used to a situation is a proper coordination between the heart and the mind.'

'I'll be only too happy to have you with us.' Mohandas had noted the determination in Polak's face.

Polak immediately resigned his position at *The Critic*, which was anyway an anti-Indian paper. Working there, Polak had always had the feeling that he was being unfair to Indians.

When Polak arrived at Phoenix, Naazar had died. *Indian Opinion* was being edited by Herbert Kitchner. Kitchner came from Rhodesia. Being a Theosophist, he had no problem settling down at Phoenix. The flat-roof house of West was ready. West and Polak, both bachelors, were living in it together. They cooked their own food, worked hard all day and slept like logs at night. Polak had no problems with any kind of work that was entrusted to him. He had access to every home in the Settlement and was always the first to volunteer his services whenever and wherever required. He was like a duck floating on Phoenix waters: the centre of all attraction yet nursing neither love nor hate for anyone in particular.

The problem still continued: such huge property and so few people living in it. Mohandas had to send money regularly. In fact, that was the only reason for him to continue at Johannesburg: Phoenix must be kept going; the people there must be allowed to work towards a transformation of their selves undisturbed. Many were the occasions when he thought of moving to Phoenix himself, but every time the thought of a greater cause led him to overlook his personal wishes.

It had been raining for a few days. The flat wooden roofs of houses had started leaking. Rooms would get filled up with water. Grass—grass of all varieties—had grown to great heights. The level of fear in the hearts of the residents was rising day by day. Polak realized that living with fear as your constant companion was not a practical proposition. So he got everyone together and handed each one of them a sword-like contraption—a long, thin strip of steel wedged into a wooden handle. They all started felling the grass. In no time, a large area was cleared of wild growth. Next the ground was pummelled level with improvised implements. A respectable settlement consisting of six or seven houses was now beginning to emerge into view.

Mohandas sent money to Phoenix at the rate of three pounds per family. The expenses of *Indian Opinion* were of course met separately. Maintenance costs were another item of expense. The compositor was paid at the prevailing rates. Mohandas wanted the settlers to learn typesetting quickly so that the salary expense on the compositor could be saved. But that proved to be a hard nut to crack. Maganlal alone had been able to master the art; the rest barely got along. Maganlal had actually mastered almost all types of printing work.

Mohandas would sometimes joke: 'Maganlal is like Hanuman; he doesn't know his own strength. He needs a Jambuwan to remind him.'

Maganlal would retort very hesitantly: 'That's you, isn't it?'

Polak's arrival on the scene had made a qualitative difference to the place. He worked with total commitment. West was taken to be more of a Director of Operations. Phoenix had acquired a new shine. The shine was, however, short-lived. One day, a message arrived from Mohandas: 'Polak must return to Johannesburg.'

Mohandas had written: 'I know that you are a man of whims, like me. I live here but my heart is always wandering around in Phoenix. You went to Phoenix; it seems, only to lose yourself in Phoenix. Ritch has completed his law studies in London and he will now be working independently. I cannot handle the work here single-handed. Please come and work with me and qualify as an attorney. As for Phoenix, we shall both finish our work here soon and shall go back to Phoenix to live together.'

The letter caused a lot of consternation at Phoenix. Why was Gandhibhai calling Polak back? West and Polak had lived together so long that they were almost like siblings. The prospect of a sudden return had shattered Polak. West asked him: 'Do you want to go?'

Polak said: 'Once I decide to trust a person, I do not create a dilemma for myself by questioning any of his decisions.'

'Don't you like the life here?'

'That's what I have precisely written to Gandhibhai in my reply. I am very happy with life here. This is precisely the kind of life I want. I wanted Phoenix to grow systematically, but I am returning following your instructions. Possibly it is best for me to become a certified attorney.'

There was nothing more West could say. The night before Polak was to leave the two spent the whole night awake. They were both worried about Phoenix.

In the morning, all Phoenix residents collected to bid Polak farewell. The womenfolk applied *tika* to his forehead with red powder and rice and made presents of fruit and dry fruit. Everyone felt as if a member of the family was going away on business. Everyone accompanied him to the outskirts of the village. Mr. West and Maganlal accompanied him to the station.

He took their hands in his own and said: 'Phoenix is my dream too. Don't let it disintegrate. God willing, I'll be back soon.'

~

XX

Mohandas knew that Polak was in love with Millie. Millie lived in England. She was not keeping well and had become rather weak. Polak did want to get married but not immediately.

After his return to Johannesburg, Polak had been invited by Mohandas to stay with him. An already well-loved man, Polak was now everybody's darling. Kastur and the kids, who were often scared of Mohandas, never had any hesitation in speaking their minds to Polak. Everyone was aware that Polak's beloved lived in England and that she wasn't keeping well. Kastur, who had now started speaking some sort of English, would often speak to Polak: 'Polak, why don't you go and get Millie? I'll see to it that she is properly fed and with Gandhibhai's hot-and-cold baths she'll be fit as a fiddle in no time at all.'

Polak would laugh and say: 'Kasturbehn, you don't know Millie. She's a real devil. Once she is here, she'll take over and throw us both out of the house.'

Kastur misunderstood him and said: 'No, no, Gandhibhai may throw me out, but he won't throw her out. I'll make friends with her ...'

In the meantime, a letter from Millie arrived. She was reaching Johannesburg. Polak was upset. For one thing, she was unwell; for another, he was Gandhibhai's guest and wouldn't know where to accommodate her. In addition, he had no means of supporting himself; how was he going to support her?

Polak went up to Mohandas and said: 'Millie wants to come. I am in no position to support her. She is also not well. What am I supposed to do?'

Gandhibhai teased: 'Look, this is a matter of two hearts coming together. How can any third entity interfere, be it Gandhibhai or Moneybhai?'

'But ...'

'No ifs and buts about it. If poverty is holding you up, every poor person will have to depart this life without ever being able to fall in love or get married. You have read Ruskin. It's not money but self-reliance that makes for happiness. You are self-reliant and need no favours from anyone.'

Polak didn't know what to say. Mohandas continued: 'Look, you are living with me, so you are a member of this family of which I am the head. The duty to provide for the members of this family is mine, not yours. You don't have to worry about it at all. You just go and prepare yourself mentally for marriage.'

Polak was still undecided. Still, he said: 'Okay, let me write to Millie.'

'Also to your father. He should also know. If you like, you can also tell him that Gandhibhai also thinks likewise. Tell him that Gandhibhai is none other than your elder brother.'

Polak dashed off letters the same day to Millie and the Senior Polak. To the latter he wrote that he had decided to get married and was asking Millie to join him in Johannesburg.

~

Preparations for the marriage were afoot. It was not so much physical preparation as mental. All talk was mostly centred on the marriage. Dresses to be made had been ordered. Mohandas was very active. Whenever he had the time, he surrounded himself with kids and told them: 'Look, you will be pulling the carriage at the wedding, with the bride in white trousseau seated in it. Polak will be dressed in a black suit and a tie and sitting next to the bride. And a hat too. Sorry I forgot about the hat.'

'What about shoes?' a child asked.

'Are shoes necessary?' Gandhi asked Polak.

They all had a good laugh. Polak was however worried. It was the perennial question:

How would he support the family? How long could he remain dependent on Gandhibhai? But when he saw Gandhibhai bubbling over with joy, he could not bring himself to say anything.

One day, Mohandas received a letter. He turned it over. The writing was quite unfamiliar to him. The letter was from London. He opened the letter and found that it was from Polak's father. Thinking that it might have been wrongly addressed or delivered, he looked more closely and found it was actually addressed to him. He read it, folded it and quietly slipped it into his pocket. It said:

> *My son, Henry Polak, is articled to you and is pursuing the study of law under your guidance. He has written to me that he is writing to his girlfriend, Millie, to join him in Johannesburg for their wedding. Millie is physically rather weak and will not be able to stand the hard life of the colony. I wish to request you to persuade Henry to drop the idea of marriage for some time. He respects your judgment. He should wait till Millie is fully recovered .*

Mohandas read the letter three or four times with short intervals and thought carefully about it. Was it right of Henry's father to make a request of this kind? Are there no weak and sick people in the colonies? England is a fortunate place that it has a high level of public health. People in the rest of the world are not so fortunate. After a lot of thought, he wrote back to Senior Polak:

> *If Millie does not keep good health in London. I think what she needs is a change of climate. There is no point in continuing at a place which doesn't agree with you. South Africa may be a colony, but it has excellent climate. Living in a loving and caring environment and leading a simple life, she will soon regain strength and be her healthy self again.*

He also wrote a letter to Millie:

> *Welcome! No more doubting and thinking; just take the plunge. We are all waiting to receive you with open arms. We will all look after you as best as we can. What however tops everything else is that here Polak will be with you. Love*

takes care of half the sickness. I and my family are here to do whatever we can. Polak may have mentioned it, or, being too shy, may have not. He waits for you with bated breath. So start at once.

Mohandas waited for Senior Polak's reply for many days. He was particularly keen to hear from him, as he wanted to talk to Henry only after he had heard from him. But Millie's telegram arrived before Senior Polak's reply. The telegram was addressed to Gandhi. It said: 'Arriving December 30, 1905.'

Mohandas carried the telegram to Polak and asked: 'Guess what message I have for you.'

Polak tried. Mohandas looked very serious.

When Polak could not take a guess for a few seconds, Mohandas said: 'Come on, give up. It's beyond you.'

Polak laughed and said: 'What's the hurry. Give me some time.'

'I know it's beyond you.'

'And if I am able to tell?'

'Then I'll have to think again.'

'Think what?'

'How to behave with you. Should I give you the good news or should I just keep quiet?'

'Ah! That means Millie is coming.'

Gandhi was overjoyed like a little boy. 'So you got it! Okay, so tell us how we are going to welcome Millie.'

'Tell me first when she is coming. And how do you know about it?'

Mohandas handed him the telegram. 'Here, her telegram.'

'You are such a riddle, Gandhibhai! The games you play! Truly, it's all between you and God! You go to Durban and set up Phoenix. You come back here and you get Millie over!'

'For me, the two are not very different.'

'I don't understand.'

'What Phoenix is to me, Millie is to you.'

'Phoenix is no less to me.'

'But she is no Millie.'

They both laughed.

~

It was the hot month of December. Mohandas and Polak were pacing the platform at the Jepp station of Johannesburg. Though the train was on time, they felt as if infinity had passed waiting for it. Finally, the train came and Millie detrained. Polak stepped forward quickly, embraced Millie and kissed her. Mohandas was looking away. When Polak remembered him, he called out: 'Gandhibhai, look here. Here's Millie.'

Gandhibhai stepped up: 'Welcome, Millie! See how impatient he was to see you. I wasn't lying, was I?'

Millie extended her hand. Mohandas took it in both his hands and shook it endearingly. Millie was sizing Mohandas up: middling height, a lean frame, brownish colour, thickset lips, a light moustache … and eyes! She kept looking at the eyes: they had a strange gleam and a soft look, as if the whole world's compassion swirled in them. Though she didn't say anything she had a feeling that this man's entire personality actually unfolded in his eyes. To see him speak and laugh, Millie felt as if she was facing a child. She had never heard such a soft and musical voice before.

'How was the journey?' Mohandas asked.

'Very good. Thank you.'

'Maybe because you were going to be with Polak. You may have seen that when a river approaches the sea, its flow becomes faster and faster. But when finally it is close to the sea, its flow slackens till it becomes almost zero.'

'I don't understand.'

'You are now very close to the sea.'

'The sea? Here?'

'No, your own, personal sea.'

She laughed. Mohandas noticed that she was beautiful, but weak and rather tired.

It was a full house. Apart from Gandhibhai, there was Kastur, the three sons—Mani, Ramdas and Devdas—and an English young man, who worked in some telephone company. Polak was already there and Millie had now joined him too. Kastur had taken to Millie like a duck to water. The house was a double-storeyed one and both storeys were now full. Millie had little problem understanding Kastur but Kastur had to struggle to make out what Millie said.

Millie arrived on December 30. Next day, Mohandas, Polak and Millie went to the Marriage Registrar's office. There was hardly any official in Johannesburg, black or white, who did not know Mohandas. As soon as Mohandas entered his office, the Registrar of Marriages promptly got up from his seat and shook hands with him. Mohandas first introduced Polak: 'Henry Polak here works with me. He is like my younger brother.' Next he introduced Millie to her. Then, laughing, he said: 'This Cupid-struck couple is here for a permanent cure for their condition. And there is only one cure: seal their marriage.'

The Registrar was uncomfortable and cast sidelong glances. They couldn't fathom the cause of his discomfort. He got up and said: 'I'll be back in a minute,' and walked out with quick paces.

The threesome sat talking. Now and then some other visitors also dropped in and made inquiries about the Registrar. Some of them waited, others just left. The empty chair was making the three nervous. It was Saturday and Saturday was half-day at the office.

Polak laughed and said: 'I think he has gone home. He must think that it's better to go home and sleep than to get us married.'

'How can he go home?' Millie objected.

'Why not?'

'He said, didn't he, that he'd be back in a moment.'

It was quite unusual for the Registrar to leave them in the lurch in this fashion. In a short while, the office would close. Mohandas thought of the Chief Magistrate, whom he knew. The Registrar worked under him. So Mohandas got up and went to see the Chief Magistrate and told him:

'Milord, my friend and articled assistant, Mr. Henry Polak is with me. He is here with his bride-to-be, Millie, for betrothal. I asked the Registrar, but he left his seat, saying that he would be back in a moment. His disappearance like this is nothing short of a magical trick. Moreover, it's Saturday today.'

The Chief Magistrate laughed a big laugh: 'You are absolutely correct. This is nothing short of a magical episode. Do you know that you are the reason why these two could not be married? The Registrar thought that this friend of yours is a coloured too. You know that Transvaal law does not permit mixed marriages. Apart from the persons getting married, the person who gets them married also becomes liable to punishment. The Registrar couldn't refuse you, so he did the next best thing: he made good his escape. Actually, he is hiding in the adjoining room.'

Mohandas too laughed. 'It would have been better if he had refused. At least we could then disabuse his mind of the misconception.'

Mohandas continued: 'If you recall, some years ago there was a religious conference held at the Africa Church. You were there too. There was a gentleman from London, a very active participant. He was Henry's father. Do you remember if he was a black?'

The Chief Magistrate tried to recollect for a moment: 'Yes,' he said, 'I now remember. Mr. Polak, wasn't it? I'm sorry, Mr. Gandhi. Please take this note. I'll join you soon. I want to be present at the happy occasion.'

Gandhibhai and the Chief Magistrate both were present at the wedding. The first man to congratulate the newly-wed couple was the Chief Magistrate. On the way back, Mohandas said to Polak and Millie: 'We have a saying in our country: "*Tukhm taaseer sohbat kaa asar.*(A person is known by the lineage and company he keeps)." My company had almost made sure today that you would both remain unmarried.'

Mohandas explained the saying, which sent them rolling with laughter. Millie said: 'So the curse of colour-discrimination had almost found a victim in our marriage too? Thank you, Gandhibhai, you have saved us.'

Mohandas put a soft hand on Millie's shoulder. She felt a cool current pass through her body.

A week later, on next Saturday, a lunch was to be arranged in honour of Millie and Polak. The decision for the lunch had been taken jointly by Polak, Mrs. Polak, Gandhibhai and Kastur. Though Kastur was not able to participate in the discussions fully, she did get the drift. Sometimes, she also offered suggestions which Mohandas translated for the benefit of the other two. It was decided to invite only fifty guests, most of them Indians. Mohandas wanted them to be introduced to Millie. They already knew Polak quite well.

Millie had been entrusted with the responsibility of getting some decent furniture for the house. The lunch had been arranged in two rooms, where the furniture was also to be placed. The eatables had mostly been prepared at home. There was a Hindu male servant called Galal who was very active in the kitchen.

Galal was a simpleton. He had seen Polak dusting and painting his room. He wanted the dining room also to be cleaned and painted in the same style. He asked Mohandas if, with his permission, he could try his hand at this work. He had asked Mohandas in the presence of Millie, but since he spoke in Gujarati, Millie didn't get it.

Mohandas gave him the permission. Galal set about by stacking the items in the room together and scraping the walls. The room was covered full of dust. Then he washed the room. The walls were now full of spots, so he took a brush and started painting them. He had actually no experience of painting. The walls were now covered with brush marks. Galal was delighted at having made the room almost like new. Gandhibhai would be too, he thought happily. When Kastur saw the work, she hit the ceiling. Galal didn't mind the scolding he got from her because he thought Kastur to be less knowledgeable in such matters than Gandhibhai. Millie could hardly suppress her laughter. When Gandhibhai appeared on the scene, Galal boasted in the presence of Millie: 'Look, Gandhibhai, I have made the room so spick and span.'

Gandhibhai almost got a heart attack. His shoulders drooped. There was hardly any time left now. The lunch was the next day at noon time.

He sat silent for a while. Then he thought of his previous secretary Dick's husband, Mac. He worked in the construction and decoration industry. He sent word to him at once. Galal was shocked to see Gandhibhai upset so much. He couldn't make out what he had done to upset Gandhibhai. He had worked like a slave, yet not only did Gandhibhai not have a word of appreciation for him; he didn't even open his mouth. He wanted to say all this to Gandhibhai, but couldn't muster enough courage.

Millie told Gandhibhai: 'It's not his fault. Even the best amongst us find it hard to distinguish between enthusiasm and skill.'

Mohandas gave a wan smile.

Several men were deployed to restore the room. Time was running out fast. Mohandas kept returning every few minutes to check how much more time was required to complete the work. The guests would start arriving any minute. Mille was setting the table in the other room. Galal was a bit subdued as a result of the previous day's scolding but it had made no difference to his sincerity. Millie had to use sign language to communicate with him. Kasturbai was busy in the kitchen. The kids were also helping Millie in laying the table. Polak and Gandhibhai stood outside to welcome the guests. Gandhibhai made frequent trips inside to check on the preparations.

One of the guests landed before time. Seeing Polak alone, he inquired: 'How come you are alone? You should have been with Mrs. Polak. Looks like Gandhibhai has already cast his spell on you.'

Mohandas was unfazed. He replied: 'Mrs. Polak is getting the room in order. Have you heard of bats, Mr. Bat-guest? Come and be pleased to hang yourself upside down.' He continued: 'Our friend, Galal, in his enthusiasm to beautify the room made it worse. People are now at work to set it right. We are actually made of the same stuff—we and our Galal.' He laughed.

'You'll have to wait just a little longer, and you'll meet Mrs. Polak and also have food prepared by Mrs. Gandhi,' Mohandas continued.

'A good joke your Galal cracked, and at the most appropriate time! A good practical joke!' said the guest.

Mohandas laughed. The room was now ready. Kastur, Millie and the kids too were now ready and stood in a line to receive the guests.

~

The expenses at Phoenix were mounting day by day. A white daughter-in-law had been added to the household. Mohandas had started an economy drive. The drive for simple living started at Durban was now being intensified. Henry was anyway a man of frugal ways. Ruskin was always present with Mohandas and Henry. It was inconceivable that Ruskin should be absent when the two were together. They would make a thorough examination of his ideas.

Simple living in a barrister's home however had its limits. One couldn't do away with the furniture. Guests would not stop coming. Simple living was exerting its pressure more on the minds. Manual labour was being promoted. A flour mill had been purchased for seven pounds. It needed two persons to run it. It had a rather heavy steel grinding wheel. Mohandas had made it a part of his daily routine to turn the wheel. Sometimes, the kids also chipped in. Kastur's daily grind was already a well settled fact. Millie and Polak were now also beginning to do their share. Though there was no compulsion for them to contribute, they were beginning to enjoy it. Gradually, the wheel-turning routine of Gandhibhai became a part of every other male's schedule too. At six-thirty in the morning, everyone was at the wheel grinding wheat. The mill worked for half an hour. Fresh flour soon turned into fresh bread. What a treat it was!

Everyone worked with a smile on his face. The house was full of laughter and jokes. Sometimes Mohandas got hold of boys from the neighbourhood and told them: 'Whatever you grind is yours to take home!'

A few turns at the wheel, and the boys would run out of breath. Pleading fatigue, they would make good their escape. After that, they made it a point to hide in corners whenever Mohandas was passing by. The boys at home, however, enjoyed the mill. For them, it had turned into a plaything. The night soil was of course cleared by the sanitation worker, but everyone had to share the house-cleaning work. This made sure that the kids got rid of their reluctance to do their own work and everyone knew the work he had to do. Actually, now everyone, from the youngest to the oldest, did his own work happily.

The biggest problem that confronted Mohandas at Johannesburg, as at Durban, was his children's education. It was still a source of constant tension between Mohandas and Kastur. The problem was still the medium, which was English. Mohandas had also called his eldest son, Harilal, from India. But nothing had really changed from Durban. Mohandas was still unsure about teaching the kids himself and, of course, there was the problem of time. He could have somehow managed time; the real problem was his half-heartedness.

When Mohandas went out for a walk, he took his kids with him, covering sometimes five miles or more. He took them along to his office too. On the way, he taught then geography or history; got them to memorize English words; taught them grammar, or multiplication tables. The medium was always Gujarati. He then asked them to repeat. The problem however was continuity.

Kastur had almost stopped talking to Mohandas on this issue. Mohandas knew this. He himself sometimes said: 'If only I could give them an hour everyday, I could turn them into ideal students.'

Harilal, a little more outspoken than others, asked: 'Why don't you, then?'

Mohandas wriggled out of that one somehow, but the question kept torturing him and making him uncomfortable. Polak too was unhappy with his decision not to send the kids to school. When Mohandas left for office, he gave the kids homework to do. The kids would complete the homework fast and then wait for the whole day. On some days Mohandas came back early and took a look at the homework; on other days, it was the day off for the kids.

One day, Polak waylaid Mohandas after dinner.

'Why don't you send the kids to school?'

'I don't consider it right that my kids should study through the medium of English. All local schools here are English-medium.'

'Your country is under the British. This place, where you live, is also a British colony. So how can you escape English?'

'If there is fire everywhere, should one not try to escape it? Should one jump into it?'

'The analogy is wrong, Gandhibhai.' When it came to argument, Polak could be as aggressive as he was polite in normal discourse.

'I believe that parents who teach their kids to think and speak in English are enemies not only of their kids but also of the country.' Mohandas spoke in all seriousness.

'I am sorry, but this amounts to playing with the lives of the kids. If they do not study English, they will be left behind in the race of life. English is a universal language. Neglecting English is neglecting your own interests in life.'

Mohandas laughed: 'I don't agree with you on this point. Is there any society in the world which dreams of progress through the language of others while giving up its own language? If there is, it is a deluded society. They must first learn Gujarati.'

'Let me ask you this. Would you be where you are today had you relied only on your mother tongue?'

'That is precisely my complaint, Mr. Polak. I was born in a slave country and I am not able to get the languages of my country to stand up to English. English continues its march trampling them underfoot. Does that mean that I should give up my attempt even within the precincts of my house?'

Polak looked at him. The pain that was in his heart was beginning to peep through his eyes. Polak did not continue the argument.

~

Evening meals dragged on till late at night. There was a lot of conversation. Kastur could speak enough words to get by. Gandhibhai was as articulate as ever. Only Polak sat glum, paying no attention to Gandhibhai. Millie had been making a note of this for some time. That day, in their room after dinner, she pointedly asked Polak: 'Why are you so standoffish these days, Henry?'

Polak made no answer. Millie also did not pursue the subject. She was satisfied that she wasn't the cause. She noted everyday that though Polak and Gandhi sat next to each other they did not exchange a single word. This was beginning to have its effect on the articulateness of others too. Everyone had a quick meal and escaped to their rooms. The custom of table-talk was beginning to languish.

One day, when everyone got up to leave the table, Kastur stopped Millie and asked in her broken English: 'What matter, Millie, what for Polak cross?'

Millie took some time getting the sense. Kastur asked again: 'Polak is cross with Gandhi. What for he cross Gandhi? What he done?'

'He has done nothing. That is why Henry is cross with Gandhibhai,' said Millie. 'Some journalist has come out with a nasty piece on Indians in an English newspaper. People, who read it, especially in England, will get the wrong impression about Indians. Gandhibhai knows this, yet he is doing nothing about it.'

'I see,' said Kastur. From her face it did not look that she was unhappy because Polak was cross with Gandhibhai; rather, she seemed to be unhappy with Gandhibhai for being so inconsiderate towards someone who cared so much for him, while he was so sweet towards others.

'He care not who love him,' she said.

Kastur was looking not at Henry but at herself.

Everyone had finished. When they got up from the dinner table and started for their rooms, Mohandas called out to Polak: 'Could you stay back? I want to have a word with you.'

Others left.

Mohandas asked Henry: 'What's the matter with you? Why are you so cross with me?'

'You know why.'

'I do? Anyway, I want hear it from your lips. Why so cross?'

'You read that article in the newspaper?'

'Yes, I did.'

'You are letting him get away with it?'

'Why are you so upset?' Mohandas' tone was full of consideration.

'It's a bunch of lies and you know it.'

'I am letting him get away with it because it is a bunch of lies. A lie and a thief have no leg to stand on,' Mohandas said in a conciliatory tone.

'No leg? But it has a sharp mind behind it,' Polak's voice was shaking in anger. 'You can't evade your responsibility using that argument. As long as you do not show it up to be what it is—a bunch of lies—it will keep haunting us as the truth. How will anyone ever get to know that it's a lie? Writings like this will create problems for Indians. If you want to protect their interests you will have to bring the truth out into the open.'

'What do you want me to do?' Mohandas' voice was soft and composed.

'Issue a statement or write an article baring the truth. You write on every other topic, then why not on this? Who knows the truth better than you? This problem relates to you and your people.'

'What I know you know too.'

'All right. So I know it but everyone else can get to know it too. That is why it's all the more necessary that it should be brought out into the open.'

Mohandas said nothing. Silence stood uncertainly between them for a while. Then, all of a sudden, Mohandas' face lit up, as if he had found a way to appease Polak.

'Let's do it this way. Since you are feeling so upset about it, you write about it, okay?'

Polak looked at Mohandas and broke into a big grin. 'Okay! You could have said the same thing earlier.' Then he shook his head and said: 'You are a difficult man to understand.'

'All right. Stop abusing me further.'

'Up to your old tricks again!'

They both laughed.

~

One day, finding the front door open, a few whites entered the Gandhi home. Gandhi had seen them earlier but wasn't familiar with them. Kastur didn't know them at all. Mohandas welcomed them.

The moment they were seated, one of them said: 'Mr. Gandhi, you keep a clean house. Generally, your houses are very dirty.' Mohandas said: 'There are really no fixed measures of cleanliness. It's really a relative thing: one thing can be dirtier than another which can be dirtier than a third thing. Sometimes, poor people can be clean and rich dirty.'

'Isn't it a habit? I mean living in unclean surroundings?'

'A habit like any other: not having a regular bath, not washing clothes regularly, finding faults with others, and many others.'

'And because of this bad habit, they carry personal diseases with them, which they propagate here.'

Mohandas tried to laugh the whole issue off. 'Do any of you know of any case of an Indian importing a personal disease which you may have caught from him?'

They looked at one another. Then one of them thought of it and said: 'The plague, of course.'

'Plague is not a personal disease. It's an epidemic caused by rats. It also came to India travelling on ships. Your countries are not quite free from rats either.'

'How can you live so many in one small room?' They were now reduced to asking irrelevant questions.

'Have you ever seen my home? One European family also lives with me. But they never thought of such absurd questions, nor did they ever ask one.'

'We were talking about other Indians.'

'It would be better if you ask them, or maybe ask their masters why they allow them so little space. Why don't they allow each member of their family a separate room to live in so that they can live and eat decently?'

'That's not the responsibility of the master.'

'If you don't even know whose responsibility it is, why are you wasting your time asking such questions?'

They now started asking even more rude questions. 'Where is Mrs. Gandhi? Doesn't she like to meet male visitors?'

'She could be busy. Couldn't she?'

They all laughed. Mohandas went inside quietly and told Kastur that some whites wanted to see her.

Mrs. Gandhi didn't say anything. She had overheard the conversation and knew what was going on. From the tone of their questions, she had guessed the purpose of the visitors.

'I have no desire to meet them,' she said.

'It's part of our culture to greet our visitors.'

'Don't try to teach me my culture. I do not like street hooligans making fun of me and my home.'

'Still.'

Kastur did not come down. Mohandas came and told them: 'She doesn't wish to see you.'

They laughed again. Mohandas looked at them and led them out.

~

For some time now, Mohandas had been experiencing the feeling that Johannesburg was taking the place of his home. His goals were of course limited: to carry out his practice, to look after his home, and to take Phoenix and *Indian Opinion* forward. He also wanted to be able to teach his kids regularly. He was conscious that by sacrificing the interests of his kids for the sake of societal interests he was being unjust to them. On occasion this consciousness became rather painful.

Kastur always told him: 'Don't expect your kids to become saints like you …'

Kastur's sarcasm, on top of the questions that kept bothering him all the time, so irritated Mohandas that he could not keep his annoyance under control. 'I cannot possibly push my kids into the abyss while I am still in my senses. I cannot put them into the course of studies that you want for them.'

Kastur, never one to give up first, would go on: 'Where is the question of not pushing them into the abyss when you have already pushed them into it? You could have at least spared Hari, who was doing nicely in India. But, no, you had to call him here. Didn't you go through the same course of studies? Which abyss, which ditch do you find yourself in?'

'But …'

'But what? Do you think I don't know what you and that Sheikh Mehtab were up to?'

Mohandas was practising hard to contain his anger. He tried to choke the anger within him on such occasions, but he wasn't always successful.

One day, Harilal said to *Bapu*: 'I want to study in Boys' School. Please get me admitted there.'

Mohandas said nothing. So Hari went to Millie and told her: 'Please tell *Bapu* to get me admitted to Boys' School.'

Millie explained to him that *Bapu* was against his studying in an English-medium school.

'But he himself studied in one.'

Millie had no answer to that one. She got out of the situation by saying: 'I'll talk to Gandhibhai about it.'

Millie spoke to Mohandas: 'Gandhibhai, Harilal is growing up. It's not right that he should grow up with aversion towards his studies.'

Mohandas said: 'I understand. I'll try to spare more time for the children's studies.'

He announced a morning schedule for the children's studies. The children were always ready on time.

~

It was around this time that the Zulu rebellion broke out. Mohandas was perplexed. He couldn't understand why the rebellion happened. The Zulus were not so strong as to challenge the authority of the British. They were not even organized. Mohandas was also not quite ready to blame the British for the rebellion. He still thought that the British were a peace-loving people and wished everyone well. Why would they fight a weak people and why would anyone fight the British? There was another dilemma which was now troubling him and was prompting him to extend help to the British government. We are their subjects, he thought, and it is our duty to help them. But would this be fair to the innocent Zulu rebels? At the same time, won't it be wrong to support the Zulu rebels, thus turning traitors against our rulers? It is true that all that the poor and weak Zulus wanted was justice. The Zulu chief did nothing wrong by refusing to pay tax. He was right so long as he was defending his own rights. But why did they turn violent? Why did they kill the sergeant who had gone to collect the tax? Did they not thus challenge the authority of the British government? Murder is no ordinary crime. Murder, murder, murder—the word reverberated in Mohandas' mind. Murdering a human, even if an enemy was unforgivable. Putting up with murder is as bad as committing a murder oneself.

Mohandas wrote a letter to the Natal Governor:

> *The Indian Ambulance Corps is ready to extend its cooperation to the British government in its difficult hour in any non-violent manner required.*

Simultaneously, Mohandas got busy with putting the Corps together. He had of course doubts whether, as it had happened the last time, their proposal would be accepted by the government at all, or it may be accepted with a delay. If the proposal was accepted, he would have to leave this house. The family would have to be sent away some place else. A well-settled home would be disrupted again. A period of hectic activity and uncertainty would begin. And the first victim of all this would be children's coaching.

He told Kastur: 'The Zulu rebels have risen in Natal again. Some six or seven years ago, we had worked with the government transporting the wounded to hospitals. We have asked for permission to go to the field of action. If it is granted, we will have to give up this house. What do you think?'

Kastur, who had been listening quietly, said: 'Tell us what we will be required to do. You have already done the thinking part.'

'The only way is for Millie and Polak to move out to a smaller house, while you and the kids move to Phoenix. Magan, West and others are there, so there won't be any problems for you.'

'When did our problems bother you? What has to be done has to be done.' She let out a long sigh and continued: 'Sometime I wonder what destiny awaits these kids. No studies for them. Street bums—that's what they are going to be.' She had a lump in her throat.

'Let me come back this time. I'll dedicate myself to this work.'

'When did you ever come back? Your path only leads you forward. You have to go, so just go!'

The letter had been sent on April 24, 1906. On June 9, *Indian Opinion* carried the news item that the government had accepted the proposal of the Indians. A team of twenty volunteers would leave first. They would be paid an allowance at the rate of a pound and six shillings per day. If the system worked, the number of stretcher bearers could later be raised up to two hundred. The team of twenty was imparted training by Captain Dray in the large hall on Pine Street provided by Miyankhan. After a fifteen-day training, the team started for Stranger on twenty-second June. The team included four Gujaratis and one Pathan. The rest were all south Indians and were all lapsed *girmitiya*s. Most of the members had served in the Boer War.

There was a place called Lager in Stranger, where the rifle column of one Col. Arnaut was camping. The team reported to Colonel Arnaut. The team was equipped with medicines and bandages. The team had to tend a number of malaria victims and cases of light injury on the very first day. That night, they had to sleep in the open under a winter sky.

The team was constantly on the move, never spending more than a day or two at one place. From Stranger they went to Otimati and from Otimati to Mapumulo. They were walking twenty kilometres a day bearing the stretchers. They had already become experts in walking bearing the stretcher without causing the slightest inconvenience to the patient they were carrying.

At Mapumulo, they reported to Dr. Savage. He was the local District Surgeon. He welcomed Mohandas and his team with great enthusiasm. Mohandas had been conferred the title of a Sergeant Major. Three Sergeants and a Corporal accompanied him. Everyone wore the uniform and decorations appropriate to his rank. Often they got no more than an hour's rest during the whole night. On the fifth of July, when they reached Mapumulo, after a twenty-four kilometre march from Otimati, they were supposed to rest for a day, but the moment they reached there, they were asked to leave immediately for Thringpost. Some of them were so tired that they were in no position to take a single step. Their feet were already full of blisters.

Mohandas spoke to the Chief Medical Officer: 'If conveyance is not arranged, my team will not be able to move an inch.'

The matter reached Colonel Sparks. He said: 'Those who are suffering from blisters or injuries to their feet can hitch a ride on the wagon. An empty wagon is starting for Thringpost shortly.'

No sooner had they reached Thringpost, they were ordered to Tugela valley the very next day. They had to leave for Tugela at three the next morning. It took them nearly twenty or twenty-two hours to reach Tugela valley.

Mohandas was surprised to see a battlefield without any battle and a rebellion without any rebels. The whole affair was totally one-sided. An occasional shot was fired from the other side. Most of the enemy personnel were unarmed. Mohandas quite failed to understand why they were letting themselves be killed so indiscriminately. Why didn't they instead stand bare-chested before the army guns? How many unarmed people would the army kill anyway? Their spotty resistance and their guerilla-type tactics were actually giving the colour of a rebellion to their self-defence strategy. There was no comparison with the Boer War, where the opponents stood face to face and where ammunition was used freely. Nothing of the sort was happening here. A tax was not paid, and a Sergeant was killed—did that deserve such heavy punishment? How many murders could one murder beget?

Mohandas was unable to grasp why his team was being made to run from place to place. Why? The white soldiers were neither being injured nor killed. It was the Zulus who were being killed and injured.

Mohandas mentioned this to the Chief Medical Officer. He had no answer. He only said: 'The white staff is just not ready to treat the Zulu wounded. Their wounds are rotting and I don't know what to do.'

'So?'

'You are a godsend. Why don't you collect whatever medicines, bandages, etc. you need and save their lives?'

The truth now dawned on Mohandas: This was no war. This was harassment and torture in the name of war. They are killing them and also worry about them. They inflict the wounds and also provide the treatment. But he thought better of speaking his mind and kept his thoughts to himself. He also had the satisfaction that he and his friends escaped, by a hair's breadth, the horrific sin of letting the innocents die a terrible death.

The Zulu soldiers were in terrible pain. The smell of rotting wounds spread all around them. No white doctors or nurses were to be seen anywhere in the vicinity. The Medical Officer had pointed out the Zulus from a distance and disappeared. White soldiers peeped from barred windows and whistled. They signalled to the ambulance team to leave the spot or they would be shot.

Mohandas told his companions: 'These are fake threats. Just ignore them and do your duty. Do not even look in their direction.'

When Mohandas and his colleagues started bandaging and dressing the wounded Zulus, the white soldiers appeared to get excited. Mohandas now knew why the white doctors and nurses did not even come near these victims. The white soldiers were shouting abuse not only at the Zulu wounded, they were also throwing the choicest epithets at the Indians: dogs, bastards, and so on. Occasionally, some soldier would get excited and point his gun at them as if to shoot. But the ambulance men carried on their work unconcerned, paying no attention whatsoever to the bizarre behaviour of the white soldiers.

Any wound that they opened to dress set their hair on end. The bodies were lacerated with whiplashes. Flesh had come off and was beginning to rot. The wounds gave out a terrible smell.

Mohandas asked a Zulu soldier: 'How did you get these wounds?'

The soldier was groaning. His face however bore a maturity which made it impossible to gauge the pain he was suffering. It certainly must have been beyond the limits of tolerance, but he did not seem in despair. To see him, one would think he was a big rock slightly chipped by a heavy blow but nevertheless quite unscathed to the naked eye. He said: 'I was given a hundred lashes for refusing to raise arms against my fellow soldiers. There is the whip. When my wounds hurt, I look at the whip, the General's whip, and think how it must have suffered too, but it can't cry. We, on the other hand, cannot help crying.'

'It's lifeless …'

'For them, we are lifeless too.'

He asked another wounded man: 'Were you shot at?'

'Yes.'

'Were you trying to escape?'

'No, we were in the white army. We were shot at in friendly fire.'

'You were with them?'

'So what if we were with them? They can't make out between friend and foe. They go by the colour. We too will go by the colour now.' He smiled a painful smile.

Since Mohandas had experience as a pharmacist, he got busy with his mortar and pestle to get the medicine ready. Then he put the bandage on. He thought of Dr. Booth. He had trained with him for a year. Many whites also came to him for the dressing of wounds. The whites too had suffered a few injuries.

During this period, Mohandas had also struck up friendship with the white officers, especially Colonel Sparks and Colonel Willy. This was ironical since these two officers were the one to oppose Mohandas' proposal at the time of the Boer War. The two officers were however so impressed with him now that they never tired of thanking him profusely on every small occasion. They actually couldn't believe that someone whose proposal they had resisted so stoutly was so generous towards them. They introduced him even to General Mackenzie. The interesting fact about them was that none of them was a professional soldier. Sparks had a law practice in Durban. The other officer owned a butcher shop. General Mackenzie had a huge farm in which he carried out farming. All of them had undergone military training and were now bent on rooting out a toothless rebellion. That was what irked Mohandas most. His mind worked like a treadmill all the time, giving him no respite. The level of barbarism seen in the Zulu rebellion hadn't been seen even during the Boer War. This was no war; this was more like dumb animals being rounded up for the hunter's gun.

The soldiers often brought news that a particular settlement had been targetted and not a soul was allowed to escape.

Another one reported that to hear the shooting you felt as if firecrackers were being set off.

The third one laughed and said that shooting was no great fun unless there was return fire from the other side.

Mohandas listened to them but ordered his team to continue working and not to listen to them as it would only interfere with their work.

Mohandas however derived great satisfaction from the fact that the arrival of his team had brought some relief to the poor Zulus. They had at least been able to put in their best efforts trying to save those who would otherwise have surely died.

~

Mohandas' process of thinking seemed to be somewhat like the movement of an insect which pauses, doubles up and then spreads itself out before continuing on its path. Mohandas' thought too picked itself up, enlarged itself and kept moving. Was it possible for a man to coexist with his body and his soul at the same time? Wasn't a living soul a threat to the body? Weren't the pleasures of the body fatal to the life of the soul? Was it possible to combine duty with pleasure? Wasn't duty a pleasure? Pleasure in fact sometimes resulted from duty. Whenever Kastur was pregnant, Mohandas was made conscious of the fact that one could neither sleep nor be of any help at home without self-control. The only solution he could think of was *brahmacharya*, or continence!

Mohandas saw a wounded man. His body was covered with wounds and they had turned gangrenous. After a lot of difficulty, his wife had secured permission to see him and she was with him now. For the first time in many days, there was a smile playing on the man's face, although not unmixed with a shadow of pain. The wife had been coming for some time, but she could only see him from a distance and went back crying. But she sat next to him. The man was telling her something in his own language while pointing out Mohandas to her. She was looking towards him with eyes which expressed praise. A little while later she came and stood before Mohandas and said something in her language. Then she bowed her head and left. Mohandas tried to read what she had said in her eyes. A silent sentence in her eyes had jumped across and communicated itself to him but had flown away before he could catch it. An echo however had been left behind: 'Whoever you are, you are God's own messenger who saved the life of my husband.' Then suddenly it struck Mohandas that this might simply be his vanity. The lady might actually be asking him why he chose to be a flunkey of those heinous white murderers. But why should she think that? She would only be concerned only with her husband, wouldn't she? It was possible that she said something about her husband. A question had flashed in Mohandas' mind when he saw the woman: Where are your kids? Then he thought maybe her husband was a hero of his tribe who had taken a vow not to have kids. He laughed at the thought. Thoughts could also play rope tricks and start touching the sky before you knew what was what. Why should he take a vow like that? After all, that couple was still so young!

Mohandas was sometimes filled with wonder how far and away man's thinking could transport him and how his own hidden face could begin to peep from behind his thinking.

This so-called war had pushed Mohandas into a deep dilemma. Was man also one of those creatures who celebrated his victory only by killing others of his species? A mighty empire uses the slightest of excuses to declare Zulus, a race of people with hearts overflowing with love and friendliness, as its enemy. Mohandas had seen guns spewing fire; he had seen crowds of innocent people turning into mountains of dead bodies. Did the victor of such a war never confront the defeat within? He seemed to be the only one being tormented by this inner tussle, the only one trying to make it yield something positive. Like a diver, he made many dives into the deep but beyond a sheet of reddish water on the surface he could see nothing. The whirls and eddies would begin to close in upon him. The harder he flailed his limbs, the tighter was the hold of the eddies on him. The only thing becoming clearer to him was that this was all a result of the conspiracy the evil in man was hatching against man's existence. If this evil power of man went on raising its sphere of influence, the sphere of humanity would go on contracting. Fear of death would shackle the feet of humanity and it would be able to do nothing beyond groaning and grumbling. The strong and the powerful would of course ensure the safety of their own existence; the weak would gain nothing except death. He decided that he would not let this happen. He would put up a single-handed fight against this fear.

There was only one way out. Release! Release from what? Release from all those thoughts which criss-crossed the jungle of your mind like narrow tracks which led you nowhere. You went this way and you went that way, but where did you end up? Move away from the physical alternatives, he told himself. They were nothing but tinsel. They would lose their shine any moment. Such thoughts were like a tyrant's army: they made a slave of you and imbued your heart with a fear that never, never left you.

Sometimes, Mohandas felt as if a basketful of snakes was within him, with snakes of all varieties—small and big, black and yellow, red and green—periodically escaping, swaying in the air and slithering away in all directions. How difficult it was to keep them in check! You asked them to listen; they wouldn't listen. You asked them to wait; they wouldn't wait. A never-ending racket, like you heard in a battlefield, kept rising within him constantly. But he wasn't going to be moved.

~

The Indian ambulance contingent was called back on July 19. Mohandas was returning as a deeply troubled man. He was alone, all alone. He wanted to break free of his attachments in a single clean break. He was finding himself unable to forget the way innocent people had been butchered, pronouncing them guilty. He went straight to Johannesburg, though his family was at Durban. He wanted to be alone so that he could restore himself to wholeness again. He had been forced into loneliness by a welter of contradictory situations. He wanted release from fear; he wanted power which would never fail in its face-off with power. He wanted *brahmacharya*, where no one could share his essence. He wanted to give up his wife's bed to take a vow of service to humanity, which would turn his arduous path into a simple one. Desires tormented him: he could feel their forked tongues slithering over his body and his mind. Sometimes, his heart cried so hard, it made him almost lose his hold on life. On such occasions, he told himself: 'Do you remember the time when carnal desire had seized you so that you had left your father to the care of your uncle and plunged into sex with your wife? What was that urge? Was it desire? Was it sin? Don't you think you killed your father? At least caused him to die? You are Parikshit. Parikshit sheltered *kaliyug* in his crown; you sheltered carnality in your heart. It is still sitting there. And you find yourself helpless before it.'

Mohandas tried to be still, to compose himself. 'If you want to be saved,' he told himself, 'the only way was to take a vow that you would never be by yourself, that there would be no personal bed for you. Start a *yajna* (a sacrificial fire) against this dynasty of serpents, like Janmejaya, and surrender your inner fire to it.'

~

Mohandas picked up the phone. It was his family doctor speaking from Durban: 'Mrs Gandhi's condition is getting worse every day. She needs help even to sit up in bed. She must be given beef soup, or she may not survive.'

Mohandas replied: 'I am not in favour, but if Mrs. Gandhi is willing, I have no objection.'

'I am not for bringing the patient into it. The decision must be yours or minc.'

'You can take a no from me.'

'If you don't let me decide the diet according to the needs of the patient, I cannot take responsibility for her life.'

Mohandas put the phone down and took the next train to Durban. He went straight up to the doctor. Kastur was there too.

The doctor told him: 'I had to give her beef soup to save her life. I had no other option.'

'Doctor, this is unfair. You have betrayed the trust I and Kastur placed on you.' Mohandas' reaction was spontaneous and impulsive.

'This is not betrayal, Mr. Gandhi. You call it betrayal, but I call it the right and the duty of a doctor who is dedicated completely to the welfare of the patient. The first duty of a doctor is to save the patient's life whichever way he can.'

Apparently, Mohandas was undisturbed, but he could not accept the giving of beef soup to Kastur. It hurt him as if he had suffered an internal injury. But at the same time, he knew that the doctor was not an insincere person. He had acted in the best interests of the patient. Moreover, he had family relations with the doctor.

This incident had however put a question mark on his ethics.

He put it to the doctor: 'What's the line of treatment going to be now? I think it must be clear that I will not allow my wife to be given beef soup, even at the risk of her death, unless of course she is agreeable to it. I have explained this already to you.'

'So long as she is under my treatment, I am within my rights to do whatever I consider to be in her best interest. If you don't agree, you are welcome to take her away. I cannot see her dying under my roof.'

'In other words, you want me to take her away immediately?'

'I most certainly don't mean that. What I do mean is that you should stop interfering in my treatment. I and my wife will do the best we can for her. But in case you refuse to relent, I have no choice but to ask you to take her away.'

The second son of Mohandas, Mani, stood outside the room, listening. Now he entered the room.

Mohandas asked Mani: 'You must have heard us. I want your opinion. She is your mother. I am of the opinion that we should take her home.'

'No, *Bapu*, mother won't have beef.'

'Come, let's also check with your mother.'

'I know, mother will never agree.'

'Still, she must be asked.'

The two of them went to Kastur. Kastur had grown so weak that asking or telling her anything was nothing short of adding to her misery. Every single word she spoke entailed the labour of transporting a big stone up a hill.

Mohandas asked her. 'I know,' he said, 'speaking is a big strain on you. You can answer just by saying yes or no. The doctor thinks you cannot get well until you are given beef. If you are ready to take beef you can stay here; otherwise we must take you home.'

Suddenly, Kastur seemed to have acquired new strength. For someone for whom each new breath was like a new birth, this was nothing short of an outburst: 'Being born as a human is a boon; I cannot allow it to be wasted. I'd rather die in your arms than allow my body to be polluted.'

'I know that human life is a priceless treasure and we cannot allow it to go waste. But there are hundreds of Hindus who have no objection to taking alcohol and meat soup as medicine.'

'I can't believe that you are speaking like this,' Kastur told Mohandas, 'let us leave this place at once. I cannot stay here a moment longer.'

Mohandas went to the doctor and told him: 'I am taking my wife away. I am sorry that after we told her about beef, she is not prepared to stay here a moment longer.'

The doctor lost his cool. 'You are a tyrant, Gandhi. It was disgraceful to speak to the patient about these things in her present condition. Though she is your wife, at present she is in no condition to be moved. She cannot walk a step. Anything can happen to her on the way. But if you still insist on taking her away in her present condition, that is up to you. If you are not ready to let her have beef soup, I am not willing to keep her here a moment longer.'

It was drizzling outside and there was a chill in the air. The station was at some distance. The toughest part however would be going from Durban station to Phoenix and from Phoenix station to the Settlement. Mohandas was conscious of the serious risk he was taking, but there was no other way. Mr. West had been informed and asked to be at the station with some conveyance. He should also bring with him six men, a bottle of warm milk and a hot water bottle.

Mohandas hired a rickshaw and put Kastur on it with Mani by her side supporting her in a lying position. Mohandas walked by the side of the rickshaw holding it in case his help was required. He kept feeling Kastur's body and also asked her every now and again: 'How are you feeling? Let us just get to Phoenix and ...'

Kastur replied: 'Don't worry about me, I'll be fine.'

As the rickshaw moved, Mohandas worried that Kastur's bones might crack. The rickshaw-puller was a native but extremely careful. Kastur was well protected with warm covering. Fortunately the drizzling had stopped, though that had not made any difference to the chill. Mani was snuggling close to *Ba.* The rickshaw pulled up outside the station. The distance to the train had to be covered on foot. For Kastur, that was completely out of the question, as she couldn't even move. There was no chance that the rickshaw might go inside the station. So Mohandas picked up Kastur in his arms and started walking. The train was at the platform. He went and laid her down in a compartment.

Bringing Kastur over to Phoenix was the easy part, but the place had no doctor, nor any hospital. They would have to depend entirely on naturopathy. There were no signs that the bleeding was going to stop, and her weakness was increasing day by day. She of course looked more alert. Mohandas had no clue what his next step should be. He looked over his books and checked his notes. They were all related to naturopathy or vegetarianism. He couldn't find anything relevant. One of the books he found said that those observing *brahmacharya* should abstain from salt as far as possible. Mohandas laughed to himself. How many *brahmachari*s of today, he told himself, would be ready to eat saltless, tasteless food? Everyone looks for pleasures of the palate. Another thing the book said was the lentil *urad* is hard to digest for a weak person.

Mohandas told Kastur: 'Avoid salt in food. It will bring peace and purity to your mind.' He continued: 'I think the cause of your bleeding is lentils. Avoid both salt and lentils for a few days and let us see the results.'

Kastur got annoyed and said: 'First, there was the doctor who wanted me to eat beef. Now you want me to give up salt and lentils. If one has to do all this in order to survive, let me rather die.'

'I am not asking you to give them up forever. Once you are normal, you can resume.'

'If I give up salt and lentils, what remains there to eat?'

'Jain saints …'

'I am not a saint.'

'Just try and give them up for a few days.'

Kastur shot back: 'Can you do it?'

Mohandas cast a glance at Kastur. For a minute, he was taken aback and his eyebrows arched. The next moment, however, he relaxed and said in a controlled voice: 'Done! For one year, no salt and no lentils for me.'

Even in her debilitated state, Kastur shrieked: 'You are a tyrant! You do all this only to hurt me. You want to give up salt and lentils to see me die.'

'How does tyranny come into it? You can't give them up, so I do. It's possible that some merit of my good deed may find its way to you. Salt is bad for those who are sworn to *brahmacharya*, and we are both sworn to it. Lentils give strength to a weak person. But why do I need to be strong?'

Kastur was unable to hold herself. She was still muttering to herself: 'All this has only one purpose: hurting me. You won't even allow me a peaceful death. O Ram! What have I done to deserve this?'

Mohandas thought it best to leave the spot.

When he returned in the evening, Kastur called him. She took him by the hand and asked him to sit by her and said: 'Please forgive me. I am sorry I told you all those nasty things. For God's sake, don't give up salt and lentils. I promise you I won't touch either. Don't punish me so hard.'

Mohandas smiled as he looked at Kastur. Kastur thought he was laughing at her. 'You can laugh all you like at me,' she said, 'but don't punish me so.'

'Not at all. I am not laughing at you, but I am happy at your decision to give up salt and lentils. To expect a sacrifice from others without making one yourself—that has been today's lesson for me. You need not feel unhappy about what I have done. Both wheels of a bicycle must move for it to run. One jammed wheel means a jammed bicycle. No salt will certainly mean lower tension for you. This is a test of truth for me; for you, it's moral support.'

'I am yet to see a man more stubborn and stone-hearted than you. What you decide you must do! You have no respect for the feelings of others.'

Kastur's sobs continued for a long time. Mohandas was unmoved.

~

The government was mighty pleased at having put down the Zulu rebellion. Mohandas was wondering what caused the government to be pleased or displeased. Possibly, it was good at finding the causes it wanted in either case. There was hardly a rebellion in the first place, and if there was no rebellion what was suppressed? There was hardly any opposition worth the name. Moreover, it hadn't been suppressed; maybe it had been crippled. The government could not be so ignorant as to believe that a rebellion could ever be fully suppressed. No one had been able to achieve that feat yet.

When someone asked Mohandas about the Zulu rebellion, he asked him this question: 'Did you ever see the rebellion happening with your own eyes?'

'No.'

Mohandas would then say: 'I did. I saw that there was no opposition. I saw Zulus falling like fruit from a tree when you throw stones at it. The kraals were burning. There was no one to look after the wounded, all of them black natives. The whites hated the black blood they bled. Their language was unintelligible. Their eyes were so expressive but they were black and therefore not trustworthy for the whites. Their eyes spoke of the waves of pain that ran like snake poison through their bodies. Their wounds had turned gangrenous. If someone washed their wounds, applied medicines and bandaged them, whole sentences began to dance in their eyes and their language changed. This was a language that everyone could understand, everyone except those who did not want to understand. Eyes are so rich in languages.'

When Gandhi spoke in this vein people did not understand what he said, or at best understood it in bits and pieces.

Members of the stretcher-bearer contingent had been awarded medals for their services by the government. The members were overjoyed.

Mohandas too had been awarded a medal. He turned it over in his hands and examined it and wondered what the purpose of the government was in giving them these medals and what the recipients of the medals thought about it.

Mohandas told his companions: 'These medals, you know, have been awarded to us in recognition of the services rendered by us to the government. But you should not look upon the medals only in this spirit. We really didn't render much of a service to the government, for it didn't really need any. We worked for those helpless, defenceless, inarticulate and unarmed people on whose foreheads the government stamped death and who had been scorched senseless by their hatred. It is the service we rendered to them that makes these medals symbols of honour for us. The signs of love that we read in their eyes, the signs they used as a language for us, are even bigger medals they awarded us …'

These words of Gandhi had brought tears to the eyes of every one of them.

~

Telegrams and letters had started piling up on his table even before Gandhibhai reached Phoenix. The Transvaal government had issued an ordinance which posed a danger to the identity of Indians. Gandhibhai had to retrace his steps at once. On the way, all kinds of questions about the ordinance and its provisions which could endanger the identity of Indians kept disturbing him. Caught in a web of hatred and tyranny, Zulus there and Indians here were like flies beating their wings in vain.

The ordinance had been published in the official gazette of August 22, 1906. On his return, Gandhi went through it and tried to find out the reactions of people to it. But when the people reacted by asking *him* questions, he said: 'Let me first try to understand it in my language. I will therefore translate it into Gujarati. If you face a legal conundrum in a foreign language and are unable to grasp it fully, or cannot grasp it at all, the thing to do is to translate it in your own language, and it will open all its secrets to you. If you don't do so, you will turn into a slave of the foreign language and will understand only that which it says.

Mohandas had already left his 14, Albmerry Street house. His German friend, Kallenbach, had a house on a hill. Ever since he had given up his own house, he was living as a guest of Kallenbach. The Kallenbach house had all the comforts one could ask for. There was an army of servants and every one of them was eager to please Gandhibhai.

It was in this house that Mohandas translated the full ordinance into Gujarati. While translating, he occupied himself exclusively with the finer points of language. When he had finished translation, he started a clause-by-clause analysis of the ordinance. As its complexities began to reveal themselves to him one by one, a cry escaped his lips. Each one of the clauses was a black coat of paint on the faces of Indians. In Natal, they had used bullets to strike the Zulus down and had burned down their kraals. Here they were using a burnished legal sword to strike at the soul of Indians. Their self-respect was being trampled underfoot. Their identity was being erased. The ordinance was writing a new chapter in the history of hatred which aimed at making the displacement of Indians a permanent reality. If the ordinance ever came into effect, it would mean death for Indians. If it did not come into effect, there would still be life for them, but this possibility was so faint it could be extinguished any moment. Petition after petition was filed, prayers were addressed ... but the result was zero. Mohandas made a declaration: 'A dignified death is any day preferable to life under such a law. I admire the Zulus; they chose death. They were killed in the name of rebellion.'

He read out the Gujarati translation to himself: 'Every Indian—man, woman or a child above eight years of age—will be required to register himself or herself in the Asiatic Registrar's office, and to obtain a certificate, in case he/she wants to settle in Transvaal.' Even convicts who are on parole are not treated like this in England, added Mohandas.

'The old permits will no longer be valid and will have to be surrendered. The Registrar will make a record of the permanent identifying marks on their bodies and their finger and thumb prints will be noted. Any one who does not present himself by the stipulated date and extend his or her full cooperation in completing the process of identification will automatically lose his right to stay in Transvaal. Their continued stay in Transvaal beyond that date will be treated as a transgression of law and such persons could be sent to jail. They could be fined or deported. These provisions would also apply to children up to sixteen years of age.'

Mohandas stood up and started pacing the room. He was feeling choked. When he recovered, he read the next sentence: 'The police will be empowered to enter any household in order to check the certificates.'

'What are we going to do?' Mohandas was alone in the room and asking himself.

'Nothing will be achieved in haste or anger. Quiet consideration is what is called for. This is going to be a long haul. We will have to prepare ourselves for much adversity and oppression.' He told himself.

Fingerprinting was a novelty in South Africa. It had been introduced in India by the British government for some criminal tribes.

Mohandas went to Mr. Henry, a police officer. 'Mr. Henry,' he said, 'Do you have any literature on fingerprinting which will tell me when and how the government collects fingerprints, and from which people?'

'Do you require this information for some lawsuit? There is actually no such practice in this country, but, I understand, your country has it.'

'You are also going to get it soon.' Mohandas laughed.

'I don't understand.'

Mohandas said nothing. Henry started hunting for the literature. He handed over whatever he could find. Mohandas read it through, sitting right there, while also taking notes. As he read, he imagined all of them being made to stand in a line and being beaten up like convicts and slaves as if they were animals. They were all being pushed into a quicksand from where no retrieval was possible.

Mohandas stood up and thanked Mr. Henry. Shaking his hand, he said: 'You will shortly have to treat me like an accused.'

'What are you saying, Mr. Gandhi!'

'I am not saying this. It's the new law which the Transvaal government is going to bring against Indians that says this. We are soon going to be declared a criminal tribe by law.'

His lips were trembling. Coming out of the room, he took a minute trying to compose himself.

~

September 11. Days were beginning to get warm. A meeting had been called at the Empire theatre, also known as the Jew theatre. Indians from all over Transvaal were gathered there. The hall was overflowing with people. Every inch of space was taken. The President of the British Indian Association, Abdul Ghani, was in the Chair. He was one of the oldest citizens of Transvaal and was Manager of the Johannesburg branch of the Mohmmad Qasim Kamruddin firm.

The first to speak was Abdul Ghani. He extended a warm welcome to all the Indians present. Then he said: 'Without taking any more of your time, I'll now request my friend and benefactor, Mr. M.K.Gandhi, Bar-at-Law, to tell us something about this black law especially how it is going to affect our entire community adversely.'

Mohandas stood up to a deafening applause from the audience. He stood for some time waiting for the applause to die down. Eventually, the applause ebbed and only the sound of a single handclap remained. It looked as if all the other handclaps had merged into it one by one.

Mohandas started:

> *My fellow countrymen! I came to Natal on a one-year* girmit. *After spending only a few days in Natal, I came over to Transvaal. Transvaal taught me brotherhood; it taught me to sacrifice my personal interests for the sake of my brothers. Tyeb Sheth and Mr. Baker were my mentors in Pretoria. In his brief speech, Mr. Abdual Ghani called me his benefactor and thus shifted his entire responsibility to me. I am like*

one of you. I am looking for the path of freedom in the deep darkness that prevails here. The only difference probably is that the excruciating agony of slavery, whether it is in Transvaal, Natal or India, makes me totally restless, for slavery is slavery, wherever it may be. Most people tend to accept their conditions as they find them. They tend to get used to them. As their conditions get worse, their capacity to tolerate them also goes on increasing, because they never defy them. They begin to feel that like all other things which they have to put up with, slavery is also something they must put up with. A dog gets an injury on his head, and he goes around with its head bowed, tolerating the pain and eventually dies. The dog dies of his head injury; man dies of slavery. My own thinking on this matter is quite different. Those who cast others in chains of slavery do not applaud their powers of tolerance—never. Rather, their powers of tolerance become the ground for tightening the chains of slavery and making them heavier. That is what is happening to us.

At this sentence, there was another round of applause.

Mohandas continued:

We are passing through a crisis of our existence. It is no ordinary crisis; there is a move afoot to wipe out our culture and our very existence. In the shape of this law, the government of Transvaal is forging a new chain of slavery for us. The conditions in which we are surviving here are already worse than slavery. Once this law comes into force, our own hands won't belong to us, our houses will no longer be ours and we will have no identity. We will be like a shapeless stain which everyone will want to be removed. Actually, even a stain has a ground which it stains; we don't even have that. You know that the moment this law comes into force, every Indian will be a proclaimed member of a criminal gang. In Natal, our franchise was taken away from us; in this colony, even that would become unnecessary. When a dog has to be killed, it is not necessary to prove that it is rabid. Give it a bad name and hang it. When a community is declared criminal by law, it becomes unnecessary to consult it before depriving it of political freedom or its civic rights. If this law is allowed to come nto force in Transvaal, it will become a precedent not only for the rest of South Africa, but also for all the other British colonies. Like the chemical that is poured into the roots of trees when they are to be destroyed, this law is also a powerful chemical the purpose of which is to finish the race of Indians. We'll be finished. There will be no trace of us left.

'We'll not allow it,' screamed the agitated audience.

Abdul Ghani got up and asked the audience to listen to Gandhi in peace: 'Please listen to Gandhibhai and give very careful consideration to what he is saying. If you don't hear him out fully, how will you give it the consideration it deserves?'

The audience settled down and Mohandas continued his speech.

It'll not do to get angry and become careless. On our shoulders lies the responsibility not only of the ten or fifteen thousand Indians living in Transvaal, but also of all the Indians spread over the whole of South Africa. This is the beginning of our exile from this land. If we give them our finger and thumb prints, we will be putting at stake our honour and the honour of our country. Any two penny-half-penny soldier will walk into our house and demand our registration certificate and dishonour our womenfolk and our kids. An enslaved person or race is as helpless and vulnerable as a lion in chains.

Someone in the audience screamed out loud: 'If anyone so much as dares to speak a word to my wife, forget about demanding the registration certificate, I'll kill him on the spot. If I am hanged for this, that's fine with me.'

One who is tied, picked up Mohandas slowly, *cannot die, nor can he kill. Have you ever thought of those hapless people who have nothing to eat, nothing to wear and nothing to lean on to save themselves from falling? Why is this black law being forced on us? What is the crime we have committed? No one has an answer to this question. Do you know what it means to humiliate innocent people like this? It means humiliating the entire community and the nation. But, despite this, we must not lose patience, we must not allow ourselves to be provoked, we must not fall victims to any accident in our haste, for if we do, it will be difficult for us to escape the attack that has been launched on us under the cover of law. We must collectively oppose this law tooth and nail. We must prepare ourselves for a prolonged battle. God also will come to our help only if we do.*

Mohandas returned to his seat. A transparent, icy silence had gripped the hall. After a while, a single handclap was heard. When Mohandas had risen to speak, he had been greeted by an avalanche of applause, which had finally been reduced to a single handclap. Exactly the reverse was now happening. Soon the entire Empire theatre was swept away by another avalanche, an overpowering chorus of solidarity.

The proceedings of the meeting had been conducted in Hindi and Gujarati. Tamil and Telugu speakers had been briefed about the proceedings in their own languages. Except some white policemen and a police sergeant, who had made themselves comfortable in the front seats right at the start of the meeting, there was no one who was now unfamiliar with the proceedings. Next, it was Haji Habib, who stood up to speak. Like the Chairman, Abdul Ghani, he too was one of the oldest inhabitants of Johannesburg. An aged man, with white beard and a Turkish cap, which was sometimes replaced by a turban, he had, by the grace of God, a booming voice. He said:

Friends, we belong to a country which never played with the honour and freedom of another country and which never eyes the wealth of another country. Our country has been happy to be left alone. We have always been grateful to God for His grace. While we came and settled down in this country, we have always observed the customs and traditions of our country. We are still alive to those traditions. Whether rich or poor, we always lived a life of honesty. We turned this country green and prosperous, some through their labour, others through trade. This is indeed the story of every colony where we have gone for business or work. Is this law the black medal awarded for this honesty? Is this law the government's way of recognizing our honesty and helplessness? I make an appeal to all of you to forget your differences and stand like a rock before this law under the leadership of Gandhibhai. This is a question of the honour and identity of our country, whose blood runs in our veins. India exists only so long as Indians exist. I swear to Allah that, though heavens may fall, I will not surrender to this law. I appeal to you that you too today take this oath …

A frenzy seemed to sweep through the hall. Shouts and cries filled the theatre. Everyone was impatient to come to the stage and make his speech. Everyone wanted to take an oath like Haji Habib.

Mohandas picked up his ears hearing Haji Abdullah swearing by Allah. He didn't expect this. Why did Haji Abdullah have to bring Allah into it in a meeting of this nature? Resolutions had been moved and passed before, but such a thing had never happened. Passing a simple resolution and swearing by the name of God were two very different things. There was no disgrace in failing to honour a resolution even after it had been passed, but if you swore by God, you were duty-bound to honour your word. In case you failed, you became a proclaimed sinner. The legal system everywhere relied on this stipulation. Going back on your word after taking an oath made you liable to punishment. It was a different matter that introducing God in such affairs made for more unity and solidarity. Mohandas had a shrewd idea that this was perhaps the motivation.

Mohandas sought the Chairman's permission to speak.

With your permission, I want to clarify what Haji Sahib has said. There are a few things which do need clarification.

After he got the permission, Mohandas said:

The oath taken by Haji Sahib in the name of Allah has ramifications that go beyond the present case. There are other angles on this issue which need to be considered.

He looked around and then continued:

Before I came to this meeting, I had no idea that we will be up against a resolution which will turn into a test of our faith and integrity. It may actually put a question mark on our personal character. We are all believers in God, though we may call him by different names. Passing a resolution of this kind is quite easy, but living up to it may be difficult. And if we fail to honour it, we will be shown up as sinners in the eyes of the entire humanity. It will be like giving a silver coat to a copper coin: it not only turns the coin into a counterfeit one; it also turns the one who does it into a criminal in the eyes of law. Swearing in the name of God and then failing to honour the word is exactly like this. The people who are present here know what is what; they are no fools. Once you swear by God, it will be difficult for you to wriggle out of your commitment by pleading misunderstanding. In that situation, God Himself will be standing between you and your oath. This black law represents a new phase in the life of Indians settled here, in which we will be required to take new decisions everyday while pushing aside the old ones. We will be facing difficulties which we cannot even imagine today. And we will have to stand firm in the face of those difficulties, oath or no oath.

Mohandas paused and then continued:

While I caution you about the oath that Habib Sahib has taken, I also want to tell you that you will have to convince everyone about your sincerity to the cause without bringing God into it. I am saying this in full possession of my senses. It's possible that some of our friends may be carried away by the heat of the moment to take the oath, but when the moment of trial comes we may find only a handful of our friends in the field. When that moment comes, I'll be left with no choice except to lay down my life rather than bow before this law. At that moment, even if I am the only one in the field, I'll stick it out till the last drop of blood in my body.

There was another surge of applause, which subsided when Mohandas added:

If you are not sure that you will have the necessary grit to stick it out in the field, please do not take the risk of being labelled a sinner by swearing in the name of Allah or Ishwar.

With those words, Mohandas returned to his seat. From the expressions on the faces of the people, one could tell that Mohandas had made sense. The Chairman stood up next and said: 'From this moment, it will be hard not to put into effect what Gandhibhai has said and yet to stay alive. It will mean compromising with the honour of our wives and daughters. As Gandhibhai spoke, I could feel a light spreading within me. I could see clearly the conditions which we are facing and those which we will face in the future. When facing humiliations becomes part of your daily routine, a firm resolve is what you need to change it. Gandhibhai has presented in graphic detail the true picture of our weak spots and of the dangers that await us. But I swear in the name of Allah, the Holy one, that, though I am a man of peace, I will have no choice except to behead the man who demands a certificate from my wife. If I am unable to do it, I will lay down my own life. There is no point in a life without honour.'

The Chairman returned to his seat, his legs shaking with anger. With that, everyone took a vow that they would rather die than surrender to the black law.

On the third day after the meeting, the Empire theatre caught fire and everything was reduced to ashes, creating a controversy of its own. The curse of the innocents and the flames it gave rise to have caused the theatre to burn down, said some. The day was not far off, said others, when this government would burn down too.

When the news reached Gandhi, he said: 'I am not interested in burning anything; nor am I interested in the gossip of these men. I am only interested in restoring the honour of my country and my countrymen. Please lend me your support.'

They all remained silent thereafter.

Meetings were being organized everywhere. More and more people were getting involved. The fear that you were in another country with another government with another set of laws had disappeared from their minds. *Indian Opinion* had single-handedly declared war on the black law. Every one, black or white, read the pages of *Indian Opinion* to find out what Gandhi's next move was going to be.

Mr. Duncan was the Colonial Secretary. An Indian delegation approached Duncan, who had already received reports on the Empire theatre meeting and the oaths that had been sworn there. Details of Mohandas' speech were also known to him.

Duncan addressed himself to Gandhi first: 'What is it you want, Mr. Gandhi?'

'Withdraw the bill,' said Mohandas without mincing words.

'The government is not prepared to do that. It wants the bill made into law.'

'But why?' asked Abdul Ghani.

'The government had a definite purpose in allowing Indians into this country. It is not ready to go back on that purpose, nor does it want to go beyond it.'

Another member of the delegation spoke up: 'You mean you are free to enter our houses and violate the privacy of our women and children, and that there are no limits that you can't cross? On the other hand, if we try to protect our interests while staying within our limits, we are accused of crossing our limits. What kind of justice is this, sir?'

Haji Habib, who had been sitting silently this far, now got up and said: 'You rule over half the world, but I want to make it clear to you that if any official of this government enters my household and demands the fingerprints of my wife or children, I'll kill the man and then kill myself.'

'What Habib Sahib has said is what every Indian will do.' Abdul Ghani lent support to Habib's point.

Mr. Duncan was amazed to hear them speak like this. He was looking at Habib's face closely to find out if these were the same Indians who till the other day dared not open their mouths before the whites. He surveyed the lot and said: 'The government is reconsidering the issue. It is possible that the clause regarding women and children may be dropped. No official will enter your houses.'

People present there were not convinced by Duncan's statement.

'What about the rest of the bill?' someone asked.

'I've told you that the government has decided to convert this bill into law.'

'May I ask what crime the Indians have committed that they are being prepared for the garbage heap? They are all peace-loving people, ready to do whatever they can for the prosperity of Transvaal. They are also subjects of the same British crown that rules over this colony.'

'I'll advise you, Mr. Gandhi, to prove your goodwill by obeying this law. I notice that more recently the tongues and the brains of people around here have acquired rather sharp edges.' He said, casting a sideways look at Mohandas, and continued: 'This will be in your best interests. Of course, if you want some minor modifications to the bill, we are ready to consider them.'

'Mr. Duncan, when the matter started, the government had refused even to entertain any discussion on it. It is some consolation that at least in the matter of women and children you are now willing to reconsider your views. But it is not enough. Our demand that the bill should be scrapped completely remains in place.'

Mohandas stood up. Duncan said: 'This is not in your best interests, Mr. Gandhi.'

Mohandas smiled and, raising a finger skyward, said: 'Let's leave it to Him, shall we?'

~

On his return from Phoenix, Mohandas had rented a small house. Unlike the earlier houses, this house was neither located in a European quarter, nor did it possess any qualities that might revolutionize the sensibility of an aesthete. When Millie returned from Phoenix, she too had to live in the same house. She found it very strange living in that house.

When Millie was in Phoenix, she lived in the same room with Kastur. Often they would keep awake the whole night and curse Mohandas: 'Couldn't he find a better place to dump us? Is this place fit for humans?' It gave them stiff muscles. That was the time when Debu, or Devdas, was still an infant. He had been crying all night. At four in the morning, Mohandas came downstairs and was pacing the space in front of their room. He overheard their conversation. He entered the room and asked: 'Do you need something?' He sounded worried.

Kastur found the opening she was looking for. She came quickly round to where he was and spoke in Gujarati: 'So you brought and dumped me here—that was fine, but tell me what has this poor, white woman done to deserve this fate? What are you punishing her for? I happen to be your wife: I'll live the way you want me to live; I'll do whatever you want me to do. Punish me anyway you like and I'll take it. Anyone who loves you, anyone who respects you, makes sure that her fate is sealed.'

Mohandas only said, in the most restrained of voices: 'Have patience. Everything will turn out fine. We have to make do and make things better with whatever is available here, but of course everything essential will be brought in. A life of service to humanity and *brahmacharya* is not a bed of roses.'

Kastur was completely unrestrained: 'Neither the kids, nor the other people living here have taken the vow of *brahmacharya*, so why are they suffering? As for "everything essential," essential would be what you would consider essential, wouldn't it? How would our needs ever turn into your needs?'

Mohandas made no reply. He continued on his round to see how the other inmates were doing.

The moment Millie had entered the house; she knew she would have to take charge. If Kastur could put up with those conditions, why couldn't she? Millie started effecting changes she thought best. She converted the kitchen into the dining room and moved the books to the front room. The latter meant more space in the living room. Of the remaining two rooms, one was allotted to Mohandas and the other one was Millie and Polak's bedroom. The rooms were so small that they barely accommodated two beds. There was a servant's quarter which Mohandas had given to an Indian young man. In Mohandas' household, of course, everyone was his or her own servant. And if someone was not used to doing his or her own work, there was always Gandhibhai to help out.

There was a verandah in the front which faced the Scottish settlement.

One day, Millie spoke to Gandhibhai: 'I want to get some curtains, carpets and a few paintings.'

'Why?'

'I wish this place to look like a home.'

'You mean it is not a home now?' Mohandas asked in a surprised tone.

'Possibly a home means different things to different people.'

'But why do you want to cover the windows with curtains? An open sky, sunrise and sunset, the clusters of houses spread all round, birds in the sky—they are before your eyes all the while. Where will you find a more natural, a more honest-to-goodness landscape?'

'Curtains of fine cotton will not make the landscape disappear. They will simply hang around the sides of doors and windows keeping out of sight this ugly and stained wood. When looking at the sky your eyes skid to this ugly specimen of wood, the sky vanishes and ugly spots cover its whole expanse. And, anyway, one cannot be looking out of the window all the time. Six o'clock and darkness descends and all that you can then see are the naked walls. The bare walls make me nervous. A couple of paintings and maybe the walls will torture me less.'

'The purpose of walls is limited, so don't allow yourself to be overwhelmed by them. Let them not come between you and nature. There is so much expanse and so much beauty in nature.'

As he spoke these words, Mohandas extended his arms towards the open window beyond which one could see the highlands. A long row of houses belonging to Scotsmen could be seen. Greenery ruled everywhere Mohandas said: 'Can we find a substitute for the beauty which God has arrayed all around us by hanging pictures on the walls of closed rooms? There is a lot of difference between the original thing and its half-baked copy, Millie.'

'I'm sorry, Gandhibhai, I cannot differentiate between God and man the way you do. If man creates a thing of beauty, I see God in it too.'

'If you believed in God, would you still make man your object of worship? Suppose God were to vanish leaving behind only man ...?' Mohandas wanted to add something but desisted and gave a smile instead.

'No, but I can experience His divine love, and feel His holy touch through man. He is present in all the beauty man creates. Actually, it is man who expounds God.'

'Doesn't that represent the limit of European thought? God explains himself in more ways than one, but the methods and the mediums he employs are different. When man runs into God, all that God does is to give a signal; that is all the explanation he provides. But be that as it may, let me not stand between you and your curtains and pictures. You can go and get them if you so wish.'

As Mohandas placed a hand on her shoulder, she felt a shiver run through her body. Mohandas stood facing the highlands, where a sea of greenery extended till the horizon.

~

XXI

The struggle was getting more intense day by day. It would be midnight by the time Mohandas returned home. To reach the modest shelter of his house, Mohandas had to walk four miles every day. Relief was however not assured even after he reached home. On many days, people would walk back four miles with him. Some continued their chatter even after they were home. The fear of possible dangers had paralysed their minds. When they got so tired that their lips could not form words, groundsheets and mattresses were unrolled on the floor and they were fast asleep the moment they stretched themselves out on them. Gandhibhai too retired to his room. Only a few hours of sleep and they would hit the road again.

A bus did go past their house, but it was for whites only. If Gandhi had asked for it, he could have got permission to travel by it, but he preferred to walk on his own two feet rather than ask for a favour. When he saw old and weak persons walking on the road, the white bus filled him with resentment.

That particular night Mohandas returned with several people in tow. It was one at night. Everyone was so tired that they could stay on their feet with difficulty. Groundsheets and mattresses were rolled out on the verandah outside and soon everyone was snoring away. When snoring stopped, it sounded like sleep stopped too, interfering with silence. Suddenly, a racket picked up outside. Sounds of pulling and pushing, shouting and groaning, etc. started streaming in. The sounds were all coming from just below Millie and Henry Polak's room. Both of them woke up and, opening the window, looked down, but they could see nothing. Just then, someone also opened the street side door below.

There were two men, who had come from a nearby village. They wanted to see Gandhibhai. 'Please call him at once,' they entreated.

Actually, what had happened was that they couldn't locate the door because of the dark. Someone was sleeping on the steps. One of the men stepped on him and he screamed. He thought they had been attacked.

Lights were put on and the people walked in. No one could sleep that night. The two men had lost their way and had been looking for Gandhi's house all night. Gandhi and his friends had assumed that they had gone back. Everyone had a good laugh, but suppose they had been real robbers?

'If you can laugh, you can win too,' said Mohandas. 'To be able to laugh before you take on the enemy means you have won half the battle.'

~

Millie was pregnant.

Whenever he had the time, Mohandas would go and sit by Millie's side and start questioning her.

'How do you feel?'

'Can you feel the baby inside you?'

'Do you think the baby can understand your feelings?'

Once he told her the story of Abhimanyu. 'We have an epic called the Mahabharata. One of the episodes in it deals with Arjuna, the mightiest hero of the epic, and his son, Abhimanyu. When Abhimanyu was still in his mother's womb, his father told her about a style of warfare called *Chakravyuha*, in which you seek to protect your object by throwing a complex circle of rings around it. Arjun explained how to gain entry into the *Chakravyuha*, but when he was explaining how to get out of it, Abhimannyu's mother dozed off. The baby could thus learn how to get into the *Chakra* but not how to leave it. The baby later went on to become a great warrior, but since he didn't know how to get out of the *Chakra*, he died at the hands of his own relatives.'

'Is it true that when the mother falls asleep, the baby also goes to sleep?'

It filled Millie with wonder to hear this kind of stuff. She would laugh and say: 'Gandhibhai, as a father of so many kids, you should know these things better than me. Why do you ask me? After all, for me this is just the first time.'

Mohandas would fall silent but would continue later: 'At the birth of my children, I was either always away from home or so busy that I had no time. When Hari was born, I was still under the shadow of the loss of my eldest. His death was a consequence of the sin that I and Kastur, more I than Kastur, had committed. My father was in death bed and I was enjoying myself in bed with my wife. This is something that I have never been able to forget. It came back to me with full force every time a child was born. At this point of my life, everything comes to a dead stop.'

Silence descended between the two. He continued after a pause: 'What can I do? When I talk about it to her, Kastur gets so annoyed.'

Millie was looking at the expression on his face …

~

It was the lull before the storm. Millie had given birth. Mohandas always found time for the child. He was so happy in its company that one would think he had found the greatest happiness of his life. To see the joy of Henry and Mohandas, one would believe a child was the central point of human love relationships.

A cry from the baby would send Mohandas scurrying to find out why it was crying. The question that bothered him was whether, considering that a baby was supposed to be above good and evil, love and hatred, etc., it suffered pain and enjoyed happiness? And if it did, how much? Maybe only as much as the body could take, for his soul was certainly pure and enlightened. Among his own sons, he had only seen Ramdas and Devdas at this young age, and only for very short times. A child was truly a storehouse of mysteries. How did a baby think? Why did it smile? How much could it understand of what it heard? What did it like or dislike? You could not understand a baby through your intellect: Could you tell when it would cry or laugh? When it would be hungry? Perhaps no one other than its mother can tell, for only she has that sensitive equipment.

Millie said: 'Gandhibhai, you know so much about the problems and mysteries of the world, but when it comes to babies you are a baby yourself.'

Sometimes he asked: 'When it suckles, how do you feel? How did it know how to suckle?'

Millie laughed and said: 'To know that, you would have to be a mother yourself. These things cannot be explained, nor easily understood, especially by men.'

When the baby began to show some signs of comprehension, started reacting to stimuli and producing a variety of sounds, Mohandas could feel that something new was taking birth within the baby, something which tugged at his innocence. Henry, on occasion, would turn a baby himself and would make Millie's life difficult by bothering her with all manner of questions. When she was by herself, Millie laughed immensely. Grown-up babies, that's what these two are, she would say.

Millie looked after the baby herself. The first nurse she hired was so inept that she left on the third day. The second nurse was so upset by the insistence of Gandhibhai and others that she should eat with the others at table that she left without even collecting her wages. So Millie could neither retain a nurse nor did she have the benefit of any experienced woman. In the matter of bringing up kids, she was of course a novice. So, all the three of them followed the kid around. Only Gandhi among them could be said to have some experience. Whenever there was a problem, he lectured Millie in a style which would give the impression that he might have brought up generations of kids. His refrain was: 'A mother should be guided by her inner voice. A mother's love is the beacon, the path and the goal, all rolled into one.' Millie laughed but kept her thoughts to herself.

The baby would not go to sleep till late at night. When Millie tried some force to make it go to sleep, Mohandas interfered: 'It doesn't want to sleep yet. Why are you trying to force it?'

Millie would get tired stroking the baby. It would close its eyes, but the moment the strokes stopped it would start looking around with its large eyes. Others enjoyed the baby's mischief, but Millie looked harassed. Her harassed looks greatly amused Mohandas and Henry. Mohandas would later explain to Millie: 'The baby is not going to adjust itself to the mum; it's the mum who will have to adjust herself to the baby. When the baby sleeps, you catch some sleep too. If you try to make it sleep forcibly according to your convenience, it will acquire such clever tricks.'

Millie did not enjoy these frequent admonitions of Mohandas, but said nothing. When she got annoyed, she just shut up. Most of the times, however, she just laughed it off.

~

Once, Mohandas had fallen seriously ill. This was around the time when he had been attacked. His white friends had then come to his help. Just after this experience, a new quality, if you like, or a transformation, if you would prefer to call it that, had changed Mohandas. He would fall into deep sleep whenever he wished, but woke up quickly and started work again.

Subsequent to the illness, Mohandas was staying with the Polaks, recuperating. The Polaks had given up the old house and had moved to a small house in the city. One day he was giving a dictation to his secretary. Millie was also sitting nearby doing some thing. Suddenly, the flow of sounds from Mohandas stopped. Startled, Millie looked up and saw that Gandhibhai had fallen into deep slumber. Millie and the secretary sat still, afraid that any movement might wake Gandhibhai up. He had just come out of his illness and was still quite weak. Suddenly, Mohandas opened his eyes and resumed the dictation precisely from the point where he had left off in the middle of a sentence. In such a situation, one normally asks for the context: 'Where was I? What was I saying?'

Mohandas caught on that the secretary was finding it difficult to pick up the clue, so he repeated the last sentence and made it easier for her. And the work continued.

During that illness, Gandhibhai had refused any medicines, which had got everyone very worried. Worried and anxious, some friends had gone to the extent of saying that Gandhibhai's stubbornness was actually responsible for his illness. Gandhibhai of course refused even to entertain the idea. He said: 'Nature strikes its own equilibrium in the body. When there is an imbalance of the elements, this is how it restores the balance. Let us keep our interference in nature's laws to the minimum.'

The whites could never make sense of Gandhi's theory.

~

Mohandas had given a lot of thought to the protest against the black law during his illness. Mr. Duncan having dismissed their petition summarily, the question now was how to fight the black law best. What should be the weapons of their war? If they adopted the weapons of their enemy, defeat was certain. He had seen during the Zulu war the consequences of adopting this strategy. If you chose the opponent's place, time and weapons to fight a war, the victory was also sure to go to the opponent. Mohandas wanted to use a new strategy. He knew that guns were not for the weak. They needed some more powerful weapons to fight their opponent. The answer that rang in his ears was: Truth! It was a strong weapon and also provided a strong foundation to your struggle. A struggle for the survival of the entire mankind rather than for one's own life! A strategy quite apart from all traditional strategies! Such a strategy could not be called war.

Mohandas published an advertisement in *Indian Opinion*. It asked the readers to suggest a name for a struggle in which there was no enmity, no malice, no bloodshed and no anger; which would use no sword and no cannon; which would be based on truth and sacrifice, and which would aim at truth and love. The winner would be given a prize. Mohandas did have a name in mind: 'passive resistance,' but it carried a British flavour. A few years ago when the British parliament had passed a statute of education, a struggle with this name had been led against it by Dr. Clifford. He wanted it to bear a name which would relate it to the soul of Indians.

There were a number of entries, but Mohandas didn't take a fancy to any one of them. Then his eyes fell on a name: '*Sadagrah*'. Mohandas jumped with joy. This was exactly what he was looking for. Look hard and you will find, they say. He had looked hard, within him and without, and found exactly what he wanted.

The entry was from Maganlal. 'This word epitomises what I've learnt from you,' his letter said. 'The prize is yours, Maganlal! But we must work on this name and polish it further. It reflects the soul of our struggle, but we have to polish it like glass so that every Indian can see his face in it.'

'*Bapu*! I got my prize when you saw in the name the image of your thought. You can polish it the way you like. This is an uncut diamond extracted from the mines of your thoughts.'

Mohandas said nothing. He seemed to have gone into deep meditation. He felt as if the word '*Sadagraha*' had been ringing in his ears from time immemorial, but Maganlal had heard it once and transcribed it on paper, something that he hadn't been able to do. Still, he was trying to catch the fleeting sounds within him. They kept eluding him. Eventually, they began to slow down. It was as if the bells were beginning to cease ringing and an incantatory chant was rising above their languishing sounds. Each letter of that word was giving the sounds a concrete shape. His eyes opened and he pronounced: '*Satyagraha*'. He repeated the word two or three times and then announced: 'The name of our struggle is s*atyagraha. Satyagraha* will guide us; *satyagraha* will take on this black law; whenever there is a crisis of thought and identity, *satyagraha* will be our weapon; *satyagraha* will be our purpose; *satyagraha* will be the magic mantra which will help us beat all ills.'

Satyagraha had no place for hatred; *satyagraha* used no physical force, *satyagraha* was the ultimate test of endurance.

~

The meeting with Mr. Duncan had yielded one positive result: the parliament had removed the provision for the fingerprinting of women before approving the bill. The rest of the bill became law. Indians were angry. Their feelings had been hurt and their hopes for the future had dimmed. But it also had a positive fallout: their spirits, instead of falling, had soared. Wherever Gandhibhai went, he had only one message to convey: 'Truth alone will win. If you lose heart, you will not only lose your victory, you will also stray from the path of truth. If you win, you get freedom. Freedom means a life of dignity and respect for all, a life with a clear identity for you.'

Mohandas was not a mesmerizing speaker, but he spoke with sincerity and a child-like innocence, which touched the hearts of the listeners. Even those who had lost all hope would feel rejuvenated at least once and would stand up with their heads held high.

At one of the meetings, Gandhi said: 'You have nothing to worry about even if this bill becomes law. Truth is on your side, and those who have truth on their side have nothing to worry about. Let them worry whose strength is not backed by truth. The strength within you and me is the strength of truth, and no one has the courage to fight it. We stand for the truth and the truth stands for us. Before we launch our struggle, we will have to exhaust all the legal options, since we do not wish to give anyone the opportunity to cast doubt on our good faith. Transvaal is still a colony of London. We still have faith in the government in London, though this faith is being tested once too often. If it becomes necessary, we will have to knock at the doors of London. This bill cannot become law without royal consent.

The people present at the meeting were in favour of sending a delegation to London. Mohandas put forward three proposals.

'Each one of us had taken an oath at the Empire theatre. We must renew that oath today and resolve that we will not allow ourselves to turn weak, nor allow any element of doubt to creep into our hearts. So long as s*atyagraha* is our weapon, we will oppose the bill no matter whether it is the Colonial Secretary or some other secretary we have to face.'

The second proposal was that if a delegation was to travel to London, the travel expenses of the delegation must be collected in advance.

The last proposal was that the number of people to be included in the delegation must be decided right away.

All the three of Mohandas' proposals were approved unanimously.

Mohandas was supposed to lead the mission ; the question was about the person who would go with him. A committee had been formed to identify the person. The committee was looking for a person who could speak and understand English but was finding it difficult to locate one. The members had spent nights discussing the issue. Though this involved no Hindu-Muslim angle, still one could not say that there was complete agreement between the communities on the issue. When the committee members could not agree on a name, they approached Mohandas and said: 'Gandhibhai, the best thing would be for you to go and hold discussions with the British government alone.'

'That's quite impossible,' retorted Mohandas. He paused for a while and said: 'I am of the view that there should be a Muslim member in the delegation. It is true that I am here to represent the interests of the entire Indian community, but a question could be raised tomorrow why interests of other groups were not taken into account when sending the delegation. That would be a matter of shame for me and for all of you too.'

After a lot of wrangling, the name of H.O. Ali was agreed upon. Ali's father was an Indian, mother a Malay. His mother tongue was Dutch, but he had mastery over both English and Dutch. He was a journalist too and had connections in the British Indian Association. Mohandas had a background in Natal Indian Congress. Ali was thus a suitable choice from every point of view.

Before the delegation left for London, a telegram was sent to the Colonial Secretary from the British Indian Association. It said: 'Indians here are filled with a deep sense of apprehension by the great urgency being displayed by the Transvaal government in getting the Asiatic Ordinance passed. If this ordinance becomes law, the status of Indians will not only become worse than what it was during the Dutch rule, it will become worse than that of the native population. The British Indian Association appeals to the British monarch not to grant approval to this ordinance. A delegation under the leadership of Mr. M.K.Gandhi is arriving in London soon to represent its case to the British government.'

On the way, Mohandas and Ali gave final shape to another petition to be presented to the British government. Lord Elgin was the Colonial Secretary. Lord Morley looked after the Indian affairs. After landing in London, the delegation first called on Dadabhai Naoroji and showed him the draft of the petition. He gave it a careful reading. As he read the draft, the golden frame of his glasses cast its shiny reflection in a geometrical shape. As long as he was reading it, their hearts were in a flutter with apprehension. After all, he was such an eminent legal luminary and might find the petition quite inadequate. That would mean a total waste of effort. Dadabhai kept nodding as he read the text, and sometime paused to reflect on what he had read. When he had finished, it was apparent that he was satisfied, though he said nothing. He handed the petition back to them, adding: 'I would recommend that before you submit this petition, you should approach a few members who are influential and independent thinkers. You should approach Lord Elgin in the company of those members.'

When they later met Sir Bhuncharji, he recommended the name of Lord Griffin for this purpose.

Griffin was unhappy with the movement which was afoot in India. He started his conversation with that topic, but when Mohandas and Ali gave him a complete picture of the situation in Transvaal, he changed his mind and said: 'I am ready to go with your delegation to see Lord Elgin. I wish you should get full justice.'

The delegation met Lord Elgin with Lord Griffin. Mohandas spoke in no uncertain terms: 'Transvaal is one of your colonies; so is India. We are all subjects of the British crown. The Asiatic Ordinance was proposed to humiliate us. If it is turned into a law, we will be bundled off into separate settlements, which will be like open jails for us. We will be forced to live the life of untouchables. We will be required to produce our fingerprints whenever asked like members of criminal tribes. We will be required to keep our registration certificates ready at all times and the police will be authorized to call for them whenever they deem it fit. Our lot will be worse than that of the natives. It was bad enough under Dutch rule; it will be worse now. It was all along being said that the British fought the Boer war for the dignity and honour of Indians. That dignity and honour lies in tatters today.'

Ali continued: 'This black law toys with our self-respect and dignity. We had been told that the government would give thought to our petition and we should wait for a reply. But far from giving us a reply, the bill was passed within two days. I am now an old man; I have eleven children, but if this law is brought into force, I'll oppose it with all the strength that I have. They may throw us all into prison, or kill us all.' Ali choked on his words.

Lord Elgin looked at Lord Griffin, who adopted a conciliatory attitude: 'I believe it is an unacceptable course of action. If the British government goes ahead and gives its approval to this illegitimate and contemptuous piece of action, it will have no face left to stand up to similar excesses by other nations. I am sure this bill will meet a forceful opposition in the House too.'

Lord Elgin was listening very carefully to their words. Finally, he spoke: 'My full sympathies are with you.'

Ali rejoined at once: 'We don't want sympathies; we want justice.'

'We have our compulsions too,' said Lord Elgin. 'We cannot exert undue pressure on the colonies beyond a certain point. Furthermore, the political situation in Transvaal is somewhat different from that of the other colonies in South Africa. Still, we'll see what can be done in the matter.'

Mohandas had realized that it would not do to meet only members of parliament and to explain their problem to them. It would be necessary to meet important people outside the parliament and to create a general atmosphere favourable to their cause. It wasn't going to be easy to prepare daily circulars on different aspects of the problem, to collect addresses of people to whom to send the circulars, and to dispatch the circulars, etc. He needed helping staff and of course money.

Mohandas was quite familiar with everything that such work entailed. He also knew that paid help was no match for volunteer help. A number of Indian students were in London at the time for higher studies, many of them quite enthusiastic about working for a cause. They had also become familiar with Mohandas and liked working with him. Mohandas often drew on their help, but of course most of the work had to be done by the two of them.

One day, an Englishman turned up to see him: 'I want to meet Mr. M.K.Gandhi,' he said.

Mohandas recognised him at once: 'Symonds! It's you! It's been ages!'

'I read in the papers that you are in London to prepare public opinion against the anti-Indian law being contemplated by the Government of Transvaal. I thought I should come and see you.'

'It is great to see you,' said Mohandas.

'I am at your service. I am ready to work even as an office attendant. You might however have heard of my extraordinary skills as a stenographer. There is absolutely no one who can compete with me.' He laughed.

'I know. I saw you working as secretary to George Farrar in South Africa. It is no joke working as a secretary to a multi-millionaire. Too much money turns a man into an eccentric. As a result, he cannot distinguish between essential and non-essential work.'

They laughed. Mohandas said: 'Once a few white men dropped in. They told me that that Indians carried plague. I told them that I had always thought it was mice that carried plague. I remembered then how you had helped the Indian victims in the plague of 1897. You were the only white person who had tended to patients irrespective of their colour and quite unafraid of the plague. I picked up this virtue from you. Today, when we are fighting another battle against colour discrimination, you appear again out of nowhere! I had no idea at all where you might be!'

Mohandas was so overpowered with emotion that he clasped Symonds in a tight embrace.

Symonds left home quite early and was at Mohandas' place before the two of them were quite ready. Typing, sticking stamps on the envelopes, posting them at the post office—he did everything by himself. Sometimes, it was quite late by the time he left, but he never showed the faintest trace of fatigue on his face. In fact, his face would be shining with happiness.

One day, while at work, Mohandas asked him: 'You haven't married yet, Symonds? What do you think about marriage?'

He laughed and said: 'Mr. Gandhi, you are more qualified to give advice on that issue. Personally I feel that marriage can prove to be a serious handicap to freedom and service. To keep all the three going would be as difficult as keeping the egos of three wives satisfied at the same time.'

Mohandas stared at him. His fingers were flying furiously on the keyboard.

~

They had been in London for a month and a half, but had received nothing but assurances. The money was almost finished. The two therefore decided to go back. The night before they were to leave Symonds worked till three in the morning, helping them to wind up. They had made so many contacts in a month and a half that tying up all the loose ends was not easy. Sorting out the papers, keeping the useful ones, destroying the others, preserving useful correspondence and taking it with them—all this constituted challenging work. Symonds of course knew everything and worked like a mechanical sorter. The amount of work he put in was simply unimaginable.

He went in the morning to bid them farewell at the ship. As the ship steamed out, he stared after it unblinking. When leaving, Mohandas had tried to give him some money. 'Look, Symonds,' he said, 'This can in no circumstances be a payment for the sacrifice and dedication that you have displayed in the struggle for justice, but it will make me very happy if you can accept the few pounds that I have as a gift from a friend. You gave up all your own work and worked for us day and night—this is something I will never forget.'

'No, Mr. Gandhi. If I accept this money from you, I shall never be able to forgive myself. I shall always be conscious that I did this service not for people who were victims of torture and injustice, not for the fulfilment of Gandhi's aims, but for money and wages. Have you ever accepted money in return for your service to mankind?'

Tears welled up in the eyes of Gandhi. His hand on Symonds's shoulder, he stood there silently for a while.

~

After a month and a half's hard labour, they were relaxing even as they took stock of the situation. Ali was more anxious of the two. He said to Gandhi: 'Gandhibhai, if this ordinance turns into law, how will our women, purdah-bound as they are, ever go to the registration office to get themselves registered? What a humiliating experience it will be for them to violate the purdah to appear before the police again and again to show their certificates! We will also have to leave our present houses and go and live in those settlements which the government will set up for us. What sort of places will they be?'

Mohandas tried to console him: 'On December 3, the Under Secretary of the Colonial Department, Winston Churchill, said in the Lower House that His Majesty was not in favour of approving this ordinance into a law. We should therefore wait and watch.'

'But nothing has so far happened. The Englishman keeps all his options open. You never know which way he will finally turn.'

'I have heard that Churchill is a man with a strong presence. Moreover, he is a Tory. If he has said something, he can be expected to stand by it. But, even so, if the British government goes ahead with its approval, we will just have to continue our struggle, won't we?'

'But how long?'

'Look, our struggle does not depend on arms and ammunition. So it will not end when the ammunition is spent. Ours is a struggle based on moral force and truth. So long as the moral force survives, so does our struggle. It will end only when our slavery does.'

'Gandhibhai, your words truly give us courage. If you hadn't been around, we wouldn't know what was what, and we'd have been crushed underfoot.'

Mohandas laughed: 'No one can help others, or protect them, as much as their conditions do. It is the struggle which generates strength, and which, in the end, becomes your armour.'

'Armour?'

'Yes, armour. You know, your shield, protection.'

They both laughed despite the fact that the ship was lurching rather violently then.

~

Like Polak, Mohandas had another articled clerk with him: Ritch. He was also in London at the time, studying law. He belonged to South Africa and it was in fact Mohandas who had sent him to London to study law. Ritch too had been running around with Mohandas and Ali. Mohandas had founded a South African British Indian Committee in London, with Ritch as its secretary. When their ship reached Madeira, they received a telegram from Ritch. Finding a telegram in the middle of an ocean is somewhat like finding a floating whale when you are swimming. Mohandas opened the envelope. The telegram said: 'February 18 STOP Lord Elgin announces in Lower House STOP Government withholds consent to South African Asiatic Ordinance.'

Mohandas sat for a while with the telegram in his hand and his eyes closed till Ali had to ask: 'Is everything fine, Gandhibhai? Is there a problem?'

Gandhibhai held out the telegram to him and said: 'Here is the good news you had been waiting for.'

Haji Ojer Ali read it and started dancing with joy. He took both Gandhi's hands in his own and kissed them: 'Gandhi, you are great! You are an angel! This news has given us Indians a new lease of life.'

Ojer Ali wasn't tired of singing praises of the British Empire: 'So great! So fair-minded! It looks after the ant as much as it looks after the lion!'

It had taken full fifteen days for the ship to reach Cape Town from Madeira.

Transvaal was categorized as a Crown Colony. A Crown Colony was a colony that maintained a representative as an ambassador in London, whose job was to advise the Colonial Secretary from time to time on affairs relating to the colony. The current Transvaal representative in London was Sir Richard Soloman, a distinguished South African lawyer. It was only after consultation with him that Lord Elgin had announced the withholding of consent to the Asiatic Ordinance.

At first, Soloman came out strongly against the proposal: 'If the British government prevents this ordinance from becoming law, the white community of South Africa will be very disappointed. The coolies have become rebellious and militant ever since Mr. Gandhi has stepped in Transvaal. The Transvaal government will find it difficult to keep them under control unless this law is brought into force. Once this law is enforced, the coolies will either leave the colony or will obey the law and desist from their rebellious activities. The government cannot allow them to be let loose like bloodthirsty, wild animals.

Lord Elgin listened to him attentively and then said: 'We are proposing autonomy for Transvaal. If the autonomous Transvaal government comes out with a law, it should have no problem in securing the royal consent. But if the British government grants consent to this ordinance, it will bring a bad name to the government. India, you know, is the most precious jewel in the British Crown.'

'But …'

'You have seen that they have the support of members of parliament like Lord Griffin. Mr. Gandhi is a great operator. I know how he is respected in India. He has converted the whole of London by the force of his logic. The British government cannot go against public opinion, because it stands or falls on public opinion. It is quite impossible for me to advise His Majesty to grant approval to this ordinance.'

Sir Richard Soloman knew when it was wise to beat a retreat. He withdrew quietly.

Mohandas wrote in *Indian Opinion*: 'We succeeded beyond all expectations. The ways of God are mysterious, but efforts made in the right direction always bear fruit. The Indians' demands were justified and conditions played themselves out accordingly. Although the results are beyond our expectations, we should not allow ourselves to be carried away. The hour of adversity is not yet over. Actually, it is keeping a step ahead of us.'

People did not like the last sentence. How can both things be true? When they returned from London, they were given a hero's welcome. Hundred of people were at the port to receive them with garlands. No one could have imagined that an ordinance passed by Transvaal parliament would be turned down by the British government as a result of the efforts of Gandhibhai and Ali.

The whites had cancelled all celebrations. Offices had struck work.

~

They had been in Johannesburg barely for a week when the British government announced autonomy for Transvaal. All of Transvaal burst into celebrations. There were fireworks. Prisoners were granted amnesty. Indians also joined the celebrations but only as much as outsiders could be expected to join them. The new parliament opened in session amidst great pomp and show. The Governor's position was now elevated to the Governor General's. The parliament was now free to make its own laws, though His Majesty was still the sanctioning authority. That was however now a formality.

The opening session was inaugurated by the Governor General. Members in resplendent dresses attended the session.

Indians had been sidelined. Leaders of the community were not invited even on formal occasions, whereas tribal chiefs were there. Indians were feeling isolated and nervous. There was no mention of Indians in any of the speeches made in the parliament.

The session started with the approval of the budget. It was followed by what Mohandas had described in his leading article of *Indian Opinion* on his return from London as adversity 'walking a step ahead of them'. British India Association was thinking along the same lines. The next item on the agenda of the house was the Asiatic Ordinance; only its title had been changed. It was now called: Asiatic Immigration Registration

Bill. One more bill was moved along side this one which was called Immigration Restriction Bill. Both bills aimed at the oppression of Asiatics, which included the Chinese, the Malay but mostly Indians. When passed, the bills would be known as TARA (Transvaal Asiatic Registration Act) and TIRA (Transvaal Immigration Registration Act) respectively. Indians saw TARA and TIRA as swords hanging over their heads, sticking in their sides and jutting up from the ground below them.

A large public meeting was organized in the Gaiety theatre on March 11, 1907. The hall was again packed to capacity. Mohandas was in his busy self again, with no time to go to Phoenix and see the family.

People stood in a long queue outside the gate. Those at the tail of the queue started leaving, as they saw no chance of their ever getting a seat. The speeches could not be heard from outside the hall. This was the second large meeting after the one at the Empire theatre.

Abdul Ghani was in the Chair once again. Seats on the stage were occupied by delegates from cities plus a few eminent persons of the Indian community. Among the latter were Mohandas and Haji Ojer Ali.

Abdul Ghani delivered the welcome speech as the Chairman:

> *I have once again the responsibility of welcoming my Indian brethren to this meeting.*
>
> *You are aware that only a few days ago, Lord Elgin had refused to grant approval to the Asiatic Bill. But the newly autonomous Transvaal government has displayed such haste in presenting the same bill under a new name that it reminds one of fortifications being built up against an imminent enemy attack. When we were welcoming our victorious delegates returning from London, we were under no illusion. We knew that the real battle was going to start now. What we didn't expect was for the government to set everything aside and give top priority to a proposal that had been rejected by the British government only a few days ago. It is now going to try to pass it into law in a space of twenty-four hours. Had it been a matter*

> *of a national calamity from which the nation had to be saved, one could understand the haste. That a wolf should be so scared of a lamb is past one's understanding. Such elaborate preparations for slaughtering a mere lamb! On one side are a quarter of a million whites, fully equipped with all possible rights, their numbers growing everyday, with no restrictions on their admission, or their trades. Yet they say that since our numbers are growing by a hundred a month, we present a serious threat to their existence! Who is a threat—the one who has power or the one who is without it? The truth is that they hate us; they hate us worse than the filthiest beast in this land.*

After touching on various aspects of the problem, Abdul Ghani finally made another point:

> *We remember that when President Kruger passed a law requiring the whites to carry passes, the whites had thrown a fit. Whites all over South Africa had risen in revolt against Kruger accusing him of trying to humiliate the entire white race. The humiliation that our race will have to undergo if this bill becomes law will be far, far more painful than the humiliation that the whites had felt when Kruger had promulgated that law.*

At the end of the meeting, a few proposals were put forward: The government to set a date on which permits would be checked in the whole of Transvaal; either permit or registration, not both; traders should get the trading licence on production of the permit. All together, seven such proposals were mooted. Each of them was separately moved and was passed by a show of hands.

People continued to let off steam for a long time. Even a worm turns, said one. This bill is like a snake bite, said another. We expect justice from King Edward. If even he fails us, there will be darkness everywhere. Whatever will happen to the sun which is said never to set in his empire, said still another.

A man, Gauri Shankar Vyas by name, said:

Whatever was said at the Empire theatre in September, burned the theatre to ashes, but the vows we had taken remained alive. If we are not ready to face jail in order to protect our honour and freedom, we should quit this country.

Khandubhai said:

You can take away all a man's possessions but you can't take away his heart and his mind. As long as our hearts and minds are free, slavery dare not come anywhere near us.

Mohandas stood up to speak at the end:

The government says that the present permit system is ineffective in preventing illegal entry of Indians. Thumb impressions are not clear; people sell their permit at one place, their certificate at another, and so on. The accusations are false. Still, if the government accepts our conditions for grant of permit, we are ready to accept their condition. The proposal to be moved here should be that we will accept permits voluntarily but not under legal coercion. The government should give up its insistence on bringing in a permit law and should instead trust us. For permits to work, both parties must be agreeable. If after this proposal is accepted we continue to court arrests and fill the jails, as Khandubhai has proposed, truth will be on our side. We will be able to tell them that we gave them no false promises and that it was they who were in the wrong and not us. I know that the final solution to this problem is courting arrests and filling up jails.

You will have to think of the jail as your home. For governments are not reasonable; they are stubborn.

Everyone stayed silent.

'If the black law is used to declare *satyagraha* illegal, what then?'

'What will happen to the non-*satyagrahi* members of organizations declared illegal? Why should they suffer?'

The third question that was raised was: 'Won't the money that was raised at the time when *satyagraha* had not even been thought of be considered unauthorized?'

The real issue of *satyagraha* tended to get lost in a maze of questions like these, though everyone was agreed that it was the only way out. Like a policeman at a crossing, the fear of annoying the government stood blocking the path of *satyagraha.*

Mohandas tried to explain the situation to them:

> *What the government wants to do is to put a dog-collar around our necks which can neither be taken off nor will allow us to rest in peace. If you find the dog-collar to be more safe and comfortable than the rigours of* satyagraha, *you should keep it on. There is no other way we can stop that collar from being tied round our necks. We have no guns or swords, and even if we did, would we be able to face a government which has the support of a power like the British Empire? We have only two choices: physical force, or violence, or developing the power of the soul, which means we go on putting up with their excesses but continue on the path to our goal. The world of violence is a strange one: you can use force and destroy the enemy, but what can you do with enmity? What can you do with hatred? Every drop of the enemy's blood will give birth to a new enemy and to hatred. Enemies will multiply all around you. Hatred will give rise to more love for hatred and violence is the greatest achievement of that hatred. You cannot measure your life goals by the number of people you have killed.*

Mohandas paused for while, trying to read the faces of the people present. Then he continued:

> *If your goal is your freedom, and the freedom of your people, can you say that making others your slaves is also part of that goal? If that is so, what is the sanctity of your goal? To kill others so that you can be free is barbarism. In earlier days, men behaved barbarically with other men, animals with other animals; now races and communities behave barbarically with other races and communities. Barbarism flourishes where power is blind and hearts have become inhuman. We must look within ourselves and see which of these we are nursing within us and which of these we want to nurse within us. We cannot adopt the path of violence even if they label us barbaric. Barbarism is not in our nature. History is a witness. At the same time, however, we cannot continue to bear the yoke of slavery. So, we are left only with one alternative:* satyagraha. Satyagraha *has the potential of helping us break out of the cage of fear. Our power is within us. Truth is what rids us of fear.*

Despite the long delivery, people held their peace. You could see from their faces that that light was beginning to dawn within them. A short period of silence later, one gentleman stood up and said: 'We are in Transvaal. The law of Transvaal is the law of our life. This law can close down our businesses. It can throw us into jails. Resorting to *satyagraha* will mean opening the doors to disaster and calamity. We will not join *satyagraha*, but we will oppose this black law with all our strength.'

Mohandas smiled and said: 'I am happy that at least on the issue of resisting this black law, we are all of one opinion. In fact, this itself should be sufficient to rid us of the fear of closed businesses and jails. For *satyagraha*, we will need to have a separate association—an organization for passive resistance. The whites will find this phrase easier to understand. I think this is the demand of the times. The most important prerequisites for *satyagraha* are mutual trust, self-discipline, harmony and unity. We must not lose our unity under any circumstances.'

As Mohandas finished what he had to say, he got up and started walking. A large number of people also got up and followed him.

The dedicated band of *satyagrahi*s was unhappy that, when the struggle entered the crucial phase, the people got divided. Mohandas could sense their unhappiness. Whenever there was an occasion, the discussion centred on how a divided force would face the struggle. Wouldn't the others take advantage of the split?

Mohandas listened to them carefully and thought about what they said. In the end, he discussed it with the *satyagrahi*s: '*Satyagraha* means *satyagraha* (insistence on truth) and not *duragraha* (stubbornness). Our goal is freedom and our method is discipline. First, you decide what you want; next, you dedicate yourself to the goal. If you have any doubts, get them cleared. A person who rejects *satyagraha* is superior to one who participates in it with doubts in his mind. Bearing ill will towards a non-*satyagrahi* also turns *satyagraha* into *duragraha,* because it means you are trying to impose your ideas on others, or that you are feeling upset by their decision not to join *satyagraha.* The strength of a *satyagrahi* lies only in *satyagraha.* The self-confidence it gives him confers on him enough soul-force to transform others. Respect for a decision that goes against you is an essential pre-requisite for a *satyagrahi.* Respect for your opponent, despite your disagreement with him, is the mark of a *satyagrahi.* For him, everyone is a near and dear one. Love for our fellow beings is the backbone of our civilization. Let's not forsake that love lest we violate *satyagraha.*

~

July 31. A meeting of the *satyagrahi*s had been organized in the grounds of a mosque in Pretoria. The time for the implementation of the black law was approaching fast. The whole of the Indian community was watching with bated breath to see the outcome. General Botha and General Smuts were two of the top authorities of the country. Though they were Boers, their voices were decisive. They too were keen to know which way the Indian animal was going to turn.

Botha and Smuts had met a couple of days before the meeting at a garden party. Placing a hand on his shoulder, Botha took Smuts aside for some side talk. There was a sea of white ladies and gentlemen dotted with black bearers. A few Indians could also be seen like ugly black spots on white faces, although on the fair faces of the ladies black moles made the men go crazy over them and they were ready to lay down for their sake not just their share of wealth in this world but also their share of the paradise hereafter.

Botha asked: 'Do you know that Gandhi is organizing a "passive resistance" meeting?'

'Are they capable of anything beyond "passive resistance"'?

'But I thought the merchants had broken away from them.'

'That's right. They are arguing that once His Majesty's government has rejected the bill, the decisions taken at the Empire theatre meeting have no meaning.'

'I don't think Gandhi is going to be swayed by such arguments. A clever fox, that's what he is. He is collecting illiterates whose lives in India were worse than those of animals. Absolute ignoramuses! The fellow can breathe life in absolute clods, I tell you. He is teaching politics to utter fools who don't even know what life means.'

'That means they could be more dangerous.'

'He thinks they have nothing to lose. When this time round most of the traders kept themselves out of his movement, he knew he had to find some other way. So he is going to have an army of monkeys this time.' Botha laughed.

Mrs. Botha appeared and intervened in their talk: 'You are at a garden party, not at a political meeting! Are all these people who are waiting for you fools, do you think?'

'Please carry on! We'll join you in a minute!'

'What the heck do you mean?'

'An important matter to discuss.' She stamped out of their presence. A faint glow lighted the area. The flowers looked as if they were covered with a transparent sheet.

'What do you think?'

'These people consider William Hosken a friend of theirs. Why not send him to the meeting? He could go and tell them clearly what the government wants and how far it is prepared to go.'

'Are you sure it won't prove counterproductive?'

'So what if it does? We will have to deal with the fallout anyway. We cannot let things drift for too long.'

'It is important that a warning is issued to them now so that the blame is not laid at our door later. We don't want to use force to teach the entire community a lesson.'

The dancing had started. Botha and Smuts went and joined the dance, but they were wondering if they were the only ones dancing. What about the others?

~

The place was overflowing with a mass of people. Transvaal had an Indian population of thirteen thousand—ten thousand in Pretoria, the rest scattered all over Transvaal. Representatives from all the places were at the meeting. Had the meeting been organized in a hall, it would be difficult to accommodate all. It would have been worse than Empire theatre. There were about two thousand people, two thousand out of ten, one-fifth of the population. The presence of such large numbers at such a meeting meant something. It meant that here was a movement against the government which drew its strength from the soul and not from the stick, the bullet, or the gun. Holding the meeting in the open was also throwing a challenge to a power which was many times your own strength. It also meant more sense and less expense. You didn't need tables and chairs; everyone sat on the ground.

The Vice President of the British India Association, Yusuf Ismail Miyan, was chairing the meeting. As the meeting was about to start, Mr. Hosken landed on the scene. Although he had not been invited and no one expected him. Everyone was taken by surprise. Mohandas sat silently.

Mr. Hosken addressed himself to the Chair:

I want to present the government's viewpoint. It's possible that it will help you arrive at a decision.

Everyone waited with bated breath to see if Mr. Hosken would be permitted to speak. Ismail Miyan looked at Mohandas, who nodded his consent.

Ismail Miyan said: 'Mr. Hosken is one of our old sympathizers. The fact that he is here today at our meeting is a guarantee that there will be no excesses committed on us. He is here to speak to us. He wants to put the government's viewpoint before us; as such, we can consider him the government's representative, but we should look on him as our friend.'

There was a slight wave of unrest in the crowd: this is our meeting; these are our people, so what's he doing here?

Mohandas tried to assure them: 'This is a public meeting. We must allow everyone who wants to speak. There is no harm in letting him speak; it will only help us understand the government's position better. As Mr. Hosken said, it might actually help us arrive at a decision.'

Mr. Hosken started his speech. An eerie silence descended all round. Mr. Hosken himself felt as if he was making his way through a rock of silence. His voice was rather low and slow when he started, like a man who needs to put in some extra effort when he first applies force to lift something heavy.

You know that I am a friend. I am also closer to you in the way you feel and think. If it were in my power, I would force your opponents to concede all your demands.

A few in the audience smiled with their heads bowed. On the stage, one could hear some indistinct utterance 'Oh, indeed!'

Mr. Hosken was continuing:

However, you cannot be unaware that the Transvaal whites are set against you, in fact, to put it more bluntly, they do not like you. I have been sent here by General Botha. He respects you. He honours your sentiments, but he has his compulsions.

No one actually laughed, but a smile did escape some lips. Hosken was not looking at those who smiled, nor was he listening to those making whispered comments to themselves. He was speaking with total concentration.

In reality, each and every European of Transvaal desires that the new law should be brought into immediate force. What can poor Mr. Botha do single-handed, even though in the heart of his hearts he is with you?

Then, with a pause, he added, as if wanting to put special emphasis on it.

You are well aware of the power that the government of Transvaal can wield and do not need to be educated about it. The Indians made every possible effort to stop the bill from becoming law and they also succeeded to an extent. But, in the end, His Majesty's Government had to give its consent. As peace-loving citizens of this nation, it now behooves you that you bow to this law and give proof of your patriotism. If there are any minor modifications you want to make in this law, General Smuts will consider them with an open mind.

At this point, Hosken looked around and then made his final statement:

My personal advice to you is that you should respect this message from General Botha. I do not need to repeat that the Government of Transvaal is firm in its determination to enforce the law. I would not wish you to follow any misguided counsel and set yourselves on a course of opposition to the government inviting inevitable ruin.

Mohandas made a word-for-word translation of Hosken's speech and explained its import to the audience. There was applause. Mr. Hosken resumed his seat, pleased with his performance.

Ahmed Cachalia stood up to speak next. This was Cachalia's first opportunity to address a public meeting. He spoke English well enough to communicate his and his Indian friends' ideas to senior English lawyers without any difficulty. He was a well-respected figure in the Indian community. There were no legal conundrums that he couldn't crack in a jiffy. He wouldn't hesitate to take on the topmost lawyers in the profession. Although a devout Muslim, he made no distinction between a Hindu and a Muslim and would not brook any misdemeanour on anyone's part, telling it to his face as as it was. He knew no fear. His attitude was: What fear? Why fear?

Cachalia gave a short speech:

> *Every Transvaal Indian now knows how many daggers, how many vials of poison the government now carries concealed in this legal trap. I listened to Mr. Hosken very carefully and so I expect you did. We know only too well how powerful the Transvaal government is. What is the worst that a powerful government can do? It can make black laws to make the life of the poor and the helpless more miserable. If it decides to flaunt more power, it will clamp us into prisons, take away our houses and property and send us out of the country. If it is still not satisfied, it will hang us. We are ready for everything, but we will not bow before this black law.*

There was no trace of anger or excitement in Cachalia's talk. Each word was spoken in a measured tone. But there was a rush of blood on the shimmering white of his face, glowing like red-hot iron. The veins of his neck and forehead bulged as he spoke. A nerve in the temple twitched incessantly. The fingers of his right hand ran across his throat muscles.

After having said this much in measured tones, his voice suddenly changed into the growl of a lion:

> *I swear by Allah that I may hang on the gallows but I will not bow to Botha's law. I also expect from everyone present here that they will not retrace their steps. Amen!*

Everyone seemed to be delighted. Mohandas sat with his eyes closed but the grin on his face looked a bit wider.

~

Kallenbach's home was situated on a small hillock. One day, Kallenbach came to Mohandas and said: 'Come, you have to go with me. You will now stay with me.'

Mohandas thought for a minute and the next minute spoke up like a child: 'Good! Let's go!'

The whole thing happened so fast that Kallenbach didn't quite grasp how Gandhi could agree with such alacrity, nor did Gandhi quite grasp how he consented so quickly to Kallenbach's request.

The house was open all sides. You had a feeling as if the sky had come down to the earth. Kallenbach found a similarity between his nature and the open surroundings of his house. Mohandas too felt delighted, although Kallenbach's fabulous lifestyle left him awestruck. There was an army of servants. While one helped him put his shoes on, another helped with the jacket. The style in which he was shaved while still lying in bed was a topic of animated talk among his friends.

One day, Mohandas asked him: 'How much do you spend on running this place?'

Kallenbach found the question unusual, but he laughed and answered: 'Oh, about a hundred pounds.'

'Do you own this place?'

'No, the rent is extra.'

Mohandas touched his body and said: 'You must make some use of this great body, or it will remain an art object; after a while not even that.'

'Suggest something, Gandhibhai.'

Kallenbach had his lunch at a European restaurant, though he had a personal cook at home. The cook's services were made use of only when the boss didn't feel like going out. Otherwise, it was always the restaurant, except of course for breakfast. The services of the cooks were mostly used when a party or a dinner was to be hosted; the rest of the time, like their boss, they too had a great time.

Kallenbach often took Mohandas with him for lunch. The restaurant was for whites only and blacks were not permitted. Other Indians often wondered how Gandhi managed to gain entry to the place. All kinds of stories were in circulation. Some said it was because of Kallenbach. Others said it was Gandhi's own influence, which was not inconsiderable. He had political influence which made people think twice. What nonsense, said others. Fear from Gandhi? A mere mosquito! Did you see that cartoon called 'Gandhi, the Martyr'? It shows Gandhi with the drum of Asiatic Ordinance slung round his neck. Piles of dry straw are stacked around him to burn him, while a white man stands nearby with a burning torch in his hand. Below it says: 'Gandhi, the Martyr! A serious menace! Must do something about him and quick!'

There were others who said: 'He is a barrister, no less! Lives like a European! Who has the courage to stop him?'

'Barristers are a dime a dozen! But a black is a black first and a white a white first!'

Kallenbach's office was located in a building called *Sacci's*. Kallenbach usually came downstairs personally to escort Mohandas, but that day Mohandas made his way to the office unexpectedly and walked to the lift. When the liftman saw him, he closed the doors of the lift and took the lift to the second floor and stayed put.

Mohandas said nothing and went back.

Kallenbach waited for some time but when Mohandas didn't turn up, he went downstairs and checked with the liftman. 'Was an Indian gentleman here in European dress?'

'Yes. A lean and thin man was trying to get into the lift. I took the lift up.'

Kallenbach wanted to give him a piece of his mind but could say nothing. Instead, he walked out quickly and proceeded to Mohandas' office. Mohandas walked fast and was in his office in a few long steps. Kallenbach knew that he would have gone to his office. When Kallenbach arrived, Mohandas was already absorbed in his work.

'I'm sorry, Gandhibhai,' said Kallenbach.

'What for?'

'The liftman stopped you from entering the lift.'

'This is a daily occurrence. He didn't actually say anything to me. He only drew my attention to the rules by taking the lift to the second floor and leaving it there. He didn't make the rules; he only carries them out.'

'Come, let's go and eat. Lunch is waiting for you.' He tried to change the topic.

'That was the last time I went there. I won't go there any more. Going there means breaking their rules and getting humiliated. Now on, you will be my guest. There are no rules here which humiliate people.' He laughed and said: 'It's possible that if we were in your position, we would also behave the same way. God has been very kind to us that it has spared us the kind of situation where we might have had to humiliate others. Though, I must say, we have not been spared quite completely. In our own country, we behave much worse than this with our own people. In fact, even in this country, we are not quite free of it.'

Kallenbach sat for a while with his eyes closed and then said: 'I'll be only too happy to eat with you.' There was a mixture of love and atonement in his voice.

'With me, you will get only routine fare to eat,' said Gandhibhai, laughing.

'Routine and tasty!' Kallenbach laughed.

~

A slow transformation was taking place in Kallenbach. He seemed to be moved by a desire to spend the greatest amount of time with Mohandas. The very presence of Mohandas seemed to fill him with thrill. Anything Mohandas said to him he treated as a sacred utterance.

Whenever Mohandas had the time, he explained the Indian way of life to Kallenbach: 'There are kings and princes and very rich people in India who live in great style, but true respect and reverence goes only to the person who gives up his worldly possessions. He is considered to be a real prince and a true noble man. People fall at his feet out of sheer reverence and without fear. There is no greater joy than renunciation. How I wish I could also partake of that joy!'

Kallenbach listened to him like a dedicated follower. The words that fell from his mouth were to him like flowers which he picked up meticulously, adding them to his treasure.

He pruned the number of his servants. One day he asked one of the servants to clean his shoes. Mohandas went and started cleaning the shoes himself. Kallenbach saw it but he didn't know what to say. That day, he made his trip to the wardrobe himself and picked out the simplest clothes. Normally, it was the butler who took out the clothes, got them ironed and helped him to put them on. When the butler came, Kallenbach told him: 'From now on, you needn't do all this. I'll be doing it myself.'

The butler was astonished. What could be wrong with the master?

Mohandas used to keep fasts; now Kallenbach also started keeping him company. When Mohandas gave up eating grain and milk, so did he. Kallenbach gave it a lot of thought but he couldn't figure out why he was doing it. He couldn't label it, but he was developing a sense of indifference which he had never known before. He found himself sinking in it to the depths of his existence.

~

Offices for issuing permits under the Asiatic law were opened all over Transvaal in 1907. The Indian community was opposing the opening of these offices. Each and every office was being picketed by volunteers who tried to explain to the applicants that, through the registration process, the Transvaal government was going to deprive them of their freedom. 'You are already poor and deprived. Economic deprivation can however be remedied but political deprivation is hard to get rid of. You can be picked up any time and thrown into jail. The honour of your wife and kids will no longer be safe. You are not criminals, but you will be forced to lead the lives of criminals. If you want to lead a life of honour and self-respect, you can do so or at least your children will be able to do so, only if you oppose this arbitrary law.'

Every volunteer had been provided with a small bag containing some snacks, some first aid material and medicines. They had clear instructions that force was not to be applied. They were only to ask for the applicants' names but if someone was not willing to give his name he was not to be pressurized.

Those who could read were given a leaflet to read. It described the problems with the law and the hardships and the hurt to the self-respect of Indians it was going to cause. It also made an appeal: Please do not allow yourself to fall a blind victim to the law. It may not do you much harm, but your next generation will be disabled permanently and become a hostage to the tyranny of this cruel law.

The appeal was followed by advice that the *satyagrahi* volunteer should also treat the policemen politely and respectfully. If the police were to indulge in abuse and foul language, or beatings, they should put up with them peacefully. If they found it difficult to put up with them, they should remove themselves from the scene. If the police want to take them into custody, they should let themselves be arrested without protest.

Every band of volunteers had a designated leader. His duty was to ensure that the instructions were strictly followed. Every volunteer was expected to follow his directions.

Boys twelve to eighteen years old were taking active part in the picketing. Even these boys had been told that if someone wanting to get registered was feeling discouraged or threatened by the picketers, one of them should escort him to the office, get him registered and then escort him back to his house. The boys followed these instructions literally. Reports of their conduct were conveyed to Gandhibhai regularly. Some people even made fun of the whole thing. Was it a protest or the wild wail of a widow, they asked. The *satyagrahi*s ignored their barbs.

The police were slowly beginning to realize that the *satyagrahi*s were more stupid than dangerous. They therefore began to take them rather lightly. They in fact laughed at them: Only Indians can be such fools, they said. Imagine them showing their opponents the way to the very office which they are supposed to picket! They are fighting the government and yet at the same time helping the government by escorting the registration aspirants to the registration office! What can one say to such fools and what punishment can one give them? You punish them and they behave as if someone else and not they themselves are being punished. This kind of attitude on the part of the *satyagrahi*s had completely puzzled the police. Protestors and agitationists usually tried to escape, hide or hit back, but nothing of the sort was in evidence here.

Mohandas and the other party leaders were keeping a close watch on the situation trying to make sure that no *satyagrahi* lost control and indulged in violence.

The *satyagrahi*s were receiving up-to-the-minute information from the registration offices. In fact, the staff of the offices itself came and gave them information on the sly: about people who got registered during the day; about government's thinking on different issues; about its strategies, and so on. Those who were getting registered had their own problems. Possibly, they would have avoided registration, but they feared the government's reaction. It could stop their business. By getting registered, they had got into another kind of problem. There was no appreciation from any quarters, but their own people had started looking down on them.

Big traders would not let them have any merchandise before interrogating them: 'How many in your family got registered?'

Sometimes, a man would try to lie his way out, but the association had a list of everyone registered and the list was available with every volunteer. To such men, the traders had only one thing to say: 'No goods available. Please try the government.'

The registration office was up to new tricks everyday. One day all the registration offices remained almost closed. Not a single person appeared for registration. The *satyagrahi*s were puzzled. A few people had always been turning up every day. Then the *satyagrahi*s discovered that registration had been arranged to be carried out at midnight in the premises of a shop and everyone was supposed to report there. So the volunteers reported there in the evening and started picketing. A little before midnight, a few people turned up for registration. The official team was already in position. The *satyagrahi*s lay down in front of them and said: 'If you carry on with registration, it will break us. We will lose heart.'

The people went back but came back by some other route. The picketers tried to stop them again but this time they did not agree.

The volunteers saw to it that the names of those who got registered at night appeared in the gazette the next day. The *satyagrahi* gazette carried the notification the next day: 'The following people got themselves registered at a shop on the night of … clandestinely…' and the roll list followed.

This incident did discourage the prospective registrants. Their number started going down. The government had to change its policy. The officials started door to door registration. The *satyagrahi*s could not trace out all the locations to be visited by them but did manage to reach a place if information became available in advance. This enraged the registration seekers, but the volunteers were patient and put up with their tirades silently.

'By seeking registration, you are letting yourself and your country down.' That was all they told them.

About five hundred people had got themelves registered clandestinely. Their names were published in headlines and they found themselves ostracized.

A *girmitiya* called Ramsunder was reported to the registration office by some people of Germiston. The complaint against him said that he was loud-mouthed and said all kinds of foul things to the registration seekers. No one in Germiston would come forward for registration till he was arrested. Ramsunder was not very educated, but he had a repertoire of couplets and verses which he could recite extempore. He had a verse for every occasion. This had made him very popular with Indians. Though a simpleton, he had made sure that the message of *satyagraha* reached each and every Indian through his verses and couplets.

It was the Christmas week. Transvaal was drowned in festivities. Indians took part in the festivities in large numbers. Ramsunder had been arrested at the behest of the Germistinians. The Indian community had rallied behind Ramsunder. The Asiatic Officer had got him arrested with the idea that it would open a flood of registrations, but just the opposite had been the result. Ramsunder had turned into a hero overnight. He was sentenced to a month's simple imprisonment. The government was so nervous that he was housed in the European wing and was allowed many relaxations. There was a stream of visitors throughout the day, carrying all kinds of delicacies for Ramsunder. Ramsunder was in great demand.

As *satyagraha* gathered steam, Indians and Chinese communities were turning into roadblocks to registration. The officials met at a meeting to consider the issue and took stock of the situation. The majority of officials were in favour of immediate arrest and imprisonment of the leaders of the *satyagraha*, but a few disagreed. They argued that by arresting a good-for-nothing fellow like Ramsunder, the police had turned him into a martyr. It was another matter that he had not been able to take advantage of the martyrdom. If the top leaders were to be arrested, they would have a hard time giving explanations to London. These leaders were already quite influential; the arrest would only make them more powerful.

'So, what are we supposed to do? If the government does nothing, we will become a laughing stock and the law and order situation will go out of hand.'

A magistrate made the suggestion: 'Let the government file a complaint. The magistrate will issue a notice to all the leaders asking them to appear before the court to explain why they should not be proceeded against under the new law. They will have to present themselves before the court. This will not lead to any agitation and the leaders will not turn into martyrs like Ramsunder. And if they don't present themselves before the court, arresting them would present no difficulty.'

Everyone liked the idea. It was put into effect and notices were issued to the leaders.

The government was expecting the leaders to run scared. It did not expect anyone to appear before the court on the stipulated date, but every single leader appeared in court on the set date. The first man to do so was Thambi Naidu.

Thambi Naidu was a Tamil speaker. He had migrated from Mauritius to South Africa when he was fourteen. His parents had been long dead and gone and he had been brought up by his elder brother and his wife. He arrived first in Cape Town with his two brothers. Leaving his brothers there, he came to Johannesburg. He could communicate in broken English. Living in Mauritius, he had also picked up Hindustani. He of course knew Mauritius Creole. Telugu and Tamil were his own languages. He had a strong body. He could work through day and night without any sign of fatigue. He could carry the heaviest load on his shoulders through the streets without a trace of any embarrassment on his face. His business was on the upswing. He had married Veerooma, a local girl. He owned three trolleys, one truck and a stable of eleven horses. Not very prosperous, he was doing better than most.

The first time he participated in a meeting was the one attended by three thousand people in Transvaal. That was the meeting at which vows to fill jails were taken. Khandubhai was the first one to take the vow. Among the people who had spoken from the dais under the leadership of Gandhibhai, Thambi Naidu was also one. People knew him quite well as he was President of the Tamil Benefit Society. His love for his country knew no bounds. It dripped from his face. His only weakness was his short temper. Though it never caused any harm to anyone, it did try the patience of people interacting with him. If he had not been short-tempered, he would have been another Cachalia providing leadership to the Transvaal struggle.

The magistrate was trying each case separately. It had already been decided that no *satyagrahi* was going to put up a defence. Everyone would accept his guilt and obey the magistrate's orders. So no one said a word in his defence and everyone was sentenced to three-month's hard labour. Only Mohandas had been awarded a two-month simple imprisonment.

When the sentence was pronounced, hundreds of Indian labourers and traders collected in the courtroom and outside. Many members of the bar were also present, most of them were white. Mohandas sought the magistrate's permission to make a submission, the magistrate responded by simply turning his gaze at him. Mohandas said: 'I have been told that my companions in Pretoria have been awarded three months hard labour and have been fined heavily. If they don't pay the fine, they have to spend another three months in jail. My crime is actually much greater than theirs. I therefore appeal to you to award me the strictest of sentences.'

The magistrate said nothing. Mohandas repeated his plea. The magistrate cast sidelong glances as if he had been caught thieving and said: 'The verdict has been delivered. What has happened at Pretoria is of no concern to you.'

A confusion prevailed in court room.

Mohandas was today standing as an accused in a court in which he normally appeared as a barrister and where his arguments were listened to with respect. Today, his arguments were being ignored, but Mohandas was finding his position as an accused more respectable than it had been as a barrister.

As soon as the verdict was pronounced, Mohandas was taken into custody. At that moment, he was the only person whose case had been decided and sentence announced. The policeman who took him into custody was a white. He looked at Mohandas as if he was a rejected commodity and told him: 'Go and sit down on that bench.'

The bench was meant for prison inmates. Mohandas went and sat down on it. It was the detention room of the court. After he was seated, the door of the detention room was locked. Mohandas sat alone for a long time. Occasionally, he got up and started pacing the room. He had to keep reminding himself again and again: 'You are a prisoner, Mr. Mohandas.'

Questions swarmed in his head. Two months! How would he ever be able to spend two months in prison? It would be full two months, unless people renegaded on their scheduled plan to fill up the jails. If the jails became full, the government might find it difficult to keep so many people in jail. Then, suddenly, Mohandas received a jolt: What was all this he was thinking? If this was what he was going to consider, why did he ever get into the business of *satyagraha* at all? And he had been talking martyrdom with the magistrate! He had been telling people that jails were His Majesty's hotels! Being guests in these hotels for the sake of the black law was an honour, a matter of ultimate bliss! So, why these questions now: How would he spend two months in jail? When would they be released? Mohandas felt everyone present in the courtroom had his eyes on him, looking at him through the bars and laughing at him. Great, Gandhibhai, great! Appearance and reality turned out to be really different with you! He found his face flushed with shame and anger: shame at himself and anger at the thoughts that were trying to weaken him.

The door opened. A police officer walked in. Without speaking, he beckoned to Mohandas to follow him. Mohandas got up and did as he had been told. He was fully dressed at the time and his mind was working fast. He was wondering what jail life would be like. Would he be living alone or would there be others with him too? He smiled at the thought. Whether you lived alone or with someone, what was the difference? A jail remained a jail. Dozens of Indians must have spent their days in this jail; did he think they came here with their friends to have a picnic? Most of them *girmitiya*s, there wouldn't be anyone even to bail them out.

The prison van stood at the gate. The police officer beckoned to him to get in. The way the police officer was using sign language,

Mohandas felt he might be dumb. He asked him in English: 'You can speak, I hope?'

'What do you mean?'

'Nothing.' Mohandas smiled.

'What is there to smile about in going to prison?' asked the policeman.

Mohandas did not make a response. The policeman pointed to a seat in the van and, this time using speech, asked him to occupy it.

Mohandas wanted to laugh loudly but maintained a serious mien. The policeman could ask him the same question again.

Inside the jail, the jailor gave him the once-over and said: 'Take off your clothes.'

'Take off my clothes?'

'Yes, take your clothes off!'

'But why?'

'Don't ask questions. You'll have to put on jail clothing.'

'Let me have it first then.'

'I told you to take off the clothes first.' Mohandas stood unmoving.

'Are you going to take off the clothes or not?' The jailer, a native, glowered at him.

Mohandas suddenly remembered. Before courting arrests, they had decided unanimously that every *satyagrahi* would follow the rules of the jail. But going stark naked couldn't possibly be a rule!

'Is it a regulation?' he asked.

The jailor fixed him with his red-hot eyes. Mohandas told himself: 'What's the point of asking these questions? For a *satyagrahi*, his goal is the uppermost. For the sake of that goal, he has to swallow every order unless the ground for opposing it has already been decided on. Mohandas started taking off his clothes one by one: outer clothes first, the jacket, the bow, the shirt, the undershirt. When they reached the trousers, his hands hesitated for a second.'

'Take them off,' the jailor screamed.

Mohandas started taking off the lower clothes but stopped at the briefs.

The jailor took a step forward: 'Are you going to take them off or are you not?'

'Let the jail clothes arrive. I'll take them off. I have no special attachment to them.'

'All the clothes off first before you get the jail clothes! This is a jail, not your bloody home! The jail rules apply here.'

'Rules?' Mohandas recalled to himself: 'Every *satyagrahi* will follow the rules, written or verbal.' He took off the briefs. Mohandas had never seen himself so naked! For the first time he experienced the difference between being naked to oneself and being naked in the presence of someone else: in the latter situation, one was more naked than naked. He closed his eyes. The thought of Kastur came fluttering across like a scrap of paper from nowhere …

The jailor was laughing. Mohandas stood in that position for a long time. The jail clothes arrived half an hour later. They were so dirty that putting them on was by itself a trial. Before they arrived he went through the torture of nakedness. He kept thinking of Digamber Jain saints: the ability to stay naked was by itself a high enough goal to achieve. But, he told himself, it is no pursuit of a high goal to which you owe your own nakedness!

While putting on the clothes, his feeling was that there couldn't be a greater torture, but he was a *satyagrahi* and couldn't even think of dressing differently from his fellow *satyagrahi*s. It would still take him some time to become a seasoned *satyagrahi*. Not till all other options had been exhausted would he be able to call himself a single-minded *satyagrahi*. He looked upon the incident as acquiring baptism into jail life. As he thought this, he couldn't help smiling.

He was next taken to another officer. This was baptism again. He was asked his name, parents' names and all other details. Identification marks on his body were checked. Then he was asked: 'Where would you like to stay?'

'With my companions.'

He was sent to a barrack-like building where his other friends were also present. They danced with joy to see Mohandas. Some of them bore whip marks on their bodies.

'What happened?' asked Mohandas.

They laughed and said: 'When you were arrested, we took out a protest march with black flags in our hands. The police did not like it and tried to disperse the procession. When they failed to disperse us, they started using whips. We made no protest against that.'

Mohandas was overwhelmed. 'You are the true *satyagrahi*s. I have still a lot to learn from you.'

One of the *satyagrahi*s said: 'We got over the whipping when they put us all together. And now, of course, all the remaining hurt is gone too ...'

Mohandas was staring at their shining faces.

The jail had two wards, one for white prisoners and the other for natives and coloureds. The *satyagrahi*s had been kept in the natives' ward. The cell was locked up at six in the evening and the guards started their rounds. The shouts and cries they gave out during their rounds were unintelligible to the *satyagrahi*s. It was some strange and frightening language. They could not see anything from their cages as the doors were of steel without bars. For air, there were vents on the top half of the doors. All the light and air they got were through these vents.

A few of them were unhappy that they had been holed up in a black hole. Their way of saying this was rather indiect, though. 'Whatever Ramsunder might have turned out to be in his later years, while in jail he did have a great time at the expense of the government!'

'What style he had! There was a stream of visitors at all hours. Food from outside, clothes of his choice, and fruit and snacks from the jail authorities!'

'And look at us! Not quite evening and we are locked up in the safe like a miser's wealth!'

Mohandas listened to the plaint patiently, but finally he had to speak. 'It's not exactly the way you think. Ramsunder was the first *satyagrahi*. The government couldn't decide how to deal with him. This time, the arrests were pre-planned. It was already decided for everyone how he was going to be dealt with. As for this jail ... how can everyone be a Ramsunder? Let me confess that I too had this sinful thought: Would I have to live out the whole sentence or could I be released earlier? I thought a lot about it and I arrived at the conclusion that a *satyagrahi* must be more balanced, trusting, stable and focused in mind than an average person. From my experience, I can now understand how easily a man can be swayed by his weakness and attraction for comforts.'

The next day, Mohandas was transferred to another jail. There were a couple of others too. They were supposed to carry their luggage on their heads or shoulders. The station was at some distance. Mohandas picked up his luggage and supported it on his head.

One of the prisoners offered to carry his luggage.

'No,' said Mohandas, 'I will carry my own luggage.'

'Look, we are used to carrying heavy weights. This is nothing.'

'Can you do my term for me? If not, why should you carry my luggage?

It is an essential part of *satyagraha* that one should do all one's work himself.'

Mohandas walked ahead with the luggage. The weight did not make any difference to his gait.

That night, Mohandas had to share his ward with some Zulu and Chinese prisoners. The place was smelly. Faced with such situations, Mohandas repeated to himself: 'A *satyagrahi* must accept everything with a positive frame of mind. Even the slightest negative thought can destroy the sacred essence of *satyagraha*.'

Mohandas placed his luggage in a corner. He had been given a plate and a few smelly blankets. He lay down to sleep but sleep evaded him and he spent his time trying to weed out the distracting thoughts from his stream of thinking. His clothes bit into his skin. A strange silence, interspersed with whisperings, pervaded the place. Incomprehensible sounds were also making their appearance here. The light was very dim.

Two men entered the room, both prisoners, though for some time Mohandas took them to be jail staff on their rounds. He said nothing. They beckoned to Mohandas but Mohandas did not move. The two were stuck to each other like railway bogeys. Mohandas didn't know what to do. For a moment, he thought of calling out to others. Then he changed his mind. You must solve your problem yourself in a peaceful frame of mind, he told himself. He closed his eyes and tried to control his emotions. The two were making obscene gestures to him.

One of them touched his body. He was already stark naked. The other, Chinese prisoner too was naked and he was doing something while blabbering in his language. Mohandas guessed that he was calling him.

Mohandas sat up in his bed and signalled them to leave. They both now tried to pull him in, but he resisted. When they couldn't get him to join, they got busy themselves.

Mohandas closed his eyes.

The next day, the Jail Superintendent appeared personally and took Mohandas with him. He was then sent to another ward.

When leaving, the Superintendent presented him a bundle of books and said: 'General Smuts has sent you these books with his compliments.'

'I can reciprocate only with compliments.' Mohandas laughed and said.

He turned over the books. They included the *Bible* and some religious books. Mohandas smiled and said: 'Prisoners do need such books rather badly.'

The Superintendent left.

~

The *satyagraha* was gathering momentum. Indians were courting arrest in substantial numbers. Some three or four days after Mohandas' arrest, group after group of jail-seekers started streaming in. Among those courting arrests, most were peddlers, hawkers and released *girmitiya*s. They lived a hand to mouth existence. When they heard that their leaders had been arrested, they came out on the streets. They had discovered a unique way of courting arrest. All peddlers and hawkers had to have a licence. Any policeman could demand the licence any time. If you were unable to produce it, you were packed off to jail. They had now collectively decided not to show the licence. This had proved to be a very effective trick. Hundreds of coolies were now in jails. Those in jail no longer had to depend on newspapers to get outside news.

Simple sentence prisoners received plain corn porridge for breakfast. You could add salt if you wanted to, but normally salt seemed to have sand mixed in it. At lunch, they were given four ounces of rice, four ounces of bread, one ounce of clarified butter and salt. Dinner was again corn porridge and a little bit of vegetable.

The food was hardly enough to satisfy their hunger. For one thing, it was barely edible and, for another, the filthy surroundings made one throw up.

The jail doctor was on his rounds. The *satyagrahi*s surrounded him and said: 'We must have spices. We can't eat without salt and spices. In India, the prisoners are allowed spices.'

'This is not India. Anyway, prisoners are not here to be feted.'

'You can at least give us pulses. Our food has no nourishment for muscles.'

The doctor was mad. 'Don't cross the limits. And keep your knowledge to yourself. You are given boiled beans twice a week in place of corn. If your digestion is sound, your body can go without food for a whole week and get its nourishment from the food eaten a week before.'

When the news reached the Superintendent, he permitted the *satyagrahi*s to cook their own food. Thambi Naidu became the Chief Cook. When adequate vegetables were not issued, Thambi would pick up a row and would not come down till full rations were issued.

~

The jail at Johannesburg had a hundred and fifty prisoners in it, all of them serving a simple sentence. As the number of *satyagrahi*s increased, screws began to be tighten on them. Now everyone was being awarded hard labour. The authorities thought that this would discourage the people and they would stop courting arrests. But the process that had started showed no signs of slackening. This never ceased to surprise the white government of that black country. Don't these people ever feel afraid, it wondered.

Ever since the day General Smuts had sent him books, the Superintendent had started listening to Gandhibhai. On Gandhibhai's request, he had allowed the *satyagrahi*s to engage in physical exercise. Their day anyway used to start with a drill exercise. Next, it was cleaning of the barracks. Those sentenced to simple imprisonment had nothing else to do. In fact, even this little bit was their own choice. There was a Pathan named Nawab Khan among the *satyagrahi*s. He had become a sort of Drill Master. After the warders had completed their drill, he took over. The commands he gave, however, were a drill more for their stomachs than for their bodies, as his style of issuing commands was such that they doubled up with laughter, holding their stomachs. 'Stand-at-ease' was issued as 'Sundalese,' triggering laughter. Not that the laughter made any impression on him: he continued with his commands.

They called his English 'Pathani English,' which gave him a swollen head.

~

Most of the newspapers published in Transvaal were owned by gold mine owners. Their editors were very eminent journalists. The editor of the *Daily Star* had been Lord Milner's Secretary. Later, he went over to London as editor of *The Times.* The editor of *The Transvaal Leader* was Albert Cartwright. In addition to their own interests, the editors were also quite conscious of the interests of the public. They had covered the public meetings of the Indians quite extensively and challengingly. This had made Cartwright a good friend of Mohandas. He lent open support to the cause of Indians in his paper.

As soon as he got to know that Gandhi had been sent to jail, he immediately called up General Smuts and said: 'I want to see you now.'

'Come right away,' said Smuts, who had picked up the phone himself.

'Yes, Mr. Editor, what can I do for you?' asked Smuts the moment Cartwright entered his office.

'You need to do nothing for me,' said Cartwright forthrightly, 'but please listen to the British Indians settled in Transvaal.'

'They are bent on picking up a fight.'

'You call it a fight? You are getting them whipped, packing them in jails yet they are putting up with everything silently. Did they ever throw a single stone at your men?'

'Why don't they speak up? Who is stopping them?'

'Their own conscience. They know that if they speak up, you will crush them as rebels. Mr. Gandhi knows it only too well.'

'This Gandhi is a pain in the neck.'

'Not at all. Have you ever tried to talk to him?'

'Will he listen at all?'

'Certainly, unless you speak against Indian interests…'

'How can we withdraw a law after it has been passed?'

'You can at least try to understand their viewpoint.'

'Why don't you mediate and help settle the issue? The government will appreciate it.'

'I'll prepare a draft on the basis of what has appeared in the papers and in their speeches. Take a look at it. I'll then take it to Mr. Gandhi. He is not a stubborn man; in fact, he is quite realistic. It's his realism which sometimes makes him stubborn.'

'I wish you good luck.'

When Albert Cartwright met Mohandas, he first stared at him for a while and then said: 'I could never imagine that one day I would have to see you as a prisoner.'

'If you would like, you can see many more like me here. This is after all His Majesty's Hotel. When someone is to be shown special honour, he is privileged with a lice-infested uniform and special hospitality. And then of course friends like you keep visiting to inquire after our well-being. I hope you are keeping well.' Mohandas laughed.

'Don't you think from a respected barrister you have turned into a jailbird?'

'You too perhaps don't think that way, or the editor of a great newspaper would not have come to see a jailbird.'

Cartwright looked at Mohandas. His face had a look of absolute normality. 'You are a barrister,' he said. 'I can't expect to outwit you. I met General Smuts and some members of the Indian community. Smuts wants a negotiated solution. The Indian leaders say they do not understand the subtleties of a negotiated settlement and there cannot be one till Gandhibhai is out of jail. So, actually both parties wanted me to see you.'

Gandhi laughed and said: 'And I was under the illusion that Albert was here to see a prisoner friend.'

'Of course. You are a friend, aren't you?'

'I will hear it from you later. Right now, why don't you tell me what the proposal is?'

'Here is a draft. Take a look.'

Mohandas read the draft word-for-word and then said: 'I'm ready to sign it.'

'That's what I expected. Nothing great about rotting in a jail.'

'Nothing very wrong either. But let me first talk to my colleagues. They have as much in stake in this struggle as I myself, or General Smuts. In any case, they have to spend their whole life here.'

'If the Indians agree to register voluntarily, the Asiatic Law, your "Black Law," will be withdrawn.'

'This draft doesn't say that. Have it added and all scope for a doubt removed.'

Cartwright's voice went a little hoarse: 'From the General's side, no changes are possible in the draft.'

'There are things which are before your eyes, yet you can't see them.'

'But I assure you that if you get registered voluntarily, the law will not have a leg to stand on.'

'Look, Mr. Cartwright, I respect your goodwill from the bottom of my heart. I quite understand that the language used in this draft is essential to maintain the authority of the government. But if there is the slightest possibility of something being completely misunderstood or misinterpreted, where is the harm in making the meaning and intention quite clear? This is an agreement. Both sides to the agreement enjoy the fullest right to make alterations. General Smuts has already fired a shot at us. What'll he get by firing another one? His announcement that from his side the agreement is unalterable takes away from its importance. It makes it a command.'

Cartwright had no answer to that.

~

Ever since Mohandas had landed in jail, Kallenbach had been completely at sea. He didn't know what to do. When he thought of all the hardships Mohandas must be facing in jail, he got very upset. He had started sleeping on the floor. He was living on a subsistence diet. He couldn't concentrate on his work. The image of Gandhi was constantly before his eyes. How would he be spending his days?

But then he would think: 'Would it really make any difference to Gandhi?'

On several occasions, he made ready to pay a visit to Gandhi, but soon his enthusiasm deserted him. He tested his courage by asking himself: 'Would I be able to see him as a prisoner?'

And he found all his courage gone.

It was beginning to get warm, but despite the fact it was January, it wasn't really hot. Suddenly, there was a call from the Jail Superintendent for Mohandas. At that time, Leuing Quinn, leader of the Chinese community, and Thambi were with Mohandas. The Chinese were also taking part in the *satyagraha.* Mohandas told them: 'Looks like something serious has come up. I may be sent to some other place. If that happens, do not get upset. Keep going.'

Quinn, Thambi and all other *satyagrahi*s who got to know came out to see him off. Their faces were lined with worry. Mohandas however looked quite unperturbed. He walked off with the warder.

The Jail Superintendent stood up to shake his hand. With him sat Mr. Vernon, Police Superintendent of Johannesburg. He was introduced to Vernon. Vernon stood up to shake his hand too. Mohandas could not understand why a Police Superintendent had to get up to shake a prisoner's hand. One could understand why the Jail Superintendent had to, but a Police Superintendent?

Gandhi was formal: 'How do you do, Mr. Vernon?'

'I'm fine, and you, Mr. Gandhi?'

'Well, here I am, standing before you …,' Gandhi gave a smile.

The Jail Superintendent signalled to him to take a seat. Mohandas said: 'Thanks, I'm fine as I am. A prisoner should know his limits.'

'Meaning?'

'I don't think any other prisoner would have the courage to sit in your presence. It would be considered sheer effrontery. At least for the time, treat me like one of them. Would you now tell me what you want of me?'

'Mr. Vernon wanted to see you.'

'Me? I hope there is no fresh problem.' He laughed and said: 'In the present circumstances, I don't think I can do anything more for anyone.'

'There is nothing you cannot do,' said Mr. Vernon, laughing. 'You will have to go to Pretoria with me.'

'Is my stay in this prison creating some danger for the government of this colony?'

'Nothing of the sort. I have received a message that I should be in Pretoria with you as soon as possible. Perhaps General Smuts wants to see you.'

'See me?' Mohandas looked at Mr. Vernon with total surprise. 'Please allow a few minutes. I want to consult my companions.'

'I regret that's not possible. The meeting is supposed to be completely confidential.'

'I don't understand.'

'Nor do I. That's all I know and that's the entire message I have received. You can change, if you so want.'

'My sentence is not yet over. Till it is, my status remains that of a prisoner.'

'Shall we move?'

Mohandas thought for a minute and then said: 'All right ...' Then he laughed and said: 'I was thinking I could at least say goodbye to my friends. After all, I'm going to meet a General, which is nothing short of going into a lion's den.'

Vernon and the Jail Superintendent laughed.

~

The journey to Pretoria wasn't really long, though they did have to take a train. It was an unusual sight for the onlookers to see a white Police Superintendent personally escorting a coloured prisoner in a first class carriage. Mohandas wanted to laugh out loud but was keeping himself in check. During the whole journey, he spoke only one sentence: 'Do forgive me, Mr. Vernon, for causing you so much embarrassment. People must be wondering.'

'No, nothing of the kind. You are a respectable man after all.'

'Thank you, but not currently.'

A government vehicle awaited them at the Pretoria station. Mohandas rode the vehicle to Smuts' office. At the office, he was led and followed by a guard. The office staff gaped: a coolie and that too a prisoner, marching towards General Smuts' chamber as if he was the ambassador of some nation! Because of the guards in the front and the rear, they couldn't satisfy their curiosity by asking questions.

Mohandas walked with a carefree gait and this annoyed the white office staff the most. If his eyes met anyone's, Mohandas greeted him with a smile.

They took it to be improper.

'He is a prisoner, but look at the way he is walking!'

'Looks like he is the troublemaker coolie leader, Gandhi.'

'Should be hanged from a sour apple tree.'

'How did General Smuts permit this coolie to appear here, and in a prisoner's clothes?'

They were letting off steam in whispered words and draping their faces in layer after layer of hatred.

Mohandas continued to greet them with smiles

General Smuts' chamber was a large one, well appointed and fully secured. Smuts himself was a giant of a man, balding and with a big face. Cheekbones were rather prominent.

When Mohandas entered the chamber, Smuts looked up from his work and was jolted to see a prison inmate walking in so confidently, but he sized up the situation quickly. Smuts had his secretary sitting with him. Mohandas looked at him and gave him a smile which seemed to indicate long familiarity. Then he said to Smuts: 'General Smuts, I'm M.K. Gandhi and I have been brought here directly from Johannesburg Jail.'

Smuts had so far given no indication that he had recognized him or that he knew him. Even after Mohandas had told him his name, he showed no reaction.

He pulled himself up a little in his chair and said: 'I was waiting for you. I hope you had a trouble-free journey.'

'Trouble is actually an invention of the mind. Governments use it to create fear and mislead. So far as possible, passive resistance has to keep it at bay. Tell me what you wanted me here for.'

Smuts was not quite ready to come to the main issue so fast. He wanted to take his time warming up to the main topic. But Mohandas' question forced him to come to it straight away.

'I had a talk with Mr. Cartwright. He is a great admirer and a supporter of your cause. It was his proposal that we should meet and talk it over. Many issues get sorted out this way. I found his argument quite logical.'

'I'd told Mr. Cartwright what I thought about the issue. I have no problems with your draft, but I want a couple of things cleared up. I do not want that an agreement should start its life with a doubt. One of our scriptures, the Gita, says: "Doubt is the leading cause of destruction."'

'I want to congratulate the Indian community. They did not lose courage or disintegrate despite your arrest.'

'The credit for their solidarity goes entirely to you. If you hadn't produced this law, the situation would not have arisen.'

'I haven't the slightest hatred for your people. Like you, I am also a barrister. As a student, I had many Indians as my friends. But I am helpless. I have a responsibility to shoulder. Europeans want this law implemented and they are all English speakers. Boers are neutral. Had they been Boers, I'd have tried to persuade them. I agree with your proposal one hundred per cent. I have also talked to General Botha. As soon as the majority of you get your registrations, the Asiatic Law will be repealed. When a new law is made, you will be consulted. I have actually developed great respect for your people after seeing their capacity for sacrifice and their peace-loving nature. I do not wish the old story to be repeated.'

'Could I have a copy of the agreement?'

'I told you that the English-speaking whites are determined to see the law enforced. You have to trust me. I am giving you my word. Please ask your people to get registered. As soon as the registrations are done, I'll start the process of reforming the law.'

Mohandas looked at Smuts' face. It was quite transparent. There was no attempt to look away or down which could indicate sleight or deception.

'I'm taking a great risk on the strength of your verbal assurance.'

'I too have taken a great risk.'

Mohandas got up. 'Please arrange to have me sent back where I came from. My friends must be waiting for me.'

Smuts laughed a big laugh. 'You are free as of this moment. Who can keep you in chains any more? I'll call the Jail Department. Your friends too will be released by tomorrow morning.' After a pause he added: 'Please go slow with your meetings. They will create problems for the government.'

'Please rest assured. If the government doesn't create problems for us, we won't create any problems for the government either. I will of course have to tell my people about this agreement: how it was arrived at, what its conditions are and how we are supposed to live up to it, and so on.'

'On those matters, of course, you can have as many meetings as you like. For me, it is enough that you have understood what I wanted to say.' Smuts looked at Gandhi with eyes which seemed to be sizing him up.

The clock on the wall showed seven in the evening. There was only one train remaining for Johannesburg. Mohandas had no money with him. He said: 'I must return to Johannesburg at once, but I haven't a single farthing in my pocket.' He was looking for pockets but found none: 'What use is money for prisoners? That's why probably there are no pockets.' And he laughed. 'What a fool I am. I was trying to look into my pockets.'

'Oh!' Smuts laughed and went through three or four of his pockets quickly.

'I am in the same boat.'

Mohandas shrugged. 'This means there is nothing that can be done except going back to jail.'

'Mr. Gandhi, you are not only a barrister; you are also a very clever man.'

'Am I the only one to fit that description?'

Smuts was taken slightly aback. Then laughed out aloud and asked his secretary: 'Have you any money with you? Mr. Gandhi needs it to go back to Johannesburg.'

'Do we have to pay?'

'We got him here.'

He only had a few pence. Mohandas took them and came out smiling. The secretary was trying to replace his wallet. The damage had left him feeling impoverished.

When Mohandas reached Johannesburg, it was already nine. On the way to Pretoria, the food had been provided officially, though he wasn't in the least inclined to eat. Now he was by himself. The few pence he had been given had been used up in the fare. He had only a penny or two left with him.

Mohandas made straight for Yusuf Mian's place. He was the party president. He had learnt that Mohandas had been whisked away to Pretoria secretly. Why and for how long, no one knew. When he saw

Gandhibhai standing in front of him, he clasped him in his embrace. 'Gandhibhai, are you all in one piece? We were eating our hearts out worrying what the devil might do to you.'

'There was nothing of the sort.'

'You went alone?'

'I'll tell you all. That is why I took the first train back. Please call a meeting of the party the first thing.'

By now, a few more people had got the news that Gandhibhai was back safe and sound. They too collected at Yusuf Mian's place. Everyone was agreed that a meeting should be called at once. There was a mosque close to Yusuf Mian's place. Most of the meetings were held in the courtyard of the mosque. So, the people present were dispatched post-haste to inform the members. In two hours, most of the members had arrived. The meeting started exactly at midnight. About a thousand people were present. Word had gone round that Gandhibhai had been taken from the jail to Pretoria and that he had somehow made it back to Johannesburg. They were all curious to get a glimpse of Gandhibhai. Everyone had his own worries. Heaven knew what treatment the government meted out to Gandhibhai!

They heaved a sigh of relief to see Mohandas. There was no sign of any injury on his body. Mohandas gave a detailed account of his talk with General Smuts and described the agreement.

After they had heard Mohandas, there was silence for a while. Then someone got up and asked: 'If General Smuts goes back on his word, what will be your reaction? This black law will continue to hang like a sword on our heads, while having got ourselves registered; we would be like puppets in the hands of our enemy. We will be handing them one more sword to try on our necks.'

Another member put it in a nutshell: 'The right thing would have been for them to repeal the Asiatic Law first and for us to get the registrations second.'

Mohandas was listening to the objections carefully. He said: 'Your objections are justified. Your suggestions are also logical. It would certainly have been better for the law to be repealed first and for us to get ourselves registered voluntarily later. But the agreement does not include this condition. When you make a compromise, you need to move from your fixed positions and to prepare the ground for a new position with mutual agreement. Horses that are tied to their stall do not get anywhere. Our basic position was that we would not accept this black law and would not get registered under its provisions. We still stick to that position. The government wants to put a stop to the entry of unauthorized Indians into Transvaal. We should appreciate this concern of the government. This was the reason why I agreed to the deal. Quinn, Thambi and others are in jail. This deal will not come into effect without their, and your, consent. But we must find a way out of this maze. And a compromise is that way out.' Everyone listened patiently. Mohandas continued after a pause: 'This agreement will impose an additional responsibility on us all. We must go and get registered voluntarily. We will also have to make sure that no Indian enters Transvaal illegally. If anyone doesn't get registered even after this agreement is signed, no legal action will be taken against him, but it will mean that he refuses to abide by the agreement. You can truly enjoy the fruits of your victory only when you are ready to fulfil your obligations under the agreement honestly and sincerely.'

As soon as Mohandas sat down after completing his statement, a Pathan jumped up and spoke in a sharp voice: 'Does the agreement include the condition that we must give fingerprints of all the ten fingers?'

'Yes and no,' explained Mohandas. 'Personally, I think we should not have the slightest hesitation in giving all the ten fingerprints. But, if there is anyone who considers giving all the ten fingerprints an insult to his honour, he would be free not to give his fingerprints.'

'Don't confuse the issue. Tell us clearly what you are going to do.' His tone was aggressive.

Mohandas said without a trace of hesitation: 'I will have no hesitation in giving all the ten fingerprints. How can I ask others to do it, if I try to shirk my own responsibility?'

'Do you have any sense of honour left ...?' He came out with a foul expletive and continued: 'Only till the other day, you weren't tired of repeating that only criminals gave their fingerprints. It was on this point that you took issue with the government. Why has the situation changed in a matter of hours?'

'I stand by what I said. It will be wrong to give our fingerprints under the pressure of the black law. But now that the situation has changed, no one should have any objection. Look at it like this: If you force me to salute you and I start saluting you out of fear, I will not only lose your respect, I will also feel diminished in my own eyes. But if I salute you out of my regard for you, it will be taken as politeness and good manners.'

The Pathan screamed: 'You are a liar. You have sold our honour by accepting fifteen thousand pounds from General Smuts. You have let the entire Asian community down. We will not allow our fingerprints to be taken; nor permit any one else to give his fingerprints. I swear by Allah that anyone who tries to do so will meet his death at my hands.'

Mohandas remained calm. 'Please don't think,' he said, 'that I don't understand the feelings of my Pathan brothers. I'd like to know if there is any one else here who thinks that I have sold his honour for money. I'll repeat that any one who does not want to give his fingerprints will not be forced to do so. I'll go with such a person myself and make sure that he gets his registration certificate without giving his fingerprints. But ...,' and here Gandhi paused for a second before continuing. 'But I do not fear death. Therefore it is meaningless to threaten me with death. It is possible that my friends here are angry with me, but I'm sure their anger will be short-lived and will pass soon. I consider it my responsibility to step forward and give my fingerprints. The day of one's death is pre-determined. If my friend here can ensure that that day is advanced, there would be nothing I'd like better. I assure you I'll bear no hatred or anger for my killer. It will not postpone the day of my death even if I do, will it? All that I can say now is that one day my killer will realize the truth of what I'm saying and will regret his action.'

There was a furore in the meeting, with some people trying to pacify the Pathan. Mohandas had to intervene again: 'Please do not upset yourself,' he said. 'God's will will prevail. Please go home. It's quite late already.'

Yusuf Mian closed the meeting. The incident had upset him particularly. The number of Pathans in Transvaal was not very large, maybe about fifty. Some of them had come at the time of the Boer War as new recruits and had later settled down in the colony. A few had come as bodyguards of traders. Actually, many of them were Mohandas' clients. Pathans were considered to be a warlike people. Death and killing held no horror for them. If a friend, a Pathan could be more loyal than a brother; if an enemy, he could be the worst of enemies. The one word they hated most was treachery.

What had hurt the Pathans most was that they would now have to give prints of all the ten fingers, something that only criminals had to do. That was what had made Mohandas corrupt in their eyes.

~

February 10, 1908. Mohandas was on the way to his office. His office was also the office of the *Satyagraha* Association. When he reached the office, Mohandas saw two or three Pathans hovering outside. One of them was Mir Alam, the one who had made the allegation of corruption against him at the meeting. Mir Alam had been Mohandas' client and usually always approached him whenever he had a problem. Mohandas was surprised to see him loitering outside his office instead of going inside to wait for him. When their eyes met, instead of greeting him he averted eye contact. This was the first time that he had consciously avoided greeting him. Mohandas therefore made the first move to which he made a cursory response. Mohandas surmised that he was still angry with him over yesterday's issue.

Mohandas said: 'Mir Alam Bhai, how are you today?'

He muttered something which Mohandas could not catch. 'What was that?' Mohandas asked which probably Mir Alam did not quite get. Mohandas guessed he might have said he was fine. What else could one say? But the usual smile was missing from Mir Alam's face. Mohandas did not like the look of things. He hadn't taken the things Mir Alam had said yesterday very seriously. Pathans are a rather hot-tempered people, he had thought, so he might have spoken in anger. But Mohandas now found his face rather discoloured with hatred and anger. Mohandas was worried at the sudden transformation of a decent man.

By then, Yusuf Mian and other companions also arrived. Some of the friends who had just been released from jail were also present. They were all supposed to go to the Asiatic Registration Office for registration, so they all set out together. The topic of their conversation was how people were not trying to see the developments in the proper perspective. Mohandas had almost forgotten about the Mir Alam episode. He was talking about the challenges ahead.

Mohandas turned around and saw Mir Alam and his friends following them. The registration was at Von Brandis Square, which was about a mile from the place. They were in front of the Arnot & Gibson shop. Suddenly, Mir Alam leapt forward and stood confronting Gandhi: 'Where are you going?' he demanded.

'To give my fingerprints and get the registration certificate. Come and join us. You register first, I'll do it second. You can give only thumb prints …'

He had barely completed his sentence when he received a full-strength blow to his head from the rear. As he fell, more blows rained on him. Kicks, fists, stick—everything was freely used.

As they hit him, they shouted: 'Traitor, cheat, you pocketed the money, didn't you?' Yusuf Mian and Thambi tried to save him but they were also beaten up. A few whites, who were passing by, saw and rushed towards the assailants and chased them as they ran. They were caught and handed over to the police, which also arrived on the spot.

When Mohandas regained consciousness, he found himself in the chamber of J.C. Gibson, partner Arnot & Gibson. A padre named Mr. Doke was bending over him. He asked 'How are you feeling now?'

With unsteady pupils and in a weak voice Mohandas said: 'I'm fine … except for some pain in the teeth and ribs. But, don't worry, I should be fine.' The next thing he asked was: 'Where is Mir Alam?'

'They have all been arrested.'

'Why? I have not filed any complaint.' Mohandas was upset. 'Please get them released.'

He continued to groan.

'All right. You are lying in a stranger's chamber. If you don't mind, I'll take you home. The police wanted to take you to hospital, but I stopped them. I've taken charge of your welfare.'

'Fine, we can go,' Mohandas said weakly. 'Please thank the police and tell them that I have gone to your house out of my own will.'

As they reached Doke's place, Mr. Chamney also arrived. He was Registrar in the Asiatic Registration office. Doke's place was on Smit Street. As they waited for the doctor, Mohandas told Chamney: 'I was coming to your office to give my fingerprints, but God willed otherwise. I met with this accident on the way. Please get my fingerprints right away. I don't want anyone else to beat me to it.'

'Please take it easy. The doctor is coming. I'll reserve the first place for you.'

'No, that will be wrong. I have vowed to get the first certificate. If I don't survive, my vow will be broken.'

Chamney left to collect the necessary papers.

Dr. Thwaites arrived as soon as Chamney left. Though in great pain, Mohandas was keeping his groans and cries under control. Whenever he moved a little, or turned over, a cry did escape him. He was talking to Mrs. Doke regularly and also talked normally to anyone who came asking how he was. The blood spots on his clothes were still in place and the collar was in fact quite red.

The doctor examined him carefully. He cleaned the wounds with warm water. In a couple of places where the skin had split he used stitches. There was a large wound on the head. Shoulders and limbs were relatively less affected. The pain in the ribs was particularly bad. A couple of ribs were broken. Dr. Thwaites wrote his prescriptions. Because of pain in the teeth and ribs, intake of food was ruled out. He could only consume liquids like milk, juice, porridge, etc.

As he was leaving, the doctor said: 'You are not to leave the bed at all. If very necessary, you can work from the bed.'

'For how long?'

'At least two months, till the ribs rejoin and the head wound heals.'

'Two months? That's a lot.'

'If you don't, you will have to live with the pain in the ribs for a long, long time. Another thing. Keep your talk to the minimum.'

'You want me to keep my mouth shut when I have visitors?'

'Yes, No more speaking for you.' Thwaites put a finger on his lips and smiled. 'Mr. Gandhi,' he said, 'The doctor is more helpless than the patient. I am helpless too.'

Mohandas smiled with some difficulty and said: 'We must appreciate each other's helplessness, mustn't we?'

Although prevented from speaking, there was no prohibition on his hands, which Mohandas now started using with a vengeance. Lying in bed, he drafted an appeal to his companions. '... Mr. and Mrs. Doke are looking after me like my own brother and sister. I am quite comfortable in this place. God willing, I should be able to resume my work very soon. Please do not vent your anger at my assailants. The fault also lay with me as I was unable to explain my reasons to them. Please do not think of any retaliatory action against them. They didn't know what they were doing. In their own understanding of things, what they did was right. In their view, what I am doing is wrong. It is natural that a wrongdoer should be punished.

'This attack was carried out by my own companions, who happened to belong to a different religion. But they were not motivated by the fact that I belonged to a different religion. That is why I make a special appeal to the Hindus that, though they may have been hurt by what happened they should not take it amiss. The blood I have shed should help strengthen the Hindu-Muslim relationship. If it doesn't, I will be forced to think that what flows in my veins is not blood but water. Amen!

'Please forget that I was ever attacked. Only remember that no Asian should be found wanting in his duty to offer his fingerprints. If there are any conscientious objectors, or there are people who find themselves opposed to the proposal in principle, their abstentions will be pardoned by the government. *Satyagraha* means exactly this: be not afraid of anyone except God; do only that which your conscience tells you; never do anything out of fear.'

Mohandas sent the appeal to the *Satyagraha* Association with the request that arrangements for its immediate publication in the newspapers might be made.

He also addressed a letter to the Attorney General: 'I do not consider Mir Alam and his friends guilty of attacking me. I hope they will all be released on my request.'

~

XXII

Chamney was back with the necessary papers. Mohandas pressed all ten of his fingertips on the ink pad and stamped the prints on the registration form. The prints were very neat. Finger, shells, vortices—everything could be seen clearly. After submitting the prints, Mohandas looked quite relieved as if a great responsibility had been carried out successfully. He lay quietly with his eyes closed for a few minutes. The ink on his fingertips was drying up. Still supine, he washed his fingers in a basin.

Mr. Chamney's eyes, slightly moist, were fixed at Mohandas. Soon, Mohandas began to snore slightly.

Doke's house had turned into a public place. Mohandas' appeal had aroused a lot of enthusiasm among the people. Visitors, mostly Indians, walked in and out all day. Basket-bearing, shabbily dressed, in mud-caked shoes, anyone from the President of the British Indian Association to, well, practically anybody just walked in without a thought for the inconvenience that might be caused to the Dokes. Everybody was welcomed in the drawing room and offered full hospitality. All Doke's time went either in entertaining the visitors or attending to Mohandas. Things had come to such a pass that anyone felt free to walk in whenever he found the time.

Entertaining Mohandas had also caused problems for the Dokes. Doke was a priest in a Baptist church. The flock was all white and they provided him with the wherewithal. Most of the flock held uncompromising views on colour and race and detested Indians. They were all unhappy with Doke's giving shelter to Gandhi. Attendance in the church was falling, affecting Doke's income.

The changes did not escape Mohandas' notice. One day, he said to Doke: 'I know that both of you are facing problems on my account. The members of your church are unhappy with you and your financial problems are multiplying.'

Doke did not allow him to continue. He said: 'Look, my friend, how much do you know about this religion of Jesus Christ? I am a humble follower of the great Jesus who mounted the cross with a smile on his face for the sake of his beliefs. His love of humanity lights up the whole world today. If the European community considers me a representative of Jesus, why shouldn't I play a part in your struggle? I'll have no complaint even if they want to punish me for doing so. By helping you, I'm doing no favour to Asians; I'm only carrying out the wish of Jesus. I'm only doing my duty towards the human race. Please have no worry on my account. It's not the whites who provide for me; it's God. It's He who provides for everyone—from the ant to the human being. I have in fact already told them that if they have any objections to my relations with Indians and Asians, they can let me go.'

Mohandas looked at Doke. His face was radiant with a glory which was not of this world and his head was bowed in the direction of the cross.

From somewhere inside, the strains of a song being sung by Doke's daughter floated in: 'Lead, kindly light ...'

~

The news of the attack on Mohandas had reached Phoenix. Whatever effect it might have had on the inmates, it was sufficient to upset Kastur and the kids considerably. The incident also had its effect on the reputation of the Settlement. *Indian Opinion* was getting flooded with letters with comments of all types, both favourable and unfavourable.

'By compromising with General Smuts Mr. Gandhi has betrayed the *satyagrahis*.'

'This is a stab on the back.'

'How are you going to prove that what Mir Alam said was wrong?'

Some also said that people should wait. It was not right to declare Gandhi guilty without giving him a hearing.

Mr. West could do little except sending the letters to Mohandas.

Kastur felt so disturbed that she asked West and Polak to make arrangements for her and the kids to go to Johannesburg.

Mr. West and Polak considered her request carefully and then said: This is a moment of crisis for the Phoenix Settlement. It would not be right to leave Phoenix at this time as it would send out a wrong signal all round. Gandhibhai may not like it.'

During this time, Gandhi had been so busy with *satyagraha* that he had not been able to send money to Phoenix. Running Phoenix Settlement and *Indian Opinion* was becoming difficult.

'But who is going to look after him there?' asked Kastur.

Polak laughed. 'His family there is a lot larger than it is in Durban,' he said. 'Currently, he is the guest of a church father, Mr. Doke. Mr. and Mrs Doke are looking after him personally. You don't need to worry at all.'

'But the Pathan may strike again! How many times I have told him to be careful, but does he listen?' She was in tears.

'Mrs. Gandhi, it's perhaps easy to kill a person who lives solely for himself. But killing someone whose business in life is to live for others is rather difficult: the killer must die several deaths himself before he can kill him,' said West, laughing. 'And Gandhi gave up living for himself a long time ago.' His voice had grown rather hoarse.

'Gandhibhai will be here as soon as he recovers. Word has come that he is showing good recovery.' Polak tried to reassure Mrs. Gandhi in a most endearing manner.

That day, Kastur, for the first time, realized what it was to be in a foreign country: alone and helpless.

Though Dr. Thwaites had advised a long period of rest to Mohandas, he was up and walking in barely ten days. Dr. Thwaites was amazed at the speed of his recovery and regaining strength. 'This is only possible through a miracle or extraordinary willpower,' he said.

Mohandas laughed and said: 'You had sentenced me to two months in bed.'

'That was for the average patient. I had no idea that you were not one of them.'

'Now, Doctor, do me a favour, will you? Please tell Doke to let me go. If he tries to stop me again, I'll not be able to resist him and everything I have done will come undone.'

Mr. Doke was listening. He laughed and said: 'When a doctor declares that your recovery is a miracle, how can I stop you? A miracle, after all, is a miracle. The miracle which helped you recover will also help you leave.'

Mohandas laughed.

Mohandas had spent barely ten days in the Doke home but the Doke family felt so close to him as if he had been living there all his life. When he was ready to leave, the Dokes didn't know how to bid farewell to this otherworldly figure, a man who remained unaffected by joy and sorrow. Mohandas laughed and said: 'Mr. Doke, I have caused you so much trouble that you should be happy that I am going. Instead, you are feeling sorry and are trying to get me to forget about all my responsibilities and continue my lazy life here. But I warn you. If I decided to stick to you, you would find it easier to get rid of a leech than me.'

The younger daughter of Doke said: 'Uncle, you liked "Lead Kindly Light," didn't you? I promise I'll sing it for you every day.'

Mohandas put his hand on her head and said: 'Please, sing it for me now so that your uncle, who has lost his way, can find it again.'

As the child sang, every eye in the room became moist. Mohandas felt light spreading all around him. Gradually, the ring of light enveloped all of them. Mohandas' eyes were beginning to close as he felt a film of moisture draw across them.

~

From the Dokes's place, Mohandas left directly for Durban. The news from Phoenix indicated to Mohandas that misunderstandings among the people of Natal were multiplying fast. These doubts were even more misleading than the ones that had been spread by the *Green*

Pamphlet. It was strange that these people thought that violence was the only way of removing these misunderstandings. Talks were completely ruled out for them. Mohandas knew that until he himself went to Durban the misunderstandings could not be cleared. He often also had the feeling that though Indians were spread all over South Africa, in good numbers in some places and not so good in some other, the fight against the Asiatic Law was confined to Transvaal only. Till this struggle spread to all the Indians in South Africa, how would Indians in other British colonies appreciate the meaning of freedom? The fight for Indian franchise had started in Natal, so Natal should also be a party to this fight. If the government succeeded in enforcing the Asiatic Law in this colony, Indians of all the colonies would eventually fall a victim to this law. For them, this was indeed an experiment …'

The sudden appearance of Mohandas in Phoenix created a dilemma for the people. They could not decide how they should welcome him: with smiling or with glum faces. His sudden appearance was nothing short of an apparition. They were under the impression that since Mohandas was under medical advice of rest for a couple of months, there was no question of seeing him before the end of two months. Kastur was very upset about this.

When Kastur saw Mohandas fit and fine, she was speechless with joy. She asked a little later: 'How did all this come about?'

'All because of love,' he said.

'Do they kill someone because of love?'

'Yes. Frustrated love is not easy to take. You need extraordinary determination to do it.'

Kastur was befuddled. 'I don't understand,' she said.

Mohandas joked: 'If you don't understand, who will?' He continued: 'Mir Alam loved, in fact loves, Gandhibhai. He thought of him as a god. You don't ask your god why he does what he does. You form your own ideas of what he should or should not be doing as a god. If he doesn't conform to those ideas, he is no longer a god; he is devil himself. The same love which made him a god for them now makes him an object of hatred. So far as I am concerned, his making me a god did not make me one, and I am no devil now. If he has punished me because he thinks I am a devil now, that's his right. The one who loves you also has the right to hate you ...'

'But why did you keep your mouth shut? Why didn't you press charges against him and get him punished?'

'There was a time when he poured all his love on me. Did I then go round telling the world about it? What should I have got him punished for? He made a god out of me then and I gave him no prizes for it; so what right did I have of getting him punished when he made a devil out of me? It's best to treat a man as a man.'

'Your meaningless philosophizing is totally beyond me. He was trying to kill you and you ask what should you have got him punished for? You can punish only your near and dear ones; for others, you have both love and forgiveness. You left us in this place while yourself you went and set yourself down in Transvaal. Anything could happen to you and all that we could do was to worry! Who is our help and support in this place?'

'The One who helps and supports everyone. Do I help and support everyone? If I am in Transvaal, Polak is here. Millie and his child are in Transvaal.'

Kastur didn't know how to explain her problem to Mohandas. He could appreciate people's problems but only when they were other people. Us, he considers a part of himself. We also must appreciate other people's problems, forgetting our own. Kastur was now speaking to herself.

~

Mohandas called a meeting of all the Indians in Durban. The move caused a commotion. A few Indians came to Mohandas and asked: 'Why are you calling this meeting?'

'Why not? How can I talk to people without calling a meeting? People in Transvaal are fighting against the Asiatic Law. Till every Indian in Transvaal makes it his own fight, how can we protect our rights?'

'That's not what people think here. They are furious. Even Dada Abdullah hasn't opened his mouth. The French businessman, Marcel, is here these days and he is going around saying that you and Ali were his guests in London and it was out of his regard for him that Lord Elgin refused approval to the Asiatic Bill. At the same time, he is also saying that you stabbed the Transvaal Indians in the back and now it is the Durban Indians who are up for betrayal.'

'That makes no difference to me. I am going to talk to Indians directly. The war of Indians in South Africa is a joint war, irrespective of whether it is fought in Transvaal, or Orange State or Natal.'

'Why don't you understand? People are upset. They think you have reached an understanding with General Smuts.'

'That issue too needs to be sorted out.'

One of the persons got up and asked: 'And if you are assaulted again?'

'So that means I should neither call a meeting, nor attend it, does it?' He laughed.

'But ...'

'No ifs and buts. You think I should desert the people who stood by me for so long just because they might attack me? When a master calls out to his servant and the servant doesn't answer out of fear, the servant loses the right to serve. What would you call a person who takes a vow of service and then quits his chosen path because he fears punishment? Service to others brings you appreciation and happiness, but it also teaches you to persevere in your chosen path despite all difficulties, adversities and neglect. If there are garlands of flowers on one side, there is the sharp edge of the sword on the other. If you think that you can collect the garlands and sidestep the sword, you are mistaken.'

His friends were now convinced that Gandhi was quite oblivious to the impending disaster. Durban was no longer what it used to be.

Mohandas was however totally at peace with himself.

~

The meeting was held at eight o'clock in the evening. Sheth Daud Mohammad was in the Chair. With his permission, Mohandas proceeded to give an account of the agreement reached with General Smuts. Questions from the audience followed. Mohandas started to answer the questions in a calm and patient manner.

A Pathan was then seen moving towards the raised platform and suddenly the lights went off. Pandemonium followed. People started running helter-skelter. There were cries and shouts. Daud Mohammad stood up on the table and shouted: 'Please keep quiet and listen to Gandhibhai. Do not get excited.'

Some people formed a security ring around Mohandas. People who were anticipating that something like thing could happen were ready for the occasion. One of them had even brought a revolver with him, which he now fired. It was dark and noisy and people were running around and hitting out crazily. Nobody could see anything, nor knew what to do. Rustomji Parsi got up quietly and, despite his bulk, started running. The police station was close by. By sheer chance, the Captain of Police, Alexander, happened to be present at the station. When he saw the breathless Rustomji, he got worried. Rustomji told him the whole story in one breath. Alexander at once dispatched a squad and told Rustomji. 'This friend of yours enjoys a good beating and makes sure that his attackers go unpunished. Someday, his own people may hang him on the Cross like Jesus.'

All that Rustomji could say was: 'So, what'll be new about it? Such people always meet such an end.'

When the police reached the spot, it formed a passageway to escort Mohandas out. He was taken to Rustomji Parsi's house, where Rustomji and Alexander were already waiting for him.

Alexander looked at Gandhi and said: 'Don't you think, Mr. Gandhi that it may be Durban or Johannesburg, people everywhere are thirsting for your blood. What is in your blood that makes it so special?'

Mohandas laughed and said: 'Love! My wife asked me the same question and I gave her the same answer.'

'I don't understand.'

'Such a simple thing and neither my wife nor the Police Superintendent of Durban can understand it. It's only because of love that people get angry with me and get so angry with me that they are hell-bent to see me get the severest punishment. Don't you think that those who love you also have a right to punish you?'

Alexander kept staring at Mohandas for a while. Then, stepping forward, he took Mohandas' hands in his own and stood there wordlessly with his eyes closed.

'Mr. Gandhi, these people will one day hang you for sure. In their eyes, what you are doing is illegal and against their philosophy of mankind.'

~

Mohandas was Rustomji Parsi's guest in Durban. Rustomji spent a restless night pacing the room. What could be the solution to this tricky problem? Why were the Pathans so mad with Gandhibhai, both in Transvaal as well as here? Johannesburg was going to be repeated in Durban, though Durban was Gandhi's hometown. Everyone in Durban, be he a Hindu, a Muslim, a Parsi or a Christian, loved Gandhibhai dearly. Ever since Marcel had come back, he had been trying his best to incite the people against Gandhibhai. He was a regular visitor to Dada Abdullah and in fact to Rustomji himself too, but he never let go a chance to pour venom on Gandhi. Rustomji always cut him short, suggesting that they talk about something else. Dada Abdullah too did not like him talking ill of Gandhibhai, but his respect for the white colour got the better of him. As a result, Marcel must be counting him as one of his supporters.

The next day, Rustomji left home rather early. Mohandas had a pile of letters to attend to. He did check on Rustomji twice but he was told that he had left home early and that he would be returning by ten. Last night's incident still weighed on Mohandas' mind. He asked himself who was right: he or they? I could well be wrong. Why is a compromise wrong in their eyes? Then he forced his mind away from the topic and tried to concentrate on the letters.

When Rustomji returned at ten o'clock, he had with him several leading members of the Pathan community. Mohandas was all bathed and ready by then. The sight of the visitors startled Mohandas at first. So this was the purpose of Rustomji's early morning foray, he thought. Then he went up to them, embraced them all and offered them seats very respectfully.

Rustomji was the one to speak first: 'Gandhibhai,' he said, 'You belong to us all. I do not wish that any one of us should carry any misunderstanding about you. We all worked together in the franchise case. What happened yesterday has hurt me deeply.'

One of the Pathans asked: 'Gandhibhai, why did you break your word and give your consent to the proposal for giving our fingerprints to the government? How did a single meeting with General Smuts change you so completely?'

'Our struggle was against the Asiatic Law. If we didn't stop it at this stage, its tentacles would have reached all the Asians living in British colonies. Our first concern was to stop the Asiatic Bill at whatever cost it was our main object and the only way of achieving this object was a compromise. That was the only hope I could see of helping the Indian and Asiatic people escape the dreadful provisions of that terrible bill.'

'If that was the case, we could have united Asians of all the colonies in a long struggle against the law.'

'Yes, I thought if that was possible. I don't think the Indians could have been united. Transvaal Indians fight their own wars, Natal Indians fight their own. They are all a scattered, unorganized lot. The Indians of Transvaal were in jail; there were some Chinese and Malay with them too—all peddlers and *girmitiya*s living a hand to mouth existence. I considered it my first duty to get them out of prison.'

'Gandhibhai, that was something we should have thought of before we started the *satyagraha*, shouldn't we?'

'I don't think so. The rich and the resourceful were sitting at home, while these people rotted in jails. Their children were crying for food, though they didn't complain, nor did their kids. They had to show solidarity, didn't they? But the rich weren't even looking towards them.'

'The message the compromise conveyed was that you had let the Indian people down.'

Mohandas laughed and said: 'Suspicion is in our blood, like a poison. I don't think any amount of explanation will get rid of it. The only way to remove it is to pray and to seek purification of your souls.'

They got up and left. Their faces showed indignation.

The people who had formed a protective ring round Mohandas the previous evening were also present at Rustomji's house the next day. Their leader was a man called Jake Moodley. Moodley was a Tamil, but he was born in Natal. He was a boxer and people, black or white, generally avoided taking him on.

Mohandas had to leave for Phoenix the same day. When Moodley got to know he came and said: 'We can't let you go alone.'

Mohandas tried to discourage them but they wouldn't listen. Mohandas said: 'Look, if you insist on coming with me despite my refusal, there is nothing I can do. But Phoenix is a wild area. Phoenix people may not be able to arrange food for you. If that happens, what are you going to eat? Phoenix people may in fact have to fast because of you.' Mohandas laughed like a child.

One of Moodley's companions said: 'Gandhibhai, such talk is not going to discourage us. We are quite capable of looking after ourselves.'

Moodlay also laughed and said: 'We can always raid other people's kitchens.'

'Phoenix is not Durban,' said Gandhi.

They all followed Gandhi like tourists. From time to time, they raised a huge cry and then continued on their way singing.

Throughout the journey, Mohandas had the feeling of something like a woodpecker pecking away in his head, but whenever he tried to pause and identify him, he just disappeared. Mohandas continued chasing him right up to Phoenix, but all through the journey the woodpecker pecked in his head and flew off the moment he tried to get hold of him.

The news of Mohandas' arrival had preceded him to Phoenix. People were worried and excited too. When they saw Mohandas accompanied by some unknown characters, their suspicions were confirmed. What they had heard was not wrong. Something had happened.

Kastur and the kids stood silently, hoping he would come out with it himself. But Mohandas said nothing on the topic. So, Hari asked: '*Bapu*, we heard that there was some trouble at the Durban meeting too?'

Mohandas laughed and said: 'This is going to be a regular happening. You'll get tired asking and I'll be tired answering your questions.' Then, turning to Kastur, he said: 'For some time, surrender your Mohandas to the society. My love for you cramps me. There is something inside me that tears at my soul: What if something happens to you? This love turns into a trial by fire for me.'

Kastur thought better not to say anything at all, although the thought was in her mind: You have renounced us already, so where is the question of our surrendering you to anyone? We don't have any right.

At night, Mohandas decided to sleep in the open instead of indoors. Kastur didn't say it herself but sent a message through West: 'Tell him to sleep indoors.'

'Why?'

'Why?' she thought. 'So much is happening and he asks why?' West put it briefly: 'Safety considerations.'

'Safety against whom? Against oneself or against others?'

'I don't understand.'

'Safety against others doesn't necessarily make you safe against yourself.'

West held his peace. Mohandas slept in the open and the people who had come with him from Durban also joined him. They took turns at keeping a watch.

Mohandas tried to persuade them: 'Go and sleep. There is no danger here. The wilds look dangerous but are actually safer than the cities.'

'If we feel sleepy, we'll go to sleep. It' so nice here, one doesn't feel like sleeping.'

A short time after Mohandas lay down to sleep, the woodpecker started again. In the surrounding silence, the pecking got louder and louder. Mohandas went and stood right where the pecking was on. There was one small question which was spawning question after question: 'Why did you get so many of them here?'

'It was their wish.'

'Yes, but how hard did you try to stop them?'

'Not hard at all.'

'Were you afraid of death?'

Mohandas had no answer. Something was knocked down somewhere and Mohandas was startled.

'See ...?' The woodpecker asked.

Mohandas sat up in his bed. Moodley was awake. 'What is it, Gandhibhai?' he asked at once.

Gandhibhai lay down again.

The woodpecker whispered in his ears again: 'Whatever happened to the faith on which you sailed across seven seas to get here?'

'I think of death merely as a transformation.'

'Why are you afraid then?'

Mohandas looked up to the sky: 'I don't know how long I have been washing myself in the waters of your faith only to rid myself of this fear.' He paused and then said: 'Fear of death? *Satyagraha* and fear? How can the two go together? Death is a celebration of transformation. Should one fear a celebration?

Mohnadas felt the pecking fading away. His eyes began to feel heavy.

He told Moodley the first thing in the morning: 'I think the fear of death had seized me that was why I let you come here with me. But I am no longer afraid of death. You may please go back. Your presence here has helped me a lot in getting rid of that fear. I am deeply grateful to you for it.'

Moodley tried to protest.

Mohandas said: 'Please do not upset yourself. Death can come in any form: it could be a flower, or a snake. No one, not you, not me, would be able to stop death. So, it's best to welcome it. *Satyagraha* means welcome to every truth. Death is the biggest truth of all. You never know when it will come and embrace you like a long-lost friend.'

Moodley and others were staring at his face like small, innocent lambs.

Mohandas made up his mind to spend some time at Phoenix. Most of the letters to *Indian Opinion* were critical of Mohandas for the compromise he had reached with General Smuts. Mohnadas wanted to establish contacts with Indians living in Transvaal and Durban using these letters as the excuse. He always said: 'A leader is a servant of the people. His conduct should be like a book open to all and sundry. Every question addressed to him is like a debt which it is his first responsibility to repay.'

So, Mohandas was replying to each of the charges levelled against him point by point.

'I agreed to a compromise,' he wrote, 'because I wanted the Indians and Asiatics settled in the British colonies to escape the poison of the Asiatic Law. But I do not have a monopoly of this compromise. Transvaal Asians can reject it, if they so want. Everything—from the agreement to the parties to the agreement—is in the dock before you. The judgment is in your hands.'

The compromise controversy in the pages of *Indian Opinion* was being followed widely by everyone—by people who could read as well as those who couldn't, the latter having it read out to them. Some agreed, some didn't, but they all helped to resolve its complexities and raise issues. People sometimes just agreed to agree and sometimes they agreed to disagree. But, by and by, more people were agreeing to agree and the number of people agreeing to disagree started going down. The numbers at the Registration Centres were beginning to rise steeply. Work in the offices was becoming unmanageable. Then there came a time when Asians, especially Indians, were through with their share of work.

Mohandas was beginning to wonder how vulnerable violence was. A little peace and it loses its grip. Had Mir Alam and his friends finished Mohandas instead of leaving him injured, had the community remained indifferent and said nothing, even forgiven Mir Alam thinking that he was capable of doing no better, they would have realized their error and all the misunderstandings would have been cleared up. As far as a *satyagrahi* is concerned, what better death could he expect than dying for the sake of truth? You cannot forgive, nor can you love, till you have cleaned your heart and mind of all hatred.

Hari came up right then and asked: '*Bapu*, are you going to Johannesburg?'

'Yes.'

'I want to come too.'

'You stay with *Ba* for now. When the time comes, I'll send for you.'

'There's nothing for me to do here. There, I will join *satyagraha*.'

'Sure, but not now. Stay here and learn the essence of service and sacrifice.'

Kastur was keeping quiet. When she saw that she was losing the game, she joined in: 'Why don't you take him with you? You must be getting bored all alone.'

'Who has the time to get bored? When I have the time, I'll join you here or will send for you. Till then, I'll be on the move all the time.'

'You have created enemies wherever you have gone. We cannot sleep peacefully any more.'

'Who says they are my enemies? They are my touchstones. They are touchstones of my love for truth, my tolerance, my love for others. They won't touch me. They in fact tell me how much untruth, intolerance and hatred have risen higher or sunk lower in me.'

'Fine,' said Kastur, 'Torture us the best you can.'

'Torture you? In fact, you should be happy that you are my partner in this scorching pursuit of truth. You are actually my face in this struggle.'

Kastur got up and left. The lump in the throat was beginning to hurt.

~

General Smuts had the reputation of the ablest leader and administrator in South Africa. He enjoyed a fairly high ranking in the list of colonial rulers. He was known as 'Slim Jenny' in the whole of South Africa. He was indeed slim, but full-bodied and tall. Many of Mohandas' friends had warned him to be cautious in his dealings with Slim Jenny. It was hard, they told him, to make out the real meaning of what he said. Only Slim Jenny knew what he meant; others could keep guessing only to discover at the end that what he meant was quite different not only from what you thought he said but also from what all others thought he said. There was some third sense which was the correct one. It could also be a fourth one. The arguments he put forward persuaded everyone that eventually he was right and everyone else wrong.

Mohandas realized this when it was too late. People generally attributed to Mohandas the ability to judge people quickly and correctly. However, when it came to agreements, Mohandas placed his trust only on trust. You give trust and in turn you receive trust.

Nearly all Indians had given their fingerprints and got themselves registered. Other Asians too had gone along. All in all, the Indians had kept their side of the deal. It was now the government's turn. General Smuts had to carry out his promise and repeal the Asiatic Law so that Transvaal Indians could withdraw their *satyagraha*. The fight was now against the black law and not against the government or against General Smuts.

On reaching Transvaal, Mohandas found out that the Asiatic Law would remain intact with both its new names and all its provisions. The only change would be that the government would extend recognition to voluntary registrations. At the end of the validity period of this registration, they would have to re-register themselves under the law. The Asiatic Law, armed to the teeth, would then be staring the Asians in the face. Mohandas was aghast. Such a great ruler and so mean an action! Mohandas thought of Albert Cartwright. He went and told him: 'You mediated on his behalf. You assured us of his cooperation. Now tell us what we should do. How de we convince the people that it was not a false agreement, that it had actually taken place and that the government was now going back on it.'

Cartwright was a journalist. He thought it over and then said: 'Mr. Gandhi, I quite fail to understand what sort of person we are dealing with. He had promised to repeal the law. But the fellow is stubborn and no one can make him budge an inch.'

'Please write the truth in your newspaper and let the people know the truth.'

Cartwright laughed: 'You may splash this in all the newspapers, but it won't make any difference to him. I don't think I'll be able to do much to help you.'

Mohandas also laughed. 'You have given me my first lesson in politics: how even a newspaper surrenders its loyalty to truth to a powerful enough ruler.'

Cartwright fumbled for a few minutes for an answer and then became silent.

Mohandas did not accept defeat. He met Hosken next and said: 'You came to our meeting with his message. What do you say now?'

Hosken wrote a letter to General Smuts. He received a short reply in a few days: 'General Smuts will take up your letter for consideration at the appropriate time.'

Mohandas had now no choice except to get back to himself. He started the process of self-analysis. Where did I go wrong? *Satyagraha* was not wrong. Trusting people was not wrong. Was there a deficiency in my own determination? He immediately called a meeting. No matter who may have been wrong, correction and atonement were possible only through the mediation of people. He made a clean breast of everything: How the talks were arranged; who were the go-betweens; how General Smuts went back on his word; how the mediators had washed their hands of the affair.

A member of the audience stood up and said: 'The other day when the Pathan tore into you and your agreement, we thought there was a conspiracy afoot to humiliate you and we went along with you. Now it appears that he was right and we were wrong. If a matter is a personal one, you are welcome to trust any one you like. It makes no difference to others. But this was a matter which concerned the entire community and all the Asians. Why should they suffer humiliation because of a personal decision made by you?'

'Because of your decision people's spirit will desert them forever,' said another.

'You know the stuff we Indians are made of. It takes us long to develop our spirit. A little jolt and it goes to pieces. You have to turn the small wave into an instantaneous storm or it simply fizzles out. Our spirit is like a feeble ocean wave.'

Having heard them all, Mohandas stood up to speak: 'I know it's in my nature to trust people. That's something that everyone needs to have, not just me. Trust which cannot stand a small jolt; I would not call trust at all. This may be a personal shortcoming with me, but my shortcomings come with my virtues. I offer myself to you as I am. I am not ready to concede that our spirit, our zeal or our determination is like a feeble wave. Every wave of the ocean has in it to become a storm. If you compare your and my spirit to a wave that dissipates quickly, you are being unfair to me and to yourself. In a long struggle like this one, ebb and tide will follow each other. However well you may know your adversary, you can never stop him from going back on his word. How many of us have loaned and borrowed money on the strength of IOUs? What can be a stronger verification than your signature or thumb impression? Still there are lawsuits and court cases; there are court decisions, decrees and confiscations. How much money and time is wasted in such activities! Can you read in someone's face if he is honest or dishonest? Who can vouch for another person's conduct? You cannot vouch for me; I cannot vouch for General Smuts. Yet everyone must have the courage to stand up against injustice, especially the victims. Our struggle is not yet at an end. A *satyagrahi*'s gaze is fixed at the truth. He does not give up the pursuit of truth under the pressure of untruth.'

Cachalia had been sitting quietly. Now he stood up and spoke a single sentence: 'We are ready for the struggle.'

Yusuf Mian, the Chairman, was also quiet. Now he looked about him and said: 'I am with you. But, in the present conditions, it won't be possible for me to continue to act as President of the Association.'

Someone moved a proposal: 'Let Cachalia be the President in place of Yusuf Mian.'

It was a fresh proposal and no one had the time to give it careful consideration. They all raised their hands and Cachalia was elected President of the *Satyagraha* Association.'

The Association started preparations for a movement under the Presidentship of Cachalia. Word was sent around that everyone should be ready to fight the arbitrary and duplicitous behaviour of the government. Registration certificates were being collected from everyone. Letters to the government all went unanswered. All complaints met with a deafening silence. In the end, the Association found itself obliged to send a final warning to General Smuts informing him of its decision. A draft was got ready. 'An agreement had been reached between General Smuts and the Indian community that if the Indians got themselves registered voluntarily, the Asiatic Law would be repealed and voluntary registrations would be accorded official approval. Since Indians and other Asians have already fulfilled their side of the deal, the government is now requested to repeal the black law as promised in the deal. The Association has sent several communications to General Smuts on this subject but he has chosen to turn a deaf ear to our requests. The matter of official approval to voluntary registrations is also hanging fire in the parliament. People's representatives of Transvaal should make the parliament aware of the increasing discontent among Indians and Asians on this account. We regret having to say that if the Asiatic Law is not repealed as per the agreement and due information is not given to us by a definite date, Indians will be obliged to make a public conflagration of the certificates.'

The draft was read out at an ordinary meeting of the Association. One of the members asked: 'Is it necessary to ask for the information to be given by a definite date?'

Another supported the point of view: 'This may lead to a hardening of the government's attitude.'

'When they read this threat, they will simply throw our letter into the dustbin, even if they were inclined to consider our demand sympathetically.'

'It might be better if we didn't send anything in writing. We could simply announce our decision.'

As many mouths, so many opinions. There seemed to be no end to the discussion. Cachalia had to intervene: 'Suppose we accept your suggestion and approach the masters with our heads bowed, bare feet and folded hands, do you think they will agree to consider our request?'

Mohandas elaborated on his point: 'This is a risk we will have to take. They may tell us we are lying. They may reject our demands on reading this sentence despite being otherwise prepared to concede them. However they may regard us, we are nevertheless human beings like them. If we believe that we can put up with any adversity to secure the rights that properly belong to us, we have no choice but to follow this path.'

Some members of the trading community kept their own counsel. Others came out in open support of the draft. War had been declared.

Some people had rather long faces.

When Cachalia reached home, he found the assistants of some white traders waiting for him. Cachalia at once guessed what was up.

'What can I do for you?' asked Cachalia.

'We want our money back,' they came to the point directly without any preface.

Cachalia knew that this was not the accepted way of demanding money invested in business. He said very politely: 'We are business partners of long standing. The conditions for the receipt of goods and payment, etc. are all set in the agreement.'

'That's fine, but when you need money, nothing else will do. We need money now, so we want our money back,' one of the white assistants said.

'I'm not in a position to return your money now.'

Another one of the assistants offered: 'You can be spared on one condition.'

'And that is?'

'Dissociate yourself from Gandhi's passive resistance like Yusuf Mian.'

'And if I don't?'

'Then we must have our money.'

'If you are arrested tomorrow, what happens to our money?'

'Therefore, we must have our money in cash.'

'Look, this is a personal matter. Whether or not I take part in *satyagraha* has nothing to do with my business. My faith, my religion, the honour of the Indian community—everything is at stake here. I am grateful to the white community for helping me in my business in every possible way. But there are limits to gratitude. All I can do is to assure you that your money is quite safe with me. I'll repay every penny I owe you before I die. If something happens to me in the meantime, you have my balance sheets and business records, and the goods in the warehouse, which you can use to claim your money.'

They paid no attention to him and left.

Cachalia's firm was declared bankrupt by the court a short while later.

When Cachalia learnt of it, he laughed and said: 'I am more of a free man now. By confiscating my property, they have released me from those chains which I myself was unable to break. There were times when I feared that the threat of confiscation of my property might make me bend before the whites and accept their condition. But I realize now that adversity has a way of equipping you to deal with it.'

Cachalia had opened a door which would lead the whites to think twice before they applied the same technique to other traders since it could affect their own business. Cachalia had made a dangerous leap, but by doing so he had saved other traders from many dangers. It had of course also done a lot to boost their courage.

The day the parliament was to pass the ordinance was also the last date of the ultimatum served by the *Satyagraha* Association. General Smuts had already reacted: 'What do these Indian rats take themselves to be? How dare they serve an ultimatum on us? They haven't yet seen what the government can do! There are a few troublemakers among them who are inciting the poor and want to see them destroyed.'

The newspapers had made a big deal of General Smuts' reaction.

~

August 16, 1908. The *satyagrahi*s were asked to gather in the compound of the Hamidiya mosque at four o'clock in the afternoon, but people had started collecting at two. People expected that the government might still see sense and make a reasonable proposal, in which case the meeting could be used for making an official announcement instead of *satyagraha.* That way, people could not complain of a wasted trip, and the meeting would have served a purpose. At the same time, people also realized that the government would not bend so easily: after all it was a government! But still, against all hope, there was a slight ray of hope.

The meeting was attended by members of all sections of the Indian community: Hindus, Muslims, Parsis, Christians, traders, *girmitiya*s, non-*girmitiya*s and so on. The ground was packed to capacity. A huge brazier, normally used for community cooking, had been placed in the middle of the ground with a fire blazing away in it. Sparks flew when the coal in it ignited. Everyone was quite assured that the fire was not likely to go out soon.

The proceedings were about to start when Mohandas saw a volunteer rushing to the site pushing his bicycle hard. Everyone's eyes turned on him. Till he arrived, everyone was swinging between hope and despair. Everyone was praying that the government might have seen sense and might have decided to honour, or to promise to honour, the sentiments of such a large number of people. The volunteer handed over a sheet of paper to the President. Everyone held his breath as it was opened: What would it say—yes or no? It was a telegram which said: 'Decision of Indian community unfortunate STOP Government unable to change decision.'

All doubts were set at rest. Some people started dancing with joy: the chance to burn the certificates had almost escaped them. There was prolonged applause. More coal had been shovelled into the brazier. The coal was igniting and the air was quaking with the heat it emitted.

Cachalia stood up. He gave a full account of the developments so far. Mohandas was asked to speak next. He said: 'If there is anyone here who might have deposited his certificate with us but, on reconsideration, wants to have it back, he can step up here and collect his certificate without the slightest hesitation. Burning your certificate is not a crime and does not make you liable to any punishment. All that it implies is that we do not accept this law and that we are now burning the registrations we made taking the government at its word, which now stands dishonoured, so that we can be free from the obligation of producing the certificates when the police ask for them. It will of course be a crime not to produce the certificate on demand. You will be disobeying a law which you refuse to accept. But even after the certificate has been burnt, if someone wants a certified copy and wants to stay within the bounds of law, he can obtain the copy from the registration office. Those who are unable to muster enough courage to face the consequences of failing to produce the certificate on demand still have an opportunity to take their certificates back. In fact, even doing this will require no less courage.' After a pause, he said: 'We should all be clear in our minds about one thing. This is not going to be a two-day war. We are in it for a long haul. Many of our friends have already withdrawn from the advancing contingent of this army. The remaining ones also have to bear the burden of their responsibilities. Please think calmly about all these facets of the problem before joining the fray.'

There was a collective cry: 'We want to have nothing to do with these certificates. Let's burn them.'

Mohandas raised his voice and asked them: 'If there is anyone who wants to speak against this motion, let him speak out without hesitation.'

Their necks swivelled towards one another for a couple of minutes as if they were screwed to their bodies. Everyone was trying to assess everyone else to see who could be against the proposal. Mir Alam sat in a corner with his friends without speaking a word. Now he stood up to speak, causing a suspenseful silence throughout the benches. What would he say? Mohandas asked: 'You have something to say, Mir Alam Bhai?'

He stood quietly for a while as if trying to find his balance. Then the words came out: 'I plead guilty. I attacked Gandhibhai.' His voice quivered. There was a sigh of relief all round. He was unable to continue for some time. Then he came and stood close to Gandhibhai and handed his certificate to him and said: 'Gandhibhai, this is my original certificate. I and my friends did not get the new certificate, under the new law, by giving our fingerprints. I got this certificate when I came here first. I have no desire to retain even this certificate.'

Gandhibhai took both his hands in his own. The audience could not decide for some time how to greet the scene: with applause or with silent appreciation. The applause started after a pause.

Yusuf Mian was the oldest among them. It had been decided that the holy task of burning the certificates should be initiated by him. Certificates dipped in kerosene were handed to him and he would drop them into the brazier with his own hands. They immediately broke into flames and a cry of joy went up. About two thousand certificates were consigned to flames.

When all the certificates had been disposed of, a man came up waving his certificate. He dipped it in the kerosene and said: 'I hereby hand this certificate to Yusuf Mian. Please burn it. I wanted to burn my certificate with everyone watching. It is a celebration for me.'

Yusuf Mian took his certificate and put it in the fire. It was reduced to ashes instantaneously. Then the man shook hands with Yusuf Mian and Gandhi and returned to his seat with his head held high as if he had beaten a mighty foe.

Another man got up. He said: 'I was unable to muster enough courage. I was suspicious that others may withdraw their certificates later. But when all the certificates are now gone, I ask if so many can go without certificates, why can't I? We will all live and die together.'

'Yes, we'll all live and die together,' chorused everyone present.

It was however life and not death that was in the air all round.

~

Another law called the Transvaal Immigration Restriction Law had been promulgated at the same time as the Asiatic Act. It was aimed mainly at Indians. Unauthorized entry into Transvaal invited three kinds of punishment: fine, imprisonment and deportation. It was up to the magistrate to decide whether one or all the three penalties were to be awarded in a case. Deportation meant expulsion of the accused outside Transvaal borders, maybe Natal or Orange Free State or the East African Portuguese colony. Indians entering Transvaal illegally were pushed outside the borders and left to fend for themselves.

While the war against the Asiatic Act was on, it was also becoming necessary to start a struggle against the Immigration Restriction Act. The question was whether they should concentrate on a single issue at a time or should start the struggle against the Immigration Restriction Act also simultaneously. Would it send out the wrong signal if they did so?

A meeting of the *Satyagraha* Association was called.

There was a difference of opinion among the members. Some thought they should carry out an open fight against the Immigration Act too.

Mohandas said: 'If we start *satyagraha* on every issue, we will only devalue it. The "insistence on truth" will turn into plain and bad insistence. There is little to gain by starting a *satyagraha* without a clear idea of our strength except defeat and humiliation.'

'On the other hand, if we do nothing, it will be interpreted to mean that that we have no problem with the law, while, in actuality, this law is a tweedledum to the Asiatic Act's tweedledee.' Most people seemed to be in agreement with this view.

'We must include the Immigration Restriction Act in our *satyagraha* programme as it is a fresh assault on our rights. We shall not put up with it.'

A leader seated on the stage added: 'If you consider yourself too weak to take on a couple of challenges to your rights, you might as well give up your struggle against the Asiatic Act too and toe the government's line in all matters.'

'We should not think of ourselves as so weak that attack after attack on our rights should leave us unmoved.'

Mohandas stood up and said: 'If all of you wish that the Immigration Restriction Act should be made part of the *satyagraha* movement, I have no objection. If you are so firm and determined in your protest, I am sure this battle will be a decisive one.'

Some people got so carried away that they wanted all anti-Indian or anti-Asian laws in all the colonies of South Africa brought into the ambit of the protest and argued that Indians all over South Africa should be persuaded to join the *satyagarah* against them.

'A good suggestion,' said others, 'We must start a protest ...'

Mohandas could see that people had failed to appreciate the spirit of *satyagraha* as well as their own strength. They were being carried away by their own rhetoric. He said: 'I can understand your feelings; so, I'm sure, does everyone else. But we must also consider the practical and moral questions associated with this issue. Taking a decision today on an issue of which we had no inkling when *satyagraha* was first started would be immoral and impractical. I am already being accused by General Smuts of being cunning, though I don't think he can cite a single example of my cunning. If we wander off, we cannot be a *satyagrahi*; you need to be able to walk a taut rope with the concentration and balancing skill of a street magician to be one.'

Everyone listened silently. Mohandas carried on after a pause: '*Satyagraha* is like the stream of the river Ganga. When it comes down from the hills, it does not go asking the springs and the cataracts to come and join it. Rather, they come and join her on their own, lending greater and greater spread to its stream. There is no *satyagraha*, and there is no *satyagrahi*, unless you join the stream.'

No one had any answer to Mohandas' argument.

~

Though the *Satyagraha* Association had taken the Immigration Restriction Law on its agenda, the question was how to conduct the movement against this law. In order to break this law, they would have to get some people to join their movement who were prohibited from entering Transvaal under this law. A relief that the Act provided, rather a clause that it included, was that anyone wishing to enter Transvaal must know at least one European language. Anyone without this qualification could not even be considered for entry. It was therefore decided that the man to be selected for entry into Transvaal must at least know English, whatever else he might or might not know. The neighbouring colonies were notified that they should send names of young men who knew English and who were ready to enter Transvaal at the risk of being jailed. Quite a few Indian young men offered themselves. The one to be selected was a Parsi gentleman. Mohandas had always carried a very special opinion about Parsis. There would be about a hundred thousand Parsis in the whole world. Despite being in such small numbers, they had always ensured an honourable place for themselves in the society. They were also known for their munificence.

The gentleman selected was Sorabji Shapurji Adajania. Mohandas was challenged even for this selection. He was asked: 'Are you sure that this man will be able to withstand government pressure?'

Mohandas did not mince words: 'I don't know Sorabji very well, but his letters gave me the impression that government pressure will not deter him.'

When Mohandas felt deeply about something, he spoke forcefully in its favour and people did not have any problem believing him. The name of Sorabji was unanimously approved.

Sorabji notified the government in advance that he would be defying the Immigration Restriction Act and enter Transvaal on a certain date, a certain time and a certain place. On the notified date, time and place Sorabji crossed the Transvaal border and made straight for the Immigration Officer and spoke to him in English. 'I am Sorabji Shapurji Adajania, a resident of Natal, and I am now entering Transvaal. You may take whatever action is required of you.'

'I know you,' said the Immigration Officer.

'I am entering Transvaal to find out how the government will react under the new law. Please satisfy yourself about my knowledge of English. If there is anything you wish to ask, I am ready to answer.'

'That won't be necessary. I am already familiar with your competence in English. We have met before.'

'I am breaking the law. You can arrest me, if you so wish.'

The officer was getting nervous. 'I have no instructions to take you into custody. You are free to go wherever you please. If the government wants to arrest you, it can do so anywhere.'

Sorabji was surprised. What kind of law was this which its protectors cannot safeguard?

Sorabji made straight for Johannesburg. The *Satyagraha* Association accorded him a rousing welcome. There was a celebration. Victory! A *satyagrahi* succeeds in entering Transvaal! The government has lost!

Mohandas tried to explain to the people: 'Not quite. Actually, government officers are not even aware of their rights under the law. Moreover, there is the arrogance of power. A *satyagrahi*, on the other hand, is fully aware of his responsibility and is ready to lay down his life for it. When the government finds out that a *satyagrahi* from Natal made a forcible entry into Transvaal and broke a cast iron law, things will begin to move. They will then not try to see what might have been wrong with the law; they will simply target the lawbreaker. Do not take it as a victory. We are miles away from a victory.'

As soon as he arrived in Johannesburg, Sorabji informed the police that he had entered Transvaal by transgressing the immigration law and that he believed that he had a right to live in Transvaal.

There was no response to his notice for many days. Sorabji went around Johannesburg without any let or hindrance. He told everyone he met very cheerfully how he had entered Transvaal, violating the immigration law, to test his right to stay in Transvaal. He wanted to test the stuff he was made of. Would he last or would he break down?

Listening to him whites were reduced to despair while Indians broke into applause. But Sorabji made no comments, either on the reaction of the whites or on the glee displayed by the Indians.

One early morning, Sorabji received a summons from the court. He had been asked to present himself in the court on July 8, 1908. The charges were not mentioned. Sorabji was in the court with Mohandas at the exact hour. The court was packed with spectators, mostly Indians and other Asians. They were eager to see the court's attitude in the Sorabji case. Sorabji had already made a public declaration that as a *satyagrahi* he considered prison to be his rightful place and that he was ready to take any risk. The final victory, he said, would belong to *satyagraha.*

The case was called. Mohandas asked the court: 'Milord! Why has my client been summoned to appear before the court?'

'You know it.'

'That doesn't help my client. If my client doesn't know the charges against him, how can he present a defence? Will the court announce its verdict without listening to the defence? If that is the case, even the summons was not required.'

The magistrate examined the summons and put off the case for the next day.

Outside, Mohandas said to Sorabji: 'Well, you escaped today.'

Sorabji laughed and said: 'I would have been happy to be sent to jail today. At least, my struggle would enter the second phase. Now I am still stuck in the first.'

Mohandas said: 'I knew only what your letters revealed to me about you. Your selection as the first *satyagrahi* was entirely based on them. I'm glad our choice turned out to be correct.'

The next day, Sorabji was let off with a warning, but was asked to present himself to the court again on July 10.

'The second phase starts tomorrow,' said Mohandas.

That made Sorabji happy like a child.

Sorabji had been handed the summons for the tenth right there. This time the summons spelled out the charges. Mohandas knew what was coming.

On the next hearing, Mohandas stood up to argue the case. The magistrate stopped him and announced his judgment: 'Sorabji Shapurji Adajania, resident of Natal, is hereby ordered to leave Transvaal in seven days.'

Sorabji whispered to Mohandas: 'Why did the magistrate allow seven days?'

'So that you can say call on your friends and relatives, consider everything carefully and decide whether or not to leave Transvaal.'

Sorabji had a good laugh. In fact, he was finding it difficult to control his laughter. When he finally succeeded, he said: 'What does the magistrate think? Will seven days transform Sorabji into a different person? These whites ...'

Back from the court, Sorabji dashed off a letter to the police Captain:

> *I have no intention of leaving Transvaal. As a British citizen, it is my birthright to take up residence in any British colony I like.*

On July 20, Sorabji was sentenced to one month's labour on charges of disobedience. Sorabji danced with joy as if a lifelong wish of his had finally been fulfilled.

~

Satyagraha started with Sorabji, who was a young man. Young men were showing greater and greater alacrity in joining Gandhi in his work, though elderly people were not exactly lagging behind. The other batch of *satyagrahi*s was being led by Daud Mohammad, who had been the President of Natal Congress. He was the first Indian businessman to land in South Africa. He was a Sunni Vohra from Surat. He had a reasonably good command of English and Dutch. He also enjoyed a good standing among white businessmen.

He always had a full house with at least fifty people for every meal. He had lost his only son, Husain, when he was still young. He not only loved his son deeply, he practically worshipped him for his sincerity and his strong belief in Hindu-Muslim parity. Currently, Daud Mohammed's wife was seriously ill.

Daud's batch included, apart from such big traders like Rustomji Parsi, people like Surendra Ram Mehta, Pragji Khandubhai Desai, Ratanji Mulji Sodha and Mohandas' own eldest son, Harilal. Harilal was the youngest of the lot. This army of *satyagrahi*s was marching on foot. The hot season had not yet started and the weather was pleasant. Daudbhai led the pack, Rustomji followed and the rear was brought up by Harilal, a downy growth just beginning to show on his face. The government had been given advance warning about the march, giving some people a cause for amusement. An Indian must beat a drum when he does something, they said. He does it when he is born; he does it when he dies. If you want to force yourself in, go ahead and do it; why shout it from the housetops?

To this, Mohandas had a reply: 'This is *satyagraha*, not burglary!' People however found it difficult to grasp that fairness and fighting can go together. The British believed that everything was fair in love and war. Gandhi however argued that love and war were both crucial to man's existence and that therefore nothing could be right in them except fairness.

When this party arrived at the border, it found that the government had made elaborate preparations for its reception. The government was in a dilemma; it couldn't decide whether to detain them or to let them go. It couldn't possibly have let them go even if it wanted to. When the party stepped forward to cross into Transvaal, the police tried to stop them.

Daudbhai signalled to everyone to continue their advance. As they did, the police issued a warning: 'One step forward and everyone will be arrested.'

'So what?' said Khandubhai. 'We will be guests in the state rest house. Doesn't Gandhibhai say that jails are His Majesty's hotels?'

The police officer's eyes fell on Harilal. He took him to be a curious onlooker who had followed the party for fun. He tried to shoo the boy off: 'Be off, kid, what are you doing here?'

'I didn't come here to be off ...' Harilal was defiant.

'Jail is no fun. You'll die of hard labour. And you aren't even a man yet.'

'What difference does that make? I am a *satyagrahi*. You are a man. Not every man is a brave man, is he?' They were finding it difficult to control their laughter.

The police officer tried to persuade Harilal: 'Look, little boy, your parents will get worried looking for you. Jail is a jail; it's not a playground.'

'I have my mother's permission. My father is in Transvaal.'

'He is Mr. Gandhi's son. He won't be easily persuaded,' said Daudbhai.

'Oh. So you are Gandhi's son!' The officer's face flamed red. He commanded the constables: 'Arrest all of them. Gandhi is the root of the trouble.'

They all sniggered.

The magistrate ordered all of them to leave Transvaal within seven days, but they all told him to his face: 'We refuse to accept your decision.'

The magistrate gritted his teeth.

Ten days later Daud Mian and his party were arrested by the Transvaal government. This time, they were neither sent to jail nor prosecuted; they were simply transported to the border and pushed across. They wandered around for three days without much food and drink. On the fourth day, they re-crossed the border into Transvaal. Everyone was Harilal's senior in age. Daud Mian was perhaps senior even to his father. When Daud Mian began to tire, Harilal took the lead. In barely a fortnight, Harilal had acquired amazing self-confidence. He never got tired, never accepted defeat and never bothered about food and drink. The more he walked, the happier he was. As he walked at the head of others, he felt he had grown up beyond his years.

The minute they crossed the Transvaal border, the police took them into custody once again. This time, the government had decided to prosecute them.

The trial took place on September 8. The hearing lasted the whole day. Mohandas was the lawyer for the accused. The court didn't seem interested in the arguments and Mohandas knew from the indifference of the court that the decision had been reached in advance.

Mohandas stopped in the middle of his arguments and said to the court: 'I have a feeling the court has already arrived at its decision in the case and my arguments are unlikely to make any difference. In the circumstances, it might be better if the verdict is announced right away.'

The magistrate did not try to refute Mohandas' allegation and went on to declare his verdict: 'On the basis of the witnesses produced and the evidence presented, it is established that the accused entered the Transvaal border with the deliberate intention of violating the immigration law. The accused are all fined fifty pounds each. If the fine is not paid within the stipulated period, the accused will have to undergo three months' hard labour.'

No one proposed that they should pay the fine.

~

The jails of Transvaal were filling up. Natal Indians were falling over one another to be the first to enter the jails. Two of these Indians were Imam Abdul Qader and Joseph Royappen. They were arrested on a charge that was too ridiculous to believe. Imam Qader was a man of such delicate upbringing that walking barefoot caused blisters in his feet. Food was his major weakness. His house was provided with every conceivable comfort. He had a Malayali wife. Royappen was a barrister one period after barrister. The two of them came so strongly under the influence of *satyagraha* that they turned into vegetable peddlers carrying vegetable baskets on their heads. Of course, the two had started on this course without mutual consultation, at different times and without any advance planning. In those days, the police were on extra alert and they asked the two for licences. Of course, being fake peddlers, they had no licences, so they were arrested. People thought the government would have sense enough to realize that a respectable man like Imam Qader would turn peddler only as a mode of frivolous protest, and that it couldn't possibly be his means of living. Similar things were also being thought and expressed about barrister Royappen.

When Royappen was arrested, Mohandas was present at the spot. The police were escorting him by train and took him into a third class carriage. Royappen was shocked: 'What? I have to travel third?' he asked.

'If you travel first or second, how will I persuade others to travel third?' asked Mohandas.

Royappen thought for a minute and then said: 'You are right' and that very moment decided that he would now always travel third.

Imam was made of different stuff. When in jail, one day he wasn't feeling well and despite his best effort wasn't able to complete the work assigned to him. When it was dinner time, he refused dinner, saying: 'Since I wasn't able to finish my work, I'll forgo my dinner,' he said.

His friends tried to persuade him to eat, whereupon he laughed and said: 'Gandhibhai wants us to maintain discipline and you want me to break it? *Satyagraha* would lose all its meaning …'

Jail authorities were especially harsh with *satyagrahi*s. Tough tasks were assigned to them like breaking stones, cleaning up or digging up stony surfaces. Sometimes the *satygrahis* would fall unconscious working but no *satyagrahi* ever refused to work. They did their work with complete honesty. If, on a particular day, the assigned work could not be completed, the next day they more than made up for it. Men like Imam would even fast on days they were not able to finish their work. They believed that having your food when your work remained unfinished was betrayal of the trust placed on you.

Troubles were mounting for the Transvaal government day after day. The jails were getting flooded with prisoners. Government expenses were mounting. General Smuts called a meeting of his officials. 'These Indian protesters are giving me a headache,' he told them. 'The jails are overflowing with them. Our expenses are going out of control. These jails were meant for local criminals who were always limited in numbers. No jail has ever been full. But these people are courting arrest with the sole purpose of filling them up. In jail, they are always creating trouble. Sometimes they give up food because they can't have ghee or some other stuff and we have to meet their demands. How long can we go on like this?'

Suggestions started pouring in. 'We must make them work hard and harder till their spirit breaks.'

'No use,' said another officer. 'They already work so hard that they often fall unconscious working but still do not quit work. If they are unable to finish their work some day, they forgo their dinner. Whatever work is assigned to them they accept gladly. They are not run-of-the-mill prisoners.'

Another officer spoke up: 'This is unacceptable. How can we allow them dictate terms to us in jail?'

'They argue that they are following the official rules in letter and spirit. If they are working against anyone's interests, it is their own. There is some secret magical trick this coolie barrister Gandhi has let them into which makes them hold up against all fear and punishment.'

Everyone looked sharply at the officer, who had the uncomfortable feeling that perhaps he had spoken out of turn.

General Smuts hated this kind of talk. 'We have not gathered here to shower praise on the courage and bravery of these people. We must find a way out of our problem. I think the way out is to deport these men back to their country. That's the only way they will bend.'

One officer wanted to make a comment but General Smuts stood up. The officer could not have his say in the presence of Smuts—a regret that the officer took a long time to overcome.

~

The deported Indians were being sent up on the ship. Some of them had their families with them, others were by themselves. The ship was going to India. The majority of those being deported was *girmitiya*s and peddlers, or freshly released *girmitiya*s and small traders. A few of them had been forced to leave their property and businesses behind. Mohandas was going round consoling and comforting every deportee individually.

'We have no money. What are we going to eat?' asked one deportee.

'Food is the government's responsibility on the ship. When you land in India, you will be met by our men.' Though the deportees accepted the answer, the thought kept troubling them that in India no one might even recognize them. Some old people might even have passed away. Those alive might have lost their vision.

A strange thing was that everyone, high or low, had been given the status of deck passengers. Many of them had big homes in Natal or Transvaal, but they too were on the deck. Mohandas went from passenger to passenger and told them: 'We appreciate the difficulties you are facing. But still we would like to know if you regret being deported on account of your association with the *satyagraha*.'

'What is going to happen to our people and our property?'

'Today you are being deported from Transvaal because you joined *satyagraha* to protect your honour. It is possible that tomorrow you might all be deported out of Transvaal without being given any reason for it. The net result will be the same. Some members of your family are staying back and they will take care of your property. But look at these *girmitiya*s and peddlers. Their families are now left without anyone to look after them. They have neither land nor property. Only either Allah or Ram …'

People listened to Mohandas. In him, they thought they had someone who tried to extract their pain out of them. Many of them said nothing. There were others who said: 'Gandhibhai, we have no regrets. God sent us here and God is taking us back. He looked after us here; He will also look after us there. If He so wishes he will bring us back here. We did whatever we did out of our own will because we believed in it and because we believed in truth and self-respect.'

They were calling out to their God—Allah or Ram. Some of them were silent; others had tears in their eyes. Some had their eyes fixed at the distant horizon.

A few traders offered to Mohandas rather hesitantly: 'We have some pounds with us. If you permit, we can distribute them among these people so that when they land in India they won't have to beg or borrow. They'll at least be saved from starvation.'

Mohandas said: 'It's indeed good that you think that way. But don't you think this will invite a blot on *satyagraha*? Word will go round that *satyagraha* is being run on money power. And, come to think of it, I don't think we have enough money to bear their expenses during their stay in India. How long will a few pounds last? Giving them false hope is like giving them a living death. I wouldn't like people who earned their living the hard way in this country to go looking for patronage in India.'

'But …'

For the first time, Mohandas turned emotional. 'Maybe,' he said, 'you would consider me a hard-hearted man, but I think goodwill matters more than money. A friendly glance and a couple of endearments will go a longer way than money. How long will ten or twenty pounds last? One who craves for money has little to do with *satyagraha*. Craving for money is another kind of force which doesn't take too long to turn into a force for evil. It's a force that isolates a man; it leaves him without love and sympathy. A man who has found love, on the other hand, will sacrifice everything for love; he will put up with every adversity for love. Let's not measure sacrifice with money.'

Everyone fell silent, their hands frozen in their pockets.

'If you really want to do something for these people, send one of you with them, someone who can see that they are fed and looked after properly, someone who can mitigate their hardships. It is quite possible that once they are aboard, they are treated like prisoners again.'

No one reacted to this proposal of Mohandas at first. Then one of them said: 'Only a few hours are left for the ship to depart. How can we arrange someone to go with them at such short notice?'

Mohandas called P.K.Naidu and asked him: 'Can you go with these poor, harried and hassled people to India?'

'Sure.'

'The ship is about to leave.'

'So what?'

'What about your clothes and food and so on?'

'The suit I am wearing will do. Food should be available on the ship.'

Mohandas couldn't take his eyes off his face. No body would have believed that any one could agree to go on such a long journey at such short notice.

Mohandas asked Rustomji: 'Do you think you could arrange things?'

Rustomji immediately set about arranging for the ticket, clothes, blankets and some money and Naidu was aboard the ship when it left. He hopped around saying his farewells before getting on to the ship, overjoyed as if he had hit a jackpot.

As the ship was about to leave, Mohandas handed a letter for Natesan to Naidu and said: 'I am sending Natesan a telegram. He will receive you at the Madras port. He is my companion as well as a true friend of these Indians. He will do whatever is in his power for these people. You must put the welfare of these people before your own. And you will have to tell the people in India how the Transvaal government is going against its own laws to deport the Indians.'

Naidu said: 'I am a true soldier and I will stand by your orders till my last breath.'

When the ship set sail, those standing on the shore watched with wet eyes. As for those on the ship, it was all they could do to keep themselves from breaking down.

~

The spirits of the *satyagrahi*s were rising in direct proportion to the severity of the crackdown on them. As a hungry man will not wait for delicacies, so the rising spirits too did not wait for the youth. Old men and children too had donned the *satyagrahi*s' robes. At first, the *satyagrahi*s were being housed together in barracks, so they could at least lend one another courage and support in times of pain and distress. Transvaal winters are biting cold and once the cold seizes you it doesn't let go of you easily. And the seizure could be life-threatening.

In the early days, the government only handed out punishment; now it was ready to take lives. Many of the prisoners had been housed in road camps, where visitors could not reach. Loneliness is the biggest curse of a jail. A few friends or companions can make life bearable. The cold in the camps was so severe that you woke up in the mornings with frozen fingers. You couldn't feel the fingers at all. If you can't work, you are no better than a rock anyway. Work is the religion of your intellect and your hands. They tortured your body, hoping that if they could control your body, your hands, your intellect and your heart would be rendered useless anyway.

Swami Nagappan must have been eighteen. He had taken the *satyagraha* route to jail, where he followed the jail rules religiously. Hard work was his faith. Every morning, he was taken to the road construction site where his job was to crush rocks into gravel for the road. He spent the nights shivering with cold. The two blankets they were provided were just enough to give them the illusion of not being exposed to the climate. Waves of cold swept over you, suffused your body, and rolled past you only to return again and soak you again. By evening, he felt his body going in pieces. When it was night, he started coughing. But he refused to give up, taking every thing as a duty, including the shivering and the coughing, the crushing of rocks and laying of the road. The pain was to him a rule of the jail.

His friends advised him: 'Speak to the jailor and get remand.'

He dismissed the suggestion with a laugh. 'A *satyagrahi* does not beg and does not retract his steps. Don't you know the things that Gandhi had to suffer? He was pulled out of the toilet and bundled into the road because a bloodthirsty native brute could not wait. Gandhi had nothing but forgiveness even for him, though the papers had come out strongly in his support. He did not want this small matter to come in the way of his main pursuit."

Like the moon as it moves into a new phase, Nagappan wasted away. When he was finally released, he was completely broken but a happy man.

He laughed and said: 'My education is now complete. I am now a seasoned *satyagrahi*.'

On his release, it was found that his lungs had caught a chill and pneumonia has seized him. An illiterate son of a *girmitiya*! He could speak Zulu and English, but, with his condition worsening, his speech became paralysed. Even Tamil was now a foreign language to him. He was always thinking of *satyagraha*. 'I am going to heaven to take up *satyagraha* there. I'll tell God not to be another General Smuts and have mercy on His people.' And he laughed his typical laughter.

When the time came for him to breathe his last, he sent for Gandhibhai. 'Gandhibhai,' he said, 'I'm sorry I couldn't finish my work. I hope I'll be able to finish it where I am going.' He was finding it difficult to breathe.

Gandhibhai's hand lay on his forehead. When he tried to remove it, Nagappan stopped him. 'I like your touch. It gives me peace and takes away my pain.'

'Nagappan,' said Gandhi, 'You have brought great glory to India.'

He smiled and said: 'When is the next batch leaving, Gandhibhai? It will have my name, won't it? I …'

Those were his last words. His hand on Gandhi's, a smile on his face, Nagappan made it to a batch which was starting on an endless journey with him as its leader.

~

Satyagraha was a war of the poor and for the poor. It was now taking the shape of a popular movement of Indians in general. It included peddlers, *girmitiya*s, released *girmitiya*s and others who had transformed themselves into their likes. Gandhi was one of them. This was his third jail term. The first time, he had been sentenced to two month's simple imprisonment but had been released early. The next time, it was a three-month term. Only a month had elapsed after the completion of the term that he had to go to jail again.

The charge against him was that he hadn't got himself a registration pass under the new law and had in fact prevented others from getting it too.

From Volksrust, Mohandas was taken to Johannesburg jail. Mohandas rose early that day. Summer had just started. All the prisoners who were to be moved were asked to leave the barracks, assemble in the grounds outside and 'fall in'. Every prisoner was required by rules to take off his cap and salute every officer, big or small. Whenever Mohandas had to take off his cap, he was reminded of the Durban incident and the magistrate's face flashed before his eyes. However, in the present situation, both the cap and its wearer belonged to them. Where was the question of freedom for a prisoner?

Another instruction followed: 'Kits on heads, everyone.'

Kits went on heads. Handcuffs were put on. The order came 'March!' and they all started marching.

Mohandas was with the other prisoners, walking on foot towards the station on the main road. Those who knew him stopped to see him in a prisoner's uniform, carrying a load on his head. Their blood boiled and tears rolled down their eyes. They wanted to speak to him, to stop him, to accompany him, but were in no position to do anything.

Mohandas was walking rather fast, which was his normal pace. A few people tried to stop him. With folded hands, Mohandas requested them to desist. In the meantime, the police too pushed them back. Three policemen walked with him—one ahead, one by his side and the third bringing up the rear. A journalist, who knew M.K. Gandhi, happened to pass by. He joined the train and asked Gandhi: 'You are a barrister; why didn't you refuse to be handcuffed?'

'I am a prisoner too.'

'How do you feel walking the road like an ordinary prisoner, carrying a head load?'

'I am happy that I am a *satyagrahi* and am doing justice to a *satyagrahi*'s creed.'

'You are a political prisoner.'

'What difference does that make? The government has the same jail for everyone and everyone is called a prisoner. There is no discrimination in that regard.' Mohandas laughed.

'You are laughing!'

'Is there a rule that a prisoner cannot laugh?'

The journalist was out of breath. Still, he persisted: 'Why don't you protest?'

'This is my protest. To put up with every torment and every inflicted torture on you in the fight against inhumanity and injustice is protest. This is my way of protesting.' The journalist was scribbling furiously.

Gandhi walked on ahead. The journalist was so tired that he thought it best to give up. Others kept up all the way to the station. When the train arrived, they all waved him goodbye as he got into a jam-packed coach along with his two guards. One guard stayed behind. So long as the train waited, the guard and others too waited on the platform.

Mohandas was first taken to the Johannesburg jail, then to Pretoria jail. Mohandas knew from his experience now that prisoners were required to strip stark naked the first thing in a jail, so this time he raised no questions and followed the jailor's instructions to the letter. Mohandas couldn't help laughing when he thought of the journalist who thought that being a political prisoner should make a difference to the jail authorities. Why would it, when everyone was just a prisoner?

Mohandas was given a pair of breeches, a shirt made of coarse cloth, a jumper, a cap, a towel, a pair of socks and a pair of front-enclosed sandals. The cap was a boat shaped object of thick cloth. The clothes he had worn in the earlier jails were taken back. Mohandas laughed and said: 'This is my Gandhi cap.'

At first the warder was a bit withdrawn and would fly off the handle without reason. If the prisoners asked for any prescribed facilities, he meted out the severest treatment to them. Mohandas put up with everything without protest. People asked him: 'You fight against the government; why don't you fight against the day-to-day excesses of these people?'

'Everyone puts up with these excesses, so I must do too. It's not in the warder's powers to change himself; nor can anyone else change him. It's the government that makes the rules and it's the government which breaks them. So it's the government that we must fight. Why fight the poor warder, who only carries out the orders? He might sometimes cherish the illusion that he is the government, but we know that he is not.'

When the warders talked amongst themselves, Gandhibhai invariably came up as a topic.

'A strange man, this Gandhi chap. He fights the government, but refuses to see us as the government.'

The withdrawn warder said: 'He fears me so much that he doesn't tangle with me at all. Then why should I tangle with him?'

'We must keep the prisoners tight. You give them an inch and they will try to take a mile.' This was an old warder, who always liked to introduce his opinion before dozing off again.

The withdrawn warder began to relax and his attitude softened. He started making concessions to Mohandas in matters like bathroom and toilet visits. But about the time when his attitude to Mohandas was undergoing change, he was transferred and his place was taken by another warder. The concessions Mohandas had earned were all legitimate, so Mohandas wasn't unduly worried.

The first thing the new warder told Mohandas was: 'Look, prisoner, I have heard all about you and I do not consider you a prisoner. You are fighting for your people. I too am a fighter, and all fighters belong to each other.'

When Mohandas was permitted out, the new warder always tried to be by his side trying to find out whatever he could about him.

'How many people do you have at home?'

Mohandas told him everything in detail. The warder would get serious and ask: 'Don't you miss your wife and kids?'

'I do, but staying away from them and missing them is all part of our struggle.'

The warder could do little but to stare at him, thinking 'What sort of man is this?'

One day, a journalist friend of Mohandas, Lichtenstein, visited the jail on some other business, but he also arranged a visit to Mohandas. He came to Mohandas' cell. The warder was also present during the visit. Lichtenstein was a white and he sat at a little distance from Mohandas.

'How are you?' he asked Mohandas.

'I am absolutely fine,' said Mohandas.

'That's your formal answer. Tell me how you are in reality.'

At first, Mohandas did not respond. Then he said: 'All that I can say is that I am being subjected to cruel treatment. Perhaps General Smuts thinks that we will withdraw our steps if he gives us such treatment. That will never happen. I will put up with all the ill treatment. In fact, it gives me peace. What gives you peace is the real service of God.' After a pause, he added: 'Please do not publish these things. I would like to tell them to the people myself when I am released.'

Mr. Lichtenstein listened to him with his eyes closed. As he left, he said: 'Mr. Gandhi, you have all my good wishes.'

~

The Director of jails was visiting. The jail had been cleaned up thoroughly and done up for the visit. Suddenly, the Director appeared in Mohandas' cell. The first thing he did was to ask his retinue to leave the cell; then he turned to Mohandas and said: 'Mr. Gandhi, I want to have a word with you.'

'I hope it's not going to be a repeat of what happened the last time,' said Mohandas. He had decided that he would not respond to any summons this time, be it from General Smuts or General Botha.'

The Director placed Lord Selbourne's order and Polak's letter before him. Mohandas knew it was Lichtenstein's doing.

'I have been asked to conduct an inquiry,' said the Director.

Mohandas read the letter carefully and said: 'I'd told these things to Lichtenstein and he seems to have passed them on to Polak. If you like,

I can repeat the things I told Lichtenstein. I did not ask for anything by way of a special privilege. I asked only for facilities which, as a human being, every prisoner should have: a bed, a pillow, blankets, books and so on.' Mohandas laughed and said: 'Maybe, Indians are both more delicate and more forbearing than the whites.'

The Director left, but now the jail officials became more solicitous of Mohandas and told him that he could ask for anything he needed without hesitation.

Mohandas said nothing except to thank them.

On the tenth day, however, a bed, a pillow and other sleeping accessories were made available to Mohandas. Till then, he had been sleeping on the floor with books for his pillow. The bed had so many bedbugs that sleep was out of the question. It took eight days for the bed to be replaced.

'There are other prisoners like me here. Did you ask them?'

A long silence was the reply.

Mohandas spent his time reading books, sitting at the door of the cell. In the beginning, he was very restless. He had so many worries and cares that he grew very upset. Then he thought out the problem carefully and tried to imbibe the lessons. Worries and cares did not originate outside you; they festered within you like bedbugs. They laid siege of you the moment they found you unoccupied. Kastur and the kids, Polak, Millie, Kallenbach—the entire horizon from Porbandar to here and now swarmed with worries and more worries. He didn't have a clue how to deal with them. Worries like molten lead filled every pore of his body.

Mohandas was worried about the people who hadn't been arrested. How was the government treating them? When he thought of Hari, he felt a proud father. So young and such a devoted *satyagrahi*!

Books seemed like a scenic island to him. Tolstoy, Emerson, Carlyle—he got all these and others from the jail library and was lost in them. He had brought Tamil Primers, the Quran, the Bible and the Gita with him.

It was the searing loneliness of the jail that had led him to strike up friendship with books.

He remembered a few poems of Raichandbhai. Sometimes he read them out or hummed them to himself and felt he was having a dialogue with Raichandbhai. He felt divine light spreading within him, helping him to see and understand himself. As he read Carlyle's book on the French Revolution, he felt the problems of his country were totally beyond the capacity of the whites to solve. Only we could solve them. How could our problems be their problems? He was convinced that when the French Revolution could not solve the problems of France, how could it solve the problems of the rest of the world? He would see the map of India emerging before his eyes, the country's sorrows rising as various colours across its face.

He would start humming the lines:

Alakh nam dhuni lagi gagan me—
Magan bhaya man mora ji
Asan mar surat dridh dhari
Diya agam ghar dera ji.
(The universe echoes with the sound of the Lord's name
And my heart is lost in ecstasy;
I have sat myself down and made up my mind
Not to stir from the Lord's presence.)

Sometimes he would actually sing the lines:

Hasata ramata prakat kari dekhi re
Maru jivyu tav lekhi re
Tenu swapna je darshan paye re
Tanu man na chare bije bhabhe re.
(I'll consider my life a success
When I see you in person laughing and playing;
Whoever can have a glimpse of you even in a dream
Can be sure nothing else will sway his mind ever again.)

On occasion, the warders would come and stand listening to him silently without trying to stop him singing. They would stand for a while and then leave quietly.

~

The incident in Volksrust jail kept coming back to him and made him restless. Kastur's figure flashed before his eyes. A telegram from West had informed him that Kastur had started bleeding again and that her condition was serious. The problem for him was how to get there. He could have been allowed to go even without paying the fine, but he had known in advance the price he might have to pay for joining the *satyagraha.* So he decided that if it was God's will that Kastur should depart this world without him holding her hand to console her as a loving husband, then so be it. Only he knew how he had been holding himself back since he had received the news and the thought made his hair stand on end. In the end, he sent West a telegram asking him to do him a favour by keeping him abreast of Kastur's condition telegraphically every day. He also indicated that this did not mean that he would be able to do anything about it; only that he would be able to draw some consolation from it. After all, he too was a human being.

Mohandas now got to know about Kastur's condition everyday. He consoled himself with the idea that, though he was not present physically, he was still able to share some of her pain in his own way.

He also wrote a letter to Kastur. He still remembered some of its contents and he went through them mentally. Although everything was now over, even the memory was so reassuring. The letter said:

> *Dear Kastur,*
>
> *I received West's letter about your condition. It made my heart sick with grief. But unfortunately I cannot come and be of service to you. I have surrendered myself totally to* satyagraha. Satyagraha *actually is surrender, so I cannot come even after*

paying the fine. But take courage, follow some discipline in your eating habits and you will be fine. But, if despite this, it is my misfortune to see you go, I assure you that my heart has so much love for you that it will never, never dry up and you will live in my heart forever. Your soul will never die, and be sure that I will never marry again.

Mohandas

He didn't remember the exact words, but what he had said in the letter was still alive in his heart. Suddenly, Mohandas grew very upset: Was it ever possible that his Kastur would leave him forever, especially in his absence. No, it wasn't possible. She would never, never do it.

He closed his eyes and started humming *Vaishnava jan to taine kahiye* … (Call him a man of God who …)

~

When he was released from jail, the question before Mohandas was where to go. He sat outside the jail for a while and tried to think of a solution. He had already given up the Johannesburg house. After Mir Alam's attack on him, he had spent about two weeks in Joseph Doke's house. During that period, Millie Polak had also given up the house in the country and moved to Johannesburg. When he had partially recovered from the attack, Mohandas had moved into Millie Polak's place. He had a lot of work to do as *satyagraha* was in progress. So he wanted a place where he could work in peace. Moreover, he was in and out of jail all the time. Four hours of sleep was all that he was getting then. So long as he was awake, every minute was spent at work, in carrying out his responsibilities and in worrying about *satyagraha*. Millie took every care of his meals. Sometimes, she told him: 'Gandhibhai, Kastur Behn and the kids think of you all the time. Hari, you have already converted into a *satyagraha* …'

'Yes,' Mohandas laughed. 'A truer *satyagrahi* than me!' Then he turned serious: 'Let's see how long it lasts.'

'We have taken a vow,' he would continue, laughing again, 'so long as we don't get justice from the government, we will continue our fight with God as our witness. Whoever can walk with us, to whatever distance, is most welcome. Your mind and your body have to be in a single line or the mind, like a wild horse, will jump into a ditch and take the body with it.'

'Why must you talk like that?' objected Millie, 'Hari is one of your true followers.'

'Millie, till date, even I am not my own true follower. I am trying, though. The fewer the complexities in his mind, the easier is the path of a *satyagrahi*. Cobwebs in the mind turn even the physical pathways of your life hard to negotiate.'

Millie thought it best not to take the topic forward.

Mohandas found that Millie's home suited him best.

He always returned late at night and that day too he had been late. He had an uneasy stomach and he wanted lemonade badly. He didn't want to turn on the lights as that would wake up everyone. He groped his way to the kitchen. He knew where things were kept as he had always been in the habit of attending to his own needs.

The house was not very organized or clean. A lot of Polak's money had gone into the fight against the government. The house was an old style one and didn't have a bathroom. The previous tenant had put up a bathroom in an area that didn't have sufficient slope for the water to flow out. As a result, sewage collected and seeped into the wall, which had made it damp. The moment it was dark, cockroaches invaded the entire house like bad characters from the streets and roamed all over the place as if there was no such thing as the rule of law.

Mohandas suddenly stepped on something soft and smooth. As he was bare-soled, the smoothness made a more immediate impact. Mohandas stood still for a moment. His first reaction was that it could be a stray piece of fish or meat. Millie had a native girl working for her and she was a non-vegetarian.

Mohandas had been out of jail only for a few days and could be back in jail any day. He was in a state of mind when even small things made a big impact.

'Thank God, it was an insect, or I should have been in jail again on charges of murder.' He smiled to himself in the dark.

Millie was awake. It was already light. It pained her to see Mohandas' face. The man had come to her seeking solace after a jail term and she couldn't provide him any. What good was a place like this?

Millie's eyes were wet. 'Why didn't you wake me up, Gandhibhai?' she asked.

'It was just lemonade I wanted. I could help myself. It would be sheer ingratitude to wake you up for such a small matter.'

Millie cleaned up the floor. It was a big cockroach which had been trampled to death. Then she gave Mohandas his lemonade. Later she took his hand and led him to bed like a child, and put him to bed with a light covering on him.

When Mohandas came out of jail, Millie was indisposed. It always upset Mohandas to see anyone unwell. Millie couldn't sleep at night. The baby was still quite small. It had to be fed, put to sleep and changed and all this made her sleep very irregular.

Mohandas asked her: 'Suppose someone took over your baby for the night, would it help you to sleep better?'

'I can't say. I only know I am completely exhausted.'

'Do you trust me?'

'And what exactly do you propose to do?' Millie laughed. There were rings round her eyes. The smile looked like a strip of paper pasted on her face.

'I am a good mother,' said Mohandas. Millie burst out laughing.

'If you hand over the child to me, I can cure it of its wakeful nights.'

'How do you expect to be able to do what I couldn't, Gandhibhai?'

'Give me a chance and see,' said Mohandas. Millie agreed.

~

Mohandas usually returned from his meetings after eleven. The first thing he did on his return was the take the baby away from Millie. When at night the baby woke up or showed signs of waking up, Mohandas gave it a drink of water. Initially, the eight-month old baby had some problem drinking from a glass but it soon got used to it. Later, it became a cakewalk. Now the baby would sleep for five or six hours at a stretch without a cheep out of it. The house was still during these hours like an uninhabited place. Even if Mohandas returned after one o'clock, he would still take away the baby. He would spread his bedding on the floor; keep a jug of water and a glass by his side and the baby's mattress and pillow beside him. This went on for two weeks. At the end of two weeks, the baby went back to his mother and Millie got her sleep back too.

Soon, Millie started regaining her health. She laughed and said: 'Gandhibhai, does Kastur Behn know you are such a great mother?'

Gandhibhai laughed too. 'You should better ask her that.'

~

Mohandas and Millie often engaged in serious discussions.

Millie was of the view that sexual relationship between men and women was very important and humans could not possibly stay away from it, as the vow of celibacy required. Mohandas argued that man's quest for perfection was more important and it involved overcoming one's imperfections and shortcomings. One must maintain one's pursuit of perfection.

Millie argued that the quest for perfection did not assist man in understanding his shortcomings; rather it only helped to suppress them. Man's imperfections were an important component of his life. Man would be incomplete without them.'

'That would be like making a sick man sicker. You should be helping him to get better and stronger.'

'I cannot accept that procreation is a sin.'

'I didn't say that, did I?'

'Maybe you didn't use those words, but what you said amounts to the same. You believe that sex is an activity dissipative of the human body.'

'Is it not?'

'Certainly not.' Millie was emphatic. 'Are you trying to say that creation is an illegitimate activity? God has allowed us only one way of producing children. There is no other way.'

'Man faces many challenges other than sex. Should man devote all his energies to the production and upbringing of babies and quit everything else?'

'That, I think, would be the ideal thing to do.'

'Maybe because it gives you momentary pleasure?'

'You are trying to tell me that *brahmacharya* (celibacy) is a greater achievement than parenthood? There is no substitute for parenthood.'

Just then someone dropped in asking for Mohandas. Mohandas got up, saying: 'I know it's not easy for you to understand this at this stage. But I'm quite convinced about it and I'm sure in time I'll be able to convince you too.'

That was where the matter ended that day.

~

XXIII

Satyagraha was turning hot and cold by turns. *Satyagrahi*s were being sent off to jails or deported. The government was beginning to realize that sending them off to jail was not going to deter the *satyagrahi*s. By deporting, the government had overstepped its rights and it lost face in several court cases. Indians too were beginning to feel the fatigue. Many homes were without food. Business had suffered. Earning members of all the families were in jails. Children were crying out for food. The number of *satyagrahi*s was going down every day. They were all agreed on one point: the final victory was going to be theirs. Where the matter hit impasse was on the question 'When?'

A new problem had in the meantime raised its head. Boers and Europeans had joined hands and were in the process of forming a union of all the continent's colonies. An influential leader of the group, a general, wanted the British to be kept out of this union, a condition which was totally unacceptable to the British. They were of the view that they would be able to do nothing without the cooperation of the British parliament—neither can form the federation nor secure autonomy for it.

It was quite clear to the Indians that if the union was formed, the condition of Indians living in the colonies would go from bad to worse. Not a single colony supported the Indian cause. They all wanted to keep the Indians down and to exploit them as much as possible. When the colonies all got together, their combined excesses would far exceed the excesses of any one of them. So the Indians decided to send a delegation of their own representatives to London along with the other delegations. The delegation included Haji Habib representing the British Indian Association and Mohandas from the *Satyagraha* Association. Both delegates knew quite well that their tiny voice was going to get lost in the roar of the Boer and British lions. Still, Haji Habib and Mohandas left Cape Town on *S.S. Kenilworth Castle* on June 21. General Botha and General Smuts had already reached London.

Haji Habib was not a *satyagrahi* himself, but was a friend of *satyagrahi*s. His ideas were however not quite identical to those of Mohandas.

In London, they met everyone, journalist or MP, whom it was possible to meet. They spared no effort in explaining their point of view to them. Lord Ampthill, Member of the House of Lords and President of the London branch of the British India Association, was working with them. He went along with them to meet the people including General Botha and General Smuts. After a lot of persuasion, General Botha agreed to meet them half way. He sent word through Mohandas to Haji Habib that he sympathized with their problems and would agree to some of their minor conditions but it would not be possible to withdraw the Asiatic Law on the Immigration Restriction Act. Even if he personally agreed to withdraw them, the European community would never consent to it. Colour bar was a matter of policy for them.

Lord Ampthill did his best to persuade Mohandas to accept Botha's proposal, even saying that if he wanted he could continue his fight for the principles.

Sheth Haji Habib was not very educated but, as a businessman of standing, he could understand English, Zulu and Dutch. He was speaking to Mohandas in Gujarati and Mohandas translated him into English for Lord Ampthill. Haji Habib said: 'I represent the largest class of Indians in Transvaal. It is also the wealthiest and the most powerful class. I accept General Botha's proposal.'

When it was Mohandas' turn to speak, he said without mincing words: 'I do not for a moment doubt that Habib Sahib represents the largest and the wealthiest class of Indians. On the other hand, I am here to give voice to the wishes of the poor and the helpless. They have neither wealth nor power. But we must say this about them: they will die fighting for their cause. They have the necessary determination to stand fast till the very end. Their fight is not for comfort and security but for self-respect and principles. We are also quite conscious of the power that Genral Botha wields. But our devotion to the vow we have taken is greater than our fear of his power. For the sake of our vow, we are ready to face any adversity we may have to.'

Lord Ampthill placed his hand on Mohandas' soldier and said: 'If you are so determined, I shall not stand in your way. In fact, I'll congratulate you. The ends you are following are true and the means you have adopted are scrupulous and humane.'

Mohandas felt blessed.

~

Mohandas got some idea of the changing political climate in India while he was still in London. He was worried when he got to know about the forces which were working against the independence of India. He was beginning to feel inclined to move to India and take on these forces, but conditions in Transvaal would not permit him to do so for now. But his worries about India were beginning to multiply. He was beginning to ask himself which was more important: the problems of India where hundreds of millions of his own brothers were trying to free themselves from the yoke of British slavery, or the problems of South Africa with which he had been wrestling for so many years? As he thought carefully about the question, he became assured that his first duty was to fulfil the responsibility he had already undertaken. It would be irresponsible to run away from it.

John Morley was the man in charge of Indian affairs. He was said to be a man of progressive thinking, but all his progressive thinking disappeared in a trice when the matter of India came up before him. He had introduced a number of reforms in India, which had ultimately resulted in the growth of communal sentiment in the country. Around this time there were also resident in London a number of revolutionaries who were pursuing a destabilizing agenda for India through the creation of lawlessness and anarchy. The question that bothered Mohandas was why the same goals could not be achieved through *satyagraha*. Why must we take resort to violence and bloodshed? Maybe the reason was that *satyagraha* demanded self-denial, which was not easy to practise. In violence and murder, it was the other person who suffered. But why couldn't one make the other person's suffering one's own?

~

Four months later, on November 13, Mohandas and Haji Habib started on the *Kildonan Castle* for Cape Town in a haze of complete failure of their London mission. Mohandas was also confronted with the black shadows of rising lawlessness and the evil consequences of the so-called reforms being implemented in India

They knew only too well that their returning bare-handed from London was going to cause deep disappointment in the Indian community. People were bound to express their disappointment in different ways. Some would be looking for the same motivation in their talks with Lord Ampthill that they had found in Mohandas' talks with Lord Smuts. Of course, Mohandas hadn't cared for such talk then, nor was he going to care for it now. For all such talk, his single answer was: *Satyagraha* was no longer an infant in need of constant care. It had survived and had been strengthened by a trial by fire. It was mature enough to find its own way around. It was the worries about his own country that had Mohandas' sole attention now. He was amazed that while so much had been happening in India, he had been blissfully ignorant about it. If the revolutionaries continued to follow the path of violence, the one to profit would be the government. He had seen the way the Boer War had played out. In India too, the question of freedom would be relegated to the background and a wave of oppression would start. *Satyagraha* too would be a victim. But when tyranny and oppression are faced with unarmed resistance, their poison does not work as effectively. The oppressor, in his rage, keeps losing his good sense. In the presence of *satyagraha* and the *satyagrahi*, the tyrant and the oppressor begin to feel frustrated and clueless. Oppression actually feeds on violence from the opponent.

~

Mohandas stood on the deck of the ship moving fast towards its destination. Haji Habib was in his cabin. He was so fatigued that he had surrendered himself completely to rest and relaxation. Occasionally, he wondered what explanation he could possibly offer for his failure and this thought filled him with great anxiety. Mohandas tried to console him by asking him why he thought that success was always the highest achievement. Failure too sometimes became the foundation of a great achievement. If you could not accept defeat unreservedly, how could you accept success unsuspectingly? Habib Miyan felt persuaded by his argument.

Mohandas watched the waves form and unform. He had the illusion that he was standing not on a deck but right on top of the waves and the waves were having a jolly time, laughing and giggling. They sometimes thrust him up and sometimes pulled him down. Rising and falling with them, he too had turned into a wave and, sailing with them across the Indian Ocean, had reached his country. His country was enveloped in smoke. So tight had the white rulers of the country stretched the rope of oppression that people could see death dancing on it. They felt choked with fear. Strange sounds were emanating from their throats. A shiver ran down Mohandas' body which turned into a convulsion. He could hear screams and cries. Mohandas stood up quickly and ran into his cabin. What was all this? Why was it happening? Was it my country calling me?

Haji Habib noticed the tension on Mohandas' face and asked: 'What's the matter, Gandhibhai?'

'Nothing much. Just wrestling with some questions that are bothering me.'

'What questions?'

'Questions relating to India that are now targeting me like arrows. I am the one asking them and I am the one who has to answer them. Every citizen of an enslaved country is a question by himself, and some day or the other he has to turn into an answer. No seeker after truth can escape these questions. Where questions cease, there is no truth left, nor freedom, nor any dreams.'

Habibbhai envisioned Mohandas' reach extending: it was out of the cabin and was now spreading in all directions.

The cabin provided a desk and a chair for writing. Mohandas was the one who used it most; Habibbhai was a rare user. Mohandas now took the chair. From the look on his face, it appeared as if he stood in the middle of a stream trying to ward off a rising storm with his hands. It was a storm of questions which was trying to overwhelm him but every time he was able to beat it back with his answers. The tussle between questions and answers was a continuous one. When his right hand got tired he started using his left hand. The questions had set up a kind of blockade around him which no sound could penetrate to reach him. He was solely by himself and within him was his whole country. He was himself the question, and he himself blocked the question by becoming its answer.

The first question was: What is the duty of newspapers? To find out the feelings of the people; to give them exposure; to expose any blemishes they may have fearlessly.

Sometimes he felt that the answers he provided to his own questions tried to fudge the issue. He would immediately pull himself up. 'Don't fudge the issue, okay?' he would tell himself.

The question of the division of Bengal disturbed him. Was the division a cause of awakening? Were the resulting disturbances justified?

Dissatisfaction is productive. A satisfied man does not feel the necessity of stepping out of himself. Before any change can take place, the ground of dissatisfaction must be ready.

What about self-rule?

You talk a lot about self-rule. You are impatient for it, but do you know what it means? You have still not arrived at any final conclusions about it. All right, so we throw the British out; is that enough to have self-rule?

Self-rule is not what you think it is. Self-rule is matter of the mind and the heart and it demands firm conviction.

And civilization?

But 'civilization' for us is actually the opposite of it for you, isn't it?

The more questions his mind spawned, the more answers it also produced. The answers then gave rise to new questions, which produced more answers. Questions were the raw material for answers and answers for questions. Many answers were incomplete and were getting impatient waiting for completion. Questions and answers were like ropes tied to Mohandas from two ends, each pulling him to its side.

Yes, I was talking about civilization …!

I would not go to the extent of saying what Edward Carpenter says in his book *Civilization: Its Cause and Cure* that civilization is a kind of disease.

Pleasure matters most in civilization. Securing yourself first … In early days, a single-pointed spear would do; now you need a five-bore pistol. If you dress in the European style, you are civilized; if you don't, you are uncivilized. He wanted to laugh, but who would he be laughing at? Himself?

Another question: Why are the British holding India?

It is because of us. Napoleon used to say: 'The British are a nation of shopkeepers.' Gladstone thought Transvaal had no trade so there was no point in holding it. Chamberlain thought otherwise. He fought a war to keep it.

President Kruger of Transvaal was asked: 'Is there gold on the moon?'

Kruger replied: 'No. Had there been gold on the moon, would the British have left the place unannexed? The British came to this country for trade. Wherever they go, they go for trade and we help them flourish. They would like to turn the entire world into their market.'

What about the situation in India?

It's not the British but the modern civilization which has India under its heels.

Mohandas had lost all awareness. He wasn't aware if Habibbhai was in the cabin; in fact he wasn't aware of himself. He seemed to be under some kind of spell.

Suddenly, he heard a voice: 'I want an answer to my question, and fast. Did India remain one country after the Muslim influx?'

Alien immigrants do not destroy the nationality of a country; they lose themselves in the melting pot of the nation. In fact, it's only when this happens that a country becomes a nation. For Hindus to believe in 'India for Hindus only' would be a pipe dream; for Muslims to believe likewise would be a delusion. One nation does not mean one religion.

Satyagraha? Is there any historical testimony for *satyagraha*?

Don't expect to find silver in a zinc mine. History literally means 'hi-story' or 'story of high people like kings and emperors'. It is a story of all the tumult and turbulence the world has gone through. So many humans have survived despite so many wars and massacres. That only shows that the world is founded not on the power of guns and weapons but on truth, mercy and the power of the human spirit. What greater proof can you ask for? You need guts to turn your canons on a milling crowd. You also need guts to let yourself be tied to the mouth of a canon with a smile on your face.

What does self-rule mean?

Rule over your self, that is your mind.

How?

Through *satyagraha*, the power of your spirit and the power of mercy.

The questions were unending; so were the answers. Mohandas' mind was ranging over the entire universe. Like a gardener's wife picking flowers, it picked the questions, handed them to Mohandas and he, like a gardener, threaded them together with the answers.

Slowly, he felt the commotion die down. All the questions had found their answers, but the answers had left some questions of their own. He was beginning to hear some other noises. His fingers were swollen. Sheets of paper were piled all around him. The questions that had been bothering him were now sleeping in those sheets like little innocent babies. He began to doze off. Outside, the sea was calm. The ship was still on course to its destination. But what was the destination? This question startled him again.

He stacked the sheets neatly and wrote on top 'Hind Swaraj'.

Some of the questions in that medley of questions and answers had reached him through letters.

On November 24, he wrote a letter to Manilal from the ship.

> *... Cape Town is still five days off. My right hand is tired writing, so I am now using my left hand. I may have to go to jail on landing, hence this letter. The secret of success in a struggle is precisely this: Be happy when going to jail and be happy when you are in jail!*
>
> *You asked me about Phoenix. We must first find out ways of discovering our soul and of serving our country. Only then will you be able to understand the phenomenon called Phoenix. To discover your soul, you must first have unwavering principles of fearlessness, truth and* brahmacharya. *The same principles will also work for the service of your country. Phoenix can help you in developing them ...'*
>
> *Bapu's blessings*

The same night, he also wrote a letter to his third son, Ramdas.

> *I am writing this to you as I'm not sure when we will meet next. Please don't be unhappy with me. I couldn't get anything for you from England because I didn't like anything. I like all things Indian. Don't get upset if I am taken to jail. In fact, you should be happy if I am. My place in this struggle is with Harilal. Be happy. Let me find all of you in good health and spirits when I join you.*

Harilal had been to jail four times. When Mohandas returned from London, he was still in jail. By then, about twenty-five thousand Indians had been sent to jail, some of them four times each. Most of them were poor and helpless folk, who had now grown poorer. They included both Transvaal and Natal Indians. Even during his London journey, Mohandas worried himself about money for feeding the *satyagrahi*s and helping their families. When Mohandas and Haji Habib reached Cape Town on November 30, they were informed that Jamshedji Tata had sent twenty-five thousand rupees for the *satyagrahi*s. When Mohandas heard the news, he closed his eyes and sat still for a few moments. When he opened his eyes, the only word he spoke was 'Ram!'

From Cape Town itself, Mohandas sent a telegram to Prof. Gopalkrishna Gokhale. It said:

> *Please convey heartfelt thanks to Mr. Tata for timely and generous help. Difficulties mounting. Prisoners in bad condition. Religious sentiments overlooked. Short on provisions. Prisoners being forced to carry buckets of excreta. Refusal punished by isolation. Leading Hindu, Muslim and Parsi personalities also in jail.*

When they landed in Cape Town, President of a South African political organization and member of Cape Town municipality, Dr. Abdul Rahman, was present to receive them. He introduced them to the others who were present.

'Habibbhai is the seniormost of us all,' said Mohandas.

'You are a young man,' said Habibbhai. Perhaps he didn't like being called senior.

'Yes, a young man of forty,' laughed Mohandas. 'I have to be young to be able to fight a battle like this, a struggle in which we are always at the receiving end. My son, Harilal, is in jail for the fourth time …'

'What is your reaction?' someone asked.

'Not too good, I'm afraid. I'll feel good when everyone from my family, including my youngest, Devdas, and his mother too are in jail. At the moment, just the two of us, father and son, have the privilege. Mani too wants to join us and I'm thinking why not? Next time, I think I should let him.'

Everyone laughed, but the laughter had a tinge of pain in it. 'You shouldn't talk like that,' said one.

'If we want to win this battle, each one of us will have to do it. It is not a wedding in the neighbourhood that one member can stand in for the whole family as a formal gesture. This is a celebration in which every one of us must participate with his or her whole being.'

No one had anything to say after that.

'What's going to be your next step?' asked someone, wanting to change the topic.

'Transvaal, if the way is clear; enjoy hard labour hospitality in His Majesty's hotel, in case it isn't.'

Mohandas and Haji Habib arrived at Johannesburg on the second of December. Nearly two thousand people had gathered at the Park station, most of them Indians and Chinese and a sprinkling of Europeans. The crowd was peaceful and disciplined. There was no room for jostling and pushing.

When Mohandas and Haji Habib got off the train, they were smothered in flowers. Cries of 'Gandhibhai, Gandhibhai' rent the air. People could barely contain their joy.

Mohandas was asked to address the gathering first, but Mohandas wanted Haji Habib to speak first. When people insisted, Gandhibhai started his speech. He first thanked the Transvaal government: 'We are grateful to the Transvaal government for permitting us to re-enter this country.' He continued: 'I hope the government will re-consider the issue of revising the constitution. The current one-sided action of the government is harming not only the Indians but is also hurting the stability of the British Empire. It is tarnishing its reputation for justice and fair play. People in England and India are well aware of this fact. The sympathies of quite a few Europeans lie with our movement. Our friends are all in good spirits and are ready to make whatever sacrifice is required of them.'

Mohandas was next taken to Feeddorp. A large meeting of Asians had been arranged there. The four-month absence of Gandhi had blurred the vision of the people and they couldn't see things clearly. With Gandhibhai's return, things were beginning to clear up again, as if a window had been opened.

~

Rustomji Parsi was in Johannesburg jail living out his six-month sentence. He was unwell. In Volksrust jail, he had been forced to take off his *sadri* and *kasti*, although for every Parsi it was a religious duty to be wearing them at the time of prayers. At the other two jails, he had been allowed to wear the cap. He was also not being given the diet that had been prescribed for him medically. In addition, he had been assigned the work of breaking stones. His vision had been deteriorating.

Mohandas wrote to Bhuncharji Bhavnagari that Rustomji was a reputed citizen of Natal and in view of his deteriorating health, Bhuncharji should use his good offices to get him permission for treatment.

~

Mr. Shetal had been a sergeant. A Brahmin by caste, he had donned the *satyagrahi*'s robes and was now housed in Deepkloof jail. He had been ordered to carry excreta buckets. Though a *satyagrahi* was not supposed to refuse even the most menial of jobs, the Brahmin in him could not bear the thought. He went on refusing and consequently his punishment went on increasing. The first time it was isolation for twenty-four hours and reduced diet. The second time, it became forty-eight hours. The third time, isolation rose to fourteen days. Shetal remained unmoved. Reduced diet meant only rice gruel. He was listening to his conscience. The jail authorities were banking on isolation and hunger to break him and to force him to obey orders. Further refusals led his rice gruel diet to be reduced to half. Then isolation was raised to twenty-eight days. He had been reduced to mere skin and bones. He had been sentenced to six months' jail. Thirty-six days of this sentence had been spent in isolation and rice gruel. With the final twenty-eight days, his prison sentence would go up to nine days over six months. When the jail authorities became aware of this, they let him out nine days in advance: He was thus spared nine days of hunger and isolation.

The *Indian Opinion* wrote: 'The *satyagrahi* did not bend; not before death; not before hunger and not before tyranny. The government did.'

It was the third week of December. Seven *satyagrahi*s crossed the border into Transvaal: Ramdhan, Samuel, Head Master Joseph, David Andrew, Clark, and Mohandas' second son Manilal. The government made no attempt to stop them. At the time, Polak was in India to garner support for the cause of South African Indians. He had been telegraphically informed about the incident. Polak was constantly kept informed about events in Transvaal. There was suspicion that the Indian government was also somehow involved in these events. The free entry of the *satyagrahi*s into Transvaal could well be followed by the arrest and deportation to India of some of them. *Satyagrahi*s were being arrested regularly at other places. Courts had put off hearings in the cases of arrested Indians. This was being interpreted as a prelude to their deportation to India at the appropriate time and had caused a lot of consternation in the Indian community.

What Mohandas could not fathom was why the government would not deport him to India. Different people had different explanations, but the most common one was the government did not want to provoke Indians. However much Gandhi might protest, his presence had a sobering effect on his followers in the movement.

Another explanation was: the pressure from London, which still stuck to a minimal code of decency.

~

Manilal had been arrested in Johannesburg on the charge of unlicenced peddling. The same charge had also been brought against Ramdhan. Both had been sentenced to three months in jail. The cell to which Manilal had been assigned already had a number of Chinese prisoners in it; quite a few of them hardened criminals. They often danced naked in Manilal's presence and indulged in obscene acts. Manilal did his best to keep himself under control. He had learnt from his father that it was possible to remain calm in times of crises. The prisoners had a single bucket of water among all of them. Whenever a prisoner wanted a drink of water, he would not use a glass or a cup, or even cupped hands to drink; rather he would put his mouth into the bucket, like an animal drinking from a waterhole. This was the last straw for Manilal. He could not bring himself to drink like a dog with his mouth in the bucket. When he could not stay thirsty any longer, he approached the Deputy Superintendent of the jail and said: 'I have been putting up with the most obscene acts of my fellow prisoners in the cell, but it is not possible for me to drink water from the bucket like an animal. And if I do not drink water, how am I going to survive?'

The Deputy Superintendent frowned and said: 'This is the first time I am hearing such a complaint. No other prisoner has ever raised this matter.'

'I am not a mere prisoner. And I have no wish to compare myself with others. I am only talking about my personal problem. We Indians cannot drink water in this fashion. Moreover, it is not a healthy practice.'

'You seem to be a querulous person. What do you think you are here for—to serve out your sentence or to build your health? You don't seem to be a sociable person; why shouldn't we put you in isolation?'

That had Manilal worried for a moment. But next he thought maybe it was all to the good as he would be rid of the nuisance and have some time to himself for reflection. 'As you wish,' he said.

He was shifted to a black hole. Here the walls seemed to him more frightening and cruel than his erstwhile fellow prisoners. They seemed to cramp not only his body but also his thinking. His voice was getting choked, his limbs were getting frozen, his heart was beginning to sink and he found himself unable to breathe. He had a feeling he had been tied up into a ball and left hanging in a ditch.

He stopped eating and kept repeating the single sentence: 'I want to see the Superintendent.'

When the Superintendent came on one of his regular rounds he was informed that a prisoner was on fast and wanted to meet him.

The Superintendent came to Manilal. 'My fault was that I refused to drink water directly from a bucket like other prisoners,' Manilal told him. 'We Indians are not used to this practice. For this single reason I was branded a querulous man and sent to this black hole.' His voice was choked.

The Superintendent immediately cancelled his isolation and ordered that Indian prisoners should be provided a separate bucket for water. Manilal was sent to a ward with Indian prisoners in it.

Rustomji was also in the same jail. When prisoners were allowed out of their cells, Manilal would go and join him. He massaged and pressed his hands and feet. After a while Rustomji was transferred to Fort jail. Time now began to hang heavy on Manilal. Earlier he used to wait for the evening. That wait had now ended.

Mohandas was receiving very discouraging news about the *satyagrahi*s. Messages that he should go and see them were also being received.

It was Sunday, usually the day on which prisoners were allowed visitors. Harilal Gandhi, Isaac Sorabjee, Mohandas' former secretary Schlesin, Rustomji Parsi and some others were all in jail. Mohandas went to the jail to see them. When it was his turn, the jailor told him: 'You cannot be allowed to see them.'

'Why not?'

'A person who has been a prisoner himself cannot be allowed to see prisoners.'

Mohandas didn't know what to do. He knew that a person who had been legally insolvent once stayed insolvent forever, but that a prisoner should stay a prisoner forever, even for his friends and relatives, was beyond him. If he were to turn prisoner again, would they be able to stop him?

This was however no time to start a controversy. It was important to find out how the prisoners were doing in jail. Kallenbach was with him. He asked Kallenbach: 'You are still free from this stigma, so why don't you go and see them? Ask them to have patience. Tell them that a true *satyagrahi* cannot afford to accept defeat. Also inform them that, having been a prisoner, I'm not being allowed to see them; but they surely cannot stop me from becoming a prisoner again.'

Kallenbach spent half an hour with the *satyagrahi*s. Over the wall was Gandhibhai. His message stirred a new wave of enthusiasm in them. They felt as if it was Gandhibhai speaking in Kallenbach's voice.

They had a message for Gandhibhai: We do not want him to be in jail again and be a prisoner. If he is in jail again, who will look after our families and who will guide the movement?

It was a depressed and defeated Gandhibhai who returned from the jail. He couldn't help thinking of the absurd argument which the authorities had used to prevent him from meeting the prisoners. Can't one who has been a prisoner see his prisoner son or his relatives in jail? There was no way he was going to accept this rule.

Still wrestling with this argument, Mohandas arrived at his office and found two women waiting for him. He knew one of them. She was Fakir, wife of Sami Naidu. The other one must be her daughter-in-law, he thought. The women stood up to greet him.

Naidu's wife was immediately off the mark: 'Gandhbhai, I have taken a vow that I shall wear no ornaments so long as this fight is on,' and, without waiting for an answer from Mohandas, she proceeded to take off her earrings, nose pin, necklace, gold bracelets and rings and placed them before him. When she proceeded to take off her *mangalsutra*, Mohandas stopped her: 'No, don't take that off. It is a mark of your husband's well-being and happiness. We want success of the *satyagraha*, but equally we also wish for your husband's happiness. But, tell us, why this awesome vow?'

'My son is going to jail. My husband is already in jail. So many Indians are in jail. What use is all this jewellery to me in such conditions?'

The other woman had been keeping quiet. She was also carrying a bundle. She now put it before Gandhibhai. It also contained her *mangalsutra.* Gandhibhai took it out and returned it to her with due respect and said: 'Never do it again, ever, dear daughter,' he said.

In front of him lay *Indian Opinion* of February 5. The front page carried a news item with the title "Royappan Arrested". It said: 'Joseph Royappan, David Andrew and Samuel Joseph have been each sentenced to three months in jail. Our congratulations! The arrest of a person like Royappan will reverberate as far as India …'

The final paragraph said: 'The Tamil community has outdone itself. Currently, it is people from this community who have been populating the jails. Most people from other communities have shown their backs. Who will follow the footsteps of Royappan and his friends?'

When the two ladies stepped out, Mohandas stood up and saluted them with a raised hand. 'The paper is right,' he muttered.

~

Around this time, Father J.J. Doke was visiting America. On his return, the Chinese, the Indians and the Europeans had got together to accord him a reception on J.P. Street. The British-Indian community had arranged for a vegetarian dinner. William Hosken was presiding over the event. He sat in the middle, flanked by Doke on the right and Mrs. Doke on the left. As President of the *Satyagraha* Association, Cachalia sat next to Doke, while the Chinese leader, Quinn, sat on the left of Mrs. Doke.

Mohandas was sitting away from them. The scene when he had been attacked by Mir Alam and he lay unconscious in the office of J.C. Gibson, partner Messrs Arnot and Gibson, with Doke bending over him as he regained consciousness, passed before his eyes and he felt himself overcome with emotion.

All the speakers had said their pieces in praise of Doke. Mohandas was the last one to be called on to speak. He stood silently for a while and then picked up slowly: 'Those were days when I hardly knew Father Doke. In fact, we hardly knew each other. I lay unconscious in Mr. Gibson's chamber. People wanted to get rid of me by putting me in a hospital. Mr. Doke asked me to go with him and I agreed. My mother was already dead; my sister lived four thousand miles away. My wife and kids were four hundred miles away in Phoenix. At that time, Mr. and Mrs. Doke looked after me like my own family. How can I ever forget that scene? Mr. Doke used to tiptoe into my room in the dead of the night to see if his patient was getting his sleep or not. He not only served me, he also did a lot to advance the sacred cause of *satyagraha*, and he did so fearlessly. Our movement could also have come to a dead stop, had Mr. Hosken and his European Committee not come to our aid. I hope the next time when he goes to London, Mr. Doke will meet Lord Crew and Lord Marlow and tell them about these experiences.'

When the function was over, Mr. and Mrs. Doke came and stood by Mohandas silently. They were looking at Mohandas as if trying to absorb the invisible rays of divine light radiating from him into their own persons.

~

A meeting of the Indian community was in progress in the Masonic Hall. A host of sympathizers and people from other communities had also joined in. The hall was packed to capacity; even exits were crowded and porticos were overflowing. Millie had also accompanied Mohandas to the meeting. In those days, Mohandas was staying with the Polaks. Polak himself was in India. Mohandas was the chief guest. His speech on that day had been especially impressive. Mohandas had now started drawing large crowds and prolonged applauses. Mohandas' meetings in those days were known only for two things: his speeches and the applause. Everything else was a filler.

When Mohandas got down from the stage, people surrounded him. He shook hands with them, spoke a sentence or two and made his way parting the crowd to the entrance gate, where Millie stood waiting for him.

Millie congratulated him on his excellent speech and asked: 'Gandhibhai, I have a question. Do you think people quite understand all your talk about *brahmacharya*?'

'Yes, I think they do. Even an illiterate man in India understands the meaning of *brahmacharya*, or rejection of unnecessary sex. Though I must say that every one of us interprets what the other person says in his own way, or failing to understand it, declares the other person a fool. The one who speaks actually does little more than provide a context.'

'I'm beginning to think that you will soon arrive at a point in your thinking when you'll start believing that the ideal situation for humanity would be one when it ceases to reproduce or becomes incapable of it.'

Mohandas said: 'Why do you always give a wrong twist to whatever I say? When you went to Phoenix the last time, for several days you made no inquiries about the child whose mom was a good friend of yours. I had to take you to her. When I asked you why, you told me that you had made no inquiries because you thought that I might take your inquiry as a rebuttal of, or a protest against, my ideas. I had laughed it off then. What do you take me for—a dictator?'

As he spoke, Mohandas was keeping his eyes fixed on a man who had been following them in a rather suspicious manner. Mohandas was completely at ease as he spoke of the events of those days while at the same time keeping an eye on their stalker.

'While returning after the visit to the child, you said on an impulse that one doesn't become wise just by turning a mother. To this day, I haven't quite grasped why and how this idea occurred to you.'

'Yes, I remember. You had then said a really nice thing. Not just turning a mother, you said, but a loving mother. True love, you said, made everyone wiser, everyone without exception. And mother's love of course was the purest and the best of them all.'

Still talking, Mohandas suddenly turned about and approached the person following them. Getting closer to him, Mohandas put his hands in his and, with Millie watching them, said something to him very sweetly and lovingly. Millie of course could not hear what he said. Both of them then walked a little distance together, speaking very softly. At the turning, the man handed something to Mohandas and disappeared into the dark.'

Millie's head was bursting with questions. 'Did Gandhibhai know the man? If he did, why didn't he introduce her to him? What was so confidential about their talk? What are these cloak-and-dagger activities of Gandhibhai?'

When Gandhibhai returned, Millie asked him: 'Something special?'

'No, the man only wanted to kill me.'

'What? He wanted to kill you? Why? Was he insane?' Millie almost shrieked.

'Calm yourself. It wasn't his fault. Actually, he felt that I was being hard on people. He thought I was a collaborator and acting with the government against the people while outwardly posing to be a friend.'

'Oh, that's terrible. We must get him arrested at once. He is unpredictable and can act against you any time. Why did you let him go? I'm sure he is not normal.'

'He is quite normal. He thinks I am out of my mind or that I am being dishonest. He may be a little misguided. I talked to him. I told him that killing even a bad man has bad consequences for the goodness of people. If you want to change a bad man, do not kill him but love him. Make him your own. He then handed the knife to me and walked away.'

Millie shrank to see the knife in Mohandas' hands. She had turned pale.

Mohandas laughed out aloud. 'He left it to me to use the knife as I wished.'

'It's not a joke,' Millie was genuinely scared. 'He could have struck at you out of the dark.'

'But he didn't. Don't worry yourself. He did perhaps want to kill me, but he neither had the courage, nor was he quite convinced himself about his reasons for killing me. I also told him that if he thought that I was so bad that it was not possible to reform me, then he could go ahead and kill me. In his heart of hearts he was not sure that this was the case. But, anyway, the whole thing is now over. He is never going to attack me again. Had I got him arrested, I would not only have made an enemy of a man unsure of himself and trapped in self-doubt; I would also have opened for him another channel to stray into. Now he is a friend and all his doubts are set at rest.' Mohandas laughed like a child.

Millie was staring at his face unbelieving that a man could laugh even in such circumstances.

~

Millie was expecting her second child. In preparation for the event, Polak had moved to a bigger house. He had finished his mission in India and was now back in Transvaal. *Satyagraha* was still in progress. People were offering themselves for arrests as peddlers. They were crossing the Transvaal border in groups of four and five. *Satyagraha* was now using guerrilla techniques. *Satyagrahi*s were forcing their way into Transvaal from every part of the border. It was not possible to seal the entire border. The police arrested them and released them in the forests. Hungry and thirsty, they would wander around in the forests for a few days but were back in Transvaal again. Mohandas had to maintain a record of all arrests and returns, with details of name, place of arrest, returned or not, etc. Inevitably, he frequently returned late at night. People from all over Africa came to see him. Those who came from far away places inevitably stayed the night, raising the pressure of work on Millie.

Mohandas didn't want the pressure of work on Millie to increase on his account. So the two decided to let it be known that Gandhibhai had moved out and was now only an irregular visitor to the place, never staying for more than a day or a day and a half at a time and spending his nights in the homes of different friends on different days.

Around this time, Millie's pet cat had given birth to a litter of six kittens. It had rattled Millie to see such a large family of cats. The kittens scampered all over the house quite unchecked while the cat sat in a corner watching them, its eyes brimming over with the same motherly love mixed with pleasure that characterizes the eyes of any human mother watching her first child at play. But Millie wanted the house to be freed from the tyranny of the cat and its kittens and couldn't think of a way. She however didn't consider it appropriate to share this problem of hers with Polak or Gandhibhai. Nor could she ask them to pack the kittens in a sack and drown them in a river or a drain. Gandhibhai considered any life more precious than perhaps his own.

One day, Millie noticed that the cat stopped feeding two of the kittens. When the two approached her, she growled at them and shooed them off. The two were constantly hungry. The motherly love that spilled from her eyes when she saw the six pussies having a run of the house disappeared from her face for these two. Millie tried to feed them milk externally, but they wouldn't agree. It looked as is they were trying to match their mother's determination not to give them her milk with an equally strong determination not to have any other. The cat of course suckled the other four siblings with great élan. The two would at first quietly watch their siblings feasting and then, when they could bear it no more, would tumble forward for a drink. Barred from drinking, one of the kittens soon died of hunger. A few days later, Millie saw the cat chewing away the front paws of the other pussies. They had been disabled.

Polak got up in the middle of the night and found Mohandas washing the wounds of the disable kittens with warm water. He woke up Millie.

Millie asked Mohandas: 'What is this you are doing?'

'Only what I should be doing. Don't you think I would do the same for an injured *satyagrahi*?'

When the cat was out scouring the area at night, Mohandas tended the wounds of the kittens as if they were human babies. Unsure how long the kittens had to live, Millie one day took the kittens and drowned them in a stream. Everyone thought it was the cat who had disposed them of.

It continued to be a topic of discussion among them for many days why the cat behaved the way she did with her kittens. No one had a plausible answer, though everyone was trying to hypothesize. Mohandas argued; 'Taking the wild animals out of their natural habitat and turning them into pets kills their natural instincts. Had these kittens been born in their natural setting, they might perhaps not have had to undergo this misery. They could have walked away anywhere. The cat also must have sensed that so large a family of hers might not be welcome in the house and that her own survival might be in danger if the kittens continued in the house. So she thought it best to get the kittens out of her way …'

'You mean a cat is more intelligent than a man?' laughed Polak.

'I think her intelligence was a gift of the danger she apprehended as imminent to her own existence. Survival is the basic instinct of every creature. What distinguishes man from other creatures is that man also seeks to protect others. Take *girmitiya*s: danger to their own survival gave them the courage to face the Smuts regime.'

Polak and Millie could think of no counter argument.

~

Before the *satyagraha* started, Mohandas had been wrestling with a question: Can *satyagraha* be associated with the western attire? Would the western attire create a block in convincing people about the truth of *satyagraha*? This question had given rise to another question: Who would be the people to be associated with *satyagraha*: businessmen or wage-earning workers? One could imagine businessmen melting away before the law-enforcers' stick; whites and natives could hardly be expected to have any interest in the movement; the wage-earners depended on their daily earnings to survive, so how could they be expected to sustain *satyagraha*? A little strictness on the part of the authorities would see their children going hungry. Did that mean that nobody would be joining *satyagraha*? When Mohandas thought back to this sequence of arguments he had had with himself, he couldn't help laughing at how his mind had worked then. After the British India Association had dissociated itself from the movement, it had become clear to Mohandas that the wage-earners alone were going to form the backbone of *satyagraha*. Illiterate though they might be, they loved their freedom more. It also became clear to Mohandas that the European attire would exercise terror on them. A barrister or an official would be fine for them in the western dress, but if one of their own appeared in the same dress, he would not be recognized as the same 'he'. Not that any particular attire was antithetical to *satyagraha*: *Satyagraha* was after all a spiritual thing. But there was just the danger that for these wage-earners, *satyagraha* may ring false in the western attire. Suddenly, Mohandas found a clue and he felt light dawn. Tamils, he thought, generally wore a *lungi* and *lungi*s could be bought off the shelf. *Girmitiya*s from Bihar wore a short-sleeved shirt, or a *ganji*. The first time Mohandas stepped out for *satyagraha*, he wore a *lungi* and a *ganji* and his head was swathed in a turban. All *satyagrahi*s, including even businessmen, were filled with renewed enthusiasm to see Gandhi attired in this way.

He now started attending court also in the same dress. The first time he went thus, he couldn't help thinking of the time when he had invited the laughter of his colleagues with his collar showering starch. That day, he had been a little self-conscious, but, today, he wasn't self-conscious or uncomfortable in the least. The fear did of course strike him once that there may be a repeat of the Durban incident. The magistrate did give him the once-over, to which Mohandas jokingly responded with: 'Milord, I am fully clothed from head to toe; in fact, even the regulation gown is in place. No turban either. The hair is of course closely cropped, but there are many bald ones among the lawyers who do not even wear a wig to the court.'

The magistrate gave a brief smile and moved on.

~

There was another challenge facing Mohandas. The well-to-do among the jailed had families, homes and resources, but most of the *satyagrahi*s were without such support. They had to leave their families behind without anyone to look after their needs, except God. Not only did they have no homes, sometimes even food was not available. *Satyagraha* followed no time schedule and no one knew how long it was going to last. Hundreds, even thousands, had set out on *satyagraha* at a single call from him and their families were reduced to moving from place to place looking for their next meal. People were hesitant to give them employment. A stint in jail made these men even more tainted in the eyes of the sahibs.

The idea that was bugging Mohandas day and night was why they could not set up an ashram (a settlement) like Phoenix in Transvaal itself. Families of the *satyagrahi*s could live there with self-respect, working with their hands for their living, and learning to live a simple but organized life. Nature could be their companion.

One day, Mohandas remarked to Kallenbach: 'When I see the poor *satyagrahi*s and their families roaming the streets, my heart breaks. I cannot think of a way to help them. They readily march off to jail for their rights, leaving their families to the care of God. What can we do to help them in return for their sacrifice?'

'I never thought of that,' said Kallenbach. 'Tell me what we should do.'

'One solution is to take them all to Phoenix, which is four hundred kilometres from here. The travel will be expensive and the people may not be ready to leave their homes. Moreover, the government would not like anything better.' Mohandas laughed and continued: 'It will also make it easier for people to spread word that I have turned traitor and joined General Smuts.'

'So?'

'Why don't we set up an ashram here like the one in Phoenix where these people can live together, work collectively and produce whatever they need? Let them build their lives with their own hands. A community that does not work with its hands remains a parasite community. The native males, the local Englishmen and the princes of India are good examples.'

'That's a great idea,' Kallenbach jumped with joy. 'Absolutely right! Maybe this way we can transform their lives and generate self-reliance and self-confidence in them.'

Mohandas laughed. 'But not without money. We'll need acres of land. With so many people living and working there, there will be needs to be met.'

'Of course! In fact, with so many people living together, there could be problems as well.' Kallenbach's eyes had a glint in them. A gleam of affection for Mohandas too had appeared in them.

'Of course, there will be problems. I was brought up in a joint family, where there were a hundred or so people at every meal. My mother cooked for everyone. I have developed a deep understanding of the differences in human nature. Where there are love and morality, you need no law and no courts. People grow up learning to help one another. Those who don't are left struggling far, far behind. For all this, you need a minimum degree of tolerance and respect for one another. My parents were experts in this field.'

'Don't you think this degree of idealism may prove a little too much for these people?'

'Not at all. We are born with these germs in us. We are never able to muster the necessary wherewithal to nurse and develop these germs like silkworms. In fact, we just ignore them as worthless stuff. If we are going to put such things as respect for one another, regular work habits, etc. in the category of idealism, what are we going to regard as ordinary qualities? All that we need to do is to create the necessary environment. If we don't do this, the germs will not survive.'

Kallenbach spoke very seriously: 'We must do something for them. I'll start looking for land. Our dream will take shape on that land. I'll lay down everything I have for this dream.'

'It's all a question of money.'

'That's not for you to worry about, Gandhibhai. I have been thinking about a farm for a long time. I want to call it "Tolstoy Farm".'

Mohandas was so overwhelmed with emotion that he embraced Kallenbach. Kallenbach felt as if a current of energy had also started flowing within him.

The financial aid given to the families of *satyagrahi*s from the trust was inadequate. Some of the families had a large number of members; others had only one or two. It was also not feasible to select only bachelors and widowers for *satyagraha*. There was also a lot of room for foul play. Sometimes, needy families did not get a fair deal. The only way of avoiding such problems was communal living, where everyone would be required to work and live honestly and truthfully. The only problem was space. If they lived in Johannesburg, all the hard-earned money would go towards paying rent. That would be like emptying a bucket where a thimbleful of water would do.

Kallenbach started looking for land. On the twenty-first mile from Johannesburg there was a small station called Lawley. Nearly a mile from the station a plot of land was available. Kallenbach looked it up and was delighted to see such a vast single unit of land. He immediately bought up eleven hundred acres of land of which he transferred a hundred acres to Mohandas free of cost and rent. The only condition was that when the plot was no longer in use, it should be handed back to Kallenbach.

The farm had about a thousand fruit trees, most of them on the land where Gandhi was to set up his ashram. The trees were laden with fruit at the time. When the breeze blew, you felt as if young kids were playing hide-and-seek. There was a small bungalow on the plot which could easily accommodate ten or twelve people. When the fruits ripened, there would be piles of oranges, plums and peaches. About five hundred yards from the bungalow there was a spring with a continuous flow of water so clean and cool that a drink left you feeling delightfully contented with life. The water had to be fetched from the spring. Everyone pitched in for this work; in fact, not only for this work but also for cooking, cleaning, collecting firewood and the rest.

At first, no one wanted to leave his home to come to the farm and everyone offered excuses. As time passed and the aims of the farm were explained to them, they started trickling in. Life on the farm was comparatively difficult but open and sociable. Slowly they began to love the place. Among them were people who had sacrificed their comforts for the *satyagraha* and others who had overlooked poverty, scarcity and hunger to offer themselves for *satyagraha*. The farm soon became a sheltering place for Hindus, Muslims, Parsis, Christians and people of other communities from Gujarat, Madras, Andhra, Bihar, etc. Among them there were forty young men, two or three elderly persons, five women and about twenty-five or thirty children. They all got together to cook and serve the meals. Everyone had his or her own tales of joy and sorrow to narrate and they shared them with one another. Sometimes, they also fell out with one another but soon got together again. Gandhibhai and Kallenbach were always there to take care of everything else.

It was unanimously decided that everyone in the farm should be served vegetarian food. There were among the inmates many Christians and Muslims who were regular meat-eaters and there was no question of their eating vegetarian food. For them it was an ethical and social issue. In any case, no one could be forced to eat against his choice, especially to eat food which he had never eaten. He would prefer to stay hungry than eat such food. But introducing meat in the menu would mean a rise in expenses and arranging for separate kitchens. Mohandas had seen the messy situation separate kitchens could land you in at the Calcutta session of the Congress. On that occasion, even co-religionists had separate kitchens.

Mohandas had no objection to meat eating. His objection was to the eating of beef. In any case, he had no authority to impose restrictions on people's diets. Prohibiting meat would have meant restricting *satyagraha* to vegetarians only. He also knew that if one kind of meat was allowed, it would not be possible to keep out other kinds. For a non-vegetarian one kind of meat was as good as another.

Prayers were said twice a day—morning and evening. Morning prayers were followed by the day's work while evening prayers meant calling it a day. Evening prayers were the time for Mohandas to put his thoughts before the inmates and to listen to theirs. In one of the evening meetings, Mohandas raised the issue of food. The Muslims agreed to eat vegetarian food without any discussion. He talked to the Christians separately: it was the first time that he was talking to the Christian women in the absence of their husbands. Mohandas said to them: 'If you wish to be served beef, we will try and arrange it, but the problem is money. Space too is a problem, and so are my feelings. My feelings however are not more important than your needs. The feelings are personal to me.'

The ladies discussed the issue among themselves and said: 'Gandhibhai, please do not worry on our account. Vegetarian food is all right with us.'

'In that case, food will be your responsibility. I and my friends will always be there to help you.' Then he laughed and said: 'My father was very good at cutting vegetables. He could cut vegetables for forty people at a time.' They all laughed.

'I am in no way inferior to him.' The laughter became louder.

A kitchen started functioning. People sat in lines to have their meals. They washed their dishes after the meals and arranged them neatly in their proper place. They took turns to clean the cooking utensils in teams of three or four.

The name Tolstoy Farm had been finally settled on. The name had been conceived by Kallenbach in advance.

Pragji Khandubhai made straight for the farm after he was released from jail. Mohandas spoke to him: 'Life will be hard for you here. You are used to an easy life. The freezing cold, the scorching sun, the hard rain and a life of hard labour—all this will not agree with you.'

Khandubhai laughed. 'You know well enough Gandhibhai this place holds no horrors for someone who has spent time in Transvaal jails.'

Blocks of houses had not been readied by then. People lived in tents. Everyone had to carry construction material like wood planks, iron sheets, etc. Blocks of wood had to be cut to different sizes as required. The houses were to be readied in the shortest possible time. The architect was Kallenbach. A Gujarati mason called Narayan had made his services available free of charge. Thambi Naidu was in charge of procurement of material. He was also in charge of cleaning and sanitation. All other work was shared by all inmates. For Pragji, this involved excessive labour. In a sense, it involved more labour than the work he had done in jail. Pragji had a delicate constitution but his will power was infinite. One day, he fell down unconscious at work. It was then decided that he should be given only light work.

Kallenbach told him: 'Please look after the work of weighing and measurement …' The school had not been started by then.

Pragji retorted: 'No, that's not the lesson Gandhibhai has taught us. A *satyagrahi* does not go down before difficulties. He fights them and licks them. That's the true *satyagraha*. No matter what happens, I am not going to show my back.'

He upped and left. A little while later, one could see him lugging a pile of wood.

The inmates were regularly commuting to Johannesburg. Though they travelled third, it still entailed a lot of expense. Hence a meeting of all the inmates was called and the accounts were placed before it. Travel was the second highest item of expenditure after food.

Mohandas said: 'Please note that if we can save the amount being spent on travel to Johannesburg we can put it to better use on other items.'

Kallenbach proposed that train expenses of only those travellers should be met who go to Johannesburg on farm business.

Everyone kept silent and the matter was closed. Though everyone had it in mind, no one could bring himself to ask: 'This means none of us would perhaps ever be able to go to Johannesburg, since none of us has any money.'

Mohandas could read their thoughts from their faces.

The next day, Mohandas got up at half past two in the morning and called out to everyone: 'Any one wishing to go to Johannesburg can join me ...'

A couple of boys turned up. Mohandas explained: 'We are all going to walk and should be in Johannesburg by six or seven o'clock. We'll leave Johannesburg at about four in the afternoon and shall be back here by eight.'

The boys were a bit hesitant. Mohandas elaborated: 'Take it as a part of *satyagraha.* Many of our friends are in jail because of *satyagraha.* Can't we do this little bit as a tribute to them?'

The boys joined him.

When they returned in the evening, they weren't feeling as tired as they had felt when leaving. Mohandas made it a usual practice: he would call out at two-thirty or three in the morning and would leave for Johannesburg with those who joined him. This soon turned into a habit and people started commuting to Johannesburg on foot. Sometime, they stayed the night there. Next morning, they would leave early and would be back in Tolstoy Farm (Ashram) while it was still quite cool. Everyone carried an umbrella, some refreshments in a bag, and a sheet or turban cloth. Eating in the marketplace was forbidden, as that would require cash. And where was the cash?

~

School had started. The pupils had been divided into two groups: one group was taught through Gujarati, the other through English. Mohandas also taught Hindi, Tamil, Urdu and other languages. Mohandas had a unique approach to teaching. He told the pupils interesting stories which the pupils then repeated to one another. This way, their errors could be corrected while their mutual bonds also became stronger. A teacher had been appointed to teach geography, history, general knowledge and arithmetic. Kallenbach taught them carpentry and shoemaking in his workshop.

School worked only in the afternoon hours. Mornings were so hectic that not only children but even adults got tired. Everyone had to join in the work of construction. This was work which involved physical labour. Mohandas was of the view that for the mind to work, the body too must work. The harder the body worked, the better did the brain function. So, you must work both ways physical as well as mental.

The teachers were quite fatigued by the afternoon. Some would even start napping in the class and had to wash their eyes to keep themselves awake. Sometimes, they would just declare a games break and would get busy playing with the pupils. That helped both of them to get over their fatigue. It was up to the teacher to decide when to have games and when to have studies. Occasionally, extracts from the Quran, the Avesta and the Gita were also taught. In fact, there was even a child from the Vora community whom his father had left with Mohandas. Before starting his lessons for the day, Mohandas used to teach him Pothi.

Boys and girls were free to mix. Mohandas wanted to do away with the unnecessary hesitation that separated the two. He often sent them to the spring to have a swim. The spring was only a short distance from the kitchen and was the source of their water supply.

~

That day the children were at the spring. A few of the kids were the bad types. Mohandas had asked them to look after the girls, as they were the senior ones. He had asked them to bathe at the same place. They were all familiar with the principles of *satyagraha*, which taught self-control. Violating self-control would be tantamount to violating purity and trust.

The kids were all excited. They all shouted their assurance that they would protect the sanctity of *satyagraha*. With their clothes in their hands, they all merrily walked towards the spring. Mohandas was keeping a constant eye on them. The kids played for a while and then it was time for a bathe. Mohandas too arrived at the spot. The kids bathed happily, changed their clothes and came back. The kids were quite happy and so was Mohandas. The children had behaved themselves.

At night, they all slept in an open verandah. Mohandas slept in the middle, and the kids spread themselves out all around him like the petals of a flower. The beds were three feet apart, so even if someone was so inclined, he could not indulge in mischief. The mental development of the pupils was following the path of controlled freedom. Kallenbach, however, was not very happy. One day he told Mohandas: 'Gandhibhai, you don't know them. Some of the boys are up to no good; they have designs.'

Mohandas laughed: 'Designs? They can be made to have good designs. They are also our kids. We must keep an eye on them, an eye of trust; but we must also keep the other eye on them, the eye that tells them that they are not free to do as they please. It is after all also our responsibility to improve them, to instil self-confidence in them and to teach them to value purity, isn't it?'

Kallenbach said nothing but he was worried by the rising sense of unrestrained freedom among the young ones.

One day, a couple of girls came to Mohandas, crying. Mohandas was puzzled and asked 'What happened? Why are you crying?'

They continued to cry though Mohandas tried hard to console them. The girls could not muster enough courage to speak out. It was with great difficulty that they were able to convey that a boy had stroked the hair of one of them in a strange way.

Mohandas felt as if he had been struck hard from behind. It had hit him harder than the blow Mir Alam had struck at him. That blow had only hit the body; this one had blown apart his inner being. He found his legs shaking even as he sat on the ground. Mohandas immediately called the boy. He was a grown up lad now.

Mohandas spoke in quiet tones: 'You have betrayed my trust. You have shattered the trust of these girls. The faith of everyone in Tolstoy Farm has been shaken. The trust that the girls' parents had placed on me, on this ashram and its inmates has been wounded.'

The boy stood quietly.

Mohnadas continued: 'Do you know that Ravana couldn't so much as lay a finger on Sita, though Ram was thousands of miles away. Why? All because of the pure soul that Sita was. He had evil designs, but he was afraid of truth and purity. You have tried to violate the purity of these innocent girls' minds.'

Other farm workers had also gathered around them.

Mohandas was continuing: 'You touched her hair, didn't you? You had sin in your mind.'

The boy only said: 'It was a mistake…'

'No. You have to leave this place.'

That shocked even the girls.

Mohandas couldn't sleep that night. It troubled him no end to think that his experiment had failed. It must be due to a deficiency in my own determination, he thought. What is it that I need to do so that these people can stand warned? What can I do to destroy this seed of sin which has been planted in the people's hearts? Mohandas had a feeling that every one of the inmates of the ashram was lying awake, that even the children were restless. When he dozed off momentarily he felt as if sparks had been sown all around the Farm and they could burst into flames any moment and set the whole Tolstoy Farm ablaze.

The next morning, Mohandas went and escorted both the girls to his room. He told them: 'Look, I know that you are innocent. I am like your mother. A mother loves her children the most and also knows what is in their best interests. It sometimes so happens that even an innocent person has to make sacrifices so that others can be rid of their sins. I am particularly grieved by the fact that it was one of my own children who did this. The fault is mine. I must also do the necessary penance. I am now asking you in the capacity of a mother if you will do what I ask you to do.'

The girls remained silent. Mohandas said: 'You didn't say anything, but my advice to you is that you should let me cut your hair. I know that your hair is your beauty, but your hair was responsible for the evil thoughts in the boy's mind. By losing your hair you will also be purged of the desire and the evil thoughts that might have percolated into your mind because of his behaviour. The boy too will be made to realize the seriousness of his error. A signal will also go out to the other boys of Tolstoy Farm. A cure has to be multi-pronged for the disease to be expelled totally from the body. And this is a disease which is capable of devouring the whole of the ashram.'

The girls started crying: '*Bapu*, please, spare our hair. What wrong have we done?'

'I know that you have done no wrong,' said Mohandas. He paused for a while and continued, 'But I need your help in eradicating this sin from its very roots, this sin the seeds of which have been sown by one of my own children. The feeling which the hair raised in the mind of that boy, it could also raise in the minds of others. The boy of course has to go. I wish that the sin should also go with him and that he should face the truth. This will be your *satyagraha*.'

The girls left his presence, crying.

The boy came to Mohandas' room at night. Mohandas was sitting quietly, his eyes closed. The boy came and stood quietly. A little time passed and then Mohandas asked his eyes still closed: 'Are you ready to leave?'

'Yes, *Bapu*!' He almost choked on his words. There was another spell of silence.

'Did you tell your *Ba*?'

'Yes.'

'What did she say?'

'She said: 'It's you duty to do as *Bapu* tells you.'

'Do you want to say something?'

No words came out for a minute. Then, trying to control himself, he said: '*Bapu*! Punish me any way you like, but don't ask the girls to cut their hair.' A soft cry escaped his lips.

'I know it's not their fault, but the sin that you committed has rubbed off on them too. Stay by yourself for a while and reflect. Their hair will soon be back to normal, but the injustice you have done them by this deed of yours you will never be able to forget.'

The boy left. Mohandas sat the whole night in the same position.

The next day, Mohandas called all the ladies on the farm to a meeting. He told them: 'You are all aware why I have called you here today. I am asking for permission to cut the hair of these two girls not because I think they are guilty. I think their minds are as pure as the water of the holy river Ganga. But an evil thought in the mind of one of my own children, belonging to my own ashram, has sullied their hair too. By cutting their hair the evil that may have arisen in the minds of the girls will also be washed away. It will also serve as a warning to those who may be nursing such evil thoughts in their minds. I am aware that the event came about because I sent the boys and the girls together to the spring for a bathe. My experiment, or my resolve, failed, and for this I also hold myself guilty. I will atone for my failure by going on a fast.'

One of the ladies said: 'Gandhibhai, what you are saying is absolutely right, but what kind of justice is this which punishes the innocent?'

'This is not about giving or receiving punishment. This is also *satyagraha*. Look at it like this: It is the British government that is at fault, yet it is we who are on *satyagraha*. Why? It is the holy going on *satyagraha* against the unholy; it is the self-sacrifice of the holy. By allowing their hair to be cut, these girls will of course be doing themselves a good turn, but they will also be helping others to rid their minds of sin. It will help them purge their conscience of evil.'

Another lady said: 'For young, unmarried girls, their hair is like feathers to a peacock, or like its song to a *koel*. Losing their hair will be for them like what losing its sweet voice is to a *koel*, or losing its feathers is to a peacock. The pain will be the same.'

'I am not unjust, nor am I a tyrant. Dadhichi protected his godhood by sacrificing his bones; the thunder made from his bones helped kill the demons. The power of those bones came from the sacrifice made by Dadhichi. The hair will grow back again, but the sacrifice they make now will help eliminate the untimely sin that is growing in their minds. If one child could have this sin in his mind, it could well be growing in the minds of other young men too. This will be a sacrifice these young girls will be making for the good of the coming generation.'

The ladies could appreciate the arguments of Mohandas but could not bring themselves to believe in them. Mohandas made a final attempt: 'The husbands of most of you are in jail. Why did you let them go to jail? Wasn't it because their sacrifice would ensure the rights of Indians and Asians in this country? Don't you love your husbands and children as much as the girls love their hair? They went to jail protesting against external oppression. The evil thoughts of man not only mean internal oppression for him, they also include those around him in their orbit of oppression. *Satyagraha* means precisely this: That we should forever be ready to sacrifice the things dearest to us in order that the society around us can be made free of oppression.'

The ladies listened to Mohandas' views. Now they had no option but to accept Gandhibhai's arguments.

There was no barber on the farm. The inmates cut each other's hair when required. Scissors, razor and other hair cutting implements were available. Mohandas stood cutting the girls' hair with his own hands as everyone watched. Each lock of hair was wet with the girls' tears. As the locks fell to the floor, every woman present broke into sobs. Mohandas however worked away quite undisturbed. The girls too seemed to have reconciled themselves to the inevitable: they also appeared quite unperturbed. When all the hair had been cut, the two girls swept up the locks into their hands and carried them before them as if some affinity still survived with them. All the women followed them. Kastur was not among those present.

When everyone had left, Kallenbach said: 'Gandhibhai, I didn't know you could be so hard-hearted when you wanted to.'

~

A kind of emotional understanding had always existed between Kallenbach and Mohandas. Kallenbach called Mohandas the Upper House, while Mohandas called Kallenbach the Lower House. That was how they always addressed each other, especially in letters.

When Kastur had fallen sick and the doctor had administered beef soup to her, Mohandas wrote a detailed report of the incident to Lower House from Phoenix. 'Lower House,' he wrote, 'when I woke up on Saturday morning, I was dreaming that the house I was sleeping in was on fire. I had got up on time to leave the house but I wasn't quite ready to lock up the house. From this dream, I concluded that Kastur was no more. Wasn't it stupid of me? In those days she was under the treatment of Dr. Nanji. On Sunday, she was much better. But we still can't be sure if she will live or not. Like a small child, she doesn't let me leave her side even for a minute. She clings to me and throws her arms around me. Next week, I have to go. I am afraid my leaving her side might mean death for her, but next week I simply must go, unless, of course, I am obliged to accept His Majesty's hospitality ...'

While staying on Tolstoy Farm, the bond between Mohandas and Kallenbach had grown stronger. They did almost everything together—

coming, going, eating, sleeping, everything was done together. Often they would work together while also carrying out a discussion. More of a debate than a discussion, actually.

There were snakes galore on the farm. Kallenbach sided with those who wanted the snakes killed. Mohandas disagreed strongly. 'No, Lower House,' he would say, 'A snake may be a dangerous reptile, but I don't favour killing it.'

That came as a surprise to Kallenbach. It was hard for any white to agree that killing a snake could be wrong. It was a creature that could bite a man resulting in his death. What mercy could there be for such a creature?

Mohnadas laughed: 'Exactly what the snake must think about us. Here's a human being, He'll kill us the moment he sees us; so bite him at the first opportunity.'

'Does a snake think?'

'Not being a snake myself, I can't answer your question accurately.' Kallenbach smiled at the answer. Mohandas continued: 'Let's switch roles for a moment. Let's assume that a snake can think and speak and knows that man can kill him. What would be its reaction in the situation?'

Kallenbach was perplexed. So that he could answer Mohandas' question, he started collecting books on snakes and started studying snakes. Soon he forgot about the question but his curiosity about snakes went on increasing. How many types of snakes are there? Which snake is poisonous and which is not? Whenever he saw a snake, he collected some farm inmates and took them to see it. He told them about its genus, about how dangerous it was, if at all, and whether it was a male or a female.

One day, Kallenbach observed that if they couldn't kill snakes, they should make friends with them.

And he made friends with a cobra. He fed him with his own hands. The inmates were frightened by this act of Kallenbach, but they also enjoyed it.

Kallenbach always enjoined on the people not to disturb a snake when it was enjoying its solitude.

One day, Upper House spoke to Kallenbach: 'Lower House,' he said, 'You do it in a spirit of friendship, but it is entirely possible that the cobra does not appreciate your friendship. You are not entirely free of fear either, or you wouldn't keep him in a cage. If it is released from the cage, neither you, nor I would have courage enough to play with it. If we can, let us develop that kind of courage. There are animals which understand friendship and enmity. In taming a cobra, you may be motivated by a sense of friendship, but it is certainly not your love for him. Our love needs to be so transparent that even a cobra can see it. Furthermore, you don't keep your friends in a cage.'

Kallenbach pondered the points made by Mohandas for several days. Meanwhile, the cobra also continued. The ashramites continued to enjoy the cobra. Mohandas' curiosity too went on mounting and he started observing the cobra's daily routine very carefully. Sometimes, the caged cobra became so harried and hassled that he started slithering hither and thither inside the cage in an attempt to break free of the cage. Sometimes, he hissed so viciously that you felt he was going to blow up the cage itself.

It was hard to say if he had developed recognition for Kallenbach, but when Kallenbach was around, he did quieten down bit by little bit.

One day, when Kallenbach arrived at his cage to feed him, he found the cage empty. The prisoner had flown the coop. Kallenbach had a good laugh, all to himself.

~

Those were days of hectic activity in Tolstoy Farm. Some people were always saying their farewells because they would be going to jail, while others were back from jail and would be trying to find their place again among their near and dear ones. One morning, the inmates saw two men coming from the direction of Transvaal, taking long strides. When they approached closer, people were taken by surprise. The court cases against these two were still in progress, so how could they be walking free. Had they run away from custody? If that was the case, that would certainly bring a bad name to *satyagraha*.

When the two saw everyone's gaze fixed at them, they laughed and said: 'Why are you all looking at us as if we are escapees from a jail?'

Mohandas said: 'Your cases are still not over and the final verdict is still awaited.'

One of them said: 'Gandhibhai, it is your *satyagraha* that has made this wonder possible.'

The other one said: 'We are here to see you and must go back by the evening train.'

Their relatives were on the Farm too. They said: 'If they are escapees, then the police are sure to come and re-arrest them. Thank God! The police are not here yet.'

Mohandas said: 'Let's first hear what they have to say then we will think of the police. If they turn out to be escapees, I will personally return them to the police.'

The two had bath and lunch and then rested for a while. Then they revealed the secret: 'The case was adjourned yesterday. The verdict will be delivered tomorrow.'

They all knew what the verdict was going to be.

Actually what had happened was that the two had told the magistrate: 'Sir, after the verdict has been announced, it will no longer be possible for us to go and see our families. If you permit us, we will go and see our relatives at the Tolstoy Farm. We will be back the day after tomorrow.'

The prosecuting lawyer opposed the request: 'How can the accused be released without bail? They have confessed their guilt and they can surely turn fugitives.'

The magistrate said: 'These two have courted arrest. These two are *satyagrahi*s. They are crazy about going to jail and serving out their punishment. I have never seen anyone before who would court arrest, would accept his guilt and then ask for the severest punishment. That is what Mr. Gandhi does, and these people are his companions.'

'But ...'

'You have done your duty. If I were to fine them and release them, I know they would not deposit the fines. They are hell bent on serving jail punishment. I order them to be released on personal bonds. The condition is that they must present themselves at the appointed time the day after tomorrow in court to receive the verdict.'

Mohandas closed his eyes. Then he said: 'I am sorry. For a moment I had forgotten what it meant to be a *satyagrahi.* I went along with the impression that you may have run away out of fear of the hard life in jail. A *satyagrahi*'s faith is his greatest asset.'

Suddenly, someone jumped up and said: 'Hurry! There are only twenty minutes left for the train to arrive.'

The two jumped up too and said to Gandhibhai: 'Gandhibhai, if we miss the train, we will miss the court tomorrow morning and we will have broken our word. We must leave now.'

'Come on, we will go with you.'

'No, you won't be able to keep pace with us. We will have to make a dash for it, and we may still miss the train.

They picked up their things and started running.

The two were running to receive their punishment and to keep a *satyagrahi*'s promise. Behind them, at some distance, walked Mohandas and two or three of his companions at a furious pace. When they were still at some distance from the Lawley station, the train steamed in. They raised their speed but the train let out its last whistle and steamed out. The Station Master looked around to see the two young men running with Mohandas and his companions rushing behind them. He signalled the train to a stop. The two made it to the train and the train left again.

Mohandas and his friends reached the place after a short while, panting profusely and bathed in sweat. The station master offered them a seat and inquired: 'Did you want to catch the train too?'

'No, we were only seeing them off. If they had missed the train, it would have brought a bad name to the *satyagrahi*s. By detaining the train for them, you have safeguarded the honour of the *satyagrahis*. How can we repay your favour?'

The station master was a white. He said: 'Living in this forest, you are fighting for your rights, even if the fight is directed against us …' He laughed and continued: 'It's our duty to do whatever we can to help you.'

Mohandas placed a hand on his shoulder and said: 'The *satyagrahis* have nothing: no money for bribes, no strength for the struggle. All they can do is self-sacrifice. Put up with everything and keep up the struggle—that's all they can do. If sometimes someone is kind enough to cooperate with us that makes our goal much easier to achieve. If it hadn't been your wish, you would not have stopped a train that had already left and there was nothing we could have done. By stopping the train, you have done so much for us that we can never thank you enough for it. Our young men were able to keep their promise and our movement was saved a lot of infamy.'

'The fact that you put up with everything without raising any questions also raises a number of ethical questions before us …,' said the station master gravely.

When they left, the station master came out to bid them goodbye and stood watching them even as they left, followed by a small swell of dust.

~

Mohandas' legal practice had almost come to a stop as it was necessary for him to stay on the Farm. He had had however a number of clients who had been greatly influenced by his thought and behaviour. He had once taken up the case of a client called Lutawan who had since been released from his *girmit*. He was now an old man plagued by breathing problems. He had been to a number of vaids and doctors. He was now convinced that only Gandhibhai could get him release from his disease just as he had helped him win his case. One day, he found out that Gandhibhai had opened a farm near the Lawley station. He asked his way to the ashram.

Arriving at the ashram, Lutawan was dumbfounded to discover that Gandhibhai still remembered his name. There must be something extraordinary about this man, he thought. He stood there with folded hands, his breathing growing heavier every minute. Gandhibhai inquired: 'You don't seem to be well, Lutawan?'

Tears welled up in his eyes. 'You know everything, Gandhibhai. I have had all kinds of treatment but to no avail. You got me release from *girmit*; please get me a release from this ailment too.'

He was from eastern part of north India and was speaking in Awadhi.

Gandhibhai laughed: 'A court case and a disease are two very different things, Lutawan. But if you want me to treat you, you will have to stay here. Another thing: do you smoke or drink?'

'I chew tobacco, but that's all.'

'You'll have to give up tobacco. There can't be any treatment without your giving it up, do you understand?'

At first, he hesitated a little, but then he consented.

Mohandas started his treatment. The treatment was so different from the other treatments he had undergone that Lutawan was convinced that he would soon be on the road to recovery. Which doctor bothered about treating a patient in this way keeping the patient with him? This was surely something special.

He had to spend the first twenty-four hours without food except a little lemon-water and honey. Every afternoon, he was given a sun bath for fifteen minutes. The weather wasn't particularly hot. Next, he was given some rice, olive oil, honey, oats and sweet oranges; sometimes also grapes. He was also given wheat coffee. In fact, every inmate was given wheat coffee once a day. Mohandas also made him sleep with him, but he slept inside the room. Within a week, strength had returned to Lutawan's body. The asthma was also showing signs of improvement. But not a day passed without his getting a coughing fit at night.

Mohandas was suspicious. He asked him: 'Do you smoke at night?'

'Not at all, Gandhibhai, not at all.'

Mohandas was worried. Why the coughing fit? He decided to investigate. He would keep awake one night. He lay in bed but the moment he started dozing off he forced open his eyes. His bed was beside the door in the verandah. Lutawan slept inside the room, a little away from the door, which was partially closed. At midnight, Lutawan got his coughing fit. Mohandas got up and opened the door. Lutawan was puffing away. One puff and he would start coughing. As the cough subsided, he had another puff. Mohandas lighted his torch. Lutawan was flabbergasted to see Mohandas standing before him. He knew at once that he had been caught red-handed. Not knowing what to do, he fell at Mohandas' feet on the spot and started crying: 'I have blundered. I have tried to cheat on a man like you, though I knew that no one can keep any secret from you. I promise never to smoke again. I had told you a lie.'

Tears rolled down his cheeks. Mohandas tried to console him.

The punishment Mohandas gave him was that he was not allowed to sleep inside the room any more. In a month's time, Lutawan showed considerable improvement in his condition.

~

Mohandas travelled to Phoenix frequently. The Phoenix of his dreams was being built and he devoted all his spare time to it.

After spending three years outside, Millie and Polak had returned to Phoenix, which had undergone considerable changes in the meantime. Polak intended to settle down in Durban. Many of the old Phoenicians had left and their places had been taken by new inmates. The farms too had undergone a lot of change. Fields had been fenced. Clearing of fields, sowing, etc. had considerably improved. People worked on their fields with complete sincerity. They grew their own vegetables. Fruit trees had grown big and had started flowering. Two or three houses were now bigger than before and had been furnished too. Curtains hung on walls and doors. A room had been constructed for the school. A white lady taught the children. She was not trained, but Mohandas liked her because he thought her heart and mind were in the right place. Kids from the ages of five to seventeen were admitted to the school. There were a few kids who had been entrusted to Mohandas' care by their parents. Kids included both boys and girls.

A few of the boys were adolescents now and naturally they were attracted towards girls, even very young girls. Mohandas knew that they were trying to grapple with the mysteries of life. Though the girls were young, the boys liked to go to their houses for playing. Mohandas had ordered a few books on the subject to raise their understanding of the problem. Mohandas asked Millie to read out portions from these books to the children. 'It will help in guiding their curiosity in the right direction, which might otherwise go into wrong channels,' he told her.

There was a book entitled *What Every Young Boy and Girl must Know.*

Millie called the boys and said: 'Read out portions of this book by turns.'

She thought this would help raise the sense of moral responsibility among the boys. The boys took great interest in the book and asked a variety of questions. Mohandas and Millie were happy that the studies were moving in the right direction.

Then one day, a boy grabbed a small girl. Mohandas asked the boy: Why did you do it?'

'I was helpless,' said the boy honestly. 'I felt like it and so I did it.'

The girls' parents were furious and withdrew the girl from the school without discussing the problem with Mohandas. Thereafter they kept a strict watch on the girl at all times. So long as they stayed in Phoenix, they never let the girl out of their sight. This was a silent vote of no-confidence on Mohandas and his programme of education.

Mohandas always maintained a cheerful exterior, but that day he appeared very slow and serious. Millie and Polak were in Phoenix. When Millie greeted Mohandas, he responded in a very absent-minded manner. Millie did not like it. Usually, when Mohandas responded to greetings there was certain warmth about it.

Millie stopped and asked: 'What's the matter, Gandhibhai? Why are you so upset? Are you feeling fine?'

Gandhibhai took Millie aside. From his face, one could tell that the light within him had gone out and the effect was clear to see from the face. He spoke in a low voice: 'Everything is finished.'

'What do you mean?'

'Yes. There's been an explosion which has shaken the whole of Phoenix.'

'Tell me what has happened,' said Millie, her voice cold with worry. Mohandas' self-confidence had never been shaken like this before. His belief in truth and his constant activity always kept him fresh and bubbling.

'Jakie has lost everything. She has been with Mani …,' he could not continue.

'Are you completely sure?' Millie was shocked.

'She has admitted it herself.'

'I don't understand it. It's not possible. You knew everything about her activities, the places she goes to, so how did it happen?'

'I also thought that I knew her well. She is a friend's daughter, like my own daughter, but apparently I was wrong.' He became silent. Then he took a long breath and said: 'When she borrowed books from me I thought she was reading them while walking around the place. But she apparently walked off and met Mani at the river where they bathed in the river together.'

'Had this been going on for sometime?'

'At least for the last few weeks. Kastur had said something once or twice and Kallenbach too had mentioned something in Johannesburg.'

A stunned silence reigned all round. Words seem to have frozen deep inside. Breathing itself was hard and hesitant. Depression, like darkness, had descended all over. Millie was thinking that if the news was broadcast, Gandhibhai's reputation will be reduced to dust. The whole world will know what was going on in Phoenix. Mohandas himself had different worries: 'Where did I go wrong? Was it in my action or in my faith? What is the solution?'

'Can't we keep this incident to ourselves?'

'Truth and sin both are like rays of the sun and their accompanying shadows. Wherever there are sun's rays, there are also shadows. You can hide neither the rays nor the shadows.'

He continued: 'Everyone knew about it; I was the only one ignorant. What can I possibly tell Jakie's family? I am the one solely responsible for the whole thing.'

'How can you possibly hold yourself responsible? What was your fault?'

'There is no one else I can blame. There is no one to blame except me. I ignored the writing on the wall.'

Millie spoke emphatically: 'You are not to blame at all.'

Her face was red with rage. 'You gave that girl all your love. You gave her your trust and your protection, and she betrayed that trust. Mani is not to blame; he is too young for that. How much would he know about a woman? She must have cajoled him into it.' She paused a little and then asked: 'What are you going to do?'

'We'll have to tell her family. There's no other way. I'll have to put up with all the censure and condemnation they are bound to fling at me. Jakie is of course very unhappy. She knows what she has done. She has been crying continuously for the last twenty-four hours.'

'Gandhibhai, I have no sympathy for her, but I feel sorry for Mani. Perhaps he didn't even know what sex is before this incident took place. What have you thought about him?'

'I don't know what to think about either of them. I have lost faith in both of them. I can't even allow them to see each other alone any more.'

Millie suddenly blurted out: 'Do you think she is pregnant?'

'Thank God! We've been spared that.'

'Oh! What a mercy!'

'I've told Jakie that I'm also responsible for this act of sin. I'll atone for it by fasting.'

'But she is a married woman.'

'Yes. Her husband, Manilal Doctor, is in Fiji, serving Indians. A very good man. A true *satyagrahi*! I have asked him to go to Mauritius after he has finished his work in Fiji. They wanted somebody who could work for them keeping their interests above his own.'

'So she can't say that she is in love with Mani. It is pure lust.'

Mohandas started pacing the room. Millie resumed her silence.

When Mohandas started his fast, Jakie joined him. All inmates gathered in the evening for prayers and sang *bhajan*s.

That was the last day of the fast. Jakie sang 'Lead kindly light …' Others sang after her. When the bhajan ended, Jakie got up from her place and came and stood in front of the inmates and said: 'I wish to confess my sin in front of all of you.'

Tears streamed down her cheeks. Everybody held his breath. Mohandas sat with his eyes closed. Jakie said: 'I am a sinner. Though married, I have indulged in sin with an innocent child. I renounce all jewellery…' and she removed every piece of jewellery from her body.

She continued: 'I renounce my hair; it was at the root of my sin.' She picked up a pair of scissors and cut down her beautiful, black and flowing hair. Kastur watched her from a distance, her face dripping disgust.

Jakie said: 'From this day on, I shall wear clothes to cover my body, not to adorn it.' And that very day she changed into white clothes.

Mohandas was reminded of the girls whose hair he had cut with his own hands. Jakie went up to Mohandas, put her hair at his feet and said: 'Mohandas uncle, I am guilty. Give me whatever punishment you will; I will accept it gladly. Please give up your fast and stop adding to my guilt.'

Mohandas continued to sit with his eyes closed as if he was in a trance. He opened his eyes a little later and asked for some lemon water. Jakie gave it to him and his fast was broken. Kastur, who sat there, got up and left.

The ashramites started singing the bhajan in unison:

Vaishnava jan to taine kahiye je peer parai jane re …

~

Mohnadas was very weak. The fast had turned him into a skeleton.

Polak and Millie, who had left for Durban in the meantime, had returned after a fortnight. Polak asked Mohandas: 'How are you, Gandhibhai?

Don't you think you have enough responsibilities on you for you to involve yourself in such petty personal matters and destroy yourself in the process?'

'So long as the individual is not reformed, how can the society be reformed? Society is bigger than the individual and the individual is bigger than the society. I cannot afford to ignore either of them. If I think only of the individual, we cannot have a healthy society; if I think only of the society, I must reckon with the fact that the individual by himself does not amount to much.'

To Millie, he said: 'Jakie admitted her guilt in the presence of all the inmates. Confession has delivered her soul of the sin. When her atonement is complete, she will be like as she was before.'

Millie smiled: 'Gandhibhai, why do you take everyone to be like yourself?'

'Why don't you go and meet her?'

'If you say so. But I don't agree with you.'

'She is there in the garden, in the back.'

Millie came back. Mohandas looked at her quizzically.

Millie said: 'There is not a shred of repentance on her face. She cut down her hair, changed her clothing, shed all jewellery, but not a shred of change in her mind. Still the same merry, carefree Jakie.'

'Millie, she admitted her guilt without pressure from any quarters.'

'The pressure was your fast.'

'That was my atonement.'

'Maybe for you, but not for her. Gandhibhai, I don't believe in showmanship. I haven't the slightest sympathy for her. What she has done is immoral.'

Mohandas was calm. He said after a while: 'Why are you so hard-hearted, Millie? How much do we know about others? What are their shortcomings, what are the various weaknesses they are hiding within? We have condemned her act, but how long shall we go on condemning the individual? To make a man a sinner for life and to hate a sinner is a greater act of sin than the act for which we hate the sinner.'

'I am not ready to look upon her as the heroine of this tragedy.'

Polak was listening to their conversation silently. He asked: 'What have you decided about Mani?'

'It is true that he was an unwitting participant in that act, but he is also to blame. He has promised to me that he shall not get married unless he has my permission. He will observe *brahmacharya* in toto.'

~

XXIV

Tolstoy Farm was now, in a way, a *satyagraha* ashram. Everyone who came to the farm or left it, was a *satyagrahi*. The families of *satyagrahi*s may not have been going to jails but they too were really part of the *satyagraha* at large. Exiled from their homes, they were leading monastic lives at the Farm. Their austere lives served as capsules of cooperation and moral support for the *satyagrahi*s. No *satyagrahi* had taken success as his aim. The aim was to keep up the fight. That was their pleasure and that was their life. No hope of an approaching victory formed the basis of their struggle. That was their daily routine. The pain of defeat held no meaning for them. For them, the struggle was like an infinitely long road on which they had to keep moving till the end arrived. They had no idea how long or how short the road was, nor did they care about it. Members of their families living on the farm too had entered into a truce with time, so they had now no reason to be impatient. Joy and sorrow now held no meaning for them. They knew that their dear ones were on *satyagraha* elsewhere and they themselves were bearing the heat of that *satyagraha* on the farm. They were like the anchor that kept them steady in the sea of struggle.

Those who had their sympathies with the *satyagrahi*s took pity on their condition: 'You call it a life? It's either jail or jungle for you.'

But there were also people who thought, even said so openly: 'Good for nothing labourer, that's what they are. Having nothing to do, they have taken shelter in the jungle, away from all responsibilities, and having a great time gorging themselves. That coolie barrister is aiding and abetting the lazy bums. To all this laziness and escapism, he has given a dignified name –*satyagraha*.'

They spat out the words 'laziness' and 'escapism' with great contempt. Mohandas knew the kind of disinformation that was being spread about the *satyagrahi*s and the Farm. He knew that the Farm was being lampooned as the 'bum headquarters.' He had only one answer to all of them: 'Why worry about those who don't know and don't want to know. The *satyagrahi* has to worry only about the truth. The peace within, self-control and faith are his true companions. He does not worry about others, nor does he depend on them. It is God who provides him shelter, and it is his soul that lights up his path. Success does not respond to your beckoning, nor do you have to wait for it. Struggles which are fought with the aim of success rarely taste success. Failure is as likely a result as success. If anything, it is even more likely. A *satyagrahi* prepares himself more for failure than for success and even accepts it as his success.'

There were occasions when such talk from Mohandas filled the inmates with despair, but when they got down to work again that despair turned into their inner strength.

Mohandas had written to almost every important Indian leader that they should come and see the conditions of Indians in South Africa with their own eyes, but no one had said 'yes' even for formality's sake. They hadn't even said that though they could not join them in their struggle, at least their sympathies were with them and that they would help in bringing their problem to the attention of the people of the world. This behaviour of theirs had not disappointed Mohandas in the least as he knew that after all this war for freedom was by a few people, of a few people and for a few people, so why should outsiders get involved in it? They had to fight this war themselves, whether they won it and lived or lost it and died.

Prof. Gopal Krishna Gokhale was in London. He was keeping an eye on the struggle of Indians in South Africa. He had even got a bill passed in the Legislative Council of India against the export of *girmitiya*s to other countries. Gokhale was the only person who had lent support to Mohandas. He wrote to Mohandas from London that he had talked to the minister for Indian affairs in the British government. He also agreed to visit South Africa to find out about the conditions there. He sent a six-week programme in which he had also included the date of his departure for India.

Mohandas was turning over Gokhale's letter again and again. He couldn't bring himself to believe that a man of Gokhale's stature was coming to South Africa to take stock of Indians' struggle. He had never been so happy before. He wouldn't have been as happy if even His Majesty had himself decided to come to South Africa at his invitation. Always during his stay in South Africa Mohandas had felt that Gokhale was standing behind him solidly. It was thanks to him that a resolution about South Africa could be placed before the Calcutta session of the Indian National Congress even after the President had declared the session closed. It was due to his intervention that Mohandas had been invited to move the resolution. Otherwise the issue of South African Indians could never have been raised on the Congress platform.

Prof. Gokhale had got to know about how the South African colonial governments looked upon his visit while he was still in London. The British minister for Indian affairs had already written to them informing them about the status of Prof. Gokhale and about how much respect the British government accorded him.

Gokhale was not keeping well. Everyone, from the British government to the *girmitiya*, was worried about his travel. Thanks to Mohandas, a number of South African Indians had become familiar with his name. The shipping company had been told that he should be given a comfortable cabin to himself.

At first, the company refused pointblank: The ship has no such cabin. He has to take the ordinary cabin.

Gokhale wrote to the minister for Indian affairs: 'Because of the state of my health, it will not be possible for me to travel by ordinary cabin. The shipping company says it has no such cabin which it can allot me. In view of this, I will have to cancel my journey unless you advise me otherwise.'

The Secretary of State then wrote to the Director of the shipping company: 'The British government accords great respect to Prof.Gokhale. All his needs should be properly taken care. No laxity in this respect should be tolerated.'

Immediately the shipping company made a cabin available. Special care was taken about his food, which was prepared separately from others.

Gokhale took care to meet everybody on the ship. He would sit and chat with them, or played indoor games with them. He would listen to their tales of joy and sorrow. Everyone soon turned a Gokhale fan. Every now and then, the Captain came to check: 'Any problems, Sir?'

Gokhale laughed and said: 'There are problems galore, but none that you could solve.'

The Captain didn't get the point. Gokhale only smiled.

Indians went all out to make Gokhale's reception an occasion to remember. They only knew that the King of India was coming and was going to end all their miseries. The decoration at the Park Station of Johannesburg would have been the envy of kings and emperors. The welcome arch had been designed by Kallenbach personally. Flowers, leaves and buntings surrounded the place. It had taken full fifteen days to decorate the station. The authorities had extended their full cooperation. All the necessary sanctions had been provided without any hitch or hesitation—the most difficult part in all official matters, more so for the class of people known as coolies. Europeans were also invited to the reception. Everyone was present at the station fired by great enthusiasm. A stage had been set up on the platform itself. Standing on it, Prof. Gokhale delivered his short speech.

Gokhale had got off the ship at Cape Town on October 22. The weather was getting warm but was still tolerable. The authorities had reserved a saloon for him. Mohandas was performing the duties of Prof. Gokhale's secretary while Kallenbach was an ordinary volunteer. Every care was being taken to see that no inconvenience was caused to Gokhale.

When Gokhale got down at Park Station, Mohandas put a copy of the programme before him. He laughed and said: 'A young man's programme for an old man like me? But, never mind, I'll try to do full justice to it.'

Mohandas at once realized that he had done a great injustice to Gokhale by having such an elaborate programme for him. 'I'm sorry,' he said, 'I should not have made such a heavy programme for you. Let me take out some of the less important items.'

'It's all right. We'll see how it goes.'

Mohandas withdrew aside and cut short the programme as much as possible.

At Johannesburg, Gokhale had put up at the Kallenbach's home. It was located on a hill called Orange Grove, five miles outside Johannesburg. The house was called Mount View. All around, nature was spread out in its full splendour. Sitting in the verandah, you felt as if you were sitting atop a hill where waves of beauty swept past you, soaking your soul. It was such a rare combination of peace and beauty that Gokhale's heart was filled with pure admiration for Kallenbach.

Another house had been taken on rent where Gokhale met the visitors. A room had been set aside for receiving special guests. Another room for Gokhale to rest and a third room served as a waiting room. Special times had been set aside for receiving dignitaries from the city. The Mayor of Johannesburg had lent his car to Prof. Gokhale.

A dinner had been arranged in honour of Prof. Gokhale. There were about four hundred guests including Europeans, Indians and natives. Europeans must have been around a hundred and fifty in number; natives were only a few. Indians had to buy a guinea ticket. Only vegetarian food had been served. It was a first and a strange experience for them all when whites and blacks, vegetarians and non-vegetarians, Hindus, Muslims, Christians, Parsis, *girmitiya*s and businessmen sat together to eat vegetarian food without any sense of discrimination. There were many among them who had worked in hotels and it was with their help that such a big occasion could be organized. Fifteen different kinds of dishes had been served.

Gokhale delivered his longest speech on the occasion of this dinner.

The day before the dinner, he asked Mohandas: 'Tell me what you want me to say in my speech. You can use me whichever way you like now, but I will hear no complaints later.'

'Say whatever you think fit.'

Kallenbach was also present.

'I'm usually particular about one thing: that I should deal with local affairs. Tell me what they are and what the order of their seriousness is.'

'Tell us what we have to do.'

'Give me in writing on a piece of paper whatever you want me to speak on. It is of course possible that I may not use a single word of what you write. I do hope you won't mind the liberty I take with your notes.'

'What a thing to say! How can I expect a learned scholar of English like you to use my vocabulary? It would be sheer impudence on my part to expect that.'

Gokhale never spoke from notes. Mohandas and Kallenbach were amazed that, though the vocabulary was new, there was not a single topic he had not included in his speech.

Two days later, there was a public meeting. The question was which language to use. Mohnadas said 'Use Hindustani'.

Gokhale said: 'If I use broken Hindi, people will laugh at me. Neither will I be able to express myself nor will people be able to understand my gibberish.'

'I also use a similar language and it has helped me to reach so many people. Neither English nor Gujarati helped me do this.'

That seemed to confuse Gokhale. Seeing his confusion, Mohandas said: 'Use Marathi'.

'Speaking in Marathi in South Africa would be even more ridiculous. And, anyway, it will have to be translated. Won't it be better if I spoke in English?'

'I think we should talk to people in their own language.'

'But how many Marathi speakers do you have here? Most of them are speakers of Hindi, Tamil and Gujarati.'

'No, that's not correct. There are many Konkanis and Johannesburg has a sizable number of Marathi speakers. They would all like to hear you speak Marathi. I'll translate your Marathi speech simultaneously into Hindustani.'

Gokhale gave a loud laugh and said: 'I know about your knowledge of Hindi. I'm afraid I can't congratulate you on it. You tell me you will translate my Marathi speech into Hindustani. Will you be kind enough to tell me where you picked up so much Marathi?'

Mohandas also laughed and said: 'My knowledge of Marathi is not very different from my knowledge of Hindi. I may not be able to speak a single word of Marathi, but I can assure you that I will be able to convey the essence of your speech to the people. If you feel that I'm making nonsense of your speech, there are others here who can translate from Marathi to Hindi and we can call them. But our request to you would be that, if not Hindi, you should speak in Marathi. People here will derive great satisfaction and pride from the fact that one of their great leader loves his mother tongue so dearly.'

'You are quite stubborn, aren't you? If you decide something, it must be done! Okay, I'm at your mercy and will do whatever you say.' Gokhale laughed.

Gokhale spoke in Marathi. Mohandas worked as the interpreter. Once Gokhale had started speaking in Marathi, he went on using Marathi in every meeting till the last one in Zanzirabad and Mohandas went on translating him into Hindustani as his interpreter.

People who did not understand Marathi felt that here was the king of India speaking in the language of his country.

Gokhale's schedule was so busy that it was looking difficult that he would be able to go to Tolstoy Farm, but Mohandas wanted him to visit the Farm at all events. He wanted him to stay there, meet the people and give his frank opinion about his experiment. With great difficulty, he was able to squeeze in two days. His saloon was brought and stationed at the Lawley station. Many members of Tolstoy Farm had already seen him.

Kallenbach, Cachalia, students of the Farm, workers, all the Gandhi kids and Kastur had travelled third to Kimberley from where they had gone to Cape Town dock, where his ship had berthed, to receive him. Mohandas was so excited by his arrival that he wanted his memories to be imprinted on every heart. At Kimberley, his saloon was also attached to the same train by which the people were returning after receiving him. Gokhale was given a warm reception at every station where the train halted. Except during his rest hours, other travellers on the train also came and saw Gokhale from time to time.

Gokhale had a dupatta which he looked after with great care. He washed and ironed it himself before draping it on his shoulders. Mohandas noticed that he never separated it from himself even for a moment. He probably took greater care of it than of himself. Mohandas mustered courage and asked him: 'Why are you so particular about this dupatta? What is so special about it?'

Prof.Gokhale touched his eyes with the dupatta and said: 'This dupatta was given to me by Justice Ranade and I consider it as his blessing to me.'

Mohnadas said: 'You can now stop worrying yourself about it. Now on, I'll take care of it.'

'No …'

'I respect you; you respect Justice Ranade. Being in his third generation, I also have some rights on him, don't I?'

Gokhale laughed and said: 'Go and practise your 'barristery' on someone else.'

No vehicle had been arranged to take Gokhale from Lawley station to the Farm. Mohandas was shocked when he got off at the station. He had been carried away by his over-enthusiasm. Gokhale was finding walking difficult. Mohandas kept on repeating the same thing: 'What a terrible host I am! How could I assume that in your state of health you will be able to walk a mile? What a terrible mistake!'

Gokhale laughed and said: 'Don't worry, Gandhi. I'll go through hell but I'll not surrender to you. You made a lot of fun of my unwillingness to walk. I still remember what you said at Calcutta.'

'I was only thinking of your health.'

'But see, I am getting the health benefit, aren't I?'

Mohandas didn't know what to say.

Gokhale spent two days on the Farm. A proper bed had been arranged for him.

Gokhale got it removed.

'This is an ashram. It should be above discrimination. I can sleep on the floor.'

Mohandas tried hard to convince him, but he said: 'Look, you have invited me to your home; now don't treat me as an outsider.'

Mohandas kept quiet. It was his' wish that he should spend a few days on the farm so that Mohandas could treat him in his own style. As long as Gokhale stayed on the farm, Mohandas made him lie down and put a mud pack on his lower abdomen, changing it frequently.

Gokhale had a good laugh. 'Your treatment,' he said, 'It is not going to get me well, but your love certainly will.'

Restrictions on Gokhale's diet had been imposed right from Johannesburg. There was a feast in Gokhale's honour. It was time for the feast, but Gokhale was still busy with his work. A stickler for punctuality, Mohandas was getting restless. He circled Gokhale several times, but Gokhale would not even raise his head. Finally, Mohandas had to speak: 'Let's go. It's time.'

'Time for what?'

'The dinner, of course.'

'So?'

'It's in your honour.'

'If it's in my honour, I should be free to eat whatever I wish, shouldn't I?'

'You will have your restricted diet.'

'Then I don't wish to come. You can go.' Smiling under his huge moustache, his eyes were fixed on the book.

'How can we go there without you?'

'There must be marriage parties where the bridegroom is missing.'

'We're getting late.' Mohandas was getting increasingly restless.

'So let it be late. I'm not going to move till you allow me to eat whatever I wish.'

Gokhale continued his reading. Finally, Mohandas had to relent. 'All right, you can have whatever you wish.'

'Is that a promise or are you kidding me?'

'It's a promise.'

Gokhale was of course all set to go. Now he got up and said: 'Okay, let's go. You know what your problem is, Mohandas? You don't understand any language other than *satyagraha.* That's why I have to speak your language with you. Now tell me, whose *satyagraha* is the bigger one, mine or yours?'

'Yours. I accept defeat.'

They both laughed.

From Johannesburg, Gokhale went to Natal and from Natal to Pretoria. Pretoria was his last and busiest stopover. His stay had been arranged at Hotel Transvaal, the finest hotel in Pretoria. In fact, this was the day for which the entire South African trip of Gokhale had been planned. He was to meet ministers and officials of the government to find a solution to the problems of the Indian community.

An important question was who would assist Gokhale during the talks. Several names were suggested but, in the end, it was Mohandas' name, that was agreed on.

Gokhale thought about it for some time and then said: 'Is it necessary that one of you should be present during the talks?'

'Not at all,' said Mohandas promptly, 'but the point is that the other party will be there with the fullest preparation. They will do their best to take advantage of your ignorance in certain matters to elicit from you a misplaced assurance, or they may raise an issue about which you may not have full information.'

Gokhale said: 'I fully appreciate your anxiety on this account, but there is also another side to it. If one of you are by my side, it is possible that they are not able to speak their minds openly and without knowledge of the true situation on their side I will not be able to help you fully, either now or later on my return to India.'

Kallenbach, Haji Habib, Daud, Cachalia and some others were also present along with Mohandas. Mohandas said: 'I agree with Prof. Gokhale. My presence or the presence of one of us at the talks with Prof. Gokhale can give a different turn to the situation.'

'So?' asked Cachalia.

'Gandhi,' said Gokhale, 'Get a note ready on the condition of Indians from the very beginning to the present times. It should contain the complete history. I shall not step outside that note. If a point does arise, I shall admit my ignorance and shall dissociate myself.'

This was a big responsibility on the shoulders of Mohandas. There were four colonies and each colony had Indian workers and businessmen as settlers. Full eighteen years of history had to be encapsulated. A full account would at least need twenty pages. Time was short. First the note would have to be prepared, then Gokhale would have to read it and finally the issues raised in the note would have to be grasped. All this could not be done easily.

Gokhale's meeting with the government's representatives was fixed for the next day. Gokhale kept an all night vigil. Others collected the facts. Mohandas prepared the notes.

Gokhale would read whatever got ready. If he had any doubts, he got them clarified straight away. Gokhale was neither taking notes nor asking for answers to his questions in writing. When the comprehensive note was ready, he read the whole thing once again and repeated his questions. He told them whatever sense he could make of what they told him.

At the end of it, everyone was badly fatigued. Their stressed minds and bodies were now beginning to relax. Everyone was yawning, but in his own way everyone was satisfied with the preparation they had made.

The meeting was attended by General Botha, General Smuts and other ministers. The talks lasted for about two hours. Gokhale replied point-by-point to the accusations of the government. They were amazed that an outsider knew so much about Transvaal and South Africa. Gokhale was not even carrying any detailed notes with him.

They had no answers to Gokhale's arguments. Gokhale said: 'At the risk of annoying his own people and putting his own life at risk, Mohandas entered into an agreement with General Smuts and took it upon himself to see that it would be honoured. The assurance that General Smuts gave of withdrawing the Asiatic Act has not been implemented to this day. Don't you think this would have created the impression that the South African government was doing this in order to lower the prestige of Gandhi in the eyes of his own people? But whether or not his prestige among his own people was lowered, it certainly has called into question your own trustworthiness. Hosken had also tried to mediate as a representative of General Botha.'

Gokhale said many things of which General Botha was not even aware. At the end of the meeting, he told Gokhale: 'Prof. Gokhale, it was an experience talking to a man like you.'

One by one, Gokhale had raised all the issues: the Asiatic Act, the Immigration Act, the three-pound tax, and so on. Gokhlale was amazed at the way the government went on giving way to him on every issue.

Gokhale came out a happy man. 'Good news for you, Gandhi,' he said the moment he came out, 'General Botha and General Smuts have agreed to all your conditions. The Asiatic Act and the Immigration Restriction Act will be repealed and the Poll Tax will also be withdrawn.'

Mohandas was quiet for a minute and then said: 'You don't know these officials as well as I do. Having been deceived by them once, I cannot be very optimistic about their assurances again. But of course I value the hopes you have expressed. It is a matter of great happiness to me that you have been able to obtain these assurances from the authorities. We will now fight to have these assurances fulfilled and you will be our major witness. This will double our strength. But I don't think I will be able to fulfil the promise I gave you of returning to India within a year.

With so many of my friends in jail, I wonder what will happen to them if I go back.'

'General Botha has made a promise to me. I don't think a man of prime ministerial rank will go back on his word. I'm sure you'll be back in twelve months. I'll not listen to any excuses in this regard.'

~

Gokhale's return journey had commenced. Kallenbach and Mohandas went up to Zanzirabad to see him off. On the way, Gokhale kept on telling them: 'We are none of us getting any younger. No one knows when we might be called to account. You have as much responsibility towards your own motherland as to the Indian brethren settled here. Love for the motherland is not comparable to any other kind of love. Patriotism is not devotion to some abstract power; it's devotion to yourself, your own people and your own land. You don't have to wait long for the rewards of patriotism, nor does it go waste ever. One person follows another and the tower of patriotism keeps rising higher and higher. This is a line which, once drawn, can never be deleted, even by death.'

The words came straight from the heart of Gokhale. To Mohandas, Gokhale looked like sitting on top of the tower of patriotism. He was reminded of the things, places and people he had seen or heard about in his own country. Kallenbach too was thrilled and his eyes were moist. He only spoke one sentence: 'Patriotism is like your own little daughter whom you have left behind. Who does not want her to be a darling of your heart?'

When, at Zanzirabad, the two of them got off the ship Gokhale held Kallenbach's hand and said: 'I see Gandhi in you and you in Gandhi.'

To Gandhi, he said: 'I'll wait for you. I must hand over the country to you before I die.' And he laughed but it sounded to be a hollow laugh. That laughter had a pain which made him restless. Mohandas felt as if both '*Ba*' and '*Bapu*' were standing before his eyes.

The feeling of Gokhale's presence, that he is here, he was here, that he will be here again, lasted for several days after he had left. A big iron ball falls on wet ground and leaves a neat round impression behind. You can't help looking at it again and again. Everyone, from the oldest to the youngest, was still living the busy hours of Gokhale. Everything was at a stop except the memory of Gokhale. When you are at a stop, you are neither busy nor quite free. You are more like a hyphen.

~

The promises that General Botha and General Smuts had given to Prof. Gokhale had created a situation of wait-and-wait for everyone. Everyone was waiting for the promises to be fulfilled. You felt as if the announcement would surely come today or maybe tomorrow. The wait would often make you inactive. It was like waiting for a train: you feel it's coming, it's coming, but it does not come. Passengers wait and wait. The *satyagraha* had not been withdrawn, but it had slowed down. The terms and conditions of the *satyagraha* were pre-decided: withdrawal of the Asiatic Act. That was all. Some people albeit thought that the terms and conditions should be enlarged and new conditions should be added. Mohandas thought that straying from your set goals meant straying from your true path of struggle. The government knew this. It used the own ideals of *satyagraha* to test the *satyagraha*. For itself, the government had set no ideals. It would use its own ideals to beat the practitioners of *satyagraha*.

People lost their patience. The government was silent on the issue of promises made to Gokhale. Admission of Indians into Transvaal had become more difficult. People could not decide what to make of the promises made by the government. Voices were beginning to rise in protest. Instead of offering explanations, the government was accusing the *satyagrahi*s of going back on their word. They were now bringing in the Immigration Restriction Act into the agreement along with the Asiatic Act. The *satyagrahi*s were cheats.

Mohandas laughed to hear all this. New definitions of cheating were being invented. To demand for your rights was now being called cheating, going back on your word and lack of honesty.

Prof. Gokhale had been promised legislation to abolish the three-pound tax within a year. Instead, General Smuts gave a speech in the House in which he said: 'The European community of Natal is opposed to the abolition of the three-pound tax. The government therefore finds itself obliged not to put this proposal into effect.'

Indians felt that this was a clear case of deception. Natal was one of the four colonies and the colonies had a federal government. If General Smuts had so desired, he could have proposed a bill on behalf of the cabinet. Instead, the government had decided to go back on its word. Going back on a promise made to a respected leader and member of the legislative council like Gokhale was not only an expression of disrespect towards him but also expressed contempt for the entire country. The question was how to face this humiliation. So the issue of the three-pound tax was also included in the agenda of the *satyagraha*.

Most of the *girmitiya*s were illiterate. Though they did not read *Indian Opinion,* they were observing the struggle from close quarters. When the government broke its promise, they did not know whom to trust or how they should raise their voice against it and where. But there was an awakening and a determination that the three-pound tax would have to go.

The government had tightened its enforcement of the Poll Tax. Trains were being checked for passengers who had not paid the tax. The train was the only means of transportation available to the *girmitiya*s.

Ram Ujagar Singh was a *girmitiya.* Evening was setting in and it was the last train for him to get home. The police were out checking Poll Tax passes. Ram Ujagar singh had not been able to arrange for the three pounds that would have got him the pass. He spent some time thinking ways of avoiding jail. Then he walked to a newsagent and put all the change he had in his pockets before him and asked him to give him any English magazine that the change could buy.

The newsagent handed him an old magazine. Turbaned head and bare feet, Ram Ujagar however wore clean clothes. He went and sat down in a corner of the compartment holding the magazine in front of him as if deeply immersed in it. His ears were however cocked for the sound of the policemen checking the passes. He was waiting to be caught any moment, and if he was caught what would happen to his wife and kids? What would they eat?

There were two of them checking the passes. Ram Ujagar held his breath. But when they came close, he kept his eyes fixed on the magazine as if lost in it. He also turned a page. One of the policemen said: 'Looks like an educated man. No use of pestering him.'

The other one said: 'Sure. Educated people don't do it …' Ram Ujagar couldn't hear the latter part of the sentence as the policemen moved up.

At home, Ram Ujagar instructed his wife: 'Put this book away in my box carefully. It saved all our lives today.'

Every *girmitiya* had a box in which he kept his savings and important papers. The magazine went into the same box.

Most *girmitiya*s had however stopped using the trains except in emergencies. If it was a question of travelling ten or fifteen miles, they always did it on foot. If caught, jail was inevitable.

Mohandas wrote to Prof. Gokhale: 'The government has broken all the promises made to you. But you need not worry. We will continue our struggle against this fraud and deception till our last breath. We will see these laws removed. It however now looks more difficult than ever that I'll be able to return within a year. It is now difficult to say when I'll be able to return, or whether I'll be able to return at all.'

Reading Mohandas' letter, Gokhale felt as if someone attending to his wound and applying salve to it had suddenly inflicted an additional cut on him. He immediately shot off a letter to Mohandas: 'Send the maximum and minimum number of soldiers in your peace army and their names immediately.'

Mohandas knew at once why Gokhale was asking for this information. He replied by return mail: 'A maximum of sixty or sixty-five and a minimum of sixteen. These sixteen are the ones who founded the Phoenix Settlement.'

He also wrote along side: 'We will be able to arrange food for these people. You need not send any financial help. Please do not allow yourself to be pressurized. Newspapers tell us that you are a victim of unjust accusations since your return to India.'

It hurt Gokhale to read the letter. He wrote a sharp letter to Mohandas: 'Like you, we also understand our responsibility towards the Indians of South Africa. You need not tell us what to do or what not to do. I had only asked you about the conditions there; I didn't ask you for your advice.'

In the same letter, he also said: 'The struggle against the government's broken promises is going to be a long one. I'm not sure how long you will be able to fight the naked force of a devilish and uncivilized government with a handful of men. But while I am here, you need not worry.'

Reading the letter, Mohandas felt as if an elder in the family was pulling him up for his misbehaviour and also at the same time patting his back for good work.

~

Tolstoy Farm lasted for three years. Mohandas had now to prepare for a new struggle subsequent to the crisis created by the broken promises of the government. Mohandas' office was in a building called Berkley Arcade. He called a meeting in his office in which Pragjibhai, Medh Cachalia, Thambi Naidu, P.K.Naidu, Imam Sahib, and many others were present. The issue was the future programme of action. Having broken its promises, the government had shed all pretence to respectability and Indians were being now persecuted in every possible way.

Pragji was the first to present his undiluted reactions: 'The government is now determined to use tyranny. In view of this attitude, a large section of Muslims has seceded from us. How can we continue the struggle in the circumstances?'

Mohandas laughed and said: 'You are with me, aren't you? That's all I need. We ten will multiply to twenty-five thousand. And if you too decide not to stand with me, there will still be me and my God. I will go from house to house, hut to hut to get the three-pound tax removed. I will wake people from their sleep; I'll see to it that this tax goes.'

They were all looking at Mohandas. His face was lighted up with the same confidence that lights up the flame of a solitary lamp in the dark.

Mohandas continued: 'I have a deep attachment with Tolstoy Farm. It was like family to me. I was the father or the head of the family. So far I have fulfilled my responsibility as a teacher of young men and children. Kallnebach, Pragji and others have helped a lot in this work. We also had to face some problems. I tried hard to see that boys and girls grow up in proximity to one another. This farm was a shelter for my *satyagrahi* friends and their families. All this became possible because of Kallenbach. Now all families will go back to their homes or will stay with me at Phoenix.'

Thambi Naidu asked: 'But why do you want to go to Phoenix?'

'The fight against the three-pound poll tax is more of a fight of the poor than the rich. People here are rich. For them and for their families, three pounds per year is hardly a big sum. A fight is best fought along side those for whom you are fighting. When I was a small kid, my mother forbade me to touch, or to play with, my friend Uka. I then felt like going and staying with Uka, but was not able to do anything of the kind then. Natal is a similar story. It is the land of *girmitiya*s. I must go and stay there. What I couldn't do then, I must do now.'

It came as a shock to everyone at first, but, by and by, they all began to see Gandhi's point.

The same day, Gandhi wrote to Prof. Gokhale:

> *I have decided to fight the three-pound poll tax war living in Natal. I built up Tolstoy Farm here, but now I have to go to Natal, though Tolstoy Farm is very dear to my heart. Between love and duty, sometimes it becomes necessary to listen to the demands of duty. I am returning the Farm to Kallenbach. By allowing me to use his land for Tolstoy Farm, Kallenbach has added a valuable experience to my store of experiences. It is your experiences, I believe, which aid your growth, not your age.*

Along with the memories of springs, fruit orchards and farms, the school for kids also moved to Phoenix.

~

Durban had the same old faces. Dada Abdullah's friend and Mohandas' enemy, Marcel Ledue, having exhausted his armoury against Gandhi, had turned back to France. Dada Abdullah spent most of his time singing praises of Allah, though he was not averse to devoting a few hours to business too. Being far removed in Phoenix, Mohandas did not meet him as frequently as before. It was a different Mohandas who had left Beach Grove, different from the one who had now returned to Phoenix: no frock coat, no shimmering silk hat and no shining shoes. One would be hard put to recognize the Mohandas who had left Beach Grove.

On his return, Mohandas made his way straight, not to Beach Grove or any other place, but to Phoenix, where Kastur and the four kids awaited his arrival. Sonja too. Mohandas had a feeling he was returning to his tribe. One journey was over; another one was beginning.

Mohandas had only one comment to make on the situation: 'The travellers in this journey are people who are born travellers. Even if they wanted to stop for a breather, they would find it difficult. Breathe as you walk—that's their motto.'

It was actually a fear that was driving them—fear for their life. Mohandas, on the other hand, told them not to take it as fear but as an inspiration.

His return was like Ram's return from exile in the forest for the inmates of Phoenix.

With his friends, Mohandas was now back to the task of restarting the struggle. Hope was tinged with a shade of hopelessness the way a tinge of darkness shades a dawn. A single thought kept springing again and again in his mind: he must get a new army ready. A new bridge would have to be laid across the river of their struggle, now stretched like an ocean. It was a stretch which they must cross if they were to save themselves from drowning.

Then a strange incident occurred. The wife of a Muslim trader of Cape Town in India decided to join her husband. The immigration authorities refused her permission to land in South Africa. The husband filed an appeal in the Supreme Court. Justice Malcolm Searle allowed the wife's claim to live with her husband, but subject to proof that the lady was actually his wife. But how was this to be proved? The only acceptable proof would be a legal one. The sum and substance of the judgment was that only Christian marriages or registered marriages were to be considered legal. All other marriages were outside the pale of law.

The problem was with Hindu, Muslim and Parsi marriages. Where was one to get written proof of these marriages, since there was no registration? The wedding rituals were all religious. Since the trader's wife had no written proof, she was sent back by the next ship. She cried and cried, but all she got was a glimpse of her husband from a distance; not even a meeting. The helpless husband stood watching the ship recede in the distance.

The judgment of the Supreme Court had the force of law and this law had put a question mark on the validity of Indian marriages, thereby handing the authorities a new weapon for throwing the Indians out of South Africa. In a sense, it had, at one stroke, declared Indian kids to be bastards and Indian wives to be mistresses.

Mohandas addressed communication after communication to the government and wrote to the newspapers protesting the decision, but there was no response from any quarter. The authorities were happy at having acquired another weapon to make the Indians dance to their tune. Time and again, Mohandas asked them if they agreed with Justice Searle's judgment or if they were contemplating any steps to nullify the effect of the judgment, but when he received no response he published all his letters in *Indian Opinion,* leading to a lot of consternation all round.

Day and night, swinging from one thought to another, from hope at one end to hopelessness at another, Mohandas had finally reached the decision that a war had been forced on him and that it was a war that he must fight on his own ground.

Mohandas called a meeting of the *Satyagraha* Association. The Association now had branches in all the colonies. He told the meeting: 'Indian wives living in South Africa are no longer wives; they have turned into concubines, thanks to Justice Searle. In fact, it is also no longer in our hands to decide whose concubine a woman is. Kids have all turned illegitimate. This verdict of Justice Searle sets at naught the religious and social traditions of Hindus, Muslims and Parsis. Any policeman can walk into your house and can treat your wife not as a wife but any way he likes, assuming her to be a prostitute. The kids will no longer be the legal heirs to the property of their parents. While this clearly humiliates the men, it leaves the women and the kids entirely at their mercy.'

One of the members got up and asked: 'Can't we file an appeal against this judgment?'

Mohandas said: 'We'll have to look into that, but I think it is the government which has to file an appeal, and that is possible only if the Attorney General comes to our help.'

'In the given circumstances, filing an appeal would mean inviting a final stamp on the illegality of Indian marriages.'

'No more appeals. Let's fight it out.'

'We don't want court verdict any more. Let there be an out-of-court verdict.'

There was no dissent.

Time was running short. Things were getting out of control. The humiliation heaped on the entire womenfolk was impossible to bear for men as well as women. Everyone was boiling with anger, but it was no longer possible or desirable to escape the heat of this anger. Though *satyagrahi*s were few in number, a decision was taken to undertake an all-out *satyagraha*.

Mohandas announced the decision at the evening prayer meeting: 'If you want to protect your honour, and the honour of your country, join the *satyagraha* with single-minded devotion; if not, forget about your family and forget that you are the protector of your family and continue payment of your existence-tax to the government. And visit only those places which you are permitted to visit.'

Kastur was still not aware of of things. When the meeting was over, she cornered Mohandas: 'Are you ever going to be rid of this *satyagraha*? It was *satyagraha* when you were at the other place; it is *satyagraha* again when you are back here.'

'Do you know that you are no longer my wife?'

That spooked Kastur. Angry, she stuttered: 'What nonsense are you talking! Who can stop me from being your wife?'

'The government of this place. It has made a law which says if a woman's marriage is not registered, she is not a wife.'

'Blast the government! Set fire to their moustaches! They can go campaigning for votes; why don't they campaign against this law?'

'Who will do the campaigning?'

'We will.'

'Do you have any idea how hard jail life is?'

'It does'nt matter. Put my name down on top of the list of *satyagrahi*s.'

Some of the women had kids. Mohandas tried to dissuade them, citing the problem of their kids. The response he got was: 'Our honour comes first, kids next.'

Mohandas knew that women going to jail could create a major problem, but it was no longer in his power to stop the fire he had started. He wasn't able to dissuade Kastur, or stop other women from joining the movement.

~

The Transvaal Sisters were the first batch of *satyagrahi*s, all of them from Tolstoy Farm and all fired by enthusiasm. They were given the responsibility of crossing the border into Transvaal. Thambi Naidu's wife was their leader with ten others, wives of N. Pillai, N.S. Pillai, Marugasa Pillai, Perumal Naidu, P.K.Naidu, K. Chinaswamy Pillai, R.S. Mudalingam, Bhawani Dayal and many others.. The question before them was whether they would continue their existence as prefixes to their husbands' names, or would achieve something on their own. There were also a couple of unmarried women with them: Minachi Pillai and Baikum Migasa Pillai. They did not face this dilemma: they had names of their own and a mission too.

These ladies had been told clearly before setting out on their campaign that they were neither to give out their names nor show their passes. They were supposed to enter Transvaal at Verniging, where the police had gathered in large numbers. Anyone trying to sneak into Transvaal without catching their eye was quickly apprehended by mounted policemen.

The Transvaal Sisters moved forward to cross the border under the policemen's eyes. The Sisters' eyes were all fixed on the policemen, waiting to see them move forward to arrest them. Or wouldn't they move at all? A few policemen did make a hesitant move but were stopped by their officer. The Transvaal Sisters crossed the border without any resistance.

It made the Sisters very unhappy that the police had humiliated them by not treating them as *satyagrahi*s.

Almost all the Sisters had their homes in Transvaal. They all made for Thambi Naidu's home and rested for a while. Almost all of them were Tamil speakers. Mrs. Naidu said: 'We are not going to be taken in by these tricks of the police. We will now peddle our goods without licence. Let's see if they arrest us or not.'

The next day, baskets on their heads, with varieties of goods for sale, the Sisters set out on their rounds in different directions but making sure that they were never very far apart from one another. The idea was that even if one of them was arrested she would blow the whistle on all others and tell the police who was peddling what and where. But not one of them proved lucky enough to be arrested and sent to jail. They peddled all day and till late in the evening. They had a good sale but returned in the evening without a single arrest to show for all their efforts.

Mohandas did not feel at all discouraged by this incident. He knew that it was a deliberate strategy of the government. It wanted to kill the struggle by ignoring it. He told the Phoenicians: 'The time has come for those of us who gave their sweat and blood to build Phoenix to go into the struggle. I was keeping them in reserve for the final thrust. Now you will all have to go to jail; only those who are running *Indian Opinion*, or are below sixteen years of age, will stay behind.'

After a pause, he added: 'Gokhaleji had asked me for the maximum and the minimum number of my companions. I had given him as the minimum number the sixteen who had helped to build up Phoenix and that meant you.'

One of them said: 'You should have sent us ahead of everyone else.'

Mohandas laughed and said: 'Sacrificing yourself is the hardest of all tasks; hence those who are asked to sacrifice themselves should be called upon to do so only when the time is right.' He continued: 'There will be no announcement in this regard and you will all keep this march a secret. When you enter Transvaal, the police will ask your names, but you will not reveal your names or your addresses. You will not answer any of their questions or tell them about your purpose. If they find out who you are, where you are from, or that you are somehow connected to me, they will follow their strategy: you will neither be arrested nor questioned. You must enter Transvaal without a permit and the Transvaal Sisters will re-enter Natal. Entering Natal is of course as big a crime as entering Transvaal …'

Before he told them his plan, Mohandas talked to each one of the Phoenicians individually, the first one being the Phoenix Sisters. Most of them were Gujaratis and were related to Mohandas. What worried Mohandas most was that they might be agreeing to his plan because of their relationship with him. His presence might itself be exerting a pressure on them. If that was the case and if later they sought release from jail by offering an apology that would be a blot on the movement, a blot that would be hard to live down. Mohandas had however not talked about it to Kastur even once out of fear that if he did she would consent at once, even if she really didn't wish it. In fact, she would put her heart and soul in it.

He had put his fears before the Phoenix Sisters in the plainest words, to which their firm response was: 'We'd rather die than offer an apology. No matter how hard the life in jail, we will live through it.'

Kastur had overheard him talking to the sisters and was furious. 'You are going around talking to everyone but not a word to me! What is it that they have and I don't?'

There was a cry of pain in those words.

'It was not at all my intention to cause you pain. Nor do I lack trust in you. In fact, I'd be happy if you went to jail. What I would however not wish is that you should go to jail on my saying. This is *satyagraha.* One goes into it out of one's own will as when making a sacrifice. The 'insistence-on-truth' (*satya* + *aagraha*) is really complete only when the 'insistence' originates within oneself. I know that you will make the sacrifice if I say so, but then the merit of the sacrifice will not be yours. If you later find the hardships too hard to bear and capitulate before them, the blame will fall on the one who sent you. If the decision is your own, so are the consequences, happy or sad.'

'If you can stand the hardships of a jail why can't I? What is it that you have and I don't? Is it that you are a man? I shall go on *satyagraha* and no one can stop me.'

'Well, if that's the way it is, you certainly must.' Mohandas continued: 'Who knows you better than I do, Kastur? But, still, as I have told the others, I must tell you too: Think once again. There's still time. You want to withdraw your name, you can still do it.'

Kastur was annoyed: 'No more thinking. I don't change my mind every now and then.'

The other Sisters too were eager to go. No one was ready to reconsider her decision.

The first name among the Phoenix Sisters was that of Kastur Bai. The next one was Jayakumar Manilal Doctor alias Jakie followed by Kashi Chhaganlal and Santosh Maganlal. Then came the men: Chhaganlal, Ravibhai, Manibhai Patel, Maganbhai Patel, Soloman Rippon, Raju Govind, Ramdas Mohandas Gandhi, Shiv Pujan Badri, B. Govinda Rajulu, Kuppusami, M. Mudaliar, Gokuldas, Hansraj, Revashankar Shondha and so on. There was also someone who was not from Phoenix: Rustomji Jeevanji. This advance party set out together from Phoenix to cross the

Natal border into Transvaal. The other inmates applied *tilak* to the *satyagrahis'* foreheads, and gave them a warm farewell. Kastur Bai was leading the group.

Kastur had large eyes and they were looking even larger today. The whole world seemed to have been subsumed in them. One could read in them a keen urge to achieve something out of the ordinary. No one else had the slightest notion about where this vanguard group was headed. They all looked like *girmitiya*s, who were often seen sporting a *tilak* on their foreheads whenever they had a marriage to attend or a festival to celebrate. They got on to a train at Durban and got off at the Volksrust station. That's where the Transvaal border started.

They were closely interrogated at the border, while they looked at the interrogators like a deaf and dumb lot. The police arrested them and sent them off to the Volksrust jail.

That was the first victory the Phoenix squad had registered.

The Transvaal Sisters had entered Transvaal from Natal. There they had hawked goods without licence. When nothing transpired, they returned to Natal hoping that this time the police would certainly not let them go. Nevertheless, their return to Natal proved to be equally uneventful. Like a stray dog lazing in the streets with closed eyes, opening them only to look at a passerby with the neck slightly raised, only to resume its former position quickly thereafter, the police too took a look at them and then looked away. They felt like screaming: 'You arrested the Phoenix Sisters at the first try; why this discrimination?'

However, arrests were scarce like birds out of season. There were none to be seen anywhere around.

The Transvaal Sisters had been told that, failing arrest, they should make for Newcastle, which was the coal-mining district of Natal, and that was what the Sisters did. Though Tamil speakers, the Sisters were however able to manage broken Hindustani. Most of the miners were also South Indians. The Sisters went and made their home among the mining families.

The Sisters slowly spread themselves among the Indian labourers, the *girmitiya*s, like weeds. They went from door to door explaining the origin and history of the three-pound tax. They told them how difficult it was for a labourer who made twelve or thirteen pounds a year to spare three pounds for Poll Tax. They chatted with women as they cooked their family meals; they sat with women helping them to crush grain even as they recounted their tale; they accosted the labourers on their way to work and explained it to them. At night, they would go and sit by the fire and start their lecture. Suppose a worker had a family of six and he could somehow manage to put together the Poll Tax amount for two, what was he supposed to do for the remaining four? Throw them into the ocean or send them home? If he had money enough to send them home, wouldn't he rather deposit the Poll Tax and buy peace at least for a year?

They also exposed the lies the government had been indulging in: 'An important man from India, called Gokhale, had come to South Africa, a man no less important than a king, a man whom even the white Viceroy of India consulted regularly. Our authorities here made a promise to him that they would withdraw the Poll Tax, but when he went back, they went back on their word. It is only for this cause that Gandhibhai has closed down his Transvaal ashram and has moved to his Phoenix ashram. He has pushed even his wife and his kids into *satyagraha*. We have also abandoned our home and hearth in Transvaal and moved to Natal. Gandhibhai has taken a vow that he won't rest till the three-pound tax is removed. He is determined that due respect is given to Gokhale and India and that Indians and Asians do not lose the respect that they have earned. But for all this to happen, your cooperation and help is necessary. You must close down the mines and join the fray.'

The words of Transvaal Sisters were beginning to take effect and soon the workers declared a strike in the mines. Everyone was taken by surprise by this unexpected development.

When Mohandas received the telegram, he neither had money nor men to come to the strikers' support. He had no idea that the Transvaal

Sisters would bring about such a miracle so soon and give birth to such a monumental movement among the workers. He set out at once for the place but by the time he reached there, the Transvaal Sisters had been arrested and the strike had intensified.

Mohandas took over the reins of the movement the moment he landed. In fact, word was even spread that Gandhi was an opportunist who never missed an opportunity for self-advancement when he saw one. In Transvaal, he was first fighting against the Asiatic Act; next, he jumped into the fight against the Immigration Restriction Act and now he was there to fight against the Poll Tax. Actually, he was loyal to no one: not to the British government, not to the traders and not to the natives. As a matter of fact, he never spared a thought for the natives.

No one, however, paid any attention to these rumours. The police were just flying kites while Mohandas and his companions stood firm like a rock.

Kastur, Kashi, Santosh and Jakie had been housed with native women. These women stank and their style of living was extremely unpleasant. They went about semi-naked, which caused the other women to turn their faces away in shame. In fact, they felt like throwing up whenever they saw them. They couldn't talk to them because of the language problem but the obscene signs they made were embarrassing enough.

Kastur had barely recovered from her illness when she joined the *satyagraha*. She was still weak and not quite up to facing the rigours of a *satyagrahi*'s life. At Phoenix, Mohandas had been keeping her on fruit juices but in jail even normal food was a rarity. Kastur demanded fruit to be supplied to her but the demand was rejected outright whereupon Kastur refused food and went on a fast. Kashi, Santosh and Jakie also joined her in the fast. Kastur was now getting weaker day by day.

On the third day, the Deputy Superintendent appeared and told her: 'Mrs. Gandhi, your demand had been forwarded to the Union government and it has been accepted. You should be grateful to them.'

'It was our right,' said Kastur, 'The government has done us no favour by conceding it.'

Kastur was now given fruits in her diet, which, though insufficient even for her, she shared with the other three Sisters. She slept on the floor. She was gradually losing her appetite and was getting weaker and weaker.

The men had been assigned to work in the orchards. They often enjoyed the fruits they gathered from the trees and tried to persuade Ramdas too to join them. He refused. If asked repeatedly, he would say: 'The jail food is good enough for me. I have no desire to eat fruit.'

One week later, they were all transferred to the Pietermaritzburg jail and that was the end of their fresh fruit feasts.

At Pietermaritzburg, women had been given the work of washing clothes while men had been given rocks to break. No food was allowed from outside and jail food was barely worth eating, but neither could they do without it. There was a reverse proportion between work and food; more work went with less food. Women were getting weaker by the day while men were a fatigued lot.

Pragjibhai and Manilal were already in Pietermaritzburg jail. Every prisoner was given an ounce of fat. The fat was so smelly that not just eating it but even watching others eat was really impossible. Even the bodies of those who ate it smelt. By this time, Phoenix Sisters had also arrived in the jail and the number of prisoners had gone up. They all got together and decided that in place of the fat the authorities be asked to provide an ounce of Porbandar ghee per person.

A demand was accordingly sent to the jail authorities.

'This is not a hotel; it's a jail. So behave like prisoners,' they were told.

The prisoners said nothing but started a fast.

Ramdas was the youngest of the lot. He too insisted on a fast. Everyone, from Kastur to Pragji, tried to discourage him but he was unmoved and went on a fast. Soon his face showed it. Prisoners however continued to work as before: breaking rocks, digging wells, levelling roads, grinding grain till their hands had blisters. As long as possible, the prisoners did not allow the fast to come in the way of their work.

One day, a native warder told Ramdas: 'I feel bad when I see you going without dinner. In fact, I can hardly sleep at night. To see you go to bed without food reminds me of my kid. He too used to go to sleep hungry when there was no food in the house. You have no such problem.'

'That's what *Bapu* has taught us. All my companions go to sleep without food.'

The warder kept quiet but also kept looking at Ramdas turning over restlessly. Sometimes he also missed his dinner in sympathy.

The white officials often said among themselves: 'How are these people surviving? We find it hard to go without tea or a cigarette even for an hour.'

'Forget about the others. I'm amazed at this boy. How's he surviving?'

Another official said: 'If something happens to Gandhi's wife or his kid, the colony will go up in flames.'

News of the fast had spread all over Pietermaritzburg town and protest meetings were being organized and resolutions passed. The authorities were beginning to show signs of nervousness. Then one day the Jail Superintendent sent for Pragji and asked him: 'What is this stuff called Porbandar ghee?'

Pragji gave him all the details including where it could be got. Three days later, the Indian prisoners started receiving Porbandar ghee.

Valliamma Mudaliar was from Johannesburg, a sixteen year old girl, tall and with large eyes. Even to set eyes on her was to be filled with delight. She started getting fever while still in jail. When her condition did not improve, she was released from jail. When Mohandas found out that a girl named Valliamma from Transvaal, but now in Natal, had been to jail on *satyagraha* and was now sick, he located her and went to see her. He was shocked to see her condition. All that one could see on her face were the two eyes like two candle flames; the rest was all skeleton.

Mohandas sat beside her. Her eyes were streaming. Mohandas held her hands in one of his hands while wiping her tears with the other.

'Valliamma,' asked Mohandas, 'Do you have any regrets that you went to jail?'

'Regrets?' repeated Valliamma in a weak and shaky voice. 'Gandhibhai, if I have to go to jail again now and even in my present condition, I'm ready to do so. You will escort me yourself, won't you?'

'And if you die while in jail?'

'I'll have no regrets. Who doesn't want to die for the sake of her motherland, especially when she has the privilege of dying in your arms?'

She was so weak she could speak no more. Mohandas' eyes were full of tears. He didn't want her to exert herself more. When Mohandas was leaving, she asked: 'You will have my name in your next list of *satyagrahi*s, won't you, Gandhibhai?'

He could not speak but he pressed her hands softly. A light wave of joy streamed through her face.

Valliamma died a few days later sending shock waves all around. For the first time people learnt how smooth and easy the road to sacrifice could be for a true *satyagrahi.*

A soft wave of pain flashed in Mohandas' mind: 'How I wish I could meet a similar death!'

The jail trip of the Phoenix party did not terminate at Maritzburg. From there, they were sent to Durban jail. Durban jail was large. Its entrance gate had massive doors like a fortress. Atop the jail was what looked like a huge dome. Its reputation for strictness was enough to keep the most disorderly of prisoners on the straight path. The plate and the pitcher that were handed to them on arrival were filthy and used. No one knew how many prisoners had used them before and how these were used. The Jail Superintendent's attention was drawn to the problem but he paid no attention. He was even asked permission to wash and clean them in case they could not be replaced. But his firm reply was 'You must use the pitcher and the plate as they are.'

All the sixteen *satyagrahi*s had been housed in a separate ward. Pragjibhai was however labelled a mischief maker and condemned to a black hole for pointing out the condition of the plates and pitchers. While the fifteen prisoners were taken to the water tap together to wash their faces, Pragjibhai was taken separately. Kastur was now extremely weak but she still went with the others. They all walked in a single file with their plates and pitchers in hand. When they had finished and were back in their cells, it was Pragjibhai's turn to come out of his cell.

As he was coming out of his cell one day, and the fellow prisoners were on their way back from their morning ablutions, Pragjibhai signalled to them that he had stopped eating. His companions also informed him that they too had gone without food.

When Pragjibhai was washing his face at the tap, a warder pushed him from behind, saying: 'Are you here to have a drink of water or to wash. All your friends are back in their cell and you are still having a merry time!'

Pragji tried telling them that he was incarcerated separately from his friends and that he was taken around on his own, but the two warders who were with him did not listen to him. A third warder also joined them soon and the three of them dragged him by his feet back to the cell, his back getting badly grazed and soaked in blood in the process. He was bundled into his cell in the same condition and locked up.

Pragji ran a high fever through the night. Rustomji, who was also in the same jail, somehow managed to visit him and told him: 'Don't worry, son, I have sent word to Gandhibhai.'

His words acted as a soothing salve on Pragji's wounds.

~

When Mohandas arrived in Newcastle, the problem before him was where to stay. Newcastle was a rather small settlement but Mohandas had a number of trader friends living there. Throughout his journey to Newcastle, Mohandas kept debating to himself where it would be best for him to put up. He knew that the Transvaal Sisters had stayed with D. Lazarus, a Tamil Christian and a former *girmitiya*. Lazarus had since got himself a plot of land and had built for himself a two or three room house on it. Mohandas made straight for his house. To see him appear suddenly at his house, Lazarus almost went into a tizzy, not knowing how to welcome him.

Mohandas knew that staying with a businessman would mean inviting economic disaster on his family, making him a victim of the government's wrath and sending the wrong signal to the other traders. No average trader would be willing to take such a risk. Only someone who had nothing to lose would be willing, for his risk-taking capacity and his courage are also greater, even if rather small in proportion to his penury. Mohandas had made up his mind to stay away from friends who could be exposed to the slightest damage because of his presence in their homes.

Mohandas told Lazarus: 'By hosting us, you are inviting trouble for yourself.'

Lazarus said: 'I'm quite ready to sacrifice the small income I have for the movement. If I have to go to jail, I'm ready for that too, but I will fight, and to my last breath, against the arbitrary laws thrust on my brethren. Our sisters are in jail so we can be free of this three-pound tax. Don't you think we too must share some of the responsibility?'

The Lazarus home soon became a place of pilgrimage for all the strikers. Everyone who wanted to join the strike made it to his home. Indeed, sometimes you saw a throng of heads in front of his house.

The strike was going full blast. Ever since the strikers had got to know that Gandhibhai was in Newcastle the distance between the Lazarus home and the strikers' crowd had ceased to exist. *Girmitiya*s assembled under the open sky in the ground in front of Lazarus' home. The assemblage of such a large number of people in the house of a single person was causing concern to Mohandas. Food had to be cooked round the clock. Mrs. Lazarus was running constantly like a machine arranging the house to welcome so many persons. But her face never lost its cheer. Whether this cheer was born out of the service she was rendering or the sacrifice she was making, or maybe both, one could not say, but one never missed the cheer.

As long as it was possible for him to do so, Lazarus continued to welcome people and to provide for them, even if it was roasted grain or a couple of rotis. People ate whatever they got happily and got down to work. But when Mohandas saw that the burden was getting beyond Lazarus' capacity to bear, he addressed a meeting: 'No one can say when this strike will be over, or whether it will be over at all. It is quite possible that it may last as long as our lives, though we can't be sure how long our own lives will last. We all know that your homes are not your own; they are owned by the mine owners. Facilities like water and light are available to you at their mercy and can be withdrawn at their will. I will advise you to sell off whatever stuff you have at home that can be sold. The stuff that cannot be sold can be left alone. You will thus at least be able to meet your food expenses. I don't think the mine owners will touch the stuff you leave at home, but if they do, let them go ahead. You need not worry. You cannot have your cake and eat it too. Get only a few clothes and blankets. If there is anyone among you who is unable or afraid to do so he is quite welcome to go back and join work. I assure you that no one will bear any ill will towards such a person or look upon him with contempt. Each one of you is free to take your own decision.'

The very next day, workers started streaming in in batches. At a single call from Mohandas, workers had given up their homes and had started gathering homeless under the sky. Their kids and their wives too were ready to lay down their lives. All roads led to Lazarus' house. The ground in front of Lazarus' house was their ultimate destination. Problems were multiplying. A big hazard was sanitation. There were many among the gathering mass of people who had been to jail on criminal charges. When these points were brought to Gandhi's notice, all that he had to say was: 'It is not for me to sit on judgment on them. My only concern at present is that they should exercise self-control and observe the rules of moral conduct.' Mohandas of course kept a close watch on them.

Everybody however seemed to appreciate the gravity of the situation and was behaving accordingly.

Slowly, the local traders started extending a helping hand. Utensils for cooking, pulses, rice, vegetables, oils and whatever other similar stuff was required were immediately made available. People were amazed to see that Lazarus, whose resources till the other day were strained to the limit, was today so overstocked with goods that he was facing a storage problem.

The problem before Mohandas was the number of strikers. Where was he going to house them? They couldn't possibly continue to stay in the Lazarus home. The whites, on the other hand, were worried about the outbreak of epidemics, though so far they had been spared this scourge.

One choice Mohandas had was to take his strikers' army in small batches to Transvaal and then get them arrested on the charge of crossing the border, landing them finally in one of 'His Majesty's hotels'. That however would have taken a long time. Moreover, courting arrest in small batches would not have had quite the same effect. It was also not possible to take five thousand strikers by train. Where would the money for the tickets come from? Taking them ticketless would have meant immoral conduct and branded the strikers as immoral forever. The Transvaal border was thirty-five miles from Newcastle. Finally, Mohandas had no choice but to opt for a foot march.

His first act after he took the decision was to consult the striking workers. 'We cannot stay here much longer. Tolstoy Farm is a mile from the Lawley station. The Farm itself is a big place, and although we have left it, we can all be accommodated there. But to reach the Farm we will have to walk thirty-five miles. Our Christian friends know that Moses had led his followers on an Exodus from Egypt. Hindus walk hundreds of miles on their pilgrimages. Muslims walk to Mecca and Medina. I am not in a position to offer you either shelter or food; instead I am asking you for peace, renunciation and sacrifice.' He paused for a while and then demanded: 'Are you ready?'

Those who were accompanied with wives and kids expressed hesitation. One could read in their faces the question: 'Walk thirty-five miles?' Mohandas had to continue relentlessly: 'Those who cannot walk, or do not wish to walk, I must ask not to waste any more of their time. Let them return to their mines and resume work.'

There was a unanimous cry: 'We shall not return. We will walk with you.'

'I'm happy,' said Mohandas, 'You have accepted my suggestion and are ready for a foot march. This march will, I assure you, one day also open the doors to the independence of your country.'

Charlestown was the border town of Natal; Volksrust that of Transvaal.

Before setting out on the march, Mohandas explained to the marchers some essential rules of how to conduct themselves. The very first rule concerned food: 'It's not easy to arrange food for four to five thousand people. Our resources are not adequate enough to provide enough food for everyone. Taking into account our resources, we shall be able to provide only a pound-and-a-half of bread and an ounce of sugar to each marcher.'

The marchers were not all an educated lot. They included all kinds of people. The majority were workers, but included some low types like thieves, killers, drunkards, adulterers and so on. Violence was a real possibility where such people were present. They could engage in fighting for food or for things like sleeping arrangement, accommodation, etc. Mohandas was however assured about one thing. As he used to say: 'The poor and the destitute have many shortcomings, but they have this quality: they are tied together by a bond of love and that is a bond they do not allow to be broken.'

Mohandas got a code of conduct ready for the marchers and announced it: No drinking by the marchers; no wasting of money on smoking and such other vices, nor asking others for such stuff. No stealing and no rioting. Everyone must stay content with whatever he is given. If Gandhibhai is arrested before they reach Tolstoy Farm, the word of the leader-designate will be final. No scuffling with the police. The police may abuse them, thrash them or indulge in other excesses; they must put up with everything. No littering, or throwing garbage on the way or at wayside halts; the march must be completed with dignity, peace and respect for the onlookers. They will have to stay under the sky and the ground below will be their bedding …

Everyone assented to the conditions by raising his hands, though a few of them did whisper to each other: 'If you are thrashed or abused, how can you possibly keep quiet?'

The other one had a reply ready: 'If Gandhibhai says so, it must be so. After all, he has many things to consider. One who leads such a huge contingent has to have a cane or a staff in hand to keep order. These rules are Gandhibhai's cane.'

They all had a good laugh.

Mohandas had sent a telegram to Kallenbach asking him to reach Newcastle immediately and Kallenbach had taken the first train. His train was to arrive at six in the morning. When the train arrived, Mohandas was at the station to receive him. They quickly embraced each other. Their eyes showed the deep feelings of long-separated friends. One could see the deep colours of love in them.

By the time they came out of the station, the sun had risen above the horizon. It was a warm winter morning. Next to Kallenbach, Mohandas looked rather small. Mohandas laughed and said: 'Seeing us together, who would believe that I am the Upper House and you the Lower one?'

'He should know that appearances are deceptive.'

They both laughed and the laughter dissolved their fatigue. Kallenbach had travelled through the night while Mohandas had to spend the whole night awake. The march from Newcastle was to start in three hours.

Mohandas explained the details: 'Four thousand men, women and kids are all set to start their march to Charlestown. There were five thousand to begin with, but we had to leave out the aged ones and then there were some who, scared of the long march, cried off. The march includes all sorts, except traders of whom there is only a sprinkling. Everyone is worried how the march will turn out, but I have full faith in the marchers. In a march of this kind, everyone is focused at the goal. I do believe everyone will exercise self-discipline.'

'Tell me, Upper House, wouldn't this be the first march of its kind in the whole world?'

'Maybe you are right. Moses of course had led a march of his followers from Egypt. I have a deep desire that people of my country too should also set out on a march for their freedom and not return till they achieve their goal.'

Kallenbach looked at Mohandas' face and said: 'Upper House, I see that even as you are closely engaged in your struggle here, you cannot stop thinking of your country. In fact, I sometimes have the feeling that you are actually fighting India's struggle here. For this to happen, you need to have unshakeable faith in your people and they need to have similar faith in you. Just the kind we have in each other.'

Kallenbach laughed and said: 'Did I say something wrong?'

Mohandas laughed and said: 'Each and every marcher has been informed of the conditions of the march and everyone has supported them as one man.'

'More important than the conditions to them is the man who has imposed them.'

'This is a special virtue about Indians. Once they make someone their own, there are no two ways about it. Everything he says goes.'

'Don't the Germans have this virtue?'

'As far as I am concerned, it is from them I have picked up this quality.'

Mohandas looked at Kallenbach meaningfully and said: 'The biggest problem we are going to face is about food.'

'You needn't worry about that. Before the marchers reach the next stop, they will find me and my workers ready to receive them. Food and stay should not be a problem at all.'

'You don't know how relieved I feel to hear that.'

'In your relief lies my relief.'

Mohandas replied by pressing Kallenbach's hand softly.

They walked for a while in silence. Then Mohandas said: 'I am now the only one out of jail. The rest are all inside. Rustomji too; otherwise he would have been a great help. He and Pragjibhai have faced a lot of harassment in jail. Even his *sadri* and *kasti* were taken from him and he had to undertake a three-day fast to get them back. Without them,he couldn't say his prayers. Pragji was dragged on the ground, which bloodied his back. When Rustomji informed me about it, I wrote to the Attorney General and action was initiated against the warders. They were prosecuted, with Polak arguing for

Pragjibhai. The court's decision was: 'The prisoner was obstreperous; hence use of force became necessary.' You have met Pragjibhai, haven't you?'

Kallenbach was worried at the turn of events the way they were taking.

Mohandas kept quiet for a while. A few minutes later, he said: 'Kastur has grown very weak. She is sick most of the time anyway. Hari, Mani and Ramdas are also in jail, Devdas alone is in Phoenix. West is handling *Indian Opinion* alone. Devdas does whatever he can to help. Had he not been so young, he too would have been in jail.' Mohandas had suddenly turned serious.

Kallenbach laughed and said: "But there are so many who are with you."

'So they are, but they are a responsibility not a comfort. I have assured them that when food is available I'll cook it for them myself. That should keep them happy, since food is one item capable of causing the maximum trouble. When we run short of food, they will look at me and forgive us.'

'No one to beat you in this game, Upper House. If you can turn non-vegetarians into vegetarians, there is no reason why you can't keep people happy by feeding them your underdone stuff.'

Mohandas turned philosophical: 'Who knows, Lower House, when this underdone stuff of mine will come to be done properly. Right now, it is actually all raw stuff.'

Kallenbach looked at Mohandas and said: 'You won't have to wait too long now.'

Mohandas was still with his old question: 'Such a long journey! So many marchers! However shall we able to feed and support them?'

'Gandhibhai, stop worrying. Do you think this Lower House of yours is going to stand by and see them starve?'

'It is that spirit of yours that keeps me going ...'

Mohandas' eyes were overflowing with love.

By ten o'clock, all the marchers were standing in rows in front of Lazarus's house, bread and sugar packed in bundles and blankets and clothes loaded on their heads or backs, as if waiting for the army commander's word to start their march. No sooner the word left the commander's lips, the march would begin. People were dressed in colourful clothes, the best clothes they had. The kids stood with their parents. Unlike in the army, of course, there was no band playing nor were there any gun salutes. Only the enthusiasm was not lacking. The army discipline was also missing. But still no one was out of step and no one showed irregular movements of hand or neck. All their faces showed commitment and devotion as if they had assembled for prayer before setting out on a pilgrimage. They were all talking among themselves but in a low voice. The kids too were talking in hushed tones after their elders. They themselves felt startled if they suddenly broke into a loud voice.

Every now and then, they would ask their parents: 'When is the *yatra* going to start, *Bapu*?'

'When Gandhibhai gives the word.'

'When will he give the word?'

'He is a busy man. He has lots of other things to do.'

'Can't he do them later?'

'Look, when we go out of the house, we have to arrange the house to be locked and lots of other things to take care of. Only then we invoke the name of God and then set out. Gandhi too must be doing the same.'

A host of white journalists were on hand. Policemen, white as well as black, were around too. The journalists were at a loss to understand how such a huge mass of people, going on a thirty-five mile long march, could be walking so quietly. And Indians, of all the people! The marchers, on their part, were wondering at the presence of these uninvited guests. What were they doing here? But as soon as their eyes fell on a policeman, their eyes started hunting for Gandhibhai. Only he could save them from these evil spirits.

Hindus, Muslims, Parsis, males, females, old men and kids—they were all walking in unison. To the onlookers, it was nothing short of a magical sight. It was as if a magician had made thousands of clay models and then breathed life into them. They were worried most about other people's kids.

'Don't let go of their hands,' they would advise one another periodically.

'Children, stay with Jhabbu uncle,' someone else would shout.

'If the policemen get nasty, take the kids with you and stand aside,' the men were telling their wives.

But the kids would not agree: 'We won't go with Jhabbu uncle; we will go with Gandhibhai.' They had this idea that Gandhibhai was their guardian angel.

The journalists understood neither their language nor the sense of what they said, but their ears were cocked in their direction.

They also talked among themselves.

'Have you ever seen a motley crowd of weak, destitute, illiterate, frightened and crippled people gather in such large numbers to attack a government without swords, bows and arrows? Have you?'

'Especially when most of the wars the coolies fight are over their religion. And here all the religions have got together.'

'And not a trace of fear on their faces.'

'And to think that these are the same people who couldn't utter a syllable in the presence of their sirdar.'

'How has this come about?'

'This Gandhi is surely a miracle man. He rid their hearts of the fear of their masters.'

'Not just the masters, the authorities too.'

'That's all nonsense. They are all taking advantage of 'white nobility'. Gandhi knows that we are God-fearing people. They are a brute, that's what they are.'

'We'd never step outside our gentlemen's code and would never do anything that we might be held answerable for on the Day of Judgment.'

One of them said: 'That's not it. Look at the entire picture analytically. First, it was Gandhi's own wife and kids who went to jail. Next he changed his own self completely. Here is the first man to change himself from a barrister to a *girmitiya.*'

'I disagree. The man is a hoax, a complete showman. He is capable of anything. Only till the other day he went around like a European trying to win over Europeans and soon had them on his side.' Quite agitated, the journalist went on: 'They are a third-rate people, traitors to their own country.'

'That's impossible. One cannot fool such a large community using only deceit and showmanship.'

'Nothing is impossible in the world of deceit and fraud.'

'But you are saying that Europeans are also with him ...'

'And what about all these people ...?'

The journalists were quite vociferous. More than anger, it was hatred that you could see in their faces. The marchers of course could not follow what they were saying, but the expressions on their faces were changing with the expressions on the faces of the journalists. Their faces had turned into mirrors of the feelings the white journalists' faces wore.

The first day's march was about to come to an end when Mohandas received an invitation from the mine owners to a meeting to be held at Durban. Mohandas knew that the meeting would prove fruitless. His advisers also advised him against attending the meeting.

Mohandas laughed and said: 'An important feature of *satyagraha* is humility and turning down an invitation for no apparent reason would not be considered humility. You may or may not accept their position—that's another matter.'

'But you may be humiliated.'

'You can be humiliated only if you have no self-esteem, if you have no confidence in your own decisions and if you have set no criteria for distinguishing truth from untruth. We have our criteria; we have the trust and confidence of our people and we are determined that we shall come out unscathed from any humiliation, neglect or harassment that we may be subjected to.'

Mohandas went into the mine owners' meeting to find the atmosphere tense and restless. Questions were fired at him the moment he took his seat.

'You are aware that we are running losses?'

'It's in your hands. You can bring the strike to a quick end, if you wish.' Mohandas minced no words.

'We are not the government. How can we?'

'But it is your government. You can argue with the government on their behalf and present their demands; you can exert pressure and get the three-pound tax removed.'

'What has the strike got to do with the three-pound tax? Tell us if the strikers have any complaints against us. How do you expect us to run somebody else's show?'

Mohandas laughed and said: 'What other weapon do the poor workers have? The three-pound tax has after all been imposed for the benefit of the mine owners. The government wants the Asiatic workers to work unquestioningly and to remain loyal and subservient to the mine owners but does not wish them to breathe free air or to air their grievances. If this strike can secure the workers relief from this tax, which has become a symbol of their slavery, what is so unjust about it?'

'Does that mean you are not going to ask the workers to return to work?'

'I would like to be excused on that account.'

'Do you know what the results could be?'

'They couldn't be any worse than what they are. I am fully aware of my responsibilities.'

'You are not the one who is going to suffer, but because of you these workers will meet a fate worse than death. Will you be able to compensate them for their losses?'

'The decision to strike was the workers' and they took it after a lot of consideration. They are fully aware of what they stand to gain or lose. For a self-respecting person, his self-respect is the biggest gain; it's also his biggest loss. They now know it fully well.'

There was a short silence after which Mohandas got up and said: 'Thank you for inviting me and listening to me. My personal advice to you will be to stand with the workers for a change. You'll see that you can win their hearts.'

The mine owners had tense faces. Not a single face turned when Mohandas left the room, though when he had arrived they had received him standing. Mohandas walked out of the room carefree like a man who had just been released of his burden, as relaxed as he usually was among his own people.

Mohandas travelled third class on his return journey. He had shed his love of first class travel along with his European dress. The railway staff had also got to know him better than before. When they saw him entering the train, the ticket examiner, the guard and others also got into the same compartment. He was offered a good seat and made comfortable in every way, though Mohandas did not quite enjoy it. He was asked if he would care for a drink. The expressions on their faces showed as if they were face to face with an all-powerful man. They wanted to talk to him but couldn't figure out where to start.

After a lot of reflection, a white official asked him: 'Are these thousands of strikers going to go all the way to Charlestown with you?'

'That's up to them. But I am with them.'

'How long will it take to get there?'

'It's a two-day march, but it will depend on how fast they move. And of course on whether the government lets them move.'

'Why don't they take a train?'

'They are poor people. They can't afford the fare.' Mohandas laughed.

The conversation continued. They wanted it to continue. One of the ticket examiners asked: 'Where did these illiterate and uncomprehending indentured labourers get this rock-like will?'

'They may lack other things but a strong will is theirs by birth. It is a will that shatters rocks and grows a crop where a blade never grew.'

'Why are you going?'

'Looking for freedom.'

'And if you don't get it?'

'Freedom is within you. You have only to awaken it. You can do it too.'

Whether any of this stuff was getting through it was hard to say but they did look suitably thrilled and excited.

Their final question was: 'You used to travel first. In fact, it was for that reason you once had to jump out of a train …'

'I did not jump. I was thrown out.'

'Why don't you travel first now?'

'I was only a barrister then. Now I am a labourer too.'

The train was at a station and they all got off.

~

Charlestown had a population of four thousand. As the march progressed, more streams of marchers joined in from different directions and the number of marchers again went up to five thousand by the time they reached Charlestown. Mohandas was keeping track of everything. The obvious result of a town of four thousand being invaded by a throng of five thousand was disorder. But no disorder followed. Women and children were accommodated in the homes of local inhabitants. The remainder made their home under the sky. The weather was pleasant and rain wasn't expected.

Dr. Brisco was the Charlestown District Health Officer. The influx of such a large number of people was causing him a headache. He called on Mohandas and said: 'Help us and we'll help you. The local European community is upset. They fear our water supply may get poisoned.'

Mohandas reassured him: 'Don't be upset. Tell us what you want us to do and we'll do it. We'll give them all help. We are not here to create trouble; in fact we are here to remove their troubles.'

'We want your help in three ways.'

'Go on.'

'No water to be spilled on the roads; no garbage to be strewn in residential areas; and your people to stay confined to the area designated for them.'

Mohandas said: 'Dr. Brisco, I'm no longer a barrister; I'm a sanitation worker. Please have no worries.'

The first to reach there were Mohandas, Kallenbach, P.K.Naidu, Thambi Naidu, Albert Christo and Miss Schlesin. The first thing Mohandas did every morning was to clean up the place, collect all garbage and either burn it or bury it deep in a pit. Others followed suit. The whole place was spick and span in no time at all.

People tried to stop Mohandas: 'Why do you have to do it yourself? There are so many of us here ...'

Gandhibhai laughed and said: 'Why do you want my status reduced? The greater your service, the greater your status. No status without service.'

The matter was thus laughed off. And the work—it was over in a jiffy.

The marchers survived on bread and sugar for two days. Many strikers arrived in Charlestown directly from their mines and towns. People dropped in at odd times. Thambi Naidu led a separate march of his group of two hundred and fifty people. About four hundred women, children and disabled men had been sent by train. Having put them on the train, Kallenbach had arrived in Charlestown with his companions ahead of them.

Kallenbach had set up a temporary open air kitchen. Utensils for cooking had been arranged by the people of the locality. The traders of Charlestown had built up a big store of vegetables, lentils, rice and other foodstuff. Mohandas was the chief cook. Many others took the clue from him and dropped in to help. The kitchen ran round the clock. Mohandas believed that all new arrivals should be greeted with a meal. It was his effort to stay in the vicinity of the kitchen all the twenty-four hours in order to make sure that no one ever went hungry.

Cooking utensils were in short supply. There was also the question of time, so instead of cooking the vegetables and the lentils separately they were mixed together. Sometimes the lentils became rather watery. Expert diving was required to locate a grain of lentil or a piece of vegetable. Sometimes the lentils were underdone; rice was burnt or came mixed with foreign particles. Mohandas personally served food to the marchers while also entertaining them with his remarks: 'I bet you have never had food as tasty as this! You can use lentils in place of water; it'll do your health a world of good. Never a swollen stomach; good walking speed and no fatigue, I promise!'

Sometimes, the comment was: 'Don't think the rice is burnt; it's only the smell of the utensil it was cooked in.'

'Hard work cooking,' he would slip in occasionally. 'Harder work eating! This is what I call instant eating, quick stuffing and quick march!'

Food had run short. The women were the last ones to eat. Mohandas accordingly made the portions smaller. The women were hungry. They looked daggers at Mohandas.

'Hungry stomach and not enough food equal an angry woman,' muttered Mohandas as he served them and smiled at them. They too couldn't help laughing. He continued: 'Look, a light stomach means you will sing better *bhajan*s. Less food for you means less work for me; after all I too must get some rest, musn't I? So many mouths to feed and each mouth must have something in it! I am like that bird in the story who couldn't muster enough food one day. There were so many chicks waiting in the nest. So what she did was to drop one grain in each mouth and off she flew! The chicks were left tweeting! When I am gone, you'll be tweeting too, tweet-tweet, won't you?'

The looks on their faces showed the contentment his words had given them.

Mohandas kept a sharp eye open for the happenings around him. After the day's long march, people had time to spare. He tried to keep them busy, but still there would be time to spare. 'An empty mind is a devil's workshop' was his favourite phrase which he often kept repeating. Despite all the hectic activity and multifarious goings-on, so far things had on the whole gone on smoothly. His experiences of Phoenix and Transvaal had taught Mohandas to be on the alert all the time.

Women who had arrived with the straggler groups could not be accommodated in private homes and had to be accommodated in the open. When it is only males who are holed up together, the animal in them may occasionally awaken but for lack of opportunities goes back to dormancy. Mohandas was worried because of the unusual situation they were in. If the animal raised its head now it would lead the man by the nose and would not go back to sleep till it got what it wanted.

And that was precisely what happened. One of the marchers made it with a woman.

When Mohandas found out, he went and checked. The two stood there with drooping heads, while others were very vocal. Mohandas told the woman to go and she was sent off to stay with some family.

The man stood there motionless.

'Throw them out,' said the people around, 'They don't deserve to be in the march.'

'Yes, the sanctity will be lost.'

Mohandas remained calm and silent. When everyone had had his say, he said: 'I know what they have done is wrong. They should not have done it. After all, they are on *satyagraha*. But let me ask you something. This case came to light, but can you say with any degree of confidence that nothing of the type happened before or will not happen again?'

No one had any answer.

Mohandas resumed: 'In my life I have seen cruel people turning kinder under the influence of their environment; I have also seen cultured people turn barbarians under the influence of adverse conditions. Shouldn't we ask why this thing came about. Are we completely free of blame?'

No one spoke. Mohandas made his final remark and left: 'It's not only in the world outside that the saint meets the devil; it must also happen within us.'

The whole day the air was heavy with everyone feeling as if a heavy weight had been hung around his neck.

~

November had started. The Transvaal Sisters had completed their three months of hard labour. Fatima Mehtab had reacted rather strongly to the sentence she had been awarded. Fatima Mehtab was the wife of Sheikh Mehtab and she lived in *purdah*. Ever since Sheikh Mehtab had fallen out with Mohandas he had started living in Durban. Later he also called his wife over from India. His contacts with Mohandas had almost ceased. Fatima's mother, Hanifa Bai and their seven year old son also lived with them. When she heard about the Transvaal Sisters that they had given up their families to embrace imprisonment, Fatima Bai also left for Volksrust with her mother and her son. Sheikh Mehtab did not like the idea. At the border, they were asked for their fingerprints which they refused to provide.The registration officials said: 'Without giving your fingerprints and acquiring a permit you cannot enter Transvaal.'

'We cannot give our fingerprints. It is against our religion.'

'Then you cannot be allowed to cross the border.'

'We must go. Our sisters and brothers are in jail there.'

The police arrested the mother and the daughter and sent the seven year old son back alone.

The next day, mother and daughter were sentenced to three months' hard labour. When Mohandas found out, he appeared in the court for their defence. His childhood friend, Sheikh Mehtab, stood in front of him. Their eyes met. They stepped forward slowly and then clasped each other in their arms. Mohandas' eyes were moist. There was a lot he wanted to ask him but all that he asked was: 'Where were you all these days?'

'Trying to overcome my shame,' he replied in the same tone.

The march resumed. Sheikh Mehtab also joined the march with his son. Now they followed Mohandas like his shadow.

~

It had rained the previous night and the cold had got worse. The clothes they were wearing were barely enough. One of the children caught cold and developed high fever. Mohandas was carrying some medicines which he administered to him with water, keeping awake all night. The march was to resume the next morning. When the time came for the march to start, the child died. The march was stalled. The child's mother however said: 'Please carry on with the march. The child had to go, so he is gone. The survivors must not wait; they must carry on. He didn't wait for us, did he?'

They buried the child, shed a couple of tears on his grave and moved on with heavy hearts and tearful eyes. The mother saved the child's clothes and put them away carefully.

Another event occurred almost immediately afterwards. The marchers were crossing a rather wobbly bridge two at a time. A woman had her child in her arms. Slightly older than the previous one, the child was rather difficult to control. When he saw water, he started jumping out of his mother's arms, and despite his mother holding him, he suddenly leapt out of her arms and fell into the water. The current was strong and in a second he was gone. Gandhi, who was up ahead in front, came running as soon as he got the word, and so did Thambi Naidu, but by that time there was no trace of the child. Either he had gone far too ahead with the current or some water animal had got him. The stream was quiet as before, as if nothing had happened. The mother kept looking high and low, shouting out the child's name. Other marchers also joined in. Thambi Naidu wanted to jump into the stream but people held him back; the current was much too strong. The child's mother also forbade him. 'He must have reached his destination by now, such a hurry he was in. Don't risk your life for him. He started and finished his march, but we still have some way to go.'

'So long as we have sisters like her, we have nothing to fear,' said Mohandas to Thambi Naidu.

The march resumed.

Phoenix had almost emptied out. Only Magan Gandhi, West and his sister and the thirteen year old Devdas had been left behind. They were running *Indian Opinion.* Devdas had familiarized himself with the press and he put in ten to twelve hours everyday in the press. *Indian Opinion* was turning into a nuisance for the government. It was in the stands every week on time and copies were sent all over South Africa, some also to foreign countries. People looked forward eagerly to read *Indian Opinion.*

The inevitable result was the arrest of West, which in turn meant a lockout in *Indian Opinion*. With neither Mohandas nor West around, who was going to bring it out? At the start of *satyagraha*, the idea had been that Maganlal Gandhi, West and his sister, who had moved in with him, will continue to stay at Phoenix. There were about a dozen kids, including Devdas. They had to be looked after. There were also the farms to look after. West's sister and Maganlal looked after the children. West looked after *Indian Opinion*. Maganlal also helped out. When West was arrested, word was sent to Sonja Schlesin, who always rushed post-haste whenever Gandhi wanted her. Sonja came and took over *Indian Opinion*. The next issue was out on the dot to the complete astonishment of people. People had known West but who knew Sonja as a journalist or an editor?

Maganlal cooked the meals for the kids; also washed, bathed and fed them. He also looked after the farms and the press. He arranged for the type and the paper. Hardest of all, he arranged the money. Gandhi was still sending most of it.

The older ones among the kids collected the mail from the station twice a day. The road was practically non-existent and animals roamed the area. Snakes could often be seen dangling from the trees. The kids carried sticks with them. Though they had outgrown fear, it was still necessary to exercise caution. The workers at the station attended to them on priority. On the day of its publication, they carried bundles of *Indian Opinion* to the station and got them booked to their destinations. For this work to be done, they never had to wait. No sooner they arrived, their work was disposed of.

In the absence of Mohandas, the Johannesburg office was being run by Polak. Millie was of course with him. They kept track of the conditions changing every minute. Sonja was constantly commuting between Phoenix and Johannesburg. She bore a major share of responsibility for *satyagraha* related activities. Kallenbach was with Gandhibhai in the march. Polak sent a daily report on the activities to Gokhale by telegram. It upset

Gokhale if he did not receive the report every day and Polak would instead receive a telegram from him.

~

The *satyagraha* was hot news in India too. People were waiting eagerly to learn about the fallout of the march. They had started trying to find out about this man Gandhi: Who was this man who could collect such large number of illiterate Indians in a foreign land and launch a march like that of the 'monkey army' (in the Ramayana)?

There were also some who opposed the idea. What do such marches achieve, they argued; this is no *satyug* (the virtuous age) that Ram collects a bunch of monkeys and scores a victory over Ravana.

Those who had seen Gandhi at the Congress session were amazed that a man who couldn't read his own speech and had to be helped out by Vacha has suddenly acquired such amazing powers.

Gokhale was quiet but worried. He had had his lesson in the untrustworthiness of governments. Such a government could easily go out of control and turn brutish. If that happened, who would save these unarmed and helpless people? He wrote to the Viceroy. As expected, the complaint was received but no result followed. For Gokhale too, the only option now was to pray to God.

The evil intentions of the government were no secret to Mohandas either. It could go to any extent to achieve its goals but was unable to find an excuse. Mohandas told his fellow travellers: 'We need to have peace without: that is needed for our security. You also need to have peace within: that shows us the right way. This march may be a storm for others, but we need to have peace so that we don't lose our way.'

The marchers had to wait for several days in Natal itself before entering Transvaal. Mohandas, Kallenbach, Thambi Naidu and others had worked on individual marchers to prepare them mentally for the sentences that awaited them. When everyone was ready, Mohandas sent a message to the government of Transvaal; 'We want to assure the government that we are not entering Transvaal with the intention of settling down there. Our move is a protest against the broken promises of Transvaal government. This has hurt our self-respect. If the government arrests us, we will be relieved of all our responsibility; if it does not, the responsibility for our entering Transvaal will lie entirely with the government. We are running an open movement and there is nothing secret about it. None of us has any personal axe to grind through this movement. We are not trying to smuggle ourselves into the country on the sly; we are making a daylight entry. Thousands of strikers are with us. That also makes it necessary to forewarn you that we cannot possibly be held responsible for how each of them behaves. Our only strength is love, nothing else. We do not know whether you have ever had to deal with it or not in the past. In the end, we would like to repeat that should you decide to withdraw the three-pound tax, or give us a sincere assurance that you would do so, the strike will be withdrawn and the workers will go back to their work. We will not bring our other demands into this struggle. This matter relates to the existence of thousands of our poor and defenceless companions.'

The situation was getting worse by the day. There was an air of uncertainty about everything. They could not wait indefinitely for the government's reply. Meeting daily expenses was becoming a serious problem. How long could they support such large numbers in Charlestown? It was therefore decided to cross into Transvaal as early as possible. Tolstoy Farm was also at some distance from the border.

Mohandas addressed the *satyagrahi*s:

> *Unless we are arrested on the way, our goal is to reach Tolstoy Farm. If arrested we will be in jail; if we reach Tolstoy Farm, we will be in paradise. The place is laden with fruit and there are cold water springs. There are hills and plains. If we walk twenty-four miles every day, it will take us several days to reach there. We will stay there till our demands are met. It will become the centre of our struggle. We will till the*

fields and produce enough for our needs. We will accept gratefully whatever nature gives us. Our friend Kallenbach will do all that needs to be done.

Everyone was happy.

The idea was that they would construct small huts with clay bricks at the Farm. This work would be done by the marchers themselves. So long as the huts were not ready, the elderly and the disabled would be accommodated in tents. The rest of them would sleep under the open sky as before, though the rains were expected to start soon.

'And what happens if the struggle is prolonged?' asked Mohandas under the breath.

'You don't worry about that so long as I am around. It's not for nothing that I am your Lower House.'

Both of them smiled.

Gandhibhai had become good friends with Dr. Brisco. When he found out that the marchers were about to leave he came to see Mohandas and said: 'Mr. Gandhi, I'd heard a lot about the dirty habits of Indians, but I am amazed that with thousands of people living together in the open I find no signs of any garbage around. Even whites living in such a small quarter would have not been able to keep it so clean. It was unthinkable that these people would maintain such cleanliness.'

Mohandas laughed: 'Dr. Brisco, it is simply a question of making up your mind. When Jesus made up his mind to mount the cross, did he have any problem? In comparison, this was a very simple matter. When your mind is clear about what you want to do or not do, determination simply follows. We are actually heirs to a very ancient civilization; only we have forsaken it. We have to start living it again in thought and in deed.'

'The Europeans of Charlestown are amazed at the conduct of these illiterate and so-called antisocial coolies. It will be hard to find in the pages of history another example of a movement so large, so peaceful and so relaxed and at the same time so disciplined.'

'I don't know about history, but there are several examples in my country. People have been going on foot on hundreds of miles long pilgrimages for thousands of years, with no controlling authority over them. Muslims go to Mecca; Moses had led the Exodus. It's true however that these pilgrimages were all inspired by religious faith. Ours is inspired by freedom.'

Dr. Brisco was carrying a large box with him. He said: 'Yours is a long journey. Five thousand people are with you including children, the elderly, the disabled … I have brought some essential medicines with me which you may need on the way. Please accept them.'

Mohandas looked at the box and laughed: 'I'll hardly be able to lift the box.' He continued: 'I greatly respect your motive in offering the medicines and that you spared so much thought for these poor and resourceless people. However, the box will have to be carried on our heads, as we all carry our own stuff. Kindly make for us a smaller package of selected medicines. As we shall mostly be camping near towns, we should have no difficulty in acquiring medicines.'

Dr. Brisco got a smaller package made consisting of medicines for about a hundred people. The rest he took back with him. Before he took his leave, he joined Mohandas in a prayer: 'May Jesus grant you success in your mission. Your mission is very close to Jesus' heart. Amen.'

The marchers had to live on bread and sugar between Charlestown and Tolstoy Farm. Arranging three pounds of bread and a hundred ounces of sugar per head for five thousand marchers was no simple matter. The only satisfactory way would be an arrangement whereby a supply of fresh bread would become available at every camping site, since it was not possible to lug around such a large supply of bread; nor would it be hygienically safe. Had the bakers been Indian, an arrangement might have been arrived at, but they were all white. Moreover, not every village had a baker; those villages which had any had very small time ones, just about enough to supply local needs. It was decided that they should contact a big baker who would make the supply by train to every camping site every morning.

Volksrust was about double the size of Charlestown and had some big time bakers. Kallenbach contacted one of them. He agreed to make the supply at no extra charge. He could have tried to exploit the difficult situation of the marchers but he didn't.

When the marchers were ready to set out, Mohandas made a last effort. Letters and telegrams had already been sent; now he called General Smuts' secretary on phone. Mohandas was aware that this move of his could well be misunderstood by both sides. From the other side, the answer could well be a blunt 'No. Go ahead and do your worst.' Still Mohandas told the secretary: 'Please tell General Smuts that we are all set to enter Transvaal. Our information is that the whites of Volksrust are all worked up. We are receiving threats everyday. Even General Smuts may not tolerate such indecent behaviour. There is still time. If the government agrees to withdraw the three-pound tax, I am prepared to call a halt. I'm not breaking the law for the fun of it; the government is forcing us to do it. I can't believe that the General will not grant us this small favour.'

The reply came within half an hour: 'The General will have nothing to do with you. You are free to do what you please; we will do what we have to do.' And he hung up. Mohandas was shocked.

Mohandas of course expected a negative response but he did not expect that the receiver to be banged down on him so rudely. A more civil response was expected from the General. They had known each other for six years. But Mohandas was not discouraged by the General's rudeness. In fact, it reinforced his determination. The road ahead was now narrow and straight like a sword's blade.

He went back to the people and announced: 'We enter Transvaal at six tomorrow morning.'

People danced with joy.

His belongings balanced on the head or on the back, every marcher stood ready and alert like a soldier. Then everyone said the prayers. The prayers made no distinction between religions. Every prayer had every religion and everyone's faith in it. As the prayers ended, everyone lurched forward like a battle-ready soldier. It was after several days that the march was heading towards its destination. Like an electric current, enthusiasm flowed through everyone's body. A mile-long stretch separated Charlestown and Volksrust. One entered Volksrust only after this stretch was crossed. When they were close to Volksrust, they learnt that a detachment of mounted police was awaiting their arrival. Mohandas signalled the marchers to stop and announced: 'You must wait here till I give you the signal.'

Mohandas walked ahead to talk to the commander of the contingent. As he was talking to him, a marcher ran across and entered the border of Transvaal. This started a commotion and a few more marchers crossed into Transvaal. The police raced their horses and surrounded the transgressing marchers on all sides.

Mohandas was at a loss to understand how such a situation could arise so suddenly. He approached the offending bunch of marchers and upbraided them: 'What made you behave so? Entering Transvaal is not the end in itself. The police had no intention of arresting us. I had gone to tell them that we were going to enter Transvaal. That's what our culture teaches us: you warn the enemy before you attack him. And this happens to be *satyagraha*. Please stand in a line. Only then shall we decide what to do next.'

The marchers went back to their original positions at the word from Mohandas. The horsemen watched. They were impressed with the way a disorderly bunch fell in like disciplined soldiers at a single word from one man.

A meeting had been held at Volksrust a couple of days before attended by a majority of the town's whites. Kallenbach was in Volksrust that day and he also turned up at the venue. The whites did not want him there and neither were they ready to listen to him on any subject whatsoever. Actually, a couple of whites rushed towards him to attack him. Kallenbach displayed his muscles to them and said: I'm an athlete trained at Sandhurst. Don't make the mistake of attacking me.' The whites stopped in their tracks.

But another white got up and said: 'I'm ready to fight a duel with you.'

'I'd have loved to accept your challenge. In fact I've fought many duels with men like you in the past. But now I've taken a vow of peace. Violence is a sign of weakness. Therefore I cannot accept your challenge. You can all go ahead and do what you like, but I will stay here and attend the meeting. All Europeans, without any exception, have been invited to this meeting. I have the leaflet if you want to see it.'

No one had any reply to Kallenbach's point.

Shamefaced, one of the whites said: 'It'd be better for you to leave. We don't want to see your face, or that of your chattering coolie.'

'But I love your faces,' said Kallenbach, smiling. 'Please do not raise your blood pressure by venting your anger on those who are not present here. Please try to understand. You are not among those few whites who do not flinch from inflicting tyranny on their fellow Europeans. You happen to have one of those in your midst today and he is telling you that the accusations you have made against Indians are false and baseless. They have no intention of overthrowing you from the seat of power. For all that they care, you can continue to occupy this seat till kingdom come. All that they want is justice for themselves. A craving for justice is an essential feature of everyone's existence. They don't even want to settle in Transvaal. All that they are doing is to protest the three-pound tax that has been imposed on them by the government wholly unfairly. They are no cowards. Indeed, they are brave. They do not wish even to cast a glance at you or your wealth. You may shoot them, but they will neither be deterred nor will they surrender. It is their aim to win your hearts by sacrifice and self-denial. You are scared of them; they are not scared of you, not in the least. This was the truth I came here to tell you. I think by telling you this I have done a service to the European community. This is the only thing I want to tell you: Please avoid sinning. Neither be a sinner nor force anyone else to be one.'

As long as Kallenbach was speaking, no one else uttered a sound. When he had said his piece, Kallenbach left the place. For a long while after he had left, they could not decide what to say or do next.

As soon as he stepped out, the white who had challenged him to a duel, accosted him and said: 'Can we be friends?'

Kallenbach laughed and said: 'Of course. Friendship is a sentiment which can make even mountains bow.'

'The things you said have touched me. If someone hits us, we can hit him back; but if we hit someone and he smiles back at you, there is nothing you can do to him.'

Kallenbach smiled: 'That was precisely what I came here to tell you all.'

The sight of the police force ranged all around them had first unnerved Mohandas. It might have launched an attack on the marchers. But nothing of the sort happened. The little disorder that had occurred had been due to the over-enthusiasm of the marchers. The unarmed army had made its entry into Transvaal and not a pebble was aimed at it by any white. In fact, a large crowd of whites had turned up to see the marchers. They had the idea that this was another of Gandhi's frauds. But when they saw thousands of marchers walk in files, their belongings strapped on their heads or backs, like disciplined soldiers, they had a hard time believing their eyes. They had come to see some fireworks, but when none happened and thousands-strong procession of marchers made a peaceful entry into Transvaal, they shrank away looking very sheepish.

They had suddenly arrived at the decision that for a solution to the problem to be reached the phenomenon of Gandhi, the coolie, must be tackled first.

Someone commented: 'A phoenix is indeed what he is. He rises from the ashes again and again.'

~

XXV

Their first stop was at Palmford, eight miles from Volksrust. It was perhaps November 6. This was the first day and it was six in the evening by the time they reached Palmford. Everyone was fatigued not so much because of the march as because of the tension caused by the uncertainty. Kallenbach and his team had arranged accommodation for them in the open. On arrival, every marcher was given a loaf of bread and sugar. Having eaten, the marchers spread out their sheets and lay down to rest. Those who couldn't sleep lay chatting among themselves.

'That was a great rescue act Gandhi performed. If the horsemen had had their way, we would have had our ribs broken.'

'I wonder what came over that chap.'

'Either he didn't hear what Gandhibhai said or he thought the first one to cross the border would win a prize.'

Everyone laughed.

'We'd been hearing that the Volksrust whites were waiting for us with their guns and would kill each one of us.'

'Not when Gandhibhai was with us. You do not put out fire with fire; you need water to do it. The gun that will fire at Gandhibhai hasn't yet been made: he is the real gun antidote.'

Another one said: 'Gandhibhai had sent Kallenbach to talk to them. I hear the whites were ready to kill the white. But Gandhi has also given him the mantra of peace and they couldn't even touch him.'

Someone somewhere was singing a *purabia* love-song and the lyric wafted over the entire area.

Some of the women had carried their small kids in their arms all the way and were now badly tired. When Mohandas saw them he realized at once that for them to walk as far as Tolstoy Farm safely was out of the question. He was also wary because of the Charlestown incident. Men and women had to eat and sleep separately; they could only walk together. The two had not been punished and the result was that they had gone back to their homes the next day with Gandhi's permission.

Mohandas told Kallenbach: 'Lower House, it does not look to me that these women can make it to Tolstoy Farm safe and sound after such a long journey.'

A few local traders were around. They reassured Mohandas: 'Don't worry about them. They can stay with us.'

Mohandas breathed a sigh of relief.

At every halt, Mohandas, Kallenbach, the two Naidus, Schlesin, et al. held consultations till late at night. The next day's programme was chalked out. Only then did they retire to sleep. That day, they had been particularly delayed; so everyone was fast asleep the moment he or she hit the bed. Gandhibhai was anyway a notorious sleeper. He could go to sleep or wake up any time he wished and would still be fresh. Every now and then someone could be heard snoring. Mohandas was the only one still awake. He had arranged his papers and was about to lie down when he saw a light moving at a distance. It seemed to be approaching him. A light burned near him too. He wondered who could be coming in the pitch dark carrying a light. When the light was close by he saw it was a white man with a lantern in his hand. Mohandas was immediately on the alert. Why should a single white man come to the midst of so many Indians so late at night? It did not take him long to grasp the situation. The light kept coming closer and closer lighting up various body parts of the people sleeping in between like a silver foil, leaving behind a deeper shade of dark. Although the light could make out the childlike simplicity of the sleeping men, the white man was paying no attention to it whatsoever.

The white man approached Mohandas with great familiarity and said: 'I have an arrest warrant for you. I have to arrest you.'

'When?'

'Right now. This very moment.'

'Right now as well as this very moment? Where are you going to take me?'

'To the nearby station. Then Volksrust.'

'I do not want my sleeping friends here to know about my arrest. I'll slink away with you quietly. If you have no objection, may I tell a couple of my friends about our future programme?'

'You may do so.'

Mohandas woke up P.K. Naidu softly. He was fast asleep and woke with a start: 'What's the matter, Gandhibhai?'

'Good news. The moment I'd been waiting for has arrived. The call has come for me. There is something I must tell you. Let nobody be woken up when I leave. You must leave this place before sunrise. Inform the people about my arrest at the next halt when food is given out unless of course someone makes a specific inquiry. If you are also arrested, let Kallenbach take your place.'

Mohandas picked his way out with the police officer in the light of the lantern. If its dim light showed up the face of a sleeping marcher, Mohandas gave him a silent, smiling salute. Naidu could see his wavering, walking shadow for some time. Then both the shadow and the light disappeared in the darkness.

~

The baker was doing a sincere job. The bread loaves would be at the halting station before the caravan reached there. The baker as well as the station master of the Volksrust station was a white. The station master took extra care to see that the loaves were loaded on to the train. At the halting station, the railway staff took care to unload the stuff and hand it over to Kallenbach's men. Sometimes, they even transported the stuff to the camping site by the official vehicle. Detailed information about the halts and the dates had been made available to the baker and the station masters.

The baker was facing pressure over the fact that, despite being a white, he was helping the coolie movement by selling them bread. His answer was:

'Every business has its own ethics. Since I have accepted the contract for delivering bread, I cannot escape my responsibility till the contract is over.'

The station master was also facing the same questions, but his answer was different: 'I cannot refuse bookings. Neither the government nor the railway company has issued any instruction to the effect that the marchers' goods are not to be booked. Further, these people are undertaking such long marches to reach their destinations, but there is no indication that they have indulged in rioting or have in any way tried to harm the European community.'

'They are filthy people. They will spread diseases.'

'I have heard that five thousand people are marching together. They spent so many days in Charlestown but there was no complaint that they abused their surroundings or spread any disease. Gandhi actually goes around saying that where there is love there is no pollution. Many whites agree with him.'

The people had no answer to that.

The police officer and Mohandas spent the night at the station. They got a train for Volksrust the next morning. As he sat in the train, Mohandas was thinking of the marchers and of how they must have started on their next lap. The travel time to Volksrust was not very long. Mohandas had refreshed himself at the station, so he was taken straight to the court in Volksrust.

The government prosecutor was not aware of the background. The sight of Mohandas unnerved him. Such a prominent barrister! He must watch what he says or the barrister might catch him out. He told the court: 'I may be allowed a week to prepare the case and to get hold of the witnesses.'

Mohandas submitted a bail application: 'I am supervising the march of thousands of people. There are hundred and twenty-two women and children among them. Hundreds of women have been entrusted to the care of the local citizens of Palmford. I have to see that they all reach their destination at Tolstoy Farm.'

The prosecutor had now recovered some of his wits. He said: 'That is Mr. Gandhi's problem. In the eyes of law, he is an accused. With thousands of coolies with him, he has broken the law and has endangered peace.'

Mohandas said: 'The court has no evidence to prove this charge. Nor was I told why I was being arrested.'

The court had a problem. Though Mohandas had been arrested, there was no definite and tenable proof against him. There seemed to be no reason to deny him bail.

In the end, the court released Mohandas on a bail of fifty pounds. By now Kallenbach had also arrived and he promptly deposited the fifty pounds. Then he took him in his car to the place where the unarmed army was advancing on its mission.

Leaving him there, Kallenbach returned to Volksrust. Arrangements had to be made for the next halt.

The cavalcade reached Standerton on Saturday. The loaves had already arrived. Local traders had turned up with canisters of marmalade and Mohandas had replaced sugar with marmalade. People were happy with the change. The traders were helping with the distribution.

A white man turned up and stood next to Mohandas without speaking a word. Mohandas was so busy distributing food that he didn't notice him, and he also didn't think it right to disturb him in his work. When the distribution work was over, the man placed his hand on Gandhi's soldier and took him aside. Everyone was now looking towards them. They couldn't understand what business a white man could possibly have here. They had learnt the day before that the police had taken Mohandas away; hence they were apprehensive. Finding Mohandas back amidst them had made them so happy that they were taking it as another slap on the face of the enemy.

Mohandas asked the white man: 'What can I do for you?'

The man laughed aloud and said: 'You are my prisoner.'

It was then that Mohandas recalled the face of the magistrate who had granted him bail the day before. It was the same man. He laughed and said: 'So that means I have been promoted. In place of an ordinary policeman, a magistrate has come to arrest me. I have a request to make to you. Please dispose of my case quickly. Please don't let it hang fire.'

Mohandas went back to the marchers and said: 'Please continue your march. I'll be back soon.'

Mohandas left with the magistrate. The taste of marmalade had suddenly turned bitter.

Many others like P.K. Naidu, Rahim Karim Khan, Biharilal Maharaj were already present in the court. Rahim Karim Khan and Biharilal Maharaj were silent workers. Mohandas was surprised that the government had found out about them. They had been picked up very quietly much in advance.

As he had promised, the magistrate took up Mohandas' case first. Mohandas repeated his old argument: 'All my friends have been arrested. The responsibility of thousands lies with me. You have seen it yourself. If I don't go back, who will take care of them? Food, stay, medicine—everything must be arranged by me.'

In place of Kallenbach, this time it was the Indian traders who were at hand to take him back. The magistrate again released Mohandas on a personal bond of fifty pounds. The marchers had barely covered three miles when Mohandas was back with them. The news travelled fast that Gandhi was back and rumours of all sorts started. One was that Gandhbhai had been locked up in jail but Gandhi, without breaking the lock, had taken the aerial route back. Another one said that Gandhi had never left the camp; it was his shadow that had accompanied the magistrate. Mohandas had to describe to everyone how he had been taken to the court and how he was bailed out and brought back by the traders. He told them that in fact some of his friends were still there.

There were some among the crowd who didn't accept his version on the ground that Gandhi did not want to advertise his extraordinary powers. But the marchers' speed had picked up and, singing *Vaishnava jan to taine kahiye*, they were pushing forward.

Incidents and rumours like these had jolted the Transvaal administration. General Smuts was restless and pacing his chamber. He had called an emergency meeting of the cabinet. Two of the ministers had arrived and one more was expected. Two officers were in attendance. When everyone had arrived, General Smuts said: 'You know that the "invaders" are in Johannesburg. Why doesn't this man Gandhi understand that he is playing with the lives of so many people? He is exploiting the sentiments of uneducated and illiterate people to spread rumours about himself. We can load these people in ships like cattle and throw them out of South Africa.'

One of the ministers said: 'I'm receiving cable after cable from the mine owners. Their mines are lying closed. Gandhi has brainwashed these people into locking up their homes and join the march. There are no other workers to be had. They are losing hundreds of thousands of pounds everyday.'

With the General's permission, one of the ministers said: 'They have walked hundreds of miles to get here. But there have been no complaints from any quarters despite our extensive inquiries. They have now been in Transvaal for many days. They are moving fifteen to twenty miles everyday like a disciplined army. They do not ask anyone for anything wherever they stay, let alone harassing them. They make their night halt in the space that is allotted to them. Next morning, they are up and on their way again after cleaning up the place and without causing anyone any harassment.

'Yes, even European citizens are impressed with their discipline.'

This was not what Smuts was expecting from his officers. Annoyed, he said: 'Stop all this. We are not here to sing praises of the marchers. They have been in Transvaal for four days now. What happens to the image of this government if they succeed in reaching their destination? Is this government so weak? These people are neither Europeans nor natives. Gandhi was arrested twice but was let out on bail both times. What's happening?'

'Their spirits are high,' said another minister.

'They are a headache to the government,' agreed the third one.

'I had thought the arrest of Gandhi will unnerve them and they might indulge in violence. With the ball in their court, we could then really go after them. That was what had happened at the time of the Zulu rebellion. But Gandhi won't let them do anything of the sort and everything is going as he wants it. A little violence could prove a blessing for the government, but these chaps neither do anything themselves nor let us do anything. All that they do is walking and more walking, as if walking will get them the kingdom of Transvaal.'

'Sir, he is a strange man, this Gandhi. He makes a fool of the strikers by telling them all kinds of negativistic things. He tells them: 'Make friends with death, then you won't fear death. Death is as certain as birth. You don't fear birth, so why do you fear death? A mouse fears the cat and runs away at the sight of it while the cat rushes towards it. If the mouse shed his fear of the cat, mouse-hunting would lose all meaning for the cat. If all the lambs lay down in front of the lion, the lion wouldn't know what to do. If the lion didn't fight the hunter, the hunter would have no reason to fight him. Fear is what motivates them all—the mouse fears the cat, the lion fears the hunter, the hunter fears the lion, and so on. All these illiterate coolies have turned philosophers. All rubbish, of course. It's the law of nature that the weak are meant to be eaten by the strong, but, by removing the fear of death from their hearts, what Gandhi has done is to diminish the value of life. They are ready to die ...'

'Enough!' General Smuts slapped his hands on his ears. 'Gandhi, Gandhi, all the time! I have no interest in knowing how Gandhi fools of the workers. Tell me how to end this impasse. Tell me how to crush this silent rebellion that is raising its head. We must tell them that enough is enough. All this drama means nothing to us. It is important that Gandhi and his friends must be put behind bars immediately. They are now on their way from Standerton to Greylingstad. They must be arrested before they reach their destination. Make it a secret operation and name it Operation Gandhi.'

The General got up and strode out of the room.

~

The pilgrimage had progressed from Standerton to Teakworth. Greylingstad was the next stop and night halt. Polak was already at Teakworth. Gokhale had been writing to Mohandas to send at least Polak to India so that he could help him to explain the worsening situation of Indians in South Africa and their continuing struggle to the people and the government. He said that he was now quite advanced in age and incapable of doing much running around. Government kept on snowballing, getting bigger and stronger, and only the heat of public opinion could make it melt.

Polak had this great virtue that wherever he went he made himself indispensable. He had lived in India and had made many good friends. Mohandas had actually written to Polak that Gokhale wanted him in India as he needed him, and that he should go. However, Polak should see him first. He also warned him that coming to Teakworth might well mean his being arrested and sent to jail instead of to India.

So Polak had come to Teakworth only for a couple of days to receive instructions from Gandhi about who to see and what to do in India.

Mohandas did not want to invite any danger by letting Polak stay there for too many days. He was getting signals every hour that the government might crack down on the marchers any time. The moment he met Polak, he took him aside for consultations so that they could finish early and he could leave right away. It was still some way to sunset and the time was three o'clock. While Mohandas and Polak walked ahead of others talking, the others could also overhear what they were saying. The two were so deeply engrossed in their talk that they did not notice a vehicle standing a little distance from where they were. The others had noticed the van and they tried to signal to Gandhi and Polak about its presence. Finally, one of the marchers went up to Gandhi and told him about the van. When Mohandas looked he saw the Immigration Officer, Mr. Chamney, walking towards him with two police officers.

Mr. Chamney took Mohandas aside and said: 'You are being arrested with immediate effect.'

'I'm grateful to the government for this kindness. This is the third time in four days that I'm being arrested.' Later, he asked: 'Have you also spared a thought about my fellow travellers?'

'The government thinks of everyone. You needn't worry about them.'

Mohandas turned to Polak: 'Take charge of this march. Your India trip is cancelled for the time being.'

'You are not allowed to deliver a speech,' said Chamney.

'I didn't know that talking to a friend would be counted as giving a speech.'

The police officer told the driver: 'Let's go.'

The vehicle moved off at a fast speed. Mohandas tried to look back. The travellers had been left far behind. Mohandas was moving at several times their speed.

Mohandas was taken to Greylingstad and from there to Heidelburg, which was the night halt. They could have spent the night at Greylingstad, but there was a danger that the confidentiality of the operation would be breached. All along the way, they could hear nothing but the sound of the vehicle. Occasionally, they would exchange a sentence or two.

Mohandas said: 'Mr. Chamney, if you had simply sent the summons to me, I'd have presented myself before the law.'

The police officer said: 'That's what everyone says.'

'Other police officers know me better.'

Mohandas looked at the police officer. A shiver seemed to run through the police officer's body.

Mr. Chamney simply shook his head. To see Chamney, one felt he was feeling more constrained than Mohandas. He would neither speak nor look at anybody.

The police officer controlled himself and said: 'You were planning to deliver a speech and incite the people to disrupt peace.'

'Had I given a speech, it would have only helped your government.'

Chamney signalled to the police officer to keep quiet. Silence reigned once again.

Mohandas knew that the government had changed its attitude. When the caravan reached Greylingstad, they found Ahmed Cachalia and Ahmed Bayat already present there. They knew that Gandhibhai had been arrested and taken to an unknown destination. The government also had plans to arrest all marchers. Polak had told everyone to be ready for arrest. Polak was still hoping to be able to go to India even if a couple of days late. He would go to Durban and catch a ship. He hadn't revealed this plan to anyone yet. Bayat and Cachalia had also brought some foodstuff with them, which had been given to the marchers right in the morning for fear that there may not be an occasion later. Fortunately, women and children had been separated. Prayer and the meal over, the marchers had set out at six in the morning.

They reached Balfour at about nine. Balfour was a railway station. Three trains stood ready at the station, with policemen all around. The situation looked serious. There was tension in the air.

The moment they reached Balfour, they were told: 'You are all under arrest. All coolies into the trains.'

Some marchers started asking questions: 'We are marchers. Why should we get into the train?'

'Where do you want to take us?'

'Where is Gandhibhai? Let him be brought here first.'

'We'll get into the trains if he says so.'

Mr. Chamney was present. The officers tried to explain to the people that had Gandhibhai been present, he would not have agreed with this argument of theirs.

'If he were here, why would we make this demand?'

'You must appreciate that if you persist with this attitude, things can go out of control. Mr. Gandhi has brought you up to this point without even a minor incident.'

But the marchers weren't ready to listen.

Chamney went to Polak and Cachalia and said: 'Please explain it to them that things could go out of our hands. You know that Mr. Gandhi cannot be brought here.'

The two approached the marchers. The marchers all shouted: 'Get Gandhibhai here.'

Polak and Cachalia explained: 'You know that before entering Transvaal, Gandhibhai had written to General Smuts and also told him on the phone that if he so wanted he could take all the marchers into custody, because they were breaking a so-called law by entering Transvaal. General Smuts told Gandhi that he would have nothing to do with him. But Gandhibhai had all along held that the foremost aim of this march was to violate the law and court arrest. It is only now that the government has agreed to his proposal. If you do not cooperate at this juncture, it will make Gandhibhai unhappy. It will be our first victory when all of you go to jail.'

The workers stood silent for a while. Then one of them moved towards the train. Soon all of them followed him and got into the train.

When Polak also proceeded toward the train, Chamney stopped him. 'Why are you going that way?'

'To be arrested.'

'The government has no intention to arrest you.'

'Why not?'

'The government is obliged to you and Mr. Cachalia for your help in arresting all these people. It would have been an impossible task without your help.'

Polak looked at Cachalia. He was fuming.

Gandhibhai had entrusted these people to my charge before he was arrested. It'll be unfair to me if you don't arrest me.'

'We can't do it. You are free to go as you please.'

Polak's face lost all colour.

Mohandas was taken to Dundee. That was where his arrest warrant had been issued. He was arrested at Teakworth on November 9, 1913 and presented before the Dundee court on the eleventh after he had been taken around for a while.

The charge was that Mr. M.K. Gandhi had instigated the indentured labour working in mines to leave Natal and make a forcible entry into

Transvaal. He had conspired with the *girmitiya*s working in the coal mines to break their *girmit.* He wanted to spread unrest in the country.

The court asked for witnesses. The prosecution instead launched a tirade against Gandhi: 'The whole world knows that Mr. Gandhi is inciting the workers. He is the one who has pulled them out of the mines.'

The magistrate said: 'The law requires evidence. There is a difference between the whole world knowing something and citing evidence.'

Mohandas intervened: 'Sir,' he said, 'the prosecution lawyer was not present on the occasion. Those who were present would be hard to persuade to give evidence against me. I seek your permission to present myself as a witness.'

The magistrate was taken aback: 'I don't quite get it,' he said.

'I am a *satyagrahi.* For me truth is God. The coal mine workers were unhappy at the three pound per person tax imposed on them. I channelized their anger and thus saved unrest from taking place. I instead turned it into *satyagraha.*'

The government prosecutor tried to say something, but the magistrate stopped him and instead asked Gandhi: 'Do you realize the implications of what you are saying?'

'I'm a barrister. I take full responsibility for whatever I say.'

The magistrate sentenced Mohandas to nine months in prison.

Mr. Chamney had let Polak go with thanks. Polak took this move as an attempt at the instance of the government to isolate him from the movement. This had caused him pain. Every single marcher had been put on the train. Gandhibhai had been arrested. But when the chance came to arrest him, he was allowed to go with thanks. Chamney's words of thanks had been like spitting on his face. One moment he was leading the movement in place of Gandhi; the next moment his condition was worse than that of an ordinary marcher.

Later, when the government came to know that Polak was going to India as an emissary of Gandhi, Chamney was hauled up.

'Why was Polak not arrested?'

Chamney said: 'It was thanks to Mr. Polak and Mr. Cachalia that a huge operation like Operation Gandhi became possible. The government had issued instructions that anyone helping in the operation was to be suitably rewarded. No other reward could possibly have been given to Polak, so the two of them were allowed to go.'

The stakes having risen, the government issued an order that Polak and the other colleagues of Gandhi may be arrested at once.

Polak had reconciled himself to his non-arrest by telling himself that in a way it was all to the good as he would now be able to join Gokhale and do the tasks that Gandhi had entrusted him with. He stood at the Charlestown station with his luggage waiting for the Durban train. He had decided that he would respond to the government's efforts to isolate him from the movement by working with redoubled energy to promote the movement in India.

The train was about to enter the platform. A police officer appeared and addressed him: 'Are you Mr. Henry Polak?'

'Yes.'

'You are under arrest.'

The train came and left. Polak took himself with his luggage to the police officer's vehicle. Kallenbach was also arrested on the same day. The two met in Volksrust jail.

Gandhibhai had been sentenced on November 11 in the Dundee court. There was another case against him pending in the Volksrust court and the date was approaching. On November 13, Mohandas was taken from Dundee to Volksrust. Kallenbach and Polak were already in Volksrust jail. At first, Mohandas was startled to see Polak, but when he saw both of them, his joy knew no bounds.

'You two have again beaten me to it. Already here?'

Mohandas already knew that the marchers had been evacuated from Transvaal in three trainloads. He was worried about them. What would be their fate?

That was the first thing he asked. 'They have probably taken all our friends to Natal. They will surely be handed over to the mine owners.'

Kallenbach laughed and said: 'Upper House, whosoever you touched turned into a *satyagrahi.* So don't worry about them. They now know how to deal with any situation. Every one of them has the confidence that Gandhibhai is by his side always.'

Polak spoke on his own: 'On that occasion, I and Cachalia were allowed to go with thanks. I had felt then that a load of garbage had been heaped on me. But when I was waiting at the Charlestown station for a train, the police appeared suddenly and took me in custody.'

Mohandas said: 'They needed workers, not lawyers. Perhaps when the government found out that Polak was a bigger worker than even the worker's worker called Mohandas; it must have felt it couldn't do without you. You could create some miracle in India. In their eyes, Kallenbach was already a villain. A villain's friend is a villain anyway. It must have thought they could dispose him of too while they were about it.' Mohandas glanced at Kallenbach lovingly.

He continued: 'This whole march business is his doing anyway. Would the march have been possible without his help? After all he is the Lower House, the most important House.'

'When you set your eyes on someone, how can he escape being noticed by others?'

They all laughed at Kallenbach's joke. Only he stayed serious.

Mohandas looked at Kallenbach: 'Have you informed your cousin of your arrest?'

'How could I?'

'She'll be waiting. You are being unfair to her. Look at Polak. His father didn't approve, but he still went ahead and married Millie.'

Kallenbach kept quiet. Mohandas took his hand in his own and kissed it. Polak was looking the other way.

~

Kallenbach and Polak were presented before the court on November 14 and November 17 respectively. Mohandas' case had already been disposed of. Evidence against him would have been hard to procure but he himself had testified against himself and, taking his testimony to be authentic, the magistrate had sentenced him.

The real problems arose in the cases of Kallenbach and Polak. How could they be sentenced without evidence? Where could they get witnesses to testify against them in such a short time? Kallenbach was ready to admit the charges that had been brought against him, but Polak wanted to go to India and therefore wanted to escape a sentence. They decided that, since it was important that Polak should go to India, they should all remain noncommittal in his case neither affirming nor denying any knowledge about his actions.

On second thoughts, Mohandas didn't quite agree that it would be the right thing to do. It would be thought that, by not testifying against him, Gandhi had rescued Polak from the sentence since he was closer to him. People could use it as an excuse for hiding the truth. His own statement would provide the excuse. The same would hold for Kallenbach. So Mohandas told the court: 'I am ready to be a witness in the case of these two accused as I was a witness in my own case.'

Kallenbach's was the first case to be presented. The court permitted Mohandas to be a witness. Despite the fact that he was a convicted criminal, He was made to stand in the witness box.

The prosecutor asked: 'What do you know about Mr. Kallenbach?'

'Mr. Kallenbach is a close friend and colleague. He was with us in the march. He extended every possible help to the marchers. Indians have a great friend in him.'

Polak's case was presented three days later. Kallenbach was presented as a witness. As already decided, he gave evasive answers.

'I was not with the marchers at that time.'

He was interrogated in diverse ways but his answers followed the same pattern. He hadn't seen anything himself. He couldn't be certain about anything. There was nothing untrue about whatever he said.

Mohandas was called to the witness box next. He testified: 'When I was arrested on November 9, Polak was with me. He had come to see me before leaving for India. He had had no connection with the march. But when I was arrested there was no one around who could lead the march. I therefore handed over the responsibility to Polak. When Polak was arrested, he was leading the march.'

The court sentenced Kallenbach and Polak to three months' hard labour each.

On the way back from the court, Polak asked Mohandas: 'Why did you change the statement?'

'By telling a lie, I could have saved you from jail, but what would have happened to the truth? It is on the strength of truth that we are daring to fight such a big power. Especially since I neither saved myself, nor Kallenbach, I thought it would not be fair to me or to you to save you.'

'What about India?'

'India can wait. There was no point in taking a lie to India with you which would have stayed on there even after you had returned.'

Polak said nothing at the moment, but the next day he said: 'Gandhibhai, you did the right thing. Had I been released on the strength of a false statement from you, my shame would have been greater than what it was when I was not arrested along with the other marchers.'

Mohandas extended a letter towards Polak. As soon as he had got to know of Polak's arrest he had written a letter to Millie. This was a copy.

Dear Millie,

You are a brave woman. I am sure you will be proud of the fact that your husband has gone to jail for a cause which is close to both your hearts. This issue of the three-pound tax is linked closely to the dignity of the helpless and speechless among us. Please do not step back from helping them even if you have to beg for them. Please show them the way. Do whatever you can for them. Do not wait for them to come to you. Please go to them. Go to them even if they insult you. Like Polak, Schlesin is also part of this struggle. Please help her. I have also told Schlesin to do whatever is possible to see that the situation remains under your control. Contact Maganlal and West for your requirements. I pray to God that He may give you the strength to come out a winner in this trial by fire.

Your brother

Gandhibhai

~

Volksrust jail was bustling with activity. New prisoners were coming in everyday and they brought new stories with them. Labourers in sugarcane farms were restless and determined to go on strike. They had coined a new slogan: 'Release King Gandhi, release the queen and let go our princes.'

Mohandas had sent a message to them telling them that there were no kings, queens or princes in their midst; everyone was a *girmitiya*. 'I can admit to being the first *girmitiya*, one who was released from the *girmit* in just a year, but everyone here is working on his *girmit*.'

Mohandas, Kallenbach and Polak went and met the prisoners at every opportunity and collected fresh information about the conditions obtaining outside the jail walls. They discussed the conditions, reflected on them and outlined plans for the future. The three had formed a kind of shadow executive inside the jail, though Kallenbach and Polak looked to Mohandas for solutions to all problems. They were of the view that they could not have the same insight into the problems of Indians that Gandhibhai had. They could at best help in advancing his programmes. But, despite this, they sometimes had prolonged discussions on policy matters.

Mohandas was amazed at the way *satyagraha* was going from strength to strength even while it was on the autopilot. All the leaders were in jail and so everyone had turned his own leader. One day, a *satyagrahi* called Harbat Singh was brought in. He was a mine worker who had been released from his *girmit* only a year ago. He was not a striker but a *satyagrahi*. He was among those people who had courted open arrest by entering Transvaal when they heard of Gandhi's arrest. A seventy year old man!

The sight of Harbat set off a chain of questions in Mohandas' mind.

Were his actions misleading innocent and illiterate people? If so, who would be responsible for the evil effects of the sin being committed in the name of *satyagraha*? How would he atone for this sin? When would he atone for it—when it is too late? Those who lay down their lives fighting, drawing their inspiration from him, will they be able to come back to life? Those who have followed the path you have shown them and suffered in consequence—gone to jails, been separated from their near and dear ones—will they ever be able to cast them out of their memory?

Mohandas pondered these questions without ever discussing them with anyone. Layers of depression were forming in his mind. And then he saw a ray of light emerge, an answer to his questions. 'Mohandas,' it said, 'ask your pure intellect. Is yours a pious aim or an impious one? Is it self-serving or does it serve others? If the answer you get makes you a sinner, then you are a sinner. You must have heard it said that without *yajna,* the earth is sure to be destroyed. *Yajna* is however not burning of firewood, nor is it offering sacrifices. This might help to purify the environment but does it help you achieve your goal? A *yajna* achieves its goal only when your bones are the firewood, your blood is the ghee and you make your thoughts pure. Only then can the earth survive. Has anyone ever achieved anything without sacrificing his own self? Those who sacrifice others so that they can survive, they make parasites of their children and sinners of themselves ...'

Mohandas went up to Harbat Singh and asked him: 'Why did you come for court arrest?'

'In protest against your arrest.'

'I had not called upon senior friends like you to join the struggle.'

'When you, your wife and your children were all in jail, what was there for me to do outside it? All I had was a small farm. If I could, I would have even asked the farm to join me.'

'The hardships you will face here you will find hard to bear. Go home. I'll try for your release.'

'Please don't do it. I will not leave the jail. I am close to the end and I'll consider myself lucky if I die in jail while I am close to you.'

Mohandas could see that his commitment far surpassed his own sympathy for him. He couldn't utter a word. His gaze was fixed at his wrinkled face which seemed to be giving out some kind of glow.

Later Mohandas was to learn that, on January 5, Harbat Singh got release not only from jail but from the bonds of life too. Hundreds of Indians joined the funeral procession. Mohandas too wanted to go but could not. He only said: 'He was lucky, his prayer was heard. I am not so lucky.'

There were many who went to jail, but Harbat Singh was the first one to be released forever while still in jail.'

~

The government was keeping a constant eye on Mohandas, Kallenbach and Polak. It worried the government that Mohandas was in jail with two whites and was in constant touch with the *satyagrahis*. The government thought of the *satyagrahis* as unarmed guerillas. They could survive anywhere, could make their appearance anywhere and could disappear as suddenly. When they were arrested they behaved like docile cows being led to their shed. The high spirits that people displayed when being arrested was becoming a cause of worry for the government. But it was a fact. What was even more painful was that some whites were also going to jail with Gandhibhai. This was also worrying the Indians. Here we are sitting at home while the whites are going to jail for us, they rued. What sort of freedom are we expecting? Freedom will come only as a result of our struggle. Others can only help. Those who came out of the jail after completing their sentences told the people all kinds of stories about Gandhibhai and the two whites. The stories only aroused their eagerness to court arrest.

General Smuts told his people: 'More than the arrest of Gandhi, it is the arrest of Kallenbach and Polak that is motivating Indians to court arrest. The arrest of Gandhi, Mrs. Gandhi and their children is bringing the Indian workers together. This is not a good sign.'

One of the officers said: 'The support of Europeans for Gandhi makes our position very untenable.'

Smuts said: 'These three must be kept in separate jails. Gandhi should be kept in a place where Indians can't meet him. He must be taught a lesson.'

'The death of Harbat Singh has made the people angry. They are bloody *girmitiya*s, spreading such stories about him which no man of common sense would ever believe. His soul has merged with Gandhi's soul, they say. Bloody shit!'

'Nonsense.'

'Let's send Gandhi to Orange Free State. Its capital, Bloemfontein, would have at most fifty Indians. The jail has either European or native prisoners only. Nobody would know Gandhi. He will die of loneliness.' Smuts smiled. His expression showed as if he had found the solution to the Gandhi problem.

What about Mr. Kallenbach and Mr. Henry Polak?'

'Do as you think fit. Only remember that they are Europeans.'

The meeting ended.

Gandhi was practically all alone in Bloemfontein jail. The officials and the prisoners were all white. The white prisoners often beat up the natives and the warders hurled abuses at them. Whenever he was around, Mohandas protested. The result was that they would indulge in obscene activities standing in front of his cell. The attitude of the jailor was stricter and even worse.

When Mohandas was sent to Bloemfontein jail, he was living on fruits. He had stopped eating cereals. The jailor refused to provide him fruit, so he often had to go hungry. Later he was provided fruits, but stale and rotten ones. Mohandas sent them back. He started losing weight. Sometimes, the jail doctor paid him a visit. As a political prisoner, he was entitled to a few such privileges. Whenever he came, the doctor engaged Gandhi in conversation and questioned him closely about vegetarianism and *satyagraha*. He listened carefully to what Mohandas had to say. When he found out that Mohandas ate only fruit and the jail authorities were unwilling to provide it to him, he prescribed, in addition to fresh fruit, dry fruit like almonds, walnuts, etc. for him. He also personally examined the food that was provided to him by the jail officials and if he wasn't satisfied with its quality would send it back and ask it to be replaced. The jail officials were upset and unhappy at his attitude.

The doctor examined his cell. It didn't have even a hole for fresh air. The doctor told the jailor that it was necessary to provide a ventilator in the room, or allow the door to be kept open, from the viewpoint of the prisoner's health.

At first, the jailor tried to reason with him: 'Why are you so anxious about a traitor coolie? If he dies, so be it. After all, General Smuts must have had something in his mind when he sent him here.'

'We can't do that. He is no ordinary prisoner.'

'Inside a jail, every prisoner is the same.'

'Every prisoner is a human being first. Mr. Gandhi is not just a prisoner.'

In the end, the jailor had to tell the doctor: 'If you force me to keep the cell door open, I'll have no choice but to resign. We will be setting up a precedent for other prisoners. They will make my life here difficult. Jail discipline will go to the dogs. The worst of the criminals will rule the roost.'

Mohandas explained to the doctor: 'I can understand the jailor's problem. He has to consider jail discipline. Please do not worry about me. I can breathe even in a hell hole' he continued with a laugh: 'I can even hold my breath for some time.'

The doctor did not insist, but he did add: 'The matter is not as simple as you think. The real reason is your colour and that you are fighting the government. If it were only a matter of rules, you wouldn't see so many white criminals roaming free around here.'

Mohandas laughed and said: 'Doctor, those who are in power sometimes think they can sweep the raging waves of a stormy ocean with a broom.'

The doctor was listening to him as if to a sermon from a church father.

~

Kallenbach had been sent to the Pretoria jail and Polak to Germiston. The marchers had been sent on the three trains not for travel but for a trial by fire. The trains took them back to Natal. They were provided neither food nor water on the way. A few children were also among the marchers. When, hungry and thirsty, they reached Natal, they were charged and arrested. But the problem before the government now was where to house so many prisoners. Jails had been designed on the basis of the local population and crime rate. The Natal government had never faced the problem of housing thousands of prisoners together before, hence it had never given any thought to the problem. New jails could not be constructed for so many prisoners; nor was the government ready to spend so much money on the prisoners. The government was also apprehensive of keeping so many Indians together at one place. What would happen if the government had to succumb to their pressure? It would have to do whatever they wished.

The coal mines had been shut down. The mine owners were very unhappy not only with the Natal government but also the Union governments of all the four colonies. The government talked to the mine owners. They made it very clear that they would have to shut down the mines. Some even went to the extent of saying that if the government was so scared of Gandhi and didn't want to displease the coolies, the day was not far when it would have to withdraw the three-pound tax and take instructions from Gandhi about how to run the government.

One of them said: 'We are getting ruined anyway, but the government too will lose all respect.'

Government representative were listening to everything but had no answers to the mine owners' accusations. The government's intention was to shift the responsibility for the mine workers to the mine owners alone.

After a lot of discussion, a way was found out. Plots of vacant land adjacent to the mines would be enclosed with stakes and netting. They would be labelled 'open jails'. The jails which were set up at Dundee and Newscastle appointed the white employees of the mines as warders of the jails. Thus the government saved itself both the expense and the responsibility. The government put all the onus of the open jails on the mine owners, saving itself all the trouble. The mine owners were already quite mad with the workers; now, in an effort to recover all their losses, they tried forcing them to work like animals. Workers, who had gone as marchers, now found themselves subjected to the use of violent methods. They were forced to work well beyond their capacity. The closed mines were opened again. The workers were already prisoners and had now turned into slaves. If one of the slaves dared to run away, he was dragged back, beaten black and blue, starved and forced to work till he collapsed. This was on top of the usual jail rigours and the rest of it.

The workers complied for a few days. Then mutual consultations started while at work and proposals were mooted. They started bonding with one another. Harassment was working as the glue that held them together. There was no formal meeting, nor was any resolution passed. Quietly a decision was taken that they would stop working and would not put up with tyranny. Work ceased. Whips came out. Streams of abuse, like a thick stream of water from an open tap, flowed at all times. Kicks came thick and fast like a fast moving piston of a railway engine. Mud was stuffed into their mouths. Sticks were pushed up their anuses. Water supply to their homes was stopped. Anyone could be picked up at any time of day or night. They were forced to indulge in obscene acts with one another. The workers put up with all the excesses and stayed calm. When the torture exceeded all limits, they repeated to themselves the oath Gandhi had given them: We will put up with everything but not leave the path of truth; we'll not allow our unity to be broken. We are *satyagrahi*s; we'll live as *satyagrahi*s and die as *satyagrahi*s. We will not retaliate.

When they were beaten and tortured, they would shut their eyes tight, clench their teeth and repeat the name of Gandhi to themselves, allowing whatever was happening to them to happen.

~

Gokhale was confined to bed. He was being kept constantly informed of the developments in Natal. From his sickbed, he made sure that the news about South Africa that he received was broadcast all over India. Sometimes he spent the entire night working. He did not allow anyone to interfere in his handling of the South African affairs, nor was anyone really interested in doing so.

But as people got to know about the conditions of Indians in South Africa, their interest grew and so did their anger. The whole country was pained to hear of the excesses being committed on its people in another land. The excesses were a subject of discussion everywhere. People were worried. People in both countries were living under British rule, so why was there this discrimination? What had happened to the famed British justice? They were not so worried about the conditions in India; they were more worried about the Indians living in South Africa. Gokhale was especially worried about the arrest and jail of Mohandas, Kastur and their children.

The oppression in South Africa aroused every Indian. The cry was: 'Let's go to Natal. Let's go to Transvaal. Let's save Gandhi. Let's save the Indians.' Their sense of helplessness however only ended up making their feelings for them deeper. How could they go?

~

Lord Hardinge was the new Viceroy. Indian delegations were meeting him regularly on this subject. Prof. Gokhale's memorandum on the conditions in South Africa reached his desk everyday. It contained the latest report from the spot.

It was the month of December. Lord Hardinge was on a tour of Madras. At a largely attended meeting on December 13, Lord Hardinge, despite being a Viceroy himself, launched an attack on the South African government. Without mincing his words, he said: 'The excesses being committed on the Indians in South Africa would be a matter of shame for any civilized society.'

It was plainly wrong for the Viceroy of the biggest British colony to criticize openly the government of another British colony, but Lord Hardinge did not stand on ceremony. In fact, he went a step ahead and declared: '*Satyagraha* against a disreputable and unjust law is perfectly justified.'

He received a letter on the subject from London, but Lord Hardinge was unmoved. Journalists asked him: 'As Viceroy, don't you regret your criticism of the government of another member of the British Empire?'

'I have only carried out my responsibility towards the people of my own colony.'

'Won't this lead to tension between the governments of two member colonies of the British Empire?'

'We did not start it. It was they who did. They committed excesses on our citizens. Isn't it their responsibility too to see that we have good relations?'

'London is annoyed?'

'Let me worry about that.'

The whole country resounded with praise for Lord Hardinge, but the white community was finding it hard to digest.

~

The mines were mostly in the north-western part of Natal, but most of the labourers were concentrated in the south. Mohandas' connections were limited to the north. People of Phoenix, Verulem, Tongaat, etc. had worked with Gandhi even during the Boer War. He did have some connections in the south but very less. He also had a few workers working for him there. The surprising thing was that the news of Gandhi's arrest had spread like wild fire in all directions. People had abandoned work in thousands and joined the protest. The protest against his arrest had started everywhere—in the east, the west, the north and the south.

When he was leaving for jail, Mohandas had told his companions: 'Our movement is headed in the right direction. If we have too many workers in the movement it will become difficult to bear their expenses. There are about sixty thousand workers in South Africa. If they all abandoned work and joined our movement, how would their families survive? How would we bear their expenses? Mine workers are enough. We know them and we have connections with them. The problem of discipline can also become serious. The bigger the crowd, the more the carelessness and more the indiscipline.'

But exactly the opposite happened. No one called upon the workers to rise, yet the workers sold off their household stuff and joined the movement. You didn't know how long the strike might last, food might or might not be available, and there might in fact be no arrangement for food; if you had some money you would at least not starve. Accommodation was no problem; you could make any place your own. It was as if floodgates had been opened. Everything came to a standstill and among those causing it most were Indian workers. The other Asiatics were anyway few in number. Work had ceased in the farms, the hotels and the shops. People had effected their own division of labour. They were strikers; they were also volunteers and leaders. Everyone had the same goal: Do or die! Everyone had assigned himself his duty. The whites were aghast to see that an untrained and unarmed army could be so disciplined.

Work had come to a stop in all the four colonies. Mounted police were everywhere. Wherever there was even a doubt of *satyagraha*, horses would come galloping. Wherever there was a cry from the workers, guns started firing. The police came and forced the workers to work. The workers lay down on the ground. The soldiers kicked them. They started rolling. Soldiers chased them. The workers groaned and cried but did not get up. They would be covered in blood but would not cry for mercy. For the police it was like trying to dislodge mountain rocks with bare hands.

The strike in Verulem was a major one. A few days ago the strikers had indulged in stone throwing. Four workers had been shot. Some workers were trying to persuade other workers to return to work but they had a single demand: 'Release Gandhibhai. Release our queen and our princes.' That day, General Lukin was present himself on horseback with his entire cavalry. He was mad because of the stone throwing that had taken place the previous day. His cavalrymen ready with their guns were waiting for his orders. One signal and they would shoot the strikers down like partridges in a hunt. The situation was getting out of control. The strikers were refusing to budge. The orders could come any moment. The strikers had refused pointblank to go back to work.

Brave Sorabjee, son of Rustomji Parsi, had arrived there from Durban around the same time. He saw the two armies ranged against each other. On one side was the state army, armed to the teeth; on the other, an army of the *satyagrahi*s, upholders of peace and unarmed. Even their hands dangled by their sides lest they may be used. Absolutely fearless of death. Sorabjee feared that if the General ordered firing, hundreds of innocent *girmitiya*s might be killed. Some may be wounded, some would die. He couldn't think of anything to do, so he rushed and got hold of the reins of Lukin's horse. The horse reared a little. Sorabjee shouted: 'Don't do it, General! Don't order fire! Hundreds will be killed. It'll be a black spot on the British sense of justice. Give me a chance. I'll try to send them back. The price of a human life is many times the price of your bullets. You can cast thousands of bullets from one mould, but you cannot cast a single human eye in your factories.'

Sorabjee was an eighteen year old boy. Sweat streaming, face fuming, yet his voice under perfect control. No trembling, no frenzy.

At first, it seemed the General would lose control. From his face, it looked as if he was going to ride his horse over the boy or to shoot him dead. The soldiers' guns, already at the ready, now took aim. At least some of them were aimed at the boy's head. The very next moment, however, the General's face seemed to mellow a little and he said: 'Young man, from the way you got hold of the reins of my horse, I can tell you are a courageous boy. But what makes you think you can do it?'

'Love.'

'Fine. Go ahead and use your weapon. We'll see.'

'This is no weapon, General. This is faith. This is trust.'

The General's taut body seemed to relax a little. The soldiers' guns too could be seen to lower a bit.

Sorabjee went back to the workers and said: 'Gandhibhai, *Ba* and their sons are in jail. You are angry with the government for putting them there, aren't you? But Gandhibhai also says, and believes in it too, that it is a call of duty. He is in jail out of his own will. So are *Ba* and the sons. His message is that you must continue working. Your abandoning work will only give strength to the bloody intentions of the whites. Please go back. Our companions in Natal were arrested because they were not on strike. All that they had done was to enter Transvaal without producing the registration certificate. These guns are aimed at you because you are on strike. The government is your enemy. It will kill you either way. Why do you want to die? Those in power can get away with injustice.'

The workers did not move an inch, but they listened to him.

Sorabjee made a last effort: 'I know Gandhibhai very closely. As a child, I have played on his lap. Gandhibhai is in jail for our freedom. His family is already in jail. When he finds out that all those for whom he took this trouble have been shot down by the authorities, do you think he will be happy or he will be sad? If those who are supposed to enjoy the fruits of freedom are themselves no more, what good will his struggle have been? Can't we give up this little defiance of ours so that Gandhi's dream may be fulfilled?'

One of the men got up and walked away, saying: 'If this will make Gandhi happy, I'm going to work.'

A few more people got up and followed him. Then everybody walked away and went straight to their workplaces.

The General got off his horse and said to Sorabjee: 'So many guns could not do it. How did you do it, young man?'

'Gandhibhai has given us only one weapon. It does not cut or kill. It does not hurt anybody's dignity, nor does it frighten anyone pointlessly. It keeps you to the straight path and inspires others to do the same. It is not bound to obey any commands, nor any authority. Nor does it command anyone. Listen to the voice within you and follow it—that's what it says. Your weapon is bound to the authority of someone else. His authority says: "Kill anyone who doesn't obey. " It is always plotting to kill and to enslave. But let a man take up this weapon once and fear goes out the door. The whole world then belongs to him and he belongs to the whole world.'

Sorab laughed a childlike laugh. The General kept watching his face for some time, then shook hands with him and turned around, mounted the horse and took off. The soldiers too fell in step behind him and went off on a trot like the horse.

~

The news of the arrests of West, Kallenbach, Polak, etc. reached Gokhale one after another. During his extreme illness, the arrest of so many of his men by a heartless and tyrannical government was sufficient to add to his misery. Only Maganlal, Cachalia, Schlesin and Millie were free. Millie was not taking part in the *satyagraha* anyway, though she was with them. They had made a division of labour among themselves. Phoenix was turning into a centre of attraction for everyone from the government to the workers. People in thousands were arriving in Phoenix, some for advice, others for shelter. The whites now saw Phoenix as the hideout of the conspirators. If they could, they would have set fire to it by now. Gokhale knew all this.

A meeting in support of the *satyagraha* in South Africa was held in Lahore. Though an Englishman, Andrews had donated all his wealth to the *satyagrahi*s of South Africa and was living with Rabindranath Tagore at Shanti Niketan. Gokhale felt that, at this time of crisis, C.F. Andrews alone could help him in bringing the situation in South Africa under control. He sent a telegram to him: 'Would it be possible for you to go to South Africa at once?'

He received a reply by return post: 'It will be a pleasure.'

Andrews asked his friend Father Pearson: 'Can you go with me to South Africa?'

Pearson too was ready. By the time they received the second telegram from Gokhale, the two friends were all packed and ready to leave for South Africa on the next ship.

~

Pressure was mounting on the South African government. The way the government had terrorized the unarmed *satygrahis*, inflicted torture on them, fired on them, rode horses through them and committed all other kinds of excesses had made it an object of worldwide condemnation. Workers from mines, farms, sugar factories, etc. were spending their nights under the open sky in the Phoenix Ashram and the nearby forests with their measly belongings with them. There was no one there to look after them except Maganlal and how much could Maganlal alone do? There was only one man they could depend on and that was Rustomji's son Sorabjee. Rustomji was in jail. In his father's absence, Sorabjee had loosened his purse strings. Medicines, food—everything was being supplied by him. The workers were each doing their bit and everyone was responsible for his own discipline.

There was a class of whites which was unhappy with the policies being followed by the government of Generals Smuts and Botha towards the Indians. They were beginning to ask among themselves: 'Where is all this going to end? How long will this round of oppression continue? Enough is enough.' General Smuts had started receiving information about the dissatisfaction building up against him. Ever since four workers had been killed in firing, the pressure on General Smuts had gone up sharply. The statement of the Indian Viceroy, Lord Hardinge, had added to his difficulties. The Viceroy had written to the London government in no uncertain terms that the manner in which helpless workers were being treated in jails was bringing disgrace to His Majesty's government. He had also made it clear that the Indian government would not stand by and watch the situation for too long. No government had the right to throw thousands of innocent citizens of another country into jails.

General Smuts' condition was like that of a snake which had stuffed too many mice in its mouth and was now neither able to swallow them nor spit them out because of his greed. Inwardly, Smuts realized that injustice was being done, but he couldn't figure out the solution. Though he knew it, yet he wasn't quite able to internalize the truth that when a welfare state restricts its policies in terms of race, religion or caste, there comes a time when either it must break free of those restrictions or see itself being crushed in the deathly embrace of those python-like restrictions. Lungs are essential not only for humans; they are also essential for a government, so that fresh air may continue to circulate. General Smuts' ears echoed with the cry of 'Be just!' but the hatred stored within him, and his commitment to the white race, created distortions in his definition of justice. When a ruler starts redefining the basic concepts according to his own convenience, his ability to do justice soon atrophies, and its condition becomes somewhat similar to that of a sheet of paper which, pressed under a paperweight, can flutter all it wants but can neither fly nor move from its fixed position.

By repeatedly assuring the white community that the three-pound tax would not be withdrawn, Smuts had allowed his own promise to sit on him like a paperweight, and now he was flailing and fluttering. What could he do? His word was hostage to the whites.

He saw only one way out. He announced the appointment of a commission under the chairmanship of Sir Richard Soloman, with two Natal whites, Ewald Esselen and Wylie, as members.

The announcement immediately raised some questions: First, who was going to talk to the commission? Who will present the Indians' case before it?

To General Smuts, this question presented itself as follows: The strikers' leaders are all in jails. Some are absconding. Who will the commission talk to? Later, everyone will ask: If everyone was in jail, who did the commission talk to? How did it prepare its report?

General Smuts spent a couple of days thinking. In the end, he asked for the commission's view on it. The commission wrote back: Let Gandhi, Kallenbach and Polak be released unconditionally. They could also have been released on parole, but the government and the commission knew well that these prisoners were not so keen to be released that they would accept any condition.

The threesome had been in jail for only nine weeks. This was the second occasion when Mohandas had been released from jail prematurely.

Each one of the three was dissatisfied with his premature release for different reasons. Ever since they had been sent to three different jails, they had no idea of what had been going on in the world outside. The question that was bothering Mohandas was: 'Is General Smuts up to his old tricks again?' On that occasion, he had to bear the consequences by himself, but this time around Kallenbach and Polak too were in the ring. If the same thing that had happened to Mohandas the last time happened to these two too, they too would fall a prey to the evil designs of General Smuts.

They all reached Durban from three different directions, at slightly different times. Schlesin had told them that Smuts had set up an inquiry commission. They also got the names of its members from her.

'So that is why we have been released,' was Mohandas' first reaction.

Polak asked: 'Gandhibhai, don't you think all the three members of the commission hate Indians?'

Kallenbach asked: 'What do the others feel about it?'

Schlesin laughed and said: 'How does that matter? Those whose opinion mattered were all in jail. Now that you are here, go ahead and form an opinion. To me, it looks like a consolation prize.'

Mohandas was serious. 'I feel the commission must include a representative of the Indians.'

They all looked at Gandhi. Nobody had thought of this.

~

Prof. Gokhale had informed them that C.F. Andrews and his friend Pearson were arriving in South Africa. Mohandas had heard of C.F. Andrews. Others also knew that, despite being an Englishman, Andrews had done more for the Indians of South Africa than anyone else had ever done or was ever likely to do.

When Kallenbach heard of this, he was delighted: 'Andrews is a great Englishman. He is most welcome.'

Mohandas laughed and said: 'Do you want us to say that you are a great German and Polak here is …' Then he turned serious and said: 'People like you are the real touchstone of my *satyagraha*. My people have always put up with torture and tyranny. In fact, till a while ago they thought that life was another name for torture and tyranny. Now they are beginning to realize that torture is slow murder. The more they realize this truth, the more they are becoming a part of this struggle. People like you are neither among the tormentors nor among the tormented like us. You are the sign of the times which announces that the darkness is lifting. You don't shape the times but you give out the signals.'

'Gandhibhai, your profundities are beyond us. Call us what you will, the tick-tock of the clock, the sign of the times or rebels against exploitation, we only know that we are today what you made of us. We are only a small part of a large sensibility. Without you, we would not have been even that.'

Mohandas laughed. 'Am I any way different? I am only a tiny drop of His compassion. I would consider myself lucky if it could soak my own little soul.'

~

The heat was at its peak. Kastur and Ramdas were to be released on December 22 after serving three months' hard labour. Mohandas, Kallenbach and Polak were at hand to receive them.

The doors of the jail opened at about eleven. Mohandas took a few apprehensive steps forward. He was worried about Kastur's condition. Her condition proved his apprehension to be right. Two female warders were supporting Kastur as she tottered towards the gate. Mohandas stepped forward and took charge of her. Ramdas too looked weak but in three months his height had shot up. Mohandas' hand touched his head as he bent to touch his feet. Kastur was hardly able to take a step on her own. Her large eyes had sunk into her face, but still looked pure as before. They had the shine of a victor's eyes. She had conquered the jail.

Kastur did not ask him how he was. She only asked: 'When were you released?'

'Barely four days before you.'

'But I'd heard yours was a longer sentence.'

Mohandas laughed and said: 'If I were not to be released before you, who'd identify you in your present condition?'

'Don't joke. Tell me the truth.' Her voice was soft but firm.

'Let's get home first.' She kept quiet after that.

Mohandas had practically brought Kastur home in his arms. He asked Ramdas, 'Looks like you didn't look after your *Ba* properly.'

'We were in separate barracks and were not allowed to meet.'

'*Ba* too perhaps couldn't look after you.'

'I can see how much you looked after yourself!' she said sarcastically.

Mohandas laughed. Kastur's condition was making him uncomfortable. He could neither laugh nor cry sincerely.

The release of Mohandas and Kastur had raised the spirits of people. Ramdas was also there and so were the wives of Chhaganlal, Manilal Doctor and Maganlal. Royappan was also out after having served his term. The Indians of Maritzburg took out a procession in their honour. Kastur was in no condition to walk so she had been put in a car while others walked. It looked like a victory procession, although there was no sign of any victory anywhere. A large number of women were also present. The men danced and sang. After passing through all the main streets, the procession turned into a reception meeting in a park.

Mohandas had come to Durban specifically for this purpose. His presence had added glamour to the occasion. People insisted on a speech from him. Mohandas tried to wriggle out of it but it was now impossible that Mohandas should be present on an occasion and allowed to go without delivering a speech. He had to speak.

> *...This may be a happy occasion but it is equally an occasion for sorrow. We are still in no condition to participate in festivities and receptions. You have welcomed my wife, my son and other satyagrahi ladies and companions for which I am deeply grateful. Some of our brothers have fallen to police bullets. Although I am present here in this reception meeting, my heart is with them. Jail was better in the sense I never got to know about the unhappy events happening outside; nor did a joyful event have any meaning.*

Somewhere a child cried. Mohandas paused. When the crying ceased, he resumed:

> *This crying child expresses the sorrow that is in our hearts. We can't even cry. I appeal to all my brothers and sisters present here that they should express their sympathy with the widows of our martyred brothers in unconventional ways. Those who drink must quit drinking. Quit bad habits like betel chewing. Ladies must give up wearing ornaments and expensive clothes. Only then can we consider ourselves worthy of sharing the sorrow of our widowed sisters. The expression of sorrow cannot go with fads and addictions except when it is fake.*

Mohandas' speech turned the festive occasion into a renunciation meeting. People made diverse resolutions. The poor women had hardly any ornaments, but they gave up whatever they had. One man threw away his little box of lime even as Mohandas watched. People were drawing inspiration from one another like heat permeating from one particle to another, giving up its coldness.

On December 22, Mohandas had sent a telegram to Gokhale informing him that the three of them had been released from jail on Thursday unconditionally and that they had told the government that it would not be possible for them to appear before the commission so long as, one, they were not given the right to be consulted before a decision was arrived at; two, Shiner or appeal judge Roziens or someone else nominated by the Indian community was not included in the commission and, three, the four thousand workers imprisoned in the open jails were not released. This decision had been taken at a meeting that day attended by six thousand people. If the demands were not met, people might go hungry or eat a minimal diet but they would start a march from Durban to Pretoria and court arrest. Some influential whites had also come to their support. People here had been astonished at the mutual cooperation, determination and goodwill displayed by the *girmitiya*s even in the absence of their leadership. People of India should extend their maximum cooperation to the movement.

The telegram was signed by Gandhi, Kallenbach and Polak.

~

The ship carrying Andrews and Pearson, *Umtali*, was to reach Durban on January 2. Mohandas, Kallenbach and Polak had already left Maritzburg to be at hand to receive them. Durban port always reminded Mohandas of the days gone by. He recalled how Dada Abdullah had come to receive him. Dada Abdullah was no more and the memory turned Mohandas sentimental. It pained him to think of Durban without Dada Abdullah, especially thinking of the port. He had set up a kind of relationship with Dada Abdullah which brought him on a par with his *Bapu*. He had also met the man called Marcel Ledue at his place. The things he said served as warnings for the future regarding Mohandas, though he did not take particular notice of him: perhaps the reason why he was never happy with Mohandas.

Mohandas stood lost for sometime in confusion expecting Dada Abdullah to appear suddenly and say: 'Hello, my white elephant.'

Kallenbach asked: 'Do you know your guests by face?'

Mohandas received a start. 'No,' he said, 'Though Henry might.'

'I have heard of him,' said Polak, 'But never met him. C.F. Andrews used to stay at Shanti Niketan. Prof. Gokhale often talked of him.'

Mohandas laughed and said: 'We might well miss each other.'

Kallenbach said: 'With your halo, who can possibly miss you? Like a *satyagrahi*'s flag, you cannot be missed even from a distance.' The three of them laughed.

Lots of passengers were disembarking, both white and black. Picking out two whites from so many of them was no easy task. As people got off the ship they made directly for their destination. Some three or four whites were left behind. They must be waiting for someone.

Kallenbach picked up courage and approached them. After a pause he asked them: 'Would you be able to tell me if two white gentlemen named Mr. Andrews and Mr. Pearson have travelled by this ship?'

One of them said promptly: 'I am Charlie Andrews and this is my friend Pearson.'

'I am Kallenbach, friend of M.K.Gandhi.'

'Prof. Gokhale had told me about you.'

'Where is Mohan?' It was for the first time that Kallenbach had heard anyone call him Mohan.

'I won't need to point him out. Because of his strange appearance, you can always make him out from a distance.'

They all laughed. By this time, Mohandas and Polak also arrived at the spot.

Kallenbach laughed and said: 'Do you still need me to introduce him?'

'Not at all. No one can miss the halo.'

'This is Mr. C.F. Andrews and this, his friend Mr. Pearson.'

'Charlie for you,' and Andrews bent down to touch Mohandas' feet. Pearson followed suit. Mohandas was at a loss to understand what was going on.

When he made sense of what had happened, Mohandas said: 'Why did you do this? I don't deserve it at all.'

Andrews said: 'I'll call you Mohan, okay? I and Pearson are both religious people, attached to the church. You are more than a mere human being to us. No mere human can achieve what you have, unless he has an element of the divine in him.'

'Not at all. I am the most ordinary of people. A storehouse of faults and foibles.' Then he changed the topic: 'This is Henry Polak, a friend and a true *karmyogi*.'

'I know them by name. You have made them your own with your blessings. I also wish that Pearson and myself may also be touched by that grace.'

Kallenbach said: 'Don't make that mistake, Charlie, or you'll never be able to go back.'

Pearson had so far been only listening and watching, occasionally passing a smile. Now he spoke for the first time: 'Mr. Kallenbach, having travelled so far, we are hardly left with any choice.'

Laughter spilled from all their faces.

The incident of Mr. Andrews and Mr. Pearson touching Mohandas' feet was played up by the newspapers the next day. Two whites touching a coolie's feet! And the coolie no other than M.K. Gandhi! They have brought disgrace to the white community. Both the whites are from India and Englishmen. The papers also published their photographs. For many days in a row, condemnatory letters to the editor kept appearing in the newspapers in protest against this humiliating piece of behaviour on the part of Charlie and Pearson.

Neither of them paid any attention to the newspapers.

The day before the three sent the telegram to Gokhale, that is, on the December 21, a public meeting was held in Durban attended by about six thousand people. Abdul Qadir presided. Addressing the meeting, Mohandas became emotional:

> *Shots were fired at those of my countrymen who shared equal partnership in the prosperity of this nation. Each shot fired at them has left a mark on my chest. I wish that all those shots that were fired at my friends had also hit my chest:*

I'd have been proud of it. I was the one who advised them to go on strike. Doesn't that advice make me their killer in a way? I have given up my European dress and donned the dress of the girmitiya. When shots are fired next, I'll be one of the girmitiyas standing in the first line to receive the bullet. This dress I wear is the outward expression of my sorrow; my fast is the internal sorrow that only I know. Every struggle which is linked to the freedom and power of the soul, along with the liberation of the body, turns into a crusade, or a jehad, *for men of every religion, every race, every class and caste.*

Reuters had forwarded the report to Gokhale too. Gokhale sent a telegram to Mohandas on the night of December 21: 'Received a summary of your speech through Reuters. After Soloman's speech, it will be a mistake to boycott the inquiry commission. You will lose the sympathy of the government of India and your sympathizers in England. Hire the best lawyer. You and Polak make your presentation before the commission. Do not miss this golden chance of presenting your grievances against your oppression. Include your complaints against Esselen and Wylie in the protest letter. Attend the commission with all your objections.'

The telegram was also shown to Charlie and Pearson. Charlie said: 'Mohan, I am in full agreement with Gokhale. We should avoid doing anything which will lose us the sympathy of our friends and well-wishers.'

'You can't be unaware of the fact that this commission has been appointed not so much to provide relief to the Indians as to give the Europeans a chance to present their case. True, the Indians also have a chance to present their case, but they are hardly in a position to relate their woes to the commission, especially those Indians who are overawed just to see the white colour.'

'We will help them.'

'There is a difference between relating your woes yourself and doing so with the help of someone else, especially when you are confronted with a completely hostile audience from which not the least sympathy is expected.'

'But should we proceed on the assumption that the commission members will completely overlook the truth?'

'Yes, I can say that confidently about Esselen and Wylie. They have their limitations. It is just not possible for them to free themselves from their prejudices against the Asians. It was Wylie who had led the protest against the ships *Courland* and *Naderi* bringing Indians into South Africa. I and my family were in one of those ships. If the Captain of police of Durban and his wife had not been present on the occasion I would not be speaking to you here today and you would not have had to take the trouble of coming all the way here to help me.' Mohandas smiled. 'And Wylie had in fact said, on assuming charge in the commission, that the three-pound tax would not be withdrawn. These people consider the interests of the European community supreme, overlooking the interests of everyone else.'

'But Wylie and Esselen are not all there is to the commission. We will be there and so will be our lawyers.'

'Probably you are right. But don't you think that if this commission had been set up to consider the interests of Indians, it would have at least one member whose sympathies lay with them? We did not suggest the name of any Asian or Indian; both names we suggested were Europeans: P. Shiner and Sir James Roziens. Could anyone say that the prestige and morality of these two gentlemen were in any way inferior to those of the gentlemen who now adorn the commission as its members?'

Charlie said,'Mohanbhai, the truth is on our side. Will it lose to their falsehood?'

'Winning will take time. And it will depend on who we are up against. So far our truth has been losing to General Smuts' falsehood. We don't have the face to tell our people that this commission will be fair; you go and testify before it.'

Charlie Andrews withdrew into silence. His expression however showed that something was bugging him that did not permit him to agree with Mohandas.

~

Marcel Campbell was a sugarcane farmer. Though a European, he was not in favour of the three-pound tax and supported the Indians' demands. He had some *girmitiya*s working on his farm, who had not joined the *satyagraha*. They said that their master supported them and therefore they would not stop working.

The *satyagrahi*s said: 'We do not know who your master is, but he must be a white. Stop working and join us.'

When the *girmitiya*s didn't agree, the *satyagrahi*s threatened them: 'We'll beat you up and your family.'

The *girmitiya*s did not budge, so the *satyagrahi*s started pushing and jostling them and dragged them out.

The incident caused Marcel Campbell deep pain. He wrote a letter to Mohandas:

> *Some people walked in and thrashed the girmitiya*s *working on my farm and forced them to stop working. I have reasons to believe that they were your men.*

Campbell had given a reception in honour of Gokhale when he was in South Africa. Fifteen thousand Indians of the County of Victoria had been invited on the occasion. This incident enraged Campbell so much that he wrote to Mohandas: 'It is not yet twelve months when your committee and fifteen thousand Indians of the Victoria County were my guests and ate at my place. This incident only shows how hollow your claims and policies are. Any movement that treats the innocent and the guilty alike can never be successful. They may have very high ideals, but the injustice implicit in their policies degrades them. People are beginning to see the weak spots in your policies. By inciting the self-satisfied but uneducated workers with your high-minded talk, by awaking in them impractical aspirations and by using their threats of violence to seek political power, you will get nowhere. This cannot be considered a wise and a farsighted policy.'

Mohandas wrote back to Campbell:

> *I notice that recent incidents have led to a misunderstanding between me and my friends. Only time and appropriate action on my part will help to remove it. On my part, all I can do now is to reassure you that no one can be, or has been, allowed to indulge in or incite violence. It is the essence of* satyagraha *that a man should avoid violence even in the most crucial circumstances. So far as the question of the hospitality that you extended to Prof. Gokhale and the Indian Committee is concerned, I have to say that, despite being deeply grateful to you for it, we cannot allow it to stand in the way of the performance of what Prof. Gokhale or the rest of us consider to be our duty …*
>
> *In your letter, you have denigrated* satyagraha *at length, but in recent years* satyagraha *has been the only way available to our society to deal with its problems, though people like you have denounced it at every step. After a lot of thought and analysis, people engaged in public service have justified this non-violent mode of struggle as correct and logical. Whether contemporary Indians are wise or foolish in pursuing this mode of struggle is something that will be decided by the future generations and not by you or us.*

Reuters got wind of this correspondence and its reporters called upon Mohandas, who was then preparing to leave for the reception ceremony being held for Andrews.

The reporter asked: 'I understand that Mr. Campbell has raised some fundamental objections to *satyagraha*.'

'No, he has only aired his personal grievance. When a person expresses his misunderstanding or annoyance at something, he is not always controlled in his language. Campbell is a friend and I have appealed to him for understanding and cooperation.'

'And if you don't get it? After all, your *satyagrahi*s have beaten up his men.'

'A *satyagrahi* can't do it. One who does it cannot be a *satyagrahi*. Campbell will continue to support us on the issue of the three-pound tax.'

'But Mr. Campbell has also appealed to you to prevent anarchy and to accept the commission and cooperate with it.'

'Our boycott of the commission is inspired not by the ill treatment meted out to the *girmitiya*s by the whites but by General Smuts' violation of the word he gave to Prof. Gokhale. If the government continues to ignore our demands in this way, we will be forced to return to our old methods.'

Mohandas was in a hurry so he left without waiting for the next question.

Mohandas could understand Gokhale's concern but he was of the view that their struggle was independent of individuals like the Viceroy, or ministers of the British Empire, or indeed of any worldly authority. His vow that in the event of the government refusing their demand they would have to restart their march to Transvaal was making Gokhale restless. It had been decided that the Soloman Commission would be boycotted in all events. The government had turned down the request for enlarging the commission. Indeed, the crisis had reached such proportions that Mohandas had to send a telegram to Gokhale not to remit the eight thousand rupees received in donations, at least for the time being, as, under martial law, the government can seize anything it wants to. The law was likely to come in effect any time.

Gokhale was in continuous touch with the Viceroy. He also kept the Viceroy informed of his correspondence with Mohandas. Mohandas had written in his telegram of December 26, 1913: 'We are trying to create a situation where we can accept the Commission and postpone our movement. Please continue your assistance. We may still be able to find a way.'

Prof. Gokhale took the telegram to the Viceroy, who listened carefully to what he had to say. Said Gokhale 'My request to you', 'is to help these people any way you can. When tension is reduced, a way out may be found.'

The Viceroy said: 'I've been told that Gandhi is going to resume the movement from the first of January. If that is true, a way out may be difficult to find.'

Gokhale had already checked this with Mohandas. He said: 'No, that's not true.' He showed the Viceroy his telegram of December 27 in which Gandhi had said: 'The movement will be held in abeyance till Mr. Robertson arrives here.'

Robertson was the Viceroy's representative who was to be dispatched to South Africa. The Viceroy had himself informed Prof. Gokhale that in view of Gandhi's assurance and his desire for a peaceful solution, Sir Benjamin Robertson would be sent to South Africa on the first of January. He would be arriving in Durban around the eleventh or twelfth of January. The telegram also said: 'I'm also requesting the Colonial Secretary to postpone the meeting of the Commission. I hope that when Robertson reaches there, Gandhi is able to have a frank meeting with him.'

Gokhale immediately sent a telegram to Gandhi: 'Hold the movement in abeyance till after a week of Robertson's arrival.'

Mohandas replied the very next day, December 30: 'I assure you that we will wait for the government's decision for one week after Sir Robertson's arrival. Since he is the Viceroy's representative, due regard will be shown to him and no action will be taken till he has had a full opportunity to study the situation.'

An unbroken chain of telegrams connected Mohandas to Gokhale and Gokhale to the Viceroy.

Transvaal was paralysed by a railway strike. The strike had been called by the white workers. It was around this time that Mohandas and Andrews had arrived in Pretoria to talk to the government. The strike had forced the government into a crisis. With Gandhi's arrival at this juncture, the government's heart had begun racing, though governments don't have hearts except maybe in their boots, which they use for forging ahead while trampling others.

The journalists too assumed that Gandhi's arrival in Pretoria at this juncture was for the purpose of exploiting the strike to strengthen his own movement. It was the second week of January, perhaps the sixteenth of the month. The *Pretoria News* reporter approached Mohandas: 'What do you think about the railway strike? How do you view it?'

Mohandas' answer was short: 'I've nothing to do with it.'

'But how do you view it?'

'How does the view of one matter who has no right to vote?'

'The government is in trouble. Are you planning to restart your movement to take advantage of it?'

Mohandas paused for a moment and then said: 'We're not like the government which goes around trying to add to the people's troubles. We're opposed to this policy.'

'I'm asking you a direct question: Why are you here at this point of time?'

'I'm giving you a direct answer: I'm not in favour of adding to the government's troubles. If necessary, we'll postpone our movement, as we'd done at the time of the strike by Rand's soldiers in Johannesburg. We'll not start any action till the matter of the railway strike is resolved.'

Reactions started flowing in.

'Gandhi is a stupid fool. It is a strange ironmonger who avoids striking when the iron is hot. How long will he go on striking cold iron?'

Mohandas had sought an appointment with Smuts and was there at the appointed time. About the demand for the expansion of the commission, Smuts had written to him: 'The commission we have constituted is quite impartial. True, we didn't consult you, but we didn't consult the farm and mine owners either.'

Had it not been for the last sentence, Mohandas would have stayed quiet or would have looked for some other way. He wrote a personal letter to Smuts:

> *Give me an opportunity to talk to you. I want to put before you certain facts which will help you in arriving at a just decision.*

Unexpectedly, Smuts agreed to meet Mohandas. When he went to see him, his first encounter was with Smuts' secretary. The secretary was a happy-faced and jocular character. He said: 'Mr. Gandhi, I don't like your people at all. If it was in my power, I wouldn't lift my little finger to help them. But what can I do? You help us so much when we are in need. How can we lock you up? If you were like those railway workers, indulging in violence, you'd have seen how we treated you. We'd beat all talk of *satyagraha* out of your heads. But you are such a hopeless lot that you can't even scratch your enemy. All the pain you cause is to yourself and your people and you still want to win! You won't step out of the bounds of your principles and limits of gentlemanly behaviour, and that's how you leave us stranded nowhere.'

At that very moment, Smuts called him in. The General was tense, apprehensive of what Gandhi might say. He listened quietly to Gandhi for some time, then got up and started pacing the room and said: 'Mr. Gandhi, you have made a eunuch out of me. Me, General Smuts, the winner of many great wars. I just don't know what weapons to use against you. Any weapon that I pick up strikes back at me. No matter what we use, a stick, a bullet, a gun, it is we and our policemen who get the worst of it. You tell me, please tell me, what weapon can I use against you? *Satyagraha*, *satyagraha* ...' He repeated the word twice or thrice in his strange way so that Mohandas at first did not get it at all. When he understood, he smiled: 'Oh, *satyagraha* is what he means!'

Mohandas spoke softly: 'There is one weapon that we will lose to ... love!'

'Oh, Gandhi, this is not a kids' school. This is government. Government, do you understand?'

'That is precisely the difficulty, General. It should be compulsory for everyone to attend school: he may be a soldier, a general or a minister. The trouble is that the weapon that we need most in every walk of life, we pack it with our books and leave it behind, and then we start looking for it here. The problem is that we can't go back and look for it now and recover it.'

'Gandhi, this is no occasion for a joke.'

'General, in fact I'm very serious. All your weapons, a gun, a bullet, even the largest bomb, have a very limited range. When a man goes out of that range, you can do nothing to him. You need a very long range weapon to get him. It should be a weapon that follows him wherever he goes and only love can do it. It is a weapon that makes both immortal—the killer as well the killed.'

General Smuts looked at him dumbfounded. Suddenly he realized that it was useless trying to talk to this man. He came to the point: 'Mr. Gandhi, we have already written to you. Our response remains the same. It's now for you to think and respond.'

Rising from his seat, Gandhi said: 'Had I been talking only to Mr. Smuts, he would perhaps have looked at this aspect of the problem. It is more difficult for General Smuts to think about these questions.'

~

Ever since Kastur had been released from jail, she had not been keeping well. Mohandas was not able to spare any time for her. Even though he was in Durban, he was constantly on the go and could not attend to her. He felt very guilty about it. Looking after Kastur was also one of his duties and he always felt guilty when he could not attend to his duty. Time and again, he got this feeling that Kastur was calling him and that she needed his attention. Will I ever be able to do anything for my people, he kept asking himself. I tried to do it for my father, but what was the final outcome? My lust pulled me away like a crocodile pulls away into the water an animal standing on bank of a river. The moment I left, death claimed him. Maybe death knew me by face and avoided me. My uncle was an unknown face. There is a constant tug-of-war between death and a faithful attendant. So long as the attendant keeps tugging, death hovers around but does not swoop. The moment he lets go or lets the rope sag, down it swoops. That was precisely what had happened. The man at the rope had allowed himself to be tied to another rope and that was what death was waiting for. *Ba* had already passed away. Death must have calculated that one who tries to pluck each fruit sometimes ends up ruining the whole crop.

The children, Kastur, myself. I hope we two also don't get caught in the same kind of equation once again. She may not be able to do anything for me or me for her. It will only be left for us to regret at leisure.

On January 17, he wrote a letter to Kallenbach from Pretoria:

> *Lower House, I worry about Kastur. I want to be able to do something for her. She needs it. She wants me by her side, but though I'm free, I'm worse than a prisoner. I'm unable to pay as much attention as I should.*

In the same letter, he wrote:

> *I want to be there, I crave to do something for her. There is nothing more important for me right now. General Smuts also knows my circumstances. If he wanted he could release me from this tension by taking a decision, but why would he?*

On January 19, Kallenbach wrote to him: ...

Mrs. Gandhi is getting better.

Mohandas felt relieved, and, with the relief, he started thinking of other things. He wrote to Kallenbach: 'People are waiting for me impatiently at Johannesburg. I thing I'll look them up while I'm about it.'

Kastur asked everyday in her own style: 'When Mr. Gandhi come?'

Kallenbach told her: 'He wants to be with you as soon as he can. He will be here any day.'

When she was informed that he would be coming via Johannesburg, she said in a detached tone: 'He say something … He do nothing.'

Kallenbach didn't quite understand, but the pain behind the words did communicate itself to him. He got up and went outside.

~

Sir Benjamin Robertson, the Viceroy's representative, had arrived on a special ship according to schedule. Mohandas and Andrews had started their activities in Pretoria without waiting for Sir Robertson. Mohandas had also had a meeting with General Smuts, although a short one. The Smuts he now saw was not the Smuts he had seen when the march had started. That Smuts had his head up in the skies; this Smuts was down on the earth. The railway strike had seen to it.

In that short meeting, Smuts had given a long lecture. He had said: 'Mr. Gandhi, that's your point of view. The prestige and the responsibilities of a government are at an altogether different plane when compared to those of individuals or communities of individuals. Any change in the structure of the commission at this point will hurt the prestige of the government. Esselen is our man. He will do what we ask him to. Colonel Wylie is one of the most respected figures in Natal. It's possible that he is anti-Indian. If the commission recommends the withdrawal of the three-pound tax, it will make the government's job a lot easier. Please help us in making our task easier. We are facing many other problems too. We wish for an honourable solution to the problems of Indians. We are ready to concede your demands; all that we need is the commission's recommendation. I am aware that you have vowed not to meet the commission. You may not meet it, but please do not write or speak against it. Please don't stop others from meeting it. This will be in the best interests of your own people. How else are you going to establish that excesses were committed on your people?'

Mohandas did not affirm or deny. He only said: '…we've no objection to waiting some more. We'll hold our activities in abeyance till then.'

General didn't get the sense. What was he supposed to understand by this utterance?

After the arrival of Sir Benjamin Robertson, meetings had multiplied. On certain occasions it was Smuts and Gandhi, at times Sir Robertson and General Smuts, sometimes Andrews and Robertson. General Botha would also put in an appearance occasionally. People were watching the meetings and the talks impatiently. Some of them thought that if Gandhi remained adamant, he might also be exiled. That would hurt the Indians more.

Gladstone, the Governor General, sent a confidential report to the Colonial Secretary every week. This report of the Governor General helped the authorities in London maintain their hold on the South African government. The Mohandas-Smuts talks had been held on January 16. Lord Gladstone sent his report on January 22, in which he wrote:

> *Chances of talks between my government and the Indian community are brightening, although it would be unwise to underestimate the difficulties that they might face. Still, I can say that ever since I took over there has never been a more positive environment than we have now.*
>
> *General Smuts and Mr. Gandhi, and General Smuts and Sir Benjamin Robertson are in constant touch. C.F. Andrews has also exchanged views with the minister. General Smuts has given them a patient hearing. The points of dispute between General Smuts and Gandhi are many and of long standing. But despite this, General Smuts treats Gandhi like a friend. Deep within him, he considers Gandhi to be an extraordinary personality. His eccentricities may create problem after problem for General Smuts, but they also fascinate him and help him know the man better.*

About Sir Benjamin, Lord Gladstone wrote:

> *He has shown great skill, a logical mind and a flair for justice. He has also established his contacts with Prime Minister General Botha along with General Smuts. In fact, he has made friends with almost all*

the ministers. His resourcefulness and firmness have impressed even Mr. Gandhi. I should rather say that Sir Benjamin has so far succeeded in keeping Gandhi within the realm of talks. It's not easy for Europeans to talk to Gandhi. People brought up in the western culture can never make out when Gandhi's conscience might start acting up and how. Often talks stall at points where we can see no scope for a stall. There is a unique mix of spirituality and intellect in Mr. Gandhi's moral and mental attitudes, which an ordinary person cannot grasp. We seem to be approaching a consensus on how to resolve the matters on a practical plane.

~

Governor General Gladstone was acting as an invisible eye between the Union government and the government in London. Neither the governments nor the *satyagrahi*s could make out what the Governor General's attitude was. In the meantime, a meeting was held between Lord Gladstone and Andrews. Gladstone's very first question was: 'How well do you know Gandhi?'

'Not too well, but recently we have had extended discussions on various topics and those discussions have given me some insight into him. It is up to Gandhi to decide how much or how little he wants to let you understand of him.'

'I don't quite get you …'

'He is guided solely by his conscience. Nothing else will have any impact on him. It is not easy therefore to understand him.'

'Does that mean that no dialogue is possible with Gandhi?'

'Certainly not. He is in fact like a child. You can talk to him on any matter and in whatever way you fancy. The only condition is that you must be transparent with him, and no subterfuge.'

'But …'

'Let me give you an example. On General Smuts' assurance, Mr. Gandhi accepted the idea of voluntary registration, and also gave up his condition of not allowing their fingerprints to be taken. It was the first time that he broke a vow he had taken. What was the net result? The Pathans thrashed him and tried to kill him. It is difficult now to persuade him to give up his vow. He knows well now the immorality of breaking a vow under the influence of false assurances. He got punished for it. That was his atonement.'

'Soloman is distressed at the lack of cooperation from Gandhi and his associates. Soloman has written to Smuts about it.'

'Is it not sufficient cooperation that he is not opposing it? He will wait for the Commission's report before taking any further action.'

He resumed after a pause: 'The two important demands of Gandhi are: the state must not interfere in the married life of Indians and recognize their marriages; second, the three-pound tax must be withdrawn. If the government concedes these two demands, he will not insist on the demand for parity in franchise. He will also not question the constitutional validity of the Commission for inquiring into the riots.'

In his report sent to the government in London after the meeting, the Governor General made a detailed mention of these facts. In addition, he also wrote: 'I am greatly impressed with Andrews. He indeed has an insight into the way Gandhi thinks.'

About Sir Robertson, he wrote: 'Sir Benjamin is a capable officer … but the subtle and sensitive way Gandhi's mind works is beyond him to grasp. I have tried to explain this to General Smuts.'

The talks between General Smuts, Mohandas, Sir Robertson and Andrews continued for about two weeks. In addition many letters were exchanged. When Sir Robertson arrived in Durban and met Mohandas, their talks never went beyond the minimum requirements of formality. A few days later, Mohandas discovered that Sir Robertson was talking to Indians in separate groups and trying to create a split in their ranks.

'It's no easy task fighting a government,' he told one group. 'How long will you carry on your *satyagraha*? And that, on a foreign land where you have no rights?'

Mohandas also received some telegrams: 'Sir Robertson is behaving like a boss. He is trying to bully people. The poor and the weak among Indians are feeling the pressure.'

Mohandas talked to Andrews. They decided that the best strategy would be to talk to Robertson directly.

Mohandas said to Robertson: 'The Viceroy's message to me through Prof. Gokhale was to have frank talks with you. I hope you agree with the Viceroy.'

Robertson was disconcerted at first, but then he smiled and said: 'What could be better?'

'Our people are scared of you. Such a big officer! They feel that you may get annoyed and do them harm. For Indians, the Viceroy and his representative are mighty people. For the *girmitiya* labourers, in fact, the Viceroy is nothing short of God. A short, sharp rebuke from you can send them scurrying.'

Mohandas' talk was making Robertson uncomfortable. Without giving him a chance to say anything, Mohandas continued: 'They wish to live happily together. They want to draw the government's attention to their difficulties by inflicting pain on themselves. Please try not to bully them or to divide them. You are in a way a representative of God to them. They think of you as their saviour. We'd be happy if that was the form you appeared before them in.'

Sir Robertson made an effort but could not utter a word. Mohandas laughed and said: 'You are of course the Viceroy's representative, but, like Andrews here, you are also a friend and companion to me.'

In parting, Sir Robertson managed a few broken sentences: 'I'm sorry… You've called me a friend, so let it be a friend.'

~

A working agreement had been arrived at between Mohandas and General Smuts on January 22, but the government had not yet forwarded a draft to him. Mohandas had sent in writing all the points that had been agreed upon. Even this working agreement had created an air of festivity around them. Even the whites were happy. The big problem before Mohandas however was how to secure the consent of the Indian community for the working agreement. Certainly, no one would want the air of festivity to end.

There were questions in his mind. Who would take General Smuts at his word? The events of 1908 had led to a loss of face which still rankled. At that time too it was a verbal agreement with General Smuts. Smuts had gone back on his word while accusing Mohandas of raising fresh issues. Mohandas had not stuck to his word. In a sense, he was responsible for the sufferings of his people. Mohandas referred to these instances and told himself: 'You still haven't learnt your lesson? You are going to trust him again? But your people will not be deceived again and again. What will you do if you are deceived again? Go on *satyagraha*? How long will those people keep going to jail on your say-so? What good are agreements which are not based on truth? Make promises and break them—that's all that these people do. How long will you trust agreements that are written on sand?

But is it not *satyagraha* if you try to arrive at the bedrock of truth even after you have been deceived time and time again?

Mohandas called a public meeting to make everything public. The day the meeting was to be held, a telegram was received from London that Andrews' mother was in her deathbed. Andrews himself had himself been working ceaselessly and was running a fever.

Andrews sat for a while with his eyes closed. Then he said: 'Mohan, my mother loves me a lot. I was thinking of paying her a visit after my return from this place. It looks it is fated otherwise.'

'Go, Charlie, go! I'll make all the arrangements. But you have a fever.'

'I have heard you too were in London when your mother died. You were a student then. Now my mother is dying when I am here. The ship will take ten to fifteen days. I don't think my mother will wait that long. The agreement here is in the final stages. How proper will it be to give up something that you may well get for something that you won't? The Gita says the world is action-dominated, not feeling-dominated. You agree, don't you? If a man like me, who has given himself completely to God, were to lose himself in his own joys and sorrows and in his feelings for his near and dear ones, whatever will happen to his other children? If it is His wish that decides whatever is to happen on this earth, good or bad, then, surely, He must also have some expectations of me. Shouldn't I fulfil those expectations?'

Mohandas took Andrews's hand in his own. 'Charlie,' he said: 'I didn't even know when my mother died. You know it, but still you won't go.' His voice was choked.

Andrews's hand was hot he came to know after touching it instantly. Mohandas moved off to arrange for a mud pack. He had a feeling his mother must be very much like his own …

~

A public meeting was held on January 23. About a thousand Indians attended. Andrews had dragged himself from his sickbed. Polak and Kallenbach were present and so was Rustomji Parsi. Imam Sahib presided. To start with, Mohandas explained the conditions of the agreement. As he mentioned the illness of Andrews' mother, his heart was heavy with sorrow. He said: 'We must take a lesson from Andrews. For a man devoted to God, service to man is God Himself. When he serves God, he serves mankind; when he serves mankind, he serves God. Instead of thinking about himself and his near and dear ones, he takes the sorrow of the entire universe upon himself. Andrews' mother is on her deathbed, but he is more worried about the agreement than his mother.' Mohandas wiped his eyes.

Mohandas spoke a mixture of English and Hindustani. He first explained all those issues that had been disturbing him for the past few days. Then he went on to say:

> *Andrews and Robertson have been present at all the discussions that have taken place between me and General Smuts. General Smuts said in so many words*

that his government was ready to accept all our conditions. But his government also wants that, since a commission had been appointed. It should also be allowed to submit its report after due inquiry. So really all that has happened is that the government has accepted in writing the principle that we should be consulted. The government has also accepted the demand that Indians would not testify before the commission in person. However, I have given no commitment on your behalf. There have been times when I have taken the liberty of making a commitment without consulting you, but on this occasion I thought it necessary to seek your consent. You are absolutely free to accept or reject the agreement. If you don't like it, you are free to throw it into the waste paper basket. A decision that does not carry the consent of those who are affected by it has no meaning.

After a pause, he said:

I sought the opinion of Andrews and other friends. Our friend Pearson is also a man of God. He prefers to stay backstage, but his advice is always available to us when we need it. Everyone is of the view that the agreement is an honourable one. Everyone agrees that we can save ourselves from lot of problems by agreeing to this proposal. If your conscience does not permit it or if the agreement goes counter to the vows we have taken, we are not under any obligation to anyone to endorse it: it may be the Indian Viceroy or it may be our respected Gokhale or it may be the local government. There is no need for us to worry, or to be afraid of what might happen in the future. So long as we have a sacred weapon like satyagraha *with us, why do we need to be afraid?*

Mohandas' speech had gone on too long. Andrews took the podium next. He said:

I am in no position to give a long speech. I think we should accept what Gandhibhai has said without any apprehensions. One may try to prove that what a true man has said is untrue, but that does not make it untrue. On the other hand, the veneer of truth on falsehood soon wears off. I am a witness to this agreement.

Kallenbach and Polak also spoke a few words each. Rustomji stood up next. With the permission of Imam Sahib, he read out the resolution:

This meeting of British Indians, having heard and understood the conditions of the working agreement between the Union government and Gandhibhai, confirms it and expresses its support for the agreement.

People welcomed the resolution with prolonged applause.

~

During this time Mohandas had almost lost all touch with his family: there had been so much running around, so many meetings and so many rounds of consultations. After the agreement with Smuts there had been some relief. On February 16, he went to Cape Town with Kastur. His work in Pretoria was over. All they had to do was to wait for the results. The Commission would submit the report and the government would bring before the parliament legislation based on it as promised.

A lady named Hobhouse lived in Cape Town. She knew Mohandas by name but had never exactly met him. She was greatly impressed with Mohandas' actions. Miss Hobhouse invited Mohandas and Kastur to her home. It was an invitation from a highly distinguished member of the city elite. When Mohandas and Kastur arrived at her place, they found that the wives of General Botha and Lord Gladstone were also present.

Miss Hobhouse introduced Mohandas and Kastur to Mrs. Botha and Lady Gladstone.

'This is Mrs. Botha and this Lady Gladstone.' Then she turned to the other side and said, 'Mr. and Mrs. M.K. Gandhi.'

'A great non-violent violent fighter,' said Mrs. Botha at once.

Mohandas smiled and said: 'I hope that's not your own opinion.'

Mrs. Botha probably didn't get the meaning.

Miss Hobhouse said: 'And Mrs. Gandhi is no less … The horrors of jail life are still pursuing her.'

Lady Gladstone said: 'My husband talks a lot about Mr. Gandhi. He also likes him a lot. I have had the occasion to meet his friends Father Andrews and Father Pearson. However, this is my first meeting with Mr. Gandhi. Andrews is a true follower of Mr. Gandhi.'

Mohandas laughed and said: 'No, Madam, I am a true follower of his.'Kastur was quiet. Mohandas summarized what others said to her from time to time.

Mohandas' eyes were fixed at Miss Hobhouse. He couldn't decide whether to talk to her or just keep watching her. He couldn't take his eyes off her during the entire visit.

Back in the hotel room, he wrote a letter to Lower House,

> *I and Kastur visited Miss Hobhouse on her invitation. I saw a divine glow on her face and didn't want to take my eyes off her. When I had met Gokhale for the first time I had a similar experience of being face to face with divinity.*

~

Kastur's condition was very unsteady. The fever kept rising and falling. When she was unwell, Mohandas didn't leave her side for a moment. The rising tide of anger and annoyance within her had in the meantime stopped growing. Kastur also did not let him leave her side for a moment. He fed her with his own hands. He helped her get off the bed. She always held on to his arms to make sure that he was by his side.

The swelling on her body was growing and when that happened she became pale and her body became still. She didn't want to eat or drink.

Their family doctor was Dr. Gole and he was called. He examined her closely. A urine test was carried out. Everything seemed to be fine and Dr. Gole was perplexed. Mohandas asked: 'If you have no objection, shall I try natural cure?'

'Sure, the aim is to cure. If Mrs. Gandhi gets better, I'll also learn something. I'll turn your pupil which, in turn, will help my patients.'

Mohandas said: 'But you doctors think the treatment you give alone deserves to be called a treatment.'

'Treatment implies cure. Any treatment that cures is a treatment.'

Mohandas spent the night changing mudpacks. In three or four days, the swelling came down. Kastur's face looked alive again.

Mohandas had to spend three sleepless nights. Many virtues marked his sleep. He could sleep waking. He could think sleeping. He could wake up from deep sleep and start working seriously, a fully awake and alert man. A chain formed and unformed in his mind. All those people who had been with him during this long period, people who had worked with him, suffered with him, some dead, some alive, they all walked into his ken one by one, stayed for a while and then took their leave. Mohandas however couldn't free himself of their presence.

'Lakshmidas, the elder brother! How much he loved him and how angry did he end up! You are no one to me and I'm no one to you, he told me. Now he is on his deathbed. What a changed man! How much he regrets the letters he wrote me! He now admits that by not sending him money I neither broke family tradition, nor did I humiliate him. His earlier thinking was just the opposite. Now in his deathbed, he wants to see me. What an irony! Andrews' mother died; Andrews couldn't go to see her despite his love for her. He was fighting for the rights of others here. Now it's my elder brother. How can I go? I started everything here. His people may forgive Andrews; mine won't ever forgive me. Maybe we are more selfish …'

~

Mohandas was trying to remember everything in retrospect: it was only the other day. Mani and Jakie! And Jakie, a married woman! Daughter of my friend, Dr. Mehta, wife of a dedicated person like Manilal Doctor! Freedom is fine: it is easy to get but hard to keep. I have said hard things sometimes. People don't like it, but I have no regrets. I did not send Mani to Phoenix because Jakie was there. Millie had seen them together so many times. I do not want him to go to Johannesburg from Kallenbach's home everyday and spend the night there and eat there. I want to see him as a mighty tree, not as a lean and thin creeper snaking up a derelict tree by the roadside.There was nothing that Raojibhai did not write about Jakie. I had no choice except to send Jakie's letter to Manilal Doctor. She—a *satyagrahi* without any self-control! It's possible I may have hurt Jakie's interests. Manilal Doctor is a saint. I know that he'll forgive her. I wish his forgiveness could do her some good. The two are so far gone in sin that I have become a sinner too. Such is the quality of sin that even if it touches you it doesn't leave you unscathed, though it may not look that way on the surface. If sin and deception had not entered their hearts, the two could have turned human even after they had once turned animal. Nothing however could be achieved. How helpless does you failure make you feel! Kastur is untouched, always watching silently. In her eyes, Jakie alone is the guilty one.

Mohandas spent hours sinking and rising in the agitation that raged in his heart. There was Harilal, always asking for forgiveness, always offering arguments. He tried to run away but the port officer caught him out. He wanted to escape as a destitute. He begged for a ticket on the ship. Kastur would not stop crying. 'You are no father to him … your heart is made of stone,' she told me. But stone or not, no one can save you if you have strayed from the right path. Is he going to stray all his life? He doesn't know that when the child strays, his parents too can't save themselves from straying. Where is the question of forgiveness then? He is deluded and wants to go to Bombay. What does he hope to get there? Here he was looked upon as the younger Gandhi. I thought he had changed his ways, but his ways were following him. Even his health ceased to matter for him. I wrote to him that if he wanted to study he would have to leave Chachi, that is, his wife, with me. He would have to live alone. I would pay his expenses. 'If you want, you can also stay with me and be my right hand. Your mother is swaying between life and death. How much she loves you! She has a sharp tongue, but that touches everyone alike. Exercise self-control. Build character. Do not always think of what you can get from others; also think of what you can give. If you did not look upon my not sending you to London as injustice on my part, your sorrow would have turned into happiness. You would have had one more chance of understanding your father. By treating it as injustice, you narrowed your choices and shut down all the doors to an understanding of the problem. Now I became the guilty one, not you. I am ready to take all the guilt upon myself … I am ready to lay down my life for you …I'll leave all my inheritance to you … but that which belongs to the society will go to the society. I know, Hari, you will never forgive me because your mind is incapable of making this distinction between what belongs to you and what belongs to the society.

Ramdas is the quiet type. He doesn't have the lust of Mani or the stubbornness of Hari. He is reasonably good at studies and looks after his health too. Debu is still too young.

Valliamma passed away on January 22, 1914. How sick she was when she was released from jail! How young she died! And how keen she was to go to jail even in her condition! Her large eyes showed no desire other than this. If I, or someone of my family, were to go the way she did, it would have done me proud. People would say: 'Look at Mohandas' family! Let's also go to jail.' But what do I have to show to the world? Hari was on his way to become a *satyagrahi* and lost his way. Nagappan, Harbat Singh … so many laid down their lives, the most costly thing they had! Many died who had many years to go still. Kastur could have died! She may still die. The desire to lay down my life for my country and people allows me no peace. It demands to know what I and my family have done for the people. All the sacrifices were made by the Tamils. I bow my head to them. I look at my people and cannot raise my head in shame. I know of course that the Tamils are my people too.

Elder brother is gone too! Mohandas' sorrow was getting too great to contain. Others could cry; he couldn't do that either. He was everything for his elder brother; now he was nothing. Whatever he was today, it was because of him. He wanted to see me from his deathbed. I too wanted to go back to him after I had completed my work here. If somehow I could reach India and fall at his feet! I couldn't serve *Bapu* to the end. As punishment, God took away from me the chance of serving my elder brother. *Ba* also passed away without giving a chance. How similar are our fates—mine and Andrews'! Both our mothers loved us, yet when *Ba* died I was in London. When his mother died, Andrews was here. And now my elder brother is dead and I am here.

When I return to India, I'll be known as the chief of widows. Those who don't know the Indian system will not understand this conflict, the conflict that is within you and doesn't ever end. I must return. When, I don't know. Leave everything to Him and set out on your journey. There is another destination that calls out to you: 'Mohandas, come back! Come back!'

Mohandas wrote:

> *When such things happen to you, they make you fearless towards death. To be in sorrow too is to be self-centred, although death is a welcome fate. If I'm ready to embrace my own death, why am I so rattled by my brother's death? We all fear our own death, so we shed tears on the death of others. In the death of my brother, I saw a Mohandas dying too. If the body is transient but the soul is immortal, why cry over the clothes wearing out?*

When Kastur called, Mohandas felt he wasn't there. He had moved out to some far away place with them all, to that boundary between the valleys of life and death where the two meet. He thought of Allahabad. How long he had stood watching that stream where the two rivers met!

The context was however very different then.

~

XXVI

The Commission's report was released in the third week of March. Mohandas read it sitting next to Kastur's bed.

'What does the report say?' Kastur asked.

Mohandas laughed and said, 'It has what you went to jail for. You came out of the jail but the jail followed you home. Now the bed is your jail.'

'The Commission had a man called Wylie who wanted to have you killed. There was another man, Esselen, wasn't there? They were both against us, weren't they?'

'Yes, but they too have decided to be just. Maybe, *satyagraha* touched their hearts too. No man is good or bad forever.'

Sitting right there, Mohandas started working on a press note for *Indian Opinion*. Occasionally, Kastur would open her eyes and see him working.

> *A very large section of the Indian community boycotted the Commission. The commission has taken serious objection to it. Lord Hardinge had also expressed his displeasure at our opposition to the Commission. His displeasure was justified. He was under an obligation to stick to his recommendation and to support the Commission. Despite all this, we believe that the Indians were wise not to testify before the Commission. A vow once taken cannot be broken lightly. That damages trust. If the satyagrahis were to testify, the whole meaning of satyagraha would be lost. We would be caught in their game. They would discount our testimony and do what they pleased. Our testimonies would have taken at least six months. There would have been at least three hundred witnesses. And wouldn't they be followed by testimonies from the whites? Apart from this, the atmosphere would have been vitiated. Then the report writing would begin. A whole session of the parliament would be taken*

up by a discussion on the report. The seeds of reconciliation sown by C.F. Andrews and his friend Pearson would have remained unsprung. Possibly, Esselen and Wylie would also not have shown the same sense of responsibility. By ignoring Lord Hardinge's advice we did the right thing. If you have a God to fear, why fear a mortal?

The Commission would probably have not made the recommendations that they have made with regard to the three-pound tax and the Indian marriages even hundreds of thousands of testimonies later. The Commission has denounced the tax severely. In the other event, it would have probably not done so. Whatever came of the testimonies offered by Mr. Angalia and some of our other Indian brothers against their own community out of ignorance and lack of understanding? The note sent by Polak to Sir Benjamin also proved ineffective. The Commission has recommended the issuance of a three-year registration certificate in place of an annual one, while we had asked for a permanent certificate. In fact, it was Angalia and others who had proposed a three-year certificate. Our demand for a permanent certificate was snowed under by their testimonies. The demand for open licences for business was also rejected because of their absurd testimonies.

The Commission has accepted that the satyagraha *was justified. All our demands were justified. The allegation against the government that it went back on its word as also been found to be correct.*

In the press note, Mohandas also described in detail the advantages that would accrue to Indians as a result of the recommendations made by the Commission with regard to the legality of the Indian marriage systems.

When he had finished the report, Mohandas said to Kastur, laughing: 'Now we can hope that you will be able to continue to be my wife. Your jail trip has had the same effect as the Indian woman's worship of the *vat* tree on the *amawasya* day.'

A thin, weak smile appeared on Kastur's face.

~

Kastur's health was in a state of flux. The eight years of *satyagraha* had not had such a devastating effect on Gandhi's life as her illness. He was beginning to suspect that she had cancer of the stomach. When the strain of her illness on his mind rose beyond a point, he wrote to Lower House: 'Kastur has some serious stomach ailment, perhaps cancer. The only treatment is *neem* water. Allopathy is unlikely to work.'

Kastur had been practically on a fast in jail for three months. The result was that she was permanently in a rage. The swelling stayed all the time, sometimes a little less, sometimes a little more.

Lying in her bed, Kastur saw that Devdas' drawer was open. She flew into a rage. Despite her extreme weakness, she screamed: 'Who opened Devdas' drawer?'

'I did,' said Mohandas, who was sitting close by.

'Why did you? What were you looking for?' She was mad with fury and her eyes swung from one side to another.

'I was looking for a bed sheet.'

'You know we don't keep bed sheets in that drawer. You are trying to save Jakie. She has wrecked my home. She has already destroyed Mani, now she is going after Devdas. She may be your friend's daughter but that does not mean father and sons should go around chasing her.'

'You have a perverted mind. Your illness is a result of this perversion,' said Mohandas, his forehead crumpled and his voice sharp and bitter.

Kastur screamed all the louder: 'You are fed up with me. You want to get rid of me. That's why you have stopped giving me food.'

Mohandas felt that the beast of anger which he thought he had laid to rest permanently was stirring within him again. He said: 'I have no sympathy with you in spite of your illness. All because of your perverted, sinful mind.'

The more Mohandas spoke, the higher was Kastur's rage. She had lost control and abuses streamed from her mouth.

Suddenly, Mohandas realized what he had said. Didn't he know how sick she was? Still he had allowed himself to lose his balance.

Mohandas came close to her and apologized: 'Please forgive me, I shouldn't have said all that. You are so ill … I'll try not to hurt you with my words in future.'

Mohandas fasted that day. He spent the whole night thinking. So what if Kastur had told him that nasty thing? Ever since she has returned, Jakie has been occupying all her thoughts. Jakie is one of the reasons for her illness.

He wanted to forget and forgive but couldn't. He wrote to Kallenbach:

> *Lower House*
>
> *Kastur neither forgets nor forgives. There is so much poison within her! I have never come across another woman with such a poisonous tongue. She has thrown wild accusations at me, baseless allegations. I have served her like a son. All my love has failed to change her basic nature. How can I complain against men like Angalia? I may still have some love for them. So if they are angry with me, I won't complain. I'm beginning to think that Kastur is my teacher. She has taught me the ephemeral nature of this world. She has taught me patience. I have learnt forgiveness from her. Self-sacrifice, love, service, renunciation—everything I have learnt from her. This incident has hurt me, but it has also given me wisdom. It has taught me to love despite everything. But I'm also beginning to believe that marriage is a curse for those who want to take the vow of service. She has of course never interfered with my work. In fact, no other woman would have put up with the changes in me that she has put up with. She is not an evil woman or a bad wife. But can a leopard change its spots? What I mean to say is that if you want to live for humanity you cannot tie yourself to a woman. The two simply do not go together. That is the reason every once in a while the beast in her raises its head.*

Kallenbach was as close to him as he was to himself. Anything he could tell himself, he could tell Kallenbach.

~

In March, Mohandas moved from Cape Town to Durban and brought Kastur with him. Jakie was still in Phoenix. When Kastur was in jail, Jakie had done a lot for her, but Kastur had not been able to develop any attachment with her despite her wish to do so. She thought of her as a sorceress whose favourite act was to cast magic spells on men. Mohandas had sent Manilal to Johannesburg to stay with Kallenbach at 'Mountview.' This had led to a further rift with Kastur. Why send out Manilal? Why not Jakie? Mohandas wanted them to live away and far apart from each other. Mohandas had seen them lying side by side more than once.

Finally, he sent a telegram to Jakie's father, Dr. Pranjeevan Mehta, asking him if he could send her to her husband in Fiji. After he had received his consent, Mohandas called Jakie and said: 'Your father and me both want you to join your husband in Fiji. He has been living there all by himself.'

'I want to lead my life in the ashram. Please let me stay here.'

'Your husband is doing a great job there. If you were doing better than him, there would have been some point in your staying here, but that is not the case. It is better that you stay with your husband. He is a social worker and a saint.'

Jakie smiled: 'I know. He is indeed a saint.'

She didn't expect that Mohandas would do this to her, but she also knew that once he had decided it, it would be impossible to make him change his mind.'

'But *Bapu* had sent me to stay with you.'

He laughed and said: 'The aim for which you'd been sent here has been achieved. The Commission has submitted its report. The Relief Act is also to be presented to the parliament soon. Besides, there are various other actions that are done best in the company of your husband. I have your father's permission. Here, you can see it if you like.'

Jakie had nothing left to say.

Mohandas persuaded Miss West to go with Jakie as far as Cape Town. Ships for Fiji left from Cape Town.

Jakie said: 'I want to go via Johannesburg.'

'No, there is a direct route to Cape Town. Miss West will go with you as far as there.'

'Why Miss West? Can't I go alone?'

'You can, but she will go with you. She will bid you farewell at Cape Town on all our behalf. I'd have gone myself but Kastur is not keeping well.' It was said very peremptorily.

'Jamanadas could go with me.'

'Mani or Jamanadas—what's the difference?'

Jakie had to go. All options had been exhausted. She couldn't stay on.

Mohandas wrote to Kallenbach:

My dear Lower House,

Love is dumb and makes no grouse. Love is blind and doesn't look at the good or bad points. Love makes up no stories. It gives freely and takes freely. Good fortune or bad, it doesn't go up or down. It never tires and is never wounded. How is your love doing in these times?

I don't know about Manilal Doctor of Fiji but our Manilal is infatuated. Manilal Doctor is basically an honest person. His pain is the pain of a jilted husband. He has dwelt on his suffering without mincing words. That is his honesty. For keeping Jakie with me, I didn't even have the excuse that she was doing better than her husband. In fact, it is now quite clear to me that she comes nowhere near him. She is a liar and full of self-praise. I'm not sorry for her and have no pity for her. She is a victim of irrepressible lust …

Yours,

Upper House

When Lower House read the letter, he sat silent for some time, ruminating. Then he muttered to himself, 'I don't know if what you did was right or wrong. As for my love, we are doing fine.' A thin layer of pain could be seen to shadow his face.

He picked up his pen to write a reply but thought better not to write an instant reply and put down the pen. There was a photograph of his on the table. His eyes settled on it. Mohandas had gone on a fast in February. The May fast had told heavily on his health. These fasts had a domestic connection too. He was now unable even to write his letters—the necessary ones were written by Maganlal. His body suffered extreme pain. The stomach seemed to have been wrung out. Mohandas was preparing himself mentally to leave the country. Kastur was now doing better than before. But another worry had taken her place. Gokhale was very ill. He was waiting for Mohandas to come back so that he could hand him his responsibilities and breathe a sigh of relief. He had written several times to Mohandas to come back and Mohandas had also expressed his willingness, but the conditions in South Africa repeatedly came in the way. He had broken his word with Kastur maybe a couple of times, but with Gokhale it had become a regular feature.

On February 27, he wrote a letter to Gokhale:

> *Charlie and Pearson are wonderful persons ... Sir Benjamin disappointed us. He could do us no good but has done a lot of harm. A weak man, lacking in sincerity. Whether knowingly or not, he has been trying to create dissensions in our ranks. If the agreement is signed in March, I'm ready to leave for India in April.*

Once again Mohandas had been unable to keep his word. Someone was whispering in his ears time and again: 'Hurry! Gokhale is waiting just for you. Hurry lest his time on this earth may be over before his work is.' He was in a hurry to get to him. He wanted to serve him and to learn from him. He wanted to be by his side in his last moments. The desire was making him restless. But Kastur? Who knows she might say the goodbyes even before Gokhale does?

At the beginning of May, Kastur showed some improvement. Mohandas wrote to Gokhale on May 6:

If Kastur keeps up her speed of recovery she should recover fully in a month's time. Then we can both come to London. The draft of the Indian Relief Act has so far not been published. It is possible that it may be June by the time we are able to leave.

Gokhale was in London for his treatment.

~

When the first reading of the Indian Relief Bill took place on June 26, 1914, Mohandas was in Cape Town. He had been invited for discussions on the draft bill. The draft was handed over to him the moment he arrived in Cape Town. He spent a whole day reading it. When he arrived at the Home Secretary's office in the afternoon to discuss it, his face had a gratified look.

In his report of July 4, Lord Gladstone wrote to the Colonial Secretary.

There were hours of discussion between General Smuts and Mr. Gandhi. Subsequently, talks were held between Home Secretary Georgess and Gandhi. They also carried out written correspondence. Gandhi returned to Durban thereafter.

While on his way to Durban, Gandhi ran into the Governor General's secretary at the station. The secretary recognized him and approached him. 'Mr. Gandhi, you look very weak. I hope you are not unwell,' he said.

'We cannot afford to be weak. Times see to it that we are always fit. The problems of living are the tonic that gives us energy. But if you meant thin, I'd agree.'

'Yes, you are right. Thin was what I meant.'

'I had a fifteen-day fast in May. A fast also has its own technology. I was rather new to it, so I fell ill. Normally fasting does not make you weak; in fact, it gives you energy. Repeated experiments have made this amply clear to me now.'

'You must be pleased with the Indian Relief Act. You fought such a long battle, without any resources … it couldn't have been easy.'

'The kind of resources we needed for our battle we had in plenty. If we had also garnered additional resources we'd have lost. That's what the government wanted—our defeat. As for being pleased, we have succeeded in achieving the goals we sought. For this, we must thank General Smuts and Mr. Governor, who saw our point of view and also the Commission, who did not allow their prejudices to stand in the way of their recommendations. There are of course still issues which cause us worry and need to be resolved.'

The Governor General had also mentioned this meeting in his report.

~

Mohandas and Kastur's return to India had been fixed for July 18. Kallenbach was to accompany them. Gokhale was in London, unwell. The idea was to look him up before returning to India.

Word was beginning to spread that Gandhibhai was going back to India and a stream of callers was beginning to build up. *Girmitiya*s, workers, peddlers, mine-workers, shopkeepers and businessmen all queued up to say just one thing: 'Please don't go.'

Someone, moist-eyed, would ask: 'Will you never come back?'

Another one said, 'Had we known that our victory would take you away from us, we'd have refused such a victory and never engaged in a battle. We'd have continued as we were.'

Gandhibhai tried to explain, 'Do not insult your victory. You have secured it after great sacrifice. Never be vain. Never hurt others with your behaviour. Never bow before injustice and, whenever the need arises, fight as one man. Most important of all, never lose your faith in God.'

They wanted to touch his feet. Mohandas stopped them from doing so. 'Let every human remain a human. Why do you demean yourself by touching my feet?'

They brought small gifts for him. Mohandas kept on refusing. They went away wiping their tears. There was only one sentence in all their lips, 'What'll happen to us now?'

There were meetings and receptions galore. Papers were publishing interviews with Mohandas and his speeches at the meetings. At these meetings, he was asked questions to which he replied peacefully and patiently. Durban, Johannesburg, Cape Town, Maritzburg—wherever he went he just had one message: '… Never let fear come near you, never desert truth and never forget your country.'

People were overwhelmed with emotion as they heard him. Would they ever be able see their country again? Mohandas embraced one, shook hands with another, blessed another with his hand on his head and went around showering thanks and love on everyone.

They were to take the ship at Cape Town. Mohandas, Kastur, the Polak couple, Schlesin, Kallenbach and Rustomji arrived in Cape Town by Imperial Mail. Mohandas had been kept so busy in Johannesburg that he couldn't even visit Tolstoy Farm. He said to Kallenbach, 'I so much wanted to visit Tolstoy Farm and Phoenix but couldn't. Why does it happen that one leaves a place and is never able to return to it again? I wonder if I'll ever be able to return to this land of my action again.'

Kallenbach felt his voice growing heavy and kept walking silently.

Cape Town station had turned into a sea of human beings. Among them were not only Indians but also whites, natives and Chinese. Mohandas and Kastur were made to sit in an open carriage and were taken to the station in a procession with others on foot. Cape Towners had never seen so many people on the streets at the same time and had never seen so many people going in a procession to see a person off. Everyone who saw joined the procession and tried to catch a glimpse of the Gandhi couple.

Some of them put their children at their feet to receive their blessings. Kastur was finding it difficult to keep her emotions under control.

Before they boarded the ship, a meeting was held with Dr. Abdul Rahman in the chair, who also delivered the farewell address. When, at the end, Mohandas stood up to speak, he stood silent for a few seconds as if trying to assimilate something within him. Then he spoke:

Twenty-one years ago, I got down at Eddington Beach in Natal as a girmitiya, *a completely ignorant and frightened young man. I didn't know anyone here. I had only heard of Dada Abdullah. He is not with us today. Like a seedling, he planted me here and made me grow. Had he been alive today, I'd have told him: 'The "white elephant" you imported into this country is going back as a black elephant fully prepared to lose himself in the crowds of his country. This country now lives in every drop of my blood. This country showed the way to freedom and you are the people who put into effect my experiments and experiences and honoured me with success. This country is rich in resources and nature is its best friend. It is being irrigated by a spring that is the blood and sweat of the Indian settlers, who have made it flower. This country has given me both blows and bouquets of love. This country has given the world men like W.P. Shiner. It has given me a brother like Kallenbach, a friend like Polak and a companion like Rustomji Parsi.*

In the end, I'd like to appeal to all those who have concern for Indians in this country that my fellow countrymen are a sincere people. They are helpless, hungry for love and poor. Please keep a humane attitude towards them, try to understand them and take a peep into their hearts. They are the diamonds of your mines and they have hearts of gold. You only need to uncover them.

Mohandas could not carry on and sat down. For a time, everyone sat in a kind of daze. When they recovered, the applause began and seemed would never end. Their eyes were moist but the clapping would not cease.

When the ship sailed, Mohandas felt he had left everything behind. The shore and the people standing on it were moving farther and farther away.

Kastur bid farewell with folded hands.

Mohandas said: 'If Hari had stayed here people would have forgotten Mohandas soon, but, poor boy, he could not recognize his own capacity for sacrifice.'

Kastur kept silent.

Mohandas wrote an editorial for *Indian Opinion* with the title "The Struggle and the Result." He began it with a verse from the Quran: 'With Allah's will, how many times have small armies vanquished big ones! Allah is only with those who carry on their struggle patiently.'

He wrote a letter to Chhaganlal. Its last line went like this :

I watered my creeper of love with my tears.

Mohandas went and stood on the deck. The waves were turning back. Perhaps they too had a country which was calling out to them. A water fowl took off on a steep flight. Mohandas smiled to see it. He showed it to Kastur and said: 'Look! How free is the bird!'

~